A. F Jenkin, N. M Herbert

The Councillors' Handbook

A. F Jenkin, N. M Herbert

The Councillors' Handbook

ISBN/EAN: 9783337301903

Printed in Europe, USA, Canada, Australia, Japan

Cover: Foto ©Andreas Hilbeck / pixelio.de

More available books at **www.hansebooks.com**

THE

COUNCILLORS' HANDBOOK:

A PRACTICAL GUIDE TO THE
ELECTION AND BUSINESS OF A COUNTY COUNCIL.

BY

NICHOLAS HERBERT

AND

A. F. JENKIN, B.A.,

Of the Inner Temple, Barrister-at-Law.

TO WHICH IS APPENDED

The full text of the Local Government Act, 1888; The County Electors Act, 1888; and the Incorporated Clauses of the Municipal Corporations Act, 1882.

LONDON:
HADDEN, BEST & CO.,
WEST HARDING STREET, FETTER LANE, E.C.,
Local Government Publishers.

1888.

PREFACE

In preparing this work on the Local Government Act, our aim has been to place before our readers a practical account of the system of county government which will be introduced by that great measure, in such a form as to be useful to all persons interested in the subject, including those who are but slightly acquainted with the system of local government in this country.

Keeping that object in view we have, although the Act deals chiefly with counties and to a certain extent with boroughs, introduced brief descriptions of the system of government in Parishes, Unions, Sanitary Districts, and other areas, in order to render thoroughly clear the relations between the new County Councils and other local authorities.

The County Councils are entirely new bodies, and will have to take over business of great complexity from various existing authorities: we have accordingly devoted an entire chapter to the proceedings of the first County Councils to be elected, and have in that chapter drawn attention to the effect of the general provisions of the Act in connection with the transfer of each class of business which the County Councils will take over from other authorities.

The provisions of the Act with regard to county finance and local boundaries are of a somewhat complicated nature, and of great importance; to each of these subjects we have devoted a separate chapter.

The number and bulk of the Statutes dealing with business which will be transacted by County Councils is so great, that the task of compression has been one of much difficulty. Our object has been to avoid going at any length into questions in respect to which legal assistance will be necessary, while endeavouring to give a summary of the practical effect of the statutes mentioned.

The Local Government Act, 1888; the County Electors Act, 1888; and portions of the Municipal Corporations Act, 1882, which are incorporated with the former measure, are given at length at the end of the work.

A copious Index has been prepared, referring not only to the body of the work, but also to the Acts, which we are hopeful will prove of use to all persons having occasion to refer to those Acts.

NICHOLAS HERBERT.
AUSTIN F. JENKIN.

7, Crown Office Row,
Temple, E.C.,
August, 1888.

CONTENTS.

CHAPTER I.

INTRODUCTION.

Establishment of County Councils. Effect of Local Government Act on existing Authorities.

IN this chapter we propose first to explain briefly the nature and constitution of the County Councils that are to be established under the Local Government Act, 1888, and secondly, to give a sketch of the system of Local Government in England and Wales existing at the time that measure was passed, and to show how that system will be altered by the Act.

The system of local government in the Metropolis is very different from that obtaining elsewhere, and it is not proposed in this work to deal with it in any detail; accordingly the account of local government in this work is not, in the absence of express statement, applicable to the Metropolis.

Establishment of County Councils.

Under the Local Government Act, 1888, a County Council will be established in each of the counties in England and Wales; but the three Ridings of Yorkshire, the three divisions of Lincolnshire, the two divisions of Sussex, and the two divisions of Suffolk are treated as independent counties, as are also the Isle of Ely and the rest of Cambridgeshire, and the Soke of Peterborough and the rest of Northamptonshire. The Metropolis, which is taken out of the counties of Surrey, Kent, and Middlesex, is made for most purposes into a county of itself, called the County of London.

The existing county boundaries will in most cases be slightly altered, and the County Council of each county will have authority throughout their county except in certain important boroughs, called County Boroughs, which will be independent of the County Councils.

County Boroughs.

All boroughs the population of which was estimated to be on the 1st June, 1888, over 50,000, or which, being counties of cities or counties of towns, had according to the census of 1881 a population exceeding 20,000, are named in the third schedule to the Act, and are to be county boroughs. The Local Government Board are empowered to create other county boroughs under certain circumstances.[1]

Constitution of County Council.

The County Council is to be somewhat similarly constituted to the Town Council of a municipal borough, and will consist accordingly of County Councillors, County Aldermen and a Chairman of the Council. The number of County Councillors for each county has, under the Act, been fixed by the Local Government Board ;[2] the number of County Aldermen is to be one-third of the number of County Councillors. For the purpose of the election of County Councillors, each county will be divided into electoral divisions, and one Councillor will be elected for each electoral division by ratepayers duly qualified by the occupation of property within that electoral division. Such ratepayers are called, where they are qualified in respect of property in a municipal borough, "Burgesses," or, if that borough is a city, "Citizens," and in other cases, "County Electors." County boroughs will not share in the election of County Councillors.

Qualification of Electors.

The qualification entitling a ratepayer to vote at an election of a County Councillor is laid down in the County Electors Act, 1888, which was passed to prepare the way for the Local Government Act, 1888. Speaking broadly, all occupiers of land or premises of a clear yearly value of £10 and upwards, and all occupiers of buildings of any value, are entitled to vote. The following table shows in a simple form the main difference between the qualification conferring the parliamentary franchise and that conferring the right to vote at the election of a County Councillor.

Description of Person	At Parliamentary election	At the election of a County Councillor
Occupier of lands or a tenement of a clear yearly value of £10.	can vote	can vote
Occupier of a building of less value	cannot vote	can vote
Owner of land, &c.	can vote	cannot vote
Lodger	can vote	cannot vote
Peers and women otherwise qualified.	cannot vote	can vote

This Table is only intended to give a general idea of the qualification, of which a more detailed and accurate account is given in Chapter VI.

[1] See *post*, p. 99. [2] See Appendix G., *post*, p. 358.

The division of the County into electoral divisions for the purposes of the first election will be made as follows. The Local Government Board have apportioned the Councillors to be elected between the boroughs in the county of sufficient population to be separately represented, and the rest of the county. Where only one County Councillor has been assigned to a borough, that borough is to be an electoral division; but where more than one County Councillor has been assigned to a borough, the Town Council will divide the borough into electoral divisions. The rest of the county will be divided into electoral divisions by the Quarter Sessions of the county.[1] Electoral Divisions.

The County Aldermen are to be chosen by the County Councillors either from their own body or from outside. The Chairman of the County Council is to be appointed by the whole Council, either from their own body or from outside. County Councillors are to hold office for three years, and will all retire together; County Aldermen will hold office for six years, one-half of their number retiring triennially; the Chairman is to hold office for one year. Should, however, a casual vacancy occur in any of these offices, the person elected to fill the vacancy will go out of office at the same time as the person whose place he takes would have gone out of office. County Aldermen and Chairman.

The County Council will be a corporate body, with a common seal, and perpetual succession. They will have power to hold property (including land), to enter into contracts, to borrow money, and to raise money by means of rates, and will transact the greater part of the non-judicial or administrative business at present in the hands of the Quarter Sessions, and also other county business. Powers of County Council

Having thus indicated the nature of the County Councils that are to be established, we may go on according to our plan to give a sketch of the existing system of Local Government, treating in turn of the Parish, the Union, the Highway Parish and Highway District, the Municipal Borough, the Sanitary Districts, and the County, and of the changes in the Government of these areas under the Act. It has been thought convenient to deal with these areas in the above order, although the Local Government Act affects only boroughs and counties to any considerable extent.

The Parish.

In very early times the country was divided into townships and analogous areas, and the inhabitants of each township

[1] As to subsequent alterations of electoral divisions, see Chapter IV.

to a certain extent managed their own affairs. Later, on the establishment of a system of church government, the country was divided into parishes, called at the present day for the sake of distinction "ecclesiastical parishes," which were usually, but not necessarily, co-extensive with townships. From the intimate connection in former times between Church and State, it naturally came about that the distinction between the township and the parish was lost sight of, and we find that, from a very early date, the parish was looked upon as the area managing its own affairs in normal cases, although townships which were not co-extensive with parishes continued in many cases to exist independently.

By an important statute of 1601 (*43 Eliz. c. 2*), upon which our modern system of poor law may be said to be based, each parish was directed to maintain its own poor. This statute was somewhat loosely construed, and considered to apply in some cases to places not strictly ecclesiastical parishes, and a subsequent statute[1] expressly extended its operation to townships and other areas in certain cases, and the term parish in dealing with poor-law was extended to include any place separately maintaining its own poor. The term parish being far more frequently employed in this sense than in any other, it has been provided by an Act passed in 1866[2] that in all statutes unless there be something in the context inconsistent therewith, the word "parish" shall, among other meanings applicable to it, signify a place for which a separate poor rate is or can be made, or for which a separate Overseer is, or can be, appointed. Those places which were anciently waste land, or which for other reasons were not included in any township or parish, and which were known as extra-parochial places, have been dealt with by recent statutes, so that, at the present time, the whole country is completely sub-divided into parishes in the sense of the above definition. Where it is necessary expressly to point out that a parish in the above sense and not in any other is meant, the phrase "poor law parish" is used, but as a rule, and in this work, the word parish used alone is always employed to mean "poor law parish."

It may be observed that, under the New Parishes Act, 1856 (*19 & 20 Vict. c. 104*), new ecclesiastical parishes may be constituted for purely ecclesiastical purposes, but such parishes,

[1] 13 & 14 Car. II. c. 12.
[2] The Poor Law Amendment Act, 1866 (*29 & 30 Vict. c. 113*) sec. 18.

which are usually called "new parishes," are of but little importance for civil purposes.

Vestry.

Such local matters as are under the control of the parish are determined, except where the parish is governed by a "select vestry," by the ratepayers of the parish in vestry assembled. A vestry meeting may be called by a notice signed by a Churchwarden, Rector, Vicar, Curate, or Overseer of the parish. At vestry meetings every ratepayer, broadly speaking, is entitled to attend and vote, and the voting, if a poll is demanded, is conducted on the following system. Every ratepayer assessed to the poor rate of the parish in respect of a rateable value of—

		less than	£50	has	one vote	
of	£50	but less than	£75	"	two votes	
"	£75	" "	£100	"	three	"
"	£100	" "	£125	"	four	"
"	£125	" "	£150	"	five	"
"	£150	and over		"	six	"

Some parishes are, however, by custom or statute, governed by a "select vestry," which is a body of limited number elected in accordance with the custom or statute, and transacting all business that in ordinary cases is transacted by the ratepayers in vestry assembled. The powers of a "select vestry" are however in some cases, particularly in the Metropolis, where many parishes are governed in this way, more extensive than the powers of an ordinary vestry. The most important matters with regard to which the parish has any direct power, besides the appointment of certain officers, are :—

1st. The adoption, in certain cases, of Acts of Parliament enabling the parish to undertake works of a public nature, namely :—

The Baths and Wash-houses Acts.
The Burial Acts.
The Lighting and Watching Act.
The Public Libraries Acts.
The Public Improvement Act.

These Acts, when adopted by a parish, are carried out by Inspectors, Boards, or Commissioners, appointed by the parish, or, in certain cases, by the Sanitary Authority.

2nd. Control to a certain extent, in certain cases, of persons and companies proposing to undertake works of a public nature in the parish ; for example, gas and water-works, and tramways.[1]

[1] See the Gas and Waterworks Facilities Act, 1870 (*33 & 34 Vict. c. 70*); the Tramways Act, 1870 (*33 & 34 Vict. c. 78*).

Parish officers. For every parish Overseers of the poor are appointed by the Justices of the Peace; where the parish is an ecclesiastical parish, the Churchwardens are *ex-officio* Overseers in addition to those appointed by the Justices. The Overseers are not in any material matter under the control of the parish, and are unpaid. In certain cases other parish officers are appointed and parish buildings are provided, namely:—

Paid Assistant Overseers.

Paid Collectors of poor rates.

In parishes whose population exceeded 2,000 according to the last census, an Order may be issued by the Local Government Board enabling a paid Vestry Clerk to be appointed, and a vestry room to be provided; and in parishes the population of which, according to the last census, exceeded 4,000, a parish office may be provided.

Poor rate. Formerly each parish provided for its own poor, the Overseers raising the necessary funds by means of the poor rate, and out of these funds maintaining and providing work for the poor. Now, however, with the exception of certain important parishes, under local Acts, and certain parishes which have been organised like unions, the poor relief is managed by Boards of Guardians within "unions," which are groups of parishes. The Overseers, however, continue to raise money in each parish by means of the poor rate. Out of the sum thus raised they pay the establishment charges of the parish, and may distribute poor relief in cases of urgent necessity; but the bulk of the money coming to their hands they hand over to the Guardians of the union and to the various other bodies who are entitled to obtain contributions from the parish out of the poor rate. Besides the poor rate, the Overseers in certain cases raise money by other distinct rates for particular purposes. On the whole the parish is at present important rather as a sub-division of other areas for the purposes of local taxation and other matters, than as an area with any large powers of self-government of its own.

The Local Government Act, 1888, makes no important or extensive change in parishes or parish government.

Unions.

As we have mentioned, parishes have, for poor law purposes been in most cases either grouped into unions or made unions of themselves. We proceed accordingly to give an account of the constitution and government of "Unions."

The system under which each parish maintained its own poor gave rise to great abuses, and in 1834 a Royal Commission was appointed to inquire into the operation of the poor law. The Commissioners recommended a radical change in the principle upon which relief should be granted, and as a means to that end, the establishment of a central authority and the grouping of parishes into larger districts for the administration of the law under a better system of government. In the same year the Poor Law Amendment Act, 1834 (*4 & 5 Will. IV. c. 76*), was passed, carrying out many of their proposals.

Under that Act the Poor Law Commissioners were established as a central authority, and given power to group parishes into unions governed by Boards of Guardians, in whose hands the whole management of the poor relief was placed. Each parish continued, however, to bear almost the whole expense of its paupers. That Act is still in force, but has been much amended.

In the year 1847 the Poor Law Commissioners ceased to exist, and were replaced by the Poor Law Board, who in their turn were succeeded by the Local Government Board, in whose hands the superintendence of poor-law administration now is. Again it was found that great hardships arose owing to the burden of supporting its own poor being cast on so small an area as the parish, and accordingly the Union Chargeability Act, 1865 (*28 & 29 Vict. c. 79*), was passed, rendering the burden of poor relief a charge on the whole union.

Board of Guardians.

At the present time, with the exception of a few unions called when necessary, for distinction, "incorporations," which are under Local Acts, all unions are constituted and governed in the following way:—The union is constituted under an Order made by the Local Government Board, or their predecessors, the Poor Law Commissioners, or the Poor Law Board, and is governed by a Board of Guardians. The ratepayers and owners of every parish in the union elect the number of Guardians allotted to their parish by the Order constituting the union or by a subsequent Order (if any) altering that number. Every occupier of property who is rated to the poor-rate of the parish, and every owner of property rated to the poor-rate in the parish, is entitled to vote in the election of Guardians, and has a number of votes according to the following scale:—[1]

[1] Poor Law Amendment Act, 1844 (*7 & 8 Vict. c. 101*), sec. 14.

If the property was assessed to the last poor rate at a rateable value of—

	less than	£50	he has	one vote
of £50	but less than	£100	„	two votes
„ £100	„	£150	„	three votes
„ £150	„	£200	„	four votes
„ £200	„	£250	„	five votes
„ £250 or over, he has six votes.				

A person may vote both as owner and occupier, even in respect of the same property, so that a person may possibly have, in all, twelve votes. Besides the elected Guardians, those Justices of the Peace who reside in any parish in the union and act for the county in which the same is situated, are *ex-officio* Guardians. The Guardians appoint such officers as are necessary for the management of the union, including always a Clerk and a Treasurer. The principal duty of the Board of Guardians is to relieve the poor of the union, but they have certain other miscellaneous duties, and they also in most cases act in the entirely different capacity of Sanitary Authority.[1]

Income of Board of Guardians.

The income of the Board of Guardians in their poor-law capacity is chiefly derived from contributions paid by the Overseers of each parish in proportion to the rateable value of their parish out of the poor rates. But, in addition, the Board of Guardians receive sums from the Treasury called "grants in aid" in respect of the following matters :—

The maintenance of pauper lunatics.

The salaries of Poor Law Medical Officers and the cost of drugs and medicine.

The salaries of Schoolmasters and Schoolmistresses in poor law schools.

The fees of Registrars of Births and Deaths.

Changes under the Local Government Act.[2]

In the organization and government of unions the Local Government Act, 1888, makes no difference except that provision is made for subdividing unions extending into more than one county for purposes of out-door relief, while leaving them entire for purposes of in-door relief. The financial position of the Guardians is, however, considerably altered.

1st. The grants in aid will be paid by the Treasury, in respect of the financial year ending in March, 1889 ; but after that will cease. The Guardians will, however, receive

---

[1] See *post*, p. 17 *et seq.*

[2] Local Government Act, 1888, secs. 24, 26, 58, 121.

equivalent grants from the County Councils of counties and the Town Councils of county boroughs in which the union is situated, in respect of pauper lunatics, Teachers in poor law schools, and Registrars of Births and Deaths; and also a new grant in respect of the school fees of pauper children sent out from the workhouse to school.

2nd. The Guardians will receive annual contributions from the same Councils, equal to the sum certified by the Local Government Board to have been expended by them during the financial year ending in March, 1888, on the salaries, remuneration, and superannuation allowances of the Officers of the union, and of district schools to which the union contributes, and on drugs and medical appliances.

The effect of this arrangement will be to carry the policy of the Union Chargeability Act, 1865, still further, and throw a part of the expense of poor relief over a still larger area than the union.

The above changes will not take place until after the financial year ending in March, 1889, but the Local Government Act, 1888, provides for the grants in aid for that year being supplemented by a contribution from the probate duty, which is to be distributed by the Local Government Board to the Guardians towards the cost of union officers.

Highway Parish and Highway District.

Highway Parish and Highway District.

We now proceed to give a short account of the Highway Parish and Highway District. Each parish in early times maintained its own highways, and it was held that in the absence of a custom to the contrary this duty fell upon every parish in the strict ecclesiastical sense. But by immemorial custom some townships or analogous districts were bound to maintain their highways independently.

The Highway Act, 1835 (*5 & 6 Will. IV. c. 50*), which was passed to regulate the repair of highways, provided that in every ecclesiastical parish or other area maintaining its own highways, a Surveyor of highways should be appointed, who should see to the repair of highways in his parish or other area. In the majority of parishes and places highways are still maintained under this Act, the expenses being met by means of a highway rate made and levied throughout the parish by the Surveyor.

Other parishes and places which formerly had to maintain their own highways are grouped, under the Highway Acts of 1862 and 1864, (*25 & 26 Vict. c. 61, and 27 & 28 Vict. c. 101*) into "Highway Districts," in which the highways are maintained by "Highway Boards" composed of representatives from the constituent parishes and places called Waywardens. In this case the expenses are defrayed out of a common fund raised by rates levied equally in each constituent parish or place, according to its rateable value. In urban sanitary districts the highways are maintained by the Urban Sanitary Authority.[1]

The name "Highway Parish" has been applied to those parishes and places that maintain their own highways under the Highway Act, 1835, and also to the constituent parishes and places of highway districts. Although highways in highway districts and urban sanitary districts are maintained by the Highway Board or Urban Sanitary Authority, the liability of the parish is not completely extinguished, but still exists to a certain extent.

The Local Government Act, 1888, makes extensive changes in highway law, which are mentioned in Chapter II. In the meantime it will be sufficient to mention that certain important highways called "Main Roads," in respect of which the highway parishes and districts have received grants both from the Treasury and from the Quarter Sessions of the county, will be entirely handed over to the management of the County Councils, and these grants will cease.

Municipal Borough.

Municipal Borough.

The next local area we have to consider is the "Municipal Borough." In early times it became customary to grant charters of incorporation to important towns, whereby rights of self-government were conferred on their inhabitants. In consequence of the great abuses which had arisen in the government of these towns, the Municipal Corporations Act, 1835 (*5 & 6 Will. IV. c. 76*), was passed dealing with the greater number of them, and providing a uniform system for their government. This Act, with various amending Acts, has since been repealed by the Municipal Corporations Act, 1882 (*45 & 46 Vict. c. 50*), under which these towns are now governed. All corporate towns to which that Act applies are called "Municipal Boroughs," and are governed by a Town Council, which consists of—

Town Council.

Councillors, the number of whom depends either upon the charter of the borough or upon a local statute.

[1] See *post*, p. 17 *et seq.*

Aldermen, the number of whom is one-third of the number of elected Councillors.

The Mayor, who is the Chairman of the Council.

The Councillors are elected by the burgesses of the borough, or if the borough is a city, the citizens of the city. Town Councillors are elected either for the whole borough, or if the borough is divided into wards, so many for each ward. The Aldermen and the Mayor are chosen by the whole Council, including the Aldermen in office. Town Councillors hold office for three years, and one-third of their number retire annually; Borough Aldermen hold office for six years, and one-half of their number retire triennially. The Mayor holds office for one year. Should, however, a casual vacancy occur in any of these offices, the person elected to fill the vacancy will go out of office at the same time as the person whose place he takes would have gone out of office.

A Town Council is not itself a corporate body, but the Mayor, Aldermen and Burgesses, or Mayor, Aldermen and Citizens, as the case may be, form a Corporation, and as this Corporation invariably acts through the Council it comes to very much the same thing as if the Town Council itself were a corporate body. The Corporation of the borough has a common seal and perpetual succession; it can hold property (including land), enter into contracts, borrow money, and raise money by means of rates.

The powers and duties of Town Councils differ greatly in different boroughs; in boroughs which have a separate Court of Quarter Sessions (known as "Quarter Sessions Boroughs") they are much more extensive than in others. Some Acts of Parliament have conferred powers on the Councils of those boroughs alone that choose to adopt the Acts, and other differences exist in consequence of local Acts, &c.

In almost all cases the Town Council of the borough act as the Sanitary Authority[1] for the borough, and where this is so there are many matters in which the Town Council may act either in their capacity of Municipal Authority or in their capacity of Sanitary Authority. In which capacity the Town Council should act in any instance must be determined according to the particular circumstances of the case. This distinction is of importance, because property is differently rated in respect of expenses incurred by the Town Council, according to the capacity in which they act.

---

[1] See *post*, p. 17 *et seq*.

We have mentioned that some boroughs have a separate Court of Quarter Sessions; others have a separate Commission of the Peace, but not a Court of Quarter Sessions, and others have neither a separate Court of Quarter Sessions nor a separate Commission of the Peace. In either of the first two cases certain non-judicial duties are, or may be, transacted by the Justices of the borough.

Changes under the Local Government Act.

The Local Government Act, 1888, makes important changes in the powers and duties of Town Councils.

Firstly. All the boroughs which are made county boroughs are almost entirely exempted from the government of the County Council. The Town Councils of these boroughs will continue to transact much the same business as at present; but such business as, in the case of a county, is transferred from the Justices to the County Council, will, if not already transacted by the Town Council, be, in most cases, transferred to them, whether such business is at present transacted by the Justices of the borough or of the county in which the borough is situated.[1] This provision will have the effect of largely increasing the business of the Town Council of a county borough without a separate Court of Quarter Sessions, but will not materially increase the business of the Town Council of a Quarter Sessions Borough.

Secondly. Almost all the business at present transacted in their capacity of Municipal Authority by the Town Council of a borough, the population of which, according to the census of 1881, was under 10,000, is transferred to the County Council.[2] Whether such a borough has a separate Court of Quarter Sessions or not, the following business will be transferred to the County Council, namely:—

Analysts, appointment of.

Contagious Diseases (Animals) Acts, and Destructive Insects Act, 1877, local execution of.

Explosives Act, local execution of.

Gas Meters, superintendence of.

Police Force, maintenance of.[3]

Weights and Measures, superintendence of.

In the case of a Quarter Sessions Borough, the population of which, according to the census of 1881 was under 10,000,

[1] Local Government Act, 1888, sec. 34.

[2] *Ib.* secs. 38, 39.

[3] The county police force will be managed by a Standing Joint Committee of the Quarter Sessions and the County Council, so that the transfer in this case is not strictly to the County Council.

the following additional business will be transferred to the County Council :—

Coroners, appointment of.

Fisheries Acts, powers under.

Locomotives, making bye-laws as to.

Lunatic Asylums, maintenance of.

Reformatory and Iudustrial Schools, maintenance of and contribution to.

Thirdly. If the Justices of a borough (other than a county borough) transact any business that, in the case of a county is transferred to the County Council, such business will be transferred from the Justices of the borough to the County Council. But where the Justices of a borough, the population of which, according to the census of 1881, exceeded 10,000, maintain a lunatic asylum, the maintenance of the asylum is transferred to the Town Council.

Borough Finance

We must now consider the financial position of a borough and the changes made by the Local Government Act in that position. The expenses of a Town Council, in its capacity of Municipal Authority, are defrayed out of the "Borough Fund." The income of the borough which is paid into the borough fund consists—

Of sums derived from the corporate property of the borough.

Of sums derived from the "Borough Rate," which is a rate assessed on all the parishes in the borough, and, as a rule, levied by the Overseers of each parish as part of the poor rate.

Of sums derived from other rates in certain cases.

Of sums received from the Treasury, inluding grants in aid of—

(i.) Police.

(ii.) Criminal prosecutions.

(iii.) The maintenance of lunatics chargeable to the borough.

Other "grants in aid," which are usually payable to the Town Council in its capacity of Sanitary Authority, may in particular cases be payable in relief of the borough fund.

The changes made by the Local Government Act, 1888, in the income of the borough are as follows :—

Changes under Local Government Act.

(1.) In county boroughs the Town Council will receive a share of the income derived from certain imperial taxes,[1] and the above-mentioned grants will be discontinued.

[1] See *post*, Chapter III. and p. 234.

(2.) In those small boroughs from which business is transferred to the County Council there will, of course, be a corresponding lightening of the borough rate. The county rate may, however, be increased.

(3.) In boroughs other than the county boroughs "grants in aid" will no longer be paid by the Treasury, but the Town Council will receive similar grants from the County Council of the county in which the borough is situated.

The Town Council of such a borough, if it has a separate Court of Quarter Sessions or a separate police force, will, in addition to these grants, further receive a share of the surplus (if any) of the proceeds of imperial taxes paid over to the county.[1]

Financial Relation of Counties and Boroughs.

The financial relations between boroughs and the counties in which they are situated remain to be discussed. The present position is as follows:—Boroughs without a separate Court of Quarter Sessions are treated as part of the county, and the county rate is levied in them exactly as in other parts of the county. But arrangements are made whereby their inhabitants are relieved from contributing to the county expenses in respect of the following matters:—

The execution of the Contagious Diseases (Animals) Acts when the Town Council execute these Acts themselves.

The maintenance of the county police when the borough maintains its own police.

Quarter Sessions Boroughs are in most cases liable to contribute to the county expenses to a certain extent. Instead, however, of the county rates being levied within them the sum they are liable to contribute to county expenses is paid over by the Town Council to the Quarter Sessions of the county. All Quarter Sessions Boroughs are liable to contribute their share of the expenses of the county in which they are situated in respect of costs arising out of the prosecution, maintenance, conveyance, transport or punishment of all offenders committed for trial from the borough to the assizes in the county.

Those Quarter Sessions Boroughs which were before the 11th July, 1832, exempt from contributions to the county rate still remain exempt therefrom, except in the case of the expenses above mentioned, but if the boundaries of a Quarter Sessions Borough thus exempt have been enlarged since the

[1] See *post*, Chapter III.

11th July, 1832, the borough is bound to contribute to the county expenses in respect of the area which has been added to the borough. Quarter Sessions Boroughs are, however, exempt from contributions to the county expenses in respect of the following matters, if they themselves transact the business independently :—

Analysts.
Contagious Diseases (Animals) Acts and the Destructive Insects Act, 1877.
Coroners' inquests.
Lunatic Asylums.
Main Roads.
Police Force (if they maintain their own.)
Special Constables.
Weights and Measures.

The principal changes in the financial relations of boroughs and counties made by the Local Government Act, 1888, are as follows :—

Changes under the Local Government Act

First. As to the county boroughs.[1] The Local Government Act, 1888, provides, that an equitable adjustment of financial relations shall be made between each county borough and the county or counties in which such borough is, according to the third Schedule to the Act, situated, by agreement between the Town Council of the borough and the County Council or Councils. In default of agreement the adjustment is to be made by Commissioners appointed under the Act.[2] When this adjustment has been made the existing liabilities of the borough to contribute towards the expenses of the county will cease, and the financial relations between the county and the borough will depend entirely upon the adjustment. In making adjustment regard must be had—

To the existing financial relations between the county and the borough ;

To the shares which the Councils of the borough and the county respectively would have received from those imperial taxes, the proceeds of which are to be handed over to County and Town Councils, if the borough had remained in the county.

To the other considerations set out in the Act.

The adjustment must provide for contribution by the

---

[1] Local Government Act, 1888, sec. 32. [2] *Ib.*, sec. 61.

borough to any expenses which may in the future be incurred by the county on behalf of the borough, particularly in the following cases.

Where separate assizes are not held for the borough the borough must contribute a proper share of the expenses of the assizes of the county.

If the borough is not a Quarter Sessions Borough, the borough must contribute towards the expenses of the Quarter Sessions, Petty Sessions, and Coroners of the county.

Existing arrangements with regard to pauper lunatic asylums are to be continued as far as possible.

The adjustment must provide for the manner in which the Town Council and County Council or Councils are to share in the proceeds of the above-mentioned taxes.

Until such an adjustment has come into operation, a payment must be made by the Town Council to the County Council, or *vice versâ*, based on the average annual amounts which during the three years before the appointed day the Town Council have contributed towards the expenses of the county, and which the Quarter Sessions have expended for the benefit of the borough respectively; but any sum so paid must be taken into account in making the adjustment, which must be made so as to take effect from the appointed day.[1] At any time after the end of five years from the date of an agreement or award making such an adjustment, a new adjustment may be made either by agreement or in default of agreement, by an arbitrator to be appointed by the Local Government Board.

Second. Those boroughs the population of which, according to the census of 1881, was under 10,000, will be liable to contribute towards county expenses in all respects, whether they have separate Courts of Quarter Sessions or not, and whether they are or are not at present exempt from such contributions, and the county rates will be levied in them exactly as in any other part of the county.[2]

Third. In those boroughs, the population of which, according to the census of 1881, was above 10,000, but which are not made county boroughs, the county rates will be levied exactly as in any other part of the county, and the absolute exemption of those Quarter Sessions Boroughs which, before July, 1832, were exempt from contributions to the county rate is done

---

[1] As to the "appointed day," see *post*, p. 33.
[2] Local Government Act, 1888, secs. 38, 39.

away with; but where a Quarter Sessions Borough with such population is wholly or partly exempt from contributing towards the costs incurred for any purpose by the county, the County Council, in assessing the parishes within that borough to county contributions, must give effect to such exemptions with two exceptions.[1]

(1.) Where any business is transferred from the Justices of the borough to the County Council, the borough will be liable to contribute towards the costs of the county in respect of such business.

(2.) Such a borough will be liable to contribute in all cases towards the costs of the county in maintaining main roads.

Sanitary Districts.

The next areas of local government to consider are the "Sanitary Districts," which, unlike parishes and boroughs, are entirely a modern creation of the legislature. Their history is briefly as follows. Sanitary Districts.

With the increase of population the peculiar needs of an urban population became felt in towns and populous places, and the importance of a proper system of drainage and water supply was recognised, and it became usual for boroughs and other places of an urban character to obtain local Acts providing for drainage, lighting, and general improvements in such places. These Acts either conferred the necessary powers on the Town Council where there was one, or created a public body for the purpose of conferring the necessary powers on them. Such bodies received various names, but have of late been called generically Improvement Commissioners. In order to secure a certain degree of uniformity in the government of areas under such local Acts, the Town Police Clauses Act, 1847 (*10 & 11 Vict. c. 89*), was passed, containing a series of provisions that might be incorporated with such Acts, but it was not until 1848 that the first general Act dealing with these matters, namely the Public Health Act, 1848 (*11 & 12 Vict. c. 63*), was passed. That Act first of all set up the Board of Health as a central authority to superintend matters connected with the public health, and then provided that the Board of Health might bring the Act into operation, either on the application of the ratepayers, or, where the death-rate was exceptionally high, without such application, in any borough, parish or other convenient district. Where the Act had been brought into operation it was carried

[1] Local Government Act, 1888, sec. 35.

out by a Local Board, consisting, where the Act was brought into operation in a borough or in a district wholly comprised in a borough, of the Town Council. Where the Act was brought into operation in a district comprising the whole or part of a borough and also places outside the borough, the Local Board consisted of members selected by the Town Council and other members elected for the places outside the borough. In other districts the Local Board consisted of members elected by owners and ratepayers of the district. The Local Boards were invested with powers of various kinds for the preservation of public health and the improvement of their district.

In 1858 the Board of Health ceased to exist and the Local Government Act, 1858 (*21 & 22 Vict. c. 98*), was passed amending the Public Health Act, 1848. That Act provided for the voluntary adoption of the Public Health Act, 1848, as amended by that Act, in various districts, and for the formation, where it was necessary, of a Local Board to carry its provisions out. The Acts were further amended, but no very material change was made in their provisions prior to 1872.

In the mean time another series of Acts had been passed dealing with the Removal of Nuisances. These Acts began with a temporary Act in 1846, and the most important of them was the Nuisances Removal Act, 1855 (*18 & 19 Vict. c. 121*). Various bodies at different times acted as local authorities in carrying out these Acts, but in 1871, the local authorities were Local Boards, Town Councils, Improvement Commissioners and elsewhere generally the Guardians of the poor, but in certain cases other bodies acted.

Again, the Sewage Utilization Act, 1865 (*28 & 29 Vict. c. 15*), enabled certain bodies to act as "Sewer Authorities," with powers connected with drainage. This Act was subsequently amended, and in 1871 the following bodies acted as Sewer Authorities, namely, Local Boards, Improvement Commissioners, Town Councils, and Parish Vestries; thus in 1871 the laws dealing with public health were of extreme complexity.

Firstly. There was no supreme central authority, but the Home Office, the Poor Law Board, and the Privy Council had different powers allotted to them, on no very clear principle, for dealing with the matter.

Secondly. There were a number of local authorities, many of them acting in different capacities under different Acts, and for districts the boundaries of which frequently intersected.

Accordingly, as a first step towards simplification, the Local Government Board was constituted by the Local Government Board Act, 1871 (*34 & 35 Vict. c. 70*), as a central authority to superintend both the working of the poor law and the laws relating to public health and local government; and then by the Public Health Act, 1872 (*35 & 36 Vict. c. 79*), a uniform system of local government was provided for the purposes of the various Acts connected with public health. This system is still in force, but not under the Public Health Act, 1872; for three years later all the above-mentioned Acts and the various Acts amending them were repealed by a consolidation statute, namely, the Public Health Act, 1875 (*38 & 39 Vict. c. 55*), since the passing of which measure few amendments have been made in the law of public health. Under that Act the whole of England and Wales, with the exception of the Metropolis, is divided into "Sanitary Districts" of two kinds, Urban Sanitary Districts and Rural Sanitary Districts, each governed by a body called the Sanitary Authority.

Urban Sanitary Districts.

Urban sanitary districts are of three kinds.

1st. Municipal Boroughs, the Town Council being the Sanitary Authority.

2nd. "Improvement Act Districts," that is to say, areas for the time being subject to the jurisdiction of any Commissioners, Trustees, or other persons invested by any Local Act with powers of town government and rating; the Commissioners, &c., being the Sanitary Authority.

3rd. Local Government Districts. These are districts subject to the jurisdiction of a Local Board constituted in pursuance of the Local Government Acts,[1] before the passing of the Public Health Act, 1875; or in pursuance of that Act; the Local Board being the Sanitary Authority.

It is provided by the Public Health Act, 1875, that the boroughs of Oxford, Cambridge, Blandford, Calne, Wenlock, Folkestone, and Newport (Isle of Wight), are not for the purpose of that Act to be deemed boroughs. Moreover it was pro-

---

[1] The Local Government Acts are—
The Public Health Act, 1848 (*11 & 12 Vict. c. 63*).
The Local Government Act, 1858 (*21 & 22 Vict. c. 98*).
The Local Government Act (1858) Amendment Act, 1861 (*24 & 25 Vict. c. 61*); and
The Local Government Act Amendment Act, 1863 (*26 & 27 Vict. c. 17*).

vided that where a borough was at the passing of that Act wholly included in a local government district, or in an improvement act district, it should be absorbed for the purposes of that Act in the larger district, and that the Local Board or Improvement Commissioners, as the case might be, should be the Sanitary Authority, so that in a few cases the Town Council of a borough does not act as Sanitary Authority for the borough.

Rural Sanitary districts.

Every union or parish under a Board of Guardians, less so much as is comprised in urban sanitary districts, is a "Rural Sanitary District." The Rural Sanitary Authority is the Board of Guardians, but *ex-officio* Guardians resident in, and elected Guardians elected for, parishes in urban districts, have no vote on matters connected with the business of the Board in its capacity of Sanitary Authority.

The Local Government Board have very full powers of dividing and altering the boundaries of local government districts and of constituting new local government districts. In some cases they can only exercise their powers by Provisional Order, requiring confirmation by Parliament, and in certain other cases they may exercise their power by an Order absolute in the first instance.[1]

Constitution of Sanitary Authority.

With regard to the constitution of the different Sanitary Authorities—

1st. We have already briefly explained the constitution of a Town Council.[2]

2nd. Improvement Commissioners are of course appointed or elected in accordance with the local Act.

3rd. Members of a Local Board are elected by the ratepayers and owners of the district voting in proportion to the rateable value of their property and on the same scale as ratepayers and owners in a parish vote in the election of Guardians of the poor.[3]

4th. The constitution of a board of Guardians which we have already explained.[4]

Business of Sanitary Authority.

The business with which a Sanitary Authority have to deal comprises the following matters under the Public Health Act, 1875, and amending Acts:—

Sewerage and Drainage.

Scavenging and Cleansing.

---

[1] See the Public Health Act, 1875, Part VIII.

[2] See *ante*, p. 10. [3] See *ante*, p. 8. [4] See *ante*, p. 7.

Water Supply.
Regulation of Cellar Dwellings and Lodging-houses.
Nuisances.
Noxious Trades.
Diseased Meat.
Infectious Diseases.
Hospitals for Infectious Diseases.
Highways and Streets.
Lighting.
Public Pleasure Grounds.
Markets.
Slaughter-houses.

Sanitary Authorities have in certain cases powers under various other Acts, *e.g.* :—

The Allotments Act.
The Artizans' Dwellings Acts.
The Baths and Wash-houses Acts.
The Burial Acts.
The Labouring Classes Lodging-houses Acts.
The Public Libraries Acts.
The Sale of Food and Drugs Act.

Expenses of Urban Sanitary Authority.

The expenses of Urban Sanitary Authorities are met—

(1.) By the income of their property and undertakings.
(2.) By rates, of which the most important are "General District Rates," "Highway Rates" and "Private Improvement Rates."

General district rates are rates levied to meet the ordinary expenditure of the Sanitary Authority which is not otherwise provided for. They are assessed by the Sanitary Authority on all property in their district rateable to the poor rate, according to its rateable value, but arable land and some other descriptions of property are assessed at only one-quarter of the rateable value of the property for the purposes of the poor rate. Highway rates are levied in certain cases only; the repairs of highways being generally defrayed out of general district rates; if levied they are made, assessed, and levied by the Sanitary Authority in the same way as a rate made by the Surveyor of a highway parish, and the above-mentioned exemption does not apply. Private improvement rates are levied to defray expenses which, under the Public Health Act, 1875, are, or may be declared, private improvement expenses. These are expenses incurred by the Sanitary Authority for the benefit of particular property or persons, as, for example, in paving a private street. They are payable only by the occupiers of the property affected.

(3.) By grants in aid made by the Treasury.

These grants in aid are in respect of main roads, and salaries of Medical Officers of Health and Inspectors of Nuisances.

Expenses of Rural Sanitary Authority.

The expenses of a Rural Sanitary Authority are met—

(1.) By income derived from their property and undertakings.

(2.) By rates chiefly of three kinds, namely, a rate levied to meet "General Expenses," rates levied to meet "Special Expenses," and "Private Improvement Rates."

General expenses are the establishment charges, &c., and other expenses not otherwise provided for, and the rate to meet general expenses is made and assessed by the Sanitary Authority on the parishes and other contributory places in their district according to their rateable value, and levied by the Overseers as part of the poor rate. Special Expenses are the expenses declared by the Public Health Act, 1875, or otherwise, to be special expenses. Rates to meet special expenses may be levied over the whole district or over particular parishes and contributory places only. They are assessed according to the rateable value of the property, but arable land and certain other kinds of property are assessed at one-quarter of their value only. They are levied by the Overseers as a separate rate. Private improvement rates are made and levied by a Rural Sanitary Authority in the same way as by an Urban Sanitary Authority.

(3.) By "grants in aid" made by the Treasury. These grants are the same as those made to Urban Sanitary Authorities, except that, as a rule, a Rural Sanitary Authority does not maintain main roads, and accordingly receives no grant in aid in respect of main roads.

Changes under the Local Government Act.[1]

The following are the principal changes made by the Local Government Act, 1888, with regard to sanitary districts and Sanitary Authorities.

Firstly. Wherever the Town Council of a borough is not the Urban Sanitary Authority for their borough, the Local Government Board are to deal with the case by Pro-

[1] Local Government Act, 1888, secs. 24, 52.

visional Order, so that in future the Town Council shall be the Sanitary Authority for their borough. The Order may involve alterations of boundaries.

Secondly. The "grants in aid" will cease to be paid by the Treasury, but the Sanitary Authority will receive equivalent grants, except for main roads, from the County Council of the county in which the sanitary district is situated.

Thirdly. A Sanitary Authority other than the Town Council of a borough with a separate Court of Quarter Sessions or a separate police force, may share in the ultimate surplus of the proceeds of the imperial taxes paid over to the county; but it is probable that these sums will be entirely absorbed in payments which must be made before any surplus is divisible between the Sanitary Authorities.

County.

County.

We have already explained briefly the nature of the County Council that is to be established in each county. It remains to give a sketch of the existing arrangements for local government in counties. The word county is a term of which it is impossible to give any satisfactory definition.

England and Wales comprises fifty-two counties in the ordinary sense of the word. These counties have existed from very early times, and their boundaries are for the most part matters of tradition. Now in addition to these counties certain cities and towns have been by charter or statute made counties of themselves. These cities and towns are, besides the City of London in the Metropolis, the cities of Bristol, Canterbury, Chester, Exeter, Gloucester, Lichfield, Lincoln, Newcastle-upon-Tyne, Norwich, Worcester, and York, and the towns of Berwick-upon-Tweed, Carmarthen, Haverfordwest, Kingston-upon-Hull, Nottingham, Poole, and Southampton. But these counties of cities and towns, which are also called counties corporate, are for some purposes considered as being part of the counties, ordinarily so called, in which they are situated. And this is the case universally for the purposes of parliamentary representation, for which purpose, therefore, the whole country is mapped out into these fifty-two counties.

Quarter Sessions

The local government of each county is at present in the hands of the Justices of the Peace, appointed by a Commission of the Peace for the county, in accordance with a practice that can be traced back to the fourteenth century.

The Commission of the Peace gives the Justices power, in general terms, to keep the peace in the county, &c., and secondly, gives any two or more Justices authority—

To inquire by jury of all offences within the bounds of the Commission;

To inspect all indictments;

To grant out process against offenders;

To hear and try all such offences when the offenders are before them;

To give judgment and inflict penalties.

The jurisdiction of the Justices of the Peace for a county is exercised partly out of Sessions, or in Petty Sessions, and partly in Quarter Sessions, which are public sessions of the Justices held quarterly.

The jurisdiction conferred on the Justices by their Commission is as we see entirely criminal; but it very early became usual in statutes to confer jurisdiction on the Justices of a civil nature, partly judicial and partly administrative; the administrative jurisdiction being generally given to the justices in Quarter Sessions assembled. Thus the jurisdiction of the Quarter Sessions is of three kinds.

(i.) Criminal jurisdiction conferred on them, by their Commission, which is beyond our province.

(ii.) Original civil and administrative jurisdiction, which comprises many matters, all of which have been conferred on them by various statutes, there being no mention of civil matters in the Commission.

(iii.) Appellate jurisdiction, which is also entirely conferred on them by statutes.

It now becomes necessary to inquire into the local extent of the jurisdiction of the Quarter Sessions of each county.

We must first point out that Yorkshire is divided into three ridings and Lincolnshire into three divisions, namely, the "parts" of Kesteven, Lindsey, and Holland, into each of which ridings and divisions a separate Commission of the Peace issues. Each of these ridings and divisions is thus, for the purposes of local government, very much in the position of an independent county, and we may, using a phrase which has been somewhat vaguely employed, call each of the remaining fifty counties, and each of these ridings and divisions, a "County at Large."

By the Commission of the Peace issuing into each county at large, Justices are appointed for the whole county; it has, however, always been a prerogative of the Crown to grant a Commission of the Peace for a smaller district within a county, either directly, or by charter, conferring on such a place the right to elect Justices. Where Justices are appointed for any such place, the Justices of the county will not as a rule be prevented from acting within it, except the Commission of the Peace or charter for that place contains express words restraining the Justices for the county from acting. However, the Justices for the county seem to be restrained from acting in certain of the more important of such places by custom alone. These places with a separate Commission of the Peace are known as liberties or franchises. They are of two classes.

1st. Certain liberties into which a Commission of the Peace always issues, and where there is accordingly a separate Quarter Sessions. Such are the Isle of Ely, the Liberty of Ripon in the West Riding of Yorkshire, and the Soke of Peterborough. In such liberties the Justices of the county at large can only exercise powers by virtue of express words in a statute.

2nd. Liberties which are so by charter. The most important class of these liberties are the corporate towns to which a separate commission of the Peace is granted by Charter.

The question of the jurisdiction of the Quarter Sessions of the county within an old corporate town not under the Municipal Corporations Act, 1882, still depends on the charter of the town.

Within a municipal borough, with a separate Court of Quarter Sessions, the Justices for the county have no jurisdiction by virtue of their Commission.

With regard, however, to the administrative business of the Quarter Sessions, as these powers are conferred by statute, the statutes generally lay down the local extent of the jurisdiction in each matter, but where the statute is silent the jurisdiction of the Quarter Sessions will be co-extensive with their jurisdiction by virtue of their Commission. For some purposes the jurisdiction of the Quarter Sessions is excluded in all boroughs, the Town Council exercising the corresponding jurisdiction within their borough. On the other hand, for many purposes, Liberties, other than Quarter Sessions Boroughs, are included in the counties in which they are situated. Moreover, for some purposes the boundaries of the county are expressly altered, and accordingly in almost every set of statutes dealing with local government the term "county" has received a special definition, and that definition has to be kept carefully in view in reading the statute.

Changes under Local Government Act.

As we have seen, under the Local Government Act, 1888, a County Council is to be established for each county at large, and also for the Isle of Ely, and for the Soke of Peterborough, which are such important liberties that they have in many statutes been treated as counties at large. Moreover, Sussex and Suffolk, which although having but one Commission of the Peace, are divided into two divisions for many purposes, are each to be treated as two counties.

We are now in a position to explain the meaning of certain expressions employed in the Local Government Act, 1888, and to give an account of the changes in county boundaries made under that Act.

The area for which a County Council is elected, and throughout which, generally speaking, the Council will have authority, is called an "administrative county."

The six counties of Yorkshire, Lincolnshire, Cambridgeshire, Northamptonshire, Suffolk, and Sussex each comprise, as we have seen, more than one administrative county. The area, consisting of all the administrative counties taken together in each one of these six counties, is termed an "entire county."

The boundaries of the administrative county of London will be the boundaries of the Metropolis, as laid down in the Metropolis Management Act, 1855 (*18 & 19 Vict. c. 120*), and this provision of course determines the boundaries of the administrative counties of Middlesex, Surrey, and Kent, where they adjoin the administrative county of London.

Elsewhere the boundaries of each administrative county will be the present boundaries of the county for the purpose of returning members to Parliament, subject, however, to the following provisions and exceptions:—

(i.) The county boroughs do not form part of any administrative county.

(ii.) Where any urban sanitary district, other than a county borough, is situated partly within and partly without the parliamentary boundaries of a county, the district is to become part of the administrative county which contains the largest portion of its population, according to the census of 1881.

(iii.) Where two administrative counties which form portions of one entire county adjoin, the boundary as existing for the county rate is to be the boundary; but if an urban sanitary district lies partly without and partly within the boundaries of such a portion, the district is to become part of the administrative county which contains the largest portion of its population, according to the census of 1881.

(iv.) The wapentake of the ainsty of York (except so much as is included in the municipal borough of York as extended by the York Extension and Improvement Act, 1884) is to become part of the administrative county of the West Riding of Yorkshire.

(v.) The Scilly Islands will not form part of the administrative county of Cornwall. The Local Government Board have power, by Provisional Order, to arrange for the local government of these Islands; but until that is done the County Council of Cornwall will exercise certain powers within them.

(vi.) Subsequent changes may be made, which are explained in Chapter IV.

Thus the whole of England and Wales, including the Metropolis, will be mapped out, subject to any future alterations, into sixty-one administrative counties and sixty-one county boroughs; all existing liberties, franchises, counties of towns and counties of cities will be either in one of these counties, or themselves an administrative county or county borough.

It may be pointed out that the county is an area of importance for other purposes besides that of local government, and the Local Government Act, 1888, makes provisions for the effect of a change in county boundaries, made by or in pursuance of that Act, on the county for other purposes.[1]

The County Council will transact most of the administrative business at present transacted by the Quarter Sessions of their county, and other county business, but the local extent of their authority will not be the same as that of the Quarter Sessions to whom they succeed, for it will extend throughout their administrative county in almost all cases, except within boroughs where the Town Council exercises the corresponding authority. Further, liberties and franchises will be for the purposes of the County Council in the county in which they are situated, and the County Council will succeed to the

---

[1] Local Government Act, 1888, sec. 59.

authority of their Quarter Sessions as they succeed to that of the Quarter Sessions of the county.

The transfer of business to the County Council from the various authorities whom they succeed, is explained in Chapter II. and the business which they will, when fully constituted, have to transact is more fully dealt with in Chapter V. The finance of a County Council is explained in Chapter III. In the meantime it may be well to give a general idea of the financial position of the County Council, as compared with that of the Quarter Sessions.

Financial effect of Local Government Act.

The expenses of the Quarter Sessions are chiefly met by rates and by contributions from other local authorities, but they have received, from the Treasury, grants in aid of the police force, the costs of criminal prosecutions, the maintenance of pauper lunatics chargeable to the county, and the maintenance of main roads.

County Councils will receive no grants in aid, properly so called, but, with the Town Councils of county boroughs, will share in the proceeds of certain imperial taxes. Out of the sums thus coming to their hands they must first make grants to Boards of Guardians, to Town Councils of boroughs, other than county boroughs, and to Sanitary Authorities, in substitution for the grants in aid which will cease to be paid, and also pay a share of their own expenses in connection with their police force, and other purposes for which grants have hitherto been received from the Treasury. Secondly, they must pay the new grant we have mentioned towards the costs of union Officers.[1] Out of the surplus they must pay certain of their expenses, of which the chief will be the maintenance of main roads, and then the ultimate surplus will be divided between the County Council and certain other local authorities.

The share of the proceeds of imperial taxes, which will in this way find its way into the hands of local authorities of various kinds, will, it is estimated, exceed the sums hitherto distributed among them in the shape of grants in aid (excluding the additional grant in aid to Quarter Sessions in respect of main roads, made during the year 1887-88) by about £3,000,000 annually, the effect of which will be, it is estimated, to lighten local rates throughout the country by about 5d. in the pound on an average. The consideration of the Excise Duties (Local Purposes) Bill, by which it is proposed to levy

---

[1] See *ante*, p.

the taxes popularly known as the Horse and Wheel Tax, have been postponed to the autumn session. Should that Bill not pass, the amount to be distributed will be reduced by the amount of these taxes, which, it is estimated, would produce about £800,000 annually, and in that case the rates would, on the same basis, be lightened by about 3½d. in the pound.

Thus we see that the Local Government Act, 1888, not only effects a great reform in the direction of rendering the governing authority in the county representative of the ratepayers, but that it will also considerably alter the incidence of taxation, distributing the burden of local expenses to a greater extent than in the past, upon the whole country.

There are a few other matters that may be mentioned in conclusion.

First, under various general Acts of Parliament there are in existence the following bodies empowered to carry out works of a public nature, and to rate the area under their control for that purpose :—

Burial Boards.

Lighting and Watching Inspectors.

Commissioners of Baths and Wash-houses.

Commissioners under the Public Libraries Acts.

Secondly, under the Elementary Education Acts, the country is divided into school districts, namely :—

The Metropolis.

Municipal Boroughs except Oxford.

The District of the Local Board of Oxford.

Parishes not included in any of the above mentioned districts.

Special adjustments of the boundaries of these areas may, however, be made for the purposes of the Education Acts, so that a school district is to a certain extent an independent area. For each school district a School Board is or may be appointed ; no change in school districts or School Boards is contemplated under the Local Government Act, 1888.

In some counties there exist old sub-divisions called Hundreds, or in some counties Wapentakes. In Sussex the hundreds are grouped into larger divisions called Rapes, and in Kent the hundreds are grouped into larger divisions called Lathes. All these divisions, at one time of great importance, have ceased to exist for any practical purpose except the maintenance in some cases of bridges and certain roads. Even where they so maintain bridges and roads they have no organization for the purpose, but special rates are levied on them for that purpose, by the Quarter Sessions of the County, and these rates will continue to be so levied by the County Councils.

CHAPTER II.

PROCEEDINGS OF THE FIRST COUNTY COUNCIL.

In the foregoing chapter the general constitution of a County Council has been explained.

Leaving for the present the details of the proceedings prior to and at elections of Councillors, we propose to give a short account of the proceedings of the first County Council elected in each county, showing the steps that must be taken to bring the Council into working order, and also how the business which the County Council will have to transact will be transferred to them from the various bodies whom they succeed.

In order to make this clear, it will in certain cases be necessary to go shortly into the history of the legislation connected with the business transferred. The law connected with the various subjects, and the powers that the County Council will have, when fully constituted, will be found in Chapter V.

First Election of County Councillors.

The first election of Councillors for each county will take place in January, 1889, not earlier than the 14th; the day being fixed in each case by the Returning Officer.[1] The Councillors must hold their first meeting on the second Thursday next after the day of election. Before proceeding to transact any business each Councillor must make the declaration accepting office required by the Municipal Corporations Act, 1882.[2] This declaration a Councillor may make before any two other Councillors, who may act in administering it before they have made their own. The Councillors will not enter upon their ordinary duties until a subsequent period;

---

[1] Local Government Act, 1888, sec. 103. As to Returning Officers, see p. 209.

[2] See Municipal Corporations Act, 1882, Eighth Schedule; *post*, p. 353.

but in the meantime they will, with the Aldermen and Chairman they elect, act as a Provisional Council.[1]

Proceedings at the First Meeting of a County Council.

At their first meeting the Councillors must elect one of their number to be Chairman of that and of the second meeting, and at the first meeting, or at some adjournment thereof, they must proceed to the election of the first County Aldermen in the same manner as if they were a fully constituted County Council.[2] Each Councillor, including the Chairman of the meeting, may vote for any number of persons not exceeding the number of Aldermen to be elected by signing and delivering, at the meeting, to the Chairman, a voting paper, containing the full names, places of abode, and descriptions of the persons for whom he votes. The Chairman of the meeting, as soon as the voting papers have been delivered to him, must openly produce and read them, or cause them to be read, and the persons, not exceeding in number the Aldermen to be elected, who have the greatest number of votes, must forthwith be declared by the Chairman to be elected. In the case of an equality of votes, the Chairman has a second or casting vote. One half of the County Aldermen so elected at that meeting will retire on the 7th November, 1891, and the remaining half on the 7th November, 1894. The half who are to retire in 1891 must be determined by the Councillors at the time of the election of the Aldermen. If the total number of Aldermen is not divisible by two, the larger half must retire in 1891.[3] The County Aldermen so elected will be summoned to attend at the second and subsequent meetings of the Council, but before acting must make the declaration above mentioned, accepting office.

Election of permanent Chairman.

At the second meeting, or some adjournment thereof, the provisional Council must elect a permanent Chairman, who will also be Chairman of the County Council after the Council enters upon its ordinary duties, and will retire on the 7th November, 1889. The Provisional Council may also at any time appoint one of their members Vice-chairman; the member of the Council so appointed will also be Vice-chairman of the County Council when fully constituted.[4]

Business of Provisional Council.

The Provisional Council will conduct business in the same way as a fully constituted County Council. Their acts may be signified under the hand of the Chairman

---

[1] Local Government Act, 1888, sec. 105.
[2] See *post*, p.
[3] Local Government Act, 1888, secs. 104, 105.
[4] *Ib.*, sec. 105.

and any two Councillors present at the meeting, and countersigned by the Officer acting as their Clerk. The Provisional Council will be entitled to the use of the buildings belonging to the Quarter Sessions of their County, provided that they do not interfere with the holding of any Court. They may also hire buildings for the transaction of their business. The Clerk of the Peace and his officers, and the officers of the Quarter Sessions, must, if required, act as officers of the Provisional Council, who may also appoint such interim officers as they may think necessary. The Provisional Council will have the same powers of levying contributions for the purposes of their costs and for the future costs of the County Council, as if they were a fully constituted County Council.[1]

The Provisional Council must make the necessary arrangements for bringing the Local Government Act, 1888, into full operation, and the Quarter Sessions of every county and liberty must assist the Provisional Council in making the necessary arrangements.[2]

Appointed day.

The Provisional Council will become a fully-constituted County Council on the "Appointed Day," and on that day must hold their first meeting as County Council, which meeting will be convened by the Chairman of the Provisional Council. The appointed day will in most cases be the 1st April, 1889. The Local Government Board may, however, appoint any other day for any county, either earlier or later. On the appointed day, the business which the County Council will have to transact will be actually transferred to them; but the Local Government Board may fix another day for the transfer of any particular business, and the day so fixed is called the appointed day, in connection with that business. After the election of County Councillors for any county, the Local Government Board must not alter the appointed day, except on the application of the Provisional Council, or, after the general appointed day, of the County Council.[3]

Committees.

A County Council has power to appoint committees, and to join with other authorities in the appointment of joint committees. As a preparation for the actual transfer of business, it will be necessary for every Provisional Council to join with the Quarter Sessions of the county in the appointment of a "Standing Joint Committee," for the purpose of taking over the management of the police, and other matters. This Committee

[1] Local Government Act, 1888, sec. 106. [2] *Ib.*, sec. 106. [3] *Ib.*, secs. 107, 109.

must consist of an equal number of Justices appointed by the Quarter Sessions, and of members of the County Council, appointed by the Council.[1] In Yorkshire, Lincolnshire, Cambridgeshire, Northamptonshire, Suffolk and Sussex it will also be necessary for the Provisional Councils of the administrative counties, into which these entire counties are divided, to join in the appointment, in each case, of a Joint Committee to take over the management of certain affairs affecting the entire county.[1] The Joint Committees thus appointed for Yorkshire and Lincolnshire will be called respectively the York and Lincoln County Committees, and will be bodies corporate with a common seal and perpetual succession.[2]

It is proposed to deal with the transfer of each description of business separately and in order, but before doing so it will be necessary to recapitulate shortly some matters which we have already explained in Chapter I., with regard to the authorities from whom business will be transferred, and also to explain the general provisions of the Local Government Act, 1888, with regard to the transfer.

Local extent of authority of a County Council.

Where the Quarter Sessions of a county have jurisdiction in any administrative matter, the area over which their jurisdiction extends depends on the exact words of the statute conferring the jurisdiction. Where business is transferred from the Quarter Sessions of a county to the County Council, the area over which the County Council will have authority will, in most cases, not be identical with the area over which the jurisdiction of the Quarter Sessions of the county, with regard to that business, extended; but the area will be changed owing to the following provisions:—

1st. Where the corresponding business in a liberty is exercised by the Quarter Sessions of that liberty the authority of the County Council of the county in which the liberty is situated will extend throughout the liberty.[3]

2nd. Where the corresponding business in a county borough is transacted by the Justices either of the borough or of the county or liberty in which the borough is situated, that business will be, with certain exceptions, transferred to the Town Council of the borough.[4]

3rd. Where the corresponding business in a borough other than a county borough is transacted by the Justices of the borough, that business will be transferred to the County Council. Any business in connection with lunatic asylums,

---

[1] See *post*, p. 109. [2] Local Government Act, 1888, sec. 64. [3] *Ib.*, sec. 48.
[4] *Ib.*, sec. 34.

however, that is transacted by the Justices of a Quarter Sessions Borough, the population of which, according to the census of 1881, was above 10,000, will be transferred to the Town Council and not to the County Council.[1]

4th. Where the corresponding business in a borough the population of which, according to the census of 1881, was under 10,000, is transacted by the Town Council, that business also is, in almost all cases, transferred to the County Council.[2]

5th. The area over which the authority of the County Council will extend will also differ from the area over which the authority of the Quarter Sessions extends, owing to alterations in the county boundaries.

When we come to take each item of business transferred to the County Councils in order, it will be necessary to inquire to what authorities the County Council really succeeds, with regard to that business. In the meantime the following are the general provisions of the Local Government Act, 1888, with regard to the transfer of business, and with regard to the transfer of property, liabilities, and officers incidental to that transfer.

Transfer of business.

If any question arises, or is about to arise, as to whether any business, power, duty or liability is or is not transferred to any County Council or Joint Committee under the Local Government Act, 1888, that question may, on the application of a Chairman of Quarter Sessions, or of a County Council, Committee, or other local authority concerned, be submitted for decision to the High Court in a summary manner.[3]

The Local Government Board, on the application of a Provisional Council or a County Council, may within six months after the day fixed for the first election of the Councillors of such Council, from time to time, make such Orders as appear to them necessary for bringing the Local Government Act, 1888, into full operation as respects the Council so applying. Such Orders may modify any provisions in that Act, or in any other Act, whether general or local and personal, so far as may appear to the Board necessary for the purpose.[4]

Adustment of property, liabilities, &c.[5]

County Councils and other authorities affected by or in consequence of the Local Government Act, 1888, may make agreements for the purpose of adjusting any property, income, debts or liabilities of such authorities affected by or in conse-

[1] Local Government Act, 1888, sec. 36. [2] *Ib.*, secs. 38, 39. [3] *Ib.*, sec. 29. [4] *Ib.*, sec. 108. [5] *Ib.*, sec. 62.

quence of the Act. Such an agreement may provide for the adjustment in the fullest manner.

In default of agreement, recourse may be had, if no other means of affecting the adjustment is provided, to arbitration, and if the parties cannot agree upon the Arbitrator, he may be appointed by the Local Government Board.

When a sum is required to be paid by a County or Town Council for the purposes of such an adjustment, it may be paid out of the county or borough fund, or out of such special fund as the Council, with the approval of the Commissioners appointed under the Act, or of the Local Government Board, may direct. Money may be borrowed by a County or Town Council for the payment of a capital sum required to be paid for the purposes of such an adjustment, without the consent of the Treasury, or any other authority; but it must be repaid within such period as the Local Government Board may sanction.

Adjustment between Kent, Middlesex, Surrey, and the Metropolis.[1]

The property, debts, and liabilities of the counties of Kent, Middlesex, and Surrey must be apportioned between the portions of these counties within the Metropolis, and the portions without the Metropolis, by agreement between the respective County Councils; or, in default of agreement, by the Commissioners appointed under the Local Government Act, 1888. The property, debts, and liabilities apportioned to the portions within the Metropolis will become the property, debts, and liabilities of the whole of the administrative county of London.

Transfer of property from Quarter Sessions.[2]

Subject to what has been said, all property held for any public uses and purposes of a county, liberty, or division of a county will, on the appointed day, vest in the County Council. This includes property held by the Quarter Sessions or any Justice or Justices, or by the Clerk of the Peace or the Treasurer, or by Commissioners. The property will be held for the same estate and subject to the same conditions and restrictions as before the transfer.

Property held by the Justices of the counties of York or Lincoln in Gaol Sessions, or by Commissioners appointed by the Justices, will be transferred to the County Committee, in the same way as if such property were held by Quarter Sessions, and the County Committee were a County Council.

The existing records of, or in custody of, the Quarter Sessions will remain in the same custody as before the transfer, and in Suffolk and Sussex such records will continue to be kept in

---

[1] Local Government Act, 1888, sec 40. [2] *Ib.*, sec. 64.

the custody of the Clerk of the Peace of East Suffolk and East Sussex respectively. Such of the records of the county of Surrey as were at the passing of the Local Government Act, 1888, in the custody of the Clerk of the Peace at Newington, will continue in his custody at Newington.[1]

The Justices of a county also may retain any pictures, chattels or property, on the ground that they have been presented to them or purchased out of their own funds, or otherwise belong to them, and are not held for the public purposes of the county. If any difference arise between the County Council and the Justices, with regard to such retention, it must be referred to the Commissioners appointed under the Local Government Act, 1888, and determined by them.

The Act does not affect property belonging to a charity, and, until the Charity Commissioners otherwise determine, the trustees or managers of a charity are to be appointed in the same way as heretofore.

Property of Borough Justices.

Property held by the Justices of a borough in connection with business transferred from them to a County Council, will not pass to the County Council, but an agreement can be come to with the County Council, or the property might be dealt with for the benefit of the borough.

Property of a Town Council.

Property held by the Town Council of a borough in connection with transferred business, will not pass to the County Council, but an agreement can be come to with the County Council, or the Town Council might deal with such property for the benefit of the borough fund.

Transfer of liabilities.[2]

All debts and liabilities incurred for the purposes of a county or liberty in a county will become debts and liabilities of the County Council. This provision applies equally to debts and liabilities incurred by the Quarter Sessions, the Clerk of the Peace, any Justice or Justices of the county, the Treasurer, or any Commissioners for county purposes. Debts and liabilities of the Justices of the Counties of York or Lincoln in Gaol Sessions, or of Commissioners, will be transferred to the County Committee, in the same way as if they were debts and liabilities of Quarter Sessions, and the County Committee were a County Council.

Liabilities of a borough.[3]

With regard to the liabilities of a Town Council or the Justices of a borough, incurred in respect of business that is

---

[1] Local Government Act, 1888, secs. 83, 118. [2] *Ib.*, sec. 64.
[3] *Ib.*, secs. 35, 36, 38, 39, 122, 124.

transferred, there is some difficulty. The effect of the Act seems to be as follows:—

An existing contract that is wholly executory will be transferred to the County Council, who may enforce it, and against whom it may be enforced. The County Council will meet their liability under such a contract out of the county fund.

A debt that is due from the Justices or Town Council will be enforceable against the County Council, but the funds to meet it must be obtained from the borough, and for this purpose the County Council could either come to an agreement with the Justices or Town Council or, if necessary, levy a rate in the borough for the express purpose of paying the debt.

A continuing contract partly executed and partly executory must be apportioned. The liability of the Justices or Town Council under the part of the contract wholly executed must be treated as a debt due from the Town Council, and that under the executory part of the contract will be treated as an executory contract entered into by the Justices or Town Council.

Existing officers.[1]

Persons who are on the appointed day officers of the Quarter Sessions, or of the Justices of the county, or any committee of the Justices, and who perform duties in respect of business transferred to the County Council, will become officers of the County Council. Such officers are called in the Local Government Act, 1888, "Existing Officers." Such existing officers will hold office by the same tenure, and upon the same conditions as heretofore; and while performing the same duties, must receive not less salaries and be entitled to not less pensions (if any) than they would have been if the Act had not been passed.

The County Council may distribute the business to be performed by such existing officers as they think fit, and may also abolish the office of any existing officer whose office they deem unnecessary.

Every existing officer whose office is abolished, or who under or in consequence of the Local Government Act, 1888, suffers any direct pecuniary loss by abolition of office, or by diminution or loss of fees or salary, is entitled to be paid compensation by the County Council to whom the powers of the authority, whose officer he was, are transferred; whether such officer is expressly mentioned in the Act or not.

[1] Local Government Act, 1888, secs. 118-120.

In determining the amount of compensation regard must be had to all the circumstances of the case, and in particular to the conditions on which the officer's appointment was made, to the nature of his office, to the duration of his service, to any additional emoluments which he acquires under or in consequence of the Local Government Act, 1888, and to any emoluments which he might have acquired if he had not refused to accept any office offered by any Council or other body acting under the Act. The compensation must not exceed the amount which under the Acts and rules relating to the Civil Service is paid to a person on abolition of office.[1]

An officer entitled to compensation must deliver to the County Council a claim signed by him, which must state the whole amount received and expended by him or his predecessors in office in every year during the period of five years next before the passing of the Local Government Act, 1888, on account of the emoluments for which he claims compensation, and also distinguish the offices in respect of which the emoluments have been received. The claim must be accompanied by a statutory declaration under the Statutory Declaration Act, 1835 (*5 & 6 Will. IV. c. 62*), that the same is a true statement according to the best of the officer's knowledge, information, and belief. The statement must be submitted to the County Council, who must forthwith take the case into consideration, and assess the just amount of compensation (if any), and forthwith inform the claimant of their decision.

The claimant, if required by any member of the Council, must attend at a meeting of the County Council, and answer upon oath, which any Justice present may administer, all questions asked by any member of the Council touching the matters set forth in his claim, and must further produce all books, papers, and documents in his possession, or under his control, relating to the same.

The claimant, if aggrieved by the decision of the Council, may, within three months after the decision, appeal to the Treasury against that decision. Again, if at least one-third of the members of the Council subscribe a protest against the amount of the compensation granted by the Council as being excessive, any subscriber to such protest may, within three months of the decision, appeal to the Treasury, whose decision in either case is final.

---

[1] See *post*, Appendix D., p. 354.

The sum payable as compensation to any person under these provisions will commence to be payable at the date fixed by the County Council on granting the compensation, or, in the case of appeal, by the Treasury, and will be a specialty debt due to him from the County Council, and enforceable in like manner as if the Council had entered into a bond to pay the same.

If a person receiving compensation under these provisions is appointed to any office under the Local Government Act, 1888, the compensation will be wholly or partially suspended during his tenure of such office.[1]

The payment of compensation to officers will be a general county purpose.[2]

Clerk of the Peace and of the County Council.[3]

A Clerk of the Peace in office on the appointed day will become Clerk of the County Council. Special arrangements are, however, made for the County of London. The Clerk of the Peace for Suffolk in office on the appointed day, will be the Clerk of the County Council of both East and West Suffolk, provided that he was already in office on the 13th August, 1888. The Clerk of the Peace for Sussex in office on the appointed day, will be the Clerk of the County Councils of both East and West Sussex, provided that he was already in office on the 13th August, 1888. The Clerk of the Gaol Sessions for Yorkshire or Lincolnshire, will be Clerk to the County Committee, provided that he was already in office on the 13th August, 1888. A Clerk of the Peace, thus becoming Clerk of a County Council, unlike any subsequent Clerk that may be appointed to this office, will, provided he was already in office on the 13th August, 1888, hold office, not during the pleasure of the Standing Joint Committee, but will hold office for his life, subject to being dismissed by the Quarter Sessions in the following cases :—

1st. If he misdemean himself in his office, he may be suspended or discharged by the Quarter Sessions, after an open inquiry in their Court upon complaint, in writing, exhibited against him.[4]

2nd. If he be guilty of misconduct otherwise than in the execution of his office, two Justices of the County may exhibit a complaint in writing against him, stating the misconduct of which he has been guilty. The Quarter Sessions,

[1] Local Government Act, 1888, sec. 120. [2] As to the meaning of general county purposes, see Chapter III. [3] Local Government Act, 1888, sec. 118.
[4] 1 Will. & Mary, c. 21, sec. 5.

after examination in open Court, if satisfied of his misconduct, and that such misconduct is such as to render him an improper person to hold office, may discharge him. In the latter case, but not where discharged for misconduct in his office, the Clerk of the Peace may appeal summarily to the Lord Chancellor.[1]

Such a Clerk will moreover have the same power of appointing and acting by a deputy as heretofore.

Transferred business.

We now proceed to deal with the business transferred to the County Councils.

Analysts.

Under the Sale of Food and Drugs Act, 1875 (*38 & 39 Vict. c. 63*), Public Analysts are or may be appointed (except in the Metropolis) by the Quarter Sessions of every county, also by the Town Council of every Quarter Sessions borough, and of every borough with a separate police force. "County" is not defined in that Act, and it does not appear that an Analyst could be appointed for a liberty. On the appointed day the business, in this respect, of the Quarter Sessions of a county will be transferred to the County Council, and to the Town Councils of county boroughs in the county, who do not already appoint Analysts.[2] Town Councils of boroughs, the population of which, according to the census of 1881 was under 10,000, will cease to appoint Analysts, and the Analysts of the county will act in these boroughs.[3] The Analysts appointed by the Town Councils of these boroughs will be entitled to compensation for loss of office.

Birds.

The County Council and the Town Councils of county boroughs will succeed the Quarter Sessions of the county in their powers under the Wild Birds Protection Acts, 1880 and 1881 (*43 & 44 Vict. c. 35, and 44 & 45 Vict. c. 51*).[4]

Bridges.

This business will be discussed later, under Highways.

Contagious Diseases (Animals) Acts.

At present the statutes directed towards the stamping out of contagious diseases among animals are put in force (except in the Metropolis) by the following Local Authorities.

---

[1] 27 & 28 Vict. c. 65.
[2] Local Government Act, 1888, secs. 3, 34.
[3] *Ib.*, secs. 38, 39.
[4] *Ib.*, sec. 3.

In counties (including the Isle of Ely and the Soke of Peterborough)—The Quarter Sessions.

In municipal boroughs—The Town Council.

In places, not municipal boroughs, with a separate police establishment—The Commissioners or other body maintaining the police.

The Privy Council have power to appoint other bodies Local Authorities in certain cases.

Liberties and franchises are included in the county which they adjoin, or if they adjoin more than one county, in that county with which they have the longest common boundary. Under the Local Government Act, 1888, the business, in this respect, of the Quarter Sessions of a county and of the Town Councils of boroughs, the population of which, according to the census of 1881, was under 10,000, will be transferred to the County Council.[1]

The Quarter Sessions of a county usually appoint an Executive Committee to carry out their duties under the Contagious Diseases (Animals) Acts, and, when this is the case, such an Executive Committee, in office on the appointed day, will continue to hold office until the expiration of one week after the County Council have appointed an Executive Committee to succeed them, and no longer. Any sub-committee of an Executive Committee in office on the appointed day, will continue in office until either the County Council or their Executive Committee, as the case may be, have appointed a sub-committee for like purposes to succeed them.[2]

These provisions do not, however, extend to Committees appointed by Town Councils, and the County Council will on the appointed day come into possession of their full power in boroughs in which they succeed the Town Council.

If a virulent outbreak of disease is in progress within the county on the general appointed day, the County Council, in order to prevent the inconvenience of a change of authority at such a moment, could apply to the Local Government Board for a postponement of the appointed day as respects this business.

The Local Authorities make regulations with regard to their districts, and they may purchase and possess land and buildings, and they also appoint Inspectors and other officers.

On the appointed day the jurisdiction of the County Council will extend into various districts at present not under the

---

[1] Local Government Act, 1888, secs 3, 39. [2] *Ib.*, sec. 112.

authority of the Quarter Sessions of the county; in which districts varying regulations may be in force. The County Council will have to consider the advisability of introducing a uniform system of regulations.

The County Council will have property vested in them that at present belongs to the Quarter Sessions of the county. They will also have to consider the advisability of arranging to take over any property which may at present belong to the Town Councils whom they succeed in connection with this business.

Inspectors appointed by Town Councils whose business is transferred to the County Council will lose office and may be entitled to compensation.

Local Authorities may enter into mutual agreements for the transfer of parts of their districts, and where such a transfer has been made of part of one county to another, the agreement will continue binding on the County Council.[1]

Coroners.[2]

At present, under the Coroners Act, 1887 (*50 & 51 Vict. c. 71*), County Coroners are elected for every county by the freeholders of the county; or, if the county is divided into coroners' districts, a County Coroner is elected for each district by the freeholders of the district. A County Coroner is paid his salary and reimbursed his lawful expenses incurred in holding inquests by the Quarter Sessions of the county, who have also power to petition the Crown for a division of their county into coroners' districts, or for the alteration of such a division.

In the Coroners Act, 1887, and in the earlier Acts dealing with Coroners, the term county includes any division or liberty of a county with a separate Court of Quarter Sessions, and for which a separate Coroner has customarily been elected; but the whole of Yorkshire and the whole of Lincolnshire are each deemed to be one county, and the business in connection with Coroners transacted elsewhere by the Quarter Sessions is in these counties transacted by the Justices at their Gaol Sessions.

For every Quarter Sessions Borough a Borough Coroner is appointed by the Town Council of the borough.

On the appointed day the Borough Coroners of Quarter Sessions Boroughs, the population of which, according to the census of 1881, was under 10,000, will cease to act or to be

---

[1] Local Government Act, 1888, sec. 50. [2] *Ib.*, secs. 3, 5, 34.

appointed, and the County Coroners will act within such boroughs. Where the county is not divided into coroners' districts, the jurisdiction of the County Coroner or Coroners will, after the appointed day, extend throughout the county including such boroughs; but where the county is divided into coroners' districts, the County Council must make an Order assigning each of such boroughs in their county to a particular district. The County Council must also compensate the Borough Coroners, who will lose their offices in consequence of the Local Government Act, 1888.

County Coroners will continue in office and will continue to act within county boroughs without a separate Court of Quarter Sessions in the same way as at present, and the Town Councils of such county boroughs must contribute towards the expenses of such Coroners.

The powers and duties of the Quarter Sessions in connection with Coroners' salaries, and the division of their county into coroners' districts, and the alteration of such districts, are in most cases transferred to the County Council. Where, however, a coroner's district is situated in two administrative counties, forming part of an entire county, the Coroner of that district will be paid by the Joint Committee, who will also have power to take steps for altering the district, so that it shall no longer lie in two administrative counties.

After the appointed day also, on the occurrence of a vacancy in the office of County Coroner, a new County Coroner will be appointed by the County Council; or, in certain cases, by a Town Council of a county borough, or a Joint Committee of the County Council and such a Town Council; or, if the Coroner's district in an entire county is situated in two administrative counties, by the Joint Committee for the county.

There are besides County Coroners and Borough Coroners certain other Coroners called Franchise Coroners, who, in some cases, are at present paid by the Quarter Sessions; where this is the case, the County Council will, after the appointed day, pay such Coroners, instead of the Quarter Sessions.

Destructive Insects Act, 1877.

This is a statute providing for the destruction of the Colorado beetle. It is, and will be, executed by the Local Authorities who enforce the Contagious Diseases (Animals) Acts. [1]

---

[1] See *ante*, p. 41.

This Act has hitherto been of no practical importance, no invasion of the Colorado beetle having occurred.

Explosives.

The Explosives Act, 1875 (*38 Vict. c. 17*), under which the manufacture and sale of explosives is regulated, is put in force (except in the Metropolis) by the following Local Authorities:—

In Quarter Sessions Boroughs—the Town Council.

In any harbour within the jurisdiction of a Harbour Authority—the Harbour Authority.

The Town Council of any borough other than a Quarter Sessions Borough, or the Improvement Commissioners of any improvement act district may, by Order of a Secretary of State, upon the application of the Town Council or Commissioners, be made a Local Authority.

Elsewhere—the Justices in Petty Sessions.

Under the Local Government Act, 1888, the business of the Justices in petty sessions is transferred to the County Council, and to the Town Councils of county boroughs, and the business of the Town Councils of boroughs, the population of which, according to the census of 1881, was under 10,000, and of Improvement Commissioners of districts of like population, is transferred to the County Council.[1]

The Local Authorities grant licences for premises used for the manufacture and storage of explosives and keep certain records of the licences granted, &c. These records the County Council will have to obtain from the authorities whom they succeed. The Local Authorities also appoint officers to inspect such premises, &c., and where such officers have been appointed by a Town Council or by Improvement Commissioners, to whose business the County Council succeed, it may be necessary to compensate them; but, as a rule, police constables have been appointed without extra pay, so that there will be no need for compensation if they cease to be so employed.

Fisheries.

The Acts providing for the protection of inland fisheries are put in force locally by Boards of Conservators, each Board having under their supervision a system of rivers that has been made into a "Fishery District." A Board of Conservators consists of members appointed by the Quarter Sessions of

[1] Local Government Act, 1888, secs. 3, 38, 39.

every county, and the Town Council of every borough which is a county of a city or county of a town, through or past whose county or borough any of the rivers run, and of certain *ex-officio* and elected members.

The term "county," under the Fisheries Acts, includes liberties with a separate Court of Quarter Sessions.

The business in this respect of the Quarter Sessions of a county, and of any liberty in the county, is transferred to the County Council and to Town Councils of county boroughs. Any business in this respect of a Town Council of a borough the population of which, according to the census of 1881, was under 10,000 is also transferred to the County Council.[1] If no county borough, not already represented on the Board of Conservators, is included in a fishery district, the County Council will be entitled to appoint a number of members of the Board of Conservators of that district, equal to the whole number appointed by all the authorities whom the Council succeed. It seems, however, that, if any river in a fishery district runs through a county borough not already represented, the Town Council of that borough will, after the appointed day, be entitled to be represented on the Board of Conservators,[2] and in such a case accordingly a new arrangement as to the number of members to be appointed by each authority entitled to be represented will have to be come to.

Gas Meters.

The bodies at present superintending and testing gas-meters, under an Act passed in 1859, for regulating measures used in the sale of gas (*22 & 23 Vict. c. 66*) are:—

In counties—The Quarter Sessions.

In counties of towns and counties of cities—The Quarter Sessions.

In boroughs.

(i.) Where the Town Council are not themselves makers or sellers of gas, and have adopted the Act—The Town Council.

(ii.) Where the Town Council are makers or sellers of gas and the Justices of the borough (if any) have adopted the Act—The Justices of the borough.

(iii.) In other boroughs, the Quarter Sessions for the county exercise jurisdiction in this matter within the borough.

---

[1] Local Government Act, 1888, secs. 3, 38, 48. [2] *Ib.*, sec. 34.

Under the Local Government Act, 1888,[1] the County Council will succeed—

To the jurisdiction of the Quarter Sessions of the county.

To the jurisdiction of the Quarter Sessions of counties of towns, and counties of cities that are not county boroughs.

To the jurisdiction of the Justices of boroughs other than county boroughs where the Justices have adopted the Act.

To the jurisdiction of the Town Councils of boroughs, the population of which, according to the census of 1881, was under 10,000.

Accordingly the Local Authorities carrying out the provisions of the Act will in future be—

In counties—The County Council.

In county boroughs, where the Town Council are not makers or sellers of gas, and where they have adopted the Act—The Town Council.

In county boroughs, where the Town Council are makers or sellers of gas and the Justices have adopted the Act—The Justices of the borough.

In other boroughs, the population of which, according to the census of 1881, was over 10,000, where the Town Council are not makers or sellers of gas and have adopted the Act—The Town Council.

In all other boroughs, including county boroughs, the County Council will act as Local Authority.

Inspectors of meters are appointed by the Local Authorities, who will accordingly, in certain cases, lose office, and be entitled to compensation.

The Local Authorities also possess models of gas meters and other apparatus used in testing. Such property at present held by the Quarter Sessions of a county will pass to the County Council. Such property at present held by the Justices or Town Council of a borough, to whose authority the County Council succeeds, will be useless to the borough, and the County Council may arrange to take it over if they think it necessary.

Highways and Bridges.

The Local Government Act, 1888, makes very considerable changes in the law of highways and bridges, and it will be

[1] Secs, 3, 34, 36, 39.

necessary to go shortly into the history of that law. From early times the inhabitants of every ecclesiastical parish have been bound in general to maintain the highways of the parish, and a failure on their part to do so has been an indictable offence. This is still the case, though the procedure against the inhabitants of a parish by indictment is at the present time practically only made use of as a legal fiction for the purpose of trying the question of liability to maintain highways. Though the ecclesiastical parish was the district commonly bound to maintain its highways, still in some cases, other areas, such as townships and hamlets, were, by custom, obliged to maintain their highways so as to relieve the rest of the parish. The parishes so bound to maintain their own highways, and the other places in the same position have been called, as we have seen, "Highway Parishes." Again, in some cases, owners of particular property were and are, by custom or otherwise, bound to maintain particular highways. The ancient practical administration of highways does not concern us, as highways are now all maintained under a series of comparatively modern statutes.

The Highway Act, 1835.

The first of the important statutes now in force is the Highway Act, 1835 (*5 & 6 Will. IV. c. 50*), under which, in many places, the highways are still maintained. The general arrangement under that Act is as follows:—

In every highway parish, a Surveyor is annually elected by the inhabitants in vestry assembled, to manage the highways in the parish. His duties comprise all practical matters connected with the highways, such as the removal of obstructions, the practical arrangement for repairs, &c. The expenses of maintenance are met by a highway rate made, assessed, and levied by the Surveyor throughout the parish.

Highway Acts of 1862 & 1864.

The next Acts of importance are the Highway Act, 1862 (*25 & 26 Vict. c. 61*), and the Highway Act, 1864 (*27 & 28 Vict. c. 101*), under which the counties first became involved in highway management. These Acts arranged for the constitution by the Quarter Sessions of "Highway Districts" formed by combining highway parishes. The management of highways in a highway district is given to the Highway Board of the district, an assembly formed by representatives from each parish, called Waywardens, elected in the same way as Surveyors under the Highway Act, 1835. These Highway Boards succeeded to all the powers of the Highway Surveyors of the various parishes within their district, except as respects rating, and Surveyors ceased to be elected in parishes within highway districts.

The incidence of the expense of highway maintenance was only slightly altered by these Acts, under which the expenses of highways in highway districts were defrayed by rates made in each parish according to the expenses incurred in the parish, except that certain expenses were declared to be district expenses, and were defrayed out of a rate made on the parishes in proportion to the rateable value of the parishes.

Highways in Urban Sanitary Districts.

In the meantime highways had, in certain cases, been made maintainable by Improvement Commissioners and in all cases, under the Public Health Act, 1848, by Local Boards of Health; and now under the Public Health Act, 1875, highways within all urban sanitary districts are maintainable by the Urban Sanitary Authorities, and are accordingly maintained by them usually out of the general district rate; though in certain cases, a special highway rate may be made.

Turnpike Roads.

We must now go back and explain the history of turnpike roads. Under the old system, by which each parish maintained its own highways, the cost of maintaining the great thoroughfares between important towns was, as traffic increased, found to press very unfairly on the parishes through which these roads passed, and, in consequence, these roads were generally very ill repaired. Accordingly it became customary to vest the repair of these roads in bodies of Commissioners or Trustees under Local Acts, giving the Commissioners or Trustees a right to exact tolls, out of the income derived from which the roads were maintained. A considerable number of general statutes dealing with the matter were also passed, and the Local Acts were generally temporary and continued by annual continuance Acts. This system reached its height between 1860 and 1870, since which time steps have been taken to wind up turnpike trusts, and on the 1st January, 1889, there will be only about 150 miles of turnpike roads left. As turnpike roads became disturnpiked, the old difficulty with regard to their maintenance by small parishes, which they happened to pass through, was again felt, although in 1870 it had been provided that disturnpiked roads passing through a highway district should be maintainable by the district at large, the expense being a district expense.[1]

Highways, &c., Act, 1878.

The last important Act is the Highways and Locomotives (Amendment) Act, 1878 (*41 & 42 Vict. c. 77*), which was passed partly in order to remedy this unfair incidence of expense. This

[1] 33 & 34 Vict. c. 73, sec. 10.

Act further involved the counties in highway management by providing that every turnpike road disturnpiked since the 31st December, 1870, should become a "Main Road," and that half the expense of keeping up main roads should be, upon the certificate of the County Surveyor that the road was properly maintained, borne by the Quarter Sessions of the county, who were also given the power to declare any road in their county a main road. The Act also provided that the entire expense with certain exceptions of maintaining highways in highway districts should fall on the district as a general district expense. The Act further provided that where a highway district coincided with a rural sanitary district the Rural Sanitary Authority might take over the highways from the Highway Board, and that the Quarter Sessions in forming new highway districts should endeavour to make them coincide with rural sanitary districts. The Quarter Sessions were also given certain powers of exercising supervision over Surveyors of Highways, Highway Boards, and Sanitary Authorities maintaining highways, which bodies received the name of Highway Authorities; the area also under the jurisdiction of each Highway Authority was called a "Highway Area." Quarter Sessions Boroughs were excluded from the operation of the Act, and accordingly the Quarter Sessions of the county do not contribute towards the expenses of disturnpiked roads within those boroughs, nor have the Quarter Sessions any power to enforce the repair of highways within a Quarter Sessions Borough by the Town Council or other Urban Sanitary Authority acting in the borough, and such an Urban Sanitary Authority is not a Highway Authority within the meaning of the Act.

Roads in South Wales.

The highways in six counties of South Wales, namely, Glamorgan, Brecknock, Radnor, Carmarthen, Cardigan, and Pembroke, are managed under certain Acts applicable to these counties only (viz., *7 & 8 Vict. c. 91*, *23 & 24 Vict. c. 68*, *41 & 42 Vict. c. 34*), and to these counties the Highway Acts of 1862, 1864, and 1878 do not apply. The system is shortly as follows:—

The more important roads are turnpike roads, and their maintenance in each county is vested in a County Roads Board, consisting of Justices appointed by the Quarter Sessions, and of certain *ex-officio* and other members, but the roads are partly managed by District Roads Boards acting under the County Roads Board. To meet the expenses the County Roads Board levy tolls, and make up any deficiency out of a county road rate levied by the Quarter Sessions of each county to meet a requisition from the County Roads Board.

For the purpose of maintaining other highways each of these counties is divided into districts, and the highways in each district are maintained by a Highway Board, consisting of the Guardians elected for any parish within the district, and of the Justices of the Peace residing, or acting at any petty sessions, within the district. The expenses are borne by a rate levied in each constituent highway parish, according to the expenses incurred in that parish ; but a County Roads Board may make any important road a "District Road," and in that case the expenses are borne by the parishes of the district according to their rateable value.

Roads in the Isle of Wight.

In the Isle of Wight the highways are maintained under Local Acts,[1] and the Highway Acts of 1862, 1864, and 1878 do not apply. The more important roads are maintained by the Isle of Wight Highway Commissioners, who levy tolls for that purpose.

Parliamentary grant in aid of main roads.

In 1882, in order further to lighten the local burden of maintaining main roads, a parliamentary grant in aid of their maintenance was made, and was afterwards continued annually. The grant was one-quarter of the whole cost, as allowed by the Quarter Sessions of the counties, of maintaining each main road, and was distributed by the Local Government Board among the local Highway Authorities. Provisions were also made whereby South Wales and Quarter Sessions Boroughs shared in the benefit of the grant.

For the year 1887-88, the grant was doubled and was one-half of the whole cost allowed by the Quarter Sessions of the counties, of maintaining each main road. The grant was equally divided between the Quarter Sessions of the county and the Highway Authority, so that one-fourth of the expense was borne by the local Highway Authority, one-fourth by the Quarter Sessions of the county, and half by the Treasury. A similar grant was made towards the maintenance of dis-turnpiked roads within Quarter Sessions boroughs equal to one-half the estimated cost of their maintenance as turnpike roads, and in South Wales the grant was made equal to the average annual amount which each county had to contribute towards the maintenance of turnpike roads since 1870.

The Isle of Wight has, however, never shared in a grant in aid of main roads.

---

[1] 53 Geo. III. ch. xcii., and 46 & 47 Vict. ch. ccxxvi.

Description of Highways.

Highways are then of the following kinds:—

(i.) Ordinary highways, in highway parishes not in highway districts, managed by elective Surveyors, and of which the expenses are defrayed by a highway rate made for the parish.

(ii.) Ordinary highways in highway districts managed by a Highway Board, and of which the expenses are defrayed out of a common fund to which the highway parishes in the district contribute in proportion to their rateable value.

(iii.) Ordinary highways in rural sanitary districts, where the Rural Sanitary Authority have taken upon themselves the business of a Highway Board, managed by the Rural Sanitary Authority and of which the expenses are defrayed as a general expense under the Public Health Act, 1875.[1]

(iv.) Ordinary highways in urban sanitary districts managed by the Sanitary Authority, and of which the expenses are defrayed either by a general district rate or a special highway rate.

(v.) A few turnpike roads.

(vi.) Main roads, managed by the Highway Authorities through whose districts they pass, under the direct supervision of the Quarter Sessions of counties, and of which the expenses are shared by the Highway Authority, the county, and the Treasury.

(vii.) Disturnpiked roads in Quarter Sessions Boroughs towards which the Sanitary Authority receives a contribution from the Treasury.

(viii.) Highways in South Wales and the Isle of Wight.

Changes under the Local Government Act[2]

On the appointed day the whole maintenance of main roads, including any bridge, carrying such a road which is repairable by the Highway Authority, will be placed in the hands of the County Council of each county.

The operation of the Highways and Locomotives (Amendment) Act, 1878, is extended to Quarter Sessions Boroughs (other than county boroughs), so that all roads within such boroughs disturnpiked since the 31st December, 1870, will on the appointed day become main roads and will be maintainable by the County Council. Main roads in county boroughs on the other hand will be entirely maintained by the Town Council.

---

[1] See *ante*, p. 22

[2] Local Government Act, 1888, secs. 11, 34, 35, 38.

Any Urban Sanitary Authority may, however, within twelve months of the appointed day, claim to retain the maintenance of a main road, within their district, in their own hands; in that case the County Council will contribute towards the maintenance, repair and reasonable improvement of the road.

On the appointed day also all the turnpike roads in South Wales will cease to be turnpike roads, and will become main roads maintainable by the County Council; County Roads Boards and District Roads Boards will cease to exist, and the County Council of each county in South Wales will succeed them exactly as if they were the Quarter Sessions of the county. The County Council will have the powers of a County Roads Board for the alteration of highway districts, the appointment of the Surveyor of a Highway Board, and for other purposes relating to Highway Boards. South Wales.[1]

In the Isle of Wight, also, tolls will after the appointed day cease to be taken, and the turnpike roads will become main roads maintainable by the County Council. Until otherwise provided, however, the Isle of Wight Highway Commissioners will continue to repair and maintain these roads and must be paid for that purpose by the County Council of Southampton. Isle of Wight.[2]

The County Council will also succeed to the supervising authority of the Quarter Sessions under the Highways and Locomotives (Amendment) Act, 1878; the Town Council of a Quarter Sessions Borough will become a Highway Authority within the meaning of that Act, and so be under the control of the County Council, as will also the Highway Boards in South Wales. Control of Highway Authorities

After the appointed day a County Council may, if they think fit, contribute towards the costs of maintenance, repair, enlargement and improvement of any highway or public footpath in their county.

The actual contracts for the repair of main roads at present existing, have been made by the various Highway Authorities, according to circumstances. These contracts will be binding on and enforceable against the County Council. Where a contract has been made with regard to a highway area not wholly in one county there may be some difficulty. No express provision seems to have been made for the adjustment of such contracts. An agreement will therefore have to be come to with the Council of the adjoining county. Existing Contracts.

[1] Local Government Act, 1888, sec. 13. [2] *Ib.*, sec. 12.

County Surveyor.

The County Surveyor will become an Officer of the County Council.

Financial arrangements for the year 1888-89.[1]

During the whole of the financial year 1888-89, all highways will be maintained by the authorities heretofore maintaining them. The County Council of every county must contribute towards the expenses of Highway Authorities in maintaining main roads during that year, a sum equal to half of the expense as allowed by their Surveyor. Where a portion of that contribution has already been paid by the Quarter Sessions the County Council will have, of course, only to complete the payment.

The Local Government Board will distribute the sum placed in their hands, in lieu of the grant in aid, in the following manner:—

(i.) They will pay to every County Authority half of the contribution made for that year by that Authority in respect of the maintenance of main roads.

(ii.) They will pay to every Highway Authority one-quarter of their whole expense, as allowed by the County Authority, in maintaining main roads.

(iii.) They will pay towards the maintenance of roads in Quarter Sessions Boroughs, disturnpiked since December 31st, 1870, one-half of the estimated annual cost for material and labour of the maintenance of such roads as turnpike roads.

(iv.) They will pay to the County Authority of each county in South Wales the average annual amount which each county has been required to pay towards the maintenance of turnpike roads since 1870.

Bridges.

The law with regard to bridges is somewhat analogous with that with regard to highways, and is intricate and highly technical. The number of statutes in force concerning the subject is large, but many of them are almost obsolete.

The law is briefly as follows:—

The inhabitants of every county, town corporate, franchise, or liberty, are bound to repair all the public bridges in their county, town, or franchise unless they can prove that some other person or body is liable.[2] Some other person or

---

[1] Local Government Act, 1888, sec. 121; County Authority means, until the appointed day, the Quarter Sessions, or in South Wales the County Roads Board; and after the appointed day, the County Council.

[2] See the Statute of Bridges (*22 Henry VIII. c. 5*), which was, however, in this respect, only declaratory of the common law.

body, or the inhabitants of some other area, may, however, by statute, custom, or by reason of their tenure of land, be liable to repair a public bridge, and in particular the inhabitants of a hundred are often by custom chargeable with the repair of bridges within their hundred.

If a person or body or the inhabitants of a district liable to repair a public bridge fail to do so, their failure is a criminal offence, and will render them liable to an indictment. An indictment of this kind is generally only made use of, of course, as a legal fiction for trying the liability to repair.

Public bridges repairable by a county or hundred are practically looked after by the Quarter Sessions of the county, who pay for the repairs out of the county rate or the hundred rate as the case may be.

Borough bridges, *i.e.*, bridges repairable by the inhabitants of a borough, are in the same way looked after by the Town Council, and the expenses are paid out of the borough fund.

Charges under Local Government Act.[1]

On the appointed day the County Council will succeed to all the powers and duties of the Quarter Sessions with regard to bridges. A County Council may also purchase or take over existing bridges not being county bridges, and may erect new bridges and maintain and repair the same. They will also be liable to repair bridges on which main roads are carried. The County Council of the Soke of Peterborough will become liable to repair bridges within their administrative county. All bridges within a county borough at present repairable by a county or hundred will become repairable by the Town Council.

Local Stamp Act, 1869 (32 & 33 Vict. c. 49).

This Act provides for the payment of local fines, fees, and penalties, in certain cases, by means of stamps. The Local Authorities under the Act are the Quarter Sessions of every county at large or liberty with a separate Court of Quarter Sessions, and the Town Council of every borough. The Local Authorities make regulations for carrying out the Act and provide dies, &c., for making the stamps. The County Council will succeed to the powers under the Act of the Quarter Sessions of their county, and of any liberty therein,[2] and in the latter case will have to consider the advisability of bringing the

[1] Local Government Act, 1888, secs. 3, 6, 34, 64.

[2] *Ib.*, sec. 3.

regulations in force and stamps in use throughout their county into uniformity. Any question arising as to the application of this Act, must be referred to the Standing Joint Committee of the County Council and the Quarter Sessions.[1]

Lunatic Asylums (Pauper).

The law on this subject is somewhat intricate, and it may be well to go shortly into its history. Pauper lunatics are provided for in two distinct ways; first, as "paupers" they are maintained by the union or parish to which they are as paupers chargeable, except where it cannot be ascertained to which union or parish they belong, in which case they are chargeable to the county, or in some cases to the borough in which they were found. Secondly, as "lunatics," asylums must be provided for them by the county, or in some cases the borough to which they belong.

Expense of maintaining a pauper lunatic.

The expense of maintaining a pauper lunatic maintained in a county or borough asylum is divided between the union or parish and county or borough as follows:—

(i.) The union or parish must pay to the authority maintaining the asylum a sufficient sum to defray the expense of the lunatic's keep, medicine, clothing, &c., and in addition, to provide for the salaries of the officers of the asylum. The Treasury make a grant to the union or parish of four shillings a week towards the maintenance of each lunatic chargeable to that union or parish.

(ii.) The county or borough is chargeable with the cost of providing and repairing the asylum and the necessary furniture. Where a lunatic is chargeable to a county or borough owing to the impossibility of discovering to what union or parish he belongs, the Treasury make a grant of four shillings a week for his maintenance to the county or borough.

After several Acts of Parliament had been passed enabling counties and boroughs to erect public lunatic asylums if they thought fit, an Act was passed, in 1845,[2] rendering the erection of lunatic asylums compulsory. This Act was repealed by The Lunatic Asylums Act, 1853 (*16 & 17 Vict. c. 97*), which is still in force and which is on the same lines as the Act of 1845. The Act of 1853 has been amended in detail by subsequent Acts, but not materially altered.

Under that Act, every county and, with certain exceptions, every Quarter Sessions Borough, is bound to provide either

---

[1] Local Government Act, 1888, sec. 30. [2] *8 & 9 Vict. c. 126.*

independently or jointly with other counties, boroughs, and bodies one or more lunatic asylums sufficient for the pauper lunatics of the county or borough.

Asylum accommodation for pauper lunatics.[1]

Asylum accommodation for the county is provided by the Quarter Sessions for the county, who may either provide an asylum for the county alone, or enter into an agreement with the Quarter Sessions of other counties, Justices or Town Councils of boroughs, and subscribers to hospitals for the joint maintenance of an asylum.

Asylum accommodation for a Quarter Sessions Borough is provided usually by the Justices of the borough, who for that purpose may either—

(i.) Provide an asylum for their borough alone ; or,
(ii.) Enter into an agreement with the Quarter Sessions of counties, the Justices or Town Councils of other boroughs, and subscribers to hospitals, for the joint maintenance of an asylum ; or
(iii.) Contract for the reception of their lunatics into some existing asylum.

The Town Council of any Quarter Sessions Borough were empowered by the Lunatic Asylums Act, 1853, to take over the duties of the Justices with regard to lunatic asylums.

Under the Act of 1845, those Quarter Sessions Boroughs for which there were not more than six Justices acting were annexed to counties, and under the Act of 1853 and subsequent Acts it has accordingly been provided :—

(i.) That every Quarter Sessions Borough, in which, on the 8th August, 1845, there were not six Justices besides a Recorder, should be annexed to a county.[2]
(ii.) That if a Quarter Sessions Borough with a larger number of Justices failed to provide a lunatic asylum in proper time, it might be annexed, by Order of a Secretary of State, to a county.[2]
(iii.) That all Quarter Sessions Boroughs having become such since the 20th August, 1853, should be considered as annexed to the county in which they were situated.[3]

Meaning of term "County" under Lunatic Asylums Act.

Both under the Act of 1845 and 1853 power was given to a Secretary of State to rectify the boundaries of a county for the purposes of the Acts, and it is provided[4] that every

[1] Lunatic Asylums Act, 1853, secs. 2–5, ; 18 & 19 Vict. c. 105, sec. 1.
[2] Lunatic Asylums Act, 1853, sec. 9.
[3] 18 & 19 Vict. c. 105, sec. 7.
[4] Lunatic Asylums Act, 1853, secs. 131, 132.

city, town, liberty, parish, place, or district not being a Quarter Sessions Borough shall, for the purposes of the Acts, be annexed to and treated and rated as part of the county in which the same is situated, or if such city, town, liberty, parish, place, or district be situate partly in one county and partly in another, then to and as part of such one of the same counties as such city, town, liberty, parish, place, or district may have been annexed to under the Act of 1845, or if not so annexed, then to and as part of such one of the same counties as one of Her Majesty's Principal Secretaries of State shall, by writing under his hand and seal, direct, and the term county is defined to mean county, riding and division bounded in accordance with the above provisions.

Costs of maintaining lunatic asylums.

The expenses of providing and maintaining a lunatic asylum are met—

(1.) In a county, by a rate levied over the whole county in accordance with the above definition.

(2.) In a Quarter Sessions Borough, out of the borough fund and borough rates.

Where a Quarter Sessions Borough does not maintain an asylum independently, it contributes to the expense of the asylum to which its lunatics are sent as follows:—

Where an agreement has been entered into with counties, other boroughs, &c,—according to the terms of the agreement.

Where the borough contracts for the reception of its lunatics into some extraneous asylum—according to the terms of the contract.

Where the borough is annexed to a county—a sum fixed by the Quarter Sessions of the county in proportion to its population.

Committee of Visitors.

The actual management of the erection of a new asylum or of the maintenance of an existing asylum is always vested in a "Committee of Visitors," who are appointed as follows:—

Where a county or borough maintains its own asylum independently, by the Quarter Sessions of the County, or the Justices of the borough; or where the Town Council of a borough acts in the matter, by the Town Council; and in the last case the Town Council may discharge the duties of the Committee of Visitors themselves, delegating, however, such powers as they think fit to a Committee who will not be technically the "Committee of Visitors."

Where an agreement between counties, boroughs, &c., has been entered into, the Committee of Visitors are appointed, so many for each authority interested, according to the terms of the agreement.

Where a Quarter Sessions Borough is annexed as above mentioned to a county, the Recorder of the borough may appoint two members of the Committee of Visitors of the county. It does not seem clear whether, if the county to which a borough is annexed has itself entered into an agreement with other counties, &c., for the maintenance of a joint asylum, the Recorder has a right to appoint two members of the Committee of Visitors of that asylum.

The provisions of the Local Government Act, 1888, with regard to lunatic asylums are as follows :— Changes the Local Government Act.[1]

The County Council succeed to the powers and duties of the Quarter Sessions of the County, and of the Justices or Town Council of a Quarter Sessions Borough, the population of which, according to the census of 1881, was under 10,000. No such borough, however, maintains an asylum independently.

Where such a borough maintains an asylum jointly with any other body, the County Council will succeed to the powers of the Justices or Town Council, to appoint members of the Committee of Visitors, and will have to pay the borough's share of the expenses. The borough will be rateable to county expenses in connection with lunatic asylums.

Where such a borough contracts for the reception of its lunatics into an extraneous asylum, the provisions of the Act are as follows :—

(i.) If the asylum is the county asylum, the contract will be determined, and the borough will be rated to the expenses of the county, and its lunatics must be sent to the asylum maintained by the county.

(ii.) If the asylum is not the county asylum, it seems that the contract will become binding on the County Council, and the expenses will be defrayed out of the "special lunatic asylums account" of the county.

If such a borough is annexed as above mentioned to the county, it seems that the borough will become rateable to the expenses of the county, and so contribute in proportion to its rateable value, and not, as heretofore, to its population.

---

[1] Local Government Act, 1888, secs. 3, 32, 34, 38, 86.

The powers and duties of the Justices of a Quarter Sessions Borough, other than a county borough, the population of which, according to the census of 1881, was over 10,000, will be transferred to the Town Council. If such a borough is under contract, however, for the reception of its lunatics into the county asylum, on the determination of the existing contract the powers and duties of the Town Council will cease and the borough will become for all purposes part of the county. If such a borough is annexed as above mentioned to the county it seems that its position will be unchanged, except that the Town Council, instead of the Recorder, will nominate two members of the Committee of Visitors of the county asylum.

The powers and duties of the Justices of a county borough with regard to lunatic asylums (if any) will be transferred to the Town Council. A county borough without a separate Court of Quarter Sessions will be placed in the position of a Quarter Sessions Borough as regards lunatics, and will be chargeable with the maintenance of any lunatic found in the borough whose settlement cannot be ascertained, and will also be bound to provide asylum accommodation for the lunatics of the borough. Existing arrangements are, however, pending a fresh arrangement, to be continued.

The former arrangements as to the boundaries of the county for the purposes of the Lunatic Asylums Acts will, it seems, continue, and the county of each County Council for lunatic asylum purposes will not be in all cases co-extensive with the county for other purposes. Accordingly they may have power to rate districts lying in other counties and also may be unable to rate districts within their own county.[1]

Some difficulty may possibly arise with regard to the consequences of the alteration of county boundaries in general on the peculiar provisions of the Lunatic Asylums Acts, and will have to be very carefully considered. Probably such a difficulty could be removed by an Order of a Secretary of State.

The Committee of Visitors in office for any asylum on the appointed day will continue in office for one week after the County Council have appointed a Committee to succeed them, or in the case of a joint asylum, the members appointed for a county will continue in office until one week after the County Council have appointed members to succeed them.[2]

---

[1] Local Government Act, 1888, sec. 50. [2] *Ib.*, sec. 111.

Music and Dancing Licences.

The Acts[1] under which these licences for music and dancing are required only apply to places within twenty miles of the Cities of London and Westminster, and accordingly affect only the whole of Middlesex and parts of Surrey, Kent, Essex, Hertford, and Bucks. The County Councils of these counties, and the Town Councils of county boroughs (besides, of course, the County Council of London) will in future grant these licences within the limits of the area affected by the Acts, instead of the Quarter Sessions. The existing licences will expire in the autumn of 1889. Rules with regard to the matter have been drawn up by the Quarter Sessions of the various counties and will, as far at any rate as regards the application for new licences, require revision.[2]

Parliamentary Registration and Election.

The County Council of each county will succeed to the duties of the Quarter Sessions with regard to the Registration of Parliamentary Voters, and making certain preparations for Parliamentary Elections. The duties at present discharged in this respect by the Clerk of the Peace will in future be discharged by him in his capacity of Clerk of the County Council, under the control of the County Council.[3]

Police.

The history of the maintenance of the police force throughout the country in its present form may be said to begin with the Lighting and Watching Act, 1833 (*3 & 4 Will. IV c. 90*), under which the inhabitants of any parish who chose to adopt the Act were empowered to elect Inspectors to provide and maintain a police force for the parish. The Municipal Corporations Act, 1835 (*5 & 6 Will. IV. c. 76*), provided that a police force for every municipal borough should be provided and maintained by the Town Council acting through a committee called the Watch Committee.

The first important Act providing for the establishment of a county police force was an Act of 1839 (*2 & 3 Vict. c. 93*) whereby the Quarter Sessions of each county were empowered, if they thought fit, to provide a police force for their county. It was also provided, that upon the establishment of county County Police.

[1] 25 Geo. II. c. 36 (made perpetual by 28 Geo. II. c. 19); 38 Vict. c. 21.
[2] Local Government Act, 1888, secs. 3, 34.
[3] *Ib.* secs. 3, 31, and see *post*, Chapter VI.

police under that Act, any police force established under Local Acts, or under the Lighting and Watching Act, 1833, should be abolished. In 1840, an amending Act (*3 & 4 Vict. c. 88*) was passed dealing chiefly with details and with the levying of the police rate, but providing also that boroughs might agree to consolidate their police force with the county police force of adjoining counties, and also that constables appointed under the Lighting and Watching Act, 1833, for parishes, or under Local Acts for towns and other places, should continue to hold office until the Chief Constable of the county should give notice that he was ready to undertake the watching of such parishes and places.

No further important general Act was passed until 1856, but in the meantime many Local Acts were passed enabling towns, other than municipal boroughs, and other populous places, to provide a local police force; usually, if in a county for which a police force had been established, partly under the control of the Chief Constable for the county. The Town Police Clauses Act, 1847 (*10 & 11 Vict. c. 89*) was passed containing clauses suitable for incorporation with such Local Acts.

In 1856, an Act (*19 & 20 Vict. c. 69*) was passed rendering the establishment of a police force in every county compulsory, and otherwise amending the law, and further providing that the Treasury should, upon the certificate of one of Her Majesty's Principal Secretaries of State that the police of any county or borough had been kept in a state of efficiency during the past year, pay a share of the expenses of their pay and clothing, provided that no payment should be made by the Treasury towards the police force of a borough with a population under 5,000, unless that force was consolidated with the county police force. That Act also provided that the Treasury should make a similar grant towards the police force of any parish or place under the Lighting and Watching Act, 1833, or a Local Act, where the population exceeded 5,000, and that the separate police establishment of such a parish or place in which the population exceeded 15,000 should not be discontinued without the approval of a Secretary of State.

Borough Police.

The police force in a borough is now maintained under the Municipal Corporations Act, 1882, which, however, did not materially alter the law.

Treasury grant in aid of Police.

The Treasury grant in aid of the police has since 1856 been extended by temporary Acts, and is now half the expense of the pay and clothing.

At the present time a separate police force must be maintained— *Existing Police establishments.*

(i.) For every county.

(ii.) For every municipal borough; although such a police force may be consolidated with the police force of the county.

(iii.) For the towns of Hove and Tunbridge Wells under Local Acts. All other local establishments, whether under the Lighting and Watching Act, 1833, or otherwise have been discontinued.

Meaning of term "County" in Police Acts.[1]

The meaning of the word county under the Acts relating to police may be explained as follows:—County means "county at large" (including the Isle of Ely and the Soke of Peterborough), and all liberties and franchises are deemed part of the county by which they are surrounded, or, if surrounded by more than one county, then of that county with which they have the longest common boundary. The Quarter Sessions of two or more neighbouring counties may, however, from time to time agree that such parts of their several counties as they think fit shall be considered as forming part of any other of the same counties. Accordingly, the Quarter Sessions have to provide a sufficient police force to watch the whole of their county, as bounded for the purposes of the Police Acts, *i.e.*, including parts of other counties transferred to them, and excluding parts of their own county transferred from them to other counties, and excluding all boroughs, and towns with a separate police force, and they may levy the police rate over the same area. Of course the Quarter Sessions of a county may, under an agreement for consolidation, have to provide for the watching of a borough, but in that case they do not rate the borough but receive a contribution from the Town Council.

Metropolitan Police District.

In the Metropolitan Police District, which consists of the parishes and places contained in the schedule to an Act of 1829 (*10 Geo. IV. c. 44*) and of other parishes and places added thereto under provisions of that Act, and of another Act of 1839 (*2 & 3 Vict. c. 47*) by Order in Council, the police are managed by the Commissioners of the Metropolitan Police and are not under local control. The Metropolitan Police District comprises parts of Middlesex, Surrey, Kent, Hertford, and Essex, and within its limits the Acts relating to county and borough police do not apply, so that the

[1] 2 & 3 Vict. c. 93, secs. 27, 28; 3 & 4 Vict. c. 88., secs. 2, 34; 19 & 20 Vict. c. 69, sec. 30; 21 & 22 Vict. c. 68.

Justices of the above-mentioned counties do not levy a police rate within its limits nor do the county constables act therein.

Changes under the Local Government Act.[1]

Under the Local Government Act, 1888, the management of the county police is transferred from the Quarter Sessions to the Standing Joint Committee of the Quarter Sessions and the County Council. The power of a Town Council of a borough, the population of which, according to the census of 1881, was under 10,000, to maintain a police force ceases, and the county police force will act in these boroughs; the constables and police officers, however, of such a borough will become officers of the Standing Joint Committee, and all provisions with regard to existing officers apply to them and also to the constables and police officers of the county police force as if they became officers of the County Council; the Metropolitan police force is, however, unaffected.

The authority of the Standing Joint Committee will extend throughout the county in accordance with the definition given above, with the addition of the small boroughs; existing agreements for the transfer of parts of counties being unaffected.[2] The general change of county boundaries under the Local Government Act, 1888, may necessitate a fresh agreement when such a change takes place in the neighbourhood of a transferred district.

The Treasury grants in aid of the police will cease, but an equivalent grant towards the pay and clothing of the police force of a borough, other than a county borough, still maintaining its own police, will be paid by the County Council. One-half of the expenses of the pay and clothing of the county police and of the police of a county borough will also be paid out of the proceeds of imperial taxes handed over to the County or Town Council; so that the grant in these cases will practically continue, though in another form. The County Councils of those counties, of which parts are included in the Metropolitan police district, will, out of the same funds, have to contribute towards the maintenance of the Metropolitan police force.[3] The Standing Joint Committee will not levy the police rate, but their expenditure will be paid out of the County Fund and provided for by the County Council.[4]

Public Buildings.[5]

On the appointed day, the following buildings will, among

---

[1] Local Government Act, 1888, secs. 9, 39.
[2] *Ib.*, sec. 50.
[3] *Ib.*, sec. 24.
[4] *Ib.*, sec. 30.
[5] *Ib.*, secs. 3, 64.

others, vest in the County Council:—Shire Halls, County Halls, Assize Courts, Judges' Lodgings, Lock-up houses, Justices' Rooms, Police Stations. The County Council may deal freely with these buildings, and may, with the consent of the Local Government Board, alienate them.

The County Council must, however, provide such accommodation and rooms as may from time to time be determined, by the Standing Joint Committee of the Quarter Sessions and the County Council, to be necessary and proper for the due transaction of business, and convenient keeping of the records and documents of the Quarter Sessions and Justices out of sessions, or of any committee of the Quarter Sessions or Justices, &c.

It may be mentioned here that all buildings and property vested in the Justices of the county palatine of Lancaster, under the Manchester Assize Courts Act, 1858 (*21 & 22 Vict. c. xxiv.*), will vest in the County Council of Lancashire; but will be under the control of a Joint Committee, to be appointed by the County Council of Lancashire and the Town Councils of all the county boroughs situated in the hundred of Salford.[1]

Race-courses.

Under the Race-courses Licensing Act, 1879 (*42 & 43 Vict. c. 18*), every race-course within a radius of ten miles from Charing Cross must at present be licensed by the Quarter Sessions of the county in which the race-course is situated. This is transferred to the County Council and to the Town Councils of county boroughs.[2] The only counties affected by this provision are Middlesex, Surrey, Kent, Essex, and Hertford. The only county boroughs within the radius are Croydon and West Ham.

Reformatory and Industrial Schools.

The law relating to these schools, as far as it concerns us, is connected with the history of the law relating to local prisons. The Prisons Act, 1865 (*28 & 29 Vict. c. 126*), regulated the establishment and maintenance of local prisons by the following authorities, called "Prison Authorities," namely:—

As respects any prison belonging to a county—The Quarter Sessions. Whether or not the Quarter Sessions of a liberty or franchise, with a separate Court of Quarter Sessions,

[1] Local Government Act, 1888, sec. 47. [2] *Ib.*, secs. 3, 34.

were a separate Prison Authority, depended on the circumstances in each case. In Yorkshire and Lincolnshire the county prisons were maintained under this Act by the Justices of the whole county in Gaol Sessions.

As respects any prison belonging to a borough—The Town Council.

There were also other Prison Authorities in particular cases.

Subsequent statutes gave the Prison Authorities power, first, to contribute towards and afterwards to erect and maintain reformatory and industrial schools. By the Prison Act, 1877 (*40 & 41 Vict. c. 21*), all prisons were handed over to the Government and made maintainable by them. The Prison Authorities were, however, kept in existence for the purposes, firstly, of arranging financial matters connected with the transfer of prisons to the Government, and, secondly, of dealing as before with reformatory and industrial schools.

Under the Local Government Act, 1888, business connected with these schools is transferred from the Quarter Sessions of a county or liberty to the County Council, and to the Town Councils of county boroughs who were not formerly Prison Authorities. The powers, duties, and liabilities also of the Town Council of Quarter Sessions Boroughs, the population of which, according to the census of 1881, was under 10,000, with regard to such schools, are transferred to the County Council. In Yorkshire and Lincolnshire this business will have to be transacted by the County Committee.[1]

Registration of Charitable Gifts, Places of Religious Worship, and Rules of Societies.

Charitable gifts secured by deed, will, or other instrument, must, in many cases, be registered with the Clerk of the Peace of the county within which the persons to be benefited reside. In future the Clerk of the Peace will act in this matter in his capacity of Clerk of the County Council, and under their control. Where the persons to be benefited reside within a county borough the registration must, after the appointed day, be made with the Town Clerk.[2]

A certificate must, in certain cases, be obtained for a place of religious worship of Protestants where more than twenty persons meet besides the family of the person on whose premises the meetings take place. The Quarter Sessions of every county

[1] Local Government Act, 1888, secs. 3, 38. [2] *Ib.*, secs. 3, 34.

keep a record of the places so certificated. This duty is transferred to the County Council and to the Town Councils of county boroughs.[1]

The rules of every loan society formed under the Loan Societies Act, 1840 (*3 & 4 Vict. c. 110*), must be registered with the Quarter Sessions of the county in which the society is formed. This business is transferred to the County Council and to the Town Councils of county boroughs.[1]

The buildings of scientific and artistic societies are exempt from rates; but to secure this exemption the rules of the society must be approved by the Chief Registrar, and a certified copy enrolled in the records of the county after confirmation by the Quarter Sessions, whose business in this respect is transferred to the County Council and to the Town Councils of county boroughs.[1]

Riot (Damages) Act, 1886 (49 & 50 Vict. c. 38).

This Act provides for the payment of compensation, out of the police rate, where property has been destroyed by a riot. The authorities who must pay the compensation are (outside the Metropolitan Police District)—

In counties—The Quarter Sessions.

In boroughs maintaining a separate police force—The Town Council.

In other towns with a separate police force—The Authority maintaining the police.

In the River Tyne within the limits of the Acts relating to the Tyne Improvement Commissioners—the Tyne Improvement Commissioners.

"County" in this Act seems to have the same meaning as under the Acts relating to the establishment of a county police force; but it is not quite clear, if damage were done by riot in a portion of a county transferred for the purposes of the Police Acts, which county would have to pay.

The duties of the Quarter Sessions of a county in this respect are transferred to the County Council.[2]

Theatre Licences.

Under an Act of 1843 (*6 & 7 Vict. c. 68*) all places, except theatres to which letters patent have been granted, used for the representation of stage plays, must be licensed, outside the limits of the Lord Chamberlain's jurisdiction, by the

---

[1] Local Government Act, 1888, secs. 3, 34.

[2] *Ib.*, sec. 3.

Justices in special sessions. Their business in this respect is transferred to the County Council and to the Town Councils of county boroughs.[1]

Weights and Measures.

The Weights and Measures Act, 1878 (*41 & 42 Vict. c. 49*), which provides for the use of a uniform system of weights and measures, and for the detection and prosecution of persons using false weights and measures, is put in force (except in the Metropolis) by the following authorities:—

In counties (including the Isle of Ely and the Soke of Peterborough)—The Quarter Sessions.

Every liberty is deemed to be included in the county by which it is surrounded, or, if surrounded by more than one county, then in that county with which it has the longest common boundary.

In boroughs—The Town Council.

The Town Council of a borough without a separate Court of Quarter Sessions need not, however, act as a Local Authority unless they choose.

Under the Local Government Act, 1888, the business of the Quarter Sessions of counties and of the Town Councils of boroughs, the population of which, according to the census of 1881, was under 10,000, is transferred to the County Council.[2]

Local Authorities, under the Weights and Measures Act, possess standard weights and measures, and apparatus for testing weights and measures. This property in the case of a small borough will become useless to the borough, and the County Council will have to consider the advisability of agreeing to take it over.

The Local Authorities also appoint Inspectors of Weights and Measures. Those appointed by the Town Councils of small boroughs will lose their office and may be entitled to compensation.

Yorkshire Registries Act, 1884.

Under this Act (*47 & 48 Vict. c. 54*) a registry office under the management of a Registrar is maintained by the Quarter Sessions in each of the Ridings of Yorkshire for the registration of title-deeds affecting land in the Riding.

The business of the Quarter Sessions in this respect is transferred to the County Council, in whom the offices, buildings, and property at the registry will vest.[3] The Registrar and his staff of officers will become officers of the County Council.

---

[1] Local Government Act, 1888, secs. 3, 34. [2] *Ib.*, sec. 3. [3] *Ib.*, sec. 46.

Title-deeds affecting land within a county borough in the Riding must be registered at the registry office of the Riding, and for this purpose Kingston-upon-Hull is deemed to be situated in the East Riding.

Additional County Business.

In conclusion we may point out that, besides the transferred business that we have discussed, the County Council, after the appointed day, will have certain entirely new county business to transact.

Under the Allotments Act, 1887 (*50 & 51 Vict. c. 48*), the County Council may, upon the petition from a Sanitary Authority, make a Provisional Order enabling that Authority to acquire land compulsorily for the purpose of providing allotments for the labouring classes.

The County Council may enforce the provisions of the Rivers Pollution Prevention Act, 1876 (*39 & 40 Vict. c. 75*); they may make bye-laws relating to their county; they may appoint Medical Officers of Health; they may oppose Bills in Parliament, and have certain new powers with regard to local boundaries, &c.

Further, the Local Government Board may from time to time make Provisional Orders (requiring confirmation by Parliament) transferring to County Councils— **Further Transfer of Powers by Provisional Orders.**[1]

(i.) Any business of Quarter Sessions or Justices, or any Committee thereof under any Local Act, which is similar in character to the business transferred to County Councils by the Local Government Act, 1888, or which relates to property transferred to a County Council by that Act.

(ii.) Business of any Government Department which relates to matters arising in the county and is of an administrative character; but the consent of that Department must first be obtained.

(iii.) Business in their county of any Commissioners of Sewers, Conservators, or other public body, except Town Councils, Sanitary Authorities, School Boards, and Boards of Guardians; but the consent of such Commissioners, Conservators, or other public body must first be obtained.

Again, Her Majesty is empowered by Order in Council to transfer to County Councils the power to levy all or any of certain licences called local taxation licences.[2]

---

[1] Local Government Act, 1888, secs. 4, 10.   [2] *Ib.*, sec. 20; and see *post*, p. 70.

CHAPTER III.

COUNTY FINANCE.

County Fund.

In this chapter we propose to give an account of the finance of the County Council.

All receipts of the County Council are to be paid into the "County Fund," and all payments are to be made out of it.

Accounts of County Fund.

The county fund is divided into several accounts, namely:—

The Exchequer Contribution Account.

The General County Account.

Special County Accounts.

(1.) To the Exchequer Contribution Account will be carried the sums paid to the Council, in respect of certain licences, and in respect of a grant from the Treasury, called the "Probate Duty Grant."

From the Exchequer Contribution Account will be paid certain grants to local authorities in the county, and if there is any surplus, a transfer will be made out of it to the General County Account, and if there be still a surplus, it will be divided between the Special County Accounts and certain local authorities.

(2.) To the General County Account are to be carried the whole or part of the surplus of the Exchequer Contribution Account, after certain payments have been made out of it, and the contributions assessed on the whole area of the county for "General County Purposes" besides sums, in certain cases, receivable from other local authorities, and miscellaneous receipts.

From the General County Account are to be paid all costs incurred in respect of general county purposes, *i.e.*, purposes declared by the Local Government Act, 1888, or any other Act to be general county purposes, and all purposes to which the whole area of the county is liable to be assessed to county contributions.

(3.) To each Special County Account are carried the transfer, if any, made thereto out of the surplus of the Exchequer

Contribution Account, after the necessary payments have been made therefrom to the General County Account, and the contributions assessed on that part of the area of the county which is liable to be assessed to the corresponding "Special County Purpose," besides sums receivable in certain cases from other Local Authorities, and miscellaneous receipts.

From each Special County Account are to be paid the expenses incurred in respect of the corresponding special county purpose, *i.e.*, the purpose for which county contributions to that Special County Account may be assessed.

The county contributions assessed for both general and special county purposes are to be raised by rates.

We propose to discuss first the Exchequer Contribution Account and its distribution, and then the raising of the additional contributions necessary for the general and special county purposes. Exchequer Contribution Account.[1]

The Commissioners of Inland Revenue will pay into the Bank of England, to an account called the Local Taxation Account, from time to time, the proceeds of the duties collected by the Commissioners in each county in respect of the certain licences called "Local Taxation Licences," of which a list is given in the first schedule to the Local Government Act, 1888.

Under the direction of the Local Government Board, the amount certified by the Commissioners of Inland Revenue to have been collected in respect of Local Taxation Licences in each county (including the county boroughs in the county) is to be paid to the County Council of that county and to the Town Councils of those county boroughs. The proportions the County Council and those Town Councils will respectively receive will depend upon the equitable adjustment of the financial arrangements between the county and those boroughs to be made in the manner explained in Chapter I.[2]

The proceeds of such licences in the financial year ending the 31st March, 1888, amounted to £3,000,000 approximately. In that year, however, no licence was required for locomotives, horses and mules, or horse-dealers. Under the Excise Duties (Local Purposes) Bill it is proposed to render a licence necessary for locomotives, horses and mules, and horse-dealers, and it is estimated that the duties on these licences (known as the Horse and Wheel Tax) will produce about £800,000.

The Commissioners of Inland Revenue will also, from time

---

[1] Local Government Act, 1888, secs. 20-27.

[2] See *ante*, p. 15.

to time, after the 31st March, 1889, pay into the Bank of England, to the Local Taxation Account, two-fifths of the proceeds of the sums collected by them in respect of probate duties. The sums so paid (called the "Probate Duty Grant") will be distributed among the several counties in England and Wales in proportion to the share which the Local Government Board certify to have been received by each county during the financial year ending the 31st March, 1888, from the grants formerly made out of the Exchequer in aid of local rates, which are to be discontinued. To the share of each of the six counties in South Wales, and of the Isle of Wight, must be added such additional sum as the Local Government Board certify to be the amount that each of these counties and the Isle of Wight would have received out of the grants in aid, if the roads maintained by the County Roads Boards or the Highway Commissioners had been main roads. The Probate Duty Grant, which is estimated to amount in all to about £1,800,000, will be divided in each county between the County Council and the Town Councils of the county boroughs in the same way as the proceeds of the Local Taxation Licences.

Thus the whole sum to be distributed out of the Local Taxation Account for the year commencing on the 1st April, 1889, is estimated, including the Horse and Wheel Tax, at about £5,600,000.

The distribution will be managed, and the share which each county is to receive will be estimated, by the Local Government Board, who may, if they think fit, vary their certificate; but, subject to such variation, their certificate is final. The sums received by a County Council in respect of the Local Taxation Licences and the Probate Duty Grant are to be paid to the county fund and carried to the Exchequer Contribution Account.

Distribution of Exchequer Contribution Account.

The sums standing to the Exchequer Contribution Account will be applied as follows:—

Firstly, in payment of the costs incurred in respect of the fund or otherwise chargeable on it, which will necessarily be small.

Secondly, in payment of the sums to be paid by the County Council in substitution for Exchequer grants,[1] namely:—

To Boards of Guardians—

(i.) Towards the remuneration of Teachers in poor law schools.

[1] Local Government Act, 1888, sec. 24.

(ii.) Towards the fees of Registrars of births and deaths.
(iii.) Towards the maintenance of pauper lunatics in asylums.
(iv.) The fees of children sent from the workhouse to a public elementary school.[1]

To Town Councils—
(i.) Towards the maintenance of lunatics chargeable to their borough.
(ii.) Towards the maintenance of borough police.

To Sanitary Authorities—
In respect of the salaries of Medical Officers of Health and inspectors of nuisances.

To Public Vaccinators—
The awards paid under Section 5 of the Vaccination Act, 1867 (*30 & 31 Vict. c. 84*).

To the Police account of the County Council—
Towards the maintenance of county police.

To the Account of the County Council, to which compensation to Clerks of the Peace, for loss of fees, under *18 & 19 Vict. c. 126*, is chargeable—
The cost of such compensation.

To the Account of the County Council to which lunatics whose settlement cannot be ascertained are chargeable—
Towards their maintenance.

To the Receiver of the Metropolitan Police—
Towards the maintenance of the police.[2]

The sum paid during the financial year ending in March, 1888, in respect of the Exchequer grants in aid, which are to be discontinued (exclusive of the grant in aid of main roads) was £2,325,311.

Thirdly, the Exchequer Contribution Account must be applied by every County Council other than the London County Council in paying to the Board of Guardians of every union in the administrative county, a sum for the costs of the officers of the union, and of district schools to which the union contributes. The sum must be the sum certified by the Local Government Board, to have been expended by the Board of Guardians, during the financial year ending

[1] This is new, no such grant having been made by the Treasury.

[2] This grant is only payable by the County Council of a county wholly or partly comprised within the Metropolitan Police District. The grant will practically be deducted from the sum paid to the County Council, and paid direct to the Receiver.

the 25th March, 1888, on the salaries, remuneration and superannuation allowances of such officers (other than Teachers in poor law schools) and on drugs and medical appliances.

If a union is not situated wholly in one administrative county, this payment must be borne by the County Council of every administrative county and the Town Council of every county borough in which any portion of the union is situated, in proportion to the rateable value of that portion, ascertained on such day as the Local Government Board may fix.

In the administrative county of London the County Council instead of making the grant made by other County Councils towards the costs of officers, will pay to the Guardians of every union wholly within their county such sums as the Local Government Board may certify to be due from the County Council in substitution for the Exchequer grants formerly made in aid of the remuneration of Poor Law Medical Officers and the costs of drugs and medical appliances and also a sum equal to fourpence a head per day for every indoor pauper maintained in that union, calculated in the manner laid down in the Local Government Act, 1888.

If a union is partly situated within the administrative county of London and partly not, the grant to the Guardians is to be the same as if the union were wholly outside the administrative county of London, and must be borne by the County Council of London and the County Council of any other county, and the Town Council of any county borough, within which any portion of the union is situated, in proportion to the rateable value of that portion.[1]

It is estimated that the total amount that will be required for these payments to the Board of Guardians, including those made by the County Council of London, will be about £1,200,000.

Fourthly, the Exchequer Contribution Account must be applied in repaying to the General County Account of the county fund, the costs on account of general county purposes, for which the whole of the county is liable to be assessed to county contributions.

The principal general county purpose is the maintenance of main roads, the cost of which throughout the country, including the turnpike roads in South Wales, is upwards of £1,000,000, annually.

The Exchequer Contribution Account must be applied to these four purposes in the above order.

---

[1] Local Government Acts, sec. 43.

If any surplus remains, and from the figures we have given it appears that a surplus of something under £1,000,000, is likely to remain for the whole country, it must be distributed between Special County Accounts of the county fund and Quarter Sessions Boroughs in the following way:—

Every Quarter Sessions Borough which is exempt from contribution to any special county purpose, that is to say, practically, every Quarter Sessions Borough the population of which, according to the Census of 1881, was above 10,000, and which, on the 13th August, 1888, had already a separate Court of Quarter Sessions, will be entitled to a share of the surplus, bearing the same proportion to the whole surplus as the rateable value of the borough bears to the rateable value of the county, according to the basis for the county rate. If, however, the borough is liable to contribute to any special county purpose, the amount the borough has to contribute will be deducted from its share of the surplus, instead of being levied in the borough by means of rates.

Each Quarter Sessions Borough having been paid its proper share, the rest of the surplus must be applied in repaying to the proper Special County Accounts the costs on account of which the whole area of the county, with the exception of such Quarter Sessions Boroughs, is liable to be assessed to county contributions.

If after these payments a surplus still remains, it must be divided, on the same principle, between boroughs other than the above-mentioned Quarter Sessions Boroughs, but which maintain a separate police force, and the Special County Accounts to which the area of the county, exclusive of all the above-mentioned boroughs, is liable to be assessed.

Should any surplus still remain, which, however, is improbable, it is, after deducting any sum the County Council may think it advisable to carry forward to the next account, to be divided according to the rateable value of their district among Sanitary Authorities other than Town Councils who have already shared in the distribution of the account.

Before giving an account of how county contributions are raised, it will be necessary to give a brief account of the law and practice relating to the poor rate. For the purpose of the relief of the poor, the occupier of real property in any parish, speaking generally, is rated in proportion to the rateable value of that property. The law with regard to the principles of rating is extremely intricate and technical, and it is beyond our scope to treat it in any detail. Rating.

A rate is a personal tax, although made in respect of real property; that is to say, the rate is not a charge on the land or other property, but the occupier is personally liable. Almost every description of real property is rateable, but the circumstances in which it stands, or the use to which it is put, may prevent its being actually rated for the time being. Thus, property that is unoccupied, *e.g.*, an empty house, is not rateable while it continues empty. Again, property in the occupation of the Crown is not rateable, nor churches, nor museums, &c., under certain circumstances. The occupier, speaking generally, is the person liable to pay the rate, and therefore it becomes important to understand the meaning of the term occupation. It is, however, almost impossible to define accurately what is the meaning of occupation. Mere legal possession does not constitute occupation; thus, an owner of land is in possesssion of minerals underneath, but if he does not dig for them he is not in occupation of them. The owner of an empty house is, in the same way, though in legal possession, not in occupation. On the other hand, without legal possession, a person may be in occupation; thus, a mere squatter on a common is in occupation of the land he uses. Occupation may be said to involve the idea of control and employment.

Should the property be rateable, it remains to inquire what its rateable value is. To ascertain this, the "gross estimated rental" must first be ascertained. The "gross estimated rental" was said by the Law Officers of the Crown, in 1859, to be "the rent at which the property might be expected to let, free of tenants' rates and taxes, and tithe commutation rent-charge, the tenant taking these burdens upon himself."[1] Thus, practically, the gross estimated rental is the rack-rent on a tenancy from year to year.

It must be pointed out that the value is taken one year with another, good and bad, and also that the increased rent which the property may be worth, owing to its being let on lease, is not taken into account.

The rateable value is the gross estimated rental, deducting therefrom the probable annual average of the repairs, insurance, and other expenses, necessary to maintain the property in a state to command such rent.

Where the property is property of a class with an ascer-

[1] Statutory definitions have since that date been given, but are consistent therewith.

tained value, such as houses, agricultural land, &c., the question of rating is comparatively simple. The principal difficulties arise with regard to such property as great country mansions, for which there is practically no means of estimating a reasonable rental, and as to public undertakings, such as railways, docks, &c.

It is impossible within the limits of the present work to deal with the many peculiar provisions and principles with regard to particular classes of property; any account that we could give within our limits must, from its very brevity, be misleading. The more practical branch of the subject being less technical, may be explained at greater length.

Valuation List.

A list of the property liable to be rated to the poor rate, with its value, is prepared in every union. This list is known as "The Valuation List;" and although prepared primarily for the purpose of enabling the Guardians to assess contributions on each parish, towards their common poor fund, it serves other purposes in connection with local taxation.

The statutes dealing with the preparation of the valuation list are—

The Union Assessment Committee Act, 1862 (*25 & 26 Vict. c. 103*).

The Union Assessment Committee Amendment Act, 1864 (*27 & 28 Vict. c. 39*).

The Union Assessment Act, 1880 (*43 & 44 Vict. c. 7*), which three statutes are called together the Union Assessment Acts, 1861 to 1880.[1]

These Acts apply to every union which is constituted under the Poor Law Amendment Act, 1834 (*4 & 5 Will. IV. c. 76*). In incorporations and unions under other Acts, the poor law authority may adopt the Union Assessment Acts, and in most cases have done so. In single parishes under Boards of Guardians, constituted under the Poor Law Amendment Act, 1834; or under a Local Act, the Local Government Board may, by Order, bring the Acts into operation; but the Acts do not apply within the Metropolis.

In unions and incorporations in which these Acts are in force, a valuation list is prepared for each parish, and the combined lists of all the parishes in the union form the valuation list for the union.

The Board of Guardians or other authority annually appoint

[1] Certain provisions on the subject are also contained in the Poor Law Amendment Act, 1868 (31 & 32 Vict. c. 122) sec. 30-32, 38.

a committee called the "Assessment Committee" of the union. Where the union is co-extensive with a municipal borough, the Clerk to the Guardians, upon the appointment of the Committee, if directed by the Board of Guardians, sends a list of the members of the Committee to the Town Council, who may then appoint additional members of the Assessment Committee; but the Town Council have no right to appoint additional members unless the Board of Guardians direct their Clerk to send them the list of members.

At the present time valuation lists have been prepared, and are in force for almost every parish in England and Wales to which the Acts are applicable.

The valuation lists in force for the time being for a union are kept in the custody of the Guardians; and a certified copy of the valuation list in force for each parish is kept by the Overseers with the rate book of the parish, and is open for inspection. In order to keep the valuation lists up to date, the Overseers from time to time prepare supplemental lists, or, if necessary, new lists. A supplemental list may be made by the Overseers whenever they think it necessary; the Assessment Committee also, may from time to time direct the preparation of new or supplemental valuation lists.

The form of every valuation list is as follows:—

Valuation List for (*the parish or place for which the list is made*), in the County of .

Name of occupier.	Name of owner.	Description of property.	Name or situation of property.	Estimated extent	Gross estimated rental.	Rateable value.

Signed this day of

A. B. } *Overseers of the Poor*
C. D. } *of the parish aforesaid.*

Where a supplemental or new list is prepared by the Overseers, they send a copy of it to the Board of Guardians, and the list itself they deposit with the rate books, &c., for inspection by any persons rateable in the parish, and give public notice of the deposit on the next Sunday, by affixing a notice of the deposit on church doors.

On the next Monday fortnight they must transmit the original list to the Board of Guardians, where it remains still open for inspection by any ratepayer or Overseer of a parish within the union.

At any time after the deposit of the list, and within 28 days of the deposit, any person aggrieved by the list may give notice of objection to the list, which notice must be sent to the Board of Guardians and to the Overseers of the parish in which the property, in respect of which the objection is made, is situated. If the grievance is in respect of property other than the objector's own property, notice must also be sent to the person liable to be rated in respect of that property. In a notice of objection the ground of objection must be stated.

The Assessment Committee hold meetings to hear objections, and whether objections are made or not, may correct and alter the list. After they have corrected the list they approve it and send a copy to the Overseers. The list so approved becomes "the valuation list in force," or if it is a supplemental list, part of the "valuation list in force," but if it has been altered by the Assessment Committee it must again be deposited with the rate book for a period of between seven and fourteen days, during which time objections may be made in the same way as before. If any objections are so made the Assessment Committee will hear them, and again, if necessary, alter and approve the list. The certified copy sent to the Overseers is kept by them with the rate book, and is open to the inspection of ratepayers in the same way as the rate book.

The Overseers of any parish in the union, with the consent of the inhabitants in vestry assembled, may appeal from the valuation list as approved by the Assessment Committee, either on the ground that their own parish is valued too high or that some other parish is valued too low. The appeal lies to the Quarter Sessions of the county or borough comprising the greatest number of parishes in the union, or in the case of equality of numbers, to the Quarter Sessions within whose jurisdiction the parish lies, in which the workhouse of the union is situated. The appeal must be made to the first sessions after the expiration of one month from the deposit of the list.

"The valuation list in force" remains in force until a new list or supplemental list has been made and approved; subject to the following provisions.

(1.) Where a poor rate is made based on the valuation list, and a person proposes to appeal against the rate, he must give 21 days' notice of his intention to appeal to the Assessment Committee, stating the grounds of his intended appeal. The Assessment Committee must hold a meeting to hear the objection, and may, if they consider the objection valid, alter the valuation list accordingly. It may be pointed out that no person may appeal against a poor rate unless he has first failed to obtain relief from the Assessment Committee. Owing apparently to careless drafting of the Union Assessment Amendment Act, 1864, the appellant against a poor rate must give notice of appeal to the Assessment Committee, whether the ground of his appeal is the unfairness of the valuation list or not; so that notice must be given even in a case where the Assessment Committee are powerless to grant relief, though whether the Assessment Committee in such a case have to go through the formality of a meeting to hear the objection seems doubtful.

(2.) If a successful appeal against the rate is made after the refusal of the Assessment Committee to give satisfactory relief to the appellant, the valuation list must be altered in accordance with the result of that appeal.

(3.) Where an appeal is made by Overseers against the valuation list, the list may be corrected by the Quarter Sessions.

Making a Poor Rate

The poor rate is actually estimated by the Overseers of each parish.

The expenses that the Overseers will have to meet are the immediate expenses of the parish, Orders for contributions from the Guardians of the Union, and Orders for contributions in certain cases from other authorities.

As far as possible the Overseers, as a rule, make poor rates for six months at a time, estimating what will be required to meet all the expenses during those six months; the rate is then calculated out in the following way:—

The total sum required is compared with the total rateable value of the parish as it appears in the valuation list, and from that comparison the Overseers decide at what rate in the pound the rate will have to be made, making an allowance for property unoccupied, and difficulties of collection, &c.

The actual sum required from each occupier is estimated in accordance with the valuation list and put in the rate book.

The rate thus prepared must be submitted by the Overseers to two or more Justices of the Peace, who must "allow" it, which they do by signing a statement at the foot of the rate book to the effect that they consent to and allow the assessment. The rate is then published, after which the Overseers or Collectors of the poor rate proceed to collect it. The form of a rate book is shown in Appendix E; it will be seen that columns 4 to 10 are copied from the valuation list.

We now proceed to give an account of a county rate, that is to say, a contribution assessed on the whole or part of their county by the County Council. County Rate

The county rate is levied by the Overseers, usually, as part of the poor rate. The County Council compute what the contribution of each parish should be, and obtain payment of that contribution in a lump sum through the Guardians and Overseers.

For the purpose of raising the county rate a basis or standard is prepared for every county save the County of London, which basis is really a list of the parishes and parts of parishes in the county, with the rateable value of each—the rateable value being calculated on the same principle as rateable value for the purpose of the poor rate. The preparation of this basis will be the duty of the County Council, and must practically be carried out by a Committee. Basis.[1]

For the purpose of obtaining the necessary information, the Committee have wide powers.

1st. The Clerk of every Union Assessment Committee must annually, in December, send to the Clerk of the County Council copies of the totals of the gross estimated rental and rateable value of the several parishes in the union, as corrected up to date by any supplemental valuation lists.[2]

2nd. The Committee may, by an Order in writing, direct Overseers of the poor, Constables, Assessors and Collectors of public rates for any parish, borough, or place within their county, and all other persons having the custody of any public or parochial rates or valuations for such parish or place, to make returns in writing to the Committee at such times and places as they may appoint, stating the rateable value of the whole or any

[1] See 15 & 16 Vict. c. 81, secs. 2-20.
[2] Union Assessment Committee Amendment Act, 1864, sec. 9.

part of the property within the parish, &c., the date of the last valuation for the assessment of such parish, and the name of the surveyor or other person or persons by whom the valuation was made. Thus the Committee can obtain full information as to any valuations that have been made, whether by a Union Assessment Committee or in any other way.

3rd. The Committee may, by Order in writing, require Overseers, Constables, Assessors and Collectors of rates, and other persons to appear before them, to produce all parochial and other rates, assessments, valuations, apportionments and other documents in their custody or power relating to the value of an assessment on all or any of the property within parishes and places liable to be assessed to the county rate, and they may examine such persons. Private persons may be summoned before the Committee and are bound to produce private accounts and documents.[1]

4th. The Committee may cause copies to be made, of the total amount assessed in each parish, &c., in respect of the assessed taxes, and the total amount of the valuation of the property on which the assessments were made, by the Clerk to the Commissioners of assessed taxes.

5th. In order to enforce the making of returns and the appearance of persons summoned to appear, it has been provided that any person failing to comply with the requisitions of the Committee is liable to a penalty not exceeding £20, which the Committee may recover before two Justices.

6th. The Committee may have an independent valuation made of any parish, &c., within the county, and the valuer appointed by them may, at all reasonable times, with his assistants, enter upon, view, examine, survey and measure the lands and other property in the parish, &c.

As soon as the Committee have prepared a basis in which there is any variation from the preceding basis, they have the basis printed and a copy sent to the Overseers of every parish and to every Justice of the county, and at the same time give notice of the time within which objections are to be sent, and of the time and place for hearing objections. The Overseers of any parish then call a vestry meeting to consider the basis. The objections having been heard and determined upon by the Committee, and their basis finally prepared, it is laid before the County Council at a meeting of which notice is given.

---

[1] Dickson *v.* Doubleday, 30 L.J. M.C. 99.

The County Council then correct and confirm the basis or refer it back to the Committee, and consider it again at an adjourned meeting.

When finally confirmed by the County Council, the basis becomes valid and binding, notwithstanding any irregularity in the making of it. A copy of the basis thus finally confirmed is sent to the Overseers of every parish and to every Justice of the Peace in the county, and the Overseers of any parish, or any inhabitant, may appeal against the basis so confirmed to the next Quarter Sessions held after the confirmation. If the grievance is the under-valuation or omission of some other parish 24 days' notice must be given to the Overseers of that parish. The Quarter Sessions may then correct the basis with regard to the matters complained of.

The Committee may revise the basis from time to time, so as to bring it into accordance with existing circumstances, and in that case they need only give notice to the parish, the valuation of which they propose to alter; upon which that parish may make objections, and the proposed revision must be confirmed by the County Council.

The expenses of the Committee will, in general, be paid out of the county fund and charged to the general county account; but in two cases their expenses in connection with a particular parish may be charged against that parish.

1st. If the Overseers of a parish neglect to make such returns in writing as they are required to do, or make a false return, the County Council may, on the report of the Committee, order the expense incurred in ascertaining the value of that parish to be charged thereon as a special contribution to the county rate.

2nd. Where the Committee have directed the whole or any part of a parish to be valued, and where, in the basis as finally allowed, such parish is assessed at a greater sum than the sum in the returns made to the Committee by the Overseers, the costs of such a valuation must be charged in the same way against that parish; unless there be a successful appeal whereby the value of that parish in the basis is reduced to or below the sum returned by the Overseers.

It must be pointed out that a new basis will be required, in most cases, in the course of the year 1889, because of the changes in county boundaries, and also owing to the fact that Quarter Sessions Boroughs will become liable to be assessed to the county rate, which they have hitherto not been.

Assessing the County Rate.[1]

The making and assessing of the county rate is a duty that will fall on the County Council; for the practical management of the finances of the county, as we have seen, a Finance Committee must be appointed. It must be remembered that the county rate is to be levied in respect of "general county purposes" and "special county purposes."

The following is a list of the principal special county purposes:—

Police;
Lunatic Asylums;
Weights and Measures;
Coroners;
Contagious Diseases (animals).

The County Council will make an estimate of the sum it will be necessary to obtain for general county purposes, and an estimate of the sum required for each special county purpose. In determining the amount of expenditure for any county purpose, general or special, a proper proportion of the cost of the officers, buildings, and establishment of the County Council may be added to the expenditure directly expended for that purpose.

The County Council will have before them the basis for the county rate, prepared for the county. Taking first the whole sum required for general county purposes, the County Council must compute the sum that each parish in their county should contribute towards those purposes, and each parish must contribute in porportion to its value, as shown in the basis. Then taking the sum required for each special county purpose, the County Council must ascertain what parishes in the county are liable to contribute in respect of that purpose, and then must compute what share of that sum each of those parishes should contribute, remembering that each must contribute in proportion to its value, as shown in the basis.

Thus, for example:—Let us suppose, for the sake of simplicity, that a county consists of five parishes, A, B, C, D, E, and that the basis shows the value of each of these parishes, as follows:—

Parish.	Rateable Value.
A	£1,000
B	£1,500
C	£2,000
D	£500
E	£10,000

[1] Local Government Act, 1888, sec. 68.

and that the total sum required for general county purposes is estimated at £62 10s. 0d., then each parish will have to contribute as follows:—

Parish.	Rateable on	£	s.	d.
A	£1,000	4	3	4
B	£1,500	6	5	0
C	£2,000	8	6	8
D	£500	2	1	8
E	£10,000	41	13	4

Now take a special county purpose, say police. Perhaps E is in a borough maintaining its own police, and, therefore, not liable to contribute towards the police of the county; and suppose that the total sum required for police purposes is £42 13s. 4d., then the parishes must contribute—

	£	s.	d.
A	8	6	8
B	12	10	0
C	16	13	4
D	4	3	4

Taking each special county purpose in turn in this way the whole sum that each parish will have to contribute will be ascertained.

This estimate must be made at the beginning of the local financial year, which for the year 1889-90 begins on the 26th March, 1889. It must show the amount that will be required for each purpose, and for each parish, for the first six months of the local financial year, and, also, what will be required for the second six months. At the end of the first six months the original estimate may be revised. Probably it may be advisable to have the estimate published in such a shape as to show what parishes have been assessed to contributions for each special county purpose, and at what rate in the pound the contributions for general county purposes, and for each special county purpose, have been assessed; but contributions for different special county purposes, which are levied over the same part of the county, might probably be treated together. [1]

Levying County Contributions.[2]

The next process after having computed the amount each parish ought to contribute, is to obtain the contribution. For this purpose the County Council will send a precept to the Board of Guardians of the union in which any parish in their county is situated, directing them to pay within a given time the contribution so computed.

[1] Local Government Act, 1888, secs. 73, 74, and see 15 & 16 Vict. c. 81.
[2] See 15 & 16 Vict. c. 81.

Two cases may arise where the whole of a parish is not liable to contribute to a county rate :—

1st. Where the parish is in two counties. In this case the value of that part of the parish which is in each county will appear in the basis for that county, and the County Council, instead of sending a precept to the Guardians of the Union in which such parish is situated must send a precept to the Overseers of that parish directing them to pay to the County Treasurer the contributions assessed on that part of the parish. It is probable that the County Council will take steps to deal with every parish which lies partly in their county and partly in another, so as to prevent their county boundary cutting any parish boundary : this case in the future will accordingly not be likely to arise.

2nd. Where a parish is partly liable to contribute towards a special county purpose, and partly not, the question is more difficult. The way in which this will ordinarily arise will be where the parish is partly situated in a borough and partly outside ; in that case the value of the part of the parish not within the borough, and the part within the borough will not appear separately in the basis. There appears to be no enactment providing how the value of each part of the parish is to be calculated. The safest course will be for the County Council to divide the value of the parish in the proportion shown by the valuation list. In this case they obtain the necessary contributions from each part, by sending precepts to the Guardians.

County Loans.[1] A County Council may borrow money on the security of their funds and revenues for the following purposes :—

(1.) For consolidating the debts of the county.

(2.) For purchasing any land, or building any building, which they are authorised by any Act to purchase or build.

(3.) For any permanent work or thing which the County Council are authorized to execute or do, and the cost of which ought, in the opinion of the Local Government Board, to be spread over a term of years.

(4.) For making advances to any persons or body in aid of the emigration or colonisation of inhabitants of the county, if they have a guarantee for the repayment of such advances from a local authority in the county, or from the Government of a colony.

---

[1] Local Government Act, 1888, secs. 69, 70.

(5.) For any purpose for which Quarter Sessions or the County Council are authorized by any Act to borrow.

The County Council must not, however, except for the purpose of discharging a loan already made, borrow money without the consent of the Local Government Board, who, before giving their consent, will take into consideration any representation made by any ratepayer or owner of property rated to county contributions. The consent of the Local Government Board will dispense with any other consent which may be required by the Acts relating to such borrowing.

If the County Council propose to borrow any sum, when their total debt, including that sum, and excluding the amount of any sinking fund, exceeds one-tenth of the annual rateable value of the rateable property in the county, according to the basis for the county rate; then that sum must not be borrowed except in pursuance of a Provisional Order made by the Local Government Board, and confirmed by Parliament.

During the period, however, which was fixed for the discharge of any loan raised by the County Council or their predecessors, the County Council may, without the consent of the Local Government Board, borrow such amount as may be required for paying off the whole or any part of such loan. If the County Council have already borrowed for the purpose of paying such a loan, and have so paid it, they may again borrow for the purpose of paying off such second loan, so that without consent of the Local Government Board, the County Council may take advantage of any rise in the price of their stock; but all money so borrowed must be repaid within the period fixed for repayment of the original loan.

The County Council may borrow for such period not exceeding thirty years, as they, with the sanction of the Local Government Board, determine in each case.

If the County Council raise a loan for any special county purpose they must charge the sums payable in respect of that loan to the corresponding Special County Account.

Every loan must be paid off, either by equal yearly or half-yearly instalments of principal, or of principal and interest combined, or by means of a sinking fund.

A County Council authorized to borrow may raise money either by one loan or several loans, and in the following ways:—

1st. By the issue of county stock under the Local Government Act, 1888.[1]

[1] Local Government Act, 1888, sec. 70.

The Local Government Board has powers to make regulations with regard to the creation, issue, transference, and redemption of county stock.

2nd. By debentures under the Local Loans Act, 1875 (*38 & 39 Vict. c. 83*).

3rd. By annuity certificates under the Local Loans Act, 1875.

Such a debenture is an instrument taking effect as a deed, and charging the county revenues, or any part of the county revenues, or any county property in such debenture mentioned, with the payment of the principal sum and interest, in the manner mentioned in the debenture.

The principal sum may be made payable to the bearer of the debenture, in which case the debenture is transferable by delivery; or the principal sum may be made payable to a person to be named therein, his executors, administrators or assigns, in which case the debenture is termed a "nominal debenture," and is transferable by writing in such manner as the County Council may direct.

There may be attached to debentures, coupons, payable to order or to bearer; or the interest on a debenture may be made payable to the owner for the time being of the debenture, or otherwise, as may be mentioned in the debenture.

A debenture may be for any sum not less than £5.

An annuity certificate issued by a County Council is an instrument taking effect as a deed, and charging the county revenues, or part of the county revenues, or any county property, with the payment of the annual sum therein mentioned, in the manner in the certificate mentioned.

Like the principal sum in a debenture, the annual sum in an annuity certificate, may be payable to bearer; or the certificate may be a nominal certificate.

An annuity certificate may be issued for any sum not less than £3.

The County Council issuing nominal debentures, or nominal annuity certificates must cause a register of such securities to be kept, in which must be entered the names and addresses, and the descriptions of the owners for the time being, of every such security, with a statement of the securities held by each person registered, and also the date at which the name of any person was entered in the register, in respect of any such security.

Any person may inspect the register at any reasonable time, upon payment of such fee, not exceeding one shilling, as the County Council may fix, and may purchase from the Registrar copies or extracts certified by him to be true copies or extracts.

The Commissioners of Inland Revenue may supply the County Council with debentures, coupons, and annuity certificates, upon such terms as may, with the sanction of the Treasury, be agreed upon.

4th. The County Council may borrow by mortgage of their revenue in accordance with the provisions of the Public Health Act, 1875 (*38 & 39 Vict. c. 55*), secs. 236, 237, if any special reason exists for so doing; but if the County Council have already borrowed by means of stock they must not borrow by mortgage for any period exceeding five years.

The mortgage must be by deed, and must truly state the date, consideration, and place of payment, and must be under the common seal of the County Council.

The County Council must, at their office, keep a register of the mortgages on each source of revenue, and within fourteen days after the date of any mortgage an entry must be made in the register of the number and date thereof, and of the parties thereto, as stated in the deed. The register must be open for public inspection during office hours free of charge.

A loan borrowed by a County Council must, as we have seen, be paid off within the time fixed at its issue, in equal yearly or half-yearly instalments, or by means of a sinking fund.

If the loan is raised by stock, the Local Government Board may make regulations for the repayment. If the loan is raised by annuity certificates they may be made terminable and limited to expire within the prescribed period.

If the loan is raised by debentures, they may be made payable in such a manner that in each year a certain number will become due and be paid off; or an annual appropriation may be made of a fixed sum to the discharge of a certain portion of the loan.

In this case the County Council must in each year raise such equal sum as will, at or before the expiration of the fixed period, pay off the whole of the loan and the interest thereon. Out of this fixed sum in each year the County Council must pay the interest due, and with the remainder pay off a corresponding amount of the principal sum secured by the debentures.

The debentures to be paid off in any year must be ascertained in such manner as may be fixed at the time of issue of the debentures, or as may thereafter be arranged.

If the debentures to be paid off are to be determined by lot, the lots must be drawn in the presence of the County Council and of any owners of debentures who choose to be present; the County Council must give not less than one month's previous notice of the time and place at which lots are to be drawn, by advertisement published at least once in each of four successive weeks in some newspaper circulating in the county.

Any fractional sum remaining over must be carried to the credit of the annual sum to be raised in the ensuing year.

Where the loan is raised by debentures, a sinking fund may be established, when the following provisions apply:—

1st. Such equal yearly or half-yearly sums must be paid into the sinking fund as, being accumulated at compound interest at the rate the Local Government Board may prescribe, will at the expiration of some period not longer than the period prescribed for the repayment of the loan, be sufficient, after payment of all expenses, to discharge the loan.

2nd. The first of such payments must be made within one year from the date of the loan.

3rd. All sums paid into the sinking fund must, without delay, be invested, and the proceeds of such investments must be re-invested.

4th. The County Council may apply the sinking fund, from time to time, in discharge of the loan, but to no other purpose.

5th. The debentures, to the payment of which the sinking fund is, for the time being, applicable, must be ascertained in the same manner as the debentures to be paid off when the payment is made by the appropriation of a fixed annual sum.

6th. Any surplus of the sinking fund, after the discharge of the loan, must be paid into some other sinking fund under the control of the County Council, or if there is no such fund, must be applied to any purpose to which the loan was applicable, as the County Council may, with the consent of the Local Government Board, think expedient.

7th. When any part of the sinking fund is invested in securities of the County Council, or is applied in paying off any part of the loan before the prescribed period, the interest which would otherwise be payable on such securities, or on such part of the loan, must be paid into the sinking fund and invested.

8th. If the annual income of the sinking fund is not less than the annual interest payable on so much of the loan as remains undischarged, the equal annual payments into the sinking fund may cease to be paid.

Accounts of County Council.[1]

The accounts of the receipts and expenditure of the County Council must be made up to the end of each local financial year, and be in the form for the time being prescribed by the Local Government Board.

The accounts of the County Treasurer must be made up half-yearly to such dates as the County Council, with the approval of the Local Government Board, may from time to time appoint.

A return must be made annually to the Local Government Board of the receipts and expenditure of the County Council in such form as the Local Government Board may direct.

The accounts of a County Council and of the County Treasurer, and of the Officers of the County Council, must be audited in accordance with secs. 247 and 250 of the Public Health Act, 1875 (*38 & 39 Vict. c. 55*), by the District Auditors appointed by the Local Government Board under the District Auditors Act, 1879 (*42 & 43 Vict. c. 6*).

The County Council must pay a stamp duty for accounts thus audited.

The District Auditor will give notice of the time and place at which he proposes to attend for the audit, and after receiving that notice the County Council must give at least fourteen days' notice of that time and place, and also of the deposit of accounts they are required to make, by advertisement in one or more local newspapers.

A copy of the accounts, duly made up and balanced, together with all rate books, account books, deeds, contracts, accounts, vouchers, and receipts, mentioned or referred to in such accounts, must be deposited in the office of the County Council and must be open during office hours to the inspection of all persons interested, for seven clear days before the audit, and all such persons may take copies or extracts free of charge.

For the purpose of the audit the District Auditor may, by summons, in writing, require the production of all books, deeds, accounts, &c., that he may deem necessary, and may require any person holding or accountable for such books, &c., to appear before him and sign a declaration as to their correctness.

---

[1] Local Government Act, 1888, sec. 71.

Any ratepayer or owner of property in the county may be present at the audit, and may make any objection to the accounts before the District Auditor, and such ratepayers and owners have the same right of appeal against allowances by a District Auditor as is given in the case of disallowances.

The District Auditor must disallow every item of account contrary to law, and surcharge the same on the person making or authorizing the making of the illegal payment; he must charge against any person accounting the amount of any deficiency he has incurred by the negligence or misconduct of that person, or of any item which ought to have been, but is not, brought into account by that person. In every case of disallowance or surcharge, he must certify the amount due from such person, and on application by any party aggrieved, must state in writing the reasons for his decision in respect of such disallowance or surcharge, and also of any allowance which he may have made.

Any person aggrieved by disallowance, may apply to the Queen's Bench Division of the High Court for a writ of *certiorari*, to remove the disallowance into that court ; or such person may appeal to the Local Government Board.

Every sum certified to be due from any person by the District Auditor, must be paid by such person to the Treasurer of the County Council within fourteen days after the same has been so certified ; unless there is an appeal. If the sum is not paid, the Auditor may recover the same.

Within fourteen days after the completion of the audit, the District Auditor must report on the accounts audited, and deliver his report to the Clerk of the County Council, who must deposit the same in their office and must publish an abstract of the accounts in one or more local newspapers.

CHAPTER IV.

BOUNDARIES.

IN this chapter it is intended to give an account of the boundaries of the various areas of importance in connection with Local Government, namely :—The parish, the union, the highway parish, the highway district, the borough, the sanitary districts, the county, the wards of boroughs and of sanitary districts, and the electoral divisions of counties.

New powers of Local Government Board.

Before going into details, we may point out that under the Local Government Act, 1888, the Local Government Board have large new powers for dealing with local boundaries. In particular they may, by a Provisional Order, requiring confirmation by Parliament, alter county and borough boundaries, which it has hitherto been impossible, generally speaking, to deal with by any means short of an Act of Parliament; they may also by such an Order unite counties and county boroughs for all or any of the purposes of the Local Government Act, 1888, or divide counties.

In certain cases the Board may, however, exercise their power, only in pursuance of a representation from a County or Town Council interested.[1]

County Councils also are given powers of dealing with local boundaries; in particular they may make Orders, requiring confirmation by the Local Government Board, dealing with parish boundaries and with the boundaries of sanitary districts, and also for converting rural sanitary districts, or parts thereof, into urban sanitary districts and *vice versâ*.[2]

Powers of County Council.

We now proceed to deal more in detail with each area which we have mentioned above.

Parish.

A parish is generally, as we have explained, either an old

[1] Local Government Act, 1888, sec. 54.
[2] *Ib.*, sec. 57.

ecclesiastical parish or a township, or some equivalent area.[1] The boundaries of ancient parishes and of townships, &c., never were definitely determined, but were matters of tradition; and so far as the boundaries of parishes have not been definitely laid down by, or in pursuance of, recent statutes they still remain matters of tradition. Where a dispute arises as to the position of a parish boundary which has remained unaffected, the question must be decided by the Courts upon such evidence of tradition as is brought before them.

The following is a brief account of the recent legislation and of the places in which records of the changes consequent upon such legislation have been kept.

Until recently certain places were extra-parochial, *i.e.*, not in any parish. By an Act of 1857 (*20 Vict. c. 19*), such extra-parochial places as were entered as extra-parochial in the census returns for 1851 were made parishes. Extra-parochial places.

The Justices of the Peace were also empowered to make other extra-parochial places into parishes by simply appointing Overseers for them. The owners and occupiers of an extra-parochial place might, with the consent of a parish, annex such a place to a parish. The annexation was effected by an Order of the Quarter Sessions of the county or borough in which the parish was situated, and such an Order might probably be found in the records of the parish or of the county.

By the Poor Law Amendment Act, 1868 (*31 & 32 Vict. c. 122*)[2] all remaining extra-parochial places were incorporated with the adjoining parish with which they had the longest common boundary, or in case of an equality of boundaries, with the parish of the lowest rateable value.

The next general Act affecting parish boundaries, dealt with detached portions of parishes. Large numbers of parishes had formerly, and many have still, outlying portions completely detached from the main body. These cases had before 1882, been dealt with in considerable numbers by the Local Government Board, under certain powers that we shall discuss subsequently. Detached parts of parishes.

By the Divided Parishes and Poor Law Amendment Act, 1882 (*45 & 46 Vict. c. 58*), those portions of divided parishes which were wholly surrounded by another parish became part of the surrounding parish, and where two or more isolated parts of different parishes adjoining each other were wholly

[1] *Ante*, p. 34. [2] Sec. 27.

surrounded by another parish, they in the same way became part of the surrounding parish. An opportunity was however given to the inhabitants of such a detached part of a parish, containing a population over 300, to apply to the Local Government Board to be made into a separate parish, but that provision had to be taken advantage of before the 1st December, 1882.

Thus apart from awards, orders and statutes dealing with particular cases, a parish retains its traditional boundaries, but it may contain additional places that were extra-parochial in 1857 or 1868, or which were detached parts of other parishes in 1882.

We now deal with the orders and awards that may have affected or defined parish boundaries.

The Justices, as we have seen, had formerly power to annex places to parishes, and their Orders may be found among the records either of the parish or county. This power is of course obsolete.

Tithe Commissioners and Inclosure Commissioners.

The Tithe Commissioners and the Inclosure Commissioners have power in certain cases to alter, define, and straighten parish boundaries.[1] The records of these bodies in connection with parish boundaries may probably be found among the parish records of the parishes affected. These powers still exist, but are not of very general importance.

Divided Parishes Acts.

Under the Divided Parishes and Poor Law Amendment Act, 1876 (*39 & 40 Vict. c. 61*), the Poor Law Act, 1879 (*42 & 43 Vict. c. 54*), and the Divided Parishes and Poor Law Amendment Act, 1882 (*45 & 46 Vict. c. 58*), the Local Government Board may deal with any parish :—

(i.) which is divided so that some portions are completely detached from others ; or

(ii.) which is divided so that part of it is divided from another part by the boundary of a municipal borough or of a county or by a river estuary or branch of the sea ; or

(iii.) which has a part nearly detached from the rest of it or otherwise so situated as to render the administration of the relief of the poor, in such part, or its local

[1] The powers of the Tithe Commissioners are contained in—6 & 7 Will. IV. c. 71, sec. 12 ; 1 Vict. c. 69, secs. 2, 3 ; 2 & 3 Vict. c. 62, secs. 34-36 ; 3 & 4 Vict. c. 15, sec. 28 ; 9 & 10 Vict. c. 73, sec. 21. The powers of the Inclosure Commissioners, in—41 Geo. III. c. 109, sec. 3 ; 6 & 7 Will. IV. c. 115, sec. 28 ; 3 & 4 Vict. c. 31, secs. 2, 3 ; 8 & 9 Vict. c. 118, sec. 39 ; 12 & 13 Vict. c. 83, secs. 1, 9 ; 15 & 16 Vict. c. 79, sec. 28.

government inconvenient in conjunction with the rest of the parish ; or

(iv.) which was before 1857 an extra-parochial place.

The Local Government Board may make separate parishes of the detached parts, or annex them to existing parishes which they adjoin. Where it is proposed to deal with a parish in this way, notice must be given to the Clerk of the Peace of the county or counties in which the parts of the parish are situated, and also published in the parishes to be affected, in the same way as other parochial notices. A local inquiry is then held by the Local Government Board, and if it is decided to deal with the case the Board make an Order and send copies thereof to the Overseers of the parishes affected. The Order, however, must not take effect till the expiration of at least three months from the day on which a copy is sent to the Overseers.

If one-tenth in number and rateable value of the persons, appearing on the poor rate in force for the time being, give notice to the Local Government Board of their objection to the Order within three months after copies have been sent to the Overseers, the Order will be provisional only, and will require confirmation by Parliament. The actual change will take place on the 25th March next after the day on which the Order, if not objected to, takes effect, or, if objected to, next after the Act of Parliament confirming the Provisional Order.

The Order of the Board may provide for an adjustment of debts and liabilities, the custody of parish records, compensation to officers deprived of employment, and decide who is to be Chairman of the vestry if a new parish is constituted.

Powers of County Council with regard to parish boundaries.[1]

Under the Local Government Act, 1888, the County Council may, whenever they are satisfied that a *primâ facie* case is made out for a proposal for the alteration of a parish boundary or for the division of a parish, or for its amalgamation with any other parish or parishes, or for the transfer of part of a parish to another parish, cause an inquiry to be made in the locality, and notice thereof to be given both locally and to certain Government Departments.

If satisfied that the proposal is desirable the County Council may make an Order for the same, which must be submitted to the Local Government Board for confirmation or alteration. Notice of the provisions of the Order must be given and copies thereof must be supplied. The procedure in the matter must

[1] Local Government Act, 1888, sec. 57

be in accordance with rules that will be prescribed by the Local Government Board.

If within three months after the first notice of the provisions of the Order is given, any number of county electors registered in any parish affected, not being less than one-sixth of the whole number, petition the Local Government Board to disallow the Order, the Local Government Board must hold a local inquiry to determine whether the Order is to be confirmed or not.

If no petition is presented, or if a petition having been presented is withdrawn, the Local Government Board must confirm the Order, but may make any necessary modifications in it. The Order may provide for all incidental arrangements in the way of adjustment of property, debts, &c.[1]

The power of the Local Government Board under the Divided Parishes Acts is, however, unaffected by these provisions.

Parish boundaries, we may point out, may cut any other boundaries save those of unions.

Union.

As a union is merely a combination of parishes the question of its boundaries in the strict sense depends merely on the boundaries of the constituent parishes.

As to the formation, dissolution, and alteration of a union by the addition or subtraction of parishes, it is sufficient to point out that the Local Government Board have full powers to form new unions and to alter and dissolve existing unions.[2]

It is contemplated by the Local Government Act, 1888, that steps will be taken to deal with unions that stretch into more than one county, so as to obviate as far as possible the inconvenience of intersecting boundaries, but the County Council will have no power in the matter beyond making a representation to the Local Government Board that an alteration is desirable. The dealing with such unions is facilitated by a provision in the Act under which a union situated in more than one county may be divided by the Local Government Board into parts, one in each county, each part being for purposes of outdoor relief an independent union, while the

---

[1] See Local Government Act, 1888, sec. 59.

[2] Poor Law Amendment Act, 1834 (*4 & 5 Will. IV. c. 76*), secs. 26, 32.
Poor Law Amendment Act, 1844 (*7 & 8 Vict. c. 101*), sec. 66.
Divided Parishes and Poor Law Amendment Act, 1876 (*39 & 40 Vict. c. 61*), sec. 11.

union will remain in its present condition for purposes of indoor relief.[1]

Highway Parish.

Highway parishes, like poor law parishes, are, for the most part, either old ecclesiastical parishes or townships, with traditional boundaries.

There are considerable difficulties as to the construction of the older Acts dealing with parishes, in connection with this subject; it appears, however, that the Act of 1857 (*20 Vict. c. 19*), dealing with extra-parochial places, did not apply to highway parishes even where they were co-extensive with poor law parishes. By the Highway Act, 1862 (*25 & 26 Vict. c. 61, sec. 3*), it is provided that where an extra-parochial place was by the Act of 1857 declared to be a parish it should, for the purposes of the Act of 1862, be deemed a highway parish, and that where, in pursuance of the same Act, a place had been annexed to an adjoining parish, such place should, for the same purposes, be deemed to be annexed to such parish.[2]

The Highway Act, 1864 (*27 & 28 Vict. c. 101*), sec. 9, provided that the Justices might deal with remaining extra-parochial places for highway purposes in the same way as for poor law purposes under the Act of 1857.

Under the Highway Acts of 1862 and 1864, the Justices were given extensive powers of combining and altering the boundaries of highway parishes, which powers are unaffected by the Local Government Act, 1888.

It seems that the provisions of the Poor Law Amendment Act, 1868, above mentioned[3] apply to highway parishes as well as to poor law parishes, though their effect, where poor law parishes and highway parishes do not coincide, seems doubtful.

Where a detached portion of a parish became annexed to the surrounding parish under the Divided Parishes and Poor Law Amendment Act, 1882,[3] and the parish to which it was annexed was also a highway parish, but not otherwise, the annexation extended to highway purposes.

Under the Divided Parishes Acts,[4] where a poor law parish dealt with by an Order of the Local Government Board, is a highway parish, the Order is deemed to have

---

[1] Local Government Act, 1888, sec. 58.

[2] The effect of this provision is very doubtful, see R. *v.* Central Wingland, 2 Q.B.D., 349.

[3] *Ante*, p. 93. [4] *Ante*, p. 94.

dealt with the parish for highway, as well as for poor law purposes. Where the parish is not a highway parish, the Board may make provisions in their Order dealing with the parish for highway purposes in the same way as for poor law purposes.

Where a County Council make an Order dealing with poor law parishes, their Order may provide for any necessary or convenient incidental change in highway parishes; but apart from such an Order, it seems that the County Council have no authority to deal with highway parishes.

Highway District.

A highway district is merely a combination of highway parishes, so that its boundaries depend upon the boundaries of the constituent highway parishes.

A highway district may be constituted, dissolved, and altered by the Quarter Sessions, but a discussion of this subject is beyond our scope, as neither the Local Government Board nor the County Council will have, in general, any power to alter the boundaries of a highway district, except incidentally of course, when dealing with urban sanitary districts or highway parishes. Where a highway district, however, lies in more than one administrative county it seems that the Local Government Board may make an Order dealing with the case. They may before the appointed day make such an Order of their own accord after local inquiry. After the appointed day they may do so upon the representation of the County Council of a county, in which any portion of the highway district is situated.

Borough.

Of the boroughs dealt with by the Municipal Corporations Act, 1835 (*5 & 6 Will. IV. c. 76*), those contained in the first sections of schedules A. and B. to that Act, were given the same boundaries as the then parliamentary boroughs corresponding with them, subject to certain provisions; and those contained in the second sections of the same schedules retained their existing boundaries subject to certain provisions. Some further general provisions were made by the Municipal Corporation Boundaries Act, 1836 (*6 & 7 Will. IV. c. 103*).

Municipal boroughs incorporated since 1835 have had their boundaries laid down in their charters, and borough boundaries have in very many cases been altered by Local Acts.

There has hitherto been no general provision under which an alteration could be effected, either directly or incidentally, in the boundaries of a municipal borough; but under the Local Government Act, 1888, it is provided that on the representation of a County or Town Council, the Local Government Board may, after local inquiry, alter the boundary of a borough by a Provisional Order requiring confirmation by Parliament. Provisions of Local Government Act.[1]

Before the appointed day the Local Government Board may exercise this power without the previous representation of the County or Town Council; but between that date and the 1st November, 1889, the Board may only act in pursuance of such a representation. After the 1st November, 1889, the Board may, however, act without any previous representation, with regard to any borough, in respect of which neither a County Council nor a Town Council has previously made any representation, but not otherwise. In their Order the Board may make all necessary incidental arrangements.

In all but a few cases boroughs are urban sanitary districts; in the few cases in which this is not so, the Local Government Board must make a Provisional Order dealing with the case, so that no such anomaly shall in future exist.[2]

Borough boundaries after the appointed day will still cut parish and union boundaries, but not the boundaries of administrative counties.

Before leaving the subject of borough boundaries, we may conveniently mention certain matters which, although not strictly questions of boundaries, are of a closely allied character. Wherever it is represented to the Local Government Board by any County or Town Council that—

(i.) The union for all or any of the purposes of the Local Government Act, 1888, of a county borough with a county is desirable; or

(ii.) That the union of any boroughs for all or any of the purposes of the Act is desirable; or

(iii.) That it is desirable to constitute any borough the population of which is not under 50,000 into a county borough;

the Board may, after local inquiry, make a Provisional Order carrying out the proposal or some similar proposal, and the Order may provide for all necessary or convenient incidental changes.

---

[1] Local Government Act, 1888, sec. 54. [2] *Ib.*, sec. 52.

Before the appointed day, the Board may make such an Order without any previous representation; between that date and the 1st November, 1889, the Board may only act in pursuance of such a representation; after that date again the Board may act in pursuance of such a representation, or without such representation with regard to any borough as respects which no previous representation has been made, but not otherwise.

Charter for a new borough.[1]

We have already alluded to the fact that a new borough may be created by Charter from the Crown; under the Municipal Corporations Act, 1882, it is provided that any inhabitant householders of any town or towns, or district may petition the Crown for a Charter of Incorporation, and that every such petition shall be referred to a Committee of the Privy Council for consideration. One month's notice of the petition and of the time when it will be taken into consideration must be published in the *London Gazette* and otherwise as the Committee may direct. If the Charter is granted, the provisions of the Municipal Corporations Act are thereby extended to the borough, and the Committee must settle a scheme providing for all necessary adjustment of powers, duties, properties, &c. Before the scheme is settled it must be referred to the Secretary of State and to the Local Government Board, and in certain cases also to the Board of Trade.

The scheme when settled by the Committee must be published in the *London Gazette*. If within one month after this publication a petition is presented against it by any local authority affected, or by not less than one-twentieth of the owners and ratepayers of the proposed borough (either in number or as respects the value of the property), and such petition is not withdrawn, the scheme will require confirmation by Parliament; in other cases the scheme may be either confirmed by Parliament or by Her Majesty by Order in Council.

Under the Local Government Act, 1888, notice of the petition for a Charter must be given to the County Council of the County in which the proposed borough is situated, and also to the Local Government Board, and the Privy Council must consider any representations made by the County Council or by that Board, together with the petition.[2]

A separate Court of Quarter Sessions for a borough may be

---

[1] Municipal Corporations Act, 1882, secs. 210-218.

[2] Local Government Act, 1888, sec. 56.

granted by the Queen, on the petition to Her Majesty in Council, of the Town Council.[1]

Hitherto, as has been explained in Chapter I., a grant of a separate Court of Quarter Sessions to a borough has materially affected the powers and duties of the Town Council and has also greatly changed the financial relations between the borough and the county in which it is situated.

The grant of a separate Court of Quarter Sessions to a borough after the 13th August, 1888, will not affect the powers, duties, or liabilities of a County Council as regards that borough, nor exempt the parishes in the borough from contributing to any purposes to which they were formerly assessed; nor will such grant impose any new powers, duties, or liabilities on the Town Council, save such as are necessary for establishing and maintaining the Court of Quarter Sessions.[2]

Her Majesty may, on the petition of the Town Council, by Order in Council, revoke the grant of a separate Court of Quarter Sessions, or by letters patent revoke the grant of a Commission of the Peace made to any borough the population of which, according to the census of 1881, was under 10,000.[3]

Sanitary District.

Urban Sanitary Districts are, as we have explained, of three kinds, namely:—

(i.) Boroughs: the boundaries of which have already been dealt with.

(ii.) Improvement Act Districts: the boundaries of which depend on Local Acts.

(iii.) Local Government Districts.

Local Government Districts were constituted under the Public Health Act of 1848 by a Provisional Order of the Board of Health, confirmed by Parliament, and accordingly these Orders may be found among the Private and Local Acts.

Local Government Districts were constituted under the Local Government Act, 1858, by a resolution of the owners and ratepayers of the district, which was published in the *London Gazette*, and also in local newspapers. Where the area made a Local Government District under that Act was not an area with known or defined boundaries, it was,

---

1 Municipal Corporations Act, 1882, secs. 162-169.

2 Local Government Act, 1888, sec. 37.

3 *Ib.*, sec. 38.

however, necessary first to obtain an Order from a Secretary of State setting out the boundaries, which Order would of course be found among the records of the Sanitary Authority.

Under the Public Health Act, 1875[1], which repealed the above-mentioned Acts, the Local Government Board, without any previous representation from the locality, may, by a Provisional Order, constitute, dissolve, and make any changes they may think fit in the boundaries of, a Local Government District; or the Board, acting in pursuance of a resolution of the owners and ratepayers of any place, may constitute that place a Local Government District, by an Order absolute in the first instance; and if the place is not a place with a known or defined boundary, the Local Government Board, on petition being made to them, may, as a preliminary step, settle the boundaries of the place.

Rural Sanitary Districts.

The boundaries of rural sanitary districts are entirely determined by those of the unions with which they (with the exception of urban districts) are co-extensive, and by the boundaries of urban sanitary districts.

Provisions of Local Government Act.[2]

Under the Local Government Act, 1888, if a *primâ facie* case is made out for the alteration of the boundary of an urban sanitary district or its division or union with other districts, or the conversion of any sanitary district or any part thereof, from a rural sanitary district into an urban district or *vice versâ*; the County Council, after local inquiry held after notice has been given in the locality and also to certain Government Departments, may make an Order for carrying out the proposal, which Order must be submitted to the Local Government Board for confirmation.

If within three months of the first notice of the provisions of the Order, the Sanitary Authority of any district affected by the Order or any number of county electors registered in that district, not less than one-sixth of the total number of electors in the district, petition the Local Government Board to disallow the Order, the Local Government Board are to hold a local inquiry and determine whether the Order is to be confirmed or not.

In other cases the Local Government Board must confirm the Order, but may introduce such modifications as they consider necessary for carrying into effect the objects of the Order.

---

[1] Secs. 270-278.

[2] *Ib.*, sec. 57.

The Local Government Board will prescribe regulations as to the manner in which notices are to be given, &c.

County.

We have explained in Chapter I. the meaning of the terms entire county and administrative county, and how the county of a County Council is, subject to certain changes, the county as at present bounded for the purposes of parliamentary elections, except in the cases in which an entire county is divided into more than one administrative county.[1]

It remains, therefore, to inquire what the boundaries of counties are for parliamentary purposes, and how the boundaries of administrative counties may, in the future, be altered. The boundaries of the counties for parliamentary purposes at present are the old traditional boundaries of the 52 counties of England and Wales, subject to certain recent alterations, the most important of which are as follows:—

Prior to 1832 many counties comprised parts isolated from the main body of the county, and in that year it was provided by the Parliamentary Boundaries Act (*2 & 3 Will. IV. c. 64*) that all such isolated parts described in Schedule M to that Act should, for parliamentary purposes, form parts of the counties to which they were annexed in that schedule; and further that all other isolated parts of counties should, for parliamentary purposes, be considered part of that county (not being a county corporate, *i.e.*, a county of a city or of a town) or of that division, riding, or part, whereby such isolated part was surrounded, or if surrounded by more than one county, then as part of that county with which such detached part had the longest common boundary.

It should be mentioned that by an Act of 1844 (*7 & 8 Vict. c. 61.*) the readjustment, thus effected for parliamentary purposes, was extended to all purposes except—

(i.) Ecclesiastical jurisdiction and patronage.

(ii.) The jurisdiction of certain Coroners already appointed at the date of that Act.

(iii.) The incidence and management of the Land Tax and Assessed Taxes.

No enactment hitherto has provided for any direct change in the boundary of a county, but the changes we have mentioned above in parish boundaries have in certain cases altered them, more especially the changes under the Divided Parishes Acts.

---

[1] *Ante*, pp. 26, 27.

The Redistribution of Seats Act, 1885 (*48 & 49 Vict. c. 23*), provided that alterations of county boundaries, incidental to the constitution of new parishes, or to the division or alteration of boundaries of parishes, made by, or in pursuance of, any Act of Parliament, that came into operation on or before the 25th March, 1885, should have effect for parliamentary purposes.

Provisions of Local Government Act.[1]

In future the Local Government Board may, on the representation of a County Council after a local inquiry, make a Provisional Order requiring confirmation in Parliament, altering county boundaries, and dividing or uniting counties for all or any of the purposes of the Local Government Act, 1888. Before the appointed day the Local Government Board may make such an Order without any such previous representation. Between the appointed day and November 1st, 1889, the Local Government Board may only make such an Order in pursuance of a previous representation. After that date again the Local Government Board may make such a Provisional Order upon the representation of a County Council, or without such previous representation in the case of a county with regard to which the County Council have made no previous representation, but not otherwise.

Electoral Divisions and Wards.

The remaining question is the division of counties, boroughs, and urban sanitary districts for election purposes. We must premise that most boroughs and many other urban sanitary districts are divided into wards; so many Councillors, Improvement Commissioners, or members of the Local Board being elected for each ward. County Councillors, as we have stated, are to be elected one for each electoral division of the county.

Electoral Divisions.[2]

Electoral Divisions must be arranged with a view to the population of each division being, so nearly as conveniently may be, equal, regard being had to a proper representation both of the rural and of the urban population and to the distribution and pursuits of such population, and to area, and to the last published census for the time being, and to evidence of any considerable change of population since such census.

Electoral Divisions must also, as far as may be reasonably practicable, be framed so that every division shall be a sanitary district or a ward of a sanitary district or a combination of

---

[1] Local Government Act, 1888, sec. 54.
[2] *Ib.*, secs. 51, 54; and see *ante*, p. 3.

sanitary districts or wards, or be comprised in one sanitary district or ward.

After the first election of County Councils, the Local Government Board may, on the representation of a County Council, alter the number of Councillors for the county and the boundaries of any electoral division of the county.

If two-thirds of a Town Council agree, a petition may be presented to the Crown by the Town Council for the division of the borough into wards, or for the alteration of an existing division; the petition will be considered in the Privy Council, and Her Majesty may, by Order in Council, provide for the division or alteration accordingly. Wards of Borough.[1]

If a *primâ facie* case is made out for the alteration of the number of wards of a sanitary district, or of the boundaries of any ward, or of the number of members of the Sanitary Authority, the County Council, within whose county the district is situated, must hold a local inquiry, and cause notice to be given, both locally and to certain Government Departments, in such manner as the Local Government Board may prescribe, and if satisfied that the proposal is desirable, the County Council may make an absolute Order carrying it into effect. Wards of Sanitary District.[2]

---

[1] Municipal Corporations Act, 1882, sec. 30.
Local Government Act, 1888, sec. 57.

CHAPTER V.

BUSINESS OF A FULLY CONSTITUTED COUNTY COUNCIL.

IN this chapter we propose to deal with the business of a fully constituted County Council. We shall first mention some matters connected with the constitution and proceedings of County Councils, and afterwards explain the business they will have to transact.

In speaking of the constitution and proceedings of a County Council we shall, as the difference in the proceedings of the two bodies is but small, take occasion to mention the corresponding matters connected with a Town Council. The matters to be considered are the number of Councillors, the office of Chairman or Mayor, the rules concerning the meetings of a Council, the appointment of Committees, and the appointment of the general officers of the Council.

Number of County Councillors.

The number of Councillors of each County Council, which is identical with the number of electoral divisions, has been, as we have seen, determined by the Local Government Board for the first election. This number may be altered from time to time by an Order of that Board made after local inquiry, on the representation of a County Council. The Order of the Local Government Board altering the number of Councillors may of course involve a corresponding alteration in the number of County Aldermen.[1]

Number of Town Councillors.

The number of Town Councillors in a borough depends, in general, on the charter of the borough, or upon a local statute. Some boroughs are divided into wards for election purposes and others not. If the Town Council are desirous of having their borough divided into wards or of obtaining an alteration in a division already made, they may, if two-thirds of the members of the Council agree, petition Her Majesty for

[1] Local Government Act, 1888, sec. 54; and see *ante*, p. 105.

such division or alteration, whereupon the petition will be taken into consideration by the Privy Council. It is believed that in connection with the division of a borough into wards, or an alteration in the existing number of wards, an alteration in the number of Town Councillors may be effected, and where an alteration in the boundaries of a borough is made in pursuance of the Local Government Act, 1888, the number of Councillors may at the same time be altered[1]; but it seems that except in these cases no alteration can be made in the number of Town Councillors by any means short of a Local Act.

Chairman and Mayor.

The Chairman of a County Council is, during his year of office, and for the next year after, a Justice of the Peace for the county, by virtue of his office. But before acting as such Justice, he must, if he has not already done so, take the oaths required by law to be taken by a Justice of the Peace, other than the oath respecting the qualification by estate.[2] The County Council may from time to time appoint a member of the Council to be Vice-Chairman, to hold office during the year of office of the Chairman, and subject to any rules made by the County Council, anything authorised or required to be done by, to, or before the Chairman, may be done by, to, or before the Vice-Chairman.[2] The Mayor of a borough also is, during his term of office, a Justice of the borough, and unless he becomes disqualified to be Mayor, he continues to be a Justice during the year after he goes out of office.[3] The Chairman of a County Council and the Mayor of a borough may receive such salary as the Council in each case think fit.[4]

The Chairman of a County Council or the Mayor of a borough may from time to time appoint an Alderman or Councillor to act as Deputy Chairman or Mayor during his illness or absence. The appointment must be signified to the Council in writing and be recorded on the minutes of the Council. The Deputy so appointed will have all the powers of Chairman or Mayor, except that he will not be a Justice of the Peace, and will not take the chair at a meeting of the Council unless specially appointed at the meeting to do so.[5]

Rules as to meetings of Council.

Rules as to meetings of a Town Council are given in the second schedule to the Municipal Corporations Act, 1882,[6]

---

[1] Local Government Act, 1888, sec. 54.
[2] *Ib.*, sec. 2.
[3] Municipal Corporations Act, 1882, sec. 155.
[4] *Ib.*, sec. 15.
[5] *Ib.*, sec. 16.
[6] See *post*, p. 350.

and are applicable also to a County Council; subject to the following modifications:—[1]

(i.) Chairman of the County Council must be substituted for Mayor.

(ii.) Clerk of the County Council must be substituted for Town Clerk.

(iii.) The 7th November must be substituted for the 9th November as the day for holding a quarterly meeting of the County Council.

(iv.) One-fourth of the whole number of the Council will be a quorum, and must be substituted for one-third in paragraph 10 of the rules.

No member of a County or Town Council may vote or take part in the discussion of any matter before the Council or before a Committee in which he has directly or indirectly, by himself or his partner, any pecuniary interest.[2] A County Councillor elected for an electoral division consisting wholly of a Quarter Sessions Borough, the population of which, according to the census of 1881, exceeded 10,000, or consisting of some part of such borough, must not act or vote in respect of any question arising before the Council as regards matters involving expenditure, on account of which the parishes in the borough are not liable to be assessed equally with the rest of the county, to county contributions.[3]

Committees.

A County Council have powers of appointing Committees of their own body and also to join with other bodies in the appointment of Joint Committees, and there are some such Committees which must be appointed.

Any County Council may appoint a Committee for any purpose, and delegate such powers as they think fit to such Committee, except that they must not delegate any power of raising money by rate or by loan. The Council appointing a Committee may make, from time to time, and vary and revoke regulations respecting the quorum and proceedings of the Committee, and as to the area (if any) within which it is to exercise its authority. Subject to such regulations, the proceedings and quorum will be such as the Committee itself may from time to time direct.

A County Council may join with any other County Council or Councils, or with any Court or Courts of Quarter Sessions, or with the Town Council or Councils of

[1] Local Government Act, 1888, sec. 75.
[2] Municipal Corporations Act, 1882, sec. 22.
[3] Local Government Act, 1888, sec. 34. [4] *Ib.*, secs. 28, 81, 82.

any county borough or county boroughs in appointing out of their respective bodies a Joint Committee for any purpose in respect of which they are jointly interested. To such a Committee, the bodies appointing it may delegate any powers that they think fit, except the power of making a rate or borrowing money. Subject to the terms of delegation, such a Joint Committee will, in respect of any matters delegated to it, have the same power in all respects as the Councils, or Councils and Courts appointing it. The members of a Joint Committee may be appointed at such times, and in such manner, and will hold office for such time, as may be fixed by the appointing bodies; but where any members of the Committee are appointed by a County Council, the Committee must not continue to exist for more than three months after the day of general election of County Councillors. The bodies appointing such a Committee may make, vary, and revoke regulations respecting the quorum and proceedings of such Committee, and as to the area (if any) within which it is to exercise its authority. Subject to such regulations the proceedings and quorum will be such as the Committee itself may direct.

The following Committees must be appointed:—

1st. A Standing Joint Committee of the County Council and Quarter Sessions of the County. This Committee must consist of an equal number of Justices appointed by the Quarter Sessions, and of members of the County Council appointed by the Council. The number of the Committee must be determined by agreement between the Quarter Sessions and the County Council, or in default of agreement, by a Secretary of State. Standing Joint Committee of County Council and Quarter Sessions.[1]

The Standing Joint Committee must elect a Chairman, and should there be an equality of votes for two or more persons, one of those persons must be elected Chairman by lot. The business of the Standing Joint Committee includes the management of the police and other matters.

2nd. A Finance Committee must be appointed by each County Council.[2] Finance Committee.

3rd. In each of the six entire counties, which comprise more than one administrative county, a Joint Committee must be appointed by the County Councils of the administrative counties comprised therein. Such a Joint Committee must, Joint Committee for entire county.[3]

---

[1] Local Government Act, 1888, sec. 30.
[2] *Ib.*, sec. 80. [3] *Ib.*, secs. 46, 64, 82.

if the business to be transacted by them so require, comprise a Joint Committee of the Quarter Sessions of the several ridings and divisions which constitute the administrative counties. If any difference arises as to the number of members or as to the mode or time of appointing such a Joint Committee, the difference must be determined by a Secretary of State.

In Yorkshire and Lincolnshire the Committee will, as we have seen, be a corporate body, called the York County Committee or the Lincoln County Committee, with a common seal and perpetual succession. These County Committees will transact business, transferred from Quarter Sessions by the Local Government Act, 1888, which has hitherto been transacted by the Justices of all the ridings and divisions at Gaol Sessions, or by any Joint Committee of the Justices, or by Commissioners appointed by the Justices, or otherwise jointly by such Justices.

In Sussex, Suffolk, Cambridgeshire, and Northamptonshire the Joint Committee will not be a corporate body, but will transact all business transferred from Quarter Sessions, which has hitherto been transacted at any General Sessions for Sussex or Suffolk, or by any joint action of the Quarter Sessions of the divisions of the county of Cambridge or of the county of Northampton, and all matters under the Local Government Act, 1888, which concern the entire county.

Any Joint Committee for an entire county appointed under these provisions will stand in reference to business transacted by them in the position, as far as circumstances admit, of a County Council for the entire county, and their expenses must be defrayed by the County Councils appointing the Committee.

Delegation of Authority of County Council.[1]

A County Council may delegate, conditionally or otherwise, any powers or duties transferred to them by or in pursuance of the Local Government Act, 1888, except any power of raising money by rate or loan, to any Sanitary Authority. They may also delegate to the Justices in Petty Sessions any of their powers and duties, except the power of raising money by rate or loan, in respect of licensing theatres, or in respect of execution, as Local Authority, of the Explosives Act, 1875, or of the Contagious Diseases (Animals) Acts.

Clerk of County Council.

We now propose to deal with certain general officers of a County Council, and of a Town Council.

Firstly, the Clerk of the County Council will also be Clerk of the Peace of the County, and as Clerk of the Peace, will have

[1] Local Government Act, 1888, sec. 28.

many duties connected with the business of the Quarter Sessions. He will be appointed by the Standing Joint Committee of the County Council and the Quarter Sessions, and will be removable at the discretion of that Committee.[1]

The Clerk of the Peace and of the County Council may be paid either by fees or by salary, or partly by fees and partly by salary. In any case the Clerk will receive fees in respect of a great number of matters. If he is paid by fees he will receive them for his own use, but if he is paid by salary the fees payable to him, except those (if any) that may be excluded (that is to say declared to be receivable by him for his own use), will be paid into the county fund.

The Standing Joint Committee may, from time to time, prepare a table of fees, and lay such table, signed by the Chairman of the Committee, before a Secretary of State, who may subscribe a declaration to the effect that such table of fees, with such modifications as he thinks proper to insert, are proper fees to be demanded; whereupon the table of fees must be sent to the Clerk, who will be bound by the table.

If the Standing Joint Committee wish to pay the Clerk by salary, in lieu of, or partly in lieu of, fees, or to alter the amount of the salary, &c., they may, from time to time, recommend to a Secretary of State that the Clerk should be so paid, or that the salary should be so altered, &c.; and, in that case, the Committee must in their recommendation state the amount of the salary that, in their opinion, should be paid, and the recommendation must be signed by the Chairman of the Committee, and transmitted to the Secretary of State, who may thereupon make an Order that the Clerk shall be paid by salary, or that the salary shall be varied. The Committee in making their recommendation may, if they wish, first recommend that any description of the business of the Clerk should not be included in fixing the salary, but that, in respect of such business, the Clerk should continue to be paid by fees. The Secretary of State in making the Order may accordingly exclude those fees.

The Joint Committee may appoint a Deputy Clerk to hold office during their pleasure; without prejudice, however, to the appointment of a Deputy Clerk for the purpose of a

---

[1] Subject to the rights of Clerks of the Peace already in office on the 13th August, 1888. See *ante*, p. 40. As to future appointments, see Local Government Act, 1888, secs. 30, 83. As to his salary and fees, see 11 & 12 Vict. c. 43, sec. 30, and 14 & 15 Vict. c. 55, secs. 9-11.

second Court or the division of the Court of Quarter Sessions for judicial business.[1]

County Treasurer.

Secondly, the County Council must appoint a Treasurer, who is removable at their pleasure.[2]

The Town Council of every borough appoint the following general officers:—

Town Clerk.

Firstly, a Town Clerk, holding office during the pleasure of the Town Council. The Town Council may also appoint a deputy to act during the absence or illness of the Town Clerk.[3]

Borough Treasurer.

Secondly, a Treasurer, also holding office during the pleasure of the Town Council.[4]

We now propose to deal with the law relating to the business to be transacted by a County Council.

Allotments.

The Allotments Act, 1887 (*50 & 51 Vict. c. 48*), enables Sanitary Authorities, under certain circumstances, to acquire land, either by purchase or hiring, for the purpose of making allotments to the labouring classes.

An Urban Sanitary Authority may acquire land for the benefit of the labouring population of their whole district, and a Rural Sanitary Authority may acquire land for the benefit of the labouring population of any parish or contributory place in their district.

A Sanitary Authority must not acquire land except at such price or rent that, in their opinion, all expenses (except such as are incurred in making public roads) incurred by the Authority in respect of the land and allotments, may reasonably be expected to be recouped out of the rents obtained in respect thereof.

Any expenses of an Urban Sanitary Authority under the Allotments Act, 1887, are payable as general expenses under the Public Health Act, 1875. The expenses of a Rural Sanitary Authority are payable as special expenses under the Public Health Act, 1875, and must be charged on the parish or contributory place for the benefit of which the expenses were incurred.

The management of allotments may be partly or wholly

[1] Local Government Act, 1888, sec. 83. This is, of course, subject to the provisions with regard to the Deputy of a Clerk of the Peace already in office on the 13th August, 1888. See *ante*, p. 40.

[2] See Local Government Act, 1888, sec. 75, and 12 Geo. II. c. 29, sec. 11.

[3] Municipal Corporations Act, 1882, sec. 17.

[4] *Ib.*, sec. 18.

delegated by a Sanitary Authority to Allotment Managers appointed by the Sanitary Authority; or, in the case of land acquired by a Rural Sanitary Authority, in certain cases to Allotment Managers elected by the Parliamentary voters registered for the parish for the benefit of which the land was acquired.

An allotment held by one person must not exceed one acre, and no building other than a toolhouse, shed, greenhouse, fowlhouse, or pigstye, must be erected on it.

If a Sanitary Authority are unable to acquire land by agreement, sufficient for allotments, at a reasonable price or rent, and subject to reasonable conditions, such Authority may petition the County Council of the county in which their district is situated for a Provisional Order authorising them to acquire land compulsorily under the provisions of the Land Clauses Consolidation Acts for the compulsory purchase and letting of land.

Before presenting such a petition the Sanitary Authority must—

1st. Publish, once at least, in each of three consecutive weeks in one of the months of September, October, or November, in some local newspaper circulated in their district, an advertisement describing shortly the purpose for which the lands are proposed to be taken, naming a place where a plan of the proposed allotments may be seen at all reasonable hours, and stating the quantity of land required.

2nd. Serve a notice in the succeeding month on every owner or reputed owner, lessee or reputed lessee, and occupier of the land; defining in each case the particular lands intended to be taken, and requiring an answer stating whether the person so served assents, dissents, or is neuter in respect of taking such lands.

The petition must be under seal, and state the lands intended to be taken and the purposes for which they are required, and the names of the owners, lessees, and occupiers who have assented, dissented, or are neuter in respect of taking such lands, or who have returned no answer to the notice.

The County Council must first be satisfied that the provisions, with regard to advertisements and notices, have been duly complied with, and if so satisfied, must take the petition into consideration. They may then either dismiss the petition or direct a local inquiry by an officer whom they may appoint for the purpose, who will have powers for the examination of witnesses, &c., similar to those of Inspectors of the Local Government Board under sec. 296 of the Public Health Act, 1875.[1]

[1] Under the Public Health Act, 1875, Inspectors of the Local Government Board are to have similar powers to those of Poor Law Inspectors. See the Poor Law Board Act, 1847 (*10 & 11 Vict. c. 109*), secs. 21, 26.

The County Council must give notice of the local inquiry and of the purport of the proposed Order by advertisement in a local newspaper in two successive weeks, and at the inquiry all persons interested may attend and make objections.

After the inquiry has been held, the County Council may make a Provisional Order, granting the prayer of the petition with such modifications as they think fit. The Provisional Order must not authorize the purchase of any park, garden, pleasure-ground or other land required for the amenity or convenience of any dwelling house, or any land which is the property of a railway or canal company and which is or may be required for the purposes of their undertaking; or of any right to coal or metalliferous ore.

In making a Provisional Order, the County Council must have regard to the extent of land held in the neighbourhood by any owner, and to the convenience of other property belonging to the same owner, and must, so far as is practicable, avoid taking an undue or inconvenient quantity of land from any one owner.

When the County Council have made a Provisional Order, the Local Government Board must, upon the application of the Council, introduce a Bill into Parliament, confirming that Order; and the Sanitary Authority petitioning for the Order will be considered as the promoters of the Order.

Analysts.

The Acts relating to Public Analysts are the Sale of Food and Drugs Act, 1875 (*38 & 39 Vict. c. 63*), the Sale of Food and Drugs Act Amendment Act, 1879 (*42 & 43 Vict. c. 30*). The object of these Acts is to provide for the detection and punishment of the adulteration of food (including drink) and drugs (including medicine both for external and internal use).

For this purpose the County Council of every county, and the Town Council of every county borough and of every other borough the population of which, according to the census of 1881, was above 10,000, and which has either a separate Court of Quarter Sessions or a separate police force, may appoint Public Analysts for their county or borough. The appointment in every case is subject to the approval of the Local Government Board, who may make such conditions as to the appointment and removal of a Public Analyst as they think fit; and no person may be appointed Public Analyst, for any place, who is engaged in any trade or business connected with the sale of food or drugs in such place.

The Local Government Board may also require such a County or Town Council to appoint Public Analysts if they neglect to do so of their own accord.

A Town Council may agree that the Analyst appointed for a neighbouring borough, or for the county in which the borough is situated, shall act also for them.

Any Medical Officer, Inspector of Nuisances, Inspector of Weights and Measures, Inspector of Markets, or Police Constable may, under the direction and at the cost, either of the authority appointing such officer, or of any Council who appoint a Public Analyst, procure samples, from time to time, of food and drugs for the purpose of analysis; and if the Analyst's report shows that an offence has been committed in respect of the substance so submitted to him, the officer may proceed against the offender summarily before Justices in Petty Sessions.

Each Analyst must make a quarterly report to the Council appointing him, showing the number of articles analysed by him, under the Acts, during the foregoing quarter, specifying the result of each analysis, and the sum paid to him in respect thereof.

Each Council appointing an analyst must transmit to the Local Government Board a certified copy of the quarterly reports.

The expenses of carrying out the Acts, *i.e.*, the Analysts' salaries or fees, the expense of prosecuting offenders, &c., will, in counties, be a special county purpose; all Quarter Sessions boroughs appointing their own Analysts, or agreeing for the employment of Analysts, will be exempt from assessment to contributions to the corresponding Special County Account. In boroughs the expense is paid out of the borough fund. All penalties recovered in respect of offences against the Acts, by an officer of a County or Town Council appointing an Analyst, must be carried to the credit of the account out of which the expenses of carrying out the Acts are paid.

Bill in Parliament (Opposing).[1]

A County Council may oppose any personal or local Bill in Parliament when they consider it necessary to do so for the

[1] Local Government Act, 1888, sec. 15. Municipal Corporations (Borough Funds) Act, 1875 (*35 & 36 Vict. c. 91*).

protection of the inhabitants of the county, and may pay the expenses incidental to such opposition out of the county fund, charging them to such account as they think fit. But the power of a County Council to incur expense in opposing a Bill is subject to the following conditions:—

1st. A resolution to oppose the Bill must be passed by an absolute majority of the whole number of the Council, at a meeting of which ten clear days' notice has been given, both by public notice of the meeting and its purpose in a local newspaper, and in the ordinary way in which notice of meeting is given.

2nd. The resolution must be published at least twice in some local newspaper or newspapers.

3rd. The resolution must receive the consent of the Local Government Board, if the Bill is in respect of matters within their jurisdiction, or in other cases of a Secretary of State. The approval of the Local Government Board, or of a Secretary of State, must not be given until the expiration of seven days after the second publication of the resolution, and in the meantime any ratepayer in the county may give notice in writing to the Local Government Board, or Secretary of State, objecting to their approval. The Local Government Board or Secretary of State may, before giving their approval, direct a local inquiry for the purpose of ascertaining whether the opposition is justifiable.

No payment may be made to any member of the Council for acting as counsel or agent in opposing the Bill, and all expenses must, before they may be paid by the Council, be examined and allowed by some person authorized by the Local Government Board or the Secretary of State, as the case may be.

Birds.

Under the Wild Birds Protection Acts, 1880 & 1881 (*43 & 44 Vict. c. 35*, and *44 & 45 Vict. c. 51*) a close time, from the 15th March to the 1st August, is provided for wild birds, and any person taking or killing wild birds during that time is liable to a penalty. A County Council or the Town Council of a county borough may apply to a Secretary of State to vary the close time in their county or borough in respect of any bird or birds, or to exempt their county or borough, or any part thereof, from the operation of the Acts as regards all or any wild birds. If the application is granted, the Order of the Secretary of State must be published in the *London Gazette.*

Bye-Laws.[1]

A County Council may make bye-laws for the good rule and government of their county, and for the prevention and suppression of nuisances not already punishable in a summary manner by virtue of any Act in force throughout the county. Such a bye-law must not be made except at a meeting at which at least two-thirds of the Council are present.

In the case of a bye-law for the good rule or government of the county, a copy sealed with the corporate seal of the County Council must be sent to a Secretary of State, and the bye-law will not come into force until the expiration of forty days after the copy is so sent. Her Majesty, with the advice of the Privy Council, may, within the forty days, wholly or partly disallow the bye-law, or may suspend its coming into force for a longer period than the forty days. Such a bye-law may impose a penalty not exceeding £5, and an offence against it may be prosecuted summarily.

If the bye-law is for the prevention and suppression of nuisances not already punishable summarily, it must be submitted to, and confirmed by, the Local Government Board, who must not confirm it—

1st. Unless notice of the intention to apply for confirmation has been given in one or more local newspapers, one month at least before making the application ; and

2nd. Unless for one month at least before making the application, a copy of the proposed bye-law has been kept at the office of the County Council, and been open, free of charge during office hours, to the inspection of ratepayers of the district to which the bye-law relates.

Such a bye-law must be under the common seal of the County Council, and may be altered and repealed by subsequent bye-laws. It may impose any penalty not exceeding £5 for each offence, and in addition, in the case of a continuing offence, a further penalty not exceeding forty shillings a day for each day after written notice of the offence has been given by the County Council. Such a bye-law must be so passed as to allow of the recovery of any sum less than the full amount of the penalty. A copy of all such bye-laws must be printed and hung up in the office of the County Council, and a copy must be delivered to any ratepayer of the district to which they relate, on his application

[1] Local Government Act, 1888, sec. 16. Municipal Corporations Act, 1882, sec. 23. Public Health Act, 1875, sec. 187.

for the same; a copy must also be transmitted to the Overseers of every parish to which such bye-laws relate, to be deposited with the public documents of the parish, and to be open to the inspection of any ratepayer of the parish at all reasonable hours.

Contagious Diseases (Animals).

The statute law with regard to the prevention of contagious diseases among animals was codified in the Contagious Diseases (Animals) Act, 1878 (*41 & 42 Vict. c. 74*), which has since been amended by three other Acts, namely:—

The Contagious Diseases (Animals) Act, 1884 (*47 Vict. c. 13*), the Contagious Diseases (Animals) Transfer of Parts of Districts Act, 1884 (*47 & 48 Vict. c. 47*), and the Contagious Diseases (Animals) Act, 1886 (*49 & 50 Vict. c. 32*).

The four Acts together are known as the Contagious Diseases (Animals) Acts, 1878 to 1886.

The working of these Acts is under the supervision of the Privy Council, who have wide powers of making, by Orders in Council, either general or local regulations for carrying out the intention of the Acts.

The general Orders in Council in force are—

The Animals Order, 1886 (No. 3446).
The Animals (Amendment) Order, 1886 (No. 3475).
The Animals Amendment Order, 1887 (No. 3513).
The Anthrax Order, 1886 (No. 3447).
The Rabies Order, 1887 (No. 3497).
The Admiralty Foreign Animals Wharves Order, 1887 (No. 317).

The Agricultural Department of the Privy Council Office have prepared a handbook of the laws and regulations relating to contagious and infectious diseases among animals, and for the details of the Acts and Orders reference must be made to that work.

The Acts and Orders provide—

1st. For the stamping out of disease that has actually broken out.

2nd. For the regulation of the conveyance and transport of animals generally.

3rd. For preventing the introduction of disease from foreign countries.

Locally the Acts and Orders are carried out, except in the Metropolis, by the following Local Authorities, namely:—

(1.) In counties—The County Council.

(2.) In boroughs the population of which, according to the census of 1881, was over 10,000—The Town Council.

(3.) In other places with a separate Police Establishment—The Commissioners maintaining the police.

(4.) For the purposes of the provisions relating to foreign animals, the Privy Council may constitute any other body a Local Authority, *e.g.*, a Harbour Authority.

Local Authorities, as also the Privy Council, appoint Inspectors to take the necessary steps to stamp out disease and repress offences against the Acts and Orders. Local Authorities must appoint a Committee, or Committees, to carry out the Acts and Orders, consisting either entirely of members of the Local Authority, or partly of such members and partly of other persons.[1] A County Council may delegate powers within the Acts and Orders to Justices of the Peace.[2]

The scheme provided by the Acts and Orders for the stamping out of disease when an outbreak occurs in the case of cattle plague, pleuro-pneumonia, foot-and-mouth disease, swine-fever, and sheep-pox is as follows:—The spot where the outbreak occurs and its immediate surroundings are declared an "infected place," either by an Inspector, a Local Authority, or the Privy Council, according to circumstances. The more distant surrounding places may then become an "infected circle," and a still larger district, including an infected place, may also be declared by the Privy Council an "infected area." Steps are then taken of more or less stringency, according to the Acts and Orders in Council, to isolate infected places, circles, and areas by such means as prohibiting or regulating the movement of animals into and out of them, and also to stamp out the disease within the infected places, circles and areas by destroying diseased animals and animals that might carry the seeds of disease in them, and also by such means as the destruction or disinfection of pens, sheds, &c., that might be dangerous.

In the case of less serious diseases a less elaborate arrangement is made, dispensing with the system of infected places and areas.

The Acts and Orders make certain regulations to be observed by railway companies, owners of vessels, &c., with respect to the transport of animals, providing for a proper cleansing of trucks, pens at railway stations, &c.

For the purpose of preventing the introduction of disease from abroad, the Acts provide—

1st. That the Privy Council may forbid the landing of animals, or any specified kind thereof, dead or alive, which are

---

[1] See *post*, p. 123.

[2] Local Government Act, 1888, sec. 28.

brought from any foreign country or from any specified part thereof.

2nd. That the Privy Council may prescribe certain ports, and at such ports certain wharves, &c., at which alone foreign animals may be landed.

3rd. That all animals landed alive for the purpose of being slaughtered, shall be slaughtered at once.

4th. That animals landed for breeding purposes, &c., shall be kept in quarantine.

The execution of the Acts and Orders in a county is a special county purpose; parishes comprised in a borough, the population of which, according to the census of 1881, was over 10,000, or in a place with a separate police establishment, are exempt from contribution to the corresponding Special County Account. Sums derived by the County Council from the sale of carcases, &c, and, subject to certain provisions, the sums derived from their undertakings under the Acts[1] must be carried to the credit of that Special County Account.

We now proceed to discuss the Acts and Orders in Council more in detail.

These matters we shall deal with in the following order:—

1st. Definitions. As many words are used throughout the Acts and Orders, in a technical sense, it may be advisable to give a list of such words, with their definitions.

2nd. The powers of the Privy Council.

3rd. The Local Authorities, and their powers.

4th. The appointment and powers of Inspectors, and the powers of constables under the Acts.

5th. Miscellaneous matters.

Definitions.

The following definitions are given in the Acts and Orders.[2]

Animals, in the Acts and General Orders, means, cattle, sheep and goats, and all other ruminating animals, and swine. The Privy Council have, however, power to bring all, or any provisions of the Acts into force with regard to any other four-footed animals, and provisions have been made by the Privy Council for horses, asses, mules,[3] and dogs.[4]

Cattle, in the Acts and General Orders, means bulls, cows, oxen, heifers and calves.

Disease, in the Acts, means Cattle-plague, *i.e.*, Rinderpest; Pleuro-pneumonia, *i.e.*, contagious Pleuro-pneumonia of cattle; Foot and-Mouth Disease; Sheep-pox; Sheep-scab. The Privy Council have the power to extend the definition of disease either generally or locally,[5] and in the Animals Order, 1886, disease includes, in addition to the above-mentioned diseases—Glanders, Farcy, and Swine-Fever. The Privy Council have also made provisions for Anthrax, in the Anthrax Order, 1886, and for Rabies, in the Rabies Order, 1887.

Diseased means, affected with disease.

---

[1] See *post*, p. 129.

[2] The Contagious Diseases (Animals) Act, 1878, sec. 5. The Animals Order, 1886, Art. 5. The Rabies Order, 1887, Art. 4.

[3] In the Animals Order, 1886. [4] In the Rabies Order, 1887.

[5] Contagious Diseases (Animals) Act, 1878, sec. 32.

Suspected means, suspected of being diseased.

Foreign, as applied to animals and things, means, brought to the United Kingdom from any other country, including the Isle of Man and the Channel Islands.

Inspector means, an Inspector appointed by the Privy Council or a Local Authority, for the purposes of the Acts.

Veterinary Inspector means, an Inspector who is a member of the Royal College of Veterinary Surgeons, or any veterinary practitioner qualified as approved by the Privy Council.

Infected Place and *Infected Area* are technical terms, and mean districts that have been duly declared such; these terms are used with the name of any particular disease to mean districts, &c., that have been declared infected places or infected areas in respect of that disease. Thus, "cattle-plague infected place" means a district that has been duly declared an infected place in respect of cattle-plague.

Infected Circle.[1]—The Privy Council may by Order provide, in respect of any particular disease, that, on any place becoming an infected place in respect of that disease, the whole space lying within half a mile of that place shall become an infected circle. The Privy Council may also make provisions for the consequences of a district becoming an infected circle. The only diseases for which this has been done are foot-and-mouth disease and swine-fever.

Powers of Privy Council

The Privy Council may make general or special Orders for an immense variety of matters connected with the contagious diseases of animals.

The following are the main powers and duties of the Privy Council in the case of particular diseases. The Privy Council may declare any place or area to be an infected place or area in respect of cattle disease, pleuro-pneumonia, foot-and-mouth disease, sheep-pox, and swine fever.[2] The Privy Council may declare any place or area which has been duly declared an infected place or area in respect of cattle plague, or any part of such place or area, to be free from such disease.[3]

The Privy Council may declare any place that has been declared an infected place in respect of pleuro-pneumonia, foot-and-mouth disease, sheep-pox, or swine fever, to be free from such disease.[4] They may also declare any area that has been declared an infected area in respect of the same disease, or any part of such area, to be free from such disease.[5]

The Privy Council may extend, alter, or contract the limits of any cattle-plague, pleuro-pneumonia, or foot-and-mouth disease infected place.[6] They may extend the limits of any sheep-pox or swine-fever infected place.[7]

The Privy Council may extend the limits of any area that has become an infected area in respect of any of the five last-mentioned diseases, but can only alter so as contract them in the case of cattle-plague.[8] This distinction is, of course, owing to a draftsman's error, and the difficulty can be got over by the Privy Council declaring part of the infected area to be free from disease.

---

[1] Contagious Diseases (Animals) Act, 1886, sec. 2.

[2] The Contagious Diseases (Animals) Act, 1878, secs. 11, 12, 17, 18, 23, 24. The Animals Order, 1886, Arts. 49, 80.

[3] Contagious Diseases (Animals) Act, 1878, sec. 14.

[4] Contagious Diseases (Animals) Act, 1886, sec. 4. Animals Order, 1886, Arts. 49, 80.

[5] Contagious Diseases (Animals) Act, 1878, secs. 20, 26. Animals Order, 1886, Arts. 49, 80.

[6] Contagious Diseases (Animals) Act, 1878, secs. 13, 17, 23. Contagious Diseases (Animals) Act, 1886, sec. 3.

[7] Animals Order, 1886, Arts. 49, 80.

[8] Contagious Diseases (Animals) Act, 1878, secs. 13, 18, 24. Animals Order, 1886, Arts. 49, 80.

Duties of Privy Council as to Cattle-plague

On the occurrence of an outbreak of cattle-plague the Privy Council, in all cases, deal with the matter themselves.[1] On receipt of information of an outbreak from an Inspector, they must inquire into the correctness of the Inspector's declaration. If satisfied of the correctness of that declaration they must, by Order, determine and declare accordingly, and must prescribe the limits of the place infected with cattle-plague.

If not satisfied of the correctness of the Inspector's declaration as regards the existence or past existence of cattle-plague, they must determine and declare accordingly, and thereupon, as from the time specified in their Order, the place comprised in the Inspector's declarations and notices ceases to be a place infected with cattle-plague.

The Privy Council must cause to be slaughtered[2] all animals affected with cattle-plague, or being or having been in the same shed or stable, herd or flock, or in contact with an animal infected with cattle-plague. They may, if they think fit, cause to be slaughtered all animals suspected of cattle-plague, or being in a cattle-plague infected place, or being in such parts of an area infected with cattle-plague as are not comprised in a place infected with cattle-plague (but in the last-mentioned case subject to such regulations as the Treasury from time to time think fit to make).

The Privy Council must, for animals slaughtered owing to an outbreak of cattle-plague, pay compensation out of money provided by Parliament, as follows:—

(i.) Where the animal slaughtered was affected with cattle-plague the compensation is one-half of the value of the animal before it became affected; but the compensation must not, in any case, exceed £20.

(ii.) In other cases the compensation is the whole value of the animal immediately before it was slaughtered; but the compensation must not in any case exceed £40.

Transfer of districts.[3]

The jurisdiction of each Local Authority extends only throughout their district, *e.g.*, the County Council will only be able to exercise their powers throughout their county. But where two neighbouring Authorities exercise the like jurisdiction under the Acts and Orders, they may make an agreement in writing for the exercise by one of them (called the Administrating Authority) of such jurisdiction within the district of the other (called the Surrendering Authority), or any part of it.

The agreement must, at the same time, provide for the payment by the Surrendering Authority to the Administrating Authority of a proportion of the expenses. The proportion must be settled with reference to the rateable value of the area surrendered, as compared with the rateable value of the original area of the district of the Administrating Authority.

Where the district of one Authority is wholly within that of another, such Authorities may agree as above, so that a Town Council may thus surrender their borough to the County Council of the county in which it is situated.

Appointment of Joint Committee.[3]

Two or more Local Authorities may also agree for the appointment out of their respective bodies of a Joint Committee consisting of such number of members with such term of office as they may determine. They may assign to such Joint Committee a district consisting of the whole, or such parts, of the districts of the appointing Authorities as they may determine.

They may delegate to such Joint Committee within their district the whole or any part of the jurisdiction of a Local Authority under the Acts and Orders. The

[1] Contagious Diseases (Animals) Act, 1878, secs. 10-15.

[2] Subject to a right to reserve an animal for observation—Contagious Diseases (Animals) Act, 1878, sec. 30.

[3] See the Contagious Diseases (Animals) Transfer of Parts of Districts Act, 1884.

expenses incurred by such a Committee must be apportioned between the appointing Authorities in proportion to the rateable value of the component areas belonging to such Authorities. No agreement for the transfer of a district or the appointment of a Joint Committee between Local Authorities will be binding without the approval of the Privy Council.

Committees appointed by a Local Authority.[1]

A Local Authority must form and keep up a Committee or Committees to carry out the Acts and Orders. Each Committee may consist wholly of members of the Local Authority, or partly thereof and partly of other persons. But such other persons must be rated occupiers of the district of the Local Authority. The Local Authority may delegate all or any of their powers to a Committee, except powers of rating; but the Privy Council in any Order made by them authorizing a Local Authority to make regulations, may provide that the power of making such regulations shall be exercised only by the Local Authority or their Executive Committee. A Local Authority may, if they think fit, appoint and designate one Committee as their Executive Committee, who will have all the powers of a Local Authority, except powers of rating, and who may, in their turn, appoint sub-committees and delegate any of their powers to them, except the power of making regulations when the Privy Council forbid the delegation of that power.

General powers of Local Authority.

A Local Authority may make such regulations with regard to their district as they may be empowered to make by Order of the Privy Council; such regulations must be published by the Local Authority in some local newspaper, and copies thereof must be sent to the Privy Council.[2] A Local Authority may purchase or take on lease, land for wharves or other places, or for the burial of carcases, in cases where there is not any ground suitable for the purpose in the possession or occupation of the owner of the animal, or any common and unenclosed land suitable and approved by the Privy Council for that purpose, or for any other purposes of the Act of 1878,[3] and may provide, erect, and fit up wharves, stations, lairs, sheds and other places for the reception, keeping, sale, slaughter and disposal of animals, &c.[4]

We shall now give a brief account of the powers and duties of the Local Authorites in the case of each disease.

Duty of Local Authority on outbreak of cattle-plague.

1st. *Cattle Disease.*—When a place has been declared a cattle-plague infected place, by an Inspector of a Local Authority, they must take all proper steps, pending the arrival of officers of the Privy Council, to enforce the observance of the law relating to cattle-plague, including the placing of constables and other officers at the entrance of an infected place. After the arrival of the Officer of the Privy Council, the Local Authority must assist him to carry into effect the law relating to cattle-plague.[5]

Local Authority may make regulations as to pleuro-pneumonia.[6]

2nd. *Pleuro-Pneumonia.*—In order to check the spread of pleuro-pneumonia, the Local Authority or their Executive Committee (but no other Committee) may make regulations for prohibiting or regulating the movement of cattle into their district from the district of any other Local Authority in England and Wales, or

---

[1] Contagious Diseases (Animals) Act, 1878, sec. 38 and 6th schedule. Contagious Diseases (Animals) Act, 1886, sec. 7.

[2] Contagious Diseases (Animals) Act, 1878, sec. 32; Animals Order, 1886, Arts. 184, 185.

[3] Contagious Diseases (Animals) Act, 1878, sec. 40.

[4] *Ib.*, sec. 39, Contagious Diseases (Animals) Act, 1886, sec. 10.

[5] Animals Order, 1886, Art. 11.

[6] Animals Order, 1886, Art. 20. Animals (Amendment) Order, 1887, Arts 3-5.

Scotland (but such regulations will not apply to cattle passing through their district by rail without untrucking) and for prohibiting and regulating the movement of cattle within their district, and the exposing for sale of any cattle at a market, sale or exhibition, &c., within their district.

Duty of Local Authority on outbreak of pleuro-pneumonia.[1]

On the receipt of information from an Inspector that an outbreak of pleuro-pneumonia has occurred, the Local Authority must, with the assistance of a Veterinary Inspector, or person qualified to be such, inquire into the correctness of the Inspector's declaration, and if satisfied that the declaration is correct, they must, by Order, determine and declare accordingly, and prescribe the limits of the place infected. They may include within those limits, places adjoining, or near the place to which the Inspector's declaration relates, and may include, in an infected place, any adjoining part of a district of another Local Authority, with the previous consent in writing of that Authority, but not otherwise.

If the Local Authority are not satisfied of the correctness of the Inspector's declaration, as regards the existence or past existence of the disease, they must, by Order, declare, and determine accordingly, and thereupon, as from the time specified in their Order, the place to which the Inspector's declaration relates, ceases to be an infected place.

The Local Authority must, without delay, report to the Privy Council the declaration of the Inspector, and their proceedings thereon, and must state whether or not it is in their opinion expedient that an infected area, comprising the infected place, shall be declared, and if so, what should, in their opinion, be the limits of that area, and whether or not there is, within that area, any place used for the holding of a market, fair, exhibition, or sale of cattle; and if so, whether or not it is, in their opinion, expedient that the holding, in that area, while infected, of a market, fair, exhibition, or sale of cattle, should be prohibited or restricted by Order of Council.

Having declared a place to be infected with pleuro-pneumonia the Loca Authority may, after the expiration of 56 days from the date of the cessation of tha disease, declare, by Order, that place to be free from such disease; but before making such a declaration they must obtain the advice and assistance of a Veterinary Inspector or of a person qualified to be such; such an Order they must, without delay, report to the Privy Council.

The Local Authority must cause all cattle affected with pleuro-pneumonia to be slaughtered within two days after the existence of the disease is known to them, and they may, if they think fit, cause any cattle being or having been in the same shed or herd, or in contact with, cattle affected with pleuro-pneumonia to be slaughtered or detained.

The Local Authority must pay compensation as follows, for cattle slaughtered under these provisions:—

(i.) Where the animal slaughtered was affected with pleuro-pneumonia the compensation is three-fourths of the value of the animal, immediately before it became so affected, but the compensation must in no case exceed £30.

(ii.) In other cases the compensation is the whole value of the animal immediately before it was slaughtered, but the compensation must in no case exceed £40.

Local Authority may make regulations as to foot-and-mouth disease.[2]

3rd. *Foot-and-Mouth Disease.*—In order to check the spread of foot-and-mouth

---

[1] Contagious Diseases (Animals) Act, 1878, secs. 16, 20, 21.
Contagious Diseases (Animals) Act, 1886, sec. 4.
Animals Order, 1886, Arts. 15-19, 21, 22, 87-89, 92-95, 174, 178.
Animals (Amendment) Order, 1887, Arts. 2, 5, 6.

[2] Animals Order, 1886, Arts. 36-38.

disease, the Local Authority or their Executive Committee (but no other Committee) may make regulations for prohibiting and regulating the movement of cattle, sheep, goats, or swine into their district from the district of any other Local Authority in England and Wales or Scotland (such a regulation will not apply to such animals passing through their district by rail without untrucking), and also prohibiting or regulating the exposing for sale of cattle, sheep, goats, or swine, at any market, sale, exhibition, &c., within five miles of any foot-and-mouth disease infected place, in England and Wales or Scotland, whether such infected place is within their own district or not; and also, if specially authorized by the Privy Council to do so, for regulating the movement of animals within their district.

Duties of Local Authority on an outbreak of foot-and-mouth disease.[1]

On the receipt of information from an Inspector that an outbreak of foot-and-mouth disease has occurred, the Local Authority must, with the advice and assistance of a Veterinary Inspector, or a person qualified to be such, inquire into the correctness of the Inspector's declaration, and if satisfied of the correctness of the Inspector's declaration, they must determine and declare accordingly, and prescribe the limits of the place infected. They may include within those limits, places adjoining or near the place to which the Inspector's declaration relates; they may also include in an infected place any adjoining part of the district of another Local Authority, with the previous consent in writing of that Authority, but not otherwise.

If the Local Authority are not satisfied of the correctness of the Inspector's declaration as regards the existence or past existence of the disease, they must by Order declare and determine accordingly; and thereupon as from the time specified in their Order, the place to which the Inspector's declaration relates, ceases to be an infected place.

The Local Authority must, without delay, report to the Privy Council, the declaration of the Inspector and their proceedings thereon, and must state whether or not it is, in their opinion, expedient that an infected area, comprising the infected place, shall be declared, and if so, what should, in their opinion, be the limits of that area, and whether or not there is, within that area, any place used for the holding of a market, fair, exhibition, or sale of cattle, sheep, goats or swine, and if so, whether or not it is, in their opinion, expedient that the holding in that area, while infected, of a market, fair, exhibition, or sale of cattle, should be prohibited or restricted by Order of Council.

Having declared a place to be a foot-and-mouth disease infected place, the Local Authority may, after the expiration of 14 days from the date of the cessation of the disease, or such longer period, not exceeding 28 days, as the Privy Council by General Order may direct, declare, by Order, that place to be free from the disease; but before declaring a place free from foot-and-mouth disease, the Local Authority must obtain the advice and assistance of a Veterinary Inspector or of a person qualified to be such; such an Order they must without delay report to the Privy Council.

Upon any place becoming a foot-and-mouth disease infected place, in pursuance of the declaration of an Inspector of a Local Authority, the whole space, lying within a distance of half a mile from any part of the infected place, becomes an infected circle. The Local Authority may, from time to time, alter and contract the limits of the infected circle, or of so much of it as is within their district; but

---

[1] Contagious Diseases (Animals) Act, 1878, secs. 22, 26.
Contagious Diseases (Animals) Act, 1886, secs. 4, 5.
Animals Order, 1886, Arts. 26-35, 39, 40, 87-89, 92, 93, 174, 178.

no land or buildings more than half a mile from the infected place must at any time be included in the infected circle; or the Local Authority may dissolve the infected circle altogether. On the infected place ceasing to be an infected place, the infected circle will, in any case, cease to exist.

The Local Authority must give notice of the existence of an infected circle by placards, &c., and they may make regulations as to the movement of cattle, sheep, and swine in, into, or out of infected circles.

The Local Authority may, if they think fit, cause cattle, sheep, goats or swine affected with foot-and-mouth disease to be slaughtered, and also any cattle, sheep, goats or swine having been in the same shed, &c., or in contact with animals affected with foot-and-mouth disease. But if the owner of the animal give notice in writing to the Local Authority or their Inspector or other Officers that he objects, the Local Authority must not proceed to slaughter it without the special authority of the Privy Council. The Local Authority must pay compensation for animals so slaughtered, as follows:—

(i.) Where the animal slaughtered was affected with foot-and-mouth disease, the compensation is one-half of the value of the animal immediately before it became so affected.

(ii.) In other cases the compensation is the whole value of the animal immediately before it was slaughtered.

4th. *Sheep-pox.*—A Local Authority has no power to make regulations with regard to this disease.

Duties of Local Authority with regard to Sheep-pox.[1]

On the receipt of information from an Inspector that an outbreak of sheep-pox has occurred, the Local Authority must inquire into the correctness of the Inspector's declaration, with the advice and assistance of a Veterinary Inspector or a person qualified to be such, and if satisfied of the correctness of the Inspector's declaration they must determine and declare accordingly, and prescribe the limits of the infected place, and they may include, within those limits, places adjoining or near the place to which the Inspector's declaration relates; and they may also include in an infected place any adjoining part of the district of another Local Authority, with the previous consent in writing of that Authority, but not otherwise.

If the Local Authority are not satisfied of the correctness of the Inspector's declaration as regards the existence or past existence of the disease, they must declare and determine accordingly; and thereupon, as from the time specified in their Order, the place to which the Inspector's declaration relates ceases to be an infected place.

The Local Authority must, without delay, report to the Privy Council the declaration of the Inspector and their proceedings thereon.

When the Local Authority have declared a place to be a sheep-pox infected place they may, at any time after the expiration of twenty-eight days from the cessation of the disease, declare, by Order, that place to be free from sheep-pox; such an Order they must report, without delay, to the Privy Council.

The Local Authority must cause all sheep affected with sheep-pox to be slaughtered within two days after the existence of the disease is known to them, and they may, if they think fit, cause any sheep, having been in the same shed, &c., or in contact with sheep affected with sheep-pox, to be slaughtered.

The Local Authority must pay compensation for sheep slaughtered as follows:—

(i.) Where the sheep was affected with sheep-pox, the compensation is half the value of the sheep immediately before it became affected; but the compensation must in no case exceed £2.

[1] Animals Order, 1886, Arts. 44-48, 92, 93, 174, 178.

(ii.) In other cases the compensation is the whole value of the sheep immediately before it was slaughtered; but the compensation must not exceed £4.

The Local Authority may make regulations as to swine fever.[1]

5th. *Swine Fever.*—In order to check the spread of swine fever, a Local Authority or their Executive Committee (but no other Committee) may make regulations prohibiting and regulating the movement of swine into their district from the district of any other Local Authority in England and Wales or Scotland (such a regulation will not apply to swine passing through their district by rail without untrucking), and also for the disinfection of vehicles used for carrying swine in their district except upon a railway.

Duties of Local Authority on an outbreak of swine fever.[2]

On the receipt of information from an Inspector that an outbreak of swine fever has occurred, the Local Authority must inquire into the correctness of the Inspector's declaration, with the advice and assistance of a Veterinary Inspector or a person qualified to be such, and if satisfied of the correctness of the Inspector's declaration they must, by Order, determine and declare accordingly, and prescribe the limits of the infected place, and they may include within those limits places adjoining or near the place to which the Inspector's declaration relates, and they may include in an infected place any adjoining part of the district of another Local Authority, with the previous consent in writing of that Authority, but not otherwise.

If the Local Authority are not satisfied of the correctness of the Inspector's declaration as regards the existence or past existence of the disease, they must by Order determine and declare accordingly; and thereupon, as from the time specified in their Order, the place to which the Inspector's declaration relates ceases to be an infected place. The Local Authority must without delay report to the Privy Council the declaration of the Inspector and their proceedings thereon.

Having declared a place to be a swine-fever infected place, the Local Authority may, after the expiration of 28 days from the cessation of the disease, declare, by Order, that place to be free from swine-fever, provided that proper steps for disinfection have been taken; such an Order they must, without delay, report to the Privy Council.

The Privy Council may, on the application of a Local Authority, by Order, direct that the provisions with regard to infected circles shall apply with regard to swine-fever within the district of that Authority. In any such district, upon a place becoming a swine-fever infected place in pursuance of the declaration of an Inspector of a Local Authority, the whole space lying within a distance of half a mile from any part of the infected place becomes a swine-fever infected circle; but the infected circle will not extend into the district of a neighbouring Local Authority, unless the provisions as to infected circles apply also in the last-mentioned district. The Local Authority may, from time to time, contract and alter the limits of a swine-fever infected area, or so much of it as is within their district; but no land or building more than half a mile from a swine-fever infected place must, at any time, be included in the infected circle; or the Local Authority may dissolve the infected circle altogether. On the swine-fever infected place ceasing to be an infected place, the infected circle will, in any case, cease to exist. The Local Authority must give public notice of the existence of a swine-fever infected circle by placards, &c.; and they may make regulations as to the movement of swine in, into, and out of swine-fever infected circles.

The Local Authority may, if they think fit, cause any swine affected with swine-

[1] Animals Order, 1886, Arts. 78, 79.
[2] Animals Order, 1886, Arts. 68-77, 87-89, 92, 93, 174, 175.

fever to be slaughtered, or any swine having been in the same pig-sty, &c., or in contact with swine affected with swine-fever.

The Local Authority must pay compensation as follows for swine so slaughtered:—

(i.) Where the pig slaughtered was affected with swine-fever, the compensation is half the value of the pig immediately before it became affected, but the compensation must in no case exceed £2.

(ii.) In other cases the compensation is the whole value of the pig immediately before slaughter, but the compensation must in no case exceed £4.

Duties of Local Authority with regard to sheep scab.[1]

6th. *Sheep Scab*—To this disease the system of infected places and areas does not apply; the Local Authority may, however, make regulations for prohibiting and regulating the movement of sheep affected with sheep-scab, &c., and must in certain cases cause the slaughter of sheep affected with sheep-scab while unlawfully exposed for sale, &c.

Duties of Local Authority with regard to glanders and farcy.[2]

7th. *Glanders and Farcy.*—To these diseases the system of infected places and areas does not apply; the Local Authority have, however, power to make regulations concerning the movement of horses, asses, and mules affected with these diseases, &c., and in certain cases to require them to be slaughtered. They may also give public notice of the outbreak of such diseases.

Duties of Local Authorities as to rabies.[3]

8ht. *Rabies.*—To this disease the system of infected places and areas does not apply. The Local Authority may, however, make regulations, among other things, for the muzzling of dogs, and the seizure and detention of stray dogs, for the seizure, detention, and disposal of dogs being at large and suspected of rabies, or having been in contact with dogs affected with rabies, &c., and for prohibiting and regulating the holding of dog shows. They may also give public warning of an outbreak of rabies, and when an outbreak has occurred, they may make further regulations.

Duties of Local Authorities as to anthrax.[4]

9th. *Anthrax.*—To this disease the system of infected places and areas does not apply; the Local Authority have, however, power to make certain regulations concerning the movement of animals affected therewith and other matters. They may also give public notice of an outbreak of this disease.

Local Authority fitting up wharves, &c.

The Local Authority may provide, erect, and fit up wharves, stations, lairs, sheds, and other places for the landing, reception, keeping, sale, slaughter, or disposal of animals, carcases, fodder, litter, dung, and other things, whether foreign or not. For the regulation of wharves and places so provided by the Local Authority, the Markets and Fairs Clauses Act, 1847 (*10 & 11 Vict. c. 14*), except sections 6-9, 51-60, inclusive, is incorporated with the Contagious Diseases (Animals) Act 1878.[5]

Markets and Fairs Clauses Act, 1847.

In looking at the Markets and Fairs Clauses Act, 1847, with reference to the contagious diseases of animals, the reader must keep in mind that the definition clause of that statute is wholly different from the definition clause in the Contagious Diseases (Animals) Act, 1878, so that the same words in the two statutes do not mean the same things.

The Local Authority may make bye-laws for the regulation of their wharves, &c.,

---

[1] Animals Order, 1886, Arts. 54, 92, 93.
[2] Animals Order, 1886, Arts. 60-63, 92, 93, 174.
[3] Rabies Order, 1887.
[4] Anthrax Order, 1886.
[5] Contagious Diseases (Animals) Act, 1878, sec. 39.
Contagious Diseases (Animals) Act, 1886, sec. 10.

and provide penalties for their breach; the bye-laws will become operative on their approval by the Privy Council. They may make such charge for the use of their wharves, &c., as may be authorized by their bye-laws; all sums received in this way must be carried to a separate account and be applied in payment of interest on money borrowed by them or their predecessors for the purposes of Part III. of the Contagious Diseases (Animals) Act, 1869 (*32 & 33 Vict. c. 70*), or of the Contagious Diseases (Animals) Act, 1878, sec. 39, and subject thereto towards the discharge of their expenses under the Acts and Orders.

The Local Authority must make such periodical returns to the Privy Council of their expenditure and receipts in respect of their wharves or other places, as the Privy Council may require.

The Privy Council may direct a reduction in the charges made by a Local Authority in a proper case.

The Local Authority may hold markets in such wharves and places, upon such days as they may appoint by their bye-laws.

Any person who there sells or exposes for sale unwholesome meat is liable to a penalty not exceeding £5, and any officer of the Local Authority appointed for that purpose may seize such unwholesome meat and carry the same before a Justice of the Peace, who will thereupon cause the same to be further examined by competent persons, and if it be found unfit for human food will order it to be destroyed; and any person obstructing such an officer in seizing or carrying away unwholesome meat, is liable to a penalty not exceeding £5. Any person obstructing or assaulting any person appointed by the Local Authority to superintend the wharf, or other place, will be liable to a penalty not exceeding 40s.

The Local Authority must provide proper weighing machines, &c., for weighing cattle, meat and loaded carts, and must appoint persons to attend to the weighing and measuring of the commodities sold.

Penalties are provided for any fraud that any person may commit in respect of weighing commodities.[1]

The Local Authority may erect slaughter-houses for the purpose of slaughtering animals. But if their slaughter-house is a nuisance they will be liable to indictment. Any officer of the Local Authority appointed for the purpose may enter the slaughter-house at any time and examine the premises, and if he finds any cattle or carcases that appear unfit for human food, he may seize such cattle or carcases and carry the same before a Justice of the Peace. The Justice will have the same further examined by competent persons, and will, if they appear to be unfit for human food, cause the same to be destroyed.

Officers of Local Authority[2]

The Local Authority must appoint in all cases at least one Veterinary Inspector; and such additional Veterinary Inspectors as the Privy Council may from time to time direct. They may also appoint such other Inspectors as they think fit.

The Privy Council may dismiss any Inspector for incompetence or misconduct. An Inspector appointed by a Local Authority has power only over those districts, within the jurisdiction of the Local Authority, by whom he is appointed. Inspectors are also appointed by the Privy Council, and their powers extend over all parts of England and Wales.

---

[1] Markets and Fairs Clauses Acts, 1847, secs. 21-30.
See also the Markets and Fairs (Weighing of Cattle) Act, 1887 (*50 & 51 Vict. c. 27*).

[2] Contagious Diseases (Animals) Act, 1878, secs. 42, 45.

Powers of Police constables.[1]

The Police of each police district or area, county, borough, town and place must execute and enforce the Acts and Orders, and their powers, for this purpose, are briefly as follows :—

(i.) Where a person is found committing, or is reasonably suspected of being engaged in committing, an offence against the Acts or Orders, a constable may without warrant stop or detain him ; and if his name and address are not known to the constable, and he fails to give them to his satisfaction, the constable may, without warrant, apprehend him ; and the constable may, whether so stopping, detaining, or apprehending the person or not, stop, detain and examine any animal, horse, ass, mule or dog, vehicle, boat or thing, to which the offence or suspected offence relates, and require the same to be forthwith taken back to, or into, any place or district wherefrom or whereout it was unlawfully removed, and execute and enforce that requisition.

(ii.) If any person obstructs or impedes a constable or other officer in the execution of the Acts or an Order in Council, or of a regulation of a Local Authority, or assists in any such obstructing or impeding, the constable or officer may, without warrant, apprehend the offender.

(iii.) A person so apprehended must be taken at once before a Justice of the Peace, but he must not be detained without warrant longer than is necessary for that purpose ; and all enactments relating to the release of persons on recognizances taken by an officer of police or constable apply to persons thus apprehended.

The foregoing provisions apply also to any person called by a constable to his assistance.

(iv.) The constable must forthwith make a report in writing to his superior officer of every case in which he stops any person, animal, horse, ass, mule, dog, vehicle, boat, or thing under these provisions, and of all his proceedings consequent thereon.

Every person having on his premises, or under his charge, an animal, horse, ass, mule, or dog afflicted with disease, must, with all practicable speed, give notice of the fact to a police constable, who must, in the case of cattle plague, give information thereof to his superior officer, who, in his turn, must transmit the information by telegraph or other rapid means to the Clerk of the Privy Council, Whitehall, London. In the case of other diseases, the constable must inform an Inspector of the Local Authority of the outbreak.

Powers of Inspectors.[2]

Inspectors have, among others, the following general powers :—

(i.) They have all the powers of constables for the place where they are acting.

(ii.) An Inspector may, at any time, enter any land or dairy or cowshed to which the Act of 1878 applies, or milk stores, or milk shop, or other building or place wherein he has reasonable grounds for supposing that disease exists or has within 56 days existed; that the carcase of a diseased or suspected animal is, or has been, kept, or has been buried, destroyed or otherwise disposed

---

[1] Contagious Diseases (Animals) Act, 1878, secs. 31, 50, 61.
Animals Order, 1886, Arts. 6, 11, 12, 23, 41, 50, 56, 57, 63-65.
Anthrax Order, 1886, Arts. 5, 6.
Rabies Order, 1887, Arts. 7, 8.

[2] Contagious Diseases (Animals) Act, 1878, sec. 51.
Animals Order, 1886, Arts. 56 and 64.
Anthrax Order, 1886, Art. 5.
Rabies Order, 1887, Art. 7.

of; that there is to be found any pen, place, vehicle, or thing, in respect whereof any person has on any occasion failed to comply with the provisions of the Acts or Orders or of a regulation of a Local Authority; or that the Acts or Orders, or a regulation of a Local Authority has not been, or is not being, complied with.

(iii.) An Inspector may at any time enter any pen, vehicle, vessel, or boat in which, in respect whereof, he has reasonable ground for supposing that the Acts or any provision of the Orders, or of the regulations of a Local Authority has not been, or is not being, complied with.

(iv.) An Inspector entering as above mentioned, must, if required by the owner, or occupier, or person in charge of the land, building, place, pen, vehicle, vessel or boat, state in writing his reasons for entering.

The following are a few of the duties of Inspectors with regard to particular diseases:—

Duties of Inspector to cattle plague.[1]

An Inspector, if it appears that cattle plague exists or has within ten days existed in a cowshed, field, or other place, must make and sign a declaration to that effect. He must serve a signed notice of that declaration on the occupier of that cowshed, field, or other place; and thereupon the cowshed, field, &c., with all lands and buildings contiguous thereto, in the same occupation, will become a cattle plague infected place, subject to the determination of the Privy Council.

The Inspector must also, unless under the circumstance it appears to him inexpedient, serve a like notice on the occupiers of all lands and buildings, any part of which lies in his judgment within one mile in any direction from the cowshed, &c., where the outbreak occurred, or on the occupiers of any of such lands and buildings. Thereupon all such lands and buildings, on the occupiers of which the Inspector serves a notice, become part of the infected place.

The Inspector must, with all practicable speed, inform the Privy Council and the Local Authority of his declaration and notices, and must send to the Privy Council his declaration and a copy of the notice (if any) that he has served upon neighbouring occupiers.

Inspector's duty as to pleuro-pneumonia.[2]

An Inspector of a Local Authority, where it appears to him that pleuro-pneumonia exists or has within 56 days existed in a cowshed, field, or other place, must forthwith make and sign a declaration thereof. He must serve a notice, signed by him, of the declaration on the occupier of that cowshed, field or other place. Thereupon that cowshed, field, or other place will become a pleuro-pneumonia infected place subject to the determination of the Local Authority. The Inspector must with all practicable speed inform the Local Authority of his declaration and notice.

Duties of Inspectors as to foot-and-mouth disease.[3]

An Inspector of a Local Authority, when it appears to him that foot-and-mouth disease exists or has within ten days existed in a cowshed, field, or other place, must forthwith make and sign a declaration thereof, and must serve a notice signed by him of the declaration on the occupier of that cowshed, field, or other place. Thereupon that cowshed, field, or other place will become a foot-and-mouth disease infected place, subject to the determination of the Local Authority.

---

[1] Contagious Diseases (Animals) Act, 1878, sec. 10.
Animals Order, 1886, Art. 8.

[2] Contagious Diseases (Animals) Act, 1878, sec. 10, 16.
Animals Order, 1886, Arts. 12, 14, 15, 87, 88, 92, 174.

[3] Contagious Diseases (Animals) Act, 1878, sec. 22.
Animals Order, 1886, Arts. 23, 25, 30, 31, 87, 88, 92, 174.

The Inspector must with all practicable speed inform the Local Authority of his declaration and notice.

Duties of Inspectors as to sheep-pox.[1]

An Inspector of a Local Authority, where it appears to him that sheep-pox exists, or has within ten days existed in a shed, field or other place, must forthwith make and sign a declaration thereof, and must serve a notice, signed by him, of the declaration on the occupier of that shed, field or other place, and thereupon that shed, field or other place will become a sheep-pox infected place, subject to the determination of the Local Authority. The Inspector must with all practicable speed inform the Local Authority and the Privy Council of his declaration and notice.

Duties of Inspectors as to swine-fever.[2]

An Inspector, where it appears to him that swine-fever exists, or has within ten days existed in a pig-sty, shed or other place, must forthwith make and sign a declaration thereof, and must serve a notice, signed by him, of the declaration on the occupier of that pig-sty, shed or other place. Thereupon that pig-sty, shed or other place will become a swine-fever infected place, subject to the determination of the Local Authority. The Inspector must with all practicable speed inform the Local Authority of his declaration and notice.

Duties of Inspectors as to sheep-scab and other diseases.[3]

An Inspector on receiving information from a police constable of the existence of sheep-scab, glanders, farcy, anthrax, or rabies, must report the same to the Local Authority.

Miscellaneous.[4]

An Order or Regulation of a Local Authority may be proved by the production of a newspaper, purporting to contain the Order or Regulation as an advertisement, or by the production of a copy of the Order or Regulation purporting to be certified by the Clerk of the Local Authority as a true copy.

An Order or Regulation so proved shall be taken to have been duly made, unless and until the contrary is proved.

No proof is required of the appointment or hand-writing of an Inspector or other Officer of the Privy Council, nor of the Clerk or Inspector or other Officer of a Local Authority.

A notice or other instrument may be served on the person to be affected thereby, either by the delivery thereof on him personally, or by the leaving thereof for him at his last known place of abode or business, or by the sending thereof through the post in a registered letter addressed to him. A notice or other instrument to be served on the occupier of any building, &c., may, except when sent by post, be addressed to him by the designation of the occupier of that building, &c., without naming him.

Where it is to be served on the occupiers of several buildings, &c., it may, except when sent by post, be addressed to them collectively by the designation of the occupiers of the several buildings, &c., without naming them, but separate copies must be served on them separately.

In order to prove the service by letter of a notice or other instrument, it is sufficient to prove that the letter was properly addressed, registered, and posted, and contained the notice or other instrument to be served.

Where a Local Authority fail to execute or enforce the provisions of the Acts or Orders of Council, the Privy Council may, by Order, empower a person

---

[1] Animals Order, 1886, Arts. 41, 43, 44, 46, 92, 174.
[2] Animals Order, 1886, Arts. 65, 67, 68, 71-73, 87, 88, 92, 174.
[3] Animals Order, 1886, Arts. 50, 52, 57, 59, 92, 174.
Anthrax Order, 1886, Arts. 6, 8. Rabies Order, 1887, Arts. 8, 10.
[4] Contagious Diseases (Animals) Act, 1878, secs. 41, 44, 55, 57, &c.

therein named, to execute and enforce their provisions, or to procure the execution and enforcement thereof.

The expenses incurred thereby, including compensation for animals slaughtered, will be expenses of the Local Authority, and must be paid to the Privy Council by the Treasurer or proper officer of the Local Authority.

In default of payment the Privy Council may appoint a person to sue for them. No proceeding may be taken against a Local Authority, nor against an Inspector or officer of the Privy Council or of a Local Authority, or any person, for any act done in pursuance or execution, or intended execution, of the Acts or Orders in Council, or Regulations of a Local Authority, or in respect of any alleged neglect, or default, in the execution of the Acts, Orders, and Regulations, unless it is commenced within four months after the act, neglect, or default complained of, or in case of a continuance of injury or damage, within four months next after the ceasing thereof.

The Local Authority may pay as part of their expenses, any expense an Inspector, or officer, or servant, or agent of theirs is put to when defendant in such an action. Proceedings for offences against the Acts may be taken and penalties recovered summarily.

Coroners.

The principal statutes dealing with the appointment and remuneration of Coroners, &c., are—an Act of 1844 (*7 & 8 Vict. c. 92*); an Act of 1860 (*23 & 24 Vict. c. 116*); the Municipal Corporations Act, 1882 (*45 & 46 Vict. c. 50*), and the Coroners Act, 1887 (*50 & 51 Vict. c. 71*).

Coroners are of four kinds:—

1st. Official Coroners, namely—Certain of the judges and others, whose position we do not propose to discuss.

2nd. Franchise Coroners, namely—Coroners for the Queen's Household, a Coroner for the Admiralty, a Coroner appointed by Her Majesty for the Duchy of Lancaster; and also Coroners appointed for a town corporate, liberty, &c., the Coroner of which has in the past been appointed otherwise than by election of the freeholders of a county, or part of a county, or by a Town Council. It should be observed that in the appointment of such a Franchise Coroner, the Local Government Act, 1888, makes no change. Some Franchise Coroners are paid out of rates, and in that case will be paid by the County Council within whose jurisdiction the franchise is situated.

3rd. County Coroners—

For every county, and for certain liberties and franchises Coroners were before the appointed day elected by freeholders of the county or liberty; or if the county was divided into districts, a County Coroner was elected for each district by the freeholders of that district. All such Coroners, as also those who, on the occurrence of a vacancy, will be appointed under the Local Government Act, 1888, to succeed them, are called County Coroners.

4th. Borough Coroners, namely—Coroners appointed for their borough by the Town Council of a Quarter Sessions borough.

The business of the County Council in connection with Coroners will comprise the appointment of County Coroners, the remuneration of County Coroners, and of such Franchise Coroners as are payable out of rates, and petitioning, if they think fit, for the division of their county into coroners' districts, or for the alteration of such a division. It must be remembered that under the Local Government Act, 1888, County Coroners will continue to act within county boroughs which have not a separate Court of Quarter Sessions.

Appointment of County Coroner.[1]

On the occurrence of a vacancy in the office of County Coroner, a writ *de coronatore eligendo* will be issued by the Lord Chancellor, or in Lancashire by the Chancellor of the Duchy of Lancaster, requiring the election of a new County Coroner. In the case of a coroner's district wholly comprised in a county borough the writ will be directed to the Town Council, who may make the appointment. In the case of a coroner's district situated in an entire county, and not wholly comprised in one administrative county, it seems that the writ will be directed to the County Councils of the administrative counties, within which such district lies, jointly; but the appointment must be made by the Joint Committee of the County Councils of the entire county; it seems, however, to be intended that the Joint Committee shall take steps to deal with any such district, so that, on the occurrence of a vacancy, or sooner, the district shall be brought wholly within one administrative county. Until that has been done, however, the Joint Committee will stand in the position of a County Council with regard to the coroners of that district. In other cases the writ will be directed to the County Council, who may, in general, make the appointment; but in the case of a coroner's district lying partly within a county borough, the Town Council may apply to the County Council for the appointment of a Joint Committee for the purposes of Coroners; and if such a Joint

[1] Local Government Act, 1888, secs. 5, 34. Coroners Act, 1887, sec. 39.

Committee has been appointed, the Coroner must be appointed by them.

County Councillors and County Aldermen are ineligible for the office of County Coroner, and it seems that a County Coroner must be a freeholder of the county.[1]

The Council or Committee appointing a County Coroner will have no power to dismiss him, but he may be removed by the High Court or the Lord Chancellor under certain circumstances. A County Coroner may appoint a deputy by writing under his hand; a duplicate of every such appointment must be sent to the Clerk of the County Council, and kept by him among the county records.

County Coroners are paid by salary, which is, or may be, fixed afresh every five years. The present period of five years, for which the salary was fixed by the Quarter Sessions, will in most cases end on the 31st December, 1889, when the County Council or Joint Committee, as the case may be, may fix the salary for the next five years. Coroner's salary.[2]

Should the County Council or Joint Committee fail to come to terms with any Coroner on the subject of his salary, the Home Secretary may fix it, taking into account all the circumstances of the case.

The County Council or Joint Committee, as the case may be, repay the Coroner, quarterly, his lawful expenses incurred in respect of inquests, namely:— Coroner's expenses.[3]

1st. Fees to medical men, namely—For attending to give evidence at any inquest whereat no post-mortem examination has been made—One Guinea. For making a post-mortem examination with or without an analysis of the contents of the stomach or intestines, and attending to give evidence thereon—Two Guineas.

2nd. Costs incurred in the removal of a dead body, where a place has been provided by a Sanitary Authority for the reception of dead bodies during the time required to conduct a post-morten examination, and the Coroner orders the removal of a dead body to, and from, such place for carrying out such examination.

3rd. Other sums according to a schedule which the Quarter Sessions have made, and which the County Council or Joint Committee may alter and vary from me to time. If the County Council or Joint Committee make a new schedule they must cause one copy to be deposited with their Clerk and one copy to be sent to every Coroner concerned.

---

[1] Coroners Act, 1887, sec. 12, which provides that "Every Coroner for a county shall be a fit person, having land in fee sufficient in the same county whereof he may answer to all manner of people." This section is taken from 14 Edw. III. st. 1, c. 8, which was repealed by the Coroners Act, 1887.

[2] 23 & 24 Vict. c. 116, sec. 4.

[3] Coroners Act, 1887, secs. 22-27.

The Coroner must lay before the County Council or Joint Committee, within four months after holding an inquest, a full account of all his expenses, accompanied by such vouchers as the County Council may direct. The County Council or Joint Committee may examine the Coroner as to the correctness of his account; but if satisfied that the account is correct they must pay him without abatement or deduction.

A County Coroner, in addition to his salary and expenses, is entitled to fees when he acts as Sheriff, and to fees for admitting to bail a person charged with manslaughter.

Coroners' districts.[1]

No specific number of Coroners is fixed for any county except for the twelve counties of Wales, in each of which there are two County Coroners; and it seems that the Lord Chancellor could issue a writ *de coronatore eligendo* for the appointment of additional Coroners if he thought fit. If, however, it is desirable to increase the number of Coroners for a county, the practice is to divide the county into districts, or if the county is already so divided, to alter the number of divisions. Such a division or alteration may also be carried out independently of an alteration in the number of Coroners for the sake of convenience.

If the County Council wish to divide their county into districts, or if it is already so divided, to alter the existing districts, they must (except in the case of those alterations which are to be made in consequence of the alteration of boundaries, &c., under the Local Government Act, 1888),[2] proceed as follows:—

The County Council must pass a resolution that a petition be presented to the Crown praying for a division or alteration, and they must fix a day on which that petition shall be further considered. The Clerk of the County Council must give notice of the resolution to every Coroner in the county, informing him of the date on which the petition is to be further considered. At the sitting of the County Council at which the petition is to be further considered they must hear every Coroner who attends; after which the petition must be drawn up, showing the boundaries of the proposed districts, and describing them, and giving the reasons upon which the petition is founded, and the Clerk of the County Council must send a copy of the petition to every Coroner for the county.

---

[1] 7 & 8 Vict. c. 92, secs. 2-7, 19, 20.

[2] See *ante*, p. 44.

The Queen, with the advice of the Privy Council, after taking such petition into consideration, and also any petition that may be presented by a Coroner for the County, may make an Order dividing the county into districts or altering such a division accordingly. The County Council must then in the case of an original division assign one of the districts to each County Coroner in office.

The County Council will order their Clerk to prepare a list of the several parishes, townships, or hundreds, as the case may be, in each district, which list is to be enrolled among the records of the county. After the division of a county into districts, the Coroner for a district remains a Coroner for the whole county, so that his acts are valid beyond his own district, but he should not hold inquests outside his own district, except in the unavoidable absence of the Coroner for the other district.

In the case of a coroner's district, in an entire county, which district is situated in more than one administrative county, the Joint Committee for the entire county may proceed in like manner with a view to bringing the district entirely within one administrative county.

Borough Coroners.[1]

Borough Coroners are appointed by the Town Council, for every Quarter Sessions borough, the population of which, according to the census of 1881, was above 10,000. Any person other than an Alderman or Councillor of the borough may be appointed, and he holds office during good behaviour. A vacancy must be filled up within ten days. A Borough Coroner may appoint a deputy.

A borough Coroner is paid no salary, but is paid the same expenses as a County Coroner (the schedule, of course, being drawn up by the Town Council), and, in addition, for every inquisition he takes in the borough, £1, and for every mile exceeding two miles, which he is compelled to travel from his usual place of abode to take such inquisition—ninepence.

Destructive Insects.

The Destructive Insects Act, 1877 *(40 & 41 Vict. c. 68)*, was passed for the purpose of preventing the introduction into Great Britain of the Colorado beetle (*doryphora decemlineata*).

The Privy Council are empowered to forbid the landing

---

[1] Municipal Corporations Act, 1882, secs. 171, 172.
Coroners Act, 1887, secs. 25, 28, 41.

of potatoes and other things likely to introduce the beetle; to direct or authorise the destruction of crops of potatoes, &c., on which the beetle is found, &c.; to prohibit the keeping and distribution of living specimens of the beetle; and to direct, in the case of the destruction of a crop, that the Local Authority, *i.e.*, the Local Authority under the Contagious Diseases (Animals) Acts, shall pay compensation. They may also direct the same Local Authorities to carry out the Act generally. The expenses would be borne in the same way as expenses of carrying out the Contagious Diseases (Animals) Acts.

Explosives.

In order to secure safety in the making, keeping, and conveyance of explosives, several Acts of Parliament have been passed.

These were consolidated and amended by the Explosives Act, 1875 *(38 Vict. c. 17).*

Under this Act the superintendence of explosives is vested partly in the Government[1] and partly in Local Authorities.

Regulations for carrying out the Act may be made in certain cases by Order in Council, in other cases by Order of a Secretary of State.

An official guide book to the Act and Orders has been published for the use of the persons interested in the Act. A series of abstracts of the Act and Orders also, specially prepared for the use of Local Authorities, and the proprietors of premises of various kinds used in the manufacture and keeping of explosives, are officially published at a nominal price.

The Explosives Act, 1875, provides that all premises used for the manufacture and keeping of explosives must be duly licensed, that certain regulations shall be observed in all such premises, and that certain regulations shall be observed in the conveyance of explosives. The Act provides also for the detection and punishment of any infringement of the Act. The Local Authorities for carrying out the Act are—in counties, the County Council, and in county boroughs and in Quarter Sessions Boroughs, the population of which, according to the census of 1881, was above 10,000, the Town Council. The Town Council of any other borough, and any Improvement

[1] The Home Office is the Government Department charged with the superintendence of explosives.

Commissioners, may, by Order of a Secretary of State made on the application of such Town Council or Improvement Commissioners, be made a Local Authority, provided that the population of their borough or district, according to the census of 1881, was over 10,000. A County Council may delegate all or any of their powers as Local Authority under the Act to the Justices in Petty Sessions.

Before proceeding to discuss the duties of a Local Authority, we will define certain terms used in the Act and other matters.

Explosives, which term has its natural meaning, have been divided into seven classes, namely :—1, Gunpowder Class, meaning gunpowder ordinarily so called (this does not include Schultz's, or E. C. powder); 2, Nitrate-mixture Class; 3 Nitro-compound Class; 4, Chlorate-mixture Class; 5, Fulminate Class; 6, Ammunition Class; and 7, Firework Class. The regulations respecting the manufacture and keeping of each class are different. Definitions.

Where an explosive falls within the description of more than one class, it is deemed to belong exclusively to the latest of classes within which the description of it falls.

Magazine and *Store*, are words not used synonymously. Magazine being used for the larger buildings, requiring a licence from a Secretary of State; and store for the smaller buildings, which may be licensed by a Local Authority. Licensed premises under the Act are of five principal kinds—Factories of explosives, Magazines of explosives, Stores of explosives, Small Firework Factories and Registered Premises.

For the establishment of a new factory or magazine, a licence must be obtained from the Secretary of State; after the draft licence has been approved by him, application must be made to the Local Authority, who must fix a time and place for hearing the applicant, and persons objecting to the application. Factories & Magazines.

The Local Authority must cause notice to be published in one or more local newspapers by the applicant of the application, and of the time and place when they will hear him, and persons objecting. If the proposed site is within one mile of an urban sanitary district, the applicant must also serve notice on the Urban Sanitary Authority (unless they are also the Local Authority), of the application, and of the time and place of hearing fixed by the Local Authority. Such notices must be published and served at least one month before the hearing of the application.

At the hearing, the Local Authority must hear any objections of which notice in writing has been sent seven clear days before the hearing, to their Clerk and to the applicant, giving the name, address, and calling of the person intending to object, and a short statement of the grounds of objection.

The costs of a frivolous objection, the Local Authority may direct to be paid to the applicant, by the person objecting.

The Local Authority may refuse the application altogether, or assent thereto, either absolutely, or upon terms requiring additional restrictions or precautions. An appeal however lies by the applicant to the Secretary of State.

The licence will not come into force until the factory is sufficiently completed according to the licence to justify the use thereof, and until the licence has been confirmed by the Secretary of State. Gunpowder factories and magazines in existence on the 14th June, 1875, or completed in accordance with a licence granted before the 25th February, 1875, are authorized by a continuing certificate, over which, and over alterations in which, the Local Authority has no power.

An alteration in a licence, or in a factory or magazine, may be authorized by an amending licence. In certain cases, the Secretary of State may grant this on his own authority, but where the alterations are important the application for the amending licence goes through the same stages as the application for a new licence.

Stores and Small Firework Factories.

For stores and small firework factories a licence may be obtained from the Local Authority without a previous application to a Secretary of State. The maximum amount of explosives allowed in a store is much smaller than that allowed in a magazine. A firework factory is not a small firework factory if there are on the premises at the same time :—

(i.) More than 100lbs. of any explosive, other than manufactured fireworks and coloured fires and stars ; or

(ii.) More than 500lbs. of manufactured fireworks either finished or partly finished ; or

(iii.) More than 25lbs. of coloured fires and stars, not made up into manufactured fireworks ;

these quantities are further reduced in certain cases.

For the establishment of a new store or small firework factory, application for a licence must be made to the Local Authority, giving the applicant's name, address, and calling, and the proposed site and construction of the store or small firework factory and the amount and description of explosives he proposes to have therein, and, in the case of a small firework factory, in any building therein.

Forms of application have been published, and may be purchased of various booksellers.

It is the duty of the Local Authority to see that the proposals in the application are in accordance with the regulations made by Order in Council; but if these regulations are observed the Local Authority have no discretion but must grant the licence on payment of such fee not exceeding 5s. as they may think fit.

The licence is valid only for the person named in it, and must be annually renewed on application by post, or otherwise, and payment of such fee, not exceeding 1s., as the Local Authority may determine, unless the circumstances have so changed that the grant of a new licence would not be permissible, in which case the Local Authority must refuse the renewal. The renewal may be by indorsement or otherwise.

The Explosives Act, 1875, provided that Gunpowder Stores established without a licence from a Local Authority in pursuance of the Gunpowder Act, 1860 (*23 & 24 Vict. c. 139*), or of any enactment repealed by that Act, for the use of any mine, quarry, colliery, or factory of safety fuzes, and in use on the 14th June, 1875, might be continued under a continuing certificate granted by a Local Authority.

Stores under a continuing certificate of this kind require no further licence, nor does the certificate require renewal, but no important alteration can be made in a store under a continuing certificate, so that if such an alteration is desired the certificate must be given up and a licence obtained. The certificate expires if the business is discontinued for twelve months. The number of stores in existence under continuing certificates is accordingly diminishing, and in 1887 there were in England and Wales only 291, as compared with 1,243 under licences.

Without a formal licence a person may register his premises for the keeping of explosives by simple application to the Local Authority, stating his name, calling, and the address of the premises, and paying such fee, not exceeding 1s., as the Local Authority may fix. Registered Premises.

The registration is valid only for the person registered, and must be renewed annually by notice to the Local Authority accompanied with such fee, not exceeding one shilling, as the Local Authority may fix.

The amount of explosives allowed to be kept on registered premises is much smaller than that allowed in a store.

Duty of Local Authority to repress offences.

It is the duty of the Local Authority to suppress all illegal dealings with explosives within their district; over factories and magazines licensed by a Secretary of State they have no control, but they must appoint Officers to inspect stores, small firework factories, and registered premises. These Officers, on producing a certificate of their authority, will have full power to enter and inspect any such places.

The Local Authority should also direct their Officers to endeavour to suppress any offences against the Act, namely :—

I. Manufacturing explosives in an unauthorized place.

The only authorized places for the manufacture of explosives are factories authorized by the Secretary of State either by licence or by a continuing certificate, and small firework factories licensed by the Local Authority.

Any person may, however, fill, for private use and not for sale, safety cartridges to an amount containing not more than 150 lbs. of gunpowder or other explosives. Safety cartridges are cartridges for small-arms of which the case can be extracted, after firing, and which are so closed as to prevent any explosion in one cartridge being communicated to other cartridges.

Any person also may make small quantities of explosives for chemical experiment but not for practical use or for sale.

Proprietors of licensed magazines and stores and registered premises have a limited power of carrying on manufactures.

Government factories also are to a great extent exempt from the provisions of the Act.

II. Keeping explosives in an unauthorized place.

The only authorized places are factories licensed by a Secretary of State, or having a continuing certificate, small firework factories licensed by a Local Authority, magazines licensed by a Secretary of State or having a continuing certificate, stores licensed by a Local Authority or having a continuing certificate, and registered premises.

In the following cases, however, explosives may be kept at unauthorized places:

(i.) Any person may keep for private use and not for sale 30 lbs. of gunpowder, and safety cartridges containing 150 lbs. gunpowder. Instead of 30 lbs. of gunpowder a person may keep 15 lbs. of any other explosive; or a person may keep partly gunpowder and partly some other explosive, but in that case the amount of gunpowder together with double the amount of the other explosive must not exceed 30 lbs; thus if a person keep 16 lbs of gunpowder he may have 7 lbs. of other explosive. Instead of gunpowder in safety cartridges the same weight of ammunition of the first division of class 6 may be kept, or a person may keep partly gunpowder in safety cartridges and partly ammunition of that class, but the whole weight must not exceed 150 lbs.

(ii.) A person may keep for private use and not for sale, if intended for immediate use, any quantity of fireworks, provided the same are kept for a period not exceeding 14 days, and in a safe and suitable place and with all due precautions.

(iii.) Carriers may keep explosives for the purpose of conveyance in accordance with the Act and regulations.

(iv.) Persons may keep any quantity of percussion caps and safety fuzes for blasting, and Railway Companies may keep fog signals.

(v.) Rockets for use in life-saving apparatus may be kept under the control of the Commissioners of the Admiralty, or the Board of Trade.

(vi.) Explosives may be kept under the control of general Lighthouse Authorities.

(vii.) Gunpowder, rockets, &c., may be kept on board ships for signalling, subject to certain conditions.

(viii.) Certain floating magazines in the Mersey, and all Government magazines, are exempt from the Act to a great extent.

III. Breach of the Act or of regulations in authorized places.

IV. Breach of the provisions restricting the sale of explosives.

V. Breach of the provisions relating to the conveyance of explosives.

To enable the Local Authority to check illegal proceedings their Officers may obtain warrants, enabling them to search any place where there is reason to suspect that offences are being committed.

Fisheries.

The principal Acts directed towards the preservation of Inland Fisheries are—

The Salmon Fishery Act, 1861 (*24 & 25 Vict. c. 109*).
The Salmon Acts Amendment Act, 1863 (*26 Vict. c. 10*).
The Salmon Fishery Act, 1865 (*28 & 29 Vict. c. 121*).
The Salmon Acts Amendment Act, 1870 (*33 & 34 Vict. c. 33*).
The Salmon Fishery Act, 1873 (*36 & 37 Vict. c. 71*).
The Salmon Fishery Act, 1876 (*39 & 40 Vict. c. 19*).
An Act of 1876 to amend the Law relating to Elver Fishing (*39 & 40 Vict. c. 34*).
The Fisheries (Dynamite) Act, 1877 (*40 & 41 Vict. c. 65*).
The Freshwater Fisheries Act, 1878 (*41 & 42 Vict. c. 39*).
The Salmon Fishery Law Amendment Act, 1879 (*42 & 43 Vict. c. 26*).
The Freshwater Fisheries Act, 1884 (*47 Vict. c. 11*).
The Freshwater Fisheries Act, 1886 (*49 Vict. c. 2*).
The Salmon and Freshwater Fisheries Act, 1886 (*49 & 50 Vict. c. 39*).

The earlier Acts applied exclusively to salmon, and although some provision had been made for trout and char in salmon rivers, the Freshwater Fisheries Act, 1878, was the first Act by which any general provision was made for trout, char, and other freshwater fish.

The objects of the Acts are to preserve the inland fisheries of England and Wales, by prohibiting certain very destructive methods of fishing, by prohibiting the destruction of immature fish, by regulating legitimate modes of fishing, by providing close time for fish, and by securing free passage in rivers for migratory fish. The supervision of fisheries is vested in the Board of Trade, who appoint two Inspectors of Fisheries.[1]

The local supervision of fisheries is provided for in the following way :—A system of rivers is formed into a fishery district.

Fishery districts are of three kinds, namely:—Salmon fishery districts.[2] Trout and char fishery districts.[3] Freshwater fish fishery districts.[4]

The fishery district is under the jurisdiction of a Board of Conservators, who consist of members appointed by the County Council of each county and by the Town Councils of county boroughs, and of other boroughs which are counties of cities or counties of towns, and the population of which, according to the census of 1881, was over 10,000, through which the rivers flow ;[5] of certain *ex-officio* members; and, in the case of a salmon fishery district, also of certain representative members of persons (if any) having common rights of fishery in waters of the district. The Boards of Conservators have wide powers to secure the proper working of the Acts. The formation of fishery districts, and the appointment of Boards of Conservators is business that will concern the County Council, and we will explain the provisions of the Acts with regard to these matters at some detail : for the provisions of the Acts with regard to forbidden methods of fishing, &c., and with regard to the powers and duties of Boards of Conservators when appointed, reference must be made to the Acts themselves, or to text-books on the subject.

Formation of new fishery districts.[6] The County Council of any county, and the Town Council of any such borough as above-mentioned, may apply in writing to the Board of Trade, to have all or any of the rivers lying wholly or partly within their county or borough formed into

---

[1] The Board of Trade were made the central authority in succession to the Home Office, by the Salmon and Freshwater Fisheries Act, 1886.

[2] Salmon Fishery Act, 1865.

[3] Freshwater Fisheries Act, 1878, which rendered the earlier Acts applicable to trout and char.

[4] Freshwater Fisheries Act, 1884, which rendered the earlier Acts applicable to all freshwater fish.

[5] It seems that the Town Council of any county borough may claim to appoint members of a Board of Conservators if any river in the fishery district flows through their borough ; Town Councils of boroughs which are also counties of cities or counties of towns, exercise this right under the Salmon Fishery Act, 1865, sec. 38.

[6] Salmon Fishery Act, 1865, secs. 4, 5. Salmon Fishery Act, 1873, secs. 5-9.

fishery districts. The application need not be restricted to those parts of rivers lying within their county or borough.

The Board of Trade may then form a fishery district by an Order determining the limits of the district and the rivers or parts of rivers in it, by reference to a map or otherwise, and they may modify, if they think fit, the suggestion of the Council as to the limits of the district, and as to the rivers to be included.

The Order must not be made until one month's notice of the intention to make it, and of the intended limits of the district has been given by advertisement, both in local newspapers and in some London daily papers.

After the Order is made it must again be advertised in a similar manner.

The Board of Trade, on the application of a Board of Conservators for a district, may alter the limits of a district. In that case, if any part of a county, or of such a borough as we have mentioned, not included in a district, is proposed to be affected, notice must be sent to the County Council or Town Council of that application. In making such an alteration the Board of Trade may form a new district.

On the formation of a new fishery district, whether on the application of a County Council or in consequence of alterations in existing districts, if the new district lies in more than one county a Joint Committee must be appointed to arrange for the appointment of the Board of Conservators. Joint-committee for a new district.[1]

The County Council of any county, or the Town Council of any such borough as above-mentioned, wholly or partly within the district, may apply (by notice in writing) to the County Council of every other county and the Town Council of any other such borough, wholly or partly within the district, to appoint at their next session a Committee of three of their number to form, with like Committees of the other Councils interested, a Joint Fishery Committee for the district.

As soon as any Council interested have thus appointed a Committee of three, the Clerk of that Council must send the names and addresses of the members of the Committee to the Clerk of each Council interested.

The Clerk of the Council who made the application, when sending his notice of the application, must name a time and

[1] Salmon Fishery Act, 1865, secs. 7-13.

place for the first meeting of the Joint Fishery Committee. The Joint Committee at their first meeting must elect a Chairman, who will also be Chairman at subsequent meetings; in his absence, however, a temporary Chairman may be elected at a subsequent meeting. The Joint Committee may adjourn from time to time, and one-third of the whole number of members appointed is a quorum.

Every question must be decided by a majority of votes of the members present and voting. The Chairman has a vote, and in the event of an equality of votes, a second or casting vote.

The proceedings of the Joint Committee will not be invalidated by reason of a vacancy or vacancies in their body.

The Joint Committee must determine the number of Conservators to be appointed on the Board for their district by the Council of each county, and of each such borough as above-mentioned in the district, and determine the Council by whom the accounts of the Board are to be audited.

Appointment of first Board of Conservators.

They must also appoint the first members of the Board for the district, distinguishing those who are to be considered as appointed by each county, and each such borough, and must fix the time and place of the first meeting of the Board.

Having completed their dispositions, they must give notice of them by post to the Clerk of each Council interested, upon which the Joint Committee will be dissolved.

If the district be wholly comprised in one administrative county, and is not partly situated within a borough which is a county of a city or county of a town, the population of which, according to the census of 1881, was over 10,000, the County Council will appoint members of the Board, without any preliminary proceedings, and there is no limit to the number of members they may appoint.

Ex-officio members of Board of Conservators.[1]

In addition to the appointed members of a Board, the following persons are *ex-officio* members.

1st. Every owner or occupier of a fishery or fisheries in the district, assessed to the poor rate on a gross estimated rental of £30 a-year; but both owner and occupier are not entitled to act as *ex-officio* members of the Board at the same time in respect of the same fishery or fisheries. If there is more than one owner or occupier of the same fishery or fisheries, any one of them may act as *ex-officio* members, but not more than one at the same time.

2nd. Every owner of lands in the fishery district of an annual value of £100 or over, and having a frontage of not less than one mile to one of the rivers in the district,

[1] Salmon Fishery Act, 1873, secs. 26-28.

who has a right to fish in the part of the river opposite his frontage, and who has paid a licence duty for fishing within the district during the last preceding fishing season.

If an owner of fisheries or lands otherwise entitled to be an *ex-officio* member of a Board is under a legal disability, some other person may act for him as follows :—

If the owner is—

i. A minor—one of his guardians or trustees, or the attorney or agent of one of his guardians or trustees, may act for him.

ii. An idiot or lunatic—the committee of his estate or the attorney or agent of such committee may act for him.

iii. A married woman—her husband, or his attorney or agent may act for her.

iv. A corporation, company, or fishing association—one of the members of the corporation, &c., or the attorney or agent of the corporation, &c., may act for them.

Every person who claims to be entitled to act as an *ex-officio* member of a Board of Conservators must, before taking his seat or acting in any way as a member of the Board, sign a declaration stating his qualification to act.

An *ex-officio* member, having made the declaration, is entitled to act only so long as his qualification continues.

In the case of the first Board of Conservators for a new district, the Board consists of the appointed members and the *ex-officio* members alone. The *ex-officio* members are permanent, but the appointed members only hold office for a year; a casual vacancy among the appointed members may be filled up by the Board.

On every subsequent Board, in the case of a salmon fishery district, there are, in addition to the appointed members and the *ex-officio* members, certain representative members, who are elected in the following case and to the following number :— Representative Members.[1]

Where in any part of a fishery district there are public or common rights of fishing, and such rights are exercised by fishermen duly licensed to fish (otherwise than with rod and line) all persons who have taken out licences to fish in such public or common waters, or both (otherwise than with rod and line), during the last preceding fishing season, are entitled to elect representative members of the Board of Conservators.

If the aggregate amount of licence duty paid for fishing in public or common waters, or both (other than licences for the use of a rod and line), does not exceed £50, one member may be elected; if the aggregate amount exceeds that sum, one additional member may be elected for every additional £50 or part of £50. Rules as to the election of representative members of the Board of Conservators are given in the Salmon Fishery Act, 1873, secs. 30-33; we may mention that the election is by voting papers distributed among the licensees entitled to vote, and that the licensees are entitled to more or fewer votes, according to the amount they have paid, and a voter may distribute his votes among the candidates as he thinks fit.

[1] Salmon Fishery Act, 1873, secs. 29-33.

Board of Conservators.

The Board of Conservators are a body corporate, with perpetual succession and a common seal, with powers to contract and to sue and be sued in a common name.

They have power to appoint water bailiffs; to issue licences for fishing; to purchase, for the purpose only of their removal, dams, fishing weirs, &c.; to take legal proceedings for prosecuting offences against the Acts and for removing illegal weirs, &c.; and generally, to improve the fishing in the waters under their jurisdiction. Their income is derived from the issue of licences, without which, fishing in their waters is illegal.

Gas Meters.

Gas meters are regulated under an Act of 1859 (*22 & 23 Vict. c. 66*), which has been amended by an Act of 1860 (*23 & 24 Vict. c. 79*), with respect to the Metropolis, by another Act of 1860 (*23 & 24 Vict. c. 146*), with respect to the date of the commencement of the Act, and by an Act of 1866 (*29 & 30 Vict. c. 82*), whereby the supervision of the Act was transferred from the Treasury to the Board of Trade.

Local Authorities.

The Act of 1859 provides for a uniform system of measuring gas, for the inspection and verification of gas meters and for the prosecution of persons using unfair gas meters, &c., and is put in force locally by Local Authorities. In counties, the County Council are the Local Authority. In county boroughs in which the Act has been adopted, the Town Council, if they are not makers or sellers of gas, are the Local Authority; if, however, the Town Council are makers or sellers of gas, the Justices of the borough are the Local Authority; if the Act has not been adopted, the County Council would apparently act within the borough. In other boroughs, the population of which, according to the census of 1881, was over 10,000, where the Town Council are not makers or sellers of gas, and in which the Act has been adopted, the Town Council are the Local Authority.

Sale of gas to be by cubic foot.

Under the Act, the sale of gas must, in all cases, be by cubic foot, and the gas must be measured by a "Meter," which has marked on it its measuring capacity at one revolution or complete action of the meter, the quantity it is intended to measure per hour, and a proper stamp.

Models and apparatus.

The Board of Trade have in their possession models of gas holders, with proper apparatus for testing meters, and verified copies of such models and apparatus are deposited in certain places; they also supervise the provision of stamps for stamping meters. The Local Authority must provide a sufficient number of copies of the models and apparatus provided by the Board of Trade, and must have these copies verified and stamped by that Board, and must provide the proper stamps for stamping meters.

Appointment of Inspectors.

The Local Authority must appoint Inspectors of meters and allot to each a separate district; no maker, repairer, or seller, of meters, or of gas, or any person employed in making, repairing or selling meters or gas, may be an Inspector of meters.

The stamps provided by the Local Authority must be in accordance with the directions of the Board of Trade, and be arranged so as to show the district of the Inspector by whom they are used. The models and stamps must be kept in the custody of the Inspector, and the Local Authority must determine when and where Inspectors are to attend for testing meters.

On his appointment, every Inspector must enter into a recognizance with the Crown for the due performance of his duties, &c., in such a sum as the Local Authority appointing him may fix.

Duties of Inspectors.

Every Inspector must attend at such times and places as the Local Authority may appoint, with the models, apparatus and stamps in his custody, for the purpose of testing meters, and must test, and, if found correct, stamp every meter submitted to him for that purpose, and deface or destroy the stamp on any meter found incorrect.

He must keep a book, and enter minutes of all such testings, with the numbers of identity and capacity marked by the manufacturer on such meters. If required he must give a certificate of stamping or defacing. The error permissible in a meter is 2 per cent. in favour of buyers, or 3 per cent. in favour of sellers, and the meter must not be capable of being made, by any contrivance that is practically prevented by good meters, to register quantities varying from the true standard measure by more than that amount; except that a meter with a measuring capacity, at one complete revolution or action of the meter, of 5 cubic feet or more, and marked "without float," must be stamped, if found correct in other respects, except that it is capable by the abstraction of water, of being made to register incorrectly against the seller.

The fees payable to an Inspector are—sixpence for every meter delivering one cubic foot in four or more complete revolutions; one shilling for every meter delivering one cubic foot in one or more revolutions, but less than four; and for other meters one shilling, and a further sum of one shilling for every cubic foot of gas delivered at one revolution beyond the first cubic foot.

Every Inspector must account quarterly to the County Council for the fees taken by him.

An Inspector duly authorized by a Justice of the Peace in writing may, at the request of any buyer or seller of gas, who shall have given 24 hours' notice in writing to the other party to the contract, at all reasonable times, enter any place within his jurisdiction where any meter is fixed or used.

He may examine and test the meter, and will have double fees, payable by the buyer or seller, as the Justice determines.

The following are offences under the Act :—

1st. Counterfeiting stamps and marks, for which the penalty is a fine not exceeding £10, nor less than 40s.

2nd. Tampering with a meter, or obstructing an Inspector, for which the penalty is a fine not exceeding £5.

3rd. Fixing or using an unstamped meter, or meter not duly marked, for which the penalty is a fine not exceeding £5.

In case of a dispute between the buyer and seller of gas by meter, or between an owner of a meter and an Inspector, the Inspector, if required by the person dissatisfied with his decision, must give his reasons in writing, and the aggrieved party may have the meter examined and re-tested by two Inspectors of neighbouring districts, to be named by a Justice of the Peace.

An appeal from decisions of Inspectors, &c., lies to Quarter Sessions.

Highways and Bridges.

Statutes relating to highways.

The business of the County Council with regard to highways and bridges is of two kinds. The County Council must themselves maintain Main Roads and certain Bridges ; and, secondly, the County Council have certain powers with regard to o dinary highways :—

The principal statutes relating to highways are—

The Highway Act, 1835 (*5 & 6 Will. IV. c. 50*).

The Highway Act, 1862 (*25 & 26 Vict. c. 61*).

The Highway Act, 1864 (*27 & 28 Vict. c. 101*).

The Highways and Locomotives Amendment Act, 1878 (*41 & 42 Vict. c. 77*).

Statutes relating to bridges.

The principal statutes relating to bridges are—

The Statute of Bridges 22 (*Henry VIII. c. 5*).

An Act of 1694 (*5 & 6 Will. & Mary, c. 11*).

An Act of 1701 (*1 Anne, st. 1, c. 18, or 1 Anne, c. 12*).

An Act of 1739 (*12 Geo. II. c. 29*).

An Act of 1741 (*14 Geo. II. c. 33*).

An Act of 1803 (*43 Geo. III. c. 59*).

An Act of 1812 (*52 Geo. III. c. 110*).

An Act of 1814 (*54 Geo. III. c. 90*).

An Act of 1815 (*55 Geo. III. c. 143*).

An Act of 1850 (*13 & 14 Vict. c. 64*).

We will deal with the powers and duties of the County Council with regard to main roads and county bridges, explaining first what highways and bridges are respectively main roads and county bridges ; secondly, what duties the County Council incur with regard to them ; thirdly, what the powers of the County Council are with regard to their ordinay maintenance; and lastly, what the powers of the County Council are, in effecting improvements.

Main Roads.

The following highways will on the appointed day be in administrative counties, main roads:—[1]

1st. Every road, in places to which the Highway Act, 1878, applied, which since the 31st December, 1870, has ceased to be a turnpike road; subject to the possibility of the roads having been dismained (*i.e.*, reduced to the position of an ordinary highway).[2]

2nd. Every road declared by the Quarter Sessions to be a main road, in pursuance of their powers under the last-mentioned Act; subject to the possibility of the road having been dismained.[3]

3rd. Every road in a Quarter Sessions Borough disturnpiked since the 31st December, 1870.[4]

4th. Turnpike roads in South Wales and the Isle of Wight.[5]

After the appointed day, any turnpike road in an administrative county ceasing to be such, will become a main road; the County Council also may declare any highway a main road; and on the other hand, the County Council may take steps to have a main road dismained.

Any Highway Authority,[6] wishing to have any highway within their district declared a main road, may apply in writing to the County Council, who may make an Order accordingly; but their Order must not take effect until the road has been placed in proper repair and condition to their satisfaction, and such an Order will be provisional only, and must be confirmed by a second Order within six months. If before the 13th August, 1890, the Town Council of a Quarter Sessions Borough make such an application, the Order may be absolute in the first instance, and if the County Council refuse the Order, the Town Council may appeal to the Local Government Board.[7]

The County Council, if desirous of reducing a main road to the position of an ordinary highway, must apply to the Local Government Board, who, if they think fit, may make a Provisional Order accordingly, which will become binding on confirmation by Parliament.[8]

---

[1] See *ante*, pp. 49-54.
[2] Highways, &c., Act, 1878, sec. 13.
[3] *Ib.*, sec. 15.
[4] Local Government Act, 1888, secs. 35, 38.
[5] *Ib.*, secs. 12, 13.
[6] As to the meaning of Highway Authority, see *ante*, pp. 50-53.
[7] Highways, &c., Act, 1878, sec. 75. Local Government Act, 1888, secs 35, 38.
[8] Highways, &c., Act, 1878, sec. 16.

Bridges repairable by County Council.[1]

Any bridge which, before the day appointed for the transfer of bridges to the County Council, was repairable by the inhabitants of a county or of a hundred, liberty, franchise, or any other division of a county of that nature, is termed a county bridge, and is repairable by the County Council. The question of liability to repair a bridge in doubtful cases is of a highly technical character and quite beyond the scope of the present work. The County Council have power to take over or purchase bridges existing on the appointed day that are not county bridges, and to erect new bridges. Such bridges will, however, apparently not become technically county bridges. The County Council must also maintain bridges, formerly repairable by Highway Authorities, which carry main roads.

The following points may be observed :—Bridges over water alone are county bridges ; bridges erected since 1803 are not county bridges unless they have been formally approved by the County Surveyor.[2] The liability to repair a county bridge erected before 1835 extends to the road for 300 feet on each side, but in the case of county bridges erected since that date the liability is confined to the actual bridge and its raised approaches, &c.[3] The power of the County Council to take over, purchase, and erect bridges is apparently not confined to bridges over water.

Duties of County Council with regard to main

The County Council must maintain the main roads in their county in a suitable state of repair for the traffic they are intended to carry, at all times of the year, and if the distance between the fences admit of it, the road kept in repair must, in general, be at least 20ft. wide.[4] The question as to how the County Council could be compelled to repair a main road is of some difficulty. It appears, however, that if a main road is out of repair any person desiring that it should be put in proper repair may complain to a Justice of the Peace, who will thereupon issue a summons to the County Council to appear by their officers before the Justices in Petty Sessions, and on the appearance, the Justices will, unless the liability of the County Council is denied, direct the County Council to appear at some subsequent Sessions, and in the meantime will obtain a report on the state of the road. If it appears from that report that the highway is out of repair, the Justices at the subsequent

---

[1] See *ante*, pp. 51, 55.
[2] 43 Geo. III. c. 59.
[3] Highway Act, 1835, sec. 21.
[4] Highway Act, 1835, sec. 80.

Sessions will make an Order for the repair within a limited time.[1]

Should the liability to repair be denied, it is doubtful what form the proceedings should take, and the question is too technical to be discussed in this work.

It should however be pointed out that, under sec. 11 of the Local Government Act, 1888, it seems that the County Council are liable to an indictment at common law.

It is also doubtful whether, if owing to the neglect of the County Council to repair a main road any person sustains special damage, for example, by a carriage accident occurring through the defective state of the road, such person would have an action against the County Council.[2]

The County Council must at all times keep county bridges, and other bridges repairable by them, in a proper state of repair. It is doubtful whether a County Council will be liable to indictment for failing to repair a county bridge, and also whether, if any person suffered special damage by reason of the neglect of the County Council to repair a bridge, such person could have an action against the County Council.[3]

Powers of County Council in repairing main roads.

We now proceed to give an account of the powers of the County Council as to the ordinary repair and maintenance of main roads. The County Council have for this purpose the powers of a Highway Board, and also the powers

---

[1] This is the proceeding given by the Highway Act, 1862, sec. 18, against a Highway Board. As against Highway Boards this proceeding has been superseded by proceedings under the Highways, &c., Act, 1878, sec. 10, which, however, is not applicable to a County Council. Technical difficulties are likely to arise if any attempt is made to bring the County Council before Justices in this way. Perhaps the case is not, apart from a denial of liability, likely to arise. Similar proceedings might perhaps be taken under the Highway Act, 1835, sec. 94; but again these do not seem exactly applicable.

[2] This question appears to depend upon whether or not the County Council would be liable to an indictment. The judgment in the Borough of Bathurst *v.* Macpherson, L.R. 4 App. Ca. 256, and the cases there quoted, lead the authors to think that a County Council will probably be held both liable to indictment and liable in an action for special damage.

[3] It seems that where the bridge was formerly repairable by the inhabitants of a county the County Council would be liable to indictment, and as a consequence to an action for special damage. See the Local Government Act, 1888, sec. 79, sub-sec. 2. But where the bridge was formerly repairable by part only of a county, as in the case of a hundred bridge, it seems that the County Council would not be thus liable, and that the inhabitants of the hundred would be liable as before to indictment, and that a person suffering special damage would have no right of action. See Note[2] *supra*, and also Mackinnon *v.* Penson, 9 Ex. 609. This would not apply to a bridge the repair of which is undertaken under sec. 6 of the Local Government Act, 1888. With regard to bridges carrying main roads, and formerly repairable by the Highway Authority, the County Council will stand in the same position as with regard to main roads.

formerly vested in the Quarter Sessions for the repair of bridges, and a few additional powers conferred by the Local Government Act, 1888.[1] Their principal powers are the following:—

County Council may contract with Highway Authority.

1st. They may enter into a contract with any Highway Authority for the maintenance of a main road by the Highway Authority, and may require a Highway Authority to undertake the repair of any main road in consideration of an annual contribution by the County Council, to be determined by agreement, or in default of agreement, by arbitration.[1]

Urban Sanitary Authority may retain main roads.

Any Urban Sanitary Authority may within twelve months after the appointed day, or in the case of a road in the district of such authority becoming a main road at any subsequent day, then within twelve months after that date, claim to retain the powers and duties of maintaining and repairing a main road within their district. In that case they will have the same powers and duties, with regard to that road, as if it were an ordinary highway vested in them, and the County Council must pay them an annual sum towards the maintenance, repair, and reasonable improvement of that road. The amount of such payment must be determined by agreement, or, in default of agreement, by arbitration of the Local Government Board.[1]

Payments to Highway Authorities.

In no case must a County Council make any payment to a Highway Authority towards expenses in connection with any road, until satisfied by the report of their Surveyor, or such other person as they may appoint, that the road has been properly maintained and repaired, or that the improvement has been properly executed, as the case may be.[1]

Enforcing repair of main road undertaken by Highway Authority.

If at any time the County Council are satisfied, on the report of their Surveyor, or other person appointed for that purpose, that any portion of a main road, the maintenance and repair of which are undertaken by a Highway Authority, is not in proper repair and condition, the County Council may cause notice to be given to such Highway Authority requiring them to place the road in proper repair and condition; and if the notice is not complied with within a reasonable time, the County Council may do everything that seems to them necessary to place the road in proper repair and condition, and the expense of so doing will be a debt due from the Highway Authority to the County Council.[1]

Contracts

2nd. The County Council may contract for the purchase

[1] Local Government Act, 1888, sec. 11.

and carriage of materials for repairing main roads for any period not exceeding three years; or generally for the repair of the road for any period not exceeding seven years.[1]

Road Materials.

3rd. The County Council have powers of obtaining road materials in various cases, sometimes making compensation and sometimes not.[2]

Removing snow, &c.

4th. The County Council may have snow and earth, &c., falling on their roads removed, and must do so, if ordered by a Justice of the Peace[3]

Finger-posts, &c.

5th. They may put up finger-posts, kerbstones, fences, mile-stones, &c.[4]

Removing trees, &c.

6th. They may order any tree or bush planted within fifteen feet from the centre of the road, to be removed by the owner or occupier of the land. If the Order is not complied with within 21 days the owner or occupier will be liable to a fine of ten shillings, recoverable summarily.[5]

7th. If it appears that a main road is injured by shade from hedges and trees, except trees planted for ornament or shelter for any hop-ground, house, building, or courtyard, or that the highway is obstructed by any hedge or tree, the County Council may summon the owner of the land on which the hedge or trees are growing, before the Justices in Special or Petty Sessions, and the Justices may make an Order for the trees and hedges to be pruned, or in case of obstruction to be removed. A copy of this Order must be left at the residence of the owner or his steward or agent, and if the Order is then not complied with within ten days, the owner will incur a penalty not exceeding forty shillings. The County Council may then have the pruning or removal done themselves, and recover the expense from the owner summarily. But no pruning is to be done except between the 31st September and the 31st March, nor is any timber to be felled.[6]

Draining Roads.

8th. The County Council may drain their roads, and for that purpose make drains through adjoining lands, paying compensation for any injury done, but if the drains are made through waste lands, no compensation need be made. If the owner or occupier or any other person interfere with drains

---

[1] 12 Geo. II. c. 29, sec. 14. 52 Geo. III. c. 110, sec. 1. Highway Act, 1864, sec. 52.

[2] 43 Geo. III. c. 59, sec. 1. 55 Geo. III. c. 143, secs. 1-4. The Highway Act, 1835, secs. 51-57. 3 Geo. IV. c. 126, secs. 97-102. 7 & 8 Geo. IV. c. 24, sec. 15. 33 & 34 Vict. c. 73, sec. 11.

[3] Highway Act, 1835, sec. 26.

[4] *Ib.*, sec. 24.

[5] *Ib.*, sec. 64.

[6] *Ib.*, secs. 65, 66; *see* the Highway Act Amendment Act, 1885 (*48 Vict c. 13*).

made by the County Council or their predecessors, without the consent of the County Council, he will be liable to reimburse the County Council all expenses they may be put to, and also to a fine not exceeding three times the amount of such expenses, which sums may be recovered summarily.[1]

Encroachments. 9th. If any person encroach upon the road by building, or putting up fences, &c., on the road, within 15 feet of the centre, he may be fined upon summary conviction, and after such conviction, the County Council may remove the obstruction and recover summarily the expense of such removal from the person encroaching.[2]

The County Council, so acting after conviction, will not be liable to an action, even if the conviction be quashed or shown to be wrong. The County Council might of course remove the obstruction in the first instance, but then they would be liable to an action if they failed to show that the building was on the highway. No adjoining owner is, however, entitled to encroach up to the fifteen feet; for the public have a free right of passage over the whole width of the highway, whatever that may be, and although any part of it may not have been kept in repair as a highway, and any encroaching obstruction may be removed by the County Council at their risk. Or, the County Council or any other person may indict the person encroaching, but of course, unless the obstruction come within fifteen feet of the centre, there is no summary remedy.[3]

Gates. 10th. Every gate across a main road must be at least ten feet wide, and the County Council may order any gate across a main road, that is not of the proper width, to be removed or enlarged, and if the proprietor of the gate fail to enlarge or remove it within 21 days of such Order, he will be liable to a fine, recoverable summarily, not exceeding ten shillings a day for every day he neglects to remove it.[4] Every railway company must maintain proper gates at level crossings, and are liable to a fine not exceeding £5 for every day they are in default, and the County Council may proceed against them summarily for the recovery of such penalty.[5]

Pit-shafts, engines, &c. 11th. It is not lawful to sink any pit or shaft, or to erect or cause to be erected any steam-engine, gin, or other like machine or any machinery attached thereto, within the distance of 25 yards,

---

[1] Highway Act, 1835, secs. 67, 68.
[2] *Ib.*, sec. 69. Highway Act, 1866, sec. 51.
[3] Keane *v.* Reynolds, 2. E. & B. 748; Chapman *v.* Robinson, 1. E. & E. 25.
[4] Highway Act, 1835, sec. 81.
[5] 2 & 3 Vict. c. 45.

nor any windmill within the distance of 50 yards, from any part of a main road, unless such pit or shaft or steam-engine, or other like engine or machinery, is within some house or other building, or behind some wall or fence sufficient to conceal or screen the same from the road, so that the same may not be dangerous to passengers, horses, or cattle.[1] But this provision does not apply to ploughing engines.[2]

No person may make, or cause to be made, any fire for calcining or burning of ironstone, limestone, bricks or clay, or the making of cokes, within the distance of 15 yards from any part of the road, unless the same is within some house or other building, or behind some wall or fence, sufficient to screen the same from the road. Any person erecting engines, &c., or burning ironstone, &c., within that distance of a road, is liable to a penalty not exceeding £5, for every day such engine, &c., is permitted to continue.[3]

12th. The County Council may also take steps to repress nuisances, &c., on a main road, and to enforce the provisions of the Highway Act, 1835, with regard to drivers, &c.[4] Nuisances, &c.

13th. If it appears to the County Council, on the report of their Surveyor, that extraordinary expenses have been incurred by them in repairing a main road by reason of damage caused by excessive weight passing along the same, or by reason of extraordinary traffic thereon, the County Council may recover in a summary manner, from any person by whose order such weight or traffic has been conducted, the amount of the expenses incurred by reason of such damage. A person, however, contemplating the use of a main road for the purposes of such traffic, may enter into an agreement with the County Council to pay them a composition in respect of such damage.[5] Excessive traffic.

For the ordinary repair of bridges, the County Council have, practically, nearly all the powers they have with regard to main roads, as far as they are applicable,[6] except that they have no power under the Local Government Act, 1888, to contract with a Highway Authority for their repair, nor to compel a Highway Authority to undertake their repair, nor have the Urban Sanitary Authority any power to take over their Powers of County Council in repairing bridges

[1] Highway Act, 1835, sec. 70.
[2] Locomotives Act, 1865 (*28 & 29 Vict. c. 83*), sec. 6.
[3] Highway Act, 1835, sec. 70.
[4] *Ib.* secs. 72, 73, 75-79.
[5] Highways and Locomotives Amendment Act, 1878, sec. 23.
[6] They have all the powers with regard to highways that they have with regard to main roads under the Highway Act, 1835. See sec. 22 of that Act.

repair. The County Council might, however, it seems, contract with a Highway Authority for the repair of a road over a bridge.[1]

The power of obtaining materials is not quite the same.[2]

They may recover the expenses caused by damage, arising through the excessive weight of a locomotive using their bridges, but not for damage caused by any other kind of excessive traffic.[3]

Power of County Council to improve main roads.

The County Council have also general powers to improve main roads subject to certain provisions. They may convert any unstoned main road into a stoned road, widen, straighten, and level any main road, and generally take steps for its improvement; and for the purpose of these improvements, the County Council may borrow money and may purchase lands under the Land Clauses Acts, but not otherwise than by agreement.[4]

Widening road.

The Justices in Petty Sessions may order a main road to be widened, if they think fit, but not so as to be more than thirty feet broad, and they may in their Order, provide in what manner the widening is to be effected. Such an Order may be conveniently resorted to if an owner of land refuses to sell, as by such an Order the owner is compelled to sell.[5]

The Order must not involve pulling down any house or building, nor taking any part of a garden, lawn, yard, court, paddock, planted walk, plantation, avenue to any house, or any enclosed ground set apart for building ground, or as a nursery for young trees. The Order may empower the County Council to treat with the persons interested in any land to be taken, as to compensation.

If the County Council fail to come to terms with such persons, they may apply to the Quarter Sessions to determine the proper compensation. The County Council must give fourteen days' notice to the persons interested, and the compensation must be settled by a jury impanelled by the Quarter Sessions. The costs of such proceedings must be borne by the person summoned, or the County Council, according as the jury awards less or more than the County Council offered.

---

1 52 Geo. III. c. 110, sec. 5.

2 3 Geo. II. c. 126; 7 & 8 Geo. II., and 33 & 35 Vict. c. 73, do not extend to bridges.

3 Locomotives Act, 1861 (*24 & 25 Vict. c. 70*), sec. 7. The Highways, &c., Act, 1878, sec. 23, does not apply.

4 Highway Act, 1864, secs. 47, 48, 53.

5 Highway Act, 1835, 82, 83.

When the County Council are repairing or widening a highway, they may make a temporary road over adjoining ground, making due compensation to the proprietors and occupiers of such adjoining ground. The compensation, in case of dispute, must be fixed by the Justices in Petty Sessions, and will be recoverable summarily.[1]

Altering the course of the road.[2]

If it becomes, in the opinion of the County Council, advisable to alter the course of a main road further than is involved in the mere cutting off of corners, the County Council must apply to two Justices of the Peace to view the road in question. If the Justices consider the scheme advantageous they will direct the County Council to affix a notice at each end of the portion of road it is proposed to deal with, to advertise the notice of the proposed alteration in a newspaper for four successive weeks, and to affix the same notice on the doors of the churches of the parishes in which the alteration is proposed. The County Council must then go before the Justices again to give proof that the notices have been properly published, and at the same time deliver a plan, verified by a surveyor, describing the proposed alteration.

The Justices must then make a certificate stating that they have viewed the highway, and giving the reasons why the proposed alteration is desirable, stating if the object be to shorten the highway, by how much the highway is shortened. This certificate, together with the plan of the alteration, must then be sent to the Clerk of the Peace of the County in which the road is situate, and read at the next Quarter Sessions, and then with the plan enrolled among the records of the Quarter Sessions, who, unless an appeal has been made, or the certificate is bad on the face of it, will make an Order for carrying into effect the proposed alteration. Any person who thinks he would be injured by the proposed alteration may appeal to the Quarter Sessions against it. He must give the County Council ten days' notice in writing of appeal, stating the grounds of such appeal. If the alteration was proposed at the instance of any person or body except the County Council, the County Council must within forty-eight hours deliver a copy of the notice of appeal to such person or body. The appeal will be heard at the Quarter Sessions before a jury.

Improving bridges

The County Council may improve and alter the situation of bridges, and for that purpose may borrow money and purchase

---

[1] Highway Act, 1835, sec. 25.
[2] *Ib.*, secs. 85-91.

land[1] but if the situation is altered, the new site must be within 200 yards of the old site, in the case, at any rate, of a county bridge.

Contributing to ordinary highways.

We now proceed to give an account of the powers of the County Council with regard to ordinary highways.

They may, if they think fit, contribute towards the costs of maintenance, repair, enlargement, and improvement of any highway or public footpath in the county.[2]

Bye-laws.

They have power to make bye-laws for any highways or main roads within their county—as to size, &c., of wheels, as to nails on wheels, as to locking wheels, as to gates on highways; and these bye-laws may be framed so as to inflict fines of not more than £2 to be recovered summarily, but not so as to impose a minimum fine. Such bye-laws will not be valid without confirmation by the Local Government Board, and one month's notice of the intention to apply for such confirmation must be published in local newspapers.[3]

Duty of County Council when ordinary highway is out of repair.[4]

If an ordinary highway is out of repair and any person desires that it should be put in repair, he may complain to the County Council, who must thereupon cause their Surveyor to investigate the matter, and if they are satisfied that the highway is out of repair, they must order the Highway Authority, whose duty it is, to execute the necessary repairs within a specified time. If the Highway Authority fail to comply with the Order, and do not show a reason for their failure, the County Council may appoint some person to do the work, and must make an Order for payment to him from the Highway Authority in default. This Order may be removed into the High Court, and enforced accordingly. If the Highway Authority deny their liability to repair, they must give notice to the Clerk of the County Council within ten days of the fact that they decline to comply with the Order until their liability to repair has been decided by a jury. In that case, the County Council must go into the matter, and either satisfy the Highway Authority by varying their Order or submit the question to a jury. In the latter case they must direct an indictment against the defaulting Highway Authority to be heard at the next assizes, and until the conclusion of the trial the Order of the County Council is suspended, and on the conclusion of the trial, if the jury find the defendants guilty, the Order will come into force again, but if the jury aquit the defendants the Order will become void.

[1] 14 Geo. II. c. 33, sec. 1; 43 Geo. III. c. 59, sec. 2; 54 George III. c. 90, secs. 1, 2. [2] Local Government Act, 1888, sec. 11.
[3] Highways, &c., Act, secs. 26, 35. [4] *Ib.*, sec. 10

Local Stamp Act, 1869.

Under this Act (*48 & 49 Vict. c. 49*) provision is made for the levy of fees and penalties in certain cases by means of stamps. Under the Act as modified by the Local Government Act, 1888, County Councils and Town Councils act as Local Authority.

Wherever all the Clerks of Special and Petty Sessions, and all the Clerks of the Justices of the Peace within the jurisdiction of a Local Authority are paid wholly or partly by salaries, a Local Authority may order that, after a fixed date, all or any of the fees, fines, and penalties payable to the County Treasurer or Borough Treasurer, as the case may be, shall be paid by means of stamps.

The Local Authority may accordingly cause dies to be made for the purpose of preparing stamps, and may make regulations concerning their use.

To these rules the approval of a Secretary of State must be obtained, and the consent of the Commissioners of Inland Revenue must also be obtained as far as relates the pattern, colour, and form of the stamps and dies, and the making and impressing of the same.

The Local Authority may by Order authorise any person to sell and distribute stamps for the purpose of the Act.

Lunatic Asylums.

The principal statutes dealing with this subject are :— Stat

The Lunatic Asylums Act, 1853 (*16 & 17 Vict. c. 97*).

An Act of 1855 (*18 & 19 Vict. c. 105*).

An Act of 1856 (*19 & 20 Vict. c. 87*).

The Lunacy Acts Amendment Act, 1862 (*25 & 26 Vict. c 111.*)

The Lunacy Acts Amendment Act, 1863 (*26 & 27 Vict. c. 110*)

The Lunacy Act Amendment Act, 1865 (*28 & 29 Vict. c. 80.*)

The general supervision of lunatic asylums throughout the country is in the hands of the Commissioners in Lunacy. We have already explained in Chapter II. the arrangements that have in the past been made with regard to lunatic asylums, the effect of the Local Government Act, 1888, on these arrangements, and also what the meaning of the term county is in the Acts dealing with the subject.[1] Past arrangements. Definition of county.

[1] *Ante*, pp. 56-60.

Duty to provide asylum.

It will be sufficient to state that it is the duty of every County Council, and of the Town Council of every county borough, and of every Quarter Sessions Borough, the population of which, according to the census of 1881, was above 10,000, and which was not on the 13th August 1888, under contract for the reception of its lunatics into the county asylum, to provide sufficient asylum accommodation for their county or borough.

A County Council or the Town Council of such a borough may at any time, if they think fit, provide further asylum accommodation. A Secretary of State, on a report from the Commissioners iu Lunacy that the asylum accommodation provided for a county, or for such a borough, is inadequate, may direct the County Council or Town Council to provide a new asylum; or may direct a Committee of Visitors of an existing asylum to enlarge it.[1]

A County Council or Town Council may either provide a new asylum for their county or borough, or may enter into an agreement with other County or Town Councils, and with subscribers to a hospital, for the erection of a joint asylum.[2]

The erection of a new asylum or the maintenance of an existing asylum is vested in a Committee of Visitors, whose appointment we have discussed in Chapter II.[3] If more than one asylum is maintained for a county, the County Council may appoint one Committee of Visitors to manage them all, and such Committee may appoint sub-committees for the management of each asylum.

The proceedings, &c., of a Committee of Visitors may be regulated in the same way as the proceedings of a Joint Committee, under sec. 8 of the Local Government Act, 1888.[4]

We may now proceed to give a brief account of the powers and duties of a Committee of Visitors.

Ordinary repairs.[5]

The Committee of Visitors carry out all ordinary repairs of the asylum, but their total expenditure for the year, in this respect, must not exceed £400. No Order must be made for repairs, nor for payment of money in respect thereof, where the expenses exceed £100, unless seven days' notice of the meeting at which the question is to be raised and of the intention to raise it has been given.

Sale and exchange of lands, &c.[6]

The Committee of Visitors, with the consent of a Secretary of State, may sell

[1] Lunatic Asylums Act, 1853, secs. 29, 30.

[2] Lunatic Asylums Act, 1853, secs. 2-5, 14-18; 18 & 19 Vict. c. 105, secs. 1-5.

[3] *Ante*, pp. 58-60.

[4] Local Government Act, 1888, sec. 86.

[5] Lunatic Asylums Act, 1853, sec. 38.

[6] Lunatic Asylums Act, 1853, secs. 40, 41.

and exchange lands and buildings, &c., and in case of a sale, the money received must be paid to the authority maintaining the asylum or shared among the authorities maintaining the asylum, if there be more than one.[1]

Contracts for the reception of lunatics.[1]

The Committee of Visitors, with the approval of a Secretary of State, may contract for the reception of lunatics from the counties and boroughs for which they act into any other asylum, or for the reception into their asylum of lunatics from elsewhere. Such a contract may be made for any period not exceeding five years, but may be renewed; it will, however, be liable to be put an end to by notice in writing from a Secretary of State.

Rules and regulations.[2]

The Committee of Visitors must make and may alter and vary general rules for the management of their asylum. These rules must be submitted to a Secretary of State for approval, and on receiving his approval, be printed and complied with; besides these general rules, the Committee of Visitors may make such regulations, not inconsistent with them, as they think fit for the management of their asylum, and these regulations must set out the number and description of the officers and servants to be kept, with their duties and salaries, the diet of the patients, and the reservation of beds for particular classes of patients.

Weekly charge for lunatics.[3]

The Committee of Visitors must fix the sum to be paid weekly for the maintenance of each pauper lunatic confined in their asylum. The sum should be calculated so as to provide for the lodging, maintenance, care, residence, clothing and other expenses requisite for each pauper lunatic, and also to provide such a surplus that the total sum received in this way shall defray the salaries of the officers and attendants; but the sum must not exceed 14s. a week; unless the Councils of the counties and boroughs to which the asylum belongs decide to make a greater charge, in which case their Order must be published in a local newspaper.

Officers.[4]

The Committee of Visitors must appoint the following officers:—A Chaplain, who must be in priests' orders, and licensed by the Bishop of the diocese, at least one resident Medical Officer, who must not be Clerk or Treasurer of the asylum, a Clerk, a Treasurer, a Superintendent, who must be resident, and must in general be a Medical Officer, and such other officers as they think fit.

Superannuation allowances.[5]

The Committee of Visitors may grant superannuation allowances to any Superintendent, Chaplain, Matron or other Officer.

The grant is entirely discretionary, and can only be given where the officer has become incapable of executing the office from confirmed sickness, age, or infirmity, or is retiring from long service and age, except that, where the offices of Superintendent and Matron are held by man and wife, and a superannuation allowance has been granted to the Superintendent, and the Matron has been an Officer for not less than 20 years, the Visitors may grant her an allowance although she has not become incapable of executing her office from sickness, age or infirmity; but if she is thereafter appointed to a public office, or to an office under the Lunacy Acts, in respect of which she receives a salary, the payment of her superannuation allowance must be suspended while she executes that office if the salary

---

[1] Lunatic Asylums Act, 1853, secs. 42, 43; 18 & 19 Vict. c. 105, sec. 10.

[2] *Ib.*, sec. 53.
Lunacy Acts Amendment Act, 1862, secs. 6, 7

[3] Lunatic Asylums Act, 1853, sec. 54.

[4] Lunatic Asylums Act, 1853, secs. 26, 55.

[5] Lunatic Asylums Act, 1853, sec. 57.
Lunacy Acts Amendment Act, 1862, secs. 12, 13.

is greater than the amount of the annuity; or diminished by the amount of such salary, if it is less.

The Officer to receive a superannuation allowance must have held office for at least 15 years; and in the case of a Matron who is the wife of a Superintendent in the above-mentioned case, 20 years.

The Officer also must be at least 50 years of age, except in the case of a Matron the wife of a Superintendent.

The annuity, which must not exceed two-thirds of the Officer's salary and other emoluments, taking into account the value of lodgings, rations or other allowances enjoyed by the Officer, must be approved by the Council of every county interested, before it can be charged against them.

Visitation of asylums.[1] Not less than two members of every Committee of Visitors must, once at least in every two months, inspect every part of their asylum, and see and examine as far as possible every lunatic therein, and the Order and Certificate for the admission of every lunatic admitted since their last visitation, and the general books kept in the asylum, and they must enter in a book kept for that purpose, any remarks that they think proper with regard to the condition and management of the asylum, and lunatics therein, and must sign the book upon every visit.

Reports.[2] The Committee of Visitors must make an annual report to the Council of every county and borough interested in the asylum, as to the state and condition of the asylum, its sufficiency for the proper accommodation of the number of lunatics requiring accommodation, the management and conduct of the Officers and servants, and the cure of the patients therein, with any observations they think fit to make. Their Clerk must transmit a copy of this report to the Commissioners in Lunacy. This report has hitherto been sent in at the end of December in every year.

Discharge of lunatic.[3] Any three Visitors, by writing under their hands, may order the discharge of any person detained in their asylum, whether such person be recovered or not. Any two Visitors may, with the advice in writing of the Medical Officer, order the discharge of any person detained, or may allow such person to be absent upon trial.

If application is made to the Committee of Visitors by any relative or friend of a pauper lunatic confined in their asylum, requiring that he should be delivered over to the custody or care of such relative or friend, any two of the Visitors may, if they think fit, discharge the lunatic, on the undertaking of such relative or friend to their satisfaction that the lunatic shall be no longer chargeable to the union, parish or county, and shall be properly taken care of.

Burial of lunatics.[4] A Committee of Visitors may enter into agreements with the proprietor of a cemetery, or with a Burial Board, for the burial of any pauper lunatic whom the Visitors may undertake to bury; they may also provide a burial ground for the asylum.

Erection or enlargement of asylum.[5] A Committee of Visitors duly authorised to superintend the erection of a new asylum or the enlargement of an old one, may prepare plans and estimates for everything necessary to be done, and enter into contracts for the execution of the

---

[1] Lunatic Asylums Act, 1853, sec. 61.
[2] Lunatic Asylums Act, 1853, sec. 62.
[3] Lunatic Asylums Act, 1853, sec. 79-81.
[4] 18 & 19 Vict. c. 105, secs. 11-13.
Lunacy Acts Amendment Act, 1862, sec. 9.
[5] Lunatic Asylums Act, 1853, sec. 31-36.
Lunacy Acts Amendment Act, 1862, sec. 4, 5 and see sec. 11.

necessary work. Such a contract may be absolute if the Committee of Visitors have been authorised by the various bodies interested to expend a certain sum, and the amount to be expended under such contracts does not exceed that sum; but in other cases the contracts will be subject to the approbation of the bodies interested.

If any of the authorities interested do not approve of the plans, estimates, and contracts, while other authorities approve, the objecting authorities must forward the plans, &c., with their objections in writing, to a Secretary of State, who must decide upon the question.

Removal of lunatics to asylums.

Pauper lunatics are sent to asylums on the Order of a Justice of the Peace (or in some cases of a Clergyman), and of an Overseer or Relieving Officer, made after calling in the assistance of a Physician.

An Order for the payment of the costs incurred in respect of a pauper lunatic by the Guardians, &c., may be made by a Justice or Justices of the Peace, according to circumstances; or such costs may be paid by the proper authority without any Order.

Expenses.

The expense of erecting and maintaining a lunatic asylum for a county is a special county purpose from contribution to which most Quarter Sessions Boroughs, the population of which, according to the census of 1881, was over 10,000, are exempt; as are also, apparently, any parts of the county which may have been annexed to another county; on the other hand, the County Council may, apparently, rate any part of another county that may have been annexed to their county.[1]

Music and Dancing Licences.

The Acts dealing with these licences are—

25 Geo. II. c. 36 (made perpetual by *28 Geo. II. c. 19*).

The Public Entertainment Act, 1875 (*38 Vict. c. 21*).

The Acts apply only to places within twenty miles of the cities of London and Westminster, and accordingly only interest the County Councils of Middlesex, Surrey, Kent, Essex, Hertford, and Bucks (and London), besides the Town Councils of the county boroughs of Croydon and West Ham

Every house, room, garden, or place kept for public dancing, music, or other public entertainment of the like kind must within the limits of the Acts be licensed by the County Council or Town Council of a county borough, within whose county or borough such house, &c., is.

The licence may be granted for music alone, or dancing alone, or for both, and will remain in force for one year.

Theatres and places licensed by letters patent, or by the

---

[1] Lunatic Asylums Act, 1853, sec. 130; and see *ante*, pp. 58-60.

Crown, or by the Lord Chamberlain, do not require licences under these Acts. The place to require a licence must be used habitually for music or dancing, though it need not be used solely for that purpose. A place merely used for dancing or music temporarily on a particular occasion need not be licensed. A place used for dancing must be licensed, though public dancers are not kept for the purpose of exhibition as performers. A place may require a licence though money is not taken at the door. A room kept by a dancing master, and to which the public is not admitted indiscriminately, need not be licensed.

Parliamentary Elections and Registration.

The powers and duties of a County Council in connection with this subject are discussed in Chapters VI. and VII.[1]

Police.

The principal Statutes dealing with this subject are—

Statutes.

An Act of 1839 (*2 & 3 Vict. c. 93*).
An Act of 1840 (*3 & 4 Vict. c. 88*).
An Act of 1844 (*7 & 8 Vict. c. 33*).
An Act of 1848 (*11 & 12 Vict. c. 101*).
The County and Borough Police Act, 1856 (*19 & 20 Vict. c. 69*).
An Act of 1857 (*20 Vict. c. 2*).
An Act of 1858 (*21 & 22 Vict. c. 68*).
An Act of 1859 (*22 & 23 Vict. c. 32*).
The Police Superannuation Act, 1865 (*28 Vict. c. 35*).
The Municipal Corporations Act, 1882 (*45 & 46 Vict. c. 50*).

Duty to maintain police force.

Under these Acts (as altered by the Local Government Act, 1888), a police force must (outside the Metropolitan Police District) be maintained for each county by the Standing Joint Committee of the County Council and the Quarter Sessions, and for every borough, the population of which, according to the census of 1881, was over 10,000, by the Town Council acting through a Committee called the Watch Committee. The police force of a borough, whether a county borough or not, may, however, be consolidated with the police force of the county in which it is situated.

The Urban Sanitary Districts of Hove and Tunbridge Wells are, broadly speaking, in the position of boroughs, with

[1] See particularly pp. 203, 204, 210.

regard to police, and in each of these districts the Sanitary Authority maintains a police force under Local Acts.

Transfer of parts of counties.[1]

We have in Chapter II. explained how the Quarter Sessions might formerly agree for the transfer of parts of their respective counties, and what the term county means under the Police Act.

The word county, in dealing with police, has still the same meaning, and the Standing Joint Committee of two or more neighbouring counties may agree for a transfer of parts of their respective counties in the same way as the Quarter Sessions formerly might.

Police districts.[2]

A county may be divided into police districts, and in that case, the expenditure in each district will be classed under the two heads, of general expenditure and local expenditure; the general expenditure must be defrayed in common by all the districts, and the local expenditure, consisting of the expenses of pay and clothing of the constables and such other expenses as the Standing Joint Committee, with the approval of the Secretary of State,[3] may direct to be included under this head, must be defrayed by each district separately, and police rates must be made and levied in each district accordingly.

The object of such a division is to provide for cases where different parts of a county are of a different nature in respect of population, &c., so that the number of constables required in some parts of the county is greater than in others.

The Standing Joint Committee may, with the approval of a Secretary of State, effect the division themselves; or Her Majesty may, by Order in Council, upon a petition from ratepayers in the county, direct that such a division shall be made, and thereupon the Standing Joint Committee must proceed to make the division.

Consolidation of county and borough police.[4]

The Joint Committee may enter into an agreement with the Town Council of any borough entitled to a separate police establishment for the consolidation of the county and borough police.

If any Town Council apply to the Standing Joint Committee

---

[1] *Ante*, p. 63.
2 & 3 Vict. c. 93, secs. 26, 27.
3 & 4 Vict. c. 88, secs. 2, 34.
21 & 22 Vict. c. 68.

[2] 3 & 4 Vict. c. 88, secs. 27, 28.
County and Borough Police Act, 1856, sec. 4.
22 & 23 Vict. c. 32, sec. 1.

[3] The Home Office is the Government Department superintending the police.

[4] 3 & 4 Vict. c. 88, secs. 14, 15.
County and Borough Police Act, 1856, sec. 5.

to consolidate the police of their borough with the county police, and the Standing Joint Committee fail to come to an agreement, the Town Council may represent that fact to a Secretary of State, who may then inquire into the proposed terms of consolidation and report upon them to Her Majesty in Council, and an Order in Council may in that case be made, consolidating the police upon such terms and conditions as may seem proper, and fixing a date upon which the Order shall come into operation. The police, after that date, will be consolidated as if by agreement. An agreement for consolidation may, with the consent of the Secretary of State, but not without, be put an end to, either by mutual consent of the parties or upon six months' notice by either. A consolidation by Order in Council may be put an end to, by Order in Council, at any time, but not otherwise.

Chief Constable.[1]

The police force for each county is under the command of a "Chief Constable," appointed by the Standing Joint Committee with the approval of a Secretary of State, and subject to dismissal by them at their discretion.

In the Act of 1839, a provision is made for the appointment of two Chief Constables for a county, when any county shall have been divided for the purpose of returning members to serve in Parliament for each division. This provision is a little difficult of application in the present state of affairs under the Redistribution of Seats Act, 1885 (*48 & 49 Vict. c. 23*). It would be unadvisable to appoint two Chief Constables for a county under that provision except in cases where it has hitherto been usual.

Where two Chief Constables are appointed, the accounts of the forces under each may be kept separate, and separate rates levied upon the district of each Chief Constable.

The Standing Joint Committee of any county may appoint, as Chief Constable, a person already holding that office for an adjoining county or counties, or part or parts of counties, with the consent of the Standing Joint Committee or Committees of the latter.

The Chief Constable must attend from time to time before the Standing Joint Committee, and report to them on such questions as they consider necessary, and must generally obey all their lawful orders.

[1] 2 & 3 Vict. c. 93, secs. 4, 17.
20 Vict. c. 2.

Petty constables and other police officers in counties are appointed by the Chief Constable, subject to the approval of two or more of the Justices of the county in Petty Sessions. The Chief Constable has unfettered power to dismiss petty constables and police officers.

Petty Constables, &c.[1]

In boroughs, constables are appointed by the Watch Committee, but where the force is consolidated with the county police, the Chief Constable may dismiss them at his discretion, and it may be provided by the agreement for consolidation, that the Chief Constable shall also appoint the borough constables.

The number of the force is determined by the Standing Joint Committee, subject to the approval of the Secretary of State. Rules and regulations with regard to pay, government, uniform, &c., of a police force may be made by a Secretary of State. The powers and duties of constables are, of course, beyond the scope of the present work.

Superannuation Fund.[2]

A superannuation fund must be established in every county, and in every borough with a separate police force; to the credit of which must be carried—

(i.) Such percentage of the pay of all constables in the county or borough, not exceeding 2½ per cent. per annum, as the Standing Joint Committee or the Watch Committee, as the case may be, may determine to deduct.

(ii.) Stoppages (if any) of a constable's pay during sickness.

(iii.) Fines imposed on constables for misconduct.

(iv.) Such portions of the fines imposed for drunkenness and for assaults on the police, by any Justice of the Peace, as the Justice shall direct.

(v.) Such portions of the moieties of fines and penalties awarded to informers (being police constables), on summary convictions, as the Justice inflicting the same may direct.

(vi.) All money arising from the sale of worn or cast clothing, supplied for the use of the police.

(vii.) In boroughs, any fees payable to a constable in the execution of his office.

(viii.) A deficiency in the superannuation fund may be made up in counties, out of the police rate; or in boroughs, out of the borough fund or borough rates.

The Grants out of the superannuation fund may be made by the Standing Joint Committee, on the recommendation of the Chief Constable, or by the Watch Committee with the approval of the Town Council, as the case may be, at the discretion of such Committee, subject to the following conditions:—

The allowance must not be granted to any constable less than 60 years of age, except upon a certificate of the Chief Constable that such constable is incapable from infirmity of mind or body of discharging the duties of his office.

The allowance may take the form of an annuity, but in that case, must not be

---

[1] 2 & 3 Vict. c. 93, secs. 2, 3, 6; Municipal Corporations Act, 1882, sec. 191.

[2] 3 & 4 Vict. c. 88, secs. 10, 11.
County and Borough Police Act, 1856, secs. 10-13; The Police Superannuation Act, 1865.

granted to any constable of less than 15 years' service; after 15 years, but less than 20 years' service, the annuity must not exceed half the constable's pay; after 20 years' service it must not exceed two-thirds of his pay, but where a constable is disabled by any accident or injury received in the actual execution of the duty of his office, he may be granted an allowance not exceeding the whole of his pay, whatever his length of service or age may be.

The Committee may, upon the recommendation of a Chief Constable, and upon his certifying that a constable, who has not served 15 years, is incapable from infirmity of mind or body to discharge the duties of his office, grant such constable a gratuity upon his retirement.

Gratuities to constables for specially meritorious services, may also in certain cases be granted, as also gratuities to the widow of a constable.

Expense of maintaining police.

The expense of maintaining a county police force is a special county purpose, and rates for the maintenance may be assessed throughout the county of the County Council as defined by the Police Acts, including all boroughs the population of which, according to the census of 1881, was under 10,000.

The payment of contributions in respect of places transferred to the county from other counties may be obtained by means of a warrant directed to the Treasurer of the county within which such transferred part lies, but if he fail to pay the sum required the County Council may themselves levy the rate. The County Council, on the other hand, may levy a rate within parts of their county transferred to other counties to meet the warrant of the County Council of such neighbouring counties.

To the credit of the Special Police Account of the county must be carried, from the Exchequer Contribution Account, one half of the expenses of the pay and clothing of the county police force. But if the Secretary of State withholds his certificate that the force has been maintained in a state of efficiency during the year ending on the last 29th of September, the County Council, instead of transferring such sum to the Special Police Account, will forfeit such sum to the Crown.

The expense of maintaining a police force for a borough is met either by the borough rates or the watch rate, according to circumstances. In county boroughs one half the expense of pay and clothing is, however, paid out of the Exchequer Contribution Account, and the Town Council is liable to forfeit an equivalent sum in case the Secretary of State withholds his certificate in the same way as a County Council.

In other boroughs maintaining a separate police force, the Town Council, unless the Secretary of State withholds his certificate, receive a grant from the County Council of the county in which that borough is situated of one half the expenses of pay and clothing.

For the purpose of enabling a Secretary of State to grant or withhold his certificate, according to the efficiency of the force, Inspectors are appointed by Her Majesty to visit and inspect the state of the police appointed for every county or borough, and upon their report the Secretary of State makes his decision.

Public Health.[1]

The County Council may appoint one or more Medical Officers of Health, who must not hold any other appointment or engage in private practice without the express written consent of the Council.

The County Council and any Sanitary Authority may from time to time make arrangements for rendering the services of such Officer or Officers available within the sanitary district; and the Officer will have within the district all the powers and duties of a Medical Officer of Health appointed by the Sanitary Authority. So long as such an arrangement is in force the Sanitary Authority need not appoint a separate Medical Officer.

Every person hereafter appointed Medical Officer of Health must be legally qualified for the practice of medicine, surgery, and midwifery; every Medical Officer of Health appointed after the 1st of January, 1892, for any county, county borough, or for any sanitary district or combination of sanitary districts containing, according to the last published census for the time being, a population over 50,000, must also be registered in the medical register as the holder of a diploma in sanitary science, public health, or State medicine under sec. 21 of the Medical Act, 1886 (*49 & 50 Vict. c. 90*); or must have been during three consecutive years preceding the year 1892 a Medical Officer of a district or combination of districts with a population, according to the census of 1881, not under 20,000, or have been before the 13th August, 1888, for not less than three years a Medical Officer or Inspector of the Local Government Board.

The Local Government Board may, however, in particular cases dispense with the requirement that a Medical Officer of Health must be legally qualified for the practice of medicine, surgery, and midwifery.

---

[1] Local Government Act, 1888, secs. 17-19.

Every Medical Officer of Health for a district in any county must send to the County Council a copy of every periodical report of which a copy is required to be sent to the Local Government Board. If it appears to the County Council from any such report that the Public Health Act, 1875, has not been properly put in force within the district to which the report relates, or that any other matter affecting the public health of the district requires to be remedied, the County Council may cause a representation to be made to the Local Government Board as to the matter.

Race-courses.

The Race-courses Licensing Act, 1879 (*42 Vict. c. 18*) applies only to race-courses within a radius of ten miles from Charing Cross, and therefore only concerns the County Councils of Middlesex, Surrey, Kent, Essex, and Hertford (besides that of the county of London), and the Town Councils of Croydon and West Ham.

Under that Act no horse-race may lawfully take place within that ten mile radius except on a licensed race-course. The licence must be obtained from the County Council of the county, or the Town Council of the county borough in which the race-course is situate, who may grant or refuse it in their discretion. The licence is valid for one year.

Reformatory and Industrial Schools.

The Statutes dealing with this subject are :—

The Industrial Schools Act, 1866 (*29 & 30 Vict. c. 118*).

The Reformatory Schools Act, 1866 (*29 & 30 Vict. c. 117*).

The Reformatory and Industrial Schools Acts Amendment Act, 1872 (*35 & 36 Vict. c. 21*).

The Prison Authorities Act, 1874 (*37 & 38 Vict. c. 47*).

Reference must, however, also be had to some of the Statutes dealing with prisons more particularly.

The Prison Act, 1865 (*28 & 29 Vict. c. 126*).

The Prison Act, 1877 (*40 & 41 Vict. c. 21*).

An industrial school means, exclusively, a school in which industrial training is provided, and in which children are lodged, clothed, and fed as well as taught ; but the term reformatory school appears to have received no definition. Inspectors of industrial schools, and of reformatory schools, are appointed by a Secretary of State.[1]

[1] The Home Office is the Government Department superintending reformatory and industrial schools.

The Managers of any industrial or reformatory school may apply for a certificate that the school is fit for the reception of children to be sent there under the Industrial Schools Acts, or the Reformatory Schools Acts; upon which the school will be inspected by the Inspector, and the certificate will be granted by a Secretary of State, if he is satisfied with the Inspector's report, and the school will become a certified industrial school, or a certified reformatory school as the case may be. The same school cannot be certified in both capacities.

The County Council or any Town Council who were a Prison Authority under the Prisons Act, 1865 (except Town Councils of Quarter Sessions Boroughs, the population of which, according to the census of 1881, was under 10,000), or the Town Council of any county borough may contribute towards an existing certified industrial or reformatory school, or towards the purchase of land, &c., for the building of a school intended to be a certified industrial or reformatory school; and such Councils may also undertake the management, erection, or maintenance of a certified industrial or reformatory school, or a school intended to be a certified industrial or reformatory school.[1]

Before the Council take into consideration the making of such a contribution, or the undertaking of such objects, they must give two months' notice by advertisement in local papers of their intention to do so. Further, where the object of their contribution or undertaking is the alteration, enlargement, rebuilding, establishment, or building of a school, or intended school, they must obtain the approval of the Secretary of State. In order to obtain such approval, they must send him full plans and particulars of the scheme.

Such a Council may contract with the managers of a certified reformatory or industrial school for the reception and maintenance therein of such children as are from time to time ordered by Justices to be sent there from the county or borough of the Council.

Such a Council may also contribute towards the ultimate disposal of any inmate of a reformatory or industrial school established by them.

Registration of Rules of Societies, &c.

The rules of every Loan Society, formed under the Loan Societies Act, 1840 *(3 & 4 Vict. c. 110)*, must be registered Loan societies

[1] The power of a Town Council, with regard to industrial schools, may, to a certain extent, cease if a School Board is elected for the borough and resolve to contribute to, or undertake the maintenance of, an industrial school. See 35 & 36 Vict. c. 21, sec. 8.

with the County Council of the county or Town Council of the county borough in which the Society is formed.[1] A transcript of the rules, duly certified by the Chief Registrar of Friendly Societies,[2] must be laid before the Council, who must confirm them, upon which the transcript must be enrolled among the records of the county. The Council have no discretion in the matter, and cannot refuse to confirm the rules.

Scientific societies.

The buildings, &c., of Scientific, Literary, and Artistic Societies are exempt from rates, but to secure this exemption they must submit their rules to the Chief Registrar of Friendly Societies, who, if he considers the Society entitled to exemption, will indorse a certificate on certain copies of the rules. The Registrar must send a certified copy to the County Council of the county, or the Town Council of the county borough in which such buildings, &c., are, and the Council must confirm the rules; upon which they must be enrolled in the records of the county. The Council has no discretion in this matter either, and cannot refuse to confirm the rules.[3]

Places of religious worship.

By 52 Geo. III. c. 155, a certificate must, it seems, be obtained for every place of religious worship of Protestants at which more than twenty persons, besides the immediate family of the persons upon whose premises such a meeting takes place, are allowed to be present; unless such place of meeting is certified to the Registrar-General, under an Act of 1855 (*18 & 19 Vict. c. 81*). The certificate may be obtained from a Bishop or Archdeacon, or from the County Council of the county, or Town Council of the county borough in which the place of worship is situated. Such a Council must keep a record of all places of worship so certified.

Charitable gifts.

Under 52 Geo. III. c. 102, charitable gifts secured by deed, will, or other instrument, must, in most cases, be registered with the County Council of the county, or the Town Council of the county borough in which the persons to be benefited reside.

For this purpose the Trustees of the charity must, within twelve months after the decease of the founder of the charity, send a memorial to the Clerk of such Council stating—

i. The name of the founder.

---

[1] Loan Societies Act, 1840, sec. 4.
[2] Friendly Societies Act, 1875 (38 & 39 Vict. c. 60). sec. 10.
[3] 6 & 7 Vict. c. 36; Friendly Societies Act, 1875 (38 & 39 Vict. c. 60), sec. 10.

ii. The property held for the purposes of the charity.
iii. The gross annual income derived from the property.
iv. The objects of the charity.
v. In whose control the instruments under which the charity was founded, &c., are.

The Clerk of the Council must keep a record of such memorials, properly indexed according to the names of the founders, or the names by which the charities are generally known.

This Act does not apply to—

i. Royal foundations.
ii. Charities under the superintendence of hospitals and schools.
iii. Queen Anne's charity.
iv. The Universities of Oxford and Cambridge and their colleges, or any charity under their control.
v. Radcliffe Infirmary at Oxford.
vi. The Colleges of Westminster, Eton, and Winchester.
vii. Cathedral or Collegiate Churches.
viii. The Charterhouse.
ix. Trinity House of Deptford-Stroud.
x. Charities for Jews.
xi. Charities for Quakers.
xii. Charities of which the accounts are annually passed in the Chancery Division of the High Court.
xiii. Charities of an annual value below £2, provided they are registered with the minister of the parish.

Riot (Damages).

Police authorities.

The Riot (Damages) Act, 1886 (*49 & 50 Vict. c. 38*) provides that where a house, &c., has been destroyed, or property injured, stolen, or destroyed by persons riotously or tumultuously assembled together, compensation must be paid by the Police Authority within whose jurisdiction the damage was done. Under that Act, as modified by the Local Government Act, 1888, the Police Authorities are (outside the Metropolis)—

In counties—the County Council.

In boroughs, with a separate police force—the Town Council.

In towns (Hove and Tunbridge Wells), maintaining a separate police force—the Authority maintaining the police.

In the river Tyne, within the limits of the Act relating to the Tyne Improvement Commissioners—The Tyne Improvement Commissioners.

Fund for paying expenses.

The compensation falls, in each case, on the fund or rate applicable to the maintenance of the police. Where a county is divided into police districts, the compensation will be an item of local expenditure.[1]

Claims for compensation must be made to the Police Authority of the district in which the damage was done, and the Police Authority must inquire into the truth thereof, and if satisfied, fix the compensation. A Secretary of State may, from time to time, make regulations respecting the making of claims, &c.; such regulations must be published in the *London Gazette*, and every Police Authority must cause the same to be published within their district, and copies thereof to be sold to any applicant at a price not exceeding sixpence. Any claim made which does not comply with such regulations will be excluded.

Amount of compensation.

In reckoning the amount of compensation regard must be had to the conduct of the applicant as respects precautions taken by him, as respects his being accessory to the riot, or as respects any provocation offered by him or otherwise. Where any person having sustained loss by reason of such damage, &c., has received, by way of insurance or otherwise, any sum to recoup him in whole or in part; the compensation paid to him must be reduced by that sum; or if such sum exceeds the compensation that would be otherwise payable, must not be paid at all. The person paying the recouping sum will, however, be entitled to compensation in his stead.

Proceedings if proper compensation is not paid.

If a person is aggrieved by the refusal of a Police Authority to pay sufficient compensation, he may bring an action against the Police Authority in respect of all or any of the matters mentioned in his claim to an amount not exceeding that mentioned therein; but if he fail to recover an amount exceeding that fixed by the Police Authority he must pay the costs of that Authority as between solicitor and client. If the claim for which the action is brought does not exceed £100, the action must be brought in the County Court.

Rivers Pollution (Prevention).

The Rivers Pollution Prevention Act, 1876 (*39 & 40 Vict. c. 75*) provides for the prevention of the pollution of rivers, and, without prejudice to any other rights which any person may have against persons polluting rivers, it declares that certain proceedings shall be offences against the Act, and it provides

[1] See *ante*, p. 167.

a summary method for restraining such offences. Any Sanitary Authority and any County Council may enforce the provisions of the Act, and for that purpose may, subject to the provisions of the Act, take proceedings in respect of any offence against the Act which causes any interference with the due flow of any stream within their district or county, or which causes the pollution of any stream within their district or county, whether such offence is committed within their district or county or not. The Local Government Board also; by Provisional Order made on the application of any County Council, or of the Town Council of any county borough interested, may constitute a Joint Committee or other body representing all the counties and county boroughs through which a river or any specified portion of a river or any tributary thereof passes, and may confer on that Committee or Body power to enforce the Act.[1] Authorities

Offences against the Act are divided into three classes according as they are against parts 1, 2 or 3 of that Act, and in respect of the first two classes any person aggrieved by the offence may take proceedings under the Act; but in respect of the third class proceedings may only be taken by a Sanitary Authority, County Council or such a Committee or Body appointed by the Local Government Board as we have mentioned, and then only with the consent of the Board. Offences.

The following proceeding is an offence against Part I. of the Act :— Offences against Part I.

Putting or knowingly permitting to be put the solid refuse of any manufactory, manufacturing process, or quarry, or any rubbish, or cinders, or any other waste or any putrid solid matter into a stream, so as to interfere with its flow, or to pollute its waters. Such a proceeding will be an offence, although by itself it may be too trifling to pollute or to interfere with the flow of a stream, if, in conjunction with the acts of other persons, or in conjunction with other acts of the same person, it leads to pollution or interference with the flow of the stream.

The following proceeding is an offence against Part II. of the Act :— Offences against Part II.

Causing or knowingly permitting any solid or liquid sewage matter to flow or fall into a stream.

If a channel was used or constructed, or in course of construction, on the 15th August, 1876, for the purpose of conveying sewage matter into a stream, any person may use the channel for that purpose, provided he takes the best practicable means to render the sewage matter harmless; such a proceeding, however, may of course be unlawful apart from the Act.

If a Sanitary Authority was on the 15th August, 1876, discharging sewage matter into a stream by a channel constructed or used for that purpose, the Local Govern-

[1] Local Government Act, 1888, sec. 14.

ment Board may, if they think fit, make an Order suspending the Act as to discharge of sewage matter by that channel for a specified time, in order to give the Sanitary Authority time to adopt means for rendering the sewage matter harmless, &c. The Board may renew such an Order from time to time.

Any person other than a Sanitary Authority may, without committing an offence against the Act, discharge sewage matter into a stream along a drain communicating with a sewer belonging to, or under the control of, a Sanitary Authority, with their sanction.

Offences against Part III.

The following proceedings are offences against Part III. of the Act :—

1st. Causing or permitting any poisonous, noxious, or polluting liquid proceeding from a factory or manufacturing process to fall into a stream.

If any channel was used or constructed, or in course of construction, on the 15th August, 1876, for the purpose of conveying such liquid in a stream, any person may use the channel, or any new channel constructed in substitution for it and having the same outfall, for that purpose, without committing an offence against the Act. Such a proceeding may, however, of course, be an offence apart from the Act.

2nd. Causing or knowingly permitting any solid matter from any mine to fall into a stream so as to interfere with its due flow.

3rd. Causing or permitting any poisonous, noxious, or polluting solid or liquid matter from any mine, except water in the same condition as that in which it has been drained or raised from the mine, to fall into a stream, unless the best practicable and available means are taken to render such matter harmless.

Proceedings against offenders against Part III.

The only bodies that may take proceedings to repress offences against Part III. of the Act are, as we have stated, County Councils, Sanitary Authorities, and a Committee or Representative Body, appointed by the Local Government Board for the purpose under the Local Government Act, 1888, and no such proceedings can be taken without the consent of the Local Government Board. If on the application of any person interested in the repression of such an offence, however, the Sanitary Authority, County Council or Committee, refuse to take proceedings or apply for consent, such person may apply to the Local Government Board, who may direct such Authority to take proceedings.

Consent of Local Government Board necessary.

The Local Government Board are guided in giving or withholding consent, by consideration of the industrial interests involved, and the circumstances of the locality ; they will not give their consent to proceedings by such an authority in a district which is the seat of a manufacturing industry, unless they are satisfied, after inquiry, that means for rendering harmless the poisonous, noxious, or polluting liquid proceeding from the processes of such manufactures, are reasonably practicable and available under all circumstances of the case, and that no material injury will be inflicted by such proceedings on the interests of such industry.

Protection for manufacturers.

Any person in a manufacturing district against whom proceedings are proposed to be taken may, notwithstanding that the Local Government Board may have consented to the proceedings, object before the Sanitary Authority, or County Council, or Committee, to such proceedings being taken. And any person may, if he applies in writing to such an authority, have an opportunity of being heard against proceedings been taken so far as they relate to his works or manufacturing processes.

In such a case the Sanitary Authority or County Council must allow him to be heard by himself, his agents and witnesses, and, after due inquiry, must determine whether they will proceed in the matter, having regard to all the considerations to which the Local Government Board ought to have regard.

If proceedings have been successfully taken under the Act by any County Council, or Sanitary Authority, or Committee, no other such authority may proceed against the same person until he has had reasonable time to carry out the Order of the Court.

Proceedings to be taken in County Court.

Proceedings to enforce the Act must be taken in the County Court, which Court may by summary Order require any person to abstain from the commission of any offence against the Act. The Court may order any person failing to perform a duty under the Act to perform it, and may insert in any Order such conditions as it may think just, and may suspend or rescind an Order upon terms, &c. The Court may obtain expert opinions on the matter, and may enforce their Order by a penalty not exceeding £50 a day for every day a person is in default.

If a person remains in default for a month, or such other period less than a month as such an Order may prescribe, the Court may appoint some other person to carry the Order into effect, and the expenses may be recovered in the County Court from the person in default.

Appeal from County Court.

Appeal from the County Court must be by special case agreed upon between the parties, or if they are unable to agree, to be settled by the Judge; but the case, however, may be removed upon terms into the High Court by leave of a Judge of the H'gh Court.

Inspector's Certificate.

A certificate granted by an Inspector of the Local Government Board, appointed for the purposes of the Act, to the effect that the means used for rendering harmless any sewage matter, or poisonous, noxious, or polluting solid or liquid matter, are the best and only practicable and available means under the circumstances of the case, is conclusive evidence of the fact in all proceedings under the Act.

Such a certificate may be granted for any period not exceeding two years, and any person aggrieved by the granting or withholding of a certificate may appeal to the Local Government Board against the decision of the Inspector, and the Board may confirm, reverse, or modify his decision, and may make such Order as to costs as may seem just.

No proceedings under the Act may be taken until the expiration of two months after written notice has been given to the offender, nor may proceedings be taken in respect of an offence in relation to which other proceedings are pending.

The Local Government Board may make Orders as to the cost of inquiries instituted by them under the Act, and their Inspectors have similar powers to Inspectors of the Local Government Board appointed under the Public Health Act, 1875.

Definition of "stream."

In conclusion, we may observe that the term stream includes rivers, streams, canals, lakes, and water-courses other than water-courses that were on the 15th August, 1876, mainly used as sewers, and which empty directly into the sea.

The Local Government Board, by Order published in the *London Gazette*, may declare such portion of the sea or of tidal waters to be a stream within the meaning of the Act, as may be determined by the Board after local inquiry and on sanitary grounds.

Theatres.

Under an Act of 1843 (*6 & 7 Vict. c. 68*) all theatres, except theatres with letters patent, must be licensed.

In parts of the Metropolis and in Brighton and Windsor the licence must be obtained from the Lord Chamberlain; elsewhere from the County Council of the county, or Town Council of the county borough in which the theatre is situated.

The licence must be granted to the actual and responsible manager for the time being; and a fee not exceeding 5s. a month, during the time the theatre is open, may be imposed for a licence granted by a County or Town Council.

The Council must make rules for insuring order and decency at the several theatres within their jurisdiction, and for regulating the time at which they shall severally be allowed to be open, and they may vary and revoke such rules; a Secretary of State also may make, vary, and revoke such rules for the like purpose.

The Council may require a manager, to whom they grant a

licence, to enter into a bond in not more than £500, with two sureties in not more than £100 each, for the observance of these rules.

Weights and Measures.

The law with regard to Weights and Measures was codified in the Weights and Measures Act, 1878 (*41 & 42 Vict. c. 49*). The objects of that Act are to secure uniformity in the units of weights and measures employed throughout Great Britain, and to provide machinery for preventing the use of false weights and measures.

The Act defines the unit of length (*i.e.*, the yard), and the unit of weight (*i.e.*, the pound), and secondly a system of derivative units, and provides that (with certain exceptions) these units alone must be used to express weights and measures for purposes of Trade.

The Act also provides that material weights and measures (*i.e.*, metal weights and foot rules, &c.) used in trade shall be of certain denominations only, and that they shall be tested and stamped, for which, means are provided in the Act.

Lastly, the Act provides for the prosecution of persons using false weights and measures.

Local Authorities.

The superintendence of the execution of the Act is in the hands of the Board of Trade, and under that body, locally, in the hands of Local Authorities, namely:—in counties, the County Council, and in boroughs, the population of which, according to the census of 1881, was over 10,000, the Town Council. The Town Council, however, of a borough without a separate Court of Quarter Session other than a county borough, need not act as Local Authority unless they choose.

Unit of length.

The unit of length is the imperial standard yard, which is defined as the distance between the centres of the two gold plugs in a certain bronze bar, when that bar is at 62 degrees Fahrenheit. This bar is deposited in the custody of the Board of Trade.

Unit of weight.

The unit of weight is the imperial pound, which is defined as the weight in vacuo of a certain platinum weight, which weight is also deposited in the custody of the Board of Trade. This definition of the standard of weight is, of course, from a scientific view unsatisfactory.

Unit of capacity.

The unit of capacity is the gallon, which is defined as containing ten imperial standard pounds weight of distilled water weighed in air against brass weights, with the water and air at 62 deg. Fahrenheit, and with the barometer at 30 inches.

The unit of capacity also is most unfortunate from a scientific point of view.

Purchasing copies.

Copies have been made of the imperial standards for determining the yard and the pound, and are called parliamentary copies of the imperial standards. Such copies are deposited at the Royal Mint, the Royal Society of London, and at other places.

Board of Trade Standards

The Board of Trade have prepared a series of "Board of Trade Standards," which are copies of the Imperial standards and standards of various derivative units and of multiples and aliquot parts of units as follows:—[1]

BOARD OF TRADE STANDARDS OF LENGTH.

100 feet	4 feet
66 feet = 1 chain of 100 links.	3 feet = 1 yard
16½ feet = 1 rod, pole or perch.	2 feet
10 feet	1 foot
6 feet = 2 yards.	$\frac{1}{12}$ foot = 1 inch
5 feet	

The inch is divided in three ways, namely, into 12 equal parts; 10 equal parts; and 16 equal parts.

BOARD OF TRADE STANDARDS OF WEIGHTS.

Denomination of Standard.	Denomination of Standard.	Denomination of Standard.
Avoirdupois Weights.	*Troy Bullion Weights.*	*Decimal Grain Weights.*
56 pounds	500 ounces	4,000 grains
28 ,,	400 ,,	2,000 ,,
14 ,,	300 ,,	1,000 ,,
7 ,,	200 ,,	500 ,,
4 ,,	100 ,,	300 ,,
2 ,,	50 ,,	200 ,,
1 pound	40 ,,	100 ,,
8 ounces	30 ,,	50 ,,
4 ,,	20 ,,	30 ,,
2 ,,	10 ,,	20 ,,
1 ounce	5 ,,	10 ,,
8 drams	4 ,,	5 ,,
4 ,,	3 ,,	3 ,,
2 ,,	2 ,,	2 ,,
1 dram	1 ounce	1 ,,
½ ,,	0·5 ,,	0·5 grain
240 grains, commonly called 10 pennyweights	0·4 ,,	0·3 ,,
	0·3 ,,	0·2 ,,
120 grains, commonly called 5 pennyweights.	0·2 ,,	0·1 ,,
	0·1 ,,	0·05 ,,

[1] Those given are the Board of Trade Standards mentioned in the schedules to the Weights and Measures Act, 1878. Other standards may be prepared and, if approved by Her Majesty, by Order in Council, will become Board of Trade Standards. A Board of Trade Standard may also, by Order in Council, be declared to be no longer a Board of Trade Standard.

Denomination of Standard.	Denomination of Standard.	Denomination of Standard.
Avoirdupois Weights.	*Troy Bullion Weights.*	*Decimal Grain Weights.*
2 grains, commonly called 3 pennyweights.	0·05 ounce	0·03 grain
	0·04 ,,	0·02 ,,
48 grains, commonly called 2 pennyweights.	0·03 ,,	0·01 ,,
	0·02 ,,	
24 grains, commonly called 1 pennyweight.	0·01 ,,	
	0·005 ,,	
	0·004 ,,	
	0·003 ,,	
	0·002 ,,	
	0·001 ,,	

In addition to these, the Board of Trade have prepared, according to the following table, a series of

STANDARDS FOR WEIGHING COINS.

Denomination of Coin.	Standard Weight.	
	Imperial Weight.	Metric Weights.
GOLD—	Grains.	Grains.
Five Pound	616·37239	39·94028
Two Pound... ...	246·54895	15·97611
Sovereign	123·27447	7·98805
Half Sovereign ...	61·63723	3·99402
SILVER—		
Crown	436·36363	28·27590
Half-Crown	218·18181	14·13795
Florin	174·54545	11·31036
Shilling	87·27272	5·65518
Sixpence	43·63636	2·82759
Groat or Fourpence ..	29·09090	1·88506
Threepence	21.81818	1·41379
Twopence	14·54545	0·94253
Penny	7·27272	0·47126
BRONZE—		
Penny	145·83333	9·44984
Halfpenny	87·50000	5·66990
Farthing	43·75000	2·83495

BOARD OF TRADE STANDARDS OF CAPACITY.

Bushel = 8 gallons.
Half-bushel = 4 gallons.
Peck = 2 gallons.
Gallon.
Half-gallon.
Quart = $\frac{1}{4}$ gallon.
Pint = $\frac{1}{8}$ gallon.
Half-pint = $\frac{1}{16}$ gallon.
Gill = $\frac{1}{32}$ gallon.
Half-gill = $\frac{1}{64}$ gallon
Quarter-gill = $\frac{1}{128}$ gallon.

It may be pointed out that the "gill" is not defined at all; except incidentally in a schedule to the Act dealing with the metric system.

The Board of Trade have, also, the following

STANDARDS OF CAPACITY FOR MEASURES USED IN THE SALE OF DRUGS,

and which are not defined anywhere :—

4 Fluid ounces.	30 Minims.
3 ,, ,,	20 ,,
2 ,, ,,	10 ,,
1 ,, ounce.	5 ,,
4 ,, drachms.	4 ,,
3 ,, ,,	3 ,,
2 ,, ,,	2 ,,
1 ,, ,,	1 ,,

In addition to these the Board of Trade have a set of Metric Standards, *i.e.*, standards of weights and measures according to the French system ; but these are not "Board of Trade Standards." The Board have also prepared authoritative tables comparing the metric with the imperial system.

Weights and measures to be uniform.

The provisions of the Act for securing uniformity in transactions are of two kinds. First, prescribing the manner in which the terms of a contract shall be expressed, and secondly for prescribing what material weights and measures are alone to be used. These provisions are for the most part incorporated from older Acts, and are difficult to construe.

It seems that every contract must be expressed in terms of the units above-mentioned, *i.e.*, the yard, pound, and gallon ; or in terms of derivative units ; or in terms of the units of the metric system. Besides the derivative units, of which Board of Trade Standards have been prepared, the Act contains definitions of the following derivative units :—

i. Of length, the furlong and the mile.
ii. Of area, the rood and the acre.
iii. Of weight, the hundredweight and ton.
iv. Of capacity, the quarter and the chaldron.

Again, the use for trade of any material weight or measure which is not of the denomination of a Board of Trade Standard and which has not been duly verified and stamped is unlawful. Thus the use of a seven foot rule in trade would be unlawful.

The real object of these provisions was to put an end to the use of customary weights and measures, and so to avoid the misunderstanding and unfairness that must result from the use of a weight or measure of a denomination of which there is no exact definition.

Duties of Local Authority.

We may now proceed to discuss the duties of a Local Authority.

Local Standards.

The Local Authority must, from time to time, provide such local standards of measure and weight (other than coin, weights)[1] as they deem requisite for the purpose of the verification of all weights and measures in use in their county or borough, and must fix the places where these standards are to be deposited. The local standards must be copies of Board of Trade standards.

They must provide from time to time proper means for testing weights and measures by comparison with the local standards, and for stamping the weights and measures verified. Where it becomes necessary to provide a new local standard, a copy must be made of a Board of Trade standard, and the Board of Trade must, free of charge, have the copy compared with a Board of Trade standard, and the local standard must be stamped by the Board of Trade as verified, and the fact of the verification must be evidenced by an indenture signed by an officer of the Board, so that each local standard has its indenture of verification.

The Local Authority must take steps to have their local standards re-verified from time to time, namely, in the case of a standard of weight, every five years at least, and in the case of a standard of length, every ten years at least, or at any other time if a local standard is damaged.

If a local standard has been damaged the re-verification must be made by the Board of Trade in the same way as the original verification. In other cases the re-verification may be made by the Board of Trade, or by local comparison.

A local comparison of a local standard is made by an Inspector of Weights and Measures for the county or borough in which such local standard is used, comparing the same, in the presence of a Justice of the Peace, with some other local standard that has been verified or re-verified by the Board of Trade, in the case of a weight within the last five years, and in the case of a measure, within the last ten years.

If on a local comparison the local standard is found correct, the Justice must sign an indorsement upon the indenture of verification of such standard, stating such local comparison and verification, and the error, if any found thereon,[2] and the indorsement so signed must be transmitted to the Board of Trade to be recorded.

Appointment of Inspectors.

Every Local Authority must appoint a sufficient number of Inspectors of Weights and Measures. If they appoint more

[1] All coin weights in use must be verified by the Board of Trade.

[2] Her Majesty may, from time to time, by Order in Council, determine the error to be tolerated in local standards.

than one they must allot to each Inspector (subject to any arrangement for a chief Inspector or Inspectors) a separate district, to be distinguished by some name, number, or mark. They may appoint different persons to be Inspectors for verification and for inspection respectively of weights and measures. A maker or seller of weights and measures must not be an Inspector.

The Local Authority must fix times and places at which each Inspector is to attend for the purpose of verification of weights and measures.

Two or more Local Authorities may combine, as regards either the whole or any part of the areas within their jurisdiction, for all or any of the purposes of this Act, upon such terms and in such manner as they may agree upon.

A Local Authority may make bye-laws, and when made alter and revoke and vary them:—

(i.) For regulating the comparison with their local standards, and the verification and stamping of weights and measures in use in their county or borough.

(ii.) For regulating the local comparison of their local standards.

(iii.) Generally for regulating the duties of their Inspectors.

The bye-laws must be approved by the Board of Trade, and must be published before such approval as the Board of Trade may direct. Such bye-laws may impose fines not exceeding £1, to be recovered summarily.

On appointment an Inspector must enter into a recognisance with the Crown (to be sued for in any court of record) in the sum of £200 for the due performance of the duties of his office, and for the due payment, at the times fixed by the Local Authority appointing him, of all fees received by him under the Act, and for the safe custody of the local standards and the stamps and appliances for verification committed to his charge, and for their due surrender immediately on his removal or other cessation from office to the person appointed to receive them.

Duties of Inspectors.

An Inspector must make the local comparisons of the local standards from time to time, and also attend at the places and times appointed by the Local Authority with the local standards in his custody, for the verification of weights and measures. He must at such times and places examine every measure or weight which is of the same denomination as one of such standards and which is brought to him for the purpose of verification by comparing it with that standard. If he find it correct he must stamp it with a stamp of verification in such manner as best to prevent fraud; and, in the case of a measure or of a weight of ¼lb. or upwards, he must further stamp on it a name, number, or mark distinguishing the district for which he acts. He must enter in a book kept by him minutes of such verification, and if required give a certificate under his hand of such stamping. He may take such fees for stamping and verification as the Local Authority may fix, on a scale not higher than is shown by the fifth schedule to the Weights and Measures Act, 1878. He must, at such times as the Local Authority may fix, pay over to their Treasurer all such fees.

Every Inspector authorised in writing under the hand of a Justice of the Peace, as also every Justice of the Peace, may at all reasonable times inspect all weights, measures, scales, balances, steel-yards, and weighing machines which are used within his jurisdiction.

Yorkshire Registries Act, 1884.

Under this Act (*47 & 48 Vict. c. 54*), every assurance or will affecting lands in any of the three Ridings of Yorkshire (including any county borough therein) must be registered.

For this purpose the County Council of each Riding must maintain a registry office; that for the North Riding being at Northallerton, that for the East Riding (in which for this purpose Kingston-upon-Hull is included), at Beverley, and that for the West Riding at Wakefield. The business of each registry must be conducted by a Registrar, assisted by a staff of Clerks, &c.

On the occurrence of a vacancy in the office of Registrar, the County Council may appoint a barrister or solicitor in actual practice, and of not less than seven years' standing, or a person who for five years has discharged the duties of Deputy Registrar for at least five years; but the appointment must be confirmed by the Lord Chancellor. A Registrar is (subject to savings for the rights of Registrars appointed before the 7th August, 1884) removable by the County Council in their discretion, or by the Lord Chancellor for misconduct.

The County Council may make rules for the conduct of business at a registry, which must however be confirmed by the Lord Chancellor.

CHAPTER VI.

QUALIFICATION AND REGISTRATION OF ELECTORS.

WE have already explained in Chapter I. that County Councillors are elected one for each electoral division of the county, and that Town Councillors are elected either at one election for the whole borough or, should the borough be divided into wards, so many for each ward of the borough.

As a preparation for the election of County Councillors and Town Councillors, lists are annually prepared of persons qualified to vote for Councillors for each county and borough. Such a list of persons qualified to vote for County Councillors is known as the Register of Electors for the county, or the County Roll, and such a list of persons qualified to vote for Town Councillors is known as the Register of Electors for the borough, or the Burgess Roll.

Every person whose name is on the register of electors in force for a county or borough is, with certain exceptions, entitled to vote at an election of Councillors for the county or borough, whether he was in the first instance entitled to have his name put on the register or not. We must therefore inquire as to the preparation of the register of electors, and the first point is, what qualification entitles a person to be entered upon that register. The qualification is the same, whether for a county or borough.

The principal statutory provisions on the subject are contained in—

The Municipal Corporations Act, 1882 *(45 & 46 Vict. c. 50)*, secs. 9, 31, 33, 63.

The Registration Act, 1885 *(48 & 49 Vict. c. 15)*.

The County Electors Act, 1888 *(51 Vict. c. 10)*.

A person on the register of electors for a borough is called a burgess, or, if the borough is a city, a citizen, and a person on the register of electors for a county who is not a burgess, is called a county elector; but the term burgess is employed in most Acts and in this work to include citizen.

Qualifications of County Electors and Burgesses.

The qualification which entitles a person to be registered as a burgess or county elector is complicated, and has been laid down in the County Electors Act, 1888, in the following way.

The "burgess qualification" which is given in the Municipal Corporations Act, 1882, is extended to the rest of the county, and in addition it is provided that the "£10 occupation qualification," obtaining for parliamentary purposes, slightly modified and made to include women and peers, shall entitle a person to be registered as a burgess or county elector.[1]

A person to be entitled to be registered as an elector (who may be either a man or a woman)[2] must have the following qualifications:—[3]

I. He must be of full age.

The exact date on which the person must have reached the age of twenty-one is uncertain. He must clearly be of full age before the lists are finally revised by the Revising Barrister, but perhaps it is necessary that he should have been of full age on the preceding 15th July.

II. He must on the 15th July be, and for the whole of the preceding twelve months, have been, in occupation in the county or borough of property of a nature to entitle him to be registered.

Such property is called "qualifying property." It must be either—

i. A house, warehouse, shop or other building, in which case the occupation may be joint or several. Building has been held to include very slight and unimportant structures, such as a tool-house and a potato-shed. The structure, however, must have some permanence and value, and have been intended to be of some utility.[4]

ii. Part of a house separately occupied for the purpose of any trade, business, or profession, or as a dwelling. A person occupying part of a house separately will not be disqualified by reason of being entitled to the joint use of some other part.[5]

iii. Land or a tenement of a clear yearly value of not less than £10; where such property is occupied jointly the yearly value must be sufficient to give £10 for each occupier, in order to confer the qualification. Qualification in respect of such property is called a £10 occupation qualification.[6]

---

[1] This appears to be the effect of s. 3 of the County Electors Act; but the meaning of that section, which was added during the progress of the Act through Parliament, is obscure. It is very probable that the section will not be held to apply to women or peers. It is worthy of remark that the section professes to deal with the £10 occupation qualification within the meaning of the Registration Act, 1885, whereas that Act contains no definition of £10 occupation qualification, except incidentally in the course of the instructions to Overseers contained in the schedules.

[2] See note. We use the masculine pronoun throughout for simplicity.

[3] Municipal Corporations Act, 1882, sec. 9; The County Electors Act, 1888, secs. 2,3, and schedule.

[4] See Morish *v.* Harris, L.R., 1 C.P. 155.

[5] Municipal Corporations Act, 1882, sec. 31; Grenaway *v.* Batchelor.

[6] See note.

The same property may, of course, serve to qualify in two ways, as conferring the £10 occupation qualification and also as coming within one of the first two heads. Thus, if a man occupy a warehouse of the clear yearly value of £10 or more, he may claim to be registered either simply as the occupier of a warehouse or as the occupier of a tenement of the clear yearly value of £10. The other conditions necessary to entitle him to be registered are, however, different in the two cases, so that he might succeed in his claim to be registered as the occupier of a warehouse and fail in respect of his £10 occupation qualification, or *vice versa*.

Where a person succeeds to qualifying property by descent, marriage, marriage settlement, devise or promotion to a benefice or office, the occupancy of the property by a predecessor in title is equivalent to the occupancy of the successor.[1]

The qualifying property need not be, throughout the twelve months constituting the period of qualification, the same property, nor in the same parish.[1] It may be pointed out that if a person occupy qualifying property within a county during part of the period of qualification and subsequently occupy property in a borough in the county for the rest of the period, or *vice-versâ*, he will be qualified neither as a burgess nor as a county elector.

If a person permits his qualifying property to be occupied as a furnished dwelling-house by some other person, by letting it or otherwise, for a period not exceeding four months, he will not lose his qualification.[2]

III. He must, during the whole of the twelve months which constitute the period of qualification, or, if the qualification is the £10 occupation qualification, during the last six months thereof, have resided in the county or borough, or within seven miles thereof.

It has been said that a man's residence is the place where he eats, drinks, or sleeps, or where his servants eat drink or sleep. And a man may have more than one residence.[3]

Although, in order to be qualified to vote, a person need not reside uninterruptedly in the county, &c., yet if he goes away and abandons the power or intention to return when it suits him, he will lose his residence there. For example, a soldier who is away with his regiment is under orders, and cannot return at his pleasure, and so loses his residence.[4]

The seven miles must be measured in a straight line from the nearest point in the county or borough, and for determining it recourse may be had to the ordnance map.[5]

In the case of a person letting his qualifying property as a furnished house, as above-mentioned, he does not lose his qualification by residing beyond the seven miles during such letting.[6]

---

[1] Municipal Corporations Act, 1882, sec. 33.
[2] The Municipal Voters Relief Act, 1885 *(48 Vict. c. 9)*.
[3] R. *v.* North Currey, 4 B. & C. 959.
R. *v.* Mayor of Exeter, L.R. 4 Q.B. 110.
[4] See Durant *v.* Carter, L.R. 9 C.P. 261.
Ford *v.* Page, L.R. 9 C.P., 269.
Ford *v.* Hart, L.R. 9 C.P. 293.
[5] Municipal Corporations Act, 1882, sec. 231.
[6] Municipal Voters Relief Act, 1885 *(48 Vict., c. 9)*.

Here we may point out that, if a person occupying qualifying property in a borough, reside more than seven miles from the borough, he will have no vote for the county in which the borough is situated, even although he may reside in the county.

IV. He must have been rated in respect of the qualifying property to all poor rates made, during the twelve months constituting the qualifying period, for the parish wherein the property is situated.

To constitute such rating it is necessary, subject to what appears below, that the occupier's name should actually appear on the rate book.[1] Where, however, a person succeeds to qualifying property as mentioned above, his name need not appear on the rate book, except in respect of any rate made after the date of his succession.[2]

Where, again, the owner of qualifying property is liable to be rated instead of the occupier, provisions are made that the Overseers shall insert the occupier's name in the rate book, but such rating is considered the rating of the occupier, and the omission of his name in such a case will not disqualify him.[3]

Again, if an occupier of qualifying property, whether the landlord is or is not liable to be rated to the poor rate in respect thereof, claims to be rated to the poor rate in respect thereof, and pays or tenders to the Overseers of the parish in which the property is situated, the full amount of the poor rate last made in respect of the property, the Overseers must put the occupier's name on the rate book, in respect of that rate. And if they fail to do so, the occupier is nevertheless deemed to be rated to that rate.[4]

A rate is considered to have been made on the date at which it is allowed by the Justices.[5]

V. He must, on or before the 20th July, have paid all poor rates, including county or borough rates, that have become payable by him in respect of the qualifying property up to the preceding 5th January.

If his qualification is a £10 occupation qualification, it does not matter whether he pays the rates himself or whether some other person pays them for him, so long as the rates are paid. But in other cases, though payment by the owner of the property, under an agreement with the occupier, or under any other agreement or obligation, is considered payment by the occupier, yet, if some person with no interest in the property pays the rates gratuitously, that will not be such payment by the occupier as to entitle him to be registered.[6] It may be observed that if a person pays a rate on behalf of any ratepayer to enable him to be registered and thereby to influence his vote, both he and the ratepayer are guilty of bribery.

---

1 Moss *v.* Michael Tidifield, 7 M. & C., 72.
2 Municipal Corporations Act, 1882, sec. 33.
3 Poor Rate Assessment and Collection Act, 1869 (*32 & 33 Vict. c. 41*), sec. 19. Parliamentary and Municipal Registration Act, 1878, s. 14.
4 Municipal Corporations Act, 1882, sec. 32.
5 Poor Rate Assessment and Collection Act, 1869 (*32 & 33 Vict. c. 41*), sec. 17.
6 R. *v.* Bridgnorth 10 A. & E. 66.
7 Representation of the People Act, 1867 (*30 & 31 Vict. c. 102*), sec. 49, and see *post*, p. 217.

Where the owner being liable for the rates, omits to pay them, such omission will disqualify the occupier.

Non-payment of an illegal rate will not disqualify, even if it is not appealed against.[1]

VI. He must, on before the 20th July, when the qualification is a £10 occupation qualification, have paid the assessed taxes that accrued on or before the preceding 5th of January.

VII. He must not be an alien.

VIII. He must not, during the twelve months constituting the qualifying period, have received union or parochial relief.

Relief to a person's children or to any one he is bound to support, is considered relief to him.[2] Relief to a man's parents does not disqualify.[3] Medical or surgical assistance or medicine received at the expense of a poor rate, will not disqualify. Nor will any person be disqualified merely because he has been removed by Order of Justices to a hospital at the cost of any local authority. Nor will a person be disqualified because his child has been admitted to and taught in any public or endowed school.[4]

IX. He must not be disqualified by any Act of Parliament, *e.g.*, owing to his having been guilty of offences against election law, &c.

Registration.

The registration of county electors and burgesses is accomplished simultaneously with the registration of parliamentary voters, and with certain modifications in the same manner.

The principal statutes dealing with the matter are—

The Parliamentary Registration Act, 1843 (*6 Vict. c. 18*).

The Representation of the People Act, 1867 (*30 & 31 Vict. c. 102*).

The Parliamentary and Municipal Registration Act, 1878 (*41 & 42 Vict. c. 26*).

The Municipal Corporations Act, 1882 (*45 & 46 Vict. c. 50*).

The Registration Act, 1885 (*48 Vict. c. 15*).

The County Electors Act, 1888.

Local Government Act, 1888, s. 76.

The above Acts, together with any other Acts dealing with the matter, are called the Registration of Electors Acts, 1843 to 1888.

Many of the provisions of the earlier enactments, which applied originally only to parliamentary registration, have been extended to the registration of county electors and burgesses.

---

[1] R. *v.* Mayor of New Windsor, 7 Q. B., 908.
[2] Poor Law Amendment Act, 1834 (*4 & 5 Will. IV. c. 76*), sec. 56.
[3] R. *v.* Ireland, L.R., 3 Q.B., 130.
[4] Medical Relief Disqualification Removal Act, 1885 (*48 & 49 Vict. c. 46*).

It may be found convenient here, in order to render the question of registration thoroughly intelligible, to summarise the qualifications that entitle a man to be registered as a parliamentary voter.

Qualification of Parliamentary Voters.[1]

The following are the qualifications of a parliamentary voter for a parliamentary borough :—

The £10 occupation qualification —

This we have already explained; but the property must be in the parliamentary borough and the residence within seven miles of the parliamentary borough; and the qualification does not extend to peers or women.

Household qualification—

i.e., occupation of a dwelling house as inhabitant occupier within the parliamentary borough, subject to certain conditions.

Lodger qualification—

i.e., occupation of lodgings in the parliamentary borough, subject to certain conditions.

Reserved rights—

i.e., certain rights existing in certain cases before the Reform Act, 1832 (*2 Will. IV. c. 45*).

The qualifications of a parliamentary voter for a county are :—

I. Ownership qualification. This may be shortly described as a qualification in respect of ownership of land, &c., as distinguished from occupation.

Subject to the various conditions, it is conferred by ownership of—

i. Any freehold of inheritance of land or tenements of the annual value of at least forty shillings.

ii. Freehold for life or lives of lands or tenements of an annual value above forty shillings, but below £5, provided that the property is in the *bonâ fide* occupation of the owner; or was acquired before the passing of the Reform Act, 1832; or was acquired by marriage, marriage settlement, descent, devise, or accession to a benefice or office.

iii. Freehold, copyhold, or any other tenure, for life, or lives, or any larger estate, of lands or tenements of a clear yearly value above £5.

iv. Leasehold originally created for a term not less than 60 years, and of a yearly value exceeding £5.

v. Leasehold of lands or tenements originally created for a term not less than 20 years, and of a yearly value of at least £50.

It must be pointed out that where a person occupies property within a parliamentary borough, of sufficient value to entitle him to be registered as an occupation voter for that borough, he will not be entitled to be registered as an ownership voter for the county in respect of that property, even although it would otherwise confer the ownership qualification.

---

[1] These qualifications are conferred by numerous Acts of Parliament; for further information, reference must be had to text-books on the subject.

II. Occupation qualification, namely:—

Fifty pounds rental qualification—

This is merely a temporary provision for certain persons entitled in 1884, and is generally absorbed in the £10 occupation qualification.

£10 occupation qualification—

This qualification is the same as the £10 occupation qualification for a county elector, except that residence is not required, and the assessed taxes need not have been paid, and that the qualification does not extend to peers and women.

Household qualification—

This is the same as in parliamentary boroughs.

Lodgers qualification—

This is the same as in parliamentary boroughs.

No person is qualified as an occupation voter for a county, in respect of property within a parliamentary borough.

The registration of electors is carried out in the following way:—First, provisional lists of electors are prepared for each parish; the lists are then revised by the Revising Barristers, subject to an appeal in certain cases to the High Court; and, finally, the various necessary rolls of electors are made up and printed.

The arrangements for the year 1888 are somewhat special, and will be explained on p. 204. The account of the process that we shall give will be applicable to future years after the establishment of County Councils.

The administrative duties connected with the preparation of the parish lists fall chiefly on the Town Clerks of parliamentary and municipal boroughs, and on the Clerks of the County Councils in counties, and in each parish on the Overseers of the poor.

The Board of Guardians of any union may, with the consent of the Overseers of any parish in their union, for which an Assistant Overseer has not been appointed, annually appoint a Registration Officer to perform the duties of Overseers in respect of the registration of voters for such parish. The same officer may be appointed for more than one parish. The Guardians will pay the officer and charge his remuneration against the poor rates of the parish or parishes for which he is appointed, and if he is appointed for more than one parish, in proportion to the number of voters registered for each parish.[1]

Instructions to Town Clerks, Clerks of the Peace and Overseers were given in schedules to the Registration Act, 1885, which are, however, now to a great extent superseded by the provisions of the County Electors Act, 1888. Instructions to these officers for the year 1888 have been issued by the Local Government Board, in the form of a circular. Under the Local Government Act, 1888, sec.

[1] County Electors Act, 1888. sec. 4.

76, the instructions, precepts and forms may, from time to time, be altered by Order in Council.

The account of the process of registration that we shall give will be confined as far as possible to the registration of county electors and burgesses: but we shall mention parliamentary registration incidentally, as far as may be necessary to render our account intelligible.

The proceedings are as follows:—

The Town Clerk of every parliamentary or municipal borough, on or within seven days before the 15th April,[1] sends a precept containing the instructions to Overseers in force for the time being modified so as to suit the particular circumstances of the case, and a sufficient number of blank forms for the necessary lists, to the Overseers of every parish within his borough. This precept instructs the Overseers to prepare the following lists of electors and parliamentary voters:— Precepts sent to Overseers.

The Occupiers List,
The Reserved Rights List,
The Old Lodgers List,
The Special Non-resident List,

and various supplementary lists of claimants, persons objected to, &c.

The Clerk of every County Council,[2] also on or within seven days before the 15th April,[3] sends a precept and blank forms to the Overseers of every parish within the county, including the parishes within the county boroughs. In those parishes which are within a parliamentary or municipal borough this precept is confined to Ownership Voters. In other parishes, the precept directs the preparation of the following lists:—

Lists of Ownership Voters,
The Occupiers List,
The Old Lodgers List,
The Special Non-resident List,

besides lists of claimants, &c., in each case.

Where a parish is situated partly within and partly without the boundary of a parliamentary county or borough, or a municipal borough, or an administrative county, each part of such parish is treated as a separate parish.[4]

On or before the 18th July, the Town Clerk, or Clerk of the County Council will also send to the Overseers the "corrupt and illegal practices list," if there is such a list."[5]

---

[1] Registration Act, 1885, sec. 7.
[2] See the County Electors Act, 1888, sec. 14.
[3] Registration Act, 1885, sec. 7.
[4] *Ib.*, sec. 9.
[5] See *post*, p. 226.

Occupiers list.[1] The Overseers prepare, on or before the 31st July, besides the exclusively parliamentary lists, the "Occupiers List," which is a list of persons entitled, in respect of the occupation of property in the parish, to be registered as parliamentary voters, or as county electors or burgesses, or both as parliamentary voters and as county electors or burgesses, as the case may be.

The occupiers list is made out in three divisions, the first division containing the names of persons entitled to be registered both as parliamentary voters (in respect of occupation), and as county electors or burgesses; the second division containing the names of persons entitled to be registered as parliamentary voters alone, and the third division containing the names of persons entitled to be registered as county electors or burgesses, but not as parliamentary voters, in respect of an occupation qualification.

Each division of the occupiers list is usually made out in the alphabetical order of the surnames;[2] but in certain cases a different order may be pursued.[3]

In any municipal borough, or in any parliamentary borough, co-extensive with, or partly co-extensive with a municipal borough, the Town Council may direct that the different divisions of the list shall be made out in the order of premises in the rate book, or as nearly thererto as will cause the order of houses in streets to be followed.

In any other parliamentary borough the Justices of the petty sessional division in which the borough is situated, or if the borough is situated in more than one petty sessional division, then the County Council, may in the same way direct the order of premises to be followed.[4]

If the parish is partly in one electoral division, ward of a borough, or polling district, and partly in another, the occupiers list must be made out in parts, in order that the final register can be conveniently made up in parts for separate use, in the several electoral divisions, wards, or polling districts.[5]

Non-Resident List.[6] The Overseers further, on or before the 31st July, prepare a list of persons qualified in all respects but residence, and who, though beyond the seven miles, yet reside within fifteen miles of the county or borough, as the case may be, as such

---

[1] Parliamentary and Municipal Registration Act, 1878, sec. 15.
[2] County Electors Act, 1888, sec. 4 (1).
[3] See also the County Electors Act, 1888, sec. 4.
[4] Representation of the People Act, 1867, sec. 34.
The Ballot Act, 1872, sec. 5.
The Parliamentary and Municipal Registration Act, 1878, sec. 21.
The County Electors Act, 1888, sec. 4.
[5] The Parliamentary and Municipal Registration Act, 1878, sec. 15.
The County Electors Act, 1888, sec. 4.
[6] Parliamentary and Municipal Registration Act, 1878, sec. 19.
Municipal Corporations Act, 1882, sec. 49.
The County Electors Act, 1888, sec. 12.

persons may be qualified to be County or Town Councillors, though not to vote. This List is called the "Special Non-resident List."

In order that the Overseers may have the requisite information for making their lists, the Registrars of births and deaths furnish them with returns of all deaths of persons of full age occurring within their parish.[1] The Overseers also obtain from the Relieving Officer of their parish information as to all persons who have, within the qualifying period, been in receipt of relief.[2]

Overseers obtain information as to rates and taxes.

The Oveerseers have also access to tax assessments, and the Assessors or Collectors of assessed taxes send them a list of all persons who, on the 20th July, have not paid the taxes that accrued on or before the 5th January.[3]

In order that ratepayers may have due warning that their rates, and that, where the qualification is the £10 occupation qualification, also the assessed taxes, must be paid to entitle them to be registered, the Overseers, on or before the 20th June, publish a notice to that effect, and if the rates that accrued in any case before the 5th January remain unpaid after the 1st June, they, on or before the 20th June, send, unless a previous demand note has been duly sent, a personal notice to each ratepayer so in arrear.

If the rates remain unpaid after the 20th July, the ratepayer ceases to be qualified to be registered as an elector. On or before the 22nd July, the Overseers make out a list of persons so disqualified and retain the same for public inspection.[4]

Publication of lists.[5]

The Overseers have written or printed a number of copies of the occupiers list and the non-resident list, which lists, together with the corrupt practices list, they, on or before 1st August, publish, by fixing them in certain public places. They also retain copies of all these lists for public inspection, and furnish copies of them, if required, for sale.

Claim to be registered.[6]

Any person whose name has been improperly omitted from the list of electors or the non-resident list thus prepared for a parish, may, on or before the 20th August, send notice to the Overseers claiming to have his name inserted. And if a person's name has been improperly inserted in the corrupt and illegal practices list, he may claim to have it omitted from that list.

---

[1] The Parliamentary and Municipal Registration Act, 1878, sec. 11.
[2] *Ib.*, sec. 12.
[3] Registration Act, 1843, sec. 12.
[4] Registration Act, 1843, sec. 11.
Representation of the People Act, 1867, secs. 28, 29.
The Parliamentary and Municipal Registration Act, 1878, sec. 10.
[5] Registration Act, 1843, secs. 13, 23-26.
Parliamentary and Municipal Registration Act, 1878, sec. 9.
Registration Act, 1885, sec. 1; County Electors Act, 1888, sec. 4.
[6] Registration Act, 1843, sec. 15.
Registration Act, 1885, sec. 3.
For forms, see *post*, p. 355.

Correction of Mistakes.[1]

Also any person entered upon such a list, concerning whom there is any mistake in such list, may, whether or not he has received notice of objection, make a declaration before a Justice of the Peace or a Commissioner to administer oaths correcting such mistake.

This declaration must be sent to the Town Clerk or Clerk of the County Council, as the case may be, on or before the 5th September, and must be indorsed by him. The declaration so indorsed is evidence before the Revising Barrister.

Objections

Any person on any list of burgesses, or of county electors in a county, may object to the name of any other person on a list of county electors or burgesses for any parish in that county.[2]

Where an objection is made, notice of such objection must be sent to the Overseers of the parish of the person objected to. At the same time notice of objection must be sent to the person objected to, specifying the ground of objection.[3]

Objections may be withdrawn either partially or wholly on notice being sent not less than seven days before the day appointed for the holding of the final court of revision of the list to which the objection relates. Objections in the case of the death of an objector may be revived on notice by any person qualified to have made the objection in the first instance. Notices of withdrawal and revival are sent, in municipal or parliamentary boroughs, to the Town Clerk, elsewhere to the Overseers. Notices are also sent to the person objected to.[4]

Lists of Claimants and persons objected to.[5]

The Overseers on or before the 25th of August make out lists of claimants and of persons objected to. These lists they publish (on or before the 25th of August) and keep copies of, for public inspection and for sale in the same way as the occupiers lists.

Inspection of documents in hands of Overseers.

The following provisions have been made with regard to the inspection of documents in the hands of the overseers.

---

[1] Parliamentary and Municipal Registration Act, 1878, secs. 24, 25, County Electors Act, 1888, sec. 6. For forms, see *post*, p. 356.

[2] County Electors Act, 1888, sec. 4.

[3] Registration Act, 1843, sec. 17.
Parliamentary and Municipal Registration Act, 1878, sec. 26.
County Voters Registration Act, 1865 (*28 Vict. c. 36*) secs. 7, 8.
For forms, see *post*, p. 355.

[4] Parliamentary and Municipal Registration Act, 1878, sec, 27.
Registration Act, 1885, sec. 1.
County Electors Act, 1888, sec. 4.

[5] Registration Act, 1843, secs. 15, 18.
Registration Act, 1885, sec. 3.

Any person may inspect copies of all lists required to be published, all original notices of claims and objections, and the lists that the Assessors or Collectors of taxes may have sent to the Overseers of those persons who are in arrears with their taxes.

Any registered elector for the county or borough in which the parish is situated may inspect the rate books and returns made by the Registrar of births and deaths.

Copies of Lists to be sent to Town Clerk and Clerk of County Council.

On or before the 25th August the Overseers of a parish in a municipal borough send, among other things, copies of the occupiers list and of the claim and objection lists for their parish to the Town Clerk of the borough in which the parish is situated, and also, if the parish is not in a Parliamentary borough, to the Clerk of the County Council. If the parish is not within a municipal borough the Overseers send copies to the Clerk of the County Council, and also, if the parish is within a parliamentary borough, to the Town Clerk of the borough.[1]

Revising Barrister.

For the purpose of the revision and correction of the lists prepared by the Overseers, Revising Barristers are appointed for every county and every parliamentary borough. The following statutes deal with the qualification and appointment of revising barristers :—

The Registration Act, 1843, secs. 28, 29.

The Registration Act, 1868, sec. 25.

The Revising Barristers Act, 1873 (*36 & 37 Vict. c. 70*), secs. 1 and 3.

The Revising Barristers Act, 1874 (*37 & 38 Vict. c. 53*).

The Revising Barristers Act, 1886 (*49 & 50 Vict. c. 42*)

The County Electors Act, 1888.

The lists for every parish in a parliamentary borough, or in a municipal borough which is as to any part co-extensive with a parliamentary borough, are revised by the Revising Barrister of the parliamentary borough. The lists for other parishes are revised by the Revising Barrister for the county, or part of a county, in which they are situated. The Revising Barristers hold open courts between the 8th September and the 12th October at convenient times and places, of which due notice is given beforehand.[2]

---

[1] County Electors Act, 1888, sec. 4.

[2] Registration Act, 1843, secs. 30-33
Registration Act, 1885, sec. 4.
The County Electors Act, 1888, secs. 4, 6.

Town Clerks, Clerks of County Councils, and Overseers attend at these Courts and produce the parish lists of county electors, burgesses, claimants, persons objected to, &c., together with rate books and returns of Registrars of deaths and Tax Collectors, the original notices of claims and objections, &c.[1]

Proceedings before Revising Barrister.[2]

In proceedings before the Revising Barrister his decision is final as to facts and as to the admissibility of evidence.

In the course of proceedings before the Revising Barrister:

1st. The Barrister must correct any mistake that is proved to him to have been made in any list; that is, any slight mistake which is not calculated to mislead.[3]

2nd. The Barrister may, at his discretion, correct any mistake that is proved to him to have been made in any claim or notice of objection, and if he exercises his discretion the High Court will not interfere.[4]

3rd. He must expunge the name of every person, whether objected to or not, whose qualification as stated in any list is insufficient in law to qualify him. But so long as the qualification is good on the face of it, he must retain the name if not objected to, even if he know, as a fact, that there can be no such qualification.[5]

4th. He must expunge the name of every person who, whether objected to or not, is proved to him to be dead.

5th. He must expunge the name of every person whose name, residence, or the nature of whose qualifying property is omitted or insufficiently described for the purpose of identification. But if the matter omitted or insufficiently described is supplied to his satisfaction before he has completed his revision of the list in question, he must reinstate the name.

6th. He must expunge the name of every person, whether objected to or not, where it is proved to him that such person was on the 31st July, incapacitated by law or statute from voting for the borough or county to which the list relates.

This provision applies to persons expressly disqualified by convicton for election offences, &c., and not to cases in which a person is disqualified merely through not having the requisite qualification.[6]

Where it appears to the Revising Barrister, that a person not named in the corrupt and illegal practices list, is subject to have his name inserted in that list, he must (whether an objection to the omission of his name from the list has been made or not), after giving such person an opportunity of making a statement, insert his name in that list, besides expunging his name from the lists of county electors, &c.

7th. Before expunging the name of any person not objected to, the Barrister, if

---

[1] Registration Act, 1843, secs. 34, 35.

[2] Parliamentary and Municipal Registration Act, 1878, sec. 28.
As to conduct of proceedings, &c., see *ib.*, secs. 29, 36, 38, 39; see also Registration Act, 1843, sec. 41, &c.

[3] See Wood *v.* Willesden, 2 C.B. 15.
Elliot *v.* St. Mary Within, 4 C.B. 76.

[4] Adams *v.* Bostock, 8 Q.B.D. 259.
James *v.* Howarth, 5 C.P.D. 225.
Pickard *v.* Baylis, S.C.P.D. 235.

[5] Smith *v.* James, L.R., 1 C.P. 138.

[6] See Hayward *v.* Smith, 5 C.P.D. 231.
Doulton *v.* Hulse, 18 Q.B.D. 421.

he thinks proper, may cause notice to be given to such person, or left at his usual or last known residence.

8th. Subject to the above provisions, the Barrister retains the name of every person not objected to, and also the name of every person objected to, unless the objector appears in person or by some person on his behalf to support his objection.

9th. If the objector appears, he must, unless he is an Overseer, prove that he gave the proper notices; and that there is a *prima facie* ground for his objection.

If he succeeds in proving so much, or if the objector be an Overseer, the name of the person objected to is expunged, unless he appears personally or by some one else on his behalf and proves his qualification.

10th. No proof can be given before the Revising Barrister of any other qualification than that which is on the list or claim.

Where a person is entered more than once as a burgess on the lists for a municipal borough, the Revising Barrister will retain one of such entries for voting, and place against the other or others a note to the effect that the person is not entitled to vote in respect of the qualification therein mentioned, as he is on the list for voting in respect of another qualification. Double Entry.[1]

The elector may, by notice in writing delivered to the Revising Barrister at the opening of his first revision court, select the entry to be retained, and in making a selection may select one entry for voting as a burgess and another for voting at a parliamentary election.

If the elector, do not so select the entry to be retained, the Revising Barrister may, it seems, select the entry to be retained at his discretion.

These provisions with regard to double entry do not extend to county electors, who may be entered in respect of as many qualifications as they have, though whether they may vote more than once at a county election for the same county seems doubtful.[2]

The Revising Barrister revises the lists of claimants separately in the same manner as the other lists; but the Revising Barrister will require *prima facie* proof of the validity of each claim, and any person may object there and then to the retention of any person's name without having given any notice.[3]

An appeal lies from the decision of a Revising Barrister to a Divisional Court of the Queen's Bench Division on a point of law. The aggrieved person intending to appeal, or some one on his behalf, must give a notice in writing to the Barrister before the rising of the Court, whereupon the Barrister, if he thinks it a proper case, must within ten days after the conclusion of the revision state the material facts and his decision thereon, in the form of a special case. Appeal from Revising Barrister.[4]

---

[1] Parliamentary and Municipal Registration Act, 1878, sec. 28.
Registration Act, 1885, secs. 4, 5.

[2] County Electors Act, 1888, sec. 7.

[3] Registration Act, 1843, sec. 39.
Registration Act, 1885, sec. 4.

[4] Registration Act, 1843, secs. 42, 43.
Parliamentary and Municipal Registration Act, 1878, secs 35, 38.
County Electors Act, 1888, sec. 6.
As to the method of conducting appeals, and as to the consolidation of appeals where they depend on the same point, see the Registration Act, 1843, secs. 44, 45, 66-70, the County Electors Act, secs. 6, &c.

The appellant, or some one on his behalf, then at the end of such case writes the declaration: "I appeal from this decision." The Barrister then endorses the statement with the name of the county and polling district or borough, and of the parish to which the same relates, and with the names and places of abode of the appellant and respondent, dates and signs the same, and delivers it to the appellant. If required he delivers another copy of the case and indorsement to the respondent. The party in whose favour the decision was given is the respondent, or if there be no such person or he decline, some other person interested and consenting, or the Overseers, or the Town Clerk, or Clerk of the County Council, may be the respondent or respondents. Moreover, the Barrister may in any case make the Town Clerk or Clerk of the County Council an additional respondent.

If the Barrister refuse to state a case, the aggrieved party may apply to the High Court for a rule calling upon the Revising Barrister to state a case. The aggrieved party must make his application for such a rule within a month of the refusal, and must support his application by affidavits.[1]

Preparation of final register.

After the lists have been revised by the Barrister he delivers the revised lists to the Clerk of the County Council of the county; or if the list relates to a borough, to the Town Clerk of the borough, who must send copies of such revised lists to the Clerk of the County Council, and from these lists the Clerks of the County Council and Town Clerks prepare and have printed the various rolls of electors necessary, arranging these lists in parts, so that the parts can be put together for use in electoral divisions, boroughs, wards of boroughs, and polling districts.[2] In making out these lists the list for each polling district is distinguished by a letter, and the name of each elector by a number, so that there is one complete set of numbers for each polling district. Each part of each register is made in alphabetical order of surnames, except that the parts of the register relating to parishes in which the lists have been made out in the order of premises, may follow the same order.

Expenses of Registration.[3]

We have next to inquire as to the application of the sums received in the course of the registration of voters from the sale of copies of lists, &c.; and as to the funds out of which the expenses are defrayed.

1st. The sums received by Overseers are applied, and their expenses defrayed as follows:—

---

[1] Parliamentary and Municipal Registration Act, 1878, sec. 37.

[2] Municipal Corporations Act, 1882, secs. 45, 48, 71.
County Electors Act, 1888, sec. 7.

[3] Registration Act, 1843, secs. 53-57.
Representation of the People Act, 1867, sec. 31.
Parliamentary Registration Act, 1868, secs. 31, 32.
Parliamentary and Municipal Registration Act, 1878, sec. 30.
Registration Act, 1885, secs. 8, 14.
County Electors Act, 1888, sec. 8.

i. In parishes not within a municipal borough the receipts are applied in the relief of the poor rate and the expenses defrayed out of the poor rate.

ii. In a parish which is in a municipal borough, and also in a parliamentary borough, the sums received and the expenses incurred in the registration of burgesses and parliamentary voters for the borough are applied in aid of, and defrayed out of, the poor rates and the borough fund respectively in equal shares.

It should be pointed out that the registration of county parliamentary voters in such a parish is conducted quite independently, and that the receipts and expenses in respect thereof are applied in aid of, and paid out of the poor rates respectively.

iii. In a parish in a municipal borough, and not in a parliamentary borough, the sums received, and the expenses incurred in the registration of burgesses and parliamentary voters for the county in respect of the occupation franchise are applied in aid of, and defrayed out of the poor rates, and in aid of, and out of the borough fund, respectively, in equal shares. The registration of other parliamentary voters for such a parish is managed quite independently in pursuance of a precept from the Clerk of the County Council, and the receipts and expenses are applied in aid of, and defrayed out of the poor rates entirely.

The Overseers of a parish must get a certificate from the Revising Barrister allowing their expenses before they can charge them in their accounts.

2nd. The expenses of the Clerk of the County Council in connection with the registration of both county electors and parliamentary voters of all kinds are defrayed out of the county fund, and the receipts are paid into the same fund; but where a Clerk of a County Council acts in the registration of parliamentary voters beyond the limits of the administrative county, a contribution must be made by the County Council of any other administrative county or the Town Council of any county borough within which he acts.[1]

3rd. The expenses of Town Clerks of parliamentary boroughs that are not as to any part co-extensive with municipal boroughs are, it seems, defrayed as follows:—

i. The receipts and expenses connected with the registration of county electors are paid into and out of the county fund.

ii. The receipts and expenses connected with the registration of parliamentary voters are respectively paid to and by the Overseers of each parish in aid of and out of the poor rate in proportion to the number of parliamentary voters registered for each parish.

Seeing that the registration of these parliamentary voters is conducted simultaneously with the registration of county electors, it will be very difficult to divide the receipts and expenses. The Town Clerk will have to lay his accounts before the County Council, who will make an Order for the amount payable to him out of the county fund, and will also grant a certificate for the payment of the contribution of the parishes in respect of the parliamentary expenses.

4th. The expenses of Town Clerks of parliamentary boroughs that comprise municipal boroughs (in this case the Town Clerk of the municipal borough acts as the Town Clerk of the parliamentary borough) will, it seems, be defrayed, and the receipts applied as follows:—

i. The receipts and expenses of so much of the area as is within both the municipa and parliamentary boundaries will be, as to one half, paid into and out of the

---

[1] See the Registration Act, 1885, sec. 14.

borough fund, and as to the other half, to or by the Overseers of the parishes, in aid of and out of the poor rate, in proportion to the number of parliamentary voters registered for the different parishes. The Orders for contributions from the various parishes will be made by the Town Council.

ii. The receipts and expenses of so much of the area as is within the limits of the parliamentary borough, but not within the limits of the municipal borough will be applied and paid as follows: -The receipts and expenses connected with the registration of county electors will be paid into and out of the borough fund. The receipts and expenses connected with the registration of parliamentary voters will be paid to and by the Overseers of the parishes in aid of and out of the poor rate in proportion to the number of parliamentary voters registered for each parish, the Orders for contributions from the parishes being made by the Town Council.

The Revising Barrister will apportion the receipts and expenses between the areas, within or without the municipal limits, but apparently he has no jurisdiction to decide how the receipts and expenses are to be apportioned between the county electors and parliamentary voters.

5th. It seems very doubtful how the receipts and expenses of Town Clerks of municipal boroughs that are not co-extensive with, or comprised in parliamentary boroughs should be applied and defrayed respectively. Perhaps the receipts and expenses should be respectively paid out of and into the county and borough fund in equal shares; but this is far from clear.

Remuneration of Revising Barristers.

Revising Barristers are paid 250 guineas each by the Treasury. The Treasury will make an Order on the County Councils for a contribution towards the expenses of the Revising Barristers for the circuit in which such county is situated; the Treasury may vary their Order, but subject to such variation, the Order is final. Boroughs do not contribute separately towards the remuneration of Revising Barristers.

Provisions for 1888.[1]

We must now point out the special provision for the year 1888.

1st. The duties of the Clerks of the Council are to be exercised by the Clerk of the Peace. Where a county boundary will be altered under the Local Government Act, 1888, *i.e.*, where any urban sanitary district is at present in two counties, the Clerks of the Peace must come to an arrangement, under which the list of county electors for the part about to be transferred can be used as part of the register of electors of the county to which it is to be transferred.

2nd. The dates for the various proceedings are altered, but the qualifying period is the same as usual, and will be reckoned up to the 15th July.

3rd. The duties that will in certain cases in future years fall on Town Clerks, are performed by the Clerks of the Peace.

4th. Special arrangements are made for the expenses of registration.

---

[1] See County Electors Act, 1888, and Local Government Act, 1888, sec. 76.

CHAPTER VII.

ELECTION OF COUNTY AND TOWN COUNCILS.

GENERAL elections of County Councillors will, after the first election in 1889, take place triennially on the 1st November in 1891, 1894, and so on. General elections of Town Councillors take place on November 1st, annually. If the 1st November be a Sunday, or day of public fast, humiliation, or thanksgiving, the election will take place the next day after, which is not Sunday, &c. General Election of Councillors.[1]

If a casual vacancy occur among the County Councillors or Town Councillors, the election to fill it up must be held on a day to be fixed by the Chairman of the County Council, or Mayor, as the case may be, within fourteen days after notice in writing of the vacancy has been given to the Chairman or Clerk of the County Council, or Mayor, or Town Clerk, as the case may be, by two county electors or burgesses, but if a vacancy occurs among the County Councillors within six months before the general election of County Councillors, it is not to be filled up till the general election. Election in case of a casual vacancy.[2]

As the proceedings at, and the law respecting, elections of County Councillors and Town Councillors are almost the same, they will be discussed together. The questions to be considered are—

The qualification of a Councillor.

The preparation for election, including the nomination of candidates.

The poll in the case of contested elections.

The law with regard to the conduct of a candidate, and the questioning of improper elections.

The acceptance, loss, and resignation of office, &c.

---

[1] Municipal Corporations Act, 1882, secs. 52, 230. Local Government Act, 1888, sec. 75.

[2] Municipal Corporations Act, 1882, secs. 40, 66. Local Government Act, 1888, sec. 75.

The principal statutory provisions on the subject are contained in—

The Ballot Act, 1872 (*35 & 36 Vict. c. 33.*)

The Municipal Corporations Act, 1882.

The Municipal Elections (Corrupt and Illegal Practices) Act, 1884 (*47 & 48 Vict. c. 70.*)

The Local Government Act, 1888.

Qualification of Councillor.[1]

A person to be qualified for the office of County Councillor must—

1st. Be qualified as a county elector of the county, or as a burgess of a borough in the administrative county, and be enrolled as such; or

2nd. Be qualified to be, and be, enrolled upon the special non-resident list for the county or for some borough in the administrative county, and be possessed of a property qualification; or

3rd. Be registered as a parliamentary voter for the county or a division of the county in respect of the ownership of property in the administrative county; or

4th. Be a peer owning property in the county.

A person to be qualified to be elected Town Councillor must—

1st. Be qualified and enrolled as a burgess of the borough; or

2nd. Be qualified to be, and be, enrolled upon the special non-resident list for the borough, and be possessed of a property qualification.

It is to be observed, that entry upon the register is not, in the case of a Councillor, conclusive, as it is in the case of an elector, but the qualification must exist in fact[2] except, perhaps, in the case of a County Councillor qualified by registration as a parliamentary voter in respect of the ownership of property, in which case the register seems to be conclusive.

The property qualification for a non-resident is as follows:—

A person to be qualified must—

1st. Have real or personal property, or both, to the value of £1000, or if the office be that of Town Councillor for a borough which has, or on the 18th August, 1882, had[3] less than four wards, £500; or

2nd. Be rated to the poor rate on the annual value of £30, or if the office be that of Town Councillor

---

[1] Municipal Corporations Act, 1882, secs. 11, 12. Local Government Act, 1888, sec. 2.

[2] Flintham v. Roxburgh, 17 Q.B.D., 44.

[3] Municipal Corporations Act, 1882, sec. 30.

for a borough which has, or on the 18th August, 1882, had, less than four wards, £15.

A person otherwise qualified to be elected Councillor is disqualified in the following cases :—

i. A person is disqualified to be elected or to be a Councillor if he holds any office or place of profit in the gift of the Council other than that of Mayor or Chairman of the Council, or, in the case of a Town Council, of Sheriff or of Elective Auditor, or, in the case of a County Council, of Coroner for the county.

ii. A person is disqualified to be elected or to be a Town Councillor if he is in holy orders, or is the regular member of a dissenting congregation, but such a person may be a County Councillor.

iii. A person is disqualified to be elected or to be a Councillor if he has, directly or indirectly, any share or interest in any contract with or on behalf of the Council, or is employed by or on behalf of the Council, or is in partnership with any person interested in such a contract or employment; but he may, without disqualification, have a share or interest in—

Any lease, sale, or purchase of any land, or any agreement for the same

Any agreement for the loan of money.

Any newspaper in which any advertisement relating to the affairs of the county or borough, or of the County or Town Council, is inserted.

Any company which contracts with the Council for the lighting or supplying with water, or insuring against fire, any part of the county or borough.

Any railway company or company incorporated by Act of Parliament or Royal Charter, or under the Companies Act, 1862.

iv. An undischarged bankrupt is disqualified to be elected or to be a Councillor.[1]

v. A person may lie under some other statutory disqualification, *e.g.*, owing to offences against election law.

The preliminary steps towards an election are as follows :— Nine days at least before the day for the election of a councillor, notice must be published as follows :—

Preparation for election of Councillors.[1]

i. Notice of the election of a Town Councillor is signed by the Town Clerk, and affixed by him on the Town

[1] Municipal Corporations Act, 1882, sec. 39.

Hall, and also if the election is a ward election, in some conspicuous place in the ward.[1]

ii. Notice of the election of a County Councillor must be signed by the Returning Officer or his deputy, and affixed by him in some conspicuous place in the electoral division for which the election is about to take place. If the electoral division is co-extensive with or comprised in a borough, the notice is signed by the Town Clerk, and affixed by him in some conspicuous place in the electoral division. In this case, it might be advisable to affix a notice on the Town Hall, whether the Town Hall happens to be within the electoral division or not.[3]

Nomination of candidates.

After the notice of election is given, every candidate for election must be nominated; a proceeding in reference to which rules are contained in schedule 3, part II. to the Municipal Corporations Act, 1882.[4] The application of these rules is extended to the cases of elections of County Councillors by the Local Government Act, 1888, sec. 75, subject to the following provisions:—

i. The Returning Officer or his deputy will perform the duties of the Mayor and of the Town Clerk; but where the election is for an electoral division co-extensive with, or wholly comprised in, a borough, the Mayor, or an Alderman appointed for that purpose, as the case may be, must act as deputy for the Returning Officer, in pursuance of a writ directed to him for that purpose from the Returning Officer; and, in that case, also, the Town Clerk must peform the duties assigned to him in the rules.

ii. Some place fixed by the Returning Officer must, except where the election is in a borough, be substituted for the Town Clerk's office, and, as respects the hearing of objections to nomination papers, for the Town Hall; but such place must, if the electoral division is the whole or part of an urban sanitary district, be in that district, and in any other case such place must be in the electoral division or in an adjoining electoral division.

iii. The period between nomination and election may be such period, not exceeding six days, as the Returning Officer may fix.

---

1 Municipal Corporations Act, 1882, sec. 54.
2 As to Returning Officer, see next page.
3 Local Government Act. 1888, s. 75.
4 See *post*, p. 351.

iv. Other obvious modifications must, of course, be made, such as the substitution of county elector for burgess, &c.

Candidates being duly nominated the election takes place as follows :— Election.[1]

- If the number of valid nominations exceeds that of vacancies the Councillors are elected from among the persons nominated, in the manner explained below—
- If the number of valid nominations is the same as that of vacancies, the persons nominated are elected.
- If the number of valid nominations is less than that of vacancies, the persons nominated are elected, and those retiring Councillors who were highest at the poll at their elections, or, if the poll was equal, those who are selected for that purpose by the Chairman of the County Council, or Mayor, as the case may be, continue in their office to make up the required number.
- If there is no valid nomination the retiring Councillors remain in office.

The last two provisions do not, of course, apply to the first election of County Councillors. At the first election an insufficient number of valid nominations will create a casual vacancy. But if there be from such a cause or any other cause a completely insufficient election, the Local Government Board will take steps to rectify matters.[2]

In the case of a contested election certain duties are performed by the Returning Officer, who, in the case of an election of a County Councillor, is appointed by the County Council. The County Returning Officer may by writing under his hand appoint a deputy for the discharge of all or any of his duties. In the case of an election for an electoral division co-extensive with or wholly comprised in a borough the Mayor or an Alderman appointed for that purpose by the Town Council must act as deputy in pursuance of a writ directed to him from the County Returning Officer. Returning Officer.[3]

In elections of Town Councillors the Mayor, or if the borough is divided into wards, an Alderman appointed by the Town Council, is Returning Officer. But if the Mayor is himself a candidate the Council may appoint a Returning Officer in his stead. At the first election of County Councillors the Sheriff will act as Returning Officer, but if he wishes to

---

[1] Municipal Corporations Act, 1882, sec. 56.
[2] Local Government Act, 1888, sec. 108.
[3] *Ib.*, s. 75.
Municipal Corporations Act, 1882, sec. 53.

stand as a candidate the Quarter Sessions will, at his request, appoint some other person.[1]

Expenses of Returning Officers.[2]

The costs of holding elections of County Councillors, as far as they are not otherwise provided for, must be paid out of the county fund. The costs must not exceed those allowed by Part I. of the first schedule to the Parliamentary Election (Returning Officers) Act, 1875 (*38 & 39 Vict. c. 82*), as amended by the Parliamentary Elections (Returning Officers) Act (1875) Amendment Act, 1886 (*49 & 50 Vict. c. 57*), or by such scale as the County Council may, from time to time, frame.

The Returning Officer must, within 21 days after the day on which the return is made of the persons elected, send a detailed account of his charges to the County Council from whom he claims payment, stating where the vouchers relating to the account may be seen. The Council may, at any time within one month from the receipt of the account, apply to the County Court for a taxation of the account; an appeal lies from the taxation of the County Court to the Queen's Bench Division of the High Court.

In order that the Returning Officer may have the materials for making up his account in time, it is provided that all claims for work, &c., under any contract made by or on behalf of the Returning Officer for the purposes of an election must be made in a detailed form, in writing, within fourteen days after the day on which the return of the persons elected is made.

Expenses of borough elections.[3]

Expenses of borough elections not otherwise provided for are payable out of the borough fund.

As a preliminary step to a contested election, the various electoral areas are, where it is necessary, divided into polling districts.

Polling districts.[4]

For the first election of County Councillors the Returning Officer may, if he thinks fit, divide any electoral division into polling districts, but the polling districts must be such that separate parts of the register of electors are made out for them.

Boroughs are divided into polling districts by the Town Councils, and subsequent divisions of electoral divisions of counties into polling districts will be made by the County Council.

Division of parliamentary county into polling districts

We may here indicate the provisions made for the division of parliamentary counties and boroughs into polling districts for the purposes of parliamentary elections. The term "parliamentary county" is defined in the Registration Act, 1885, as meaning a county returning a member or members to serve in Parliament,

---

[1] Local Government Act, 1888, sec. 103.

[2] Local Government Act, 1888, secs. 75, 103.
Parliamentary Elections (Returning Officers) Act, 1875, secs. 4-7.
Parliamentary Elections (Returning Officers) Act (1875) Amendment Act, 1886.

[3] Municipal Corporations Act, 1882, sec. 140, and 5th schedule.

[4] Local Government Act, 1888, sec. 103.
Municipal Corporations Act, 1882, s. 64.

[5] Representation of the People Act, 1867, sec. 34.
Corrupt and Illegal Practices Prevention Act, 1883 (*46 & 47 Vict. c. 51*) sec. 47.
Registration Act, 1885, secs. 14, 15.

and where a county is divided for the purpose of such return, as meaning a division of such county. Every parliamentary county within the meaning of this definition has been divided into polling districts by the Quarter Sessions. After the appointed day these districts may from time to time be altered by the County Council having authority for this purpose in that parliamentary county. County boroughs are considered for this purpose as situated in the counties of County Councils to which they are assigned in schedule 3 to the Local Government Act, 1888, and where a parliamentary county is wholly comprised within the county of one County Council in that sense it may be divided into polling districts by such County Council; but where a parliamentary county is situated in more than one county of a County Council it must be divided by the County Council of that county within which the greater part of it is situated. In the latter case, however a Joint Committee may be appointed by the County Councils of the various counties into which the parliamentary county extends to take the division into consideration, and the County Council with authority to make the division may act on their report.

Division of parliamentary borough into polling districts[1]

The division of a parliamentary borough into polling districts is effected by the following bodies:—

i. If any part of the parliamentary borough is co-extensive with or comprised in a municipal borough—the Town Council.

ii. If no part of the parliamentary borough is comprised in a municipal borough, but the parliamentary borough is situated wholly in one petty sessional division—the Justices of that division in Petty Sessions.

iii. In other cases—the County Council.

Contested election.

If a contested election is about to take place, the Returning Officer, at least four days before, gives public notice of the situation, division, and allotment of polling places for taking the poll at the election, and of the description of persons entitled to vote at the election, and at each polling station. In the case of a ward election in a borough, this duty, however, falls on the Mayor instead of the Returning Alderman.

It will also be the duty of the Returning Officer, or, in the case of a ward election in a borough, of the mayor, to provide suitable rooms for polling stations, and to provide every polling station with a ballot box, and ballot papers, and screened compartments for voting and other necessaries, and also with copies of such parts of the register of electors as contain the names of the electors allotted to vote at such polling station.[2]

The method of conducting the poll is laid down in the Ballot Act, 1872, as modified by the Municipal Corporations

[1] Representation of the People Act, 1867, sec. 34.
Ballot Act, 1872, sec. 5.
Registration Act, 1885, sec. 13.
Local Government Act, 1888, sec. 3.

[2] Ballot Act, 1872, sec. 8.
Municipal Corporations Act, 1882, schedule 3, Part III.
Local Government Act, 1888, sec. 75.

Act, 1882, sec. 58, and the Local Government Act, 1888. The hours of poll are from 8 a.m. till 8 p.m.[1] Rules for the conduct of the election are given in a schedule to the Ballot Act. It must, however, be observed that, while the Ballot Act, 1872, itself must be strictly complied with, the rules are merely directory, so that it is not every breach of these rules that would form a ground for questioning the election or the validity of a vote.[2] The following is a brief account of the proceedings at the poll :—

Proceedings at the Poll.[3]

The Returning Officer appoints a Presiding Officer for each station to keep order, &c. Each candidate may apparently appoint an agent on his behalf at each polling station.[4] Each ballot paper contains a list of the candidates described as in their respective nomination papers, and arranged alphabetically.

Before any person is admitted to vote, the Presiding Officer must, if required by two electors, or by a candidate or his agent, put to any person offering to vote, on his presenting himself to vote, one or both of the following questions :—

i. Are you the person enrolled in the register of electors for this electoral division, borough, or ward, as follows?—(*reading the whole entry from the Register.*)

ii. Have you already voted at the present election?—(*add in the case of a ward election in a borough*, "in this or any other ward?")[5]

Immediately before a ballot paper is delivered to an elector, it is marked on with the official mark, either on both sides, or stamped or perforated in such a manner as to show on both sides. The number, name, and description of the elector, as stated in the copy of the register of electors, is then called out, and the number of the elector is marked on the counterfoil, and a mark is placed in the register of electors, against the number of the elector, to denote that he has received a ballot paper, but without showing the particular ballot paper which he has received. The elector on receiving the ballot paper goes into one of the compartments in the polling station, and there marks his paper, and folds it up so as to conceal his vote, and then puts his paper, so folded up, into the ballot box.

If any elector is blind, or unable from physical causes to vote in the manner prescribed; or if any elector is of the Jewish persuasion, and objects (the poll being on Saturday) on religious grounds to vote in the manner prescribed; or if any voter declares that he is unable to read; then the Presiding Officer, upon the application of the elector, and in the presence of the candidates' agents, must cause the vote of an elector in such a position to be marked on a ballot paper for him, and the ballot paper to be placed in the ballot box, and the name and number of every elector whose vote is so marked, is entered on a list called "The list of votes marked by the Presiding Officer."

A voter unable to read must have a declaration of inability to read in the

---

[1] Election (Hours of Poll) Act, 1885 (*48 Vict. c. 10*).

[2] Ballot Act, 1872, sec. 13.

[3] See Ballot Act, 1872, secs. 1, 8-10, and Schedules 1 and 2.
Municipal Corporations Act, 1882, sec. 58, and Schedule 3, Part III
Local Government Act, 1888, sec. 75.

[4] See Municipal Corporations Act, 1882, sec. 58. Ballot Act, 1872, Schedule 1, rule 57, and see Clementson *v.* Mason, L.R. 10 C.P., 209.

[5] See Municipal Corporations Act, 1882, sec. 59.

form given in schedule 2 to the Ballot Act, 1872, read over to him, and sign it with his mark before he will be allowed to vote.

If a person, representing himself to be a particular elector named on the register of electors, applies for a ballot paper after another person has voted as such elector, the applicant is, upon duly answering the questions permitted to be asked of voters at the time of polling, entitled to mark a ballot paper in the same manner as any other voter, but the ballot paper, which is called a tendered ballot paper, is of a different colour to the other ballot papers, and instead of being put into the ballot box must be given to the Presiding Officer. The Presiding Officer indorses it with the name of the voter, and his number in the roll of electors, and sets it aside in a separate packet. The name of the voter, and his number on the register of electors, is entered on a list called the tendered votes list.

If a voter accidentally spoils his ballot paper, he may deliver the spoilt ballot paper to the Presiding Officer, and on satisfying him that the ballot paper was spoilt by inadvertence, may obtain another ballot paper in place of it, and the spoilt ballot paper must be immediately cancelled.

The Presiding Officer of each station, as soon as practicable after the close of the poll, makes up in the presence of the candidates' agents, into separate packets, sealed with his own seal, and the seals of such of the candidates' agents as desire to affix their seals—

i. Each ballot box in use at his station, unopened, but with the key attached;
ii. The unused and spoilt ballot papers placed together;
iii. The tendered ballot papers;
iv. The marked copies of the register of electors;
v. The counterfoils of the ballot papers;
vi. The tendered votes list;
vii. The list of votes marked by the Presiding Officer;
viii. A statement of the number of voters whose votes are so marked under the heads of "physical incapacity," "Jews," and "unable to read;"
ix. The declarations of inability to read.

It is not quite certain that all these packets need be separate. In the schedule to the Ballot Act, packets 4 and 5 are spoken of together, and packets 6, 7, 8, and 9 are also spoken of together; but it may be best to keep them separate. These packets the Presiding Officer delivers to the Returning Officer.

The packets must be accompanied by a statement made by the Presiding Officer, showing the number of ballot papers entrusted to him, and accounting for them under the heads of ballot papers in the ballot box, unused, spoilt, and tendered ballot papers, which statement is called the ballot paper account.

Counting the votes.[1]

The Returning Officer must count the votes as soon after the close of the poll as practicable. The candidates may appoint agents to attend the counting. Notice in writing of the appointment must be given to the Returning Officer at least one clear day before the opening of the poll, giving the name and address of the agent. The Returning Officer must give notice in writing, to the agents so appointed, of the time and place at which he will begin to count the votes.

The Returning Officer, his assistants, the agents of the candidates and the candidates are the only persons who have a right to be present at the counting.

[1] Municipal Corporations Act, 1882, sec. 58. Ballot Act, 1872, Schedule 1.

The first step in the counting is for the Returning Officer to mix together all the ballot papers without showing the numbers on them, at the same time counting the number in each ballot box. The Returning Officer then proceeds with the counting. He indorses as "rejected," any ballot paper he considers invalid and adds to the indorsement "rejection objected to," if the agent of any candidate object to his rejection of the paper.

The counting is proceeded with as far as possible continuously, excluding however the hours between seven p.m. and nine a.m., except by arrangement with the agents, so that, except by such arrangement, the counting will begin the day after the poll.

During the night the ballot papers and other documents are placed in security under the seal of the Returning Officer and such of the candidates' agents as desire to affix their seal.

On the completion of the counting the Returning Officer seals up in separate packets the counted and rejected ballot papers. He must not unseal the packet of tendered ballot papers, the marked copy of the register of electors, or the counterfoils of the ballot papers.

The ballot paper account he checks by comparing it with the number of ballot papers recorded by him, and with the unused and spoilt ballot papers and the tendered votes. He re-seals, after examination, each packet which he unseals, and then forwards to the Clerk of the County Council, or if the election is an election of a Town Councillor, to the Town Clerk, all the packets of ballot papers in his possession, the ballot paper accounts, the tendered votes lists, the lists of votes marked by the Presiding Officer, the statements relating thereto, the declaration of inability to read, the packets of counterfoils, and the marked copies of the registers.

On each packet he indorses a description of its contents, the date of the election to which they relate and the name of the county or borough for which the election was held.

The Clerk of the County Council or Town Clerk, as the case may be, retains all these documents for a year, and then, unless otherwise directed by the Order of one of the High Courts, or of a County Court, or of an Election Court, or of the County Council, or the Town Council, as the case may be, will cause them to be destroyed.

If an election is uncontested the Returning Officer publishes a list of the persons elected before 11 a.m. on the day of election. If the election is contested, the Returning Officer gives public notice, as soon as possible after the counting of the votes, of the candidates elected and of the number of votes given for each candidate, whether elected or not.[1] In the case of the election of a County Councillor, he makes a formal return of the candidate elected to be Clerk of the County Council.

It seems that the election, however, is over as soon as the Returning Officer has ascertained the number of votes given for each candidate, and that his omission to give notice of election

---

[1] Municipal Corporations Act, 1882, secs. 57, 58.
Ballot Act, 1872, 1st schedule, sec. 45.

will not affect the validity thereof,[1] but the candidate elected will have to make a declaration before he may act.[2]

Qualification of Aldermen.

The next matter to consider is the election of Aldermen. The qualification of an Alderman is the same as that of a Councillor.[3]

Election of Aldermen.[4]

General elections of County Aldermen take place on the 7th November, of Borough Aldermen on the 9th November, every three years. The years in which elections of County Aldermen will take place, are 1891, 1894, &c. The years in which a general election of Borough Aldermen takes place depend on the particular circumstances of the case. If the 7th or 9th November be a Sunday or day of public fast, humiliation or thanksgiving, the general election of Aldermen takes place on the next day after that is not a Sunday, &c. If a casual vacancy occur in the office of Alderman the election must be held on a day to be fixed by the Chairman of the County Council or the Mayor, as the case may be, within 14 days after notice in writing of the vacancy has been given to the Chairman or Mayor or to the Clerk of the Council or Town Clerk.

At an election of County Aldermen, County Councillors alone have a vote, County Aldermen having none. At an election of Borough Aldermen, the Aldermen in office may vote. An outgoing Alderman, even if Mayor elect, has no vote. In the case of an equality of votes the Chairman of the meeting, even if not entitled to a vote in the first instance, has a casting vote. There is no nomination of Aldermen, and the election is conducted in this way:—Every person entitled to vote may vote for any number of persons not exceeding the number of vacancies, by signing and delivering at the meeting to the Chairman a voting paper containing the full names, places of abode, and descriptions of the persons for whom he votes.

The Chairman of the meeting, as soon as all the voting papers have been delivered to him, must openly produce and read them or cause them to be read, and then deliver them to the Clerk of the County Council or Town Clerk, as the case may be, to be kept for twelve months. The persons, not exceeding in number the vacancies to be filled, who have the greatest number of votes, are declared by the Chairman to be, and thereupon are elected.

---

[1] See R. *v.* Mayor of Bangor, 18 Q.B.D., 349.
[2] See *post*, p. 226.
[3] Municipal Corporations Act, 1882, sec. 14.
[4] *Ib.*, sec. 60, 66, 230; Local Government Act, 1888, secs. 2, 75.

Election of Chairman of County Council or Mayor.[1]

It remains to consider the election of the Chairman of a County Council or the Mayor of a borough.

The qualification of the Chairman or Mayor is the same as that of a Councillor. The ordinary election of the Chairman of a County Council takes place on the 7th November, and the ordinary election of the Mayor of a borough on the 9th November annually. This election must be the first business transacted at the meeting of the Council on that date, taking place before the election of Aldermen. Should a casual vacancy occur, the election must take place on a day to be fixed by the Clerk of the Council or the Town Clerk, as the case may be, within 14 days after notice in writing has been given him of the vacancy.

A County Alderman in office may vote at the election of the Chairman of County Council, but an outgoing Alderman has no vote. Borough Aldermen, including the outgoing Aldermen, may vote at the election of the Mayor. The Chairman of the meeting, even if not entitled to vote in the first instance, has a casting vote.

Prevention of corruption at elections, &c.[2]

We have now to deal with the provisions of the legislature intended to secure against corruption at elections, of members of County and Town Councils and the means by which an election wrongfully conducted may be petitioned against. The provisions of the legislature directed against corruption are of two kinds; the first directed against corruption in the ordinary sense of the word, the second laying down a series of regulations dealing with the conduct and legitimate expenses of candidates, offences against which are placed, to a certain extent, on the same footing as wilful corruption.

Offences against these provisions are divided into four classes.

1st. Corrupt practices.

2nd. Illegal practices.

3rd. Illegal payment, employment, and hiring.

4th. Offences not classed under any of these heads, but which subject the offenders to various penalties.

Election Petitions.[3]

An election may be questioned by petition, which is heard

---

[1] Municipal Corporations Act, sec. 15, 61, 66.
Local Government Act, 1888, sec. 75.

[2] Municipal Corporations Act, 1882, secs. 77, 81, 85, 86.
Municipal Elections (Corrupt and Illegal Practices) Act, 1884.

[3] Municipal Corporations Act, 1882, secs. 87-104.
Municipal Elections (Corrupt and Illegal Practices) Act, 1884., secs. 25-33.

in a special Court constituted for that purpose, called an Election Court, which will, besides inquiring into the validity of an election, report on any offences that may have been committed in the course of it. That report will entail some of the consequences of conviction of the offenders.

Consequences of offences against election law.

The consequences of corrupt practices, illegal practices, and other offences are of three kinds :—

1st. They subject the offender to a penalty.

2nd. They may, on an election petition, either invalidate the election entirely, creating a vacancy, or invalidate the election of the candidate elected alone, resulting in the election of some other candidate.

3rd. They either on conviction, or on the report of an Election Court, subject the offender to certain disqualifications.

Election agency.

It must be borne in mind that a candidate is in general responsible for the acts of his agents. A candidate may appoint agents expressly, either in writing or verbally; but a recognition or adoption on his part of a person's acts will be enough to cause that person to be deemed his agent. Some points in which the law concerning election agency differs from that concerning ordinary agency may be pointed out.

(1.) The Court will require much less evidence to establish the agency than in ordinary cases.

(2.) The candidate will be liable for acts of the agent outside the range of his authority, and even contrary to his express instructions, unless it is shown that the agent has intentionally acted unfairly towards the candidate, or has been in league with his opponents.

(3.) A candidate's agent can delegate his authority.

Offences against election law.

We proceed now, first, to give a list of the offences against election law; secondly, to show the consequences of these offences; and thirdly, to give the rules that must guide a candidate in his candidature.

The following are corrupt practices:—

1st. Bribery.

An elaborate definition of bribery is given in the Corrupt Practices Prevention Act, 1854 (*17 & 18 Vict. c. 102*), secs. 2, 3, and added to by the Representation of the People Act, 1867 (*30 & 31 Vict. c. 102*), sec. 49. The definition is very sweeping, but is in accordance with the ordinary meaning of the word. The following points may however be noticed.

Both the briber and the bribed are guilty of bribery.

It is bribery where the bribe is offered to a person not a voter in order to induce him to endeavour to procure votes.

2nd. Personation; or aiding, abetting, counselling, or procuring the commission of the offence of personation.

A person is guilty of personation who, at an election, applies for a ballot paper in the name of some other person, whether that name be that of a person living or dead, or of a fictitious person, or who, having voted once at any such election, applies at the same election for a ballot paper in his own name.

3rd. Treating.

Treating is corruptly giving or paying for meat, drink, or entertainment in order to influence voters.

4th. Undue influence.

Every person is guilty of "undue influence" who, by force, threats, or fraud influences or endeavours to influence a voter.

5th. Making a false return or declaration of election expenses.

This last offence also subjects the candidate guilty of it to the punishment for perjury.

The following are Illegal Practices :—

1st. Contracting or paying for the conveyance of electors to or from the poll.

2nd. Contracting or paying for the exhibition of election placards, &c., contrary to law.

3rd. Contracting or paying for the use of committee-rooms in excess of the lawful number.

4th. Paying or incurring expenses in excess of the maximum allowed. This is an illegal practice on the part of a candidate or his agent alone.

5th. Inducing or procuring a person to vote who is prohibited from voting.

A person to be guilty of an illegal practice under this head must know of the prohibition.

An election will not be invalidated for illegal practices under this head committed without the knowledge or consent of the candidate, nor will the candidate suffer any incapacity.

6th. Publishing a false statement of the withdrawal of a candidate for the purpose of procuring the election of another candidate. An election will not be invalidated for illegal practices under this head, committed without the knowledge or consent of the candidate, nor will the candidate suffer any incapacity.

7th. A candidate printing or publishing a placard without the name and address of the printer and publisher on it, is guilty of an illegal practice.

8th. Where an offence of illegal payment, employment, or hiring is committed by a candidate, or with his knowledge or consent, he is guilty of an illegal practice.

9th. Failure to pay election expenses within twenty-one days after the day of election. But if this provision is contravened without the sanction or connivance of the candidate, such an illegal practice will not invalidate the election, nor will the candidate suffer any incapacity.

10th. Failure on the part of a candidate to make the proper return of his expenses and the proper declaration respecting them within the proper time.

The following matters constitute the offence of Illegal Payment :—

1st. Providing money for any payment contrary to the provisions of the Municipal Elections (Corrupt and Illegal Practices) Act, 1884.

2nd. Corruptly inducing any person to withdraw from being a candidate in consideration of payment or promise of payment, or withdrawing from being a candidate in pursuance of such inducement.

3rd. Paying or contracting for bands of music, torches, flags, cockades, ribbon, or other marks of distinction in connection with an election ; the person receiving payment or undertaking the contract will be also guilty of illegal payment.

The following proceedings are illegal hiring:—

1st. Letting, lending, or employing for the conveyance of electors to or from the poll any public stage or hackney carriage, or any horse or any other animal kept or used for drawing the same, or any carriage or horse or other animal kept for the purpose of being let out for hire ; thus a cab proprietor must not lend his cabs gratuitously even, for conveying electors to or from the poll. The person so letting, lending or employing his conveyances, &c., will not be guilty of illegal hiring unless he knows that they are to be used for the purpose of conveying electors to or from the poll.

2nd. A person is guilty of illegal hiring who hires, borrows, or uses, for conveying electors to or from the poll, a conveyance or animal which he knows the owner is prohibited to let or lend for that purpose. Illegal hiring of this nature will of course frequently be also an illegal practice.

3rd. Hiring or using, or permitting to be hired or used, any premises licensed for the sale of intoxicating liquors, or used as a refreshment room, or club premises where liquor is supplied, as a committee room, or for holding meetings, except in certain cases.

The following proceeding is illegal employment :—

Employing persons for payment in promoting an election beyond those persons legally employed as clerks and messengers and polling agents.

The consequences of corrupt practices, illegal practices, &c., are of three kinds :— Consequences of offences against Election Law.

1st. The offender is liable to punishment.

2nd. The election may be set aside.

3rd. The offender, and in certain cases, the candidate, even if innocent, is subject to certain incapacities.

The penalties are as follows :—

i. Penalties for corrupt practices.

A person guilty of a corrupt practice, other than personation, or abetting, counselling, or procuring the commission of the offence of personation, is guilty of a misdemeanour and is liable on conviction on indictment to imprisonment with or without hard labour, for a term not exceeding one year, or to a fine not exceeding £200.[1]

A person guilty of personation, or of aiding, abetting, counselling or procuring the commission of the offence of personation, is guilty of a felony and is liable on conviction on indictment to imprisonment with or without hard labour, for a term not exceeding two years.

ii. Penalties for illegal practices.

A person guilty of illegal practices is liable on summary conviction to a fine not exceeding £100.

iii. Penalty for illegal payment, hiring, or employment.

A person guilty of these offences is liable to a fine not exceeding £100 on summary conviction.

---

[1] See Corrupt and Illegal Practices Prevention Act, 1883, sec. 6.

The principal disqualifications consequent upon corrupt practices, illegal practices, &c., are as follows :—

1st. Disqualification for corrupt practices.[1]

A person convicted on indictment or reported by an Election Court to have been guilty of corrupt practices, is, during a period of seven years from the date of his conviction, incapable—

i. Of being registered as an elector or voting at an election in the United Kingdom, whether parliamentary or for any public office.

ii. Of holding any public or judicial office.

Pubic Office includes :—

The office of Councillor, Alderman, Chairman of a County Council or Mayor of a borough.

Any office under the Crown.

Any office under a County or Town Council, *e.g.*, Clerk of the County Council or Town Clerk.

Any office under the Poor Laws, the Education Laws, or the Public Health Acts.

Judicial office, includes besides other judicial offices, those of Justice of the Peace and Revising Barrister.

iii. Of sitting in the House of Commons.

Further, a person reported by an Election Court to have been guilty of corrupt practices, is incapable of ever holding any public office in the county or borough, at an election in respect of which the offence was committed.

If it is reported by an Election Court that a candidate has been guilty by his agents of corrupt practices, the candidate will be incapacitated from holding the office of Councillor, Chairman, Alderman, Mayor, or Elective Auditor for the county or borough in an election for an office in which the offence was committed.

2nd. Disqualifications for illegal practices.

A person summarily convicted, or a candidate reported by an Election Court to have been guilty of illegal practices, is incapable, for five years from the date of the conviction or of the report, of holding any public office in the county or borough in which the offence was committed.

Further, if an Election Court report that a candidate was guilty by his agents of an illegal practice, the candidate will be incapable of holding the office of Councillor, Chairman, Alderman, or Mayor, for the county or borough, for which the election was held, during the period for which he was elected to serve, or if he had been elected, would have served.

Exoneration of persons in certain cases.

In order to protect persons who may have been guilty of a breach of the regulations concerning proceedings at elections through inadvertance, the following provisions have been made :—

1st. Where any act or omission would otherwise be an illegal practice, payment, employment, or hiring, any person who would be subject to any penalty or disqualification in consequence of such act or omission, may apply to the High Court or to an Election Court for an Order allowing such act or omission to be an exception from the provisions that would otherwise make it an illegal practice, payment, hiring or employment, and thereupon such person will be released from the consequences of the act or omission.

---

[1] See Corrupt and Illegal Practices Prevention Act, 1883, secs. 6, 64.

The person so applying must show that he has given proper notice of the application in the county or borough for which the election was held, and that the act or omission came from inadvertance, or from accidental miscalculation, or from some other reasonable cause of a like nature, and in any case, did not arise from any want of good faith.

It seems that any interested party will be heard in opposition to the application.

2nd. An Election Court in making its report concerning offences may so mitigate it as to relieve the candidate from the consequences that would ensue.[1]

3rd. A candidate failing to make a proper return of expenses through inadvertence, &c., may apply to the High Court or to the County Court, or to an Election Court for an Order relieving him from the consequences.[2]

The following rules may be laid down with regard to the expenditure and conduct of a candidate at an election :— Candidate's conduct.

I.—The expense incurred by a candidate for the office of County or Town Councillor, or on his behalf, must not exceed £25 where the number of electors in the area for which he is standing does not exceed 500, but where the number of electors exceeds 500, an additional threepence for every elector in excess of that number is allowed. Expenses.

Where there are joint candidates at an election their maximum expenditure is reduced—if there are two such candidates, by one-fourth; if there are more than two by one-third. Candidates are considered joint candidates if they conduct their candidature together, but the mere employment of the same agent, committee room, &c., will not constitute candidates joint candidates where they really are essentially conducting their candidature separately.

A candidate for the office of Alderman, Chairman of a County Council, or Mayor must incur no expense in his candidature.

II.—Only one committee room may be hired for the purposes of the candidature where the number of electors for the area for which the candidate is standing is under 2,000, but an additional committee room is allowed for every 2,000, and incomplete part of 2,000 electors in excess of such number; *e.g.*, if there are 5,000 electors, one committee room is allowed for the first 2,000, one for the second 2,000, and one for the remaining 1,000, or three in all. Any number of additional rooms may, however, be used gratuitously. Committee Rooms.

No premises licensed for the sale of intoxicating liquors, or on which refreshment of any kind is supplied, may be used as a committee room, nor any premises where any intoxicating liquor is supplied to members of a club, society, or association; this, however, does not apply to a separate part of such premises ordinarily let for chambers or offices, or the holding

[1] See *post*, p. 225. [2] See *post*, p. 223.

of public meetings, or arbitrations, where such part has a separate entrance and no direct communication with any part of the premises in which intoxicating liquor, &c., is sold or supplied.

Clerks and Messengers.

III.—No person must be employed for remuneration in promoting the candidature of any person at an election, except—

i. Two persons as clerks or messengers if the number of electors in the area for which the candidate is standing is below 2,000; but if the number of electors exceed 2,000, one additional clerk or messenger is allowed for every 1,000 and incomplete part of 1,000 electors above the first 2,000.

ii. One polling agent for each polling station.

These provisions do not apply to any engagement or employment for carrying into effect a contract *bonâ fide* made with any person in the ordinary way of business. An elector employed as above-mentioned must not vote.

Conveying voters to and from the poll.

IV.—The hiring of any kind of carriage or conveyance, or of horses or other animals to convey voters to or from the poll is forbidden.

The employment, even gratuitously, of carriages usually let for hire is forbidden; but any person may lend a private carriage gratuitously, and any elector or electors, at their own cost, may hire a carriage to convey him or them to and from the poll.

Music, Torches, &c.

V.—No contract or payment may be made in connection with a candidature, for bands of music, torches, flags, banners, cockades, ribbons, or other marks of distinction.

Advertisements

VI.—No payment to, or contract with, any elector may be made, respecting the use of any house, land, building or premises for the exhibition of any address, bill, or notice, or in any way, on account of the exhibition of any address, bill or notice; but this does not apply to the case of a contract with an elector whose ordinary business such advertisement is.

Return of Election expenses.

VII.—Within twenty-eight days after the election of a Councillor, every candidate at such election must send to the Clerk of the County Council or Town Clerk, as the case may be, a return of all expenses incurred by such candidate or his agent, on account of, or in respect of, the conduct or management of such election, vouched (except in the case of sums under £1), by bills stating the particulars, and by receipts. This return must be accompanied by a declaration by the candidate, made before a Justice of the Peace, in the following form, or to the like effect:—

I, , having been a candidate at the election of councillor for the electoral division [or borough, or ward] of , on the day of , [and my agents] do hereby solemnly and sincerely declare that I have paid for my expenses at the said election, and that except as aforesaid, I have not, and to the best of my knowledge and belief, no person, nor any club, society, or association, has on my behalf made any payment, or given, promised, or offered any reward, office, employment, or valuable consideration, or incurred any liability on account of, or in respect of, the conduct or management of the said election.

And I further solemnly and sincerely declare that, except as aforesaid, no money, security, or equivalent for money, has to my knowledge or belief been paid, advanced, given, or deposited by anyone to, or in the hands of, myself, or any other person, for the purpose of defraying any expenses incurred on my behalf on account of, or in respect of, the conduct or management of the said election.

And I further solemnly and sincerely declare that I will not at any future time make, or be a party to the making or giving of any payment reward, office, employment, or valuable consideration for the purpose of defraying any such expenses as last mentioned, or provide, or be a party to the providing of any money, security, or equivalent for money, for the purpose of defraying any such expenses. Signature of declarant, C. D.

Signed and declared by the above-named declarant, on the day of before me. (Signed) E. F., Justice of the Peace for .

In order that the candidate may have, in proper time, the materials for making up the return, the following provisions have been made :—

(1.) Every claim made by any person in respect of any expenses incurred by or on behalf of a candidate at an election of a Councillor on account of, or in respect of, the conduct or management of such election, must be sent in within fourteen days after the day of election, and if not so sent in, is barred and must not be paid, and all expenses incurred in such an election must be paid within twenty-one days after the day of election.

(2.) Every agent of a candidate at an election of a Councillor must, within twenty-three days after the day of election, make a return to the candidate in writing of all expenses incurred by such agent, on account of or in respect of the conduct or management of such election, and if he fails to do so he will be liable on summary conviction to a fine not exceeding £50.

The County Court for the district in which the election was held, or the High Court, or an Election Court may, however, on the application either of the candidate or a creditor, allow any claim to be sent in and any expenses to be paid after the expiration of the proper time. In such a case a return of any sum so paid must forthwith after payment be sent to the Clerk of the County Council or Town Clerk as the case may be.

The return and declaration sent in to the Clerk of the County Council or Town Clerk are kept at his office, and are at all reasonable times, during the twelve months next after they are received by him, open to inspection by any person on the payment of one shilling. The Clerk of the County Council or Town Clerk, as the case may be, must, on demand, furnish copies thereof or of any part thereof at the price of twopence for every seventy-two words. After the expiration of the twelve months the Clerk of the County Council or Town Clerk, as the case may be, may cause the return and declarations to be destroyed, or, if the candidate so require, must return the same to him.

Election petitions.

The question of the procedure in the case of an election petition must next be inquired into. As it is not advisable to present an election petition without adequate legal assistance, it is intended to discuss this question here very briefly. Rules for the procedure have been drawn up by the Judges.

Grounds of petition.

An election may be questioned by election petition on the following grounds :—

That the election was wholly invalidated by general bribery, treating, undue influence, or personation.

That the election of the candidate returned was invalidated by corrupt or illegal practices.

That the person whose election is questioned was, at time of the election, disqualified.

That he was not duly elected by a majority of lawful votes.

Partie petition and time of presenting petition.

The petition may be presented by any four persons who voted or had a right to vote at the election, or by any person alleging himself to have been a candidate.

The petition must be presented within the following time :—

i. In most cases within twenty-one days after the day on which the election was held.

ii. If the petition complains of the election on the ground of corrupt practices and specifically alleges that a payment of money or other reward has been made or promised since the election by a person elected, or on his account, or with his connivance, in pursuance or furtherance of corrupt practices, the petition may be presented at any time within 28 days after the date of the alleged payment or promise; whether or not another petition has been previously presented or tried.

iii. If the petition complains of the election on the ground of an illegal practice, it may be presented at any time within 14 days after the day on which the Clerk of the County Council or Town Clerk receives the return and declaration respecting election expenses by the candidate whose election is questioned, or where there is an authorized excuse for failing to make the return and declaration, then, within the same time after the date of the allowance of the excuse.

v. If a petition complains of the election on the ground of an illegal practice, whether the illegal practice is or is not also a corrupt practice, and specifically alleges a payment of money or other act made or done since the election by the candidate elected or by an agent of the candidate, or with the sanction of the candidate in pursuance or furtherance of such illegal practice, it may be presented at any time within 28 days after the date of such payment or act; whether or not any other petition has been previously presented or tried.

Any person whose election is questioned, and any Returning Officer of whose conduct the petition complains, may be made a respondent.

At the time of presenting a petition, or within three days after, the petitioner must give security for costs to such amount, not exceeding £500, as the High Court or a Judge thereof, on summons, may direct. The security must be given either by deposit of money or by recognisance entered into by sureties. Security for costs.

Within five days after the presentation of the petition the petitioner must serve notice on the respondent of the presentation of the petition and of the nature of the proposed security, and a copy of the petition. The respondent may object within five days of the notice to any recognisance, and if the objection is allowed the petitioner has five days more to make the security good by the deposit of a sum of money.

On the expiration of the time for making objections or, if an objection is made, on the objection being disallowed or removed, the petition is at issue.

Election petitions are tried before an Election Court consisting of a barrister, duly qualified and appointed, sitting without a jury. The trial is in open Court, and at least seven days' notice must be given of the time and place of trial.

The Election Court has two duties to perform :—

First—To decide whether the person whose election is complained of, or any and what other person, was duly elected, or whether the election was void. The determination is certified in writing to the High Court and the determination so certified is final.

Second—Where the petition is on the ground of corrupt or illegal practices, the Election Court will report to the High Court on the subject as follows :—

i. Whether a corrupt or illegal practice has or has not been proved to have been committed by or with the knowledge of any candidate at the election, and the nature of the corrupt or illegal practice.

ii. The names of all persons proved at the trial to have been guilty of any corrupt or illegal practice.

The consequences of a report that corrupt or illegal practices have been committed, are, as we have stated, as regards the disqualification of the guilty persons, practically the same as the consequences of a conviction. In order, therefore, to relieve persons acting *bonâ fide*, the Court may report—

That the corrupt and illegal practices mentioned in the report were committed without the sanction or connivance of the candidate.

That all reasonable means to prevent the commission of such offences were taken by or on behalf of the candidate.

That the offences mentioned in the report were of a trivial, unimportant and limited character.

That in all other respects the election was free from any corrupt or illegal practice on the part of such candidate or his agents.

If the Election Court so report, the election will not be set aside, nor will the candidate suffer any incapacity.

Corrupt and Illegal Practices List [1]

It may be mentioned here that it is the duty of the Town Clerk in every municipal borough, and apparently also of the Clerk of the County Council in every county, to make out annually in July a list containing the names and descriptions of all persons who, although otherwise qualified to be enrolled as burgesses or county

[1] Municipal Elections (Corrupt and Illegal Practices) Act, 1881, sec. 24.

electors, have become, by reason of conviction for offences against election law, or by reason of the report of an Election Court of voting at an election for a Town Council or County Council, stating in the list the particular offence of which each person has been found guilty.

This list is known as the Corrupt and Illegal Practices List, and for the purpose of making it the Town Clerk or Clerk of the County Council must examine the reports of Election Courts. The list is afterwards sent to the Overseers and dealt with in the manner we have described in the foregoing chapter.

Acceptance and resignation of office.

It remains to deal with the acceptance and resignation of office, and also with the consequences of a person's becoming disqualified during office.

A person elected to the office of Councillor, Alderman, Chairman of a County Council, or Mayor of a borough must, before acting in the office, make the declaration accepting office required by the Municipal Corporations Act, 1882.[1] This declaration may be made before two members of the County Council or the Clerk of the County Council, or before two members of the Town Council or the Town Clerk, as the case may be; and members of a Council may act in administering the declaration before they have made their own.

The declaration must be made, in the case of an office in a County Council, within ten days, and in the case of an office in a Town Council, within five days, after notice of election; and if not made in proper time the office will be thereby vacated. Non-acceptance of office in a Town Council subjects the person elected to a fine; and non-acceptance of office in a County Council subjects the person elected to a fine, provided he assented to his nomination, but not otherwise. The following persons are, however, exempt from serving on County or Town Councils.

- Persons disabled by lunacy or inability of mind, or deafness, blindness, or other permanent infirmity of body.
- Persons above the age of sixty-five; but the exemption must be claimed within five days of election.
- Persons having within five years before the day of their election, either served in the same office, or paid the fine for non-acceptance but the exemption must be claimed within five days.
- Military, naval, or marine officers in Her Majesty' service on full or half pay, and officers, and other persons employed and residing in any of Her Majesty's dockyards, victualling establishments, arsenals, barracks, or other naval or military establishments.
- Registrars of births and deaths.
- Registrars of marriages.
- Commissioners, officers, clerks, or other persons, acting in the management or service of the customs.

---

[1] Municipal Corporations Act, 1882, secs. 34, 35, 41.
For Forms of Declaration see *ib.*, Eighth Schedule, *post*, p. 353.

Officers of excise, and persons employed in collection or management of revenue of excise.

The Postmaster-General and officers of the Post Office.

Inspectors under the Factory and Workshops Act, 1878 (*41 & 42 Vict. c. 16*).

Medical Practitioners registered under the Medical Act, 1858 (*21 & 22 Vict. c. 90*)

Dentists under the Dentists Act, 1878 (*41 & 42 Vict. c. 33*).

Men enrolled and officers and non-commissioned officers appointed under the Reserve Force Act, 1867 (*30 & 31 Vict. c. 110*).

Persons excused on the ground of conscientious scruples.

The fine for non-acceptance may be determined by bye-law, but so that it does not in the case of—

Mayor or Chairman, exceed £100.

In other cases, £50.

If no bye-law has been made, the fine will be—

In the case of Mayor or Chairman, £50.

In other cases, £25.

A person who acts in office before making the declaration incurs a penalty for each act, not exceeding £50;

Vacancies

The next question is, how vacancies in the Council may arise by the disqualification of a person during his tenure of office.

If a Councillor, &c., loses his qualification during his office by ceasing to be enrolled and entitled to be enrolled as an elector, or as a non-resident, or in the last case by losing his property qualification, or by his acceptance of a contract, or place of profit disqualifying him, the office remains in fact full, and the office must be declared vacant by the High Court by *quo warranto* before there can be another election, and before his authority can be determined.[1] However, if any person, after becoming disqalified, acts in office, he will be liable to a fine for each offence, not exceeding £50, recoverable by action.[2]

If a member of a Council is adjudged bankrupt, or compounds by deed with his creditors, or makes an arrangement or composition with his creditors under the Bankruptcy Act, by deed or otherwise, or is (except in case of illness) continuously absent from the county or borough, being Chairman of a County Council or Mayor, for more than two months, or being County Alderman or County Councillor, for more than twelve months, or, being Town Councillor or Borough Alderman, for more than six months, he becomes disqualified, and ceases to hold office. In this case the Council must declare the office vacant, and signify the same by notice, signed by three members of the Council, and countersigned by the Clerk of the County Council or Town Clerk, as the case may be, and fixed, in the case of a borough on the Town Hall, and in other cases, in a proper place, and thereupon the office will become vacant. If a person becomes disqualified by absence, he will be liable to the same fine as for non-acceptance of office.[3]

---

[1] Municipal Corporations Act, sec. 39.

[2] See Municipal Corporations Act, 1882, sec. 225.
See R. *v.* Phippen and Ricketts, 7 A. & E. 966.
R. *v.* Ricketts, 7 L.J., Q.B. 71.
R. *v.* Chester, 25 L.J., Q.B. 61.

[3] Municipal Corporations Act, 1882, sec. 41.

Where an office becomes vacant owing to a conviction for offences against election law, or in consequence of the report of an Election Court, it seems that the vacancy is complete on the conviction, or on the making of a report.

Resignation.

Any person may resign his office by writing delivered by him to the Clerk of the County Council or Town Clerk, as the case may be, and thereupon the office will become vacant, and the person resigning will be liable to the same fine as for non-acceptance of office.[2]

Failure to hold Election on proper day.[3]

If an election is not held on the proper day or, in the case of filling up a casual vacancy, within the appointed time, it may be held on the next day after that day, or after the expiration of the appointed time; but if that day also is passed over, application must be made to the High Court for a mandamus to hold the election on some subsequent day to be fixed by the Court.

If an ordinary election is not held on the proper day, the persons who should have gone out of office will continue to hold office until the election is actually held.

[1] Municipal Corporations Act, 1882, sec. 36.
[2] See Municipal Corporations Act, 1882, sec. 70.

CHAPTER VIII.

CONCLUSION.

Brief Summary of the Government of a Borough and of the provisions of the Local Government Act with respect to the Metropolis.

IN our concluding chapter we propose, first to sum up what we have stated with regard to boroughs in the course of the work, and to give a brief account of borough finance, and secondly, to give the shortest possible sketch of the system of local government in the Metropolis.

Boroughs may, after the appointed day, be divided into three classes, namely, county boroughs; other boroughs, the population of which according to the census of 1881, was over 10,000; and boroughs the population of which, according to that census, was under 10,000.

Again, a borough, belonging to any one of these classes, may or may not have had, on the 13th August, 1888, a separate Court of Quarter Sessions, and the powers and duties of the Town Council will differ accordingly.

The constitution of the Town Council is in all cases alike; in Chapters VI. and VII. we have sufficiently discussed the qualification and registration of burgesses and the election of members of a Town Council; in Chapter V. we have shown how the proceedings of a Town Council are conducted. We now proceed to mention the business transacted by the Town Council, which we have incidentally discussed.

Business of Town Council of a county borough.

The Town Council of a county borough transact, or will, after the appointed day transact, the following business—

(1.) They act as Sanitary Authority under the Allotments Act, 1887, but with regard to them, the Local Government Board transact the business which in other cases is transacted by the County Council.[1]

(2.) They appoint Public Analysts.[2]

---

[1] *Ante*, pp. 112-114. [2] *Ante*, p. 114.

(3.) They may oppose and also promote Bills in Parliament.[1]

(4.) They have certain powers under the Wild Birds Protection Acts, 1880 and 1881.[2]

(5.) They make bye-laws for the borough.[3]

(6.) They act as Local Authority under the Contagious Diseases (Animals) Acts, and the Destructive Insects Acts, 1877.[4]

(7.) If the borough has a separate Court of Quarter Sessions, the Town Council appoint a Borough Coroner. In the case of a county borough without a separate Court of Quarter Sessions, if the district of a County Coroner is wholly within the borough, the writ for his election will issue to the Town Council, who will appoint him. If the district of a County Coroner is partly within and partly without a county borough, the writ will issue to the County Council; but if the Town Council so require, a Joint Committee of the Town Council and the County Council may be formed to appoint the Coroner.[5]

(8.) The Town Council are a Local Authority under the Explosives Act, 1875.[6]

(9.) They have a right to appoint members of Boards of Conservators of Fisheries.[7]

(10.) The Town Council are a Local Authority under the Act of 1859, with regard to gas meters, if that Act has been adopted in the borough, except where they themselves are makers or sellers of gas, in which latter case the Justices of the borough must act.[8]

(11.) As Urban Sanitary Authority, the Town Council must maintain all highways in the borough. There is no distinction between main roads and other highways in a county borough. They must also maintain all borough bridges formerly maintainable by them, and also all public bridges within the boundaries of their borough, which were before the appointed day repairable by the county or a hundred, &c.[9]

(12.) The Town Council are a Local Authority under the Local Stamp Act, 1869.[10]

---

1 *Ante*, p. 115, and see the Municipal Corporations (Borough Funds) Act, 1875.

2 *Ante*, p. 116.

3 *Ante*, p. 117, and see the Municipal Corporations Act, 1882, sec. 23.

4 *Ante*, pp. 118-133, 138.

5 *Ante*, pp. 43, 133-137.

6 *Ante*, pp. 138-143.

7 *Ante*, pp. 45, 143-148.

8 *Ante*, pp. 46, 148-150.

9 *Ante*, pp. 47-55, 150.

10 *Ante*, p. 161.

(13.) The Town Council must provide asylum accommodation for the lunatics of the borough, and will be chargeable with the costs of any pauper lunatics who may be found in the borough and whose settlement cannot be ascertained. Any existing arrangements with regard to lunatic asylums that the borough may have made before passing of the Local Government Act, 1888, are, however, to remain as far as possible unaltered.[1]

(14.) The Town Council of a county borough within twenty miles of London and Westminster, must grant music and dancing licences. This only, therefore, applies to Croydon and West Ham.[2]

(15.) The Town Council have to superintend the registration of parliamentary occupation voters within their borough, and if the borough is as to any part co-extensive with a parliamentary borough they have power to divide the parliamentary borough into polling districts.[3]

(16.) The Town Council must maintain a police force under the Municipal Corporations Act, 1882, but their police force may be consolidated with that of the county in which the borough is situated or of a county which the borough adjoins.[4]

(17.) The Town Council of a county borough within ten miles of Charing Cross would have to license any race-course within the boundaries of their borough.[5]

(18.) The Town Council may contribute towards or erect Reformatory and Industrial Schools.[6]

(19.) The Town Council must undertake the registration of Charitable Gifts, Places of Religious Worship and Rules of Societies.[7]

(20.) They are, if they maintain a separate police force, a Police Authority under the Riot (Damages) Act, 1886.[8]

(21.) They enforce the Rivers Pollution Prevention Act, 1876, as Sanitary Authority.[9]

(22.) The Town Council must grant Theatre Licences.[10]

(23.) They act as Local Authority under the Weights and Measures Act.[11]

In addition, of course, the Town Council transact much other business as Sanitary Authority, &c., into which it is beyond our scope to enter.

---

1 *Ante*, pp. 56-60, 161-165.
2 *Ante*, p. 165.
3 *Ante*, pp. 203, 204, 210, 211.
4 *Ante*, pp. 61-64, 166-171.
5 *Ante*, p. 172.
6 *Ante*, pp. 65, 172.
7 *Ante*, p. 173.
8 *Ante*, p. 175.
9 *Ante*, pp. 176-180.
10 *Ante*, p. 180.
11 *Ante*, pp. 181-187.

Business of Town Council of Quarter Sessions Borough, with population over 10,000.

The Town Council of a Quarter Sessions Borough, which is not a county borough, and the population of which, according to the census of 1881, was above 10,000, will transact all the above-mentioned business subject to the following exceptions and provisions, which, however, may require some modification in the case of a county of a city or of a town:—

(i.) They act as Sanitary Authority under the Allotments Act, 1888, but apply to the County Council for a Provisional Order enabling them to purchase land compulsorily.

(ii.) They appoint their own Coroner in every instance.

(iii.) They appoint members of Boards of Conservators of Fishery District only if their borough is a county of a city or county of a town.

(iv.) If the Town Council are makers or sellers of gas the County Council act as Local Authority with regard to gas-meters, whether there are any borough Justices or not.

(v.) They, as Urban Sanitary Authority, maintain their highways in the borough but not main roads passing through their borough; if, however, they choose they may, in certain cases, undertake the management of main roads within their borough and will receive a contribution from the County Council in respect thereof; as Highway Authority, they will be subject to the supervision of the County Council.

(vi.) They must provide asylum accommodation for their pauper lunatics, and may do so jointly with other authorities or alone. The borough may, however, have been annexed to a county, in which case their position is unaltered, subject to any fresh agreement that may be entered into If, however, on the appointed day such a borough was under contract for the reception of its lunatics into a county asylum, on that contract coming to an end the powers and duties of the Town Council with regard to lunatics will entirely cease.

(vii.) The Town Council in no case grant music and dancing licences.

(viii.) They will not in any case license theatres, or act in the registration of charitable gifts, &c.

Business of Town Council of a borough with population over 10,000, without separate Quarter Sessions.

The Town Council of a borough without a separate Court of Quarter Sessions, but with a population, according to the census of 1881, exceeding 10,000, transact the following business, which we have incidentally discussed:—

1. They act as Sanitary Authority under the Allotments Act, 1887.[1]

---

[1] *Ante*, pp. 112-114.

(2.) They appoint Public Analysts where the borough has a separate police force.[1]

(3.) They may oppose and promote Bills in Parliament.[2]

(4.) They may make bye-laws.[3]

(5.) They act as Local Authority under the Contagious Diseases (Animals) Acts and the Destructive Insects Act, 1877.[4]

(6.) They may be made a Local Authority under the Explosives Act on application to a Secretary of State.[5]

(7.) They may act as Local Authority in connection with gas-meters, if they are not themselves makers and sellers of gas, and the Act of 1859 has been adopted for the borough.[6]

(8.) They, as Urban Sanitary Authority, maintain highways, but not main roads, unless they take them over under the provisions of the Local Government Act, 1888, in which case they receive a contribution from the County Council.[7]

(9.) They superintend the registration of Parliamentary occupation voters, and if any part of their borough is co-extensive with a parliamentary borough, they have power to divide the parliamentary borough into polling districts.[8]

(10.) They maintain a police force under the Municipal Corporations Act, 1882, but, of course, such a force may be consolidated with the police force of the county.[9]

(11.) If they maintain a separate police force, they are a Police Authority under the Riot (Damages) Act, 1886.[10]

(12.) They act as Sanitary Authority under the Rivers Pollution Prevention Act, 1876.[11]

(13.) They may act as Local Authority under the Weights and Measures Act, 1878.[12]

In addition, of course, the Town Council will have much other business to transact as Sanitary Authority, &c., into which it is beyond our scope to enter.

Business of Town Council of a borough with a population under 10,000

The most important business which the Town Council of a borough, the population of which, according to the census of 1881, was under 10,000, transact, devolves upon them in their capacity of Sanitary Authority; in their capacity of Municipal Authority they may, however, oppose and promote Bills in

[1] *Ante*, p. 114.

[2] *Ante*, p. 115, and see the Municipal Corporations (Borough Funds) Act, 1875.

[3] *Ante*, p. 117, and see the Municipal Corporations Act, 1882, sec. 23.

[4] *Ante*, pp. 118-133, 138.

[5] *Ante*, pp. 138-143.

[6] *Ante*, pp. 46, 148-150.

[7] *Ante*, pp. 47-55, 150-151, 160.

[8] *Ante* pp. 203, 204, 210, 211.

[9] *Ante*, pp. 61-64, 166-171.

[10] *Ante*, p. 175.

[11] *Ante*, pp. 176-180.

[12] *Ante*, pp. 181-187.

Parliament, make bye-laws, and they act in Parliamentary registration, &c.

Borough Finance

We now proceed to give a brief account of the finance of a borough.

Share of county borough in the Local Taxation Account.

The Town Council of a county borough will receive their share of the Local Taxation Account under the direction of the Local Government Board. Their share, as compared with that of the County Council of the county in which the borough is situated, will depend upon the equitable adjustment which is to be made of the financial relations of the county borough and the county.[1] The sums thus received must, as in a county, be carried to a separate account, called the Exchequer Contribution Account, and applied first in the payment of the costs in respect thereof or charged thereon, and, secondly, in the payment of the local grants substituted for parliamentary grants in aid, in the same way as the Exchequer Contribution Account of a county. Thus they will make the grants to Boards of Guardians for teachers in poor law schools, &c. They will transfer to the proper accounts of the borough fund, or of their general district fund, as Sanitary Authority, the sums payable in substitution for the existing grants in respect of the salaries of their Medical Officers of Health and Inspectors of Nuisances, the maintenance of pauper lunatics chargeable to their borough, and the maintenance of their police force, and if the Secretary of State withhold his report that the police force is efficient, they will forfeit a portion of the Exchequer Contribution Account. In West Ham and Croydon the Town Councils will have to contribute towards the Metropolitan police. Thirdly, the Town Council must make the same payments to Boards of Guardians for the costs of the officers of the unions and of district schools as a County Council.

The surplus of the Exchequer Contribution Account may then be carried to the borough fund or applied in aid of any rate, or rates, levied over the whole area of the borough by the Town Council, whether acting in their capacity of Municipal or of Sanitary Authority, as the Town Council may determine.[2] The other funds required the Town Council raise by means of rates which we shall discuss later.

Grants payable to boroughs with a population over 10,000, other than county boroughs.[3]

The Town Council of a borough, the population of which, according to the census of 1881, was over 10,000, will receive either in their capacity of Municipal or of Sanitary Authority

[1] *Ante*, p. 15. [2] *Ante*, pp. 70-74; Local Government Act, 188, sec. 34.
[3] *Ante*, pp. 70-74

grants from the County Council, in respect of the salaries of their Medical Officers of Health and Inspectors of Nuisances, in aid of any lunatics who, if the borough has a separate Court of Quarter Sessions, are chargeable to the borough, and in aid of their police force, if the Secretary of State reports that the force was efficient.

In addition they may receive from the County Council a share of the surplus (if any) of the Exchequer Contribution Account, if the borough has a separate Court of Quarter Sessions, or if there is a separate police force for the borough.

Whatever other funds are necessary must be raised by means of rates.

Grants payable to boroughs with a population under 10,000.[1]

The Town Councils of boroughs, the population of which, according to the census of 1881, was under 10,000, will receive grants from the County Council in aid of the salaries of their Medical Officers of Health, and a share of the ultimate surplus of the Exchequer Contribution Account, if there should be such a surplus, which, however, is very improbable. Such other funds as they may require they must levy by rates.

Borough Fund.[2]

A Town Council, as we have seen, acts in the capacity both of Municipal Authority and of Sanitary Authority. The accounts of the Town Council in their two capacities must be kept distinct; in which capacity the Town Council should act with regard to any business, depends on the particular circumstances of the case.

All receipts of the Town Council, in their capacity of Municipal Authority are paid into the borough fund, and all their expenses in that capacity are paid out of that fund. There is no general name for the fund in the hands of the Town Council as Sanitary Authority.

Borough Rates.[3]

To meet any deficiency in the borough fund the Town Council may levy a borough rate. For the purpose of the borough rate the Town Council may, if they consider the valuation lists in the parishes within the borough unfair, make a fresh valuation of the parishes in their borough. If they make such a valuation it will, like the basis for the county rate, show only the value of each parish and part of a parish in the borough. The borough rate is generally levied as part of the poor rate, and therefore as between occupiers of property in the same parish, the rate must be levied in the proportion indicated by the valuation list.

---

[1] *Ante*, pp. 70-74. [2] Municipal Corporations Act, 1882, secs. 139-143.
[3] Municipal Corporations Act, 1882, secs. 144, 149.

If the Town Council determine to make a fresh valuation they have powers for obtaining the necessary information somewhat similar to those of the Committee of a County Council appointed for the preparation of the basis for the county rate.

The sum required to be levied by means of the borough rate in each parish or part of a parish in the borough, must be calculated in accordance with the valuation upon which the Town Council determine to act, but it appears that this estimate need not be published.

The Town Council obtain payment of the contribution due from each parish by a warrant issued by the Mayor, signed by him and sealed with the corporate seal, and directed to the Overseers, who then levy the rate as part of the poor rate.

If, however, part of a parish is within a borough and part not, the Overseers may levy the necessary contributions on the part of the parish liable, as part of the poor rate, or as a separate rate of the nature of a poor rate.

In certain boroughs, however, there are peculiar provisions in force enabling the Town Council to levy the borough rate independently, by means of their own officers.

Watch rate, &c.[1]

In addition to the borough rate, the Town Council may, in certain cases, levy other rates in aid of the borough fund, of which, perhaps, the most important is a watch rate, which, in certain cases, is levied to meet the expenses of the police force of the borough. The watch rate is made, assessed, and levied in much the same way as the borough rate, except that it must be levied as a separate rate, where part only of a parish is liable to be assessed to it.

Rates levied by Town Council as Sanitary Authority.[2]

As Sanitary Authority, the Town Council of a borough levy general district rates, private improvement rates, and, in some cases, other independent rates.

The question as to what expenses should be charged on general district rates, private improvement rates, and other rates respectively is beyond our scope.

It should be observed that, as far as expenses payable out of general district rates are concerned, an Urban Sanitary Authority may divide their district for rating purposes, and charge expenses incurred for the benefit of a particular part of their district on that part alone.

The Sanitary Authority before making a general district rate must prepare an estimate of the sums required, showing the several sums required for each purpose, the rateable value

[1] Municipal Corporations Act, 1882, secs. 197-200.
[2] See Public Health Act, 1875, secs. 207-228.

of the property assessed, and the rate in the pound necessary for each purpose. On final approval this estimate must be entered in the rate book.

In estimating the rateable value of property the Sanitary Authority are bound by the valuation list, but certain descriptions of property must be assessed at only one quarter of their value as shown by the valuation list.

A general district rate is thus actually assessed on the property in the district by the Sanitary Authority, and not upon parishes. The Sanitary Authority may make such arrangements as they think fit for its collection.

Private improvement rates, &c., are made, assessed, and levied in certain cases to meet the expenses incurred for the benefit of particular property.

Loans to Town Councils

A Town Council may borrow money in certain cases in either capacity, with the approval of the Local Government Board, and the accounts of the Town Council in either capacity are audited by Borough Auditors, who are three in number; two being elected by the burgesses, and one appointed by the Mayor.

The Metropolis

In conclusion we propose to give the shortest possible account of the system of Local Government in the Metropolis.

The Metropolis, which under the Local Government Act, 1888, will become the County of London, consists of the City of London; twenty-three parishes contained in schedule A. to the Metropolis Management Act, 1855 (*18 & 19 Vict. c. 120*), to which, under the Metropolis Management Amendment Act, 1885 (*48 & 49 Vict. c. 33*), and the Metropolis Management (Battersea and Wandsworth) Act, 1887 (*50 & 51 Vict. c. 17*), have been added four more, all of which we shall call the parishes in schedule A.; certain parishes contained in schedule B. to that Act, as amended by the two Acts referred to, which we shall call the parishes in schedule B.; and eight places of a peculiar nature, such as the Inns of Court, contained in schedule C. to that Act, which we shall call the places in schedule C.

The City of London is governed by the Corporation of the Mayor, Commonalty, and Citizens of the City, acting through the Common Council, the constitution of which is still based upon old charters. For the transaction of certain business, the Common Council appoint a body, called the Commissioners of Sewers for the City of London. The business of the Common Council and the Commissioners of Sewers is not materially affected by the Local Government Act, 1888, but such powers and duties as in the case of a Quarter

Sessions Borough, are transferred from the Justices to the Town Council, are transferred from the Quarter Sessions or Justices of the City, to the Common Council.

The parishes in Schedules A. and B. are each governed by a Vestry, consisting of members elected by the ratepayers and holding office for three years, one third retiring annually. These Vestries are not materially affected by the Local Government Act, 1888.

The parishes contained in Schedule B. are grouped into fourteen districts,[1] each under the government of a District Board of Works, consisting of members elected by the Vestries of the constituent parishes, and who also hold office for three years, one-third retiring annually.

The powers and duties of the District Boards and the Vestries of the parishes contained in Schedule A. are very nearly the same; the Vestries of the parishes in Schedule B. having but unimportant duties beyond that of electing members of the District Boards. The District Boards and the Vestries of the parishes in Schedule A. occupy a position analogous in many respects to that of an Urban Sanitary Authority; their business comprises drainage, highway maintenance, the appointment of Medical Officers of Health, the removal of nuisances, &c. District Boards and Vestries in the Metropolis will not be much affected by the Local Government Act, 1888.

The supreme authority in the Metropolis is the Metropolitan Board of Works, which is a body consisting of members appointed by the Common Council and by the Vestries of the parishes in Schedule A., and by the District Boards of Works. This body will be abolished by the Local Government Act, 1888, and will be succeeded by the County Council of London.

The Metropolis has hitherto been in the counties of Middlesex, Surrey and Kent, and the Quarter Sessions and the Justices of these counties have exercised certain powers in those parts of the Metropolis within their respective jurisdictions.

Under the Local Government Act, 1888, such of their powers and duties as in other cases are transferred to a County Council are in the Metropolis transferred to the County Council of London, as are also all the powers and duties of the Justices and Quarter Sessions of the City of London,

---

[1] In the schedule itself there are sixteen districts, but two were dissolved under the Metropolis Management Amendment Act, 1885, and the Metropolis Management (Battersea and Wandsworth) Act, 1887; the parishes in them being practically transferred to schedule A.

which, in the case of a Quarter Sessions Borough, are transferred to the County Council.

The County Council of London will be a body closely resembling any other County Council. Each parliamentary borough in the Metropolis, or if it is divided into divisions, each division of such borough, will be an electoral division, and the number of County Councillors returned for each electoral division is to be double the number of members returned to Parliament for such borough or division. The number of Aldermen is to be only one-sixth of the number of Councillors.

The qualification of a county elector is to be the same as elsewhere, except that he must reside within fifteen miles of the county and need not reside, as in other cases, within seven.

The County Council will succeed to—

The Quarter Sessions and Justices of Surrey, Kent and Middlesex.

The Metropolitan Board of Works.

The Quarter Sessions and Justices of the City of London.

We proceed to give a summary of such of the future business of the County Council, the Common Council and other Authorities in the Metropolis, as we have had occasion to discuss.

1st. The Allotments Act, 1887, does not apply to the Metropolis.

2nd. Public Analysts will be appointed, as in the past, by the Vestries and District Boards, and in the City of London, by the Commissioners of Sewers.

3rd. The County Council of London might act under the Wild Birds Protection Acts.

4th. The County Council has power to make bye-laws both under the Local Government Act, 1888, and as successors of the Metropolitan Board of Works.

5th. The County Council will act as Local Authority under the Contagious Diseases (Animals) Act and the Destructive Insects Act, 1877, except within the City of London and liberties thereof, where the Common Council will continue to be the Local Authority; but the Common Council act as Local Authority throughout the Metropolis with regard to foreign animals.

6th. The County Council will appoint Coroners.

7th. The County Council will act as Local Authority under the Explosives Act, 1875, throughout the Metropolis, as successors to the Metropolitan Board of Works and the Court of the Lord Mayor and Aldermen of the City of London.

8th. No part of the Metropolis is included in a Fishery district.

9th. The County Council will superintend gas-meters as successors to the Metropolitan Board of Works.

10th. Ordinary Highways will continue to be maintained in the Metropolis by the Vestries and District Board of Works, and in the City of London by the Commissioners of Sewers.

The County Council will, however, maintain main roads in the Metropolis, subject to the right of the Vestries, District Board of Works and Commissioners of Sewers to claim to retain the management of them.

The County Council will, as successors of the Metropolitan Board of Works, have varied and extensive powers of superintending ordinary highways.

12th. The County Council of London will have to provide asylum accommodation for the lunatics of the Metropolis with the exception of the City of London. The Common Council must provide lunatic asylum accommodation for the lunatics of the City.

13th. The County Council will grant music and dancing licences.

14th. The arrangements with regard to parliamentary registration, &c., in the Metropolis are peculiar.

15th. Within the Metropolitan police district, which extends beyond the limits of the Metropolis, the police force is under the control of the Commissioners of the Police of the Metropolis, and the County Council of London will have no power in the matter. There is, also, a separate City Police force, to which again the general Police Acts do not apply.

16th. Medical Officers of Health in the Metropolis are appointed by the Vestries, the District Boards of Works, and by the Commissioners of Sewers of the City of London. The County Council may, if they think fit, appoint Medical Officers of Health under the Local Government Act, 1888, sec. 17.

17th. The County Council, as successors to the Justices of Surrey, Kent, and Middlesex, and of the City of London, may contribute towards and erect and maintain industrial and reformatory schools

18th. The County Council must act in the registration of Rules of Societies, &c.

19th. The Police Authorities under the Riot (Damages) Act, 1886, in the Metropolis are in the City—the Common Council; in the Metropolitan Police District—the Receiver for the Metropolitan Police District.

20th. It seems that the Rivers Pollution Prevention Act, 1876, might be enforced by the County Council of London; but with regard to the Thames and the Lea, special provisions are contained in that Act.

21st. The County Council will grant theatre licences outside the jurisdiction of the Lord Chamberlain.

22nd. The County Council will act as Local Authority under the Weights and Measures Act, 1878, outside the City of London. Within the City the Common Council act, subject to certain rights granted by charter to the Master, Wardens, and Commonalty of the mystery of Founders of the City of London.

Into the question of the finance of the County Council of London it is beyond the scope of this work to enter. We may, however, mention that the County Council will receive their share of the Local Taxation Account, and will carry the sum so received to an Exchequer Contribution Account, out of which they must pay grants in substitution for Parliamentary grants in aid, and also a sum to the Board of Guardians of every Union wholly within the Metropolis of 4d. a head per diem for every indoor pauper, which grant is in lieu of the grant towards officers in other Unions. To the Guardians of a Union partly within the Metropolis they must pay their share of the sum payable, in respect of officers, &c., in the ordinary way.

APPENDICES.

COUNTY ELECTORS ACT, 1888.

[51 VICT. CH. 10.]

An Act to provide for the Qualification and Registration of Electors for the purposes of Local Government in England and Wales. [*16th May, 1888.*]

WHEREAS it is expedient to make provision with respect to the qualification and registration of electors of any representative bodies (in this Act referred to as "county authorities") which may be established under any Act of the present session of Parliament for the purposes of local government in counties in England :

Be it therefore enacted by the Queen's most Excellent Majesty, by and with the advice and consent of the Lords Spiritual and Temporal, and Commons, in this present Parliament assembled, and by the authority of the same, as follows ;

Short title and construction. 48 & 49 Vict c. 15.

Sect. 1.—This Act may be cited as the County Electors Act, 1888.

The Registration Act, 1885, and the Parliamentary Registration Acts within the meaning of that Act, are in this Act referred to as the Registration of Electors Acts, and together with this Act may be cited as the Registration of Electors Acts, 1843 to 1888.

This Act shall be construed as one with the Registration of Electors Acts.

Extension of burgess franchise to county electors outside municipal boroughs. 45 & 46 Vict c. 50.

Sect. 2.—(1.) For the purpose of the election of county authorities in England, the burgess qualification, that is to say, the qualification enacted by section nine of the Municipal Corporations Act, 1882, shall extend to every part of a county not within the limits of a borough, and a person possessing in any part of a county outside the limits of a borough such burgess qualification, shall be entitled to be registered under this Act as a county elector in the parish in which the qualifying property is situate.

(2.) Sections nine, thirty-one, thirty-three, and sixty-three of the Municipal Corporations Act, 1882, and any enactments of that or any other Act affecting the same, shall extend to so much of every county as is not comprised within the limits of a municipal borough in like manner as if they were herein re-enacted, with the substitution of "county" for "borough" and of "county elector" for "burgess," and with the other necessary modifications.

Occupation of land of the value of £10 to qualify.

Sect. 3.—Every person who is entitled to be registered as a voter in respect of a ten pounds occupation qualification within the meaning of the provisions of the Registration Act, 1885, which are set out in the schedule to this Act, shall be entitled to be registered as a county elector, and to be enrolled as a burgess, in respect of such qualification, in like manner in all respects as if the sections of the Municipal Corporations Act, 1882, relating to a burgess qualification included the said ten pounds occupation qualification.

Registration of county electors. 41 & 42 Vict. c. 26.

Sect. 4.—(1.) The Registration of Electors Acts shall, so far as circumstances admit, apply to the enrolment of burgesses in a municipal borough to which the Parliamentary and Municipal Registration Act, 1878, does not apply, and to the registration of county electors within the meaning of this Act ; and the lists of burgesses, and of county electors, and of occupation voters for parliamentary elections, shall, so far as practicable, be made out and revised together ; and the Registration of Electors Acts shall accordingly—

(*a.*) apply to every such municipal borough in like manner as if it were a borough to which sub-section two of section six of the Registration Act, 1885, applied (sub-section one of which section is hereby repealed), and revising assessors for such borough shall not be elected ; and

(*b.*) apply to every parish not situate in a municipal borough, in like manner as if such parish were a municipal borough to which the Parliamentary and Municipal Registration Act, 1878, applies, and the said lists of county electors and of occupation voters for parliamentary elections in such parish shall be made out in divisions, as provided in the said Act :

Provided that a person whose name appears in any list of county electors or burgesses in a county may object to the name of any other person on a list of county electors or burgesses for a parish in that county, and may oppose the claim of a person to have his name inscribed in any such list.

(2.) In the construction of the Registration of Electors Acts for the purpose of their application to a parish not situate in a municipal borough, there shall be made the variations following, and such other variations as may be necessary for carrying into effect the application, that is to say :—

(*a.*) Where such parish is not within a parliamentary borough, "parliamentary county" shall be substituted for "parliamentary borough ;"

(*b.*) Where such parish is not within a parliamentary borough, the clerk of the peace shall perform the duties of and be substituted for the town clerk ; but any notice required to be given to the town clerk by section twenty-seven of the Parliamentary and Municipal Registration Act, 1878, relating to the withdrawal and revival of objections, shall be given to the overseers and not to the clerk of the peace ;

(*c.*) County elector shall be substituted for burgess ;

(*d.*) Section nine of the Parliamentary and Municipal Registration Act, 1878, shall not apply to any parish which is not wholly situate in an urban district ;

(*e.*) Where such parish is not within a parliamentary borough section twenty-one of the Parliamentary and Municipal Registration Act, 1878, shall not apply, and the lists and register of voters shall be made out alphabetically, but shall be framed in parts for polling districts and electoral divisions and for urban districts and for wards of urban and rural districts in such a manner that the parts may be conveniently compiled or put together to serve as lists for polling districts, and elections in urban districts and as electoral division or ward lists ;

(*f.*) Where such parish is within a parliamentary borough—

(i.) the overseers shall send to the clerk of the peace for the county two copies of the lists of voters at the same time at which they send copies to the town clerk ; and

(ii.) the town clerk shall cause to be printed such number of copies of the revised lists as the clerk of the peace may require, and shall transmit the same to the clerk of the peace, who shall deal with the same as with other lists of county electors in his county ; but,

(iii.) save as aforesaid, the clerk of the peace shall not act in relation to the registration of county electors in the said parish, and the town clerk of the parliamentary borough shall be the town clerk within the meaning of the Registration of Electors Acts and this Act in relation to such parish, and shall include in his precept to the overseers proper directions respecting the registration of the county electors within the meaning of this Act.

(*g.*) The lists of occupation voters and county electors shall be revised by the revising barrister for the parliamentary borough or county in which such parish is situate, and the revising barrister for revising the county electors lists for the whole or any part of an electoral division of any county shall, if so required by the county council, hold a court in that electoral division or at some convenient place in a division adjoining thereto.

(*h.*) The guardians of a union which is not wholly comprised in an urban

51 Vict. c. 10, s. 4.

district may, with the consent of the overseers of any parish or parishes within their union for which an assistant overseer has not been appointed, annually appoint a fit person to act as registration officer for such parish or parishes, and may remove any such person, and fill up any vacancy caused by death, resignation, or otherwise. Such registration officer shall perform all the duties of overseers of the parish or parishes for which he is appointed in respect of the registration of county electors and parliamentary voters, and the provisions of the Registration of Electors Acts relating to overseers, including those providing for penalties, shall apply to him accordingly:

Provided that his remuneration shall be fixed and paid by the guardians of the union, and charged on the poor rates of the parish or parishes for which he is appointed, and (if he acts for more than one parish) in proportion to the number of persons on the registers made during the year of his appointment of county electors and parliamentary voters for each parish.

(3.) Notwithstanding anything in this Act contained, where a municipal borough or an urban district is co-extensive with any electoral division or divisions of a parliamentary county, the lists of voters may be directed by the county authority to be made out according to the order in which the qualifying premises appear in the rate book, and section twenty-one of the Parliamentary and Municipal Registration Act, 1878, shall apply to such borough or urban district, and where lists of voters are so made out nothing in this Act shall require such part of the county register as consists of these lists to be arranged alphabetically.

Making out of lists and registers in metropolis.

Sect. 5. After the year one thousand eight hundred and eighty-eight in every part of the metropolis, and in every part of a parliamentary borough, the whole or greater part of which is situate in the metropolis, the lists and registers of parliamentary voters, and of county electors, shall, unless the local authority otherwise direct, be arranged in the same order in which the qualifying premises appear in the rate book for the parish in which those premises are situate, or as nearly thereto as will cause those lists and registers to record the qualifying premises in successive order in the street or other place in which they are situate.

For the purpose of this section "metropolis" means the city of London and the parishes and places mentioned in Schedules (A), (B), and (C) of the Metropolis Management Act, 1855. (18 & 19 Vict. c. 120.)

Revision of electoral lists.

Sect. 6.—(1.) The lists of parliamentary voters, and of burgesses, and of county electors, shall be revised between the eighth day of September and the twelfth day of October both inclusive, and shall be revised as soon as possible after the seventh day of September, and the eighth day of September shall be substituted in the Acts relating to the registration of parliamentary voters for the fifteenth day of September; and the declarations under section ten of the County Voters Registration Act, 1865, and section twenty-four of the Parliamentary and Municipal Registration Act, 1878, shall be sent to the clerk of the peace or town clerk on or before the fifth day of September. (28 & 29 Vict. c. 36. 41 & 42 Vict. c. 26.)

(2.) In sections sixty-two and sixty-three of the Parliamentary Voters Registration Act, 1843 (relating to appeals from revising barristers in England), "the Michaelmas sittings of the High Court of Justice" shall be substituted for "the Michaelmas term," and forthwith after the fourth day of the Michaelmas sittings a court or courts shall sit for the purpose of hearing such appeals, and those appeals shall be heard and determined continuously and without delay, and any statement by the barrister for the purpose of any such appeal made in pursuance of section forty-two of the said Act may be made at any time within ten days after the conclusion of the revision, so that it be made not less than four days before the first day of the said Michaelmas sittings, and the statement need not be read in open court, but shall be submitted to the appellant, who, if he approves the same, shall sign the same as directed by the said section, and return the same to the barrister. (6 & 7 Vict. c. 18.)

Roll of county electors.

Sect. 7.—(1.) The clerk of the peace of every county shall make up a register of all persons registered as burgesses or county electors in the county, both for the county and for each electoral division into which the county is divided for the purpose of election of the county authority, and such number of copies as the clerk of the peace may require of the list of burgesses as revised shall be delivered by the town clerk to such clerk of the peace for the purpose of making up such register. 51 Vict. c. 10, s. 7.

(2.) The Registration of Electors Acts, and sections forty-five, forty-eight, and seventy-one of the Municipal Corporations Act, 1882, shall apply, for the purposes of this section, with the substitution of clerk of the peace for town clerk, and of county register and division register for burgess roll and ward roll respectively, and of electoral division for ward, and of county fund for borough fund. 45 & 46 Vict. c. 50.

(3.) If district councils are established under any Act of the present session of Parliament, the clerk of every such council, not being the council of a borough, shall make up a register of all persons registered as county electors in his district, and where there are wards in a district, of all county electors in each ward, and he shall obtain from the clerk of the peace a sufficient number of copies of the lists of the county electors so registered as may be required for the purpose of making up such register and supplying the same to the public, and the above-mentioned Acts and sections shall apply for that purpose, with the substitution of "clerk of the district council" for "town clerk," and of "district register" for "burgess roll" respectively;

(4.) Provided that nothing in this section shall prevent a county elector from being registered in more than one division register.

(5.) Where in pursuance of section four of the Registration Act, 1885, the revising barrister has power to erase the name of any person as a parliamentary voter from division one of the occupiers list, such barrister, in lieu of erasing the name, shall place an asterisk or other mark against the name, and, in printing such lists, the name shall be numbered consecutively with the other names, but an asterisk or other mark shall be printed against the name, and a person against whose name such asterisk or other mark is placed shall not be entitled to vote in respect of such entry at a parliamentary election, but shall have the same right of voting at an election of a county authority as he would have if no such mark were placed against his name. 48 & 49 Vict. c. 15.

(6.) If under any Act of the present session of Parliament establishing a council for a county any portion of another county is added to that county for the purpose of such election, such portion of the county register as relates to the electors having qualifying property in the said part so added shall be deemed to be part of the county register of the county for which such council is elected, and the clerk of the peace and other officers shall take such steps as may be necessary for giving effect to these enactments.

Sect. 8.—(1.) All expenses properly incurred and all sums received in carrying into effect the provisions of this Act and the Registration of Electors Acts with respect to county electors— Expenses.

(*a*.) if incurred or received by overseers, shall be respectively paid and applied as expenses and receipts of overseers under the Registration of Electors Acts in the case of the lists of parliamentary voters; and

(*b*.) if incurred or received by the clerk of the peace or town clerk, shall be paid out of or into the county or borough fund; and such expenses shall include all proper and reasonable fees and charges made and charged by him for the trouble, care, and attention of such clerk in the performance of the services and duties imposed on him by the said provisions.

Sect. 9. Every barrister appointed to revise any list of voters under the Parliamentary Voters Registration Act, 1843, shall be paid the sum of two hundred and fifty guineas by way of remuneration to him, and in satisfaction of his travelling and other expenses, and every such barrister, after the termination of his last sitting, shall forward his appointment to the Commissioners of Her Majesty's Treasury, who shall make an order for the payment of the above sum to every such barrister. Remuneration of revising barristers and contribution by county authorities.

51 Vict. c. 10, s. 9.

49 & 50 Vict. c. 42.

The maximum amount to be paid to an additional barrister in pursuance of the Revising Barristers Act, 1886, shall not exceed the amount authorised by this section to be paid to a revising barrister.

The sums so paid to a revising barrister or an assistant barrister shall be payable partly out of moneys provided by Parliament and partly by the county authorities, as hereinafter mentioned.

(1.) There shall be annually paid by the county authority of every county out of the county fund into Her Majesty's Exchequer such sum as the Treasury certify to be one-half of the cost incurred for the payment of revising barristers at the then last revision of the lists of parliamentary electors, burgesses, and county electors in that county.

(2.) The Treasury shall yearly ascertain the total cost of the revising barristers appointed for all the counties and boroughs on any circuit, and shall divide one-half of such cost among the counties comprised in such circuit in proportion to the number of burgesses and county electors in each county, and certify the amount which under such apportionment is due under this section from each county. The Treasury may vary such certificate if they think fit, but unless it is so varied the certificate shall be final.

(3.) So much of any Act as requires a payment out of the borough fund of any borough to a revising barrister, in respect of the revision of the burgess lists, shall be repealed, without prejudice to any payment or liability previously made or incurred.

Perpetuation of 49 & 50 Vict. c. 42. Repeal of 6 & 7 Vict. c. 18, s. 59.

Sect. 10.—(1.) Section four of the Revising Barristers Act, 1886, is hereby repealed, and that Act, as amended by this Act, shall be perpetual.

(2.) So long as a separate commission of assize is issued for the county of Surrey, that county shall be deemed to be a circuit within the meaning of section two, as well as of section one of the Revising Barristers Act, 1886.

(3.) An application to appoint an additional barrister under the said Act may be made at any time after the first day of September.

(4.) Section fifty-nine of the Parliamentary Voters Registration Act, 1843, is hereby repealed.

Application of provisions of Act respecting county fund.

Sect. 11.—(1.) In the event of a county authority being established under any Act of the present session, the provisions of this Act with respect to county authority, county, and county fund shall refer to the said county authority and to the county and county fund of such authority, and in the case of any borough which, for the purposes of the said Act, is a county of itself, to the council of the borough and to the borough and borough fund.

(2.) In the event of a county authority not being established under any Act during the present session, the sums directed by this Act to be paid out of and into the county fund shall be paid by or under the direction of the local authority of every county quarter sessional area within the meaning of the Registration Act, 1885, in like manner as expenses or receipts of the clerk of the peace for such area under the Registration of Electors Acts, and by and under the direction of the council of every municipal borough which is also a parliamentary borough out of and into the borough fund, and the amount to be paid for revising barristers shall be apportioned between such quarter sessional areas and boroughs upon the principles above mentioned in this Act.

48 & 49 Vict. c. 15.

Separate list of persons residing within fifteen miles of county.

Sect. 12. A list of persons occupying property in a county, and residing within fifteen miles, but more than seven miles from the county, shall be made out in accordance with section forty-nine of the Municipal Corporations Act, 1882, and that section shall apply as if it were herein re-enacted, with the substitution of "county" for "borough," and of "county elector" for "burgess," and of "clerk of the peace" for "town clerk."

Precepts by clerk of the peace.

Sect. 13. All precepts, notices, and forms required for the purposes of the Registration of Electors Acts shall be altered in such manner as may be declared by Her Majesty in Council to be necessary for carrying into effect this Act, and clerks of the peace and town clerks shall alter their precepts and forms accordingly, and if clerks of the peace or town clerks have sent out precepts to the overseers before the passing of this Act, they shall send to them such supplemental precepts as are necessary or desirable for instructing them to carry into effect this Act. 51 Vict. c. 10, s. 13.

Sect. 14. In this Act, unless the context otherwise requires,— Definitions.

The expressions "urban district" and "rural district" respectively mean an urban or rural sanitary district, also any urban or rural district under any Act of the present session of Parliament;

The expression "clerk of the peace" means, in the event of the establishment of a county authority, the person acting as clerk of that authority, and such person shall act as clerk of the peace throughout the whole county of such authority, both for the purposes of this Act and of the Registration of Electors Acts; subject nevertheless—

(*a*) to the provisions of the Registration Act, 1885, respecting the case of any parliamentary county extending into more county quarter sessional areas than one, and

(*b*) to the proviso that where at the passing of this Act any clerk of the peace acts as clerk of the peace under the Registration of Electors Acts he shall continue so to act, but shall act as deputy of the person acting as clerk of the peace by virtue of this Act.

Sect. 15. In the year one thousand eight hundred and eighty-eight, notwithstanding anything in this Act or the enactments applied by this Act, the revision of the lists of parliamentary voters and county electors may be later than the twelfth day of October, so that it be not later than the thirty-first day of October, and the register of county electors shall be completed on or before the thirty-first day of December in the said year, and shall come into operation on the first day of January one thousand eight hundred and eighty-nine, and shall continue in operation until the next register of county electors comes in operation. Transitory provisions as to the year 1888.

In the year one thousand eight hundred and eighty-eight, notwithstanding anything in this Act or the enactments thereby applied, the clerk of the peace in a county may, if he thinks fit, instead of directing the occupiers list to be made out in three divisions as provided by the Registration of Electors Acts, direct the overseers to make supplemental lists containing the names which would otherwise be contained in division two and division three of the occupiers list respectively, and the names so contained in the supplemental list corresponding to division two shall be struck by the revising barrister out of division one of the list, and the supplemental list corresponding to division two or division three shall be treated as if it were division two or three of the said list, as the case may be.

SCHEDULE.

Section 3.

Registration Act, 1885.

DEFINITION OF TEN POUNDS OCCUPATION QUALIFICATION.

A person entitled to be registered as a voter in respect of a ten pounds occupation qualification in a borough, municipal or parliamentary— Ten pounds occupation qualification.

(*a*.) must during the whole twelve months immediately preceding the fifteenth day of July have been an occupier as owner or tenant of some land or tenement in a parish [or township] of the clear yearly value of not less than ten pounds; and

(*b*.) must have resided in or within seven miles of the borough during six months immediately preceding the fifteenth day of July; and

51 Vict c. 10, s. 3.

(*c*.) Such person, or some one else, must during the said twelve months have been rated to all poor rates made in respect of such land or tenement ; and

(*d*.) All sums due in respect of the said land or tenement on account of any poor rate made and allowed during the twelve months immediately preceding the fifth day of January next before the registration, or on account of any assessed taxes due before the said fifth day of January, must have been paid on or before the twentieth day of July.

If two or more persons jointly are such occupiers as above mentioned, and the value of the land or tenement is such as to give ten pounds or more for each occupier, each of such occupiers is entitled to be registered as a voter.

If a person has occupied in the borough different lands or tenements of the requisite value in immediate succession during the said twelve months, he is entitled in respect of the occupation thereof to be registered as a voter in the parish [or township] in which the last occupied land or tenement is situate.

Appendix C.

LOCAL GOVERNMENT (ENGLAND AND WALES) ACT, 1888.

[51 & 52 VICT. CH. 41.]

An Act to amend the Laws relating to Local Government in England and Wales, and for other purposes connected therewith.

[13th August, 1888.]

BE it enacted by the Queen's most Excellent Majesty, by and with the advice and consent of the Lords Spiritual and Temporal, and Commons, in this present Parliament assembled, and by the authority of the same, as follows:

PART I.

COUNTY COUNCILS.

Constitution of County Council.

Sect. 1. A council shall be established in every administrative county as defined by this Act, and be entrusted with the management of the administrative and financial business of that county, and shall consist of the chairman, aldermen, and councillors. Establishment of county council.

Sect. 2.—(1.) The council of a county and the members thereof shall be constituted and elected and conduct their proceedings in like manner, and be in the like position in all respects, as the council of a borough divided into wards, subject nevertheless to the provisions of this Act, and in particular to the following provisions, that is to say:— Composition and election of council and position of chairman.

(2.) As respects the aldermen or councillors—

(*a.*) clerks in holy orders and other ministers of religion shall not be disqualified for being elected and being aldermen or councillors;

(*b.*) a person shall be qualified to be an alderman or councillor who, though not qualified in manner provided by the Municipal Corporations Act, 1882, as applied by this Act, is a peer owning property in the county, or is registered as a parliamentary voter in respect of the ownership of property of whatsoever tenure situate in the county; 45 & 46 Vict. c. 50.

(*c.*) the aldermen shall be called county aldermen, and the councillors shall be called county councillors; and a county alderman shall not, as such, vote in the election of a county alderman;

(*d.*) the county councillors shall be elected for a term of three years, and shall then retire together, and their places shall be filled by a new election; and

(*e.*) the divisions of the county for the purpose of the election of county councillors, shall be called electoral divisions and not wards, and one county councillor only shall be elected for each electoral division:

(3.) As respects the number of the county councillors, and the boundaries of the electoral divisions in every county—

51 & 52 Vict. c. 41, s. 2.

(*a.*) the number of the county councillors, and their apportionment between each of the boroughs which have sufficient population to return one councillor and the rest of the county, shall be such as the Local Government Board may determine; and

(*b.*) any borough returning one councillor only shall be an electoral division; and

(*c.*) in the rest of the county the electoral divisions shall be such as in the case of a borough returning more than one councillor the council of the borough, and in the rest of the county the quarter sessions for the county, may determine, subject in either case to the directions enacted by this Act; and in the case of elections after the first, to any alterations made, in accordance with the said directions, in manner in this Act mentioned:

45 & 46 Vict. c. 50.

51 & 52 Vict. c. 10.

(4.) As respects the electors of the county councillors—
the persons entitled to vote at their election shall be, in a borough, the burgesses enrolled in pursuance of the Municipal Corporations Act, 1882, and the Acts amending the same, and elsewhere the persons registered as county electors under the County Electors Act, 1888:

(5.) As respects the chairman of the county council—

(*a.*) he shall be called chairman instead of mayor; and

(*b.*) he shall, by virtue of his office, be a justice of the peace for the county; but before acting as such justice he shall, if he has not already done so, take the oaths required by law to be taken by a justice of the peace other than the oath respecting the qualification by estate.

(6.) The county council may from time to time appoint a member of the council to be vice-chairman, to hold office during the term of office of the chairman, and, subject to any rules made from time to time by the county council, anything authorised or required to be done by, to, or before the chairman may be done by, to, or before such vice-chairman.

Powers of County Council.

Transfer to county council of administrative business of quarter sessions.

Sect. 3. There shall be transferred to the council of each county on and after the appointed day, the administrative business of the justices of the county in quarter sessions assembled, that is to say, all business done by the quarter sessions or any committee appointed by the quarter sessions, in respect of the several matters following, namely,—

(i.) The making, assessing, and levying of county, police, hundred, and all rates, and the application and expenditure thereof, and the making of orders for the payment of sums payable out of any such rate or out of the county stock or county fund, and the preparation and revision of the basis or standard for the county rate;

(ii.) The borrowing of money;

(iii.) The passing of the accounts of and the discharge of the county treasurer;

(iv.) Shire halls, county halls, assize courts, judges lodgings, lock-up houses, court houses, justices rooms, police stations, and county buildings, works, and property, subject as to the use of buildings by the quarter sessions and the justices to the provisions of this Act respecting the joint committee of quarter sessions and the county council;

(v.) The licensing under any general Act of houses and other places for music or for dancing, and the granting of licences under the Racecourses Licensing Act, 1879;

42 & 43 Vict. c. 18.

(vi.) The provision, enlargement, maintenance, management, and visitation of and other dealing with asylums for pauper lunatics;

(vii.) The establishment and maintenance of and the contribution to reformatory and industrial schools;

(viii.) Bridges and roads repairable with bridges, and any powers vested by the Highways and Locomotives (Amendment) Act, 1878, in the county authority;

41 & 42 Vict. c. 77.

(ix.) The tables of fees to be taken by and the costs to be allowed to any inspector, analyst, or person holding any office in the county other than the clerk of the peace and the clerks of the justices;

(x.) The appointment, removal, and determination of salaries, of the county treasurer, the county surveyor, the public analysts, any officer under the Explosives Act, 1875, and any officers whose remuneration is paid out of the county rate other than the clerk of the peace and the clerks of the justices; 51 & 52 Vict. c. 41, s. 3. 38 & 39 Vict. c. 17.

(xi.) The salary of any coroner whose salary is payable out of the county rate, the fees, allowances, and disbursements allowed to be paid by any such coroner, and the division of the county into coroners' districts, and the assignment of such districts;

(xii.) The division of the county into polling districts for the purposes of parliamentary elections, the appointment of places of election, the places of holding courts for the revision of the lists of voters, and the costs of and other matters to be done for the registration of parliamentary voters;

(xiii.) The execution as local authority of the Acts relating to contagious diseases of animals, to destructive insects, to fish conservancy, to wild birds, to weights and measures, and to gas meters, and of the Local Stamp Act, 1869; 32 & 33 Vict. c. 49.

(xiv.) Any matters arising under the Riot (Damages) Act, 1886; 49 & 50 Vict. c. 38.

(xv.) The registration of rules of scientific societies under the Act of the session of the sixth and seventh years of the reign of Her present Majesty, chapter thirty-six; the registration of charitable gifts under the Act of the session of the fifty-second year of the reign of George the Third, chapter one hundred and two; the certifying and recording of places of religious worship under the Act of the session of the fifty-second year of the reign of George the Third, chapter one hundred and fifty-five; the confirmation and record of the rules of loan societies under the Act of the session of the third and fourth years of the reign of Her present Majesty, chapter one hundred and ten; and

(xvi.) Any other business transferred by this Act.

Sect. 4. Where it appears to the Local Government Board that any powers, duties, or liabilities of any quarter sessions or justices, or any committee thereof, under any local Act are similar in character to the powers, duties, and liabilities transferred to county councils by this Act, or relate to property transferred to a county council by this Act, the Board may, if they think fit, make a Provisional Order for transferring such powers, duties, and liabilities to the county council. Transfer of certain powers under local Acts.

Sect. 5.—(1.) After the appointed day a coroner for a county shall not be elected by the freeholders of the county, and on any vacancy occurring in the office of a coroner for a county, who is elected to that office in pursuance of a writ *de coronatore eligendo*, a like writ for the election of a successor shall be directed to the county council of the county instead of to the sheriff, and the county council shall thereupon appoint a fit person, not being a county alderman or county councillor, to fill such office, and in the case of a county divided into coroners districts shall assign him a district; and any person so appointed shall have like powers and duties, and be entitled to like remuneration, as if he had been elected coroner for the county by the freeholders thereof. Appointment of coroners by county council.

(2.) Where the district of any such coroner is situate wholly within any administrative county, the council of that county shall, subject as hereinafter mentioned, appoint the coroner.

(3.) Where the district of any such coroner is situate partly in one and partly in another administrative county forming part of an entire county, the joint committee for the entire county may arrange for the alteration in manner provided by law of the district, so that, on the next avoidance of the office of coroner of that district, or at any earlier time fixed by the joint committee when the alteration is made, the coroner's district shall not be situate in more than one administrative county.

(4.) Until such arrangement is made, the joint committee for the entire county shall appoint the coroner for the said district, and the amount payable in respect of the salary, fees, and expenses of such coroner shall be defrayed in like manner as costs of the joint committee are directed by this Act to be defrayed.

(5.) Nothing in this Act respecting the appointment of a coroner shall alter the jurisdiction of a coroner for the entire county, or any power of removing such coroner, whether by writ *de coronatore exonerando* or otherwise, and all writs for

51 & 52 Vict. c. 41, s. 5. the election or removal of a coroner shall be altered so as to give effect to this section.

50 & 51 Vict. c. 71. (6.) Sections eleven and fourteen of the First Schedule of the Coroners Act, 1887, and any other enactment relating to the election of a coroner for a county by the freeholders of such county or any district thereof, are hereby repealed as from the appointed day, without prejudice to anything done or suffered, or any legal proceeding commenced or penalty incurred before such repeal takes effect.

(7.) A person who holds the office of coroner shall not be qualified to be elected as a county alderman or county councillor for the county for which he is a coroner.

Power of council as to bridges.

Sect. 6. The county council shall have power to purchase, or take over on terms to be agreed on, existing bridges not being at present county bridges, and to erect new bridges, and to maintain, repair, and improve any bridges so purchased, taken over, or erected.

Transfer to county council of certain powers of justices out of session.

Sect. 7. There shall be transferred to the county council on and after the appointed day the business of the justices of the county out of session—

(*a.*) in respect of the licensing of houses or places for the public performance of stage plays, and

38 & 39 Vict. c. 17. (*b.*) in respect of the execution as local authority of the Explosives Act, 1875.

Reservation of business to quarter sessions.

Sect. 8.—(1.) Nothing in this Act shall transfer to a county council any business of the quarter sessions or justices in relation to appeals by any overseers or persons against the basis or standard for the county rate or against that or any other rate.

(2.) All business of the quarter sessions or any committee thereof not transferred by or in pursuance of this Act to the county council shall be reserved to and transacted by the quarter sessions or committee thereof in the same manner, as far as circumstances admit, as if this Act had not passed.

Powers as to police.

Sect. 9.—(1.) The powers, duties, and liabilities of quarter sessions and of justices out of session with respect to the county police shall, on and after the appointed day, vest in and attach to the quarter sessions and the county council jointly, and be exercised and discharged through the standing joint committee of the quarter sessions and county council appointed as hereinafter mentioned:

19 & 20 Vict. c. 19. (2.) Provided that the powers conferred by section seven of the County and Borough Police Act, 1856, which requires constables to perform, in addition to their ordinary duties, such duties connected with the police as the quarter sessions may direct or require, shall continue to be exercised by the quarter sessions as well as by the said standing joint committee, and may also be exercised by the county council; and the said section shall be construed as if the county council and the said standing joint committee were therein mentioned as well as the quarter sessions.

(3.) Nothing in this Act shall affect the powers, duties, and liabilities of justices of the peace as conservators of the peace, or the obligation of the chief constable or other constables to obey their lawful orders given in that behalf.

Transfer to county council of power of certain Government departments and other authorities.

Sect. 10. (1.) After the passing of this Act it shall be lawful for the Local Government Board to make from time to time a Provisional Order for transferring to county councils—

(*a.*) any such powers, duties, and liabilities of Her Majesty's Privy Council, a Secretary of State, the Board of Trade, the Local Government Board, or the Education Department, or any other Government department, as are conferred by or in pursuance of any statute and appear to relate to matters arising within the county, and to be of an administrative character: also

(*b.*) any such powers, duties, and liabilities arising within the county, of any commissioners of sewers, conservators, or other public body, corporate or unincorporate (not being the corporation of a municipal borough or an urban or rural authority, or a school board, and not being a board of guardians) as are conferred by or in pursuance of any statute;

and such Order shall make such exceptions and modifications as appear to be expedient, and also such provisions as appear necessary or proper for carrying into effect such transfer, and for that purpose may transfer any power vested in Her Majesty in Council: 51 & 52 Vict. c. 41, s. 10.

(2.) Provided that before any such Order is made, the draft thereof shall be approved, if it relates to the powers, duties, or liabilities of a Secretary of State, or the Board of Trade, or any other Government department, by such Secretary of State, Board, or department, and approved, if it affects the powers, duties, or liabilities of any commissioners, conservators, or body, corporate or unincorporate, by such commissioners, conservators, or body; and every such Provisional Order shall be of no effect until it is confirmed by Parliament.

(3.) If any such powers, duties, or liabilities as are referred to in any Provisional Order under this section arise within two or more counties, they may be transferred to the county councils of such two or more counties jointly, and may be exercised and discharged by a joint committee of such councils.

(4.) The Act of Parliament confirming any Provisional Order made under this section shall be a public general Act.

Entire maintenance of main roads by county council. 41 & 42 Vict. c. 77.

Sect. 11.—(1.) Every road in a county, which is for the time being a main road within the meaning of the Highways and Locomotives (Amendment) Act, 1878, inclusive of every bridge carrying such road if repairable by the highway authority, shall, after the appointed day, be wholly maintained and repaired by the council of the county in which the road is situate, and such council, for the purpose of the maintenance, repair, improvement, and enlargement of, and other dealing with such road, shall have the same powers and be subject to the same duties as a highway board, and may further exercise any powers vested in the council for the purpose of the maintenance and repair of bridges, and the enactments relating to highways and bridges shall apply accordingly; and the county council shall have the same powers as a highway board for preventing and removing obstructions, and for asserting the right of the public to the use and enjoyment of the roadside wastes; and the execution of this section shall be a general county purpose, and the costs thereof shall be charged to the general county account.

(2.) Provided that any urban authority may, within twelve months after the appointed day, or in case of a road in the district of such authority becoming a main road at any subsequent date then within twelve months after that date, claim to retain the powers and duties of maintaining and repairing a main road within the district of such authority, and thereupon they shall be entitled to retain the same, and, for the purpose of the maintenance, repair, improvement, and enlargement of, and other dealing with such road, shall have the same powers and be subject to the same duties as if such road were an ordinary road vested in them, and the council shall make to such authority an annual payment towards the costs of the maintenance and repair, and reasonable improvement connected with the maintenance and repair of such road.

(3.) The amount of such payment shall be such annual sum as may be from time to time agreed on, or in the absence of agreement may be determined by arbitration of the Local Government Board.

(4.) The county council and any district council may from time to time contract for the undertaking by the district council of the maintenance, repair, improvement, and enlargement of, and other dealing with any main road, and, if the county council so require, the district council shall undertake the same, and such undertaking shall be in consideration of such annual payment by the county council for the costs of the undertaking as may from time to time be agreed upon, or, in case of difference, be determined by arbitration of the Local Government Board; and for the purposes of such undertaking the district council shall have the same powers and be subject to the same duties and liabilities as if the road were an ordinary road vested in them.

(5.) Provided that in no case shall a county council make any payment to a district council towards the costs of such undertaking as respects any road, or towards the costs of the maintenance, repair, or improvement of any road by an urban authority, until the county council are satisfied by the report of their

51 & 52 Vict. c. 41, s. 11. surveyor, or such other person as the county council may appoint for the purpose, that the road has been properly maintained and repaired, or that the improvement or enlargement of or other dealing with the road, as the case may be, has been properly executed.

(6.) A main road and the materials thereof, and all drains belonging thereto, shall, except where the urban authority retain the powers and duties of maintaining and repairing such road, vest in the county council, and where any sewer or other drain is used for any purpose in connexion with the drainage of any main road, the county council shall continue to have the right of using such sewer or drain for such purpose, and if any difference arises between a county council and any highway or sanitary authority as respects the authority in whom the drain is vested, or as to the use of any sewer or other drain, the council or the highway or sanitary authority may require such difference to be referred to arbitration, and the same shall be referred to arbitration in manner provided by this Act.

(7.) Where a county council declare a road to be a main road, such declaration shall not take effect until the road has been placed in proper repair and condition to the satisfaction of the county council.

(8.) If at any time the county council are satisfied, on the report of their surveyor or other person appointed by them for the purpose, that any portion of a main road, the maintenance and repair of which are undertaken by any district council, is not in proper repair and condition, the county council may cause notice to be given to such district council, requiring them to place the road in proper repair and condition; and, if such notice is not complied with within a reasonable time, the county council may do everything that seems to them necessary to place the road in proper repair and condition, and the expenses of so doing shall be a debt of the said district council to the county council.

(9.) If any difference arises under this section between a county council and a district council as to the refusal of the county council to make a payment under this section to the district council in respect of any undertaking or road, or as to a road having been placed in proper repair and condition previously to its becoming a main road, or as to any notice given to the district council by the county council to place a road in proper repair and condition, such difference shall, if either council so require, be referred to the arbitration of the Local Government Board.

(10.) The county council may, if they think fit, contribute towards the costs of the maintenance, repair, enlargement, and improvement of any highway or public footpath in the county, although the same is not a main road.

(11.) Every authority having any power or duty to light the roads in their district shall have the same power and duty to light any main road in their district.

(12.) Anything authorised or required by law to be done by or to a highway or road authority shall, as respects a main road maintained by a county council, be authorised or required to be done by or to that council; and every authority having any power to break up any road in their district for the purpose of sewerage or otherwise shall have the like power of breaking up any main road in their district, but if the road is broken up the authority shall repair it to the satisfaction of the county council maintaining such road, and if it is not repaired to the satisfaction of the county council, that council may cause the necessary repairs to be done and may charge the costs against the authority, and the same shall be a debt due from the authority to the council.

41 & 42 Vict. c. 77. (13.) Section twenty of the Highways and Locomotives (Amendment) Act, 1878, shall apply as if it were herein re-enacted and in terms made applicable to this section.

Roads and tolls in Isle of Wight. **Sect. 12.** (1.) After the appointed day, tolls shall cease to be taken on any road maintained and repaired by the Isle of Wight Highway Commissioners, under the Isle of Wight Highway Acts, 1813 and 1883, and after such day the Highways and Locomotives (Amendment) Act, 1878, as amended by this Act, shall apply to the Isle of Wight, and to every such road above mentioned, in like manner as if it were ceasing within the meaning of the said Act to be a turnpike road, and the Act of the session of the forty-fourth and forty-fifth years of the reign of Her present Majesty, chapter seventy-two, shall be repealed. 51 & 52 Vict. c. 41, s. 12. 44 & 45 Vict. c 72.

(2.) Until provision is otherwise made by Parliament, or by a Provisional Order confirmed by Parliament, the repair and maintenance of the said roads shall continue to be undertaken by the said commissioners, and the county council for the county of Southampton shall pay such commissioners, in respect of the said repairs and maintenance, and of the expenses of the commissioners, such sums as may be agreed upon, or, in case of difference, be settled by arbitration under this Act, and the provisions of this Act with respect to main roads shall apply as if the commissioners were a district council who had undertaken the maintenance and repair of such roads.

Adaptation of Act to South Wales roads. 7 & 8 Vict. c. 91.

Sect. 13.—(1.) After the appointed day no county road rate shall be levied, and tolls shall cease to be taken on any road maintained and repaired by a county roads board in South Wales, in pursuance of the South Wales Turnpike Trusts Act, 1844, and the Acts amending the same, and after such day the Highways and Locomotives (Amendment) Act, 1878, as amended by this Act shall apply to every county in South Wales as if the highway districts in that county had been constituted under the Highway Act, 1862, and the Highway Act, 1864, or one of those Acts, and shall apply to every such road as above-mentioned, in like manner as if it were ceasing, within the meaning of the said Act, to be a turnpike road. 25 & 26 Vict. c. 61. 27 & 28 Vict. c. 101.

(2.) On the appointed day every county roads board and district roads board in each county shall cease to exist, and the property, debts, and liabilities of any such board shall be transferred to the county council, and that council shall be the successors of the county and district roads boards, and the provisions of this Act, with respect to the transfer of the property, debts, and liabilities of quarter sessions to county councils, and with respect to the officers and servants of quarter sessions, shall apply as if they were herein re-enacted and made applicable to the property, debts, liabilities, and officers of the said county and district roads boards.

(3.) For the following purposes (that is to say):

(*a.*) For giving effect to the said transfer of the property, debts, and liabilities, and for controlling the officers and servants transferred by this section to the county council,. and otherwise winding up the affairs of the county and district roads boards; and

(*b.*) For the purpose of the appointment of the surveyor of a highway board, the alteration of a highway district, and other purposes relating to highway boards:

the county council of every county in South Wales shall have all the powers of a county roads board in a county under the South Wales Turnpike Trusts Act, 1844, and the Acts amending the same, so, however, that nothing shall confer on the county council any power to levy any toll or county road rate.

Power to county council to enforce provisions of 39 & 40 Vict. c. 75.

Sect. 14.—(1.) On and after the appointed day a county council shall have power, in addition to any other authority, to enforce the provisions of the Rivers Pollution Prevention Act, 1876 (subject to the restrictions in that Act contained), in relation to so much of any stream as is situate within, or passes through or by, any part of their county, and for that purpose they shall have the same powers and duties as if they were a sanitary authority within the meaning of that Act, or any other authority having power to enforce the provisions of that Act, and the county were their district.

(2.) Any county council shall have power to contribute towards the costs of any prosecution under the said Act instituted by any other county council or by any urban or rural authority.

(3.) The Local Government Board, by Provisional Order made on the application of the council of any of the counties concerned, may constitute a joint committee or other body representing all the administrative counties through or by which a river, or any specified portion of a river, or any tributary thereof,

51 & 52 Vict. c. 41. s. 14. passes, and may confer on such committee or body all of the powers of a sanitary authority under the Rivers Pollution Prevention Act, 1876, or such of them as may be specified in the Order; and the Order may contain such provisions respecting the constitution and proceedings of the said committee or body as may seem proper, and may provide for the payment of the expenses of such committee or body by the administrative counties represented by it, and for the audit of the accounts of such committee or body, and their officers.

Council to have power to oppose Bills in Parliament.

Sect. 15. The county council of an administrative county shall have the same powers of opposing Bills in Parliament, and of prosecuting or defending any legal proceedings necessary for the promotion or protection of the interests of the inhabitants of the county, as are conferred on the council of a municipal borough by the Act of the thirty-fifth and thirty-sixth years of Victoria, chapter ninety-one; and subject as herein-after provided the provisions of that Act shall extend to a county council as if such council were included in the expression "governing body," and the administrative county were the district in the said Act mentioned.

Provided that—

(*a.*) No consent of owners and ratepayers shall be required for any proceedings under this section;

(*b.*) This section shall not empower a county council to promote any Bill in Parliament, or to incur or charge any expense in relation thereto.

Power of county council to make bye-laws. 45 & 46 Vict. c. 50. 38 & 39 Vict. c. 55.

Sect. 16.—(1.) A county council shall have the same power of making bye-laws in relation to their county, or to any specified part or parts thereof, as the council of a borough have of making bye-laws in relation to their borough under section twenty-three of the Municipal Corporations Act, 1882, and section one hundred and eighty-seven of the Public Health Act, 1875, shall apply to such bye-laws:

(2.) Provided that bye-laws made under the powers of this section shall not be of any force or effect within any borough.

Power of county councils to appoint medical officer of health.

Sect. 17.—(1.) The council of any county may, if they see fit, appoint and pay a medical officer of health, or medical officers of health, who shall not hold any other appointment or engage in private practice without express written consent of the council.

(2.) The county council and any district council may from time to time make and carry into effect arrangements for rendering the services of such officer or officers regularly available in the district of the district council, on such terms as to the contribution by the district council to the salary of the medical officer, or otherwise, as may be agreed, and the medical officer shall have within such district all the powers and duties of a medical officer appointed by a district council.

(3.) So long as such an arrangement is in force, the obligation of the district council under the Public Health Act, 1875, to appoint a medical officer of health shall be deemed to be satisfied without the appointment of a separate medical officer.

Qualification of medical officers of health.

Sect. 18.—(1.) Except where the Local Government Board, for reasons brought to their notice, may see fit in particular cases specially to allow, no person shall hereafter be appointed the medical officer of health of any county or county district, or combination of county districts, or the deputy of any such officer, unless he be legally qualified for the practice of medicine, surgery, and midwifery.

(2.) No person shall after the first day of January one thousand eight hundred and ninety-two be appointed the medical officer of health of any county or of any such district or combination of districts, as contained, according to the last published census for the time being, a population of fifty thousand or more inhabitants, unless he is qualified as above-mentioned, and also either is registered in the medical register as the holder of a diploma in sanitary science, public health, or State medicine under section twenty-one of the Medical Act, 1886, or has been during three consecutive years preceding the year one thousand eight hundred and ninety-two a medical officer of a district or combination of districts, with a population according to the last published census of not less than

49 & 50 Vict. c. 48.

twenty thousand, or has before the passing of this Act been for not less than three years a medical officer or inspector of the Local Government Board. 51 & 52 Vict. c. 41, s. 18.

Sect. 19.—(1.) Every medical officer of health for a district in any county shall send to the county council a copy of every periodical report of which a copy is for the time being required by the regulations of the Local Government Board to be sent to the Board, and if a medical officer fails to send such copy the county council may refuse to pay any contribution, which otherwise the council would in pursuance of this Act pay, towards the salary of such medical officer. Power of county council as to report of medical officer of health.

(2.) If it appears to the county council from any such report that the Public Health Act, 1875, has not been properly put in force within the district to which the report relates, or that any other matter affecting the public health of the district requires to be remedied, the council may cause a representation to be made to the Local Government Board on the matter.

Financial Relations between Exchequer and County, and Contributions by County for Costs of Union Officers.

Sect. 20.—(1.) After the financial year ending on the thirty-first day of March next after the passing of this Act, the Commissioners of Inland Revenue shall from time to time, in such manner and under such regulations as the Treasury from time to time prescribe, pay into the Bank of England to such account (in this Act referred to as the Local Taxation Account) as may be fixed by the regulations, such sums as may be ascertained in manner provided by the regulations to be the proceeds of the duties collected by those Commissioners in each administrative county in England and Wales on the licences (in this Act referred to as local taxation licences) specified in the First Schedule to this Act, and for the purposes of this section all penalties and forfeitures recovered in respect of the said duties shall be considered as part of the proceeds of the duties. Payment to county council of proceeds of duties on local taxation licences.

(2.) The amount ascertained as aforesaid to have been collected in each county in respect of duties on local taxation licences shall, from time to time, be certified by the Commissioners of Inland Revenue, and paid under the direction of the Local Government Board out of the Local Taxation Account to the council of such county. The Commissioners may, if they think fit, vary such certificate, but unless so varied, their certificate shall be conclusive.

(3.) It shall be lawful for Her Majesty the Queen from time to time by Order in Council made on the recommendation of the Treasury to transfer to county councils as from the date specified in the Order the power to levy the duties on all or any of the local taxation licences, and after such date every county council and their officers shall (subject nevertheless to any exceptions and modifications contained in the Order) have within their county, for the purpose of levying the duties transferred, the same powers, duties, and liabilities as the Commissioners of Inland Revenue and their officers have with respect to the duties transferred, and to the issue and cancellation of licences on which the duties are imposed, and other matters under the Acts relating to those duties and licences, and all enactments relating to those duties and licences, and to punishments and penalties connected therewith, shall apply accordingly.

(4.) Provided as follows:—

(i.) All penalties and forfeitures recovered by a county council in pursuance of this section shall, instead of being paid to the Exchequer, be paid to the county fund, and carried to the same account as the duties.

(ii.) The county council shall have, as respects the said duties and licences, the power given by the said Acts to the Treasury for the restoration of any forfeiture, and the mitigation or remission of any penalty or any part thereof.

(iii.) Nothing in this section shall confer on the county council any special privileges of the Crown as respects legal proceedings.

(5.) On a transfer under this section of the power to levy the duties on any licence—

(*a*.) the county council shall provide for issuing, in different parts of their county, their licence for the same purpose, so as to enable persons to obtain it near their residences; and

51 & 52 Vict. c. 41, s. 20.

(*b*.) if such licence has operation in any place in the United Kingdom outside the county in which it is issued, the licence of a county council for the same purpose shall continue to have the like operation outside the county in such place.

Grant to county council of portion of probate duty.

Sect. 21. After the financial year ending the thirty-first day of March next after the passing of this Act, the Commissioners of Inland Revenue shall, from time to time, in such manner and under such regulations as the Treasury may from time to time prescribe, pay into the Bank of England to the Local Taxation Account, such sums as may be ascertained in manner provided by the regulations to be four fifth parts of one half of the proceeds of the sums collected by them in respect of the probate duties, and for the purpose of this section "probate duties" means the stamp duties charged on the affidavit required from persons applying for probate or letters of administration in England, Wales, or Ireland, and on the inventory exhibited and recorded in Scotland, and also the stamp duties charged on such accounts of personal and movable property as are specified in section thirty-eight of the Customs and Inland Revenue Act, 1881, and also includes the proceeds of all penalties and forfeitures recovered in relation to such stamp duties.

44 & 45 Vict. c. 12.

Distribution of probate duty grant.

Sect. 22.—(1.) The sums paid in pursuance of this Act to the Local Taxation Account, in respect of the proceeds of the probate duties (in this Act referred to as the "probate duty grant"), shall, until Parliament otherwise determine, be distributed among the several counties in England and Wales in proportion to the share which the Local Government Board certify to have been received by each county during the financial year ending the thirty-first day of March next before the passing of this Act out of the grants heretofore made out of the Exchequer in aid of local rates, which will cease to be granted after the passing of this Act, and the share to be so certified shall be estimated in such manner as the Local Government Board direct.

(2.) In the case of the six counties of South Wales and the Isle of Wight there shall be added to the amount actually received out of such grants as aforesaid such additional sum as the Local Government Board certify to be the amount which each of the said counties and the Isle of Wight would have received, if the roads maintained by the county roads boards or the highway commissioners had been main roads.

(3.) The proportion to be paid to each county shall from time to time be paid under the direction of the Local Government Board to the county council out of the Local Taxation Account. The Board may, if they think proper, vary their certificate, but unless it is so varied, their certificate shall be conclusive.

Application of duties on local taxation licences and probate duty grant.

Sect. 23.—(1.) All sums from time to time received by a county council in respect of—

(*a*.) the duties on the local taxation licences, whether collected by the Commissioners of Inland Revenue or by the county council; and

(*b*.) the probate duty grant,

shall be paid to the county fund and carried to a separate account, in this Act referred to as the Exchequer Contribution Account.

(2.) All sums for the time being standing to the Exchequer Contribution Account shall be applied—

(i.) in paying the costs incurred in respect thereof, or otherwise chargeable thereon; and

(ii.) in payment of the sums required by this Act to be paid by the county council in substitution for local grants; and

(iii.) in payment of the grant required by this Act to be made by the county council in respect of costs of union officers; and

(iv.) in repaying to the general county account of the county fund the costs on account of general county purposes for which the whole of the area of the county is liable to be assessed to county contributions;

and shall be so applied in the order above mentioned.

(3.) If any surplus remains after paying the above costs and sums, such proportion of the surplus, as the total rateable value of the area of each quarter sessions borough exempt from contributing to any special county purpose, bears to the rateable value of the whole county, shall be paid to the council of that borough, and the remainder shall be applied as follows:— 51 & 52 Vict. c. 14, s. 23.

(4.) It shall first be applied towards repaying to the proper special accounts of the county fund, the costs on account of which the area of the county, exclusive of such quarter sessions boroughs, is liable to be assessed to county contributions.

(5.) Provided that where any of the said quarter sessions boroughs to which a payment of a proportion of the surplus is made as aforesaid is liable to be assessed to county contributions for any of such last-mentioned costs, there shall be deducted from the amount payable to the council of that borough in respect of the said surplus, such sum as would have been raised within the area of the borough if the amount of such costs had been raised by county contributions.

(6.) If there remains any sum after repaying the said costs to the said accounts of the county fund, such residue shall be divided as follows, that is to say, such proportion thereof, as the total rateable value of the area of each borough maintaining a separate police force under the County and Borough Police Acts, and not being a quarter sessions borough above-mentioned, bears to the rateable value of the whole county, after deduction of the rateable value of every quarter sessions borough above-mentioned, shall be paid to the council of the borough, and the rest shall be applied towards repaying to the proper special accounts of the county fund the costs of the police, and other costs on account of which the area of the county, exclusive of all the said boroughs, is liable to be assessed to county contributions. Where a town, not being a borough, maintains its own police and receives any payment from the county council in pursuance of this Act towards the pay and clothing of such police, this enactment shall apply to such town as if it were a borough, and as if the sanitary authority therein were the council of the borough.

(7.) If any balance remains after all the above payments are made, and is in excess of what the county council consider necessary to carry forward to the next account, such excess shall be divided among the district councils other than the councils of quarter sessions or other boroughs to whom portions of the surplus have been paid under the foregoing provisions of this section, and shall be so divided in proportion to the rateable value of the area of each district.

(8.) Where any part of a county is situate within the Metropolitan Police district, this section shall apply as if that part were the area of a borough maintaining a separate police force, save that the sum which would be payable to such borough shall be paid to the district councils of the county districts wholly or partly situate in such part, and shall be divided among such district councils in proportion to the rateable value of the area of each district, or of so much thereof as is within the Metropolitan Police district.

(9.) All sums paid in pursuance of this section shall be carried, if paid to the council of a borough, to the borough fund, and if paid to a district council other than the council of a borough, to the district fund, and shall be applied to purposes for which the whole of the borough or district is liable to be rated.

(10.) The rateable value for the purpose of this section shall be determined according to the standard or basis for county contributions for the time being.

Sect. 24. Whereas certain grants heretofore made out of the Exchequer in aid of local rates (in this Act referred to as local grants) will by reason of the duties on the local taxation licences and the probate duty grant being by this Act made payable to local authorities, cease, it is therefore hereby enacted as follows:— Payments by county council in substitution for annual local grants out of Exchequer in aid of local rates.

(1.) So much of any enactment as requires or authorises payment out of the Exchequer of any local grant in substitution for which the county council is required by this Act to make any payment is hereby repealed as from the thirty-first day of March next after the passing of this Act without prejudice to any right accrued before that day.

(2.) In substitution for local grants, the council of each county shall from time

51 & 52 Vict. c. 41, s. 24. to time as from the said day pay out of the county fund and charge to the Exchequer Contribution Account the following sums, that is to say—

(*a.*) they shall pay to the guardians for every poor law union or officer for any other area wholly or partly in the county (as the case may be) such sums as the Local Government Board from time to time certify to be due from the said council in substitution for the local grants towards the remuneration of teachers in poor law schools, and for payments to public vaccinators under section five of the Vaccination Act, 1867; and

30 & 31 Vict. c. 84. (*b.*) they shall pay to the guardians of every poor law union the school fees paid for pauper children sent from a workhouse to a public elementary school outside the workhouse; and

(*c.*) they shall pay to every local authority, for any area wholly or partly in the county, by whom a medical officer of health or inspector of nuisances is paid, one half of the salary of such officer, where his qualification, appointment, salary, and tenure of office are in accordance with the regulations made by order under the Public Health Act, 1875, or any Act repealed by that Act, but if the Local Government Board certify to the council that such medical officer has failed to send to the Local Government Board such report and returns as are for the time being required by the regulations respecting the duties of such officer made by order of the Board under any of the said Acts, a sum equal to such half of the salary shall be forfeited to the Crown, and the council shall pay the same into Her Majesty's Exchequer and not to the said local authority; and

38 & 39 Vict. c. 55.

(*d.*) they shall pay to the guardians paying the registrars of births and deaths for any district wholly or partly in the county a sum equal to the amount paid out of local grants towards the remuneration of the registrars paid by those guardians during the financial year ending on the thirty-first day of March next after the passing of this Act; and

(*e.*) they shall transfer to that account of the county fund to which the maintenance of any pauper lunatic chargeable to the county is charged, a sum equal to four shillings a week for each such pauper lunatic, for whom the net charge upon the county council, after deducting any amount received by the county council for the maintenance of such lunatic from any source other than local rates, is equal to or exceeds four shillings a week throughout the period of maintenance for which the sum is so transferred; and

(*f.*) they shall pay to the guardians of every poor law union wholly or partly in the county a sum equal to four shillings a week for each pauper lunatic chargeable to that union, and maintained in an asylum, registered hospital, or licensed house, for whom the net charge upon the guardians, after deducting any amount received by them for the maintenance of such lunatic from any source other than local rates, is equal to or exceeds four shillings a week throughout the period of maintenance for which the sum is so paid; and

(*g.*) they shall pay to the council of each borough to which the maintenance of any pauper lunatic is chargeable, a sum equal to four shillings a week for each such pauper lunatic for whom the net charge upon the council of the borough, after deducting any amount received by them for the maintenance of such lunatic from any source other than local rates, is equal to or exceeds four shillings a week throughout the period of maintenance for which the sum is so paid; and

(*h.*) they shall transfer to that account of the county fund to which the compensation payable to the clerk of the peace of a county, or any other officer of quarter sessions for the county, under section 18 of the Act of the session of the eighteenth and nineteenth years of the reign of Her present Majesty, chapter one hundred and twenty-six is charged, the amount of such compensation; and

(*i.*) they shall, subject to the provisions of this Act, transfer to the police account of the county fund a sum equal to one half of the costs of the pay and clothing of the police of the county during the preceding year; and (*j*.) they shall, subject to the provisions of this Act, pay to the council of each borough maintaining a separate police force under the County and Borough Police Acts, one half of the costs of the pay and clothing of the police of that borough during the preceding year; and — 51 & 52 Vict. c. 41, s. 24.

(*k*.) they shall, if within their county sums are raised by rates for the purpose of the metropolitan police, pay to the receiver for the metropolitan police district in each year, a sum bearing such proportion to the sum actually raised in the same year by rates from the parishes in that county for the said purpose as a Secretary of State certifies to be the proportion which would have been contributed out of the Exchequer under the arrangement in force during the financial year next before the passing of this Act.

(3.) A reference in sections one hundred and eighty-nine and one hundred and ninety-one of the Public Health Act, 1875, to officers any portion of whose salary is paid out of moneys provided by Parliament shall be construed to refer to those officers in respect of whose salaries payment is made by a county council in pursuance of this section.

(4.) Where any payment towards the pay and clothing of the police of any town has been made in pursuance of section eighteen of the County and Borough Police Act, 1856, which authorises such payment to be made until the discontinuance of the police, the like payment shall, notwithstanding anything in this section, be made by the county council to the authority of such town until such discontinuance. — 19 & 20 Vict. c. 69.

(5.) Where a sum is payable under this section to the guardians, authority, or officer of a union or other area, and such union or area is situate in more administrative counties than one, a proportionate part only of the sum otherwise payable shall be paid by the council of each of such counties to the guardians, authority, or officer, and the Local Government Board shall certify the proportionate part due from the council of each such county.

(6.) The guardians, authority, or officer to whom a sum is payable under this section on the certificate of the Local Government Board, shall submit to the Board their claim to the payment in such manner, and produce such evidence and comply with such rules as the Board from time to time require or make, and the Board shall fix the amount due on the like principles, and may impose the like conditions for the payment thereof as before the passing of this Act.

(7.) The Local Government Board may, if they think fit, vary a certificate granted for the purposes of this section, but, unless so varied, it shall be conclusive.

Sect. 25.—(1.) If a Secretary of State withholds as respects the police of any county, his certificate under the County and Borough Police Act, 1856, that the police of the county has been maintained in a state of efficiency in point of numbers and discipline during the year ending on the twenty-ninth day of September then last past, the council of that county, in lieu of transferring any sum under the foregoing provisions of this Act to the police account of the county fund, shall forfeit to the Crown and shall pay into Her Majesty's Exchequer out of the county fund, and shall charge to the Exchequer Contribution Account of that fund, such sum as the Secretary of State certifies to be in his opinion equivalent to one half of the cost of the pay and clothing of the police of the county during the said year. — As to Secretary of State's power respecting efficiency of police.

(2.) If a Secretary of State withholds, as respects the police of any borough, his certificate under the County and Borough Police Act, 1856, that the police of the borough has been maintained in a state of efficiency in point of numbers and discipline for the year ending on the twenty-ninth day of September then last past, no payment shall be made by the county council to the council of the borough in respect of one half of the costs of the pay and clothing of the police of that borough during the said year, and such amount as a Secretary of State certifies to be in his opinion the equivalent of such one half shall be transferred by the county council from the Exchequer Contribution Account to the general county account and applied to the general purposes of the county. — 19 & 20 Vict. c. 69.

51 & 52 Vict. c. 41, s. 26.

Grant by county council towards costs of officers of union.

Sect. 26.—(1.) After the thirty-first day of March next after the passing of this Act, every county council, other than the London county council, shall grant to the guardians of every poor law union wholly or partly in their county, an annual sum for the costs of the officers of the union and of district schools to which the union contributes; and, until Parliament otherwise determine, the said annual sum shall be such sum as the Local Government Board certify to have been expended by the guardians of each poor law union during the financial year ending the twenty-fifth day of March next before the passing of this Act, on the salaries, remuneration, and superannuation allowances of the said officers (other than teachers in poor law schools), and on drugs and medical appliances.

(2.) Where a poor law union is situate in more counties than one, the payment under this section to the guardians of the union shall be borne by the counties in which each portion of such union is situate, in proportion to the rateable value of that portion, ascertained on such day as the Local Government Board may fix.

Supplemental provisions as to local taxation account and Exchequer contribution account

Sect. 27.—(1.) When a county council are required under the provisions of this or any other Act to pay any sum into Her Majesty's Exchequer, or to the Treasury, or to the receiver for the metropolitan police district, such sum shall be deducted from the amount payable under the provisions of this Act out of the Local Taxation Account to such county council, and instead of being paid to the county council, shall be paid into Her Majesty's Exchequer, or to the receiver for the metropolitan police district, as the case requires.

(2.) The account of the receipts and expenditure of the Local Taxation Account shall be audited as a public account by the Comptroller and Auditor-General in accordance with such regulations as the Treasury may from time to time make.

(3.) If at any time in any financial year the moneys standing to the Local Taxation Account are insufficient to meet such sums as the Local Government Board consider proper for the time being to pay thereout, the Local Government Board may borrow temporarily on the security of the said account and of moneys becoming payable thereto such sums as they require for the purpose of meeting such deficiency, and the Bank of England may lend such sums, but all sums so borrowed shall be repaid with the interest thereon during the same financial year out of moneys payable to the said account.

General Provisions as to Transfer.

General provisions as to powers transferred to county council.

Sect. 28.—(1.) The county council shall, as respects the business by this Act transferred to them from quarter sessions or the justices out of sessions, be subject to the provisions and limitations in this Act specified, but, save as aforesaid, shall have and be subject to all the powers, duties, and liabilities, which the quarter sessions, or any committee thereof, or any justice or justices had or were subject to in respect of the business so transferred.

(2.) The county council shall, with the exceptions hereinafter mentioned, have power to delegate, with or without any restrictions or conditions as they may think fit, any powers or duties transferred to them by or in pursuance of this Act, either to any committee of the county council appointed in pursuance of this Act, or to any district council in this Act mentioned; the county council may also, without prejudice to any other power whether to appoint committees or otherwise, delegate to the justices of the county sitting in petty sessions any power or duty transferred by this Act to the county council in respect of the licensing of houses or places for the public performance of stage plays, and in respect of the execution as local authority of the Explosives Act, 1875, or of the Act relating to contagious diseases of animals.

38 & 39 Vict. c. 17.

(3.) Provided that the county council shall not under this section delegate any power of raising money by rate or loan.

Summary proceeding for determination of questions as to transfer of powers

Sect. 29. If any question arises, or is about to arise, as to whether any business, power, duty, or liability is or is not transferred to any county council or joint committee under this Act, that question, without prejudice to any other mode of trying it, may, on the application of a chairman of quarter sessions, or of the county council, committee, or other local authority concerned, be submitted for decision to the High Court of Justice in such summary manner as subject to any rules of court may be directed by the court; and the court, after hearing such parties and taking such evidence (if any) as it thinks just, shall decide the question.

51 & 52 Vict. c. 41, s. 29.

Standing joint committee of quarter sessions and county council for the purpose of police, clerk of the peace, officers, &c.

Sect. 30.—(1.) For the purpose of the police, and the clerk of the peace, and of clerks of the justices, and joint officers, and of matters required to be determined jointly by the quarter sessions and the council of a county, there shall be a standing joint committee of the quarter sessions and the county council, consisting of such equal number of justices appointed by the quarter sessions and of members of the county council appointed by that council, as may from time to time be arranged between the quarter sessions and the council, and in default of arrangement such number taken equally from the quarter sessions and the council as may be directed by a Secretary of State.

(2.) The joint committee shall elect a chairman, and, in the case of an equality of votes for two or more persons as chairman, one of those persons shall be elected by lot.

(3.) Any matter arising under this Act with respect to the police, or to the clerk of the peace, or to clerks of the justices, or to officers who serve both the quarter sessions or justices and the county council, or to the provision of accommodation for the quarter sessions or justices out of session or to the use by them or the police or the said clerks of any buildings, rooms, or premises, or to the application of the Local Stamp Act, 1869, to any sums received by clerks to justices, or with respect to anything incidental to the above-mentioned matters, and any other matter requiring to be determined jointly by the quarter sessions and county council, shall be referred to and determined by the joint committee under this section; and all such expenditure as the said joint committee determine to be required for the purposes of the matters above in this section mentioned, shall be paid out of the county fund, and the council of the county shall provide for such payment accordingly.

32 & 33 Vict. c. 49.

PART II.

Application of Act to Boroughs, the Metropolis, and certain Special Counties.

Application of Act to Boroughs.

Certain large boroughs named in the schedule to be county boroughs.

Sect. 31. Each of the boroughs named in the Third Schedule to this Act being a borough which on the first day of June one thousand eight hundred and eighty-eight, either had a population of not less than fifty thousand, or was a county of itself shall, from and after the appointed day, be for the purposes of this Act an administrative county of itself, and is in this Act referred to as a county borough.

Provided that for all other purposes a county borough shall continue to be part of the county (if any) in which it is situate at the passing of this Act, and if a separate commission of assize, oyer and terminer, or gaol delivery is not directed to be executed within the borough, the borough shall, for the purposes of any such commission, and of the service of jurors, and the making of jury lists, be part of the county in which it is specified in the said schedule to be deemed for the purposes of this Act to be situate.

Adjustment of financial relations between counties and county boroughs.

Sect. 32.—(1.) An equitable adjustment respecting the distribution of the proceeds of the local taxation licences, and probate duty grant, and respecting all other financial relations, if any, between each county and each county borough,

51 & 52 Vict. c. 41, s. 32.

specified in the said schedule as being deemed for the purposes of this Act to be situate in that county, shall be made by agreement, within twelve months after the appointed day, between the councils of each county and each borough, and in default of any such agreement, by the Commissioners appointed under this Act; and such adjustment shall provide, in the case of any expenses which may in future be incurred by the county wholly or partly on behalf of the borough for the liability of such borough to contribute, and save as provided by this Act, any existing liability to contribute or to incur expense shall, after the appointed day, cease, and an equitable provision for such cessation shall be made in the adjustment.

(2.) Where a county borough is specified in the said schedule as being deemed for the purposes of this Act to be situate in more than one county, the necessary adjustment shall be made between the counties.

(3.) In such adjustment regard shall be had to the existing property, debts, and liabilities (if any) connected with the financial relations of the county and borough, and to the consideration that the county is not to be placed in any worse financial position by reason of the boroughs therein being constituted county boroughs, and that a county borough is not to be placed in a worse financial position than it would have been in if it had remained part of the county and had shared in the division of the sums received by a county in respect of the licence duties and the probate duty grant, as provided by this Act, and to the amount of benefit and value of the services which the borough receives in return for existing contributions, if any, and to all the circumstances of each case which it appears equitable to consider, subject nevertheless to the following provisions:—

(*a.*) Where separate commissions of assize, oyer and terminer, and gaol delivery are not directed to be executed in a county borough, the borough council shall contribute a proper share of the costs of and incidental to the assizes of the county:

(*b.*) If the borough is not at the passing of this Act a quarter sessions borough, the borough council shall contribute a proper share of the costs of and incidental to the quarter sessions and petty sessions of the county, and of and incidental to the coroners of the county or any franchise therein, and if a grant of a court of quarter sessions is hereafter made to the borough, the borough shall redeem the liability to such contribution, on such terms as may be agreed upon, or, in default of agreement, may be determined by arbitration under this Act:

(*c.*) Where any portion of the costs of building and furnishing any county lunatic asylum has been contributed by a county borough, then, until a new arrangement is made between the county and borough councils, the borough council shall contribute in respect of the lunatic asylums for the time being of the county the like amount as would if this Act had not passed have been contributed by the borough; and the county council shall provide accommodation for and maintain pauper lunatics sent from the borough on the like terms as before the passing of this Act; and the borough council may, if they so desire, appoint to be members of the commtttee of visitors of any such asylum such number of members of the council as may be agreed upon, or in default of agreement be determined by the Commissioners under this Act, but such appointment shall be in substitution for any appointment made on the part of the borough under any existing law or arrangement. Any new arrangement may be made between the county council and all the borough councils concerned with respect to any such lunatic asylum, and if any such new arrangement is made, the borough and county councils may carry into effect any adjustment of property, debts, and liabilities which is the subject of such arrangement. If any council desires to make a new arrangement, and any or all of the other councils refuse to agree to the same, the matter shall be referred to the Commissioners under this Act, or, after they have ceased to hold office, to arbitration under this Act.

(*d.*) Each county borough shall be liable for the maintenance of pauper lunatics in like manner as any other county.

(4.) In the adjustment of any financial relations other than the distribution of the proceeds of the licences and probate duty grant, no borough wholly or partially exempt from contributing to any object shall be rendered liable so to contribute or to contribute in greater proportion than at present. 51 & 52 Vict. c. 41, s. 32.

(5.) The provisions of Part III. of this Act with respect to the adjustment of property, income, debts, liabilities, and expenses, and to borrowing for the purpose, shall apply as if the Commissioners under this Act were the arbitrator in that Part mentioned.

(6.) Provided that at any time after the end of five years from the date of an agreement or award adjusting the financial relations of any county and borough, if the council of either the county or borough satisfy the Local Government Board that the adjustment has become inequitable, and that the councils are unable to agree on a new adjustment, the board shall appoint an arbitrator; and such arbitrator shall proceed to make a new equitable adjustment as if he were the Commissioners under this Act, and the provisions of this Act shall apply accordingly. Any new adjustment made by agreement, or by the award of an arbitrator under this section, may after the expiration of five years from the date of such agreement or award, be altered either by agreement or by arbitration as above mentioned.

(7.) Until any adjustment in pursuance of this section has come into operation, the county or borough council shall pay out of the county or borough fund to the borough or county council, as the case may be, the average annual amount which during the three years next before the appointed day has been expended by the county for the benefit of the borough, or contributed by the borough to the county, as the case may be, but any sum so paid shall be taken into account in the making of the adjustment, and the adjustment shall be made so as to take effect as from the appointed day.

(8.) Any contribution by a county borough to the county in pursuance of this section shall be required and made in accordance with section one hundred and fifty three of the Municipal Corporation Act, 1882, and that section, except so far as relates to the appointment of an arbitrator, shall apply in like manner as if every such borough were a quarter sessions borough situate in the county.

(9.) Expressions in this section relating to contributions by a borough to a county shall be construed to include any sum raised by the assessment of the parishes or hereditaments in the borough to the county rate.

Sect. 33.—(1.) Nothing in this Act with respect to county boroughs shall prevent the continuance of one police force for any county borough and any county, or the consolidation of the police forces of any county borough and any county, in like manner as heretofore, but where the provisions of this Act affect the arrangement with respect to the consolidated police force for a county and borough, an adjustment shall be made between the council of the borough and county in accordance with the provisions of this Act. The foregoing provisions of this section shall apply to boroughs which are not county boroughs in like manner as if they were re-enacted and in terms made applicable to those boroughs. Provisions as to police and rateable value in county boroughs.

(2.) Where, for the purpose of calculating any contribution or payment to be made under this Act, it is necessary to ascertain the rateable value of both a county and a county borough, such rateable value shall be ascertained and fixed by a joint committee composed of representatives of all the councils concerned, and such committee shall for that purpose have all the powers and jurisdiction of quarter sessions and of a committee of justices appointed under the County Rate Act, 1852, and the Acts amending the same, and the number of representatives for the county and each county borough respectively shall be settled by agreement, or in default of agreement by the Local Government Board. 15 & 16 Vict. c. 81.

Sect. 34.—(1.) The mayor, aldermen, and burgesses of each county borough acting by the council shall, subject as in this Act mentioned, have and be subject to all the powers, duties, and liabilities of a county council under this Act (in so far as they are not already in possession of or subject to the same), and in particular shall, subject to the provisions of this Act as to adjustment between counties and county boroughs, be entitled to receive the like sums out of the Local Application of Act with modifications to county boroughs.

51 & 52 Vict. c. 41, s. 34. Taxation Account, and be bound to make the like payments in substitution for local grants and the like grants in respect of the costs of the officers of unions and of districts schools as in the case of a county council, so far as the circumstances make such payments applicable, and all the provisions of this Act (including those with respect to the forfeiture on the withholding by a Secretary of State of his certificate as respects the police of the county) shall accordingly, so far as circumstances admit, apply in the case of every such borough, with the necessary modifications, and in particular with the following modifications:—

(*a.*) The county borough shall be substituted for the county, and borough fund shall be substituted for county fund, and town clerk shall be substituted for clerk of the peace and clerk of the council:

(*b.*) A reference to two or more counties shall include a reference to county boroughs as well as counties.

(*c.*) Such powers, duties, and liabilities of the court of quarter sessions or justices as in the case of a county are transferred to the county council shall be transferred to the council of the county borough, whether the same are vested in or attached to the court of quarter sessions or justices of the borough or of the county in which the borough is situate:

(*d.*) In the case of the duties collected by the Commissioners of Inland Revenue in respect of the licences for trade carts, locomotives, horses, mules, and horse-dealers under any Act of the present session, those Commissioners shall certify the amount collected in each county in like manner as if the county included each county borough specified in the Third Schedule to this Act as deemed to be situate in that county, and the amount as so ascertained shall be divided between the said boroughs, and the residue of the said county in proportion to rateable value as fixed by the joint committee in pursuance of this Act, and until such value is fixed in proportion to rateable value according to the standard or basis for county contributions for the time being, and the share so ascertained shall be paid in like manner as if it had been collected in the county borough or in the residue of the county, as the case may be:

(*e.*) Any sum standing to the Exchequer contribution account of a county borough which remains after payment of the grant required to be made in respect of the costs of union officers shall be carried to the borough fund, or be applied in aid of such rate leviable over the whole of the borough as the council may determine, and the provisions respecting the payment of the same to the general county account of the county fund, and the subsequent application and division thereof, shall not apply.

(2.) On the appointed day there shall be transferred to the mayor, aldermen, and burgesses of each county borough all such bridges and approaches thereto, or parts thereof, situate within the borough as were previously repairable by the county or any hundred therein, and the costs of the council in repairing such bridges and approaches, or parts thereof, and in repairing any roads in the borough which by virtue of this Act or any Act applied by this Act are main roads, shall be payable out of the borough fund.

(3.) The provisions of this Act with respect to—

(*a.*) the constitution, election, proceedings, or position of the county council or the chairman thereof,

(*b.*) the county treasurer, county surveyor, and other county officers,

(*c.*) the standing joint committee of the justices and the council, or

(*d.*) coroners, or

(*e.*) gas meters, or

(*f.*) the transfer to the council of powers relating to county and other rates, and the preparation or revision of the basis or standard for the county rate;

shall not apply to county boroughs, nor shall Part IV. of this Act relating to finance apply, save so far as is expressly provided in that Part.

(4.) Provided that where the district of any county coroner is wholly situate within a county borough, the coroner for that district shall be appointed by the council of that borough, and the writ for his election may be issued to that council instead of to the county council, and where the district of any county coroner is situate partly within and partly without a county borough, the writ for the election of such coroner shall be issued to the county council, but if there is a joint committee of the county and borough council for the purpose, the question of the person to be elected shall be referred to that joint committee, and the county council shall appoint the person recommended by the majority of such committee. 51 & 52 Vict. c. 41, s. 34.

(5.) If the council of a county borough so require, a joint committee shall from time to time be appointed for the purposes of coroners, consisting of such number of members of the county and borough councils as may be agreed upon, or in default of agreement may be determined by a Secretary of State.

(6.) Nothing in this Act shall transfer to the council of any borough any power in relation to the division of the county into polling districts for the purpose of a parliamentary election for the county, the appointment of places of election for the county, the places of holding courts for the revision of the list of voters, and the costs of, and other matters to be done for, the registration of parliamentary voters for the county.

(7.) The powers and duties of the county authority under the Allotments Act, 1887, shall, as respects the borough, continue to be exercised and performed by the Local Government Board. 50 & 51 Vict. c. 48.

(8.) This Act and the Municipal Corporations Act, 1882, shall be construed so as to give effect to the provisions of this section. 45 & 46 Vict c. 50.

Application of Act to larger quarter sessions boroughs not county counties.

Sect. 35. In the case of a quarter sessions borough, not being one of the boroughs named in the Third Schedule to this Act, but containing, according to the census of one thousand eight hundred and eighty-one, a population of ten thousand or upwards, the following provisions shall, on and after the appointed day, apply:

(1.) Nothing in this Act shall transfer to the county council any power of the council of the borough as local authority under any Act, or (save as in this Act expressly mentioned) alter the powers, duties, and liabilities of the council of the borough under the Municipal Corporations Act, 1882, but subject to the above provisions and to the savings herein-after contained, the borough shall form part of the county for the purposes of this Act, and the parishes in the borough shall, subject to the exemptions herein-after mentioned, be liable to be assessed to county contributions in like manner as the rest of the county.

(2.) Where such borough is at the passing of this Act exempt, in whole or in part, from contributing towards costs incurred for any purpose for which the quarter sessions of the county in which the borough is situate are authorised to incur cost the parishes in the borough shall not, save as in this Act expressly mentioned, be assessed by the county council to county contributions in respect of costs incurred for any such purpose, nor in the case of a partial exemption, be so assessed for any larger sum than such as will give effect to that exemption, but this exemption shall not extend to any costs incurred for the purpose of any powers, duties, or liabilities of the justices of the borough, which will by virtue of this Act be exercised or discharged by the county council nor to any costs of or incidental to the assizes of the county.

(3.) Notwithstanding the last enactment the borough shall, for the purposes of the provisions of the Highways and Locomotives (Amendment) Act, 1878, respecting main roads, form part of the county, and the costs of maintaining, repairing, improving, enlarging, or otherwise dealing with any main road in the borough shall be paid out of the county fund, and the payment of the costs incurred in the execution of the provisions of this Act with respect to main roads shall be a general county purpose for which the parishes of the borough may be assessed to county contributions: 41 & 42 Vict. c. 77.

(4.) Provided that—

(a.) the borough shall be deemed to be an urban sanitary district within the meaning of the Highways and Locomotives (Amendment) Act, 1878; and the council of the borough shall have the power under the Highways and Locomotives (Amendment) Act, 1878, of making bye-laws respecting 41 & 42 Vict. c. 77.

51 & 52 Vict. c. 41, s. 35.

locomotives, and authorising locomotives to be used on any road within the borough, save that if any difference is made by such bye-laws or authority between any main road maintained by the county council and the other roads in the borough, such authority and bye-laws shall require the approval of the county council; and

(*b.*) the council of the borough shall have power as an urban authority to claim, in accordance with this Act, to retain the powers and duties of maintaining and repairing any main road in the borough; and

(*c.*) the council of the borough may within two years after the passing of this Act apply to the county council to declare such roads in the borough as are mentioned in the application to be main roads within the meaning of the Highways and Locomotives (Amendment) Act, 1878, and the county council shall consider such application and inquire whether such roads are or ought to be main roads within the meaning of the said Act, and shall make or refuse the declaration accordingly, and if the county council refuse to make the declaration, the council of the borough may within a reasonable time after such refusal apply to the Local Government Board, and that Board shall have power, if after a local inquiry they think it just so to do, to make the said declaration, which shall have the same effect as if made by the county council.

(5.) The payment of the costs of assizes and sessions shall be a general county purpose for which the parishes in the borough may be assessed to county contributions, and all costs of prosecutions mentioned in section one hundred and sixty-nine of the Municipal Corporations Act, 1882, shall be paid out of the county fund.

45 & 46 Vict. c. 50.

(6.) The county councillors elected for an electoral division consisting wholly of such borough, or of some part of such borough, shall not act or vote in respect of any question arising before the county council as regards matters involving expenditure on account of which the parishes in the borough are not, for the time being, liable to be assessed equally with the rest of the county to county contributions.

(7.) The county council and the council of any such borough may agree for the cessation in whole or in part of any exemption under this section of the parishes in the borough from assessment to county contributions, in consideration either of payment by the county council of a capital sum, or of an annual payment, or of a transfer of property or liabilities, or of the county council undertaking in substitution for the council of the borough any powers or duties, or partly for one consideration and partly for another, or in any other manner, according as may be determined.

(8.) A borough which is a county of a city or a county of a town shall, for the purposes of this section, be deemed to be situate in and form part of the county which it adjoins, or if it adjoins more than one county, then in and of the county of which it forms part for the purposes of parliamentary elections.

General application of Act to boroughs with separate commission of the peace.

Sect. 36.—(1.) Where a borough has a separate commission of the peace, whether a quarter sessions borough or not (and is not a borough named in the Third Schedule to this Act), then, subject to the provisions of this Act, all such powers, duties, and liabilities of the court of quarter sessions or justices of the borough, as in the case of the county are by this Act transferred to the county council, shall cease, and the county council shall have those powers, duties, and liabilities within the area of the borough in like manner as in the rest of the county;

(2.) Provided that such powers, duties, or liabilities, so far as they are under the Acts relating to pauper lunatics, shall, save as otherwise provided by this Act, be transferred to the council of the borough and not to the county council, and the provisions of this Act with respect to the transfer to a county council shall apply with the necessary modifications to such transfer to the council of the borough.

Sect. 37. The grant after the passing of this Act of a court of quarter sessions to any borough not being a county borough, shall not affect the powers, duties, or liabilities of the county council as respects the area of that borough, nor exempt the parishes in the borough from being assessed to county contributions for any purpose to which such parishes were previously liable to be assessed, and shall not confer or impose on the mayor, aldermen, and burgesses, or the council of such borough, any powers, duties, or liabilities further than such as are necessary for establishing and maintaining the court of quarter sessions in the borough.

51 & 52 Vict. c. 41, s. 37.

Application of Act to quarter sessions boroughs hereafter created.

Sect. 38. Where a borough having a separate court of quarter sessions contained according to the census of one thousand eight hundred and eighty-one a population of less than ten thousand, the following provisions shall after the appointed day apply:—

Application of Act to smaller quarter sessions boroughs with population under 10,000.

(1.) There shall be transferred to the county council the powers, duties and liabilities of the council and justices of the borough as regards the provision, enlargement, maintenance, management, and visitation of and other dealing with asylums for pauper lunatics:

(2.) There shall be transferred to the county council the powers, duties, and liabilities of the council of the borough—

(*a.*) as regards coroners; and

(*b.*) as regards the appointment of analysts under the Acts relating to the sale of food and drugs; and

(*c.*) under the Acts relating to—

(i.) reformatory and industrial schools; and

(ii.) fish conservancy; and

(iii.) explosives; and

(*d.*) under the Highways and Locomotives (Amendment) Act, 1878;

Provided that the transfer by this section—

(*a.*) shall be subject to the provisions in this Act for the protection of existing officers and the continuance of existing contracts; and

(*b.*) shall not, save as respects the coroners, affect the powers, duties, and liabilities of the council of the borough under the Municipal Corporations Act, 1882:

(3.) The borough shall be an urban sanitary district within the meaning of the Highways and Locomotives (Amendment) Act, 1878: 41 & 42 Vict. c. 77.

(4.) The council of the borough may within two years after the passing of this Act, apply to the county council to declare such roads in the borough as are mentioned in the application to be main roads within the meaning of the Highways and Locomotives (Amendment) Act, 1878, and the county council shall consider such application, and inquire whether such roads are, or ought to be, main roads within the meaning of the said Act, and shall make or refuse the declaration accordingly, and if the county council refuse the declaration, the council of the borough may, within a reasonable time after such refusal, apply to the Local Government Board, and that Board, after a local inquiry, shall have power, if they think it just so to do, to make the said declaration, which shall have the same effect as if it had been made by the county council:

(5.) The area of the borough shall for the purposes of the above-mentioned Acts and all other administrative purposes of the county council be included in the county, as if the borough had not a separate court of quarter sessions, and accordingly shall be subject to the authority of the county council and the county coroners, and may be annexed by the county council to a coroner's district of the county, and the parishes in the borough shall be liable to be assessed to all county contributions:

(6.) Any property, debts, or liabilities of the county or of any borough affected by this or the next succeeding section (including the charge to be made for lunatics which but for this Act would have been maintainable by the borough) may be adjusted in manner provided by Part Three of this Act:

(7.) It shall be lawful for Her Majesty the Queen, on petition from the council of any borough to which this or the next succeeding section applies, by Order in Council, to revoke the grant of a court of quarter sessions to the borough,

51 & 52 Vict. c. 41, s. 38.

and by letters patent to revoke the grant of a commission of the peace for the borough, and to make such provision as to Her Majesty seems proper for the protection of interests existing at the date of the revocation, and after the date of the revocation all enactments and laws relating to courts of quarter sessions and justices and their jurisdiction shall apply, as if such court of quarter sessions or commission of the peace, as the case may be, did not exist:

(8.) A borough which is a county of a city or a county of a town shall, for the purposes of this and the next succeeding section, and if Her Majesty revokes the grant of a court of quarter sessions or a commission of the peace to such borough, then also for all purposes of quarter sessions and justices, be deemed to be situate in and form part of the county of which it forms part for the purpose of parliamentary elections:

(9.) Where this section applies to a cinque port it shall apply also to all the members thereof, and those members when not situate in a quarter sessions borough shall form part of the county for all purposes.

Application of Act to all boroughs with population under 10,000.

Sect. 39.—(1.) Where a borough, whether with or without a separate court of quarter sessions, contained according to the census of one thousand eight hundred and eighty-one a population of less than ten thousand, then after the appointed day all powers, duties, and liabilities of the mayor, aldermen, and burgesses, or council of the borough, or the watch committee of the borough in relation—

(*a.*) to the police force of the borough, or

(*b.*) to the appointment of analysts under the Acts relating to the sale of foods and drugs, or

41 & 42 Vict. c. 74. 47 & 48 Vict. cc. 13, 47. 49 & 50 Vict. c. 32. 40 & 41 Vict. c. 68.

(*c.*) to the execution of the Contagious Diseases (Animals) Acts, 1878 to 1886, or the Destructive Insects Act, 1877, or

(*d.*) to gas meters, or

(*e.*) to weights and measures, if the council exercise any jurisdiction in relation thereto,

shall cease, and, subject to the provisions of this Act as to the members of the police force holding office on the said day, the area of the borough shall, for all purposes of the Acts relating to the county police force, or other matters above in this section mentioned, form part of the county in like manner as if it were not a borough;

41 & 42 Vict. c. 74. 49 & 50 Vict. c. 32.

(2.) Provided that nothing in this section shall transfer to the county council any powers, duties, or liabilities under section thirty-four of the Contagious Diseases (Animals) Act, 1878, as amended by section nine of the Contagious Diseases (Animals) Act, 1886.

(3.) The urban authority for any borough or town with such population as above in this section mentioned shall cease to be the local authority under the Acts relating to explosives, and the county council shall have the like authority under the said Acts in the said borough or town as they have in the rest of their county.

Application of Act to Metropolis.

Application of Act to Metropolis as county of London.

Sect. 40. In the application of this Act to the Metropolis, the following provisions shall have effect:—

(1.) The Metropolis shall, on and after the appointed day, be an administrative county for the purposes of this Act by the name of the administrative county of London.

(2.) Such portion of the administrative county of London as forms part of the counties of Middlesex, Surrey, and Kent, shall on and after the appointed day be severed from those counties, and form a separate county for all non-administrative purposes by the name of the county of London; and it shall be lawful for Her Majesty the Queen to appoint a sheriff of that county, and to grant a commission of the peace and court of quarter sessions to that county; and, subject to the provisions of this Act, all enactments, laws, and usages with respect to counties in England and Wales, and to sheriffs, justices, and quarter sessions shall, so far as circumstances admit, apply to the county of London : 51 & 52 Vict. c. 41, s. 40.

(3.) Provided that, for the purpose of the jurisdiction of the justices under such commission, and of such court, as well as other non-administrative purposes, the county of the city of London shall continue a separate county, but if and when the mayor, commonalty, and citizens of the city assent to jurisdiction being conferred therein on such justices and court may by commission under the Great Seal be made subject to the jurisdiction thereof.

(4.) The number of the county councillors for the administrative county of London shall be double the number of members which at the passing of this Act, the parliamentary boroughs in the Metropolis are authorised by law to return to serve in Parliament ; and each such borough, or if it is divided into divisions, each division thereof, shall be an electoral division for the purposes of this Act, and the number of county councillors elected for each such electoral division, shall be double the number of members of Parliament which such borough or division is at the passing of this Act entitled to return to serve in Parliament :

(5.) Provided that the number of county aldermen in the administrative county of London, shall not exceed one-sixth of the whole number of county councillors.

(6.) The provisions of this Act with respect to the powers, duties, and liabilities of county councils, and the transfer of property, debts, and liabilities of counties to county councils, shall apply to the administrative county of London in like manner, so nearly as circumstances admit, as if the quarter sessions, justices, and clerks of the peace of the counties of Middlesex, Surrey, and Kent had been, so far as regards the metropolis, the quarter sessions, justices, and clerk of the peace for the administrative county of London :

(7.) Provided that any property, debts, or liabilities of the county of Kent shall not, by reason only of this enactment, be vested in the county council of London, but such property, debts, and liabilities, and also the property, debts, and liabilities of the counties of Middlesex and Surrey, shall be apportioned between the portions of those counties situate within the Metropolis and the portions situate outside the Metropolis in such manner as may be determined by agreement between the respective county councils, or in default of agreement by the Commissioners under this Act, and the property, debts, and liabilities apportioned to the portions within the Metropolis shall be the property, debts, and liabilities of the whole of the administrative county of London.

(8.) There shall also be transferred to the London county council the powers, duties, and liabilities of the Metropolitan Board of Works, and after the appointed day that board shall cease to exist, and the property, debts, and liabilities thereof shall be transferred to the London county council, and that council shall be in law the successors of the Metropolitan Board of Works.

(9.) If the London county council borrow for the purposes of this Act they shall borrow in accordance with the provisions of the Acts relating to the Metropolitan Board of Works, but save as aforesaid, Part Four of this Act shall apply to the London county council when acting as successors of the Metropolitan Board of Works, and the costs incurred when so acting shall be paid out of the county fund, and the payment thereof shall be a general county purpose.

Sect. 41.—(1.) Of the powers, duties, and liabilities of the court of quarter sessions and justices of the city of London— Position of city of London, and application of Highway Acts.

(*a.*) such of them as would, if the city were a quarter sessions borough, with a population exceeding ten thousand, be exercised by virtue of this or any other Act by the council of the borough, shall be transferred to the mayor, commonalty, and citizens of the city acting by the council (in this Act referred to as the common council) ; and

51 & 52 Vict. c. 41, s. 41.

(*b*.) such of them as would, in the said case, be by virtue of this Act exercised and discharged by the county council shall cease, and the county council shall, subject to the provisions of this Act, have those powers, duties, and liabilities within the City of London in like manner as within the rest of the administrative county of London.

(2.) The provisions of this Act with respect to the transfer to a county council shall apply with the necessary modifications to such transfer to the common council, and the common council shall be entitled to receive from the London county council in respect of each pauper lunatic, the same amount as is required by this Act to be paid by any other county council to the council of a borough.

(3.) Where at the passing of this Act the Metropolitan Board of Works or the quarter sessions of Middlesex are authorised to incur costs for any purpose, and the common council of the city are not liable to contribute to such costs, the parishes in the city of London shall not, save as in this Act expressly mentioned, be liable to be assessed to county contributions in respect of costs incurred by the county council for such purpose, but this exemption shall not extend to any costs incurred for the purpose of any powers, duties, or liabilities of the quarter sessions or justices of the city of London, which will be exercised and discharged by the London county council.

41 & 42 Vict. c. 77.

(4.) The provisions of the Highways and Locomotives (Amendment) Act, 1878, with respect to main roads, as amended by this Act, shall extend to the Metropolis in like manner as if the expression "urban sanitary district" in that Act included, as respects the Metropolis, the city of London, and a parish in Schedule A., and a district in Schedule B. of the Metropolis Management Act, 1855, as amended by subsequent Acts, and as if the Commissioners of Sewers, or vestry, or district board (as the case may be) were the urban sanitary authority: Provided that—

18 & 19 Vict. c. 120.

(*a*.) in the city of London the common council shall have the power under the Highways and Locomotives (Amendment) Act, 1878, of making bye-laws respecting locomotives, and authorising locomotives to be used on any road within the city, save that if any difference is made by such bye-laws or authority between any main road maintained by the county council and the other roads in the city, such authority and bye-laws shall require the approval of the county council; and

(*b*.) the common council in the city of London, and in any other part of the Metropolis, the vestry, or district board, shall be deemed to be a district council and an urban authority within the meaning of the provisions of this Act with respect to main roads, and may accordingly claim to retain the power of maintaining and repairing a main road, and in such case shall have all such powers and duties of maintaining, repairing, improving and enlarging, and otherwise dealing with the main road as they would have if it were an ordinary highway repairable by them, and such powers and duties shall in the city of London be discharged by the Commissioners of Sewers.

(5.) The payment of the costs of assizes and sessions shall be a general county purpose for which the parishes in the city may be assessed to county contributions, and all such costs of prosecutions in the city as are by law payable out of the county rate shall be paid out of the county fund.

(6.) The county councillors elected for the city, shall not act or vote in respect of any question arising before the county council as regards matters involving expenditure on account of which the parishes in the city are not for the time being liable to be assessed equally with the rest of the administrative county to county contributions.

(7.) The London county council, and the common council of the city of London may agree for the cessation in whole or in part of any exemption under this section from assessment, in consideration either of payment by the county council of a capital sum, or of an annual payment, or of a transfer of property or liabilities, or of the county council undertaking, in substitution for the common council, any powers or duties, or partly for one consideration and partly for another, or in any other manner, according as may be determined.

(8.) The sheriffs of the City of London shall not have any authority except in the city. 51 & 52 Vict. c. 41, s. 41.

Arrangements for paid chairman and sitting of quarter sessions for London.

Sect. 42.—(1.) If the London county council petitions Her Majesty the Queen in that behalf, it shall be lawful for Her Majesty from time to time to appoint a barrister of not less than ten years' standing to be paid chairman or deputy chairman, or one of the paid deputy chairmen, as the case may be, of the quarter sessions for the county of London.

(2.) Any person so appointed shall hold office during good behaviour, and shall by virtue of his office be a justice of the peace for the county of London.

(3.) There shall be paid to him out of the county fund as a general county purpose such yearly salary, not exceeding that stated in the petition in consequence of which the appointment was made, as Her Majesty directs.

(4.) Such chairman or deputy chairman shall not, during his office, be eligible to serve in Parliament, and shall not during his continuance in office practise as a barrister.

(5.) Where there is any such paid chairman or deputy chairman of the quarter sessions, the court may be held before such chairman or deputy chairman alone.

(6.) Separate courts of quarter sessions may be held at different parts of he county of London at the same time if so directed by the county council with the approval of a Secretary of State, and every court of general sessions of the peace for the county of London and every adjournment thereof shall have the same jurisdiction in all respects, including the power of hearing and determining appeals, as if such court were quarter sessions.

(7.) The London county council may from time to time submit to a Secretary of State a scheme for regulating the holding of courts of quarter sessions in London either at any one place or at different places, and in the latter case either at the same time or at different times, and for determining the legal character of each sessions so held, that is to say, whether quarter, general, original, or adjourned sessions, or otherwise, and for making such regulations respecting committals for trial, recognisances, depositions, and other matters as are necessary or proper for giving effect to the scheme, and such scheme, when approved by a Secretary of State, shall be published in the *London Gazette*, and thereupon shall have effect as if it were enacted in this Act.

(8.) Until the quarter sessions for the county of London constitute special sessional divisions, every petty sessional division of the counties of Middlesex, Surrey, and Kent existing at the appointed day, or so much of such division as is situate in the county of London, shall form a special or petty sessional division of the county of London.

(9.) Where any special or petty sessional division of the counties of Middlesex, Surrey, and Kent, existing at the appointed day, is situate partly within and partly without the county of London, so much thereof as is situate without the said county shall, until any alteration is made by the quarter sessions for the county of Middlesex, Surrey, or Kent, as the case may be, be a special or petty sessional division of that county.

(10.) The quarter sessions for the county of London shall be substituted for the general assessment sessions under the Valuation (Metropolis) Act, 1869, and have all the jurisdiction vested in those sessions, and shall exercise the same within the same area. Upon the hearing of any appeals in relation to property in the city of London, such two members of the court of quarter sessions of the city of London as may be appointed by that court for the purpose, shall be entitled to attend and sit as members of the quarter sessions for the county of London. 32 & 33 Vict. c.67.

(11.) The enactments respecting the times for holding sessions of the peace for the county of Middlesex, and the appointment and payment of any assistant judge or deputy assistant judge, or of a person to preside in a second court at any sessions in the county of Middlesex, shall cease to apply to the county of Middlesex. 7 & 8 Vict. c. 71 22 & 23 Vict. c. 37 & 38 Vict. c. 7.

(12.) Quarter sessions for the counties of Middlesex, Surrey, and Kent respectively may be held, and the justices of each of those counties may hold special

51 & 52 Vict. c. 41, s. 42.

and petty sessions for any division of such county, and appoint a petty sessional or occasional court house, at any place in the county of London, and for all purposes relating to such sessions or any business transacted at such court house, such place shall be deemed to be within the county and division for which the justices holding the same are justices, but no jurors shall be summoned for such sessions from within the county of London.

(13.) Nothing in this Act shall alter the powers or duties of the justices, quarter sessions, recorder, or common serjeant of the city of London, further or otherwise than is expressly provided or than the powers and duties of the justices or quarter sessions of any county are altered.

(14.) Provided that from and after the appointed day the rights claimed by the court of common council to appoint to the offices of common serjeant, and judge of the City of London Court shall cease, and in any future vacancy in each of the said offices, it shall be lawful for Her Majesty the Queen to appoint a duly qualified barrister to be such common serjeant or judge; and from and after the next vacancy no recorder shall exercise any judicial functions unless he is appointed by Her Majesty to exercise such functions.

Grant by London county council to poor law unions.

Sect. 43.—(1.) In the administrative county of London the county council—

(*a.*) shall pay to the guardians for every poor law union wholly in the county such sums as the Local Government Board from time to time certify to be due from the said council in substitution for the local grants towards the remuneration of poor law medical officers, and towards the cost of drugs and medical appliances; and

(*b.*) shall grant to the guardians of every poor law union wholly in their county an amount equal to fourpence a day per head for every indoor pauper maintained in that union, and such grant, during the five local financial years beginning on the appointed day, shall be reckoned according to the average number of indoor paupers so maintained during the five financial years ending on the twenty-fifth day of March next before the passing of this Act, and shall, after the end of the said five local financial years, unless Parliament otherwise determine, continue to be reckoned in accordance with the same average number; and

(*c.*) shall pay to the guardians of every poor law union, a portion of which only is situate in their county, such proportion of the annual sum which is, under the other provisions of this Act, payable by the county council of a county to the guardians of that union, as the rateable value of the portion within the administrative county of London bears to the rest of the union.

(2.) For the purposes of this section the expression "indoor pauper" includes all paupers maintained in a workhouse, and all paupers maintained in any district school, separate school, separate infirmary, sick asylum, hospital for infectious diseases, or institution for the deaf, dumb, blind, or idiots, or in any certified school under the Act of the session of the twenty-fifth and twenty-sixth years of the reign of Her Majesty, chapter forty-three, and includes any children boarded out, whether within or without the limits of the union, and in the metropolitan asylum district includes all inmates of any asylum for imbeciles provided by the managers of that district, but excludes paupers relieved in casual wards, and such number of indoor paupers in a workhouse or in a district or separate school or in a separate infirmary or asylum, as exceeded the number prescribed by the Local Government Board for that workhouse, school, infirmary or asylum, and also excludes paupers maintained for part only of a day: Provided always, that any paupers maintained under any contract or agreement in a workhouse other than that of the union to which they are chargeable, shall be included only in the number of indoor paupers of the union to which they are so chargeable.

(3.) The average number of paupers shall be estimated in such manner as the Local Government Board direct, and shall be certified by the Board. The Board may, if they think proper, vary their certificate, but unless it is so varied, their certificate shall be conclusive.

Sect. 44. On an after the appointed day all powers and duties of the clerk to the managers of the metropolitan asylums district under the Valuation (Metropolis) Act, 1869, shall be transferred to the clerk of the county council of London, and the said Act shall be construed as if the county council were substituted therein for the managers of the metropolitan asylums district.

51 & 52 Vict. c. 41, s. 44.

Transfer of duties under 32 & 33 Vict. c. 67 of clerk of metropolitan asylum managers

Sect. 45. On and after the appointed day, the powers, duties, and liabilities of justices out of session in the Metropolis, in relation to the licensing of slaughter-houses for the purpose of the slaughtering of cattle for butchers meat, and of cow-houses and places for the keeping of cows, shall be transferred to the county council of London.

Adjustment of law as to slaughter-houses in the metropolis

Application of Act to Special Counties and to Liberties.

Sect. 46. For the purposes of this Act there shall be enacted the provisions following; that is to say,

Application of Act to certain special counties.

(1.)—(*a.*) The ridings of Yorkshire and the divisions of Lincolnshire shall respectively be separate administrative counties.

(*b.*) The eastern and western divisions of Sussex, under the County of Sussex Act, 1865, and the eastern and western divisions of Suffolk, shall respectively be separate administrative counties for the purposes of this Act.

28 & 29 Vict. c. 37.

(*c.*) The Isle of Ely, and the residue of the county of Cambridge, shall be respectively separate administrative counties for the purposes of this Act, and are in this Act referred to as divisions of the county of Cambridge.

(*d.*) The soke of Peterborough and the residue of the county of Northampton shall be respectively separate administrative counties for the purposes of this Act, and are in this Act referred to as divisions of the county of Northampton.

(2.)—(*a.*) In the case of the county of York and the county of Lincoln respectively, the administrative business which would, if this Act had not passed, have been transacted by the justices of all the ridings and divisions at their gaol sessions, or by any joint committee of the justices of such ridings or divisions, or by any commissioners appointed by the justices, or otherwise jointly by such justices, shall be transacted by a joint committee of the county councils of the three ridings or three divisions, as the case may be, appointed in manner provided by this Act with respect to joint committees of county councils.

(*b.*) The administrative business which would, if this Act had not passed, have been transacted by any general sessions of the peace for the county of Sussex or Suffolk, or by any joint action of the quarter sessions of the divisions of the county of Cambridge, or the county of Northampton, and all matters under this Act which concern the two divisions of Sussex, Suffolk, Cambridge or Northampton jointly, shall be transacted by a joint committee of the respective county councils concerned, appointed in manner provided by this Act with respect to joint committees of county councils.

(*c.*) A joint committee formed in pursuance of this section shall, if the business transacted by them so require, comprise a joint committee of the quarter sessions of the several ridings and divisions.

(*d.*) If any difference arises as to the number of members, or the mode or time of appointing a joint committee under this section, the difference shall be determined by a Secretary of State.

(3.) A joint committee formed in pursuance of this section shall, in respect of the business to be transacted by them, stand in the same position as if the entire county were not divided for the purposes of county councils, and as if the committee were the county council of the entire county, and the provisions of this Act shall, so nearly as circumstances admit, apply accordingly, and all costs or sums payable by the joint committee shall be apportioned by the joint committee between the several administrative counties in such manner as is provided by law, or by the practice heretofore adopted, or in such other manner as may be from time to time agreed upon by the councils of the several administrative counties, or in default of agreement may, upon the application of any of such councils, be determined by arbitration in

51 & 52 Vict. c. 41, s. 46.

manner provided by this Act; and each county council shall pay the sum so apportioned to the treasurer of the joint committee, and the sum so paid shall be deemed to be paid for general county purposes.

(4.) The powers, duties, and liabilities of the county authority, under the Yorkshire Registries Act, 1884, and the Acts amending the same, shall, after the appointed day, be transferred to the county council, and the expression "county authority," in those Acts shall mean, as respects each riding, the county council of that riding.

(5.) In the application of this Act to Lancashire, the provisions of this Act with respect to county rates shall apply to the special rates levied in Lancashire for the purposes of the salary or pension of any chairman of quarter sessions or stipendiary justice, or for any assize courts, and such rates shall continue to be levied within the respective areas within which they would have been levied if this Act had not passed, and, subject as aforesaid, the position and salary of any such chairman or justice shall not be affected by any provision of this Act.

(6.) From and after the appointed day the right of the mayor, commonalty, and citizens of the city of London to elect the sheriff of Middlesex shall cease, and it shall be lawful for Her Majesty the Queen to appoint a sheriff of the county of Middlesex, and the law relating to sheriffs shall apply in the case of the county of Middlesex in like manner as in the case of any other county.

(7.) In this section "administrative business" means such business as is by this Act transferred from quarter sessions or juctices, or any committee thereof, to county councils.

Saving for Manchester Assize Courts Act, 1858, 21 & 22 Vict. c. 24.

Sect. 47.—(1.) Notwithstanding anything in this Act, the courts of assize at Manchester, with the lodgings for Her Majesty's judges, offices, lockups, and all other property vested in the justices of the peace of the county palatine of Lancaster by the Manchester Assize Courts Act, 1858, shall be vested in the county council of the said county palatine, and shall be under the control and management of a joint committee of members of the said county council, and of the council of every county borough locally situate in the hundred of Salford, and that joint committee shall have and exercise all such powers and rights (except the power of levying, imposing, or assessing a rate or of borrowing money) as are conferred on the said justices by the said Act; and the hundred of Salford (including every borough locally situate therein) shall continue liable to contribute towards expenses incurred under the authority of the said Act.

(2.) The numbers of members of a joint committee appointed for the purposes of this section shall not exceed twelve, and the quorum requisite for the transaction of business shall be three.

(3.) Any disagreement as to the number of members of the committee or as to the proportions in which the several councils are to be represented thereon, shall be settled by a Secretary of State.

Merger of liberties in county.

Sect. 48.—(1.) For all purposes of this Act, every liberty and franchise of a county, wholly or partly exempt from contribution to the county rate, shall, save as may be otherwise provided by or in pursuance of this Act, form part of the county of which it forms part for the purposes of parliamentary elections.

(2.) The provisions of this Act with respect to the transfer to the county council of the powers, duties, and liabilities of the quarter sessions and justices of a county, and of their property, debts, and liabilities, whether vested in or attaching to the clerk of the peace or any justice or justices or otherwise on behalf of the county, shall apply to every such liberty and franchise as above mentioned in like manner in all respects as if they were herein re-enacted and in terms made applicable to such liberty and franchise; and the county council shall have and exercise in every such liberty and franchise the powers and duties transferred to them by this Act from the quarter sessions and justices of the county;

(3.) Provided that where at the passing of this Act the police force in such liberty or franchise is under the control of the quarter sessions for such liberty or franchise, there shall be one police force for the whole administrative county under the county council, and the quarter sessions of such liberty or franchise shall appoint such number of the members of the standing joint committee under this Act as may be agreed upon by the county council, the quarter sessions of the county, and the quarter sessions of the liberty or franchise, or in default of agreement may be determined by a Secretary of State. 51 & 52 Vict. c. 41, s. 48.

(4.) The Cinque Ports and two ancient towns and their members shall for all purposes of the county council and of the powers and duties of quarter sessions and justices out of sessions under this Act form part of the county in which they are respectively situate without prejudice nevertheless to the position of any such port, town, or member as a quarter sessions borough under the Municipal Corporations Act, 1882, as amended by this Act, and without prejudice to the existing privileges of such ports, towns, and members as respects matters which are not affected by this Act. 45 & 46 Vict. c. 50.

Power to make Provisional Order for Scilly Islands.

Sect. 49.—(1.) It shall be lawful for the Local Government Board to make a Provisional Order for regulating the application of this Act to the Scilly Islands, and for providing for the exercise and performance in those islands of the powers and duties both of county councils and also of authorities under the Acts relating to highways and the Public Health Act, 1875, and the Acts amending the same, and for the application to the islands of any provisions of any Act touching local government, and any such Order may provide for the establishment of councils and other local authorities separate from those in the county of Cornwall, and for the contribution by the Scilly Islands to the county council of Cornwall in respect of costs incurred by the county council for matters specified in the said Order as benefiting the Scilly Islands, and such Order may also provide for all matters which appear to the Local Government Board necessary or proper for carrying the Order into full effect.

(2.) Any such Order shall not be in force until it is confirmed by Parliament.

(3.) Subject to the provisions of a Provisional Order under this Act, the county council of Cornwall shall have no greater powers or duties in the Scilly Islands than the quarter sessions of Cornwall have hitherto in fact exercised or performed therein, and the Scilly Islands shall not be included for the purposes of this Act in any electoral division of the county of Cornwall.

PART III.

Boundaries.

Boundary of county for first election.

Sect. 50.—(1.) The first council elected under this Act for any administrative county shall, subject as herein-after mentioned, be elected for the county at large as bounded at the passing of this Act for the purpose of the election of members to serve in Parliament for the county: Provided always, that—

(*a.*) This enactment shall not apply to the boundary between two administrative counties which are portions of one entire county, and in case of those administrative counties, the boundary between the portions, as existing for the purposes of county rate, shall, subject to any change made by or in pursuance of this Act, be the boundary of the administrative county for which the council is elected; and,

(*b.*) Where any urban sanitary district is situate partly within and partly without the boundary of such county, the district shall be deemed to be within that county which contains the largest portion of the population of the district, according to the census of one thousand eight hundred and eighty-one.

(*c.*) Where any portion of an administrative county has before the passing of this Act been transferred to another administrative county for the purposes of the

51 & 52 Vict. c. 41, s. 50.

Acts relating to the police or Contagious Diseases (Animals) or otherwise, nothing in this Act shall affect such transfer.

47 & 48 Vict. c. 232.

(*d.*) The wapentake of the ainsty of York (except so much as is included in the municipal borough of York as extended by the York Extension and Improvement Act, 1884) shall for all purposes of this Act be deemed to be part of the west riding of the county of York.

(2.) The county council elected under this Act shall have for the purposes of this Act authority throughout the administrative county for which it is elected, and the administrative county as bounded for the purpose of the election shall, subject to alterations made in manner herein-after mentioned, be for all the purposes of this Act the county of such county council.

(3.) If any difference arises as to the county which contains the largest portion of the population of any such district as above in this section mentioned, such difference shall be referred to the Local Government Board, whose decision shall be final.

(4.) This section applies to an administrative county within the meaning of this Act, save that it shall not apply to the administrative county of London, nor to any county borough, and any place which, though forming part of any such borough for the purposes of the election of members to serve in Parliament, is not within the municipal boundary of such borough shall, nothwithstanding anything in the foregoing provisions of this section, form, for the purposes of this section, part of the county in which such place is situate.

Directions for constitution of electoral divisions.

Sect. 51. In the constitution of electoral divisions of a county, whether for the first election or for subsequent elections, the following directions shall be observed—

(1.) The divisions shall be arranged with a view to the population of each division being, so nearly as conveniently may be, equal, regard being had to a proper representation both of the rural and of the urban population, and to the distribution and pursuits of such population, and to area, and to the last published census for the time being, and to evidence of any considerable change of population since such census;

(2.) Electoral divisions shall, so far as may be reasonably practicable, be framed so that every division shall be a county district or ward, or a combination of county districts or wards, or be comprised in one county district or ward, but where an electoral division is a portion of a county district or ward, and such portion has not a defined area for which a separate list or part of a list of voters is made under the Acts relating to the registration of electors, such portion shall, until a new register of electors is made, continue to be part of the district or ward of which it has been treated as being part in the then current register of electors;

(3.) Whenever under the provisions of this section a county district is divided into two or more portions, every such portion shall (as far as possible) consist of an entire parish or of a combination of entire parishes;

(4.) In determining the electoral divisions for the first election, the foregoing provisions shall apply as if, where a rural sanitary district is situate in more than one county, each portion of the district which is situate in the same county were a county district, and any such portion may be combined with a county district, or portion of a county district, although not adjoining;

(5.) The electoral divisions for the first election shall be fixed on or before the eighth day of November next after the passing of this Act.

Provisional order as respects boroughs and urban sanitary districts in same area.

Sect. 52.—(1.) The Local Government Board shall make provisional orders for dealing with every case where the council of a borough is not the urban sanitary authority for the whole of the area of such borough, and the area of the borough is either co-extensive with or is wholly or partly comprised in any urban sanitary district, and such order shall determine whether the area of the borough or of the sanitary district, or an area comprising both the borough and the urban sanitary district, or a portion of such united area, shall, whether with or without any adjoining area, be the area of the county district for the purposes of this

Act, so, however, that in either case the order shall provide for the council of the borough becoming the district council, and the order may for that purpose alter the boundaries of the borough, and may, if need be, alter the boundaries of the county; and if the population exceeds fifty thousand, the order may constitute the borough into a county borough, and make such provision as may be necessary for carrying this Act into effect as respect such county borough; and the provisions of this Act respecting county boroughs shall, subject to the provisions of the order, apply. 51 & 52 Vict. c. 41, s. 52.

(2.) Where certain members of the sanitary authority for any such urban sanitary district are appointed by a university or any colleges therein, the order may provide for the appointment by such university or colleges of members on the district council.

(3.) A provisional order under this section shall not be of any effect until it is confirmed by Parliament.

Sect. 53.—(1.) Every report made by the Boundary Commissioners under the Local Government (Boundaries) Act, 1887, shall be laid before the council of any administrative county or county borough affected by that report. **Consideration of alterations of boundaries by county councils.**

(2.) It shall be the duty of the council to take into consideration such report, and to make such representations to the Local Government Board as they think expedient for adjusting the boundaries of their county, and of other areas of local government partly situate in their county, with a view of securing that no such area shall be situate in more than one county.

Sect. 54.—(1.) Whenever it is represented by the council of any county or borough to the Local Government Board— **Future alterations of boundaries.**

(*a.*) that the alteration of the boundary of any county or borough is desirable; or

(*b.*) that the union, for all or any of the purposes of this Act, of a county borough with a county is desirable; or

(*c.*) that the union, for all or any of the purposes of this Act, of any counties or boroughs or the division of any county is desirable; or

(*d.*) that it is desirable to constitute any borough having a population of not less than fifty thousand into a county borough; or

(*e.*) that the alteration of the boundary of any electoral division of a county, or of the number of county councillors and electoral divisions in a county, is desirable; or

(*f.*) that the alteration of any area of local government partly situate in their county or borough is desirable.

the Local Government Board shall, unless for special reasons they think that the representation ought not to be entertained, cause to be made a local inquiry, and may make an order for the proposal contained in such representation, or for such other proposal as they may deem expedient, or may refuse such order, and if they make the order may by such order divide or alter any electoral division.

(2.) Provided that in default of such representation by the council of any county or borough before the first day of November one thousand eight hundred and eighty-nine, the Local Government Board may cause such local inquiry to be made, and thereupon may make such order as they may deem expedient.

(3.) Provided that if the order alters the boundary of a county or borough, or provides for the union of a county borough with a county, or for the union of any counties or boroughs, or for the division of any county, or for constituting a borough into a county borough, it shall be provisional only, and shall not have effect unless confirmed by Parliament.

(4.) Where such order alters the boundary of a borough, it may, as consequential upon such alteration, do all or any of the following things, increase or decrease the number of the wards in the borough, and alter the boundaries of such wards, and alter the apportionment of the number of councillors among the wards, and alter the total number of councillors, and in such case, make the proportionate alteration in the number of aldermen.

(5.) At any time before the appointed day, the Local Government Board may

51 & 52 Vict. c. 41, s. 55.

make an order in pursuance of this section without any such representation as in this section mentioned.

Contents of provisional order amalgamating two county boroughs.

Sect. 55.—(1.) Where the Local Government Board make a Provisional Order for uniting two county boroughs, such Order may make them one borough and one county for the purposes of this Act.

(2.) Such Order, and also any other Order under this Act for uniting boroughs, whether county boroughs or not, may also contain such provisions as may seem necessary or proper for regulating the division of the combined borough into wards, the number of councillors to be elected for each ward, and the first election of the council of the combined borough, and for providing for the clerks of the peace, coroners, town clerks, and officers of the boroughs, and the application to them of the provisions of this Act as to existing officers, and for providing for all matters incidental to or consequential on the union of the boroughs.

(3.) When any such Provisional Order is confirmed, it shall be lawful for Her Majesty to grant a commission of the peace and court of quarter sessions to the combined borough in like manner as to any other borough under the Municipal Corporations Act, 1882, and the Provisional Order may contain such provisions as appear necessary or proper for regulating all matters incidental to such grant, and to the changes caused by the union of the boroughs in matters connected with such commission or court or otherwise with the administration of justice.

Procedure for charter of new borough.

Sect. 56. Where a petition is presented to Her Majesty the Queen by the inhabitant householders of any town or towns or district, in pursuance of the Municipal Corporations Act, 1882, for the grant of a charter of incorporation, notice of such petition shall be given to the county council of the county in which such town, towns, or district is or are situate, and shall also be sent to the Local Government Board, and the Privy Council shall consider any representations made by such county council or the Local Government Board, together with the petition for such charter.

Future alteration of county districts and parishes and wards and future establishment of urban districts.

Sect. 57.—(1.) Whenever a county council is satisfied that a *primâ facie* case is made out as respects any county district not a borough, or as respects any parish, for a proposal for all or any of the following things; that is to say—

(*a.*) the alteration or definition of the boundary thereof:

(*b.*) the division thereof or the union thereof with any other such district or districts, parish or parishes, or the transfer of part of a parish to another parish;

(*c.*) the conversion of any such district or part thereof, if it is a rural district, into an urban district, and if it is an urban district, into a rural district, or the transfer of the whole or any part of any such district from one district to another, and the formation of new urban or rural districts;

(*d.*) The division of an urban district into wards; and

(*e.*) The alteration of the number of wards, or of the boundaries of any ward, or of the number of members of any district council, or of the apportionment of such members among the wards,

the county council may cause such inquiry to be made in the locality, and such notice to be given, both in the locality, and to the Local Government Board, Education Department, or other Government department as may be prescribed, and such other inquiry and notices (if any) as they think fit, and if satisfied that such proposal is desirable, may make an order for the same accordingly.

(2.) Notice of the provisions of the order shall be given, and copies thereof shall be supplied in the prescribed manner, and otherwise as the county council think fit, and if it relates to the division of a district into wards, or the alteration of the number of wards or of the boundaries of a ward, or of the number of the members of a district council, or of the apportionment of the members among the wards, shall come into operation upon being finally approved by the county council.

(3.) In any other case the order shall be submitted to the Local Government Board; and if within three months after such notice of the provisions of the order as the Local Government Board determine to be the first notice, the council of any district affected by the order, or any number of county electors registered in that district or in any ward of that district, not being less than one-sixth of the total number of electors in that district or ward, or if the order relates only to a parish, any number of county electors registered in that parish, not being less than one-sixth of the total number of electors in that parish, petition the Local Government Board to disallow the order, the Local Government Board shall cause to be made a local inquiry, and determine whether the order is to be confirmed or not. 51 & 52 Vict. c. 41, s. 57.

(4.) If any such petition is not presented, or being presented is withdrawn, the Local Government Board shall confirm the order.

(5.) The Local Government Board, on confirming an order, may make such modifications therein as they consider necessary for carrying into effect the objects of the order.

(6.) An order under this section, when confirmed by the Local Government Board, shall be forthwith laid upon the table of both Houses of Parliament, if Parliament be then sitting, and, if not, forthwith after the then next meeting of Parliament.

(7.) This section shall be in addition to, and not in derogation of, any power of the Local Government Board in respect of the union or division or alteration of parishes.

Sect. 58. The Local Government Board, where it appears expedient so to do with reference to any poor law union which is situate in more than one county, instead of dissolving the union may by order provide that the same shall continue to be one union for the purposes of indoor paupers or any of those purposes, and shall be divided into two or more poor law unions for the purpose of outdoor relief, and may by the order make such provisions as seem expedient for determining all other matters in relation to which such union is to be one union or two or more unions.

Additional power of Local Government Board as to unions.

Sect. 59.—(1.) A scheme or order under this Act may make such administrative and judicial arrangements incidental to or consequential on any alteration of boundaries, authorities, or other matters made by the scheme or order as may seem expedient.

Supplemental provisions as to alteration of areas.

(2.) A place which is part of an administrative county for the purposes of this Act shall, subject as in this Act mentioned, form part of that county for all purposes, whether sheriff, lieutenant, custos rotulorum, justices, militia, coroner, or other; Provided that—

(*a*.) Notwithstanding this enactment, each of the entire counties of York, Lincoln, Sussex, Suffolk, Northampton, and Cambridge shall continue to be one county for the said purposes so far as it is one county at the passing of this Act; and

(*b*.) This enactment shall not affect the existing powers or privileges of any city or borough as respects the sheriff, lieutenant, militia, justices, or coroner; but, if any county borough is, at the passing of this Act, a part of any county for any of the above purposes, nothing in this Act shall prevent the same from continuing to be part of that county for that purpose; and

(*c*.) This enactment shall not affect parliamentary elections nor the right to vote at the election of a member to serve in Parliament, nor land tax, tithes, or tithe rentcharge, nor the area within which any bishop, parson, or other ecclesiastical person has any cure of souls or jurisdiction.

(3.) For the purposes of parliamentary elections, and of the registration of voters for such elections, the sheriff, clerk of the peace, and council of the county in which any place is comprised at the passing of this Act for the purpose of parliamentary elections shall, save as otherwise provided by the scheme or order, or by the County Electors Act, 1888, or this Act, continue to have the same powers, duties, and liabilities as they would have had if no alteration of boundary had taken place. 51 & 52 Vict. c. 10.

(4.) Any scheme or order made in pursuance of this Act may, so far as may

51 & 52 Vict. c. 41, s. 59.

seem necessary or proper for the purposes of the scheme or order, provide for all or any of the following matters, that is to say,

(*a.*) may provide for the abolition, restriction, or establishment, or extension of the jurisdiction of any local authority in or over any part of the area affected by the scheme or order, and for the adjustment or alteration of the boundaries of such area, and for the constitution of the local authorities therein, and may deal with the powers and duties of any council, local authorities, quarter sessions, justices of the peace, coroners, sheriff, lieutenant, custos rotulorum, clerk of the peace, and other officer therein, and with the costs of any such authorities, sessions, persons, or officers as aforesaid, and may determine the status of any such area as a component part of any larger area, and provide for the election of representatives in such area, and may extend to any altered area the provisions of any local Act which were previously in force in a portion of the area; and

(*b.*) may make temporary provision for meeting the debts and liabilities of the various authorities affected by the scheme or order, for the management of their property, and for regulating the duties, position, and remuneration of officers affected by the scheme or order, and applying to them the provisions of this Act as to existing officers: and

(*c.*) may provide for the transfer of any writs, process, records, and documents relating to or to be executed in any part of the area affected by the scheme or order, and for determining questions arising from such transfer; and

(*d.*) may provide for all matters which appear necessary or proper for bringing into operation and giving full effect to the scheme or order; and

(*e.*) may adjust any property, debts, and liabilities affected by the scheme or order.

(5.) Where an alteration of boundaries of a county is made by this Act an order for any of the above-mentioned matters may, if it appears to the Local Government Board desirable, be made by that Board, but such order, if petitioned against by any council, sessions, or local authority affected thereby, within three months after notice of such order is given in accordance with this Act, shall be provisional only, unless the petition is withdrawn or the order is confirmed by Parliament.

(6.) A scheme or order may be made for amending any scheme or order previously made in pursuance of this Act, and may be made by the same authority and after the same procedure as the original scheme or order. Where a provision of this Act respecting a scheme or order requires the scheme or order to be laid before Parliament, or to be confirmed by Parliament, either in every case or if it is petitioned against, such scheme or order may amend any local and personal Act.

General provision as to alteration of boundaries.

Sect. 60.—In every alteration of boundaries effected under the authority of this Act, care shall be taken that, so far as practicable, the boundaries of an area of local government shall not intersect the boundaries of any other area of local government.

Appointment of commissioners.

Sect. 61.—(1.) For the purposes of this Act the Right Honourable Edward Henry, Earl of Derby, the Right Honourable George John Shaw Lefevre, John Lloyd Wharton, Esquire, Francis Mowatt, Esquire, C.B., and Joseph J. Henley, Esquire, shall be appointed Commissioners.

(2.) If a vacancy occurs in the office of any of the Commissioners by reason of death, resignation, incapacity, or otherwise, it shall be lawful for Her Majesty the Queen, under Her Royal Sign Manual, to appoint some other person to fill the vacancy, and so from time to time as often as occasion requires.

(3.) The Commissioners may, from time to time, with the assent of the Treasury as to number, appoint or employ such number of officers and persons as they may think necessary for the purpose of the execution of their duties under this Act, and may remove any officer or person so appointed or employed.

(4.) There shall be paid to any officer or person appointed or employed under this section, such salaries or other remuneration as the Treasury may assign, and that remuneration and all expenses of the Commissioners, incurred with the sanction of the Treasury in the execution of this Act, shall be paid out of moneys provided by Parliament. 51 & 52 Vict. c. 41, s. 61.

(5.) On holding any inquiry for the purposes of this Act, any Commissioner or officer of the Commissioners shall have the same powers as an inspector of the Local Government Board has on holding a local inquiry under the Public Health Act, 1875. 38 & 39 Vict. c. 55.

(6.) There shall be paid to the Commissioners by the councils of the counties and county boroughs whose financial relations are adjusted by the Commissioners in pursuance of this Act, such amounts as the Treasury may fix as necessary for the payment of the costs of such adjustment, including a proper share of the salaries and remuneration of the officers and persons appointed or employed by such Commissioners, and such amounts shall be paid into the Exchequer, and the amount so paid shall be included as part of the adjustment.

(7.) The authority of the Commissioners shall extend to the settlement and the determination by them, on such terms and in such manner as they, in their absolute discretion, think most just and fit, of the matters referred to them, and also of all such matters and questions as are, in their judgment, incidental thereto or consequent thereon, to the end that their award or awards may effect a final settlement, and until a final settlement is made the authority of the Commissioners shall extend to determine the proportions in which payments are to be made to the councils of counties and county boroughs out of the Local Taxation Account, and all payments so made shall be taken into account in the making of the adjustment.

(8.) Every award, order, and other instrument made by or proceeding from the Commissioners shall be binding and conclusive to and for all intents and purposes, and shall have the like effect as if it had been made by a judge of the High Court of Justice in England, and shall be acted on, obeyed, executed, and enforced by all sheriffs and other officers and persons accordingly. No such award, order, or other instrument shall be removable by any writ or process into any of Her Majesty's Courts, and the Commissioners proceedings or acts shall not be liable to be interfered with or questioned by or in any court, or elsewhere, by way of mandamus, prohibition, injuction, or otherwise.

(9.) The costs of and attending the inquiry and award shall be borne and paid by the parties out of the fund or rate applicable to their general expenses, in such proportions as the Commissioners may direct, and the Commissioners may order the taxation of any costs in such manner as they may see fit.

(10.) The powers of the Commissioners shall, unless continued by Parliament, cease on the last day of December one thousand eight hundred and ninety.

Sect. 62.—(1.) Any councils and other authorities affected by this Act or by any scheme, order, or other thing made or done in pursuance of this Act, may from time to time make agreements for the purpose of adjusting any property, income, debts, liabilities, and expenses, so far as affected by this Act or such scheme, order, or thing, of the parties to the agreement, and the agreement and any other agreement authorised by this Act to be made for the purpose of the adjustment of any property, debts, liabilities, or financial relations, may provide for the transfer or retention of any property, debts, and liabilities, with or without any conditions, and for the joint use of any property, and for the transfer of any duties, and for payment by either party to the agreement in respect of property, debts, duties, and liabilities so transferred or retained, or of such joint user, and in respect of the salary, remuneration, or compensation payable to any officer or person, and that either by way of a capital sum, or of a terminable annuity for a period not exceeding that allowed by the commissioners under this Act or the Local Government Board. Adjustment of property and liabilities.

(2.) In default of an agreement as to any matter requiring adjustment for the purpose of this Act, or any matter which, in case of difference, is to be referred to arbitration, then, if no other mode of making such adjustment or determining such difference is provided by this Act, such adjustment or difference may be made or determined by an arbitrator appointed by the parties, or in case of difference as to the appointment, appointed by the Local Government Board.

51 & 52 Vict. c. 41, s. 62.

8 & 9 Vict. c. 18.

(3.) An arbitrator appointed under this Act shall be deemed to be an arbitrator within the meaning of the Lands Clauses Consolidation Act, 1845, and the Acts amending the same, and the provisions of those Acts with respect to an arbitration shall apply accordingly; and, further, the arbitrator may state a special case, and notwithstanding anything in the said Acts, shall determine the amount of the costs, and shall have power to disallow as costs in the arbitration the costs of any witness whom he considers to have been called unnecessarily, and any other costs which he considers to have been incurred unnecessarily.

(4.) Any award or order made by the Commissioners or any arbitrator under this Act may provide for any matter for which an agreement might have provided.

(5.) Any sum required to be paid for the purpose of adjustment, or of any award or order made by the Commissioners, or an arbitrator under this Act, may be paid out of the county or borough fund or out of such other special fund as the council, with the approval of the Commissioners under this Act or of the Local Government Board, may direct.

(6.) The payment of any capital sum required to be paid for the purposes of the adjustment or of an agreement under this Act, or of any award or order made upon any arbitration under this Act, shall be a purpose for which a council may borrow under this Act, or in the case of a borough council, under the Municipal Corporations Act, 1882, or any local Act, and such sum may be borrowed on the security of all or any of the funds, rates, and revenues of the council, and either by the creation of stock or in any other manner in which they are for the time being authorised to borrow, and such sum may be borrowed without the consent of the Treasury or any other authority, so that it be repaid within such period as the Local Government Board may sanction, by such method as is mentioned in Part Four of this Act for paying off a loan, or, if the sum is raised by stock under a local Act, by such method as is directed by that Act.

(7.) Any capital sum paid to any council for the purpose of any adjustment, or in pursuance of any order or award of an arbitrator under this Act shall be treated as capital, and applied, with the sanction of the Local Government Board, either in the repayment of debt for or any other purpose for which capital money may be applied.

A bitration by Local Government Board. 31 & 32 Vict. c. 119.

Sect. 63. Where the Local Government Board are required in pursuance of this Act to decide any difference or other matter referred to arbitration in pursuance of this Act, the provisions of the Regulation of Railways Act, 1868, respecting arbitrations by the Board of Trade, and the enactments amending those provisions, shall apply as if they were herein re-enacted, and in terms made applicable to the Local Government Board and the decision of differences and matters under this Act.

PART IV.

FINANCE.

Property Funds and Costs of County Council.

Transfer of county property and liabilities.

Sect 64.—(1.) On and after the appointed day all property of the quarter sessions of a county, or held by the clerk of the peace, or any justice or justices of a county, or treasurer, or commissioners, or otherwise for any public uses and purposes of a county, or any division thereof, shall pass to and vest in and be held in trust for the council of the county, subject to all debts and liabilities affecting it, and shall be held by the county council for the same estate, interest, and purposes, and subject to the same covenants, conditions, and restrictions, for and subject to which that property is or would have been held if this Act had not passed, so far as those purposes are not modified by this Act. Provided that—

(*a.*) the existing records of or in the custody of the court of quarter sessions shall, subject to any order of that court, remain in the same custody in which they would have been if this Act had not passed; and 51 & 52 Vict. c. 41, s. 64.

(*b.*) where any property belongs to a charity, nothing in this Act shall affect the trust of such charity, and until otherwise directed by the Charity Commissioners for England and Wales, the trustees or managers of the charity shall be appointed in like manner as if this Act had not passed; and

(*c.*) the justices of any county may retain any pictures, chattels, or property on the ground that the same have been presented to them or purchased out of their own funds or otherwise belong to them, and are not held for public purposes of the county, and any difference arising between the county council and the justices with respect to any such retention shall be referred to and determined by the Commissioners under this Act.

(2.) On and after the appointed day all debts and liabilities of the quarter sessions, or of the clerk of the peace, or any justice or justices, or treasurer, or commissioners, incurred for county purposes, shall become debts and liabilities of the county council, and shall, subject to the provisions of this Act, be defrayed by them out of the like property and funds out of which they would have been defrayed if this Act had not passed.

(3.) The county council shall have full power to manage, alter, and enlarge, and, with the consent of the Local Government Board, to alienate any land or buildings transferred by this section, or otherwise vested in the council, but shall provide such accommodation and rooms, and such furniture, books, and other things as may from time to time be determined by the standing joint committee of quarter sessions and the county council, to be necessary or proper for the due transaction of the business, and convenient keeping of the records and documents, of the quarter sessions and justices out of sessions, or of any committee of such quarter sessions or justices.

(4.) This section shall apply, with the necessary modifications, to the administrative counties of Sussex and Suffolk.

(5.) This section shall apply in the case of the property, debts, and liabilites of the justices of all the ridings and divisions of the counties of York or Lincoln at their gaol sessions, or of commissioners appointed by the justices, in like manner as if it were herein re-enacted with the substitution of gaol sessions or commissioners for quarter sessions, and of clerk of gaol sessions for clerk of the peace, and as if the joint committee of the councils of the three ridings or divisions were the council of the county; and the said joint committee shall, for the purposes of the said property, debts and liabilities, and for the transaction of the administrative business and execution of their duties under this Act, be a body corporate, with perpetual succession and a common seal, by the name of the county committee, with the prefix of the name of the county, and with power to acquire and hold land for the purposes of their constitution without licence in mortmain.

(6.) The county council of the soke of Peterborough shall be liable to repair the county bridges in the soke, and if any costs are incurred by the county council of the county of Northampton for the benefit of the soke, an adjustment thereof shall be made by agreement, or by arbitration in manner provided by this Act.

Sect. 65.—(1.) A county council may, from time to time, for the purpose of any of their powers and duties, including those which are to be executed through the standing joint committee, acquire, purchase, or take on lease, or exchange any lands or any easements or rights over or in land, whether situate within or without the county, and may acquire, hire, erect, and furnish such halls, buildings, and offices as they may from time to time require, whether within or without their county. Power to acquire lands.

(2.) For the purpose of the purchase, taking on lease, or exchange of such lands, sections one hundred and seventy-six, one hundred and seventy-seven, and one hundred and seventy-eight of the Public Health Act, 1875, shall apply as if they were herein re-enacted, and in terms made applicable to the county council.

(3.) Where the county council, with the consent of the Local Government

51 & 52 Vict. c. 41, s. 65.

Board, sell any land, the proceeds of such sale shall be applied in such manner as the said Board sanction towards the discharge of any loan of the council, or otherwise for any purpose for which capital may be applied by the council.

Costs of justices to be payable one of county fund.

Sect. 66. All costs incurred by the quarter sessions or the justices out of session of a county, and all costs incurred by any justice, police officer, or constable, in defending any legal proceedings taken against him in respect of any order made, or act done, in the execution of his duty as such justice, police officer, or constable shall, to such amount as may be sanctioned by the standing joint committee of the county council and quarter sessions, and, so far as they are not otherwise provided for, be paid out of the county fund of the county, and the council of the county shall provide for such payment accordingly.

Adjustment of law as respects costs ordered by quarter sessions or justices to be paid.

Sect. 67. Any order of a court of quarter sessions, or of any justices or justice out of session, for the payment by the county treasurer of costs in criminal proceedings or of costs under the Act of the forty-eighth year of the reign of King George the Third, chapter seventy-five, shall be obeyed by the county treasurer in like manner as heretofore, and the county council shall cause the treasurer, or some other person on his behalf, to attend at every court of quarter sessions for the purpose of paying such sums as may be ordered by the court to be so paid.

Funds of county council.

Sect. 68.—(1.) All receipts of the county council, whether for general or special county purposes, shall be carried to the county fund, and all payments for general or special county purposes shall be made in the first instance out of that fund.

(2.) In this Act the expression "general county purposes" means all purposes declared by this or any other Act to be general county purposes, and all purposes for contributions to which the county council are for the time being authorised by law to assess the whole area of their administrative county, and the expression "general county account" means the account of the county fund to which the contributions so raised are carried, and any costs incurred for a general county purpose shall be general expenses, and all costs incurred by the county council in the execution of their duties which are not by law made special expenses shall be general expenses.

(3.) In this Act the expression "special county purposes" means any purposes from contribution to which any portion of the county is for the time being exempt, and also includes any purposes where the expenditure involved is by law restricted to a hundred, division, or other limited part of the county, and the expression "special county account" means any account of the county fund to which contributions for special county purposes are carried, and any costs incurred for a special county purpose shall be special expenses.

(4.) If the moneys standing to the general county account of the county fund are insufficient to meet the expenditure for general county purposes, county contributions may be levied to meet the deficiency on the whole administrative county, and shall be assessed on all the parishes in the county.

(5.) If the moneys standing to any special county account of the county fund are insufficient to meet the expenditure for the special county purposes chargeable to that account, county contributions may be levied to meet the deficiency on any parishes in the county liable to be assessed to county contributions for those purposes.

(6.) Any precept for county contributions may include as separate items a contribution for general county purposes, and a contribution for any special county purpose or purposes, and subject as in this or any other Act mentioned, county contributions, whether for general or special county purposes, which are liable to be assessed on the parishes, shall be assessed on such parishes in proportion to the annual value thereof, as determined by the standard or basis for the county rate, and all enactments applying to such standard or basis or to county rate shall (save as altered by this Act) apply so far as may be, consistently with the tenor thereof, to county contributions, and those enactments shall extend to all parishes within any borough which are liable under this Act to be assessed to county contributions.

(7.) The county council shall keep such accounts as will prevent the whole administrative county from being charged with expenditure properly payable by a portion only of the county, and will prevent any sums raised in a portion only of the county being applied in reduction of expenditure properly payable by the whole or a larger part of the county, and will further secure any such exemption as above in this section mentioned, and will prevent any sums by law specifically applicable to any particular purpose from being applied to any other purpose. 51 & 52 Vict. c. 41, s. 68.

(8.) In determining the amount of expenditure for any particular county purpose, general or special, a proper proportion of the cost of the officers and buildings and establishment of the county council may be added to the expenditure directly expended for that purpose.

(9.) County contributions may be made retrospective in order to raise money for the payment of costs incurred, or having become payable at any time within six months before the demand of the contributions.

Sect. 69.—(1.) The county council may from time to time, with the consent of the Local Government Board, borrow, on the security of the county fund, and of any revenues of the council, or on either such fund or revenues, or any part of the revenues, such sums as may be required for the following purposes, or any of them, that is to say; Borrowing by county council.

(*a.*) for consolidating the debts of the county; and

(*b.*) for purchasing any land or building any building, which the council are authorised by any Act to purchase or build: and

(*c.*) for any permanent work or other thing which the county council are authorised to execute or do, and the cost of which ought, in the opinion of the Local Government Board, to be spread over a term of years; and

(*d.*) for making advances (which they are hereby authorised to make) to any persons or bodies of persons, corporate or unincorporate, in aid of the emigration or colonisation of inhabitants of the county, with a guarantee for repayment of such advances from any local authority in the county, or the Government of any colony; and

(*e.*) for any purpose for which quarter sessions or the county council are authorised by any Act to borrow,

but neither the transfer of powers by this Act nor anything else in this Act shall confer on the county council any power to borrow without the consent above mentioned, and that consent shall dispense with the necessity of obtaining any other consent which may be required by the Acts relating to such borrowing, and the Local Government Board, before giving their consent, shall take into consideration any representation made by any ratepayer or owner of property rated to the county fund.

(2.) Provided that where the total debt of the county council, after deducting the amount of any sinking fund, exceeds, or if the proposed loan is borrowed will exceed, the amount of one tenth of the annual rateable value of the rateable property in the county, ascertained according to the standard or basis for the county rate, the amount shall not be borrowed, except in pursuance of a provisional order made by the Local Government Board and confirmed by Parliament.

(3.) A county council may also, from time to time, without any consent of the Local Government Board, during the period which was fixed for the discharge of any loan raised by them under this Act or transferred to them by this Act, borrow on the like security such amount as may be required for the purpose of paying off the whole or any part of such loan, or if any part of such loan has been repaid otherwise than by capital money for re-borrowing the amount so re-paid, and for the purpose of this section, "capital money" includes any instalments, annual appropriations, and sinking fund and the proceeds of the sale of land or other property, but does not include money previously borrowed for the purpose of repaying a loan.

(4.) All money reborrowed shall be repaid within the period fixed for the discharge of the original loan, and every loan for reborrowing shall for the purpose of the ultimate discharge be deemed to form part of the same loan as the original

51 & 52 Vict. c. 41, s. 69.

loan, and the obligations of the council with respect to the discharge of the original loan shall not be in any way affected by means of the reborrowing.

(5.) A loan under this section shall be repaid within such period, not exceeding thirty years as the county council, with the consent of the Local Government Board, determine in each case.

(6.) The county council shall pay off every loan either by equal yearly or half yearly instalments of principal, or of principal and interest combined, or by means of a sinking fund set apart, invested, and applied in accordance with the Local Loans Act, 1875, and the Acts amending the same.

38 & 39 Vict. c. 83.

(7.) Where a loan is raised for any special county purpose, the council shall take care that the sums payable in respect of the loan are charged to the special account to which the expenditure for that purpose is chargeable.

(8.) Where the county council are authorised to borrow any money on loan they may raise such money either as one loan or several loans, and either by stock issued under this Act, or by debentures or annuity certificates under the Local Loans Act, 1875, and the Acts amending the same, or, if special reasons exist for so borrowing, by mortgage, in accordance with sections two hundred and thirty-six and two hundred and thirty-seven of the Public Health Act, 1875.

38 & 39 Vict. c. 55.

(9.) Provided that where a county council have borrowed by means of stock they shall not borrow by way of mortgage except for a period not exceeding five years.

(10.) Where the county council borrow by debentures such debentures may be for any amount not less than five pounds.

(11.) The provisions of this section which authorise advances in aid of the emigration or colonization of inhabitants of the county, and borrowing for those advances, except the provisions respecting the total debt, shall extend to the councils of boroughs mentioned in the Third Schedule to this Act.

(12.) Nothing in this section shall be taken to empower the Cheshire County Council to borrow on the security of any revenue estimated to accrue from the surplus funds of the River Weaver Navigation.

Issue of county stock.

Sect. 70.—(1.) County stock may be created, issued, transferred, dealt with, and redeemed in such manner and in accordance with such regulations as the Local Government Board may from time to time prescribe.

(2.) Without prejudice to the generality of the above power, such regulations may provide for the discharge of any loan raised by such stock, and in the case of consolidation of debt for extending or varying the times within which loans may be discharged, and may provide for the consent of limited owners and for the application of the Acts relating to stamp duties and to cheques and for the disposal of unclaimed dividends, and may apply for the purposes of this section, with or without modifications, any enactments of the Local Loans Act, 1875, and the Acts amending the same, and of any Act relating to stock issued by the Metropolitan Board of Works, or by the corporation of any municipal borough.

(3.) Such regulations shall be laid before each House of Parliament for not less than thirty days during which such House sits, and if either House during such thirty days resolves that such regulations ought not to be proceeded with the same shall be of no effect, without prejudice nevertheless to the making of further regulations.

(4.) If no such resolution is passed it shall be lawful for Her Majesty by Order in Council to confirm such regulations, and the same when so confirmed shall be deemed to have been duly made and to be within the powers of this Act, and shall be of the same force as if they were enacted in this Act.

Audit of accounts of county council.

Sect. 71.—(1.) The accounts of the receipts and expenditure of county councils shall be made up to the end of each local financial year as defined by this Act, and be in the form for the time being prescribed by the Local Government Board.

(2.) The provisions of the Municipal Corporations Act, 1882, with respect to the return to the Local Government Board of the accounts of a council of a borough and to the accounts of the treasurer of the borough, and to the inspection and abstract thereof shall apply to the accounts of a county council, and of the treasurer and officers of such council, and the said provisions respecting the return to the Local Government Board shall extend to the return to that Board of a printed copy of the abstract of the said accounts. 51 & 52 Vict. c. 41, s. 17.

(3.) The accounts of a county council and of a county treasurer and officers of such council, shall be audited by the district auditors appointed by the Local Government Board in like manner as accounts of an urban authority and their officers under sections two hundred and forty-seven and two hundred and fifty of the Public Health Act, 1875, and those sections and all enactments amending them or applying to audit by district auditors, including the enactments imposing penalties and providing for the recovery of sums, shall apply in like manner as if, so far as they relate to an audit of the accounts of an urban authority and the officers of such authority, they were herein re-enacted with the necessary modifications, and accordingly all ratepayers and owners of property in the county shall have the like rights, and there shall be the same appeal as in the case of such audit. Provided that the First Schedule to the District Auditors Act, 1879, shall be modified in manner described in the Second Schedule to this Act. 38 & 39 Vict. c. 55. 42 & 43 Vict. c. 6.

Sect. 72. After the appointed day the Local Government Board shall exercise, as regards any county borough, or other borough, the powers conferred by Part V. of the Municipal Corporations Act, 1882, relating to corporate property and liabilities, as respects the approval of loans and of the alienation of property, and other matters therein mentioned, and that Part shall, as respects any transactions commenced after the appointed day, be construed as if "Local Government Board" were throughout that Part substituted for "Treasury."

Adaptation of Part V. of 45 & 46 Vict. c. 50 as to corporate property and liabilities.

Local Financial Year and Annual Budget.

Sect. 73.—(1.) After the appointed day, not being more than three years after the passing of this Act, the local financial year shall be the twelve months ending the thirty-first day of March, and the accounts of the receipts and expenditure of every county council shall be made up for that year, but until the appointed day the local financial year shall be the twelve months ending the twenty-fifth day of March, and the said accounts shall be made up for that year.

Fixing of local financial year and consequent adjustments

(2.) All enactments relating to accounts of local authorities, or the audit thereof, or to returns touching their receipts and expenditure, or to meetings, or other matters, shall be modified so far as is necessary for adapting them to the provisions of this section, and the Local Government Board shall from time to time give such orders and make such arrangements as appear to the Board to be necessary or proper for affecting such adaptation, and giving effect to the provisions of this section.

Sect. 74.—(1.) At the beginning of every local financial year, every county council shall cause to be submitted to them an estimate of the receipts and expenses of such council during that financial year, whether on account of property, contributions, rates, loans, or otherwise.

Annual budget of county councils

(2.) The council shall estimate the amount which will require to be raised in the first six months, and in the second six months of the said financial year by means of contributions.

(3.) If at the expiration of the first six months of such financial year it appears to the council that the amount of the contribution or rate estimated at the commencement of the year will be larger than is necessary or will be insufficient, the council may revise the estimate and alter accordingly the amount of the contribution or rate.

51 & 52 Vict. c. 41, s. 75.

PART V.

SUPPLEMENTAL.

Application of Acts.

Application of 45 & 46 Vict. c. 50, to county councils and this Act. 47 & 48 Vict. c. 70.

Sect. 75. For the purpose of the provisions of this Act with respect to county councils, and to the chairmen, members, committees, and officers of such councils, and otherwise for the purpose of carrying this Act into effect, the following portions of the Municipal Corporations Act, 1882, namely, Part Two, Part Three, Part Four (as amended by the Municipal Elections (Corrupt Practices) Act, 1884), section one hundred and twenty-four, in Part Five, Part Twelve, Part Thirteen, the Second Schedule, Part Two and Part Three of the Third Schedule, and Part One of the Eighth Schedule shall, so far as the same are unrepealed and are consistent with the provisions of this Act, apply as if they were herein re-enacted with the enactments amending the same in such terms and with such modifications as are necessary to make them applicable to the said councils and their chairmen, members, committees, and officers, and to the other provisions of this Act.

Provided as follows :—

(1.) In a year in which county councillors are elected, the elections of those councillors, and of councillors of a borough, shall be conducted together.

(2.) Such person as the county council may appoint shall be the returning officer for the election of county councillors of the county council, in substitution for the mayor, and for the aldermen assigned for that purpose by the council.

(3.) The returning officer, without prejudice to any other power, may by writing under his hand appoint a fit person to be his deputy for all or any of the purposes relating to the election of any such councillor, and may by himself or such deputy exercise any powers and do any things which a returning officer is authorised or required to exercise or do in relation to such election, and shall for the purposes of the election have all the powers of the sheriff.

(4.) A reference in this Act, or in the enactments applied by this Act, to the returning officer or to the mayor or to the alderman shall, so far as relates to the election of any such councillor, be construed to refer to the returning officer, and any such deputy as above mentioned.

(5.) A reference in the said enactments to the town clerk so far as respects the election of any such councillor shall be construed to refer to the returning officer or his deputy, and as respects matters subsequent to the election, shall be construed to refer to the clerk of the county council.

(6.) In a borough the returning officer for the purpose of the election of councillors of the borough shall continue to be the same as heretofore, and where an electoral division of the county is co-extensive with or wholly comprised in such borough, shall at the election in such division of a councillor of the county council act as the returning officer in pursuance of a writ directed to him from the county returning officer, and so far as respects that election shall follow the instructions of, and return the names of the persons elected to the county returning officer in like manner as if he were a deputy returning officer. and any decision of an objection shall be subject to revision by the county returning officer accordingly, and a reference in the said enactments to the town clerk shall, as respects the borough, be construed to refer to the town clerk.

(7.) Some place fixed by the returning officer shall, except where the election is in a borough, be substituted for the town clerk's office, and, as respects the hearing of objections to nomination papers, for the town hall, but such place shall, if the electoral division is the whole or part of an urban district, be in that district, and in any other case shall be in the electoral division or in an adjoining electoral division.

(8.) The returning officer shall forthwith after the election of county councillors for the county return the names of the persons elected to the clerk of the county council. 51 & 52 Vict. c. 41, s. 75.

(9.) The period between the nomination and election may be such period, not exceeding six days, as the returning officer may fix.

(10.) An outgoing alderman shall not as alderman vote in the election of a chairman.

(11.) The hours of the poll shall be those fixed by the Elections (Hours of Poll) Act, 1885. 48 & 49 Vict. c. 10.

(12.) Section eleven of the Municipal Corporations Act, 1882, with respect to the qualification of a county councillor by reason of his being entered in the separate non-resident list, shall include, for the purposes of this Act, all persons entered in such separate list in any municipal borough by reason of occupation of property in the borough, and all persons entered in such separate list for any part of a county not in a municipal borough by reason of the occupation of property in that part.

(13.) The seventh of November shall be substituted for the ninth of November as the ordinary day of election of the chairman and of county aldermen, and as the day for holding a quarterly meeting of the county council.

(14.) Ten days shall be substituted for five days in section thirty-four of the Municipal Corporations Act, 1882, as the time within which a person elected to a corporate office is to accept that office, and twelve months shall be substituted for six months in section thirty-nine of the said Act, as the period of absence which disqualifies an alderman or councillor.

(15.) The quorum of the council shall be one-fourth of the whole number of the council, and one-fourth shall, for the purposes of this section, be substituted for one-third in paragraph ten of the second schedule to the Municipal Corporations Act, 1882.

(16.) Nothing in the Municipal Corporations Act, 1882, as applied by this section—

(*a.*) shall alter the application of any fine, penalty, or forfeiture recoverable in a summary manner; or,

(*b.*) shall apply any of the provisions of the Municipal Corporations Act, 1882, with reference to boundaries or the alteration of wards or borough auditors, nor any of the following provisions, namely, sub-section five of section fifteen, section sixteen, section two hundred and fifty one, or section two hundred and fifty-seven; or

(*c.*) shall render any person elected to a corporate office without his consent to his nomination being previously obtained liable to pay a fine on non-acceptance of office, or render a chairman or deputy chairman disqualified as such by reason of absence; or

(*d.*) shall authorise or require a returning officer to hold an election of a councillor to fill a casual vacancy in the representation of an electoral division where the vacancy occurs within six months before the time fixed by this Act for a new election of a councillor to represent such electoral division; or

(*e.*) shall apply to a county council section seventeen of the said Act with respect to the town clerk, nor, unless the county council so resolve, section eighteen respecting the treasurer, but, if the county council so resolve, section eighteen shall supersede the existing enactments with respect to the county treasurer; or,

(*f.*) shall require the acts and proceedings of the standing joint committee of the county council and quarter sessions to be submitted to the county council for their approval; or

(*g.*) shall prevent the use of schools and public rooms for the purpose of taking the poll at elections under this Act, but section six of the Ballot Act, 1872, shall apply in the case of elections under this Act, and the returning officer may, in addition to using such rooms free of charge for taking the poll, use 35 & 36 Vict. c. 33.

51 & 52 Vict. c. 41, s. 75. the same free of charge for hearing objections to nomination papers and for counting votes.

(17.) All costs properly incurred in relation to the holding of elections of councillors of county councils, so far as not otherwise provided for by law, shall be paid out of the county fund as general expenses.

38 & 39 Vict c. 84. 48 & 49 Vict c. 62. (18.) The said costs shall not exceed those allowed by Part I. of the First Schedule to the Parliamentary Elections (Returning Officers) Act, 1875, as amended by the Parliamentary Elections (Returning Officers) Act, 1885, or by such scale as the county council may from time to time frame.

49 & 50 Vict. c. 57. (19.) Sections four, five, six, and seven of the Parliamentary Elections (Returning Officers) Act, 1875, as amended by the Parliamentary Elections (Returning Officers) Act (1875) Amendment Act, 1886, shall apply as if they were herein re-enacted with the necessary modifications, and in particular with the substitution of the county council for the person from whom payment is claimed, and of one month for the period of fourteen days within which application may be made for taxation.

(20.) A county council shall, on the request of the returning officer, prior to a poll being taken at any election of a councillor of such council, advance to him such sum not exceeding ten pounds for every thousand electors at the election as he may require.

(21.) The meeting of a county council, or of any committee thereof, may be held at such place either within or without their county, as the council from time to time direct.

Amendment of 51 & 52 Vict. c. 10. **Sect. 76.**—(1.) The provisions of section four of the County Electors Act, 1888, with respect to the framing of the lists and register of voters in parts shall extend to parishes situate within a parliamentary borough.

(2.) In the provisions of section four of the said Act with respect to making out the lists of voters according to the order in which the qualifying premises appear in the rate book, the county authority shall mean the county council.

(3.) The names of the parliamentary electors and county electors in the lists in each polling district may be numbered consecutively, and such portion of those lists as consists of the names of parliamentary electors may be taken to form the register for the purpose of parliamentary elections, and such portion of those lists as contains the names of county electors may be taken to form the register of county electors.

(4.) For the purpose of the provisions of the Acts relating to the appointment of revising barristers, and of section nine of the County Electors Act, 1888, the county of Surrey and such portion of the county of London as is situate south of the Thames shall be deemed to be separate counties forming part of the south-eastern circuit; and such portion of the administrative county of London as is situate north of the Thames shall be deemed to form part of the county of Middlesex; and the county of Middlesex, inclusive of that portion, shall be deemed to be a separate county on a circuit; but any sum payable by the London county council in respect of either of the said portions of the county, shall be paid as for a general county purpose.

(5.) The provisions of section eleven of the County Electors Act, 1888, with respect to the payment of the sums therein mentioned shall apply to the payment of the said sums in the year one thousand eight hundred and eighty-eight in like manner as if a county authority had not been established under this Act.

51 & 52 Vict. c. 10 (6.) It is hereby declared that nothing in section twelve of the County Electors Act, 1888, applies to any person occupying property within a borough.

(7.) It shall be lawful for Her Majesty the Queen, by Order in Council, from time to time to alter the instructions, precepts, notices, and forms under the Registration of Electors Acts, in such manner as appears to Her Majesty necessary for carrying into effect this Act and the County Electors Act, 1888, and any other Act for the time being in force amending or affecting the Acts mentioned in this sub-section, and the instructions, precepts, notices, and forms specified in any such Order in Council shall be observed and be valid in law, and clerks of the peace, and town clerks, and other officers shall act accordingly.

(8.) The provisions of section six of the said County Electors Act, 1888, requiring the statement of the barrister for the purpose of an appeal to be made not less than four days before the first day of the Michaelmas sittings shall not apply in the year one thousand eight hundred and eighty-eight.

51 & 52 Vict. c. 41, s. 76.

Residential qualification of county electors in administrative County of London.

Sect. 77. A person who is entitled to be registered as a county elector in respect of any qualification in the administrative county of London, in all respects except that of residence, and is resident beyond seven miles but within fifteen miles of the county, shall be entitled to be registered as a county elector.

Construction of Acts referring to business transferred.

Sect. 78.—(1.) All enactments in any Act, whether general or local and personal, relating to any business, powers, duties or liabilities transferred by or in pursuance of this Act from any authority to a county council, either alone or jointly with the quarter sessions, or to any joint committee, shall, subject to the provisions of this Act, and so far as circumstances admit, be construed as if—

(*a.*) any reference therein to the said authority or to any committee or member thereof or to any meeting thereof (so far as it relates to the business, powers, duties, or liabilities transferred) referred to the county council or to a committee or member thereof or to a meeting thereof, as the case requires, and as if—

(*b.*) a reference to any clerk or officer of such authority referred to the clerk or officer of a county council or committee thereof, as the case requires,

and all the said enactments shall be construed with such modifications as may be necessary for carrying this Act into effect.

(2.) Provided that the transfer of powers and duties enacted by this Act shall not authorise any county council or any committee or member thereof—

(*a.*) to exercise any of the powers of a court of record; or

(*b.*) to administer an oath; or

(*c.*) to exercise any jurisdiction under the Summary Jurisdiction Acts, or perform any judicial business, or otherwise act as justices or a justice of the peace;

but this enactment shall be without prejudice to the position of the chairman of the county council as justice of the peace during his term of office.

(3.) Where under any such enactment as in this section mentioned, any powers, duties, or liabilites are to be exercised or discharged after any presentment or in any particular manner, or at any particular meeting, or subject to any other conditions, the county council may, by the standing orders for the regulation of their proceedings, provide for the exercise and discharge of those powers, duties, and liabilities without any such prior presentment or in a different manner, or at any meeting of the council fixed by the standing orders, or without such other conditions; and until such standing orders take effect shall exercise and discharge them in the like manner, and at the like time, and subject to the like conditions, so nearly as circumstances admit; and a presentment by a grand jury in relation to any such powers, duties, or liabilities, shall cease to be made otherwise than by way of indictment.

(4.) For the purposes of this section the expression "authority" means a Secretary of State, the Board of Trade, the Local Government Board, and any Government Department, also any commissioners, conservators, or public body, corporate or unincorporate, specified in a Provisional Order transferring any powers, duties, or liabilities to the county council, also any quarter sessions and any justices, also the Metropolitan Board of Works, or other local authority mentioned in this Act; and the expression "member of an authority" includes, where the authority are quarter sessions or justices, any justice, and the expression "meeting of an authority" includes a court of quarter sessions, and the assembly of justices in special or petty sessions; and the expression "clerk of an authority" includes in relation to any quarter sessions or justices, the clerk of the peace or the clerk to a justice as the case requires.

This section shall apply as if a joint committee were a committee of the county council.

51 & 52 Vict. c. 41, s. 79.

Proceedings of Councils and Committees.

Incorporation of county council.

Sect. 79.—(1.) The council of each county shall be a body corporate by the name of the county council with the addition of the name of the administrative county, and shall have perpetual succession and a common seal and power to acquire and hold land for the purposes of their constitution without licence in mortmain.

(2.) All duties and liabilities of the inhabitants of a county shall become and be duties and liabilites of the council of such county.

(3.) Where any enactment (whether relating to lunatic asylums or bridges, or other county purposes, or to quarter sessions) requires or authorises land to be conveyed or granted to, or any contract or agreement to be made in the name of, the clerk of the peace, or any justice or justices or other person, on behalf of the county or quarter sessions, or justices of the county, such land shall be conveyed or granted to, and such contract and agreement shall be made with, the council of the administrative county concerned.

Payments out of fund and finance committee of county council.

Sect. 80.—(1.) All payments to and out of the county fund shall be made to and by the county treasurer, and all payments out of the fund shall, unless made in pursuance of the specific requirement of an Act of Parliament or of an order of a competent court, be made in pursuance of an order of the council signed by three members of the finance committee present at the meeting of the council and countersigned by the clerk of the council, and the same order may include several payments. Moreover all cheques for payment of moneys issued in pursuance of such order shall be countersigned by the clerk of the council or by a deputy approved by the council.

(2.) Any such order may be removed into the High Court of Justice by writ of certiorari, and may be wholly or partly disallowed or confirmed on motion and hearing with or without costs, according to the judgment and discretion of the court.

(3.) Every county council shall from time to time appoint a finance committee for regulating and controlling the finance of their county; and an order for the payment of a sum out of the county fund, whether on account of capital or income, shall not be made by a county council, except in pursuance of a resolution of the council passed on the recommendation of the finance committee, and (subject to the provisions of this Act respecting the standing joint committee) any costs, debt, or liability exceeding fifty pounds shall not be incurred except upon a resolution of the council passed on an estimate submitted by the finance committee.

(4.) The notice of the meeting at which any resolution for the payment of a sum out of the county fund (otherwise than for ordinary periodical payments), or any resolution for incurring any costs, debt, or liability exceeding fifty pounds will be proposed, shall state the amount of the said sum, costs, debt, or liability, and the purpose for which they are to be paid or incurred.

(5.) This section shall not apply to county boroughs.

Appointment of joint committees.

Sect. 81.—(1.) Any county council or councils, and any court or courts of quarter sessions, may from time to time join in appointing out of their respective bodies a joint committee for any purpose in respect of which they are jointly interested.

(2.) Any council or court taking part in the appointment of any joint committee under this section, may from time to time delegate to the committee any power which such council or court might exercise for the purpose for which the committee is appointed.

(3.) Provided that nothing in this section shall authorise a council to delegate to a committee any power of making a rate or borrowing any money.

(4.) Subject to the terms of delegation, any such joint committee shall, in respect of any matter delegated to it, have the same power in all respects as the councils and courts appointing it, or any of them, as the case may be.

(5.) The members of a joint committee appointed under this Act shall be appointed at such times and in such manner as may be from time to time fixed by the council or court who appointed them, and shall hold office for such time as may be fixed by the council or court who appointed them, so that where any members of the committee were appointed by the county council, such committee do not continue for more than three months after any triennial election of councillors of such county council. 51 & 52 Vict. c. 41, s. 81.

(6.) The costs of a joint committee shall be defrayed by the council by whom any of its members were appointed, or if appointed by more than one council in the proportion agreed to by them; and the accounts of such joint committee and their officers shall, for the purposes of the provisions of this Act, be deemed to be accounts of the county council and their officers.

(7.) This section shall apply to the councils of county boroughs in like manner as to councils of administrative counties, and a standing joint committee may be appointed for two or more administrative counties, inclusive of county boroughs, and the members of such joint committee shall be appointed by the several quarter sessions and councils in such proportion and manner as they respectively may arrange, and in default of arrangement as may be directed by a Secretary of State.

(8.) This section shall apply to the standing joint committees.

Sect. 82.—(1.) A county council appointing under this Act any committee may from time to time make, vary, and revoke regulations respecting the quorum and proceedings of such committee, and as to the area (if any) within which it is to exercise its authority; and subject to such regulations the proceedings and quorum and the place of meeting whether within or without the county, shall be such as the committee may from time to time direct, and the chairman at any meeting of the committee shall have a second or casting vote. Proceedings of committees.

(2.) Every committee shall report its proceedings to the council by whom it was appointed, but to the extent to which the council so direct, the acts and proceedings of the committee shall not be required by the provisions of the Municipal Corporations Act, 1882, to be submitted to the council for their approval.

(3.) In the case of a joint committee the councils and courts appointing the joint committee shall jointly have the powers given by this section, and the provisions of this section shall apply accordingly.

Officers.

Sect. 83. Subject to the provisions of this Act for the protection of clerks of the peace holding office at the passing of this Act, the following provisions shall have effect:— Clerk of the peace and of county council.

(1.) The clerk of the peace of a county, besides acting as clerk of the peace of that county, shall also (subject to the provisions of this Act as respects particular counties) be the clerk of the county council, and in that capacity is referred to in this Act as the clerk of the county council.

(2.) He shall be from time to time appointed by the standing joint committee of the county council and the quarter sessions, and may be removed by that joint committee.

(3.) He shall, subject to the directions of the custos rotulorum or the quarter sessions or the county council, as the case may require, have charge of and be responsible for the records and documents of the county.

(4.) The joint committee may appoint a deputy clerk to hold office during their pleasure, and to act in lieu of such clerk in case of his death, illness, or absence, or in such other cases as may be determined by the joint committee, and wherever the deputy so acts, all things authorised or required to be done by, to, or before the clerk of the peace, or clerk of the county council, may be done by, to, or before any such deputy; without prejudice to the appointment of a deputy clerk for the purpose of a second court on the division of the court of quarter sessions for judicial business.

51 & 52 Vict. c. 41, s. 83

(5.) The council shall pay to the clerk of the peace in respect of his services as clerk of the peace and as clerk of the county council, such salary as may be from time to time fixed under the enactments relating thereto, and all fees and costs payable to the clerk of the peace which are not excluded when the salary of the clerk of the peace is fixed shall be paid to the county fund, and for the purpose of the enactments relating to such salary and fees, the standing joint committee of the county council and the quarter sessions shall be substituted for the quarter sessions and the local authority respectively.

(6.) The clerk of the peace, when acting in relation to any business of the county council, and when acting under the Acts relating to the registration of parliamentary voters, or to the deposit of plans or documents, or to jury lists, or to any registration matters, shall act under the direction of the county council, and all enactments relating to such business, registration, or deposit, shall be construed as if clerk of the county council were therein substituted for clerk of the peace.

(7.) The office of clerk of the peace of each of the administrative counties of Sussex and Suffolk shall be a separate office; but nothing in this Act shall prevent the same person from being appointed to both such offices; and the justices in general sessions assembled for the entire county of Sussex or Suffolk may from time to time appoint the person who is clerk of the peace for either administrative county to be clerk of the peace of such general sessions, and may remove such clerk, and the remuneration to be paid to such clerk shall be determined jointly by the standing joint committees for the administrative counties.

(8.) The existing records of the county of Sussex and of the county of Suffolk shall, subject to the order of quarter sessions, continue to be kept by the clerk of the peace of East Sussex and by the clerk of the peace for East Suffolk respectively.

(9.) This section shall apply to the clerks of the peace and deputy clerks of the peace of the county of Lancaster, in like manner as it applies to clerks of the peace of any other county, but the appointment of any such deputy clerk of the peace may be discontinued if the standing joint committee think fit.

(10.) The joint committee of the councils of the three ridings or divisions of Yorkshire and Lincolnshire may from time to time appoint a clerk of such joint committee, and may from time to time remove such clerk.

(11.) The clerk of the peace for the county of London shall be a separate officer from the clerk of the county council for the administrative county of London, and

(*a.*) the clerk of the peace shall, subject to the directions of the quarter sessions, have charge of and be responsible for the records and documents of those sessions and of the justices out of session, and the clerk of the county council shall, subject to the directions of the council, have charge of and be responsible for all other documents of the county; and

(*b.*) the council may from time to time appoint a deputy clerk of the council, and the foregoing provisions of this section with respect to the deputy clerk shall apply; and

(*c.*) the council shall pay to the clerk of the council such salary as may be from time to time fixed by them.

(12.) The county council shall cause their clerk or other officer from time to time to send to a Secretary of State or the Local Government Board such returns and information as may from time to time be required by either House of Parliament.

(13.) Provided always, that no paid clerk or other paid official in the permanent employment of a county council who is required to devote his whole time to such employment shall be eligible to serve in Parliament.

Appointment of the justices' clerks and clerks of committees.

Sect. 84.—(1.) The salaried clerk of every petty sessional division shall be from time to time appointed, and removed, as heretofore.

(2.) The county council shall pay to the salaried clerks of petty sessional divisions such salaries as may be fixed under the enactments relating to those clerks, and all fees and costs payable to such clerks which are not excluded in the fixing of their salaries shall be paid into the county fund, and in the enactments relating to such salaries and fees the standing joint committee shall be substituted for the quarter sessions justices and the local authority respectively. 51 & 52 Vict. c. 41, s. 84.

Regulations for Bicycles, &c.

Sect. 85.—(1.) The provisions of section twenty-six, sub-section five, of the Highways and Locomotives (Amendment) Act, 1878, and section twenty-three, sub-section one, of the Municipal Corporations Act, 1882, in so far as it gives power to the council to make bye-laws regulating the use of carriages herein referred to, and all other provisions of any public or private Acts, in so far as they give power to any local authority to make bye-laws for regulating the use of bicycles, tricycles, velocipedes, and other similar machines, are hereby repealed, and bicycles, tricycles, velocipedes, and other similar machines are hereby declared to be carriages within the meaning of the Highway Acts; and the following additional regulations shall be observed by any person or persons riding or being upon such carriage:—

(*a.*) During the period between one hour after sunset and one hour before sunrise, every person riding or being upon such carriage shall carry attached to the carriage a lamp, which shall be so constructed and placed as to exhibit a light in the direction in which he is proceeding, and so lighted and kept lighted, as to afford adequate means of signalling the approach or position of the carriage;

(*b.*) Upon overtaking any cart or carriage, or any horse, mule, or other beast of burden, or any foot passenger, being on or proceeding along the carriage way, every such person shall within a reasonable distance from and before passing such cart or carriage, horse, mule, or other beast of burden, or such foot passenger, by sounding a bell or whistle, or otherwise, give audible and sufficient warning of the approach of the carriage.

(2.) Any person summarily convicted of offending against the regulations made by this section, shall for each and every such offence, forfeit and pay any sum not exceeding forty shillings.

Adaptation of Acts.

Sect. 86. For the purpose of adapting the Acts relating to pauper lunatic asylums to the provisions of this Act, the following provisions shall have effect:— Adaptation of Lunatic Asylum Acts.

(1.) The accounts of the committee of visitors and of their officers shall, for the purposes of the provisions of this Act with respect to accounts of a county council and their officers, and the audit thereof, be deemed to be accounts of the council and officers.

(2.) Nothing in this Act shall transfer to the county council or any members thereof the jurisdiction of quarter sessions or any justices in relation to the removal, reception, or detention of a lunatic into or in an asylum, or to making orders respecting the payment otherwise than out of the county fund of charges incurred on account of any pauper lunatic, or respecting any property of any such lunatic, or respecting his settlement or chargeability, or in relation to any appeal touching the said matters.

(3.) Where at the passing of this Act the recorder or justices or council of a borough appoint members of the committee of visitors of any lunatic asylum, then—

(*a.*) if the representatives of that borough on the county council are entitled to vote for the appointment by that council of visitors of that asylum, such recorder or justices or council shall cease to have power to appoint the said members; and

(*b.*) if the representatives of the borough are not so entitled to vote, the said power of appointment by the recorder or justices shall be transferred to the council of the borough.

51 & 52 Vict. c. 41, s. 86.

(4.) Where at the passing of this Act a borough with a separate court of quarter sessions not being a county borough, but containing, according to the census of one thousand eight hundred and eighty-one, a population of ten thousand or upwards, contracts with the quarter sessions of the county in which the borough is situate for the reception of the lunatics of the borough in the asylum of the county, such borough shall, on the determination of such contract, cease to have power to build a lunatic asylum, and subject to the enactments providing for an additional charge for the maintenance of lunatics in cases where no contribution has been made towards the cost of building and furnishing an asylum, shall be liable to contribute to the county rate of the county in respect of such lunatic asylum in like manner as the rest of the county.

(5.) Any asylum provided in whole or in part at the cost of a county shall for the purposes of this Act be included in the expression "county lunatic asylum."

(6.) Where there is more than one county lunatic asylum, the county council may from time to time appoint one committee for the management and control of all the county lunatic asylums, and such committee shall be the committee of each asylum within the meaning of the Acts relating to pauper lunatic asylums, and shall from time to time appoint a sub-committee for each separate asylum, and may delegate to that sub-committee such powers and duties as the committee from time to time think fit.

(7.) The said committee may, subject to any directions given by the county council, provide that a uniform charge shall be made for the maintenance of lunatics in the several county asylums, and that for that purpose any surplus arising on the accounts of one asylum shall be applied to meet the deficit arising on the accounts of another asylum.

(8.) The provisions of this Act with respect to the proceedings of committees of county councils shall apply to the proceedings of the committee of visitors for a lunatic asylum, and the chairman of such committee may be elected accordingly.

Application of provisions of 38 & 39 Vict. c. 55, as to local inquiries and provisional orders.

Sect. 87.—(1.) Where the Local Government Board are authorised by this Act to make any inquiry, to determine any difference, to make or confirm any order, to frame any scheme, or to give any consent, sanction, or approval to any matter, or otherwise to act under this Act, they may cause to be made a local inquiry, and in that case, and also in a case where they are required by this Act to cause to be made a local inquiry, sections two hundred and ninety-three to two hundred and ninety-six, both inclusive, of the Public Health Act, 1875, shall apply as if they were herein re-enacted, and in terms made applicable to this Act.

(2.) Sections two hundred and ninety-seven and two hundred and ninety-eight of the Public Health Act, 1875 (which relate to the making of provisional orders by the Local Government Board), shall apply for the purposes of this Act as if they were herein re-enacted, and in terms made applicable thereto.

(3) Provided that, where a provisional order transfers to county councils generally any powers, duties, or liabilities of Her Majesty's Privy Council, a Secretary of State, the Local Government Board, or other Government department, it shall not be necessary to hold a local inquiry nor to advertise in any local newspaper.

(4.) Where any matter is authorised or required by this Act to be prescribed, and no other provision is made declaring how the same is to be prescribed, the same shall be prescribed from time to time by the Local Government Board.

(5.) Where the Board cause any local inquiry to be held under this Act, the costs incurred in relation to such inquiry, including the salary of any inspector or officer of the Board engaged in such inquiry, not exceeding three guineas a day, shall be paid by the councils and other authorities concerned in such inquiry, or by such of them and in such proportions as the Board may direct, and the Board may certify the amount of the costs incurred, and any sum so certified and directed by the Board to be paid by any council or authority shall be a debt to the Crown from such council or authority.

Sect 88. In the administrative county of London the following provisions shall have effect: 51 & 52 Vict. c. 41, s. 88.

Adaptation of Act to Metropolis.

(*a.*) The county council may from time to time appoint any fit person to be deputy chairman, and to hold office during the term of office of the chairman, and may pay to such deputy chairman such remuneration as the county council may from time to time think fit;

(*b.*) Subject to any rules from time to time made by the county council, anything authorised or required to be done by, to, or before the chairman, may be done by, to, or before such deputy chairman;

(*c.*) Section one hundred and ninety-one of the Public Health Act, 1875, shall apply to the Metropolis in like manner as if the Commissioners of Sewers in the City of London, and every vestry of a parish in Schedule A., and district board of a district in Schedule B. to the Metropolis Management Act, 1855, or under any Act amending the same, were a local authority within the meaning of that section, and as if any medical officer hereafter appointed by such commissioners, vestry, or district board were appointed under the said Act, and the provisions of this Act with respect to the qualification of a medical officer or to the payment by a county council of a portion of the salary of a medical officer shall apply accordingly. 38 & 39 Vict. c. 55. 18 & 19 Vict. c. 120.

Adjustment of law as regards courts, juries, sittings and legal proceedings in Middlesex and London. 4 & 5 Will. 4. c. 36. 6 Geo. 4. c. 50.

Sect. 89.—(1.) The Central Criminal Court Act, 1834, shall be construed as if the county of London were throughout mentioned therein as well as the county of Middlesex.

(2.) The County Juries Act, 1825, and the Acts amending the same, shall apply to the county of London in like manner as they apply to the county of Middlesex, and persons shall be qualified to serve as jurors, and lists of jurors shall be made out in like manner, so nearly as circumstances admit, as in that county; and the present exemption of inhabitants of the liberty and city of Westminster from serving on juries at quarter sessions for the county of Middlesex shall cease; but nothing in this section shall alter the qualifications of persons to serve as jurors within the city of London.

(3.) Subject to rules of court made by the authority having power to make rules for the Supreme Court of Judicature, the county of London and the county of Middlesex shall be deemed to be one county for the purpose of all legal proceedings, civil or criminal, in the Supreme Court or Central Criminal Court, or any other court except the court of quarter sessions, and also for the purpose of the sittings of the Supreme Court, Central Criminal Court, or such other court as aforesaid, or of any judge of any such courts, and also for the purpose of any jury, and of any court of assize, oyer and terminer, and gaol delivery; and all enactments, rules, orders, and documents referring to Middlesex shall be construed so as to give effect to this section; and rules of court may be from time to time made for the purpose of carrying this section into effect, and for regulating the issue of precepts to the sheriffs of the counties of London and Middlesex for the return of jurors, and the jurors so returned shall have the same powers, duties, and liabilities as if the two counties were one county.

Special provisions as to adjustment in the Metropolis. 40 & 41 Vict. c. 99.

Sect. 90. In the adjustment of the property, debts, and liabilities between the counties of Surrey and Middlesex respectively, and the county of London, the annual sums payable by the counties of Surrey and Middlesex respectively in respect of certain bridges in pursuance of the Metropolis Toll Bridges Act, 1877, shall be deemed to be liabilities which shall be taken into consideration upon such adjustment.

Adjustment as regards the Militia Acts. 45 & 46 Vict. c. 49.

Sect. 91. The Acts relating to the general and local militia of the rest of England and Wales shall apply to the whole of the county of London in like manner as they apply to any county at large; and accordingly Her Majesty shall from time to time appoint a lieutenant of the county of London, provided that nothing in this section shall affect sec. 50 of the Militia Act, 1882.

Savings.

51 & 52 Vict. c. 41, s. 92.

Saving for votes at any Parliamentary elections

Sect. 92.—(1.) Nothing in this Act, nor anything done in pursuance of this Act, shall alter the limits of any parliamentary borough or parliamentary county, or the right of any person to be registered as a voter at any parliamentary election.

(2.) Where by virtue of the provisions of this Act with respect to the county of London, or to urban sanitary districts situate partly within and partly without the boundary of a county, a place situate in a parliamentary county becomes part of the county of a council other than the council having authority over the largest part of the parliamentary county, that is to say, the part which contains the largest number of occupation voters, then, for the purpose of making out and revising the lists of voters, of conducting any parliamentary election, of polling districts, and assigning polling places, and for all purposes of and incidental to such matters, including the payment of expenses, such place shall be deemed to be part of the same county as the said largest part of the said parliamentary county, and the sheriff, council, clerk of the peace, authorities, and officers of that county shall have authority accordingly in the said place, and the provisions of the Registration Act, 1885, with respect to parliamentary counties extending into more county quarter sessional areas than one, shall apply with the necessary modifications.

48 & 49 Vict c. 15.

(3.) Provided that the clerk of the peace who receives from the revising barrister the lists of voters in any such place shall supply to any other clerk of the peace or other officer such number of revised lists as he may require for the purpose of making up a register of county electors.

Saving for Metropolitan and City Police.

Sect. 93.—(1.) Nothing in this Act shall alter the metropolitan police district, nor (save as is expressly provided with respect to contributions in substitution for local grants) affect the metropolitan police force, or the raising of money for the same, and nothing in this Act shall affect the police of the City of London.

(2.) Nothing in this Act shall authorise any county council to raise any sum for the purposes of any police force by any contribution or rate levied within the metropolitan police district; and nothing in this Act shall alter the authority under the Riot (Damages) Act, 1886, within the metropolitan police district or the City of London.

49 & 50 Vict. c. 38.

Saving for metropolitan common poor fund.

Sect. 94. The grant made by the county council of London in respect of indoor paupers shall be in addition to any payment made out of the metropolitan common poor fund, and nothing in this Act shall affect the enactments relating to the fund.

Saving as to Middlesex, Surrey, and Kent.

Sect. 95.—(1.) Any enactment providing that any magistrate, commissioner, or other officer shall be a justice of the peace for Middlesex, shall be construed to refer to the county of London as well as the county of Middlesex.

(2.) Where any enactment, deed, instrument, or document refers to the county of Middlesex, Surrey, or Kent, such enactment, deed, instrument, or document shall be construed to apply to the same area to which it would have applied if this Act had not passed, except where such application is inconsistent with this Act, or where the object of such enactment, deed, instrument, or document requires that it shall be construed to apply to the county of London.

Saving for Middlesex Land Registry.

Sect. 96. Nothing in this Act shall alter the area to which the enactments relating to the registration of land in the county of Middlesex apply, and any reference in those enactments or in any deed, instrument, or document made or issued under or for the purpose of those enactments, to the county of Middlesex, shall be construed to apply to the same area to which it would have applied if this Act had not passed.

Saving as to liability for main roads.

Sect. 97. Nothing in this Act with respect to main roads shall alter the liability of any person or body of persons, corporate or unincorporate, not being a highway authority, to maintain and repair any road or part of a road.

Sect. 98. Notwithstanding anything in the foregoing sections of this Act, the Commissioners of Inland Revenue and the Commissioners of Customs, and the officers of those Commissioners respectively, shall have the same powers in relation to any articles subject to any duty of customs or excise, manufactured, imported, kept for sale, or sold, and any premises where the same may be, and to any machinery, apparatus, vessels, utensils, or conveyances used in connexion therewith or the removal thereof, and in relation to the person manufacturing, importing, keeping for sale, or having the custody of the same, as they would have had if this Act had not passed, and any licences transferred in pursuance of this Act had continued to be granted by the Commissioners of Inland Revenue.

51 & 52 Vict. c. 41, s. 98.

Saving for powers of Commissioners of Inland Revenue and Customs.

Definitions.

Sect. 99. All notices and documents required by this Act to be in writing may be in writing or print, or partly in writing and partly in print, and for the purposes of this section "print" includes any mechanical mode of reproduction.

Definition of "written."

Sect. 100. In this Act, if not inconsistent with the context, the following terms have the meanings herein-after respectively assigned to them; that is to say:

Interpretation of certain terms in the Act.

The expression "county" does not include a county of a city or county of a town:

The expression "entire county" means, in the case of a county divided into administrative counties, the whole of the county formed by those administrative counties.

The expression "division of a county," in the provisions of this Act respecting the property of quarter sessions, includes any hundred, lathe, wapentake, or other like division:

The expression "administrative county," means the area for which a county council is elected in pursuance of this Act, but does not (except where expressly mentioned) include a county borough:

The expression "Metropolis" means the city of London and the parishes and places mentioned in Schedules A., B., and C. to the Metropolis Management Act, 1855, as amended by subsequent Acts:

18 & 19 Vict. c. 120.

The expression "borough" means any place for the time being subject to the Municipal Corporations Act, 1882, and any reference to the mayor, aldermen, and burgesses of a borough shall include a reference to the mayor, aldermen, and citizens of a city:

45 & 46 Vict. c. 50.

The expression "quarter sessions borough" means a borough having a separate court of quarter sessions and includes a county of a city and a county of a town, subject to the Municipal Corporations Act, 1882:

The expression "quarter sessions" as respects any county, riding, division, or liberty, means the justices in quarter or general sessions assembled, and includes justices assembled in gaol sessions, annual general sessions, and adjourned sessions, and as respects any borough, means any court of quarter or general sessions held for the borough or for any county of a city or town consisting of the borough, whether held by the recorder, or by justices, and as respects the city of London, means the court of the mayor and aldermen in the inner chamber:

The expression "parish" means a place for which a separate overseer is or can be appointed, and where part of a parish is situate within, and part of it without, any county, borough, urban sanitary district, or other area, means each such part:

The expressions "parliamentary county," and "parliamentary election," and "parliamentary voters," have the same meaning as in the Registration Act, 1885, and the Acts therein referred to:

48 & 49 Vict. c. 15.

The expression "Secretary of State" means one of Her Majesty's Principal Secretaries of State:

The expression "Treasury" means the Commissioners of Her Majesty's Treasury:

51 & 52 Vict. c. 41, s. 100. The expression "Bank of England" means the Governor and Company of the Bank of England:

The expression "existing" means existing at the time specified in the enactment in which the expression is used, and if no such time is expressed, then at the day appointed to be for the purpose of such enactment the appointed day:

4 & 5 W. 4, c. 76. The expression "guardians" means guardians elected under the Poor Law Amendment Act, 1834, and the Acts amending the same, and includes guardians or other bodies of persons performing under any local Act the like functions to guardians under the Poor Law Amendment Act, 1834:

The expression "poor law union" means any parish or union of parishes for which there is a separate board of guardians:

The expressions "district council" and "county district" mean respectively any district council established for purposes of local government under an Act of any future session of Parliament, and the district under the management of such council, and until such council is established, mean respectively—

(*a.*) as regards the provisions of this Act relating to highways and main roads, a highway authority and highway area; and

38 & 39 Vict. c. 55. (*b.*) save as aforesaid, an urban or rural sanitary authority within the meaning of the Public Health Act, 1875, and the district of such authority:

The expression "highway area" means, as the case may require, an urban sanitary district, a highway district, or a highway parish not included within any highway or urban sanitary district:

The expression "highway authority" means, as respects an urban sanitary district, the urban sanitary authority, and as respects a highway district, the highway board, or authority having the powers of a highway board, and as respects a highway parish, the surveyor or surveyors of highways or other officers performing similar duties:

The expression "urban authority" means, until the establishment of district councils as aforesaid, an urban sanitary authority; and after their establishment, the district council of an urban county district:

The expression "rural authority" means, until the establishment of district councils as aforesaid, a rural sanitary authority; and, after their establishment, the district council of a rural county district:

The expression "person" includes any body of persons, whether corporate or unincorporate:

Any expression referring to the value of any parish, borough, or area as ascertained by the standard or basis for the county rate or contributions shall, where any rateable value has been fixed by agreement between the councils of any county and county boroughs be that value, and subject thereto shall, in the case of any parish, borough, or area for which there is no such standard or basis, refer to the total rateable value as determined by the last valuation lists, or if there is no valuation list, by the last poor rates for such parish or the parishes comprised in such borough or area; and where an area is authorised or directed by this Act to be assessed to any contributions or rates, the same shall, unless otherwise provided by law, be assessed according to the standard or basis for the county rate:

The expression "property" includes all property, real and personal, and all estates, interests, easements, and rights, whether equitable or legal, in, to, and out of property real and personal, including things in action, and registers, books, and documents: and when used in relation to any quarter sessions, clerk of the peace, justices, board, sanitary authority, or other authority, includes any property which on the appointed day belongs to, or is vested in, or held in trust for, or would but for this Act have, on or after that day, belonged to, or been vested in, or held in trust for, such quarter sessions, clerk of the peace, justices, board, sanitary authority, or other authority; and the expression "property" shall further include, in the case of the county of

Chester, any surplus revenue of the River Weaver Trust; which is or would but for this Act be payable to the quarter sessions: 51 & 52 Vict. c. 41, s. 100.

The expression "powers" includes rights, jurisdiction, capacities, privileges, and immunities:

The expression "duties" includes responsibilities and obligations:

The expression "liabilities" includes liability to any proceeding for enforcing any duty or for punishing the breach of any duty, and includes all debts and liabilities to which any authority are or would but for this Act be liable or subject to, whether accrued due at the date of the transfer or subsequently accruing, and includes any obligation to carry or apply any money to any sinking fund or to any particular purpose:

The expression "powers, duties, and liabilities," includes all powers, duties, and liabilities conferred or imposed by or arising under any local and personal Act:

The expression "expenses" includes costs and charges:

The expression "costs" includes charges and expenses:

The costs of assizes and of quarter and petty sessions include such of the following costs as are applicable, that is to say, the costs of maintaining and providing the courts and offices and the judges' lodgings, the salaries and remuneration of a chairman of quarter sessions, clerks of assize, clerks of the peace, clerks of the justices, and other officers, the costs of the jury lists, the costs of rewards ordered to be paid by the court, the costs of prosecutions including the costs of the defendant's witnesses, and all other costs incidental to the assizes, quarter sessions, petty sessions, or the judges, but nothing shall require a quarter sessions borough to contribute towards the costs of prosecutions at assizes except in the case of prisoners committed for trial from the borough:

The expression "assizes" includes the Central Criminal Court:

The expression "pension" includes any superannuation allowance, gratuity, or other payment made on the retirement of any officer:

The expression "office" includes any place, situation, or employment, and the expression "officer" shall be construed accordingly:

The expression "the divisions of Lincolnshire" means the parts of Holland, the parts of Kesteven, and the parts of Lindsey:

The expression "County and Borough Police Act, 1856," means the Act of the session of the nineteenth and twentieth years of the reign of Her present Majesty, chapter sixty-nine, intituled "An Act to render more effectual the police in counties and boroughs in England and Wales," and the expression "County and Borough Police Acts" means the County and Borough Police Act, 1856, and the Acts therein recited: 19 & 20 Vict. c. 69.

The expression "main road" when used in relation to the district of any highway or road authority, means so much of the main road as is situate within the district of such authority.

In relation to the election of county councillors, the day of nomination shall be deemed to be the day on which the names of the persons nominated are fixed on the Town Hall or other conspicuous place.

Sect. 101. This Act shall not extend to Scotland or Ireland. Extent of Act.

Sect. 102. This Act may be cited as the Local Government Act, 1888. Short title.

PART VI.

Transitory Provisions.

First Election of County Councillors.

Sect. 103.—(1.) The first election of county councillors under this Act shall

51 & 52 Vict. c. 41, s. 103. be held in the month of January next after the passing of this Act on such day in each county not earlier than the fourteenth day of January as the returning officer for that county may fix, and the returning officer shall publish notice of such day in the preceding month of December, and the day so fixed shall be deemed for the purposes of the first election to be the ordinary day of election of county councillors.

(2.) The sheriff of each county shall be the returning officer for such first election, but if the sheriff desires to be a candidate at such election the county quarter sessions on his application may appoint another person to be the returning officer, and the person so appointed shall, for the purpose of such election, have the powers and duties of the sheriff.

(3.) At the first election, the returning officer may, if it appears to him necessary, divide an electoral division into polling districts, so however that every polling district shall be any area or a combination of areas for which separate parts of the register of electors are made out, and he shall settle and give proper notice of the places at which the poll for each electoral division, or district of a division, shall be taken.

(4.) The clerk of the peace who will by virtue of this Act become the clerk o the county council when elected, shall make up the county register and division registers of the county electors for the purposes of the first election, and shall deliver the same to the returning officer, and every clerk of the peace who has in his custody any revised lists of electors required for making up such registers, shall supply to the above-mentioned clerk of the peace such number of copies of those lists as he may require for the purpose of making up the said registers.

(5.) The returning officer shall send to the clerk of the peace, who will by virtue of this Act become the clerk of the county council, the names of the persons elected, and shall send to each person elected a county councillor notice of his election, accompanied by a summons to attend the first meeting of the provisional council fixed by this Act at such time and place as the returning officer may fix.

(6.) The costs properly incurred by the returning officer in reference to the first election, and in reference to such first meeting of the provisional council, shall be defrayed as expenses of the county council, and may be taxed on an application made by or by direction of the provisional council.

(7.) In the administrative county of London, the returning officer for the first election shall be such fit person as the Local Government Board may appoint, and such returning officer shall, for the purposes of such election, have the powers and duties of the sheriff, and any sheriff, under-sheriff, officer of the London School Board, or other public officer having authority in the Metropolis, and being in possession of any ballot boxes or other fittings or arrangements for an election shall permit such returning officer to use the same for the purposes of such first election.

(8.) Such returning officer shall make up the county register and division registers of the county electors for the purposes of the first elections, and shall make them up out of the lists of voters made out in the year one thousand eight hundred and eighty-eight for the City of London, and for such portions of the counties of Middlesex, Surrey, and Kent, as are comprised in the Metropolis, and shall make the necessary alteration in the forms of those lists, and the secondary of the City of London, and the town clerks within the meaning of the Registration Acts for the parliamentary boroughs in the administrative county of London, and the clerks of the peace of Middlesex, Surrey, and Kent, shall deliver to the said returning officer such number of copies of the revised lists of electors as he may require. The returning officer for the administrative county of London shall send the names of the persons elected to the clerk of the Metropolitan Board of Works.

(9.) The court of quarter sessions in any county, and the Metropolitan Board of Works in the Metropolis, shall advance to the returning officer such sum as is authorised by this Act to be advanced by county councils to returning officers for the purposes of an election.

(10.) The sheriff having authority in any administrative county, or the largest part thereof, shall for the purposes of this Act be deemed to be the sheriff of that county.

51 & 52 Vict. c. 41, s 103.

Retirement of first county councillors.

Sect. 104.—(1.) The county councillors of a county council elected at the first election shall retire from office on the ordinary day of election in the third year after the passing of this Act, and their places shall be filled by election.

(2.) Of the first county aldermen one half shall retire on the ordinary day of election of county aldermen in the third year next after the passing of this Act, and the one half who are so to retire shall be determined by ballot by the provisional councillors at the time of the election of the county aldermen: Provided that where the total number of aldermen is not divisible by two the larger half shall first retire.

(3.) The remaining half of the county aldermen shall retire on the ordinary day of election of county aldermen in the sixth year next after the passing of this Act.

(4.) In this section the word "year" shall be construed to mean calendar year.

Preliminary action of county councillors as provisional council.

Sect. 105.—(1.) The members of a county council first elected under this Act shall not enter on their ordinary duties or become the county council until the first day of April next after their election, or such other day as on the application of the provisional council the Local Government Board may appoint.

(2.) Such members shall, on the second Thursday next after the day fixed for the first election, and thenceforward from time to time until the day above mentioned in this section, meet and act as a provisional council for arranging to bring this Act into operation.

(3.) The provisional councillors shall at their first meeting elect one of their number to be chairman of that meeting and of the second meeting, and shall then at that meeting, or some adjournment thereof, proceed to elect the county aldermen in like manner as if they were a fully constituted county council, and such county aldermen shall be summoned to attend at the second meeting of the provisional council, and shall form part of the provisional council both for the election of chairman and all other purposes.

(4.) The provisional council shall, at their second meeting, or some adjournment thereof, proceed to elect as their chairman a person qualified to be chairman of the county council, and may from time to time fill any vacancy in the office of such chairman, and the person elected chairman shall be chairman of the provisional council, and also on and after the appointed day of the county council, and the term of office of such chairman shall end on the next ordinary day of election of chairman.

(5.) This enactment shall extend to the vice-chairman and deputy chairman.

First proceedings of provisional council.

Sect. 106.—(1.) The provisional council after disposing of the preliminary business shall proceed to provide for bringing the various provisions of this Act into full operation on the appointed day or days, and to make the necessary arrangements with the quarter sessions, and with reference to the distribution of duties among the different officers, and to provide for all matters which appear necessary or proper for enabling the county council as constituted under this Act to execute their duties, and for giving full effect to this Act.

(2.) The provisions of this Act, and the enactments applied by this Act with respect to the proceedings of the county council, shall apply to the proceedings of the provisional council, and any act of the provisional council may be signified under the hand of the chairman and any two members of the councillors present at the meeting, and countersigned by the officer acting as their clerk.

(3.) The provisional council of a county shall be entitled to use the buildings belonging to the quarter sessions of that county, so that they do not interfere with the holding of any court, and the clerk of the peace and his officers, and the officers of the quarter sessions shall, if required, act as the officers of such provisional council, and further the provisional council may from time to time hire such buildings and appoint such interim officers as appear to them necessary for the performance of their duties, and the costs incurred in the hiring of such buildings and payment of such officers or otherwise in the performance of their duties shall be defrayed as costs properly incurred by the county council.

51 & 52 Vict. c. 41, s. 106

(4.) There shall be paid out of the county rate to the clerk of the peace of the county, such reasonable remuneration as the court of quarter sessions may award for extra services rendered by him in bringing this Act into operation, and in acting as clerk of the county council, until his salary for acting as such clerk is fixed in manner provided by this Act.

(5.) In the metropolis the foregoing provisions with respect to the use of buildings and the action of officers shall apply as if the Metropolitan Board of Works were the quarter sessions of the county, and as if any quarter sessions for the counties of Middlesex, and Surrey were the quarter sessions of the county of London, but the provisional council for the administrative county of London shall make arrangements with the provisional councils of Middlesex and Surrey as respects the use of buildings and the employment of the clerk of the peace and his officers and the officers of the quarter sessions.

(6.) The provisional council shall have the same power of levying contributions for the purpose of their costs and for the future costs of the county council as they would have if they were constituted a county council under this Act.

(7.) The quarter sessions of every county and liberty, and in the metropolis the Metropolitan Board of Works, shall, by the appointment of committees, or the holding of sessions and meetings, and otherwise, make such provisions as are necessary or proper for making arrangements with the provisional council for carrying this Act into effect; and the quarter sessions may, after the appointed day, meet in like manner as if this Act had not passed, for the purpose of receiving reports from the committees and county officers for the period subsequent to the last quarter sessions and prior to the appointed day, and for making the ordinary quarterly payments, the usual sessional orders, and otherwise concluding and winding up the business of the county.

General Provision as to First Elections.

Casual vacancies at first elections.

Sect. 107.—(1.) If at the first election a person is elected a county councillor for more than one electoral division of a county his choice as to the division for which he will serve shall be made by writing addressed to the returning officer, and if not so made, the returning officer shall, on or before the day for the first meeting of the provisional council, determine the division for which such person shall sit.

(2.) Any casual vacancy arising at the first election from a person being elected for more than one electoral division or being elected a county alderman or from a failure of election or otherwise, may be filled in like manner as a casual vacancy in the county council may be filled, and the sheriff or other officer authorised to act as returning officer at the first election shall be the returning officer at any election held to fill a casual vacancy before the appointed day.

(3.) Such number of members as have been elected for a county council at the first election shall subject to any order of the Local Government Board to the contrary under this Act proceed to act as a provisional council under this Act, notwithstanding any vacancy or vacancies arising from failure of election or otherwise.

(4.) In case of equality of votes at the first or second meeting of a provisional county council, the chairman of the meeting shall have a second or casting vote, and where on the selection of the chairman of the meeting an equal number of votes is given to two or more persons, the meeting shall determine by lot which of those persons shall be the chairman.

(5.) The first meeting of the county council shall be held on the day appointed for the council coming into office, and shall be convened by the chairman of the provisional county council.

(6.) Such first meeting, and also the first meeting of the provisional county council, shall be convened in like manner as meetings of the county council are required by this Act, and the enactments applied by this Act, to be convened, and as if the person convening the same were the chairman.

Sect. 108.—(1.) If from any cause there is no returning officer able to act in any county at the first election of a county council, or no register of electors properly made up, or no proper election takes place, or an election of an insufficient number of persons takes place, or any difficulty arises as respects the holding of the first election of county councillors, or as to the first meeting of a provisional council, the Local Government Board may by order appoint a returning officer or other officer, and do any matter or thing which appears to them necessary for the proper holding of the first election, and for the proper holding of the first meeting of the provisional council, and may, if it appears to them necessary, direct a new election to be held, and fix the dates requisite for such new election. Any such order may modify the provisions of this Act and the enactments applied by this Act so far as may appear to the Board necessary for the proper holding of the first election and first meeting of the provisional council.

51 & 52 Vict. c. 41, s. 108.

Power of Local Government Board to remedy defects.

(2.) The Local Government Board in the case of the first election may also authorise an electoral division to return two or more members, in any case where the difficulties arising out of the registers of voters and the population of any area appear to render it necessary, and may also authorise portions of two or more county districts, or wards for which a separate register can be made, to be united for the purpose of an electoral division.

(3.) The Local Government Board, on the application of a county council or provisional council, may within six months after the day fixed for the first election of the councillors of such council, from time to time, make such orders as appear to them necessary for bringing this Act into full operation as respects the council so applying, and such orders may modify any enactment in this or any other Act, whether general or local and personal, so far as may appear to the Board necessary for the said purpose.

(4.) The Local Government Board may also, if satisfied that an election cannot properly be held for any county council by reason of the electoral divisions not having been duly made, cause such steps to be taken as they consider necessary for constituting such electoral divisions and making up the registers of electors.

Appointed Day.

Sect. 109.—(1.) Subject as in this Act mentioned, the appointed day for the purposes of this Act shall in each county be the first day of April next after the passing thereof, or such other day, earlier or later, as the Local Government Board (but after the election of county councillors for such county on the application of the provisional council or county council) may appoint, either generally or with reference to any particular provision of this Act, and different days may be appointed for different purposes and different provisions of this Act, whether contained in the same section or in different sections, or for different counties.

(2.) Any enactment of this Act authorising anything to be done by the Commissioners of Inland Revenue or the Local Government Board, or relating to the registration of electors, or to the elections, or to any matter required to be done for the purpose of bringing this Act into operation on the appointed day, shall come into effect on the passing of this Act; but, save as aforesaid, and save so far as there may be anything in the context inconsistent therewith, any enactment of this Act shall come into operation on the appointed day.

Transitional Proceedings.

Sect. 110.—(1.) Every rate and precept for contributions made before the appointed day may be levied and collected, and proceedings for the enforcement thereof taken in like manner as nearly as may be as if this Act had not passed.

Current rates, jury lists, &c.

(2.) The accounts of all receipts and expenditure before the appointed day shall be audited, and disallowances, surcharges, and penalties recovered and enforced, and other consequential proceedings had in like manner as nearly as may be as if this Act had not passed, and every officer whose duty it is to make up any accounts, or to account for any portion of the receipts or expenditure in any account, shall, until the audit is completed, be deemed for the purpose of such audit to continue

51 & 52 Vict. c. 41, s. 110.

in office and be bound to perform the same duties and render the same accounts, and be subject to the same liabilities as before the appointed day.

(3.) In the counties of Middlesex, Kent, and Surrey, the lists of jurors in force on the appointed day shall continue in force until the lists which are next made come into force, and all jurors summoned before the appointed day shall attend after that day as if summoned in accordance with this Act.

(4.) All proceedings, legal and other, commenced before the appointed day, may be carried on in like manner, as nearly as may be, as if this Act had not passed, and may be so carried on by the county council in substitution for the authorities by whom such proceedings were commenced. Every legal proceeding commenced before the appointed day may be amended in such manner as may appear necessary or proper in order to bring the same into conformity with the provisions of this Act.

(5.) Every militiaman enlisted before the appointed day shall continue liable to serve in the same corps as if this Act had not passed.

Transitory provisions as to lunatic asylums.

Sect. 111.—(1.) Any committee for providing an asylum for pauper lunatics, or any committee of visitors of an asylum for pauper lunatics holding office on the day fixed for the first election of county councillors under this Act, shall continue to hold office until the expiration of one week after the county council have elected a committee for the like purposes and no longer.

(2.) Any committee elected by the county council shall come into office at the expiration of the said week, and shall be deemed to be a continuance of the old committee of visitors elected by the quarter sessions.

(3.) All visitors of an asylum appointed on behalf of a borough or subscribers who are visitors at the date of the first election of the county council under this Act shall continue to be such visitors until the annual election of visitors which happens next after such election.

(4.) Anything done in pursuance of the enactments relating to pauper lunatics by the quarter sessions or any committee thereof before the appointment of any committee by the county council shall have effect as if it had been done by the county council or by a committee elected by the county council.

(5.) Where there is a joint committee of visitors for two or more counties or boroughs, this section shall apply to each portion of the committee appointed by the justices of any such county, or by the justices or council of any such borough, in like manner as if it were a separate committee.

Transitory provisions as to Contagious Diseases (Animals) Acts.

Sect. 112.—(1.) Every executive committee appointed by the quarter sessions under the Contagious Diseases (Animals) Acts, and holding office on the appointed day, shall continue to hold office until the expiration of one week after the county council shall have appointed a committee for the like purpose, and no longer.

(2.) An executive committee appointed by the county council shall come into office at the expiration of the said week, and shall be deemed to be a continuance of the outgoing executive committee.

(3.) Every sub-committee of an executive committee under the said Acts holding office on the appointed day shall continue in office until a sub-committee for the like purposes shall be appointed by the county council, or by the executive committee appointed by the county council.

(4.) Every committee and sub-committee continued in office by virtue of this section shall, during such continuance, have all such powers as it would have had if this Act had not been passed.

Transitory Provisions as to Metropolis.

Transitory provision as to sheriffs of London and Middlesex.

Sect. 113.—(1.) The first sheriffs appointed by Her Majesty for the county of Middlesex and for the county of London may be nominated and appointed at the same time as the sheriff of any other county in England, and each of such sheriffs when appointed may make the declaration, and shall enter upon office, in like manner and at the like time as any other sheriff.

(2.) Upon the first sheriff of Middlesex so entering into office, the sheriffs of London shall cease to have jurisdiction in the county of Middlesex. 51 & 52 Vict. c. 41, s. 113.

(3.) Upon the first sheriff of the county of London so entering into office, the area which will become that county shall, for the purpose of the sheriff, be considered to be the county of London, and the sheriffs of the City of London shall cease to have any jurisdiction in the said area, and the sheriffs of Surrey and Kent shall cease to have any jurisdiction within the said area.

(4.) Provided that for the purpose of any sessions of the peace held by the justices of the counties of Middlesex, Surrey, and Kent, after the sheriff has so entered into office but prior to the date at which the justices of the county of London will come into office, the sheriffs of Middlesex, Surrey, and Kent shall continue to act and have jurisdiction as such sheriffs throughout those portions of the Metropolis which originally formed part of those counties.

(5.) Lists of prisoners, writs, process, and particulars, and all records, jury lists, books, and matters appertaining to the county of Middlesex, and to such parts of the counties of Surrey and Kent as are included in the Metropolis, shall be delivered, turned over, transferred, and signed in like manner in all respects, so nearly as circumstances admit, as is required to be done upon a new sheriff coming into office, in like manner as if the sheriff of Middlesex appointed by Her Majesty were as respects such part of the county as will after the appointed day be the county of Middlesex, the new sheriff in succession to the sheriffs of London, and as if the sheriff of the county of London appointed by Her Majesty were, as respects the area of the Metropolis exclusive of the City, the successor to the sheriffs of London, Surrey, and Kent.

(6.) If any question arises as to the delivery, turning over, transfer, or signature under this section, or any other matter relating to the change in the office of sheriff in the Metropolis, such question shall be referred to the Lord High Chancellor, whose decision shall be final.

Sect. 114.—(1.) The persons who at the passing of this Act are coroners for any district which becomes wholly or partly by virtue of this Act part of the county of London, shall continue to act for such districts until otherwise directed as herein-after mentioned, and while so continuing to act shall, as respects such part of their district as is within the county of London be deemed to be coroners for the county of London, and the amount payable in respect of the salaries, fees, and expenses of any such coroners, where the district is partly within and partly without the county of London, shall be apportioned between the counties in which such district is situate. As to existing coroners for Middlesex, Surrey, and Kent.

(2.) In the case of any coroner's district being situate partly within and partly without the county of London, the county councils of the counties in which such district is situate shall arrange for the alteration in manner provided by law of the district, so that on the next avoidance of the office of coroner, or any earlier date fixed when the alteration is made, the coroner's districts shall not be situate in more than one county.

(3.) For purposes of this Act respecting compensation, the coroners shall be deemed to be officers of the quarter sessions of the county for which they are coroners.

Sect. 115.—(1.) A commission of the peace for the county of London may be issued at any time after the passing of this Act, which shall be provisional until the appointed day, and the justices acting under such commission shall until the appointed day act provisionally for the purpose of bringing this Act into operation, and may from time to time be convened, and meet and conduct their proceedings in like manner in all respects as if they were the justices of a county, and they shall proceed to make such arrangements as appear necessary or proper for bringing this Act into operation, and may for that purpose appoint any committee or committees, either alone or jointly with any quarter sessions or provisional council. As to commission of the peace for London.

(2.) Nothing in this section shall confer on such justices any power to act as justices or as quarter sessions, nor any judicial jurisdiction, nor constitute any part

51 & 52 Vict. c 41, s. 115.

of the Metropolis a county for the purposes of justices and quarter sessions until the appointed day.

(3.) Any sessions of the peace held after the appointed day may be convened by the said justices acting provisionally before the said day, and the first sessions of the peace held after the appointed day shall be deemed to be legally held, although no justice there present has taken the oaths required by law to be taken by justices of the peace, and any justice may nevertheless take the oaths at such sessions.

(4.) The clerk of the peace for Middlesex holding office at the passing of this Act shall act as the clerk to the said justices for the county of London when acting provisionally in pursuance of this Act.

(5.) The fees payable to the clerk of the peace and clerks of the justices, and other officers and authorities in Middlesex, at the passing of this Act, shall be the first fees which may be taken in the county of London by the clerk of the peace, the clerks to the justices, and other officers and authorities in the county of London, and may continue to be taken until they are abolished or altered in manner provided by law with respect to the abolition and alteration of such fees.

As to places for holding quarter sessions.

Sect. 116. Until a scheme respecting the holding of courts of quarter sessions in the county of London comes into force, the following regulations shall be observed :—

(*a.*) Courts of quarter sessions for the trial of persons charged with offences shall be held at Clerkenwell and Newington, and courts of quarter sessions for appeals and other business shall be held at the places in London at which sessions are usually held at present, or at such of the said places as the county council may from time to time appoint ; and courts of quarter sessions for the said purposes shall be respectively held at the same times, as nearly as may be, at each such place as heretofore ;

(*b.*) Cases triable at quarter sessions for the county of London shall (save as otherwise directed by the court of quarter sessions) be heard and determined, if they arose on the north side of the River Thames, at Clerkenwell, and if they arose on the south side of the River Thames, at Newington ; and persons shall be committed for trial, and bail and recognisances shall be taken, and depositions, recognisances, documents, and things transmitted in such manner as appears necessary for carrying into effect this section, but a committal for trial or recognisance shall not be invalidated, nor shall the powers of the quarter sessions be affected by any disregard of this enactment, and every court of quarter sessions held in and for the county of London at whatever place such court is held shall have complete power to hear and determine any case arising in the county of London, notwithstanding an objection that the case ought to be heard and determined at the sessions held at another place in the county of London ;

(*c.*) Every sessions shall, as the circumstances require, be deemed to be quarter or general sessions, and if held at different places to be original sessions or adjourned sessions, and if held simultaneously at two or more places to be divided courts of the same sessions ;

(*d.*) Every matter, civil or criminal, arising before the appointed day which would have been heard, tried, determined, or otherwise dealt with by any court or quarter sessions or assessment sessions, or any justices or otherwise, may be heard, tried, determined, and dealt with in like manner as if this Act had come into operation before the said matter arose, and recognisances existing at the appointed day shall have effect and be enforced in like manner, so nearly as circumstances admit, as they would have been if this Act had not passed ; and where any trial, motion, or other matter has been adjourned from any previous court of quarter sessions, assessment sessions, special sessions, or petty sessions, and would if this Act had previously come into operation have been heard, determined, or otherwise dealt with at sessions held under this Act, the same shall be heard and determined and otherwise dealt with at the sessions held under this Act in like manner as if the same were held by the same justices by whom the same would have been held if this Act had not passed. 51 & 52 Vict. c. 41, s. 116.

As to existing justices in metropolis.

Sect. 117.—(1.) Nothing in this Act shall prevent a person who is an existing justice of the peace for any of the counties of Middlesex, Surrey, or Kent, from continuing to be a justice of the peace for that county, and every such person and also every person who at the appointed day is a justice of the peace for the liberty and city of Westminster, the liberty of the Tower of London, or any liberty which by virtue of this Act becomes part of the county of London, shall, if and so long as he is resident or occupies property in the county of London, be a justice of the peace for that county in like manner as if he were assigned by a commission of the peace, but a person shall not after the passing of this Act be named in any commission as a justice of the peace for any liberty which by virtue of this Act becomes part of the county of London.

(2.) Provided always, that the provisions of this section shall not apply to any justice of the peace of the counties of Surrey, Kent, or Middlesex, or either of them, so long as he shall hold any office connected with any court of quarter sessions of the county of London.

(3.) The persons who at the passing of this Act are members of a visiting committee of any prison situated in the county of London shall continue to form such visiting committee until a new visiting committee has been appointed in accordance with a rule of the Secretary of State.

(4.) Where a person is a justice of the peace in and for the county of London by reason of his being personally declared by this Act to be a justice of the peace in and for the county of London, the Lord High Chancellor shall have the same power of removing such person from being a justice of the peace as if he were named in a commission of the peace.

(5.) The existing assistant judge of the court of the sessions of the peace for the county of Middlesex shall cease to be chairman of that court, and shall be the first chairman of the court of quarter sessions of the county of London, and while he holds his office he shall receive such salary, not less that what he has hitherto received, as Her Majesty, on the petition of the county council, may assign, and the enactments respecting the appointment and payment of a deputy assistant judge or of a person to preside at a second court at any sessions in the county of Middlesex shall apply to the county of London, and upon the said assistant judge ceasing to hold office shall be repealed.

(6.) Nothing in this Act shall affect existing deputy lieutenants appointed by the Constable of the Tower of London as Lord Lieutenant of the Tower Hamlets.

Existing Officers.

Existing clerks of the peace and other officers.

Sect. 118.—(1.) A person holding office at the appointed day as clerk of the peace of a county, besides continuing to be such clerk of the peace shall, subject to the provisions respecting certain counties in this Act mentioned, become the clerk of the county council, and if appointed before the passing of this Act shall, notwithstanding anything in this Act, hold his offices by the same tenure and have the same power of appointing and acting by a deputy as heretofore in his capacity of clerk of the peace.

(2.) A person holding office at the passing of this Act as clerk of the peace, clerk of the general assessment sessions, or salaried clerk of a petty sessional division, shall be deemed to be an existing officer within the meaning of the provisions of this Act relating to compensation to existing officers who suffer pecuniary loss.

(3.) The person who at the appointed day is clerk of the peace for Sussex, if he held office at the passing of this Act, shall be clerk of the peace for East Sussex and clerk of the peace for West Sussex, and clerk of the peace for the justices of Sussex in general sessions assembled.

(4.) Such person shall also be clerk of the county council for East Sussex, and clerk of the county council for West Sussex, and shall, notwithstanding anything in this Act, hold his offices by the same tenure and have the same power of

51 & 52 Vict. c. 41, s. 118.

appointing and acting by a deputy as heretofore in his capacity of clerk of the peace.

(5.) The person who at the appointed day is clerk of the peace for Suffolk, if he held office at the passing of this Act, shall be clerk of the peace for East Suffolk and clerk of the peace for West Suffolk, and clerk of the peace for the justices of Suffolk in general sessions assembled.

(6.) Such person shall also be clerk of the county council for East Suffolk and clerk of the county council for West Suffolk; and shall, notwithstanding anything in this Act, hold his offices by the same tenure and have the same power of appointing and acting by a deputy as heretofore.

(7.) This section shall apply to the persons holding office at the appointed day as clerk of the peace and deputy clerks of the peace for the county of Lancaster, in like manner as it applies to clerks of the peace of other counties.

(8.) The person who, at the appointed day, is clerk of the peace for Middlesex, if he held office at the passing of this Act, shall continue to be that clerk, and, subject to the provisions of this Act, shall also be the first clerk of the peace for the county of London, and shall, notwithstanding anything in this Act, hold the office of clerk of the peace for each of the said counties by the same tenure and have the same power of appointing and acting by a deputy as heretofore.

(9.) The person who, at the appointed day, is the clerk of the gaol sessions in Yorkshire or Lincolnshire shall, if he holds office at the passing of this Act, continue to be that clerk, and shall also be the first clerk of the joint committee for the county councils of the three ridings or divisions of those counties, and shall hold that office by the same tenure and have the same power (if any) of acting by a deputy as heretofore.

(10.) If the person who at the appointed day is clerk of the peace for Surrey held office at the passing of this Act, then so long as he holds that office,—

(*a.*) He shall, besides continuing to be that clerk, continue to be clerk of the peace at any quarter sessions held for the county of London at Newington, and be, for the purpose of all business transacted at those quarter sessions, deemed to be the clerk of the peace for the county of London, and as such shall have the same power of appointing and acting by a deputy as heretofore in his capacity of clerk of the peace for Surrey; and

(*b.*) Such of the records of the county of Surrey as at the passing of this Act are in his custody at Newington, and, if this Act had not passed, would have remained in that custody, shall, subject to any order of the court of quarter sessions, continue to be kept in his custody at Newington.

(11.) The persons who at the appointed day are salaried clerks for the petty sessional divisions, wholly or in part in the county of London shall, if appointed before the passing of this Act, be as to so much of such divisions as are in the county of London, the first salaried clerks of the petty sessional divisions of the county of London, and as to so much of such divisions as are not in the county of London, such persons shall also be the first salaried clerks of the petty sessional divisions of the counties in which such parts are situate.

(12.) In the case of any of the following persons who, by virtue of this Act, become clerk of the peace for the county of London or salaried clerks of petty sessional divisions for the county of London, or who, for the purpose of all business transacted at the quarter sessions, held for the county of London at Newington, is to be deemed to be the clerk of the peace for the county of London, or who become clerk of the peace for East Sussex and clerk of the peace for West Sussex, or clerk of the peace for East Suffolk, and clerk of the peace West Suffolk, their services as such clerks after the appointed day in the county of London, or in the administrative counties of East Sussex and West Sussex, or East Suffolk and West Suffolk, respectively, shall be deemed to be a continuous service with their service as clerks of the peace and clerks of petty sessional divisions in the counties of Middlesex, Surrey, and Kent respectively, and clerk of the peace for Sussex and Suffolk respectively.

(13.) All persons who at the appointed day hold office as county treasurer, county auditor, county solicitor, or county surveyor, or are officers (whether inspectors of weights and measures, public analysts, inspectors of petroleum or explosives, or other) of the quarter sessions or justices of the county, or of the assessment sessions in the metropolis, or any committee of such justices or any committee of visitors for lunatic asylums, or are servants under such sessions or justices and perform any duties in respect of the business transferred by or in pursuance of this Act to the county council, shall become the officers and servants of the county council. 51 & 52 Vict. c. 41, s. 118.

(14.) All persons who at the appointed day are officers and servants of the Metropolitan Board of Works shall become the officers and servants of the London county council.

(15.) Every person who, on the appointed day, is the chief or other constable of the police force of any county, or is an officer or servant employed in connexion with that force, shall, after the said day, be chief or other constable of the police force of the same county under the standing joint committee appointed in pursuance of this Act, or be an officer or servant of a county council appointing a portion of such joint committee, as the case may be.

(16.) Where any constable at the appointed day belongs to the police force of any borough the council of which will by virtue of this Act cease to maintain a separate police force, such constable shall, after the said day, become a constable of the county police force, and the provisions of this Act with respect to officers of any authority who become officers of the county council shall apply to such constable, with the substitution of the standing joint committee for the county council.

Sect. 119.—(1.) The officers and servants of the quarter sessions or general assessment sessions, or justices, or any committee of such sessions, or justices, or of any committee of visitors for lunatic asylums, or of the Metropolitan Board of Works, or other authority, who held office at the passing of this Act, and who by virtue of this Act become officers and servants of a county council (in this Act referred to as existing officers), shall hold their offices by the same tenure and upon the same terms and conditions as if this Act had not passed, and while performing the same duties, shall receive no less salaries or remuneration, and be entitled to not less pensions (if any), than they would have if this Act had not passed, and where any such officer can only be removed with the consent of a Secretary of State or the Local Government Board, such consent shall be part of the tenure of his office. **As to officers transferred to county councils.**

(2.) The county council may distribute the business to be performed by existing officers in such manner as the council may think just, and every existing officer shall perform such duties in relation to that business as may be directed by the council.

(3.) The county council may abolish the office of any existing officer whose office they may deem unnecessary, but such officer shall be entitled to compensation under this Act.

(4.) The provisions of this section shall apply to the chief and other constables of any police force, and to any officers employed in connexion with such force, in like manner as if they were herein re-enacted with the substitutions of the standing joint committee under this Act for the county council.

Sect. 120.—(1.) Every existing officer declared by this Act to be entitled to compensation, and every other existing officer, whether before mentioned in this Act or not, who by virtue of this Act, or anything done in pursuance of or in consequence of this Act, suffers any direct pecuniary loss by abolition of office or by diminution or loss of fees or salary, shall be entitled to have compensation paid to him for such pecuniary loss by the county council, to whom the powers of the authority, whose officer he was, are transferred under this Act, regard being had to the conditions on which his appointment was made, to the nature of his office or employment, to the duration of his service, to any additional emoluments which he acquires by virtue of this Act or of anything done in pursuance of or in consequence of this Act, and to the emoluments which he might have acquired if he had not refused to accept any office offered by any council or other body acting under this Act, and to all the other circumstances of **Compensation to existing officers.**

51 & 52 Vict. c. 41, s. 120.

the case, and the compensation shall not exceed the amount which, under the Acts and rules relating to Her Majesty's Civil Service, is paid to a person on abolition of office.

(2.) Every person who is entitled to compensation, as above mentioned, shall deliver to the county council a claim under his hand setting forth the whole amount received and expended by him or his predecessors in office, in every year during the period of five years next before the passing of this Act, on account of the emoluments for which he claims compensation, distinguishing the offices in respect of which the same have been received, and accompanied by a statutory declaration under the Statutory Declaration Act, 1835, that the same is a true statement according to the best of his knowledge, information, and belief.

5 & 6 Will. 4, c. 62.

(3.) Such statement shall be submitted to the county council, who shall forthwith take the same into consideration, and assess the just amount of compensation (if any), and shall forthwith inform the claimant of their decision.

(4.) If a claimaint is aggrieved by the refusal of the county council to grant any compensation, or by the amount of compensation assessed, or if not less than one-third of the members of such council subscribe a protest against the amount of the compensation as being excessive, the claimant or any subscriber to such protest (as the case may be) may, within three months after the decision of the council, appeal to the Treasury, who shall consider the case and determine whether any compensation, and if so, what amount ought to be granted to the claimant and such determination shall be final.

(5.) Any claimant under this section, if so required by any member of the county council, shall attend at a meeting of the council and answer upon oath, which any justice present may administer, all questions asked by any member of the council touching the matters set forth in his claim, and shall further produce all books, papers, and documents in his possession or under his control relating to such claim.

(6.) The sum payable as compensation to any person in pursuance of this section shall commence to be payable at the date fixed by the council on granting the compensation, or, in case of appeal, by the Treasury, and shall be a speciality debt due to him from the county council, and may be enforced accordingly in like manner as if the council had entered into a bond to pay the same.

(7.) If a person receiving compensation in pursuance of this section is appointed to any office under the same or any other county council, or by virtue of this Act, or anything done in pursuance of or in consequence of this Act, receives any increase of emoluments of the office held by him, he shall not, while receiving the emoluments of that office, receive any greater amount of his compensation, if any, than, with the emoluments of the said office, is equal to the emoluments for which compensation was granted to him, and if the emoluments of the office he holds are equal to or greater than the emoluments for which compensation was granted, his compensation shall be suspended while he holds such office.

(8.) All expenses incurred by a county council in pursuance of this section shall be paid out of the county fund, as a payment for general county purposes.

Temporary Provision as to Grant from Exchequer.

Grant and application of part of probate duty and of horse and wheel tax during the year ending 31st March, 1889.

Sect. 121.—(1.) In the financial year ending the thirty-first day of March one thousand eight hundred and eighty-nine the Commissioners of Inland Revenue shall from time to time, in such manner and under such regulations as the Treasury from time to time make, pay into the Bank of England to the Local Taxation Account—

(*a.*) such sum as may be ascertained in manner provided by the said regulations to be four fifth parts of one third of the proceeds of the sums collected by them in the said year in respect of the probate duties, and for the purpose of this section, the expression "probate duties" means the stamp duties charged on the affidavit required from persons applying for probate or letters of administration in England, Wales, or Ireland, and on the inventory exhibited and recorded in Scotland, and the stamp duties charged on such accounts of personal and moveable property as are specified in section thirty-eight of the Customs and Inland Revenue Act, 1881, and includes the proceeds of all penalties and forfeitures recovered in relation to such stamp duties; and 51 & 52 Vict. c. 41, s. 121. — 44 & 45 Vict. c. 12.

(*b.*) such sum as may be ascertained in manner provided by the regulations to be the proceeds of the sums collected by them in the said year in respect of the duties on licences for trade carts, locomotives, horses, mules, and horse dealers under any Act of the present session.

(2.) The sums so paid shall be distributed by the Local Government Board as follows, that is to say,

(i.) in paying to every county, highway, and other local authority who have heretofore received out of moneys provided by Parliament a contribution to the cost of roads, or to the successors of such authority, sums calculated in like manner and according to the like scale and regulations as in the financial year ending on the thirty-first day of March one thousand eight hundred and eighty-eight;

(ii.) if the amount received by the local taxation account from the duties on licences for trade carts, locomotives, horses, mules and horse dealers under any Act of the present Session, exceeds the sum so payable to county and highway or other local authorities, the excess shall be divided between the metropolis and quarter sessions boroughs, in proportion to their rateable value, as ascertained by the valuation lists, or where there is no valuation list by the last poor rate;

(iii.) the share of the excess distributed to the metropolis shall be divided between the Commissioners of Sewers in the city of London and the vestries and district boards in the parishes in Schedule A and the districts in Schedule B to the Metropolis Management Act, 1855, as amended by subsequent Acts, according to rateable value as ascertained by the last valuation lists, and the share distributed to quarter sessions boroughs shall be paid to the councils of such boroughs; 18 & 19 Vict. c. 120.

(iv.) if any payment is made under the foregoing provisions of this section respecting roads to the council of any quarter sessions borough, or to any authority for a highway area wholly or partly situate in such borough, or to the highway authority of any parish or district in the metropolis, the share of such quarter sessions borough, parish, or district in the distribution of the balance shall be reduced by the amount of the said payment, and, if less than that amount, shall not be paid, and any sum arising from such reduction or non-payment shall be added to the balance and distributed accordingly;

(v.) any sum payable in pursuance of this section to a county authority or the council of any borough, not being a highway authority, shall be paid to the county or borough fund as the case may be, but any other sum payable under the provisions of this section respecting roads, or respecting the division of the excess to any highway authority, commissioners of sewers, vestry, or district board, shall be applied in aid of the costs of the roads maintained by such authority, commissioners, vestry, or board;

(vi.) any balance remaining after the above payments shall be divided among the counties in England and Wales, in accordance with the provisions of this Act with respect to the division of the probate duty grant, and for the purpose of such division the metropolis shall be deemed to be a county, and the share assigned to each county on such division shall be applied towards paying to the guardians of each poor law union wholly or partly situate in the county such sum as is directed by this Act to be annually paid by the county council of such county to such guardians;

(vii.) any balance remaining after the payment to the guardians of such union shall be paid to the county council of the county upon its coming into office, and, if there is any county borough in the county, the sum so paid shall be included in the adjustment under this Act between the councils of the county and borough.

(3.) Every local authority shall produce to the Local Government Board such

51 & 52 Vict. c. 41, s. 121.

evidence and comply with such rules as the Board may require or make for the purpose of effecting the distribution under this section.

(4.) A certificate of the Local Government Board of the sum due to any authority under this section may be varied by that Board, and unless so varied shall be final.

(5.) The Treasury may, from time to time during the financial year ending on the thirty-first day of March next after the passing of this Act, issue out of the Consolidated Fund or the growing produce thereof and pay to the Local Taxation Account such sums as appear to them to be required for the purpose of paying the highway authorities and county authorities such sums in respect of main roads as have been paid to them in previous years out of moneys provided by Parliament; and the sums so issued shall be treated as an advance, and shall be repaid to the Consolidated Fund out of the Local Taxation Account before any balance is distributed in manner provided by this section.

Savings.

Saving for existing securities and discharge of debts.

Sect. 122.—(1.) Nothing in this Act shall prejudicially affect any securities granted before the passing of this Act on the credit of any rate or of any property by this Act transferred to a county council; and all such securities, as well as all unsecured debts, liabilities, and obligations incurred by any authority in the exercise of any powers or in relation to any property transferred from them to the county council under this Act shall be discharged, paid, and satisfied by such council

(2.) Where for the purpose of satisfying any such security or any debt or liability, it is necessary to continue the levy of any rate or the exercise of any power which would have existed but for the provisions of this Act, such rate may continue to be levied and power to be exercised either by the authority who otherwise would have levied or exercised the same or by the county council as the case may require.

(3.) It shall be the duty of every authority whose powers, duties, and liabilities are transferred to any council by this Act to liquidate so far as practicable before the appointed day, all current debts and liabilities incurred by such authority.

Saving for existing bye-laws.

Sect. 123. All such bye-laws, orders, and regulations of the Privy Council, Secretary of State, Board of Trade, Local Government Board, or Government department, or of any quarter sessions, council of a borough, the Metropolitan Board of Works, or other authority, whose powers and duties are transferred by or in pursuance of this Act to any county council, as are in force at the time of the transfer, shall, so far as they relate to or are in pursuance of the powers and duties transferred, continue in force as if they had been made by such council, subject, nevertheless to revocation or alteration by such council in the manner in which bye-laws can be made by such council, and also to any exceptions or modifications which may be made at the time of the transfer.

Saving for pending actions, contracts, &c.

Sect. 124.—(1.) If at the date of the transfer in this section mentioned any action or proceeding, or any cause of action or proceeding, is pending or existing by or against any authority in relation to any powers, duties, liabilities, or property by this Act transferred to the county council, the same shall not be in anywise prejudicially affected by reason of the passing of this Act, but may be continued, prosecuted, and enforced by or against such council as successors of the said authority in like manner as if this Act had not been passed.

(2.) All contracts, deeds, bonds, agreements, and other instruments entered into or made and subsisting at the time of the transfer in this section mentioned, and affecting any such powers, duties, liabilities, or property of any authority as are by this Act transferred to a county council, shall be of as full force and effect against or in favour of the council, and may be enforced as fully and effectually, as if, instead of the authority, the said council had been a party thereto.

(3.) All contracts or agreements which prior to the appointed day have been made by the clerk of the peace or any justice or justices or otherwise on behalf of a county, or any division or part of a county, shall have effect as if the council of that county had been named therein instead of the clerk of the peace or such justice or justices, and may be enforced by or against the county council accordingly. 51 & 52 Vict. c. 41, s. 124.

(4.) This section shall apply in the case of a committee of any authority in like manner as if the committee were such authority, and the committee of a county council were that council, and as if contracts and agreements by any such committee appointed by quarter sessions were contracts and agreements on behalf of a county.

Saving for charters, local Acts, &c.

Sect. 125. Save so far as may be necessary to give effect to this Act or any scheme or order or other thing made or done thereunder, nothing in this Act shall prejudicially alter or affect the powers, rights, privileges, or immunities of any municipal corporation, or the operation of any municipal charter, local Act of Parliament, or order confirmed by Parliament, which immediately before the passing of this Act was in force.

Repeals.

Repeal of Acts.

Sect. 126. All enactments inconsistent with this Act are hereby repealed; Provided that—

(1.) Any enactment or document referring to any Act or enactment hereby repealed shall be construed to refer to this Act, or to the corresponding enactment in this Act:

(2.) This repeal shall not affect—

(*a.*) The past operation of any enactment hereby repealed, nor anything duly done or suffered under any enactment hereby repealed; or

(*b.*) Any right, privilege, obligation, or liability acquired, accrued, or incurred under or in accordance with any enactment hereby repealed; or

(*c.*) Any penalty, forfeiture, or punishment incurred in respect of any offence committed against any enactment hereby repealed; or

(*d.*) Any power, investigation, legal proceeding, or remedy in respect of any such right, privilege, obligation, liability, penalty, forfeiture, or punishment as aforesaid; and any such power, investigation, legal proceeding, and remedy may be exercised and carried on as if this Act had not passed.

SCHEDULES.

FIRST SCHEDULE.

Section 20.

Local Taxation Licences.

Licences for the sale of intoxicating liquor for consumption on the premises;

Retailers of spirits (publicans).
Retailers of spirits, occasional licences.
Retailers of beer.
Retailers of beer, occasional licences.
Retailers of beer and wine.
Retailers of cider.
Retailers of wine.
Retailers of wine, occasional licences.
Retailers of sweets.

Licences for the sale of intoxicating liquor by retail, by persons not licensed to deal therein, for consumption off the premises;

Retailers of beer.
Retailers of beer and wine.
Retailers of cider.
Retailers of wine.
Retailers of sweets
Retailers of table beer.

51 & 52 Vict. c. 41, s. 20.

Local Taxation Licences.—*continued.*

Licences to deal in game.

Licences for—

Beer dealers.	Carriages.
Spirit dealers.	Trade carts.
Sweets dealers.	Locomotives.
Wine dealers.	Horses and mules.
Refreshment house keepers.	Horse dealers.
Dogs.	Armorial bearings.
Killing game.	Male servants.
Guns.	Hawkers.
Appraisers.	House agents.
Auctioneers.	Pawnbrokers.
Tobacco dealers.	Plate dealers.

Section 71.

SECOND SCHEDULE.

Alteration of Schedule to District Auditors Act, 1879.
(42 & 43 Vict. c. 6.)

The following scale shall, until otherwise determined by Parliament, be substituted for so much of the scale set forth in the First Schedule to the District Auditors Act, 1879, as relates to expenditure amounting to £100,000 and upwards.

Where the Total of the Expenditure comprised in the Financial Statement is	The Sum shall be
£100,000 and under £150,000	£50.
£150,000 and under £200,000	£60.
£200,000 and upwards.	£15 in addition for every £50,000 or part thereof.

Sections 31, 34, 35, 36, 69.

THIRD SCHEDULE.

County Boroughs.

Name of Borough.	Name of County in which, for the purpose of this Act, the Borough is deemed to be situate.
Barrow	Lancaster.
Bath	Somerset.
Birkenhead	Chester.
Birmingham	Warwick.
Blackburn	Lancaster.
Bolton	Lancaster.
Bootle-cum-Linacre ...	Lancaster.
Bradford	York, West Riding.
Brighton	Sussex.
Bristol	Gloucester and Somerset.
Burnley	Lancaster.
Bury	Lancaster.
Canterbury	Kent.
Cardiff	Glamorgan.
Chester	Chester.

Name of Borough.	Name of County in which, for the purpose of this Act, the Borough is deemed to be situate.
Coventry	Warwick.
Croydon	Surrey.
Derby	Derby.
Devonport	Devon.
Dudley	Worcester.
Exeter	Devon.
Gateshead	Durham.
Gloucester	Gloucester.
Great Yarmouth	Norfolk and Suffolk.
Halifax	York, West Riding.
Hanley	Stafford.
Hastings	Sussex.
Huddersfield	York, West Riding.
Ipswich	Suffolk.
Kingston-upon-Hull ...	York, East Riding.
Leeds	York, West Riding.
Leicester	Leicester.
Lincoln	Lincoln (parts of Lindsey).
Liverpool	Lancaster.
Manchester	Lancaster.
Middlesbrough	York, North Riding.
Newcastle-upon-Tyne ...	Northumberland.
Northampton	Northampton.
Norwich	Norfolk.
Nottingham	Nottingham.
Oldham	Lancaster.
Plymouth	Devon.
Portsmouth	Hants.
Preston	Lancaster.
Reading	Berks.
Rochdale	Lancaster.
St. Helen's...	Lancaster.
Salford	Lancaster.
Sheffield	York, West Riding.
Southampton	Hants.
South Shields	Durham.
Stockport	Chester and Lancaster.
Sunderland	Durham.
Swansea	Glamorgan.
Walsall	Stafford.
West Bromwich	Stafford.
West Ham	Essex.
Wigan	Lancaster.
Wolverhampton	Stafford.
Worcester	Worcester.
York	York, North, East, and West Ridings.

NOTE.—The title of the corporation of each of the above boroughs shall be, if it is a city, the mayor, aldermen, and citizens of the city; and if it is not a city, the mayor, aldermen, and burgesses of the borough, with the addition in each case of the name of the place.

Appendix C.

THE MUNICIPAL CORPORATIONS ACT, 1882.
[45 & 46 VICT. CH. 50.]

Sections referred to in Sec. 75 of the Local Government Act, 1888.

PART II.

CONSTITUTION AND GOVERNMENT OF BOROUGH

Corporate Name.

Name of municipal corporation.

Sect. 8. The municipal corporation of a borough shall bear the name of the mayor, aldermen, and burgesses of the borough, or, in the case of a city, the mayor, aldermen, and citizens of the city.

Burgesses.

Qualification of burgess.

Sect. 9.—(1.) A person shall not be deemed a burgess for any purpose of this Act unless he is enrolled as a burgess.

(2.) A person shall not be entitled to be enrolled as a burgess unless he is qualified as follows:

(*a.*) Is of full age; and

(*b.*) Is on the fifteenth of July in any year, and has been during the whole of the then last preceding twelve months, in occupation, joint or several, of any house, warehouse, counting-house, shop, or other building (in this Act referred to as qualifying property) in the borough; and

(*c.*) Has during the whole of those twelve months resided in the borough, or within seven miles thereof; and

(*d.*) Has been rated in respect of the qualifying property to all poor rates made during those twelve months for the parish wherein the property is situate; and

(*e.*) Has on or before the twentieth of the same July paid all such rates, including borough rates (if any), as have become payable by him in respect of the qualifying property up to the then last preceding fifth of January.

(3.) Every person so qualified shall be entitled to be enrolled as a burgess, unless he—

(*a.*) Is an alien; or

(*b.*) Has within the twelve months aforesaid received union or parochial relief or other alms; or

(*c.*) Is disentitled under any Act of Parliament.

Council; Mayor, Aldermen, and Councillors.

Constitution of council.

Sect. 10.—(1.) The municipal corporation of a borough shall be capable of acting by the council of the borough, and the council shall exercise all powers vested in the corporation by this Act or otherwise.

(2.) The council shall consist of the mayor, aldermen, and councillors.

Qualification of councillor.

Sect. 11.—(1.) The councillors shall be fit persons elected by the burgesses.

(2.) A person shall not be qualified to be elected or to be a councillor, unless he—

(*a.*) Is enrolled and entitled to be enrolled as a burgess; or (*b.*) Being entitled to be so enrolled in all respects except that of residence, is resident beyond seven miles but within fifteen miles of the borough, and is entered in the separate non-resident list directed by this Act to be made; and 45 & 46 Vict. c. 50, s. 11.

(*c.*) In either of those cases, is seised or possessed of real or personal property or both, to the value or amount, in the case of a borough having four or more wards, of one thousand pounds, and in the case of any other borough, of five hundred pounds, or is rated to the poor rate in the borough, in the case of a borough having four or more wards, on the annual value of thirty pounds, and in the case of any other borough of fifteen pounds.

(3.) Provided, that every person shall be qualified to be elected and to be a councillor, who is, at the time of election, qualified to elect to the office of councillor; which last-mentioned qualification for being elected shall be alternative for and shall not repeal or take away any other qualification.

(4.) But if a person qualified under the last foregoing proviso ceases for six months to reside in the borough, he shall cease to be qualified under that proviso, and his office shall become vacant, unless he was at the time of his election and continues to be qualified in some other manner.

Sect. 12.—(1.) A person shall be disqualified for being elected and for being a councillor, if and while he— Disqualifications for being councillor.

(*a.*) Is an elective auditor or a revising assessor, or holds any office or place of profit, other than that of mayor or sheriff, in the gift or disposal of the council; or

(*b.*) Is in holy orders, or the regular minister of a dissenting congregation; or

(*c.*) Has directly or indirectly, by himself or his partner, any share or interest in any contract or employment with, by, or on behalf of the council:

(2.) But a person shall not be so disqualified, or be deemed to have any share or interest in such a contract or employment, by reason only of his having any share or interest in—

(*a.*) Any lease, sale, or purchase of land, or any agreement for the same; or

(*b.*) Any agreement for the loan of money, or any security for the payment of money only; or

(*c.*) Any newspaper in which any advertisement relating to the affairs of the borough or council is inserted; or

(*d.*) Any company which contracts with the council for lighting or supplying with water or insuring against fire any part of the borough; or

(*e.*) Any railway company, or any company incorporated by Act of Parliament or Royal charter, or under the Companies Act, 1862. 25 & 26 Vict. c. 89.

Sect. 13.—(1.) The term of office of a councillor shall be three years. Term of office and rotation of councillors.

(2.) On the ordinary day of election of councillors in every year one third of the whole number of councillors for the borough or for the ward, as the case may be, shall go out of office, and their places shall be filled by election.

(3.) The third to go out shall be the councillors who have been longest in office without re-election.

Sect. 14.—(1.) The aldermen shall be fit persons elected by the council. Number, term of office, and rotation of aldermen.

(2.) The number of aldermen shall be one third of the number of councillors.

(3.) A person shall not be qualified to be elected or to be an alderman unless he is a councillor or qualified to be a councillor.

(4.) If a councillor is elected to, and accepts, the office of alderman he vacates his office of councillor.

(5.) The term of office of an alderman shall be six years.

(6.) On the ordinary day of election of aldermen in every third year one half of the whole number of aldermen shall go out of office, and their places shall be filled by election.

(7.) The half to go out shall be those who have been aldermen for the longest time without re-election.

45 & 46 Vict. c. 50, s. 15

Qualification, term of office, salary, precedence, and powers of mayor.

Sect. 15.—(1.) The mayor shall be a fit person elected by the council from among the aldermen or councillors or persons qualified to be such.

(2.) An outgoing alderman is eligible.

(3.) The term of office of the mayor shall be one year, but he shall continue in office until his successor has accepted office and made and subscribed the required declaration.

(4.) He may receive such remuneration as the council think reasonable.

(5.) He shall, subject to the provisions of this Act respecting justices, have precedence in all places in the borough.

(6.) The mayor of a borough named in the schedules to the Municipal Corporations Act, 1835, shall be capable in law to do and suffer all acts which the chief officer of the borough might at the passing of that Act lawfully do or suffer, as far as the same were not altered or annulled by that Act, or have not been altered or annulled by any subsequent Act.

Power of mayor to appoint deputy.

Sect. 16.—(1.) The mayor may from time to time appoint an alderman or councillor to act as deputy mayor during the illness or absence of the mayor.

(2.) The appointment shall be signified to the council in writing and be recorded in their minutes.

(3.) A deputy mayor may, while acting as such, do all acts which the mayor as such might do, except that he shall not take the chair at a meeting of the council unless specially appointed by the meeting to do so, and shall not, unless he is a justice, act as a justice or in any judicial capacity.

Officers of Council.

The town clerk and deputy.

Sect. 17.—(1.) The council shall from time to time appoint a fit person, not a member of the council, to be the town clerk of the borough.

(2.) The town clerk shall hold office during the pleasure of the council.

(3.) He shall have the charge and custody of, and be responsible for, the charters, deeds, records, and documents of the borough, and they shall be kept as the council direct.

(4.) A vacancy in the office shall be filled within twenty-one days after its occurrence.

(5.) In case of the illness or absence of the town clerk, the council may appoint a deputy town clerk, to hold office during their pleasure.

(6.) All things required or authorized by law to be done by or to the town clerk may be done by or to the deputy town clerk.

The treasurer.

Sect. 18.—(1.) The council shall from time to time appoint a fit person, not a member of the council, to be the treasurer of the borough.

(2.) The treasurer shall hold office during the pleasure of the council.

(3.) A vacancy in the office shall be filled within twenty-one days after its occurrence.

(4.) The offices of town clerk and treasurer shall not be held by the same person.

Other borough officers.

Sect. 19. The council shall from time to time appoint such other officers as have been usually appointed in the borough, or as the council think necessary, and may at any time discontinue the appointment of any officer appearing to them not necessary to be re-appointed.

Security by and remuneration of officers.

Sect. 20. The council shall require every officer appointed by them to give such security as they think proper for the due execution of his office, and shall allow him such remuneration as they think reasonable.

Accountability of officers

Sect. 21.—(1.) Every officer appointed by the council shall at such times during the continuance of his office, or within three months after his ceasing to hold it, and in such manner as the council direct, deliver to the council, or as they direct, a true account in writing of all matters committed to his charge, and of his receipts and payments, with vouchers, and a list of persons from whom money is due for purposes of this Act in connexion with his office, shewing the amount due from each.

(2.) Every such officer shall pay all money due from him to the treasurer, or as the council direct. 45 & 46 Vict. c. 50, s. 21.

(3.) If any such officer—

(a.) Refuses or wilfully neglects to deliver any account or list which he ought to deliver, or any voucher relating thereto, or to make any payment which he ought to make; or

(b.) After three days notice in writing, signed by the town clerk or by three members of the council, given or left at his usual or last known place of abode, refuses or wilfully neglects to deliver to the council, or as they direct, any book or document which he ought so to deliver, or to give satisfaction respecting it to the council or as they direct;

a court of summary jurisdiction having jurisdiction where the officer is or resides may, by summary order, require him to make such delivery or payment, or to give such satisfaction.

(4.) But nothing in this section shall affect any remedy by action against any such officer or his surety, except that the officer shall not be both sued by action and proceeded against summarily for the same cause.

Meetings and Proceedings of Council; Committees.

Quarterly and other meetings of council; appointment of committees, minutes, &c.

Sect. 22.—(1.) The rules in the Second Schedule shall be observed.

(2.) The council may from time to time appoint out of their own body such and so many committees, either of a general or special nature, and consisting of such number of persons, as they think fit, for any purposes which, in the opinion of the council, would be better regulated and managed by means of such committees; but the acts of every such committee shall be submitted to the council for their approval.

(3.) A member of the council shall not vote or take part in the discussion of any matter before the council, or a committee, in which he has, directly or indirectly, by himself or by his partner, any pecuniary interest.

(4.) No act or proceeding of the council, or of a committee, shall be questioned on account of any vacancy in their body.

(5.) A minute of proceedings at a meeting of the council, or of a committee, signed at the same or the next ensuing meeting, by the mayor, or by a member of the council, or of the committee, describing himself as, or appearing to be, chairman of the meeting at which the minute is signed, shall be received in evidence without further proof.

(6.) Until the contrary is proved, every meeting of the council, or of a committee, in respect of the proceedings whereof a minute has been so made, shall be deemed to have been duly convened and held, and all the members of the meeting shall be deemed to have been duly qualified; and where the proceedings are proceedings of a committee, the committee shall be deemed to have been duly constituted, and to have had power to deal with the matters referred to in the minutes.

Bye-laws.

Power of council to make bye-laws.

Sect. 23.—(1.) The council may, from time to time, make such bye-laws as to them seem meet for the good rule and government of the borough, and for prevention and suppression of nuisances not already punishable in a summary manner by virtue of any Act in force throughout the borough, and may thereby appoint such fines, not exceeding in any case five pounds, as they deem necessary for the prevention and suppression of offences against the same.

(2.) Such a bye-law shall not be made unless at least two thirds of the whole number of the council are present.

(3.) Such a bye-law shall not come into force until the expiration of forty days after a copy thereof has been fixed on the town hall.

(4.) Such a bye-law shall not come into force until the expiration of forty days after a copy thereof, sealed with the corporate seal, has been sent to the Secretary of State; and if within those forty days the Queen, with the advice of Her Privy

45 & 46 Vict. 50, s. 23. Council, disallows the bye-law or part thereof, the bye-law or part disallowed shall not come into force; but it shall be lawful for the Queen, at any time within those forty days, to enlarge the time within which the bye-law shall not come into force, and in that case the bye-law shall not come into force until after the expiration of that enlarged time.

(5.) Any offence against such a bye-law may be prosecuted summarily.

38 & 39 Vict. c. 55. (6.) Nothing in this section shall interfere with the operation of section one hundred and eighty-seven of the Public Health Act, 1875; and that section shall have effect as if this section were therein referred to, instead of section ninety of the Municipal Corporations Act, 1835; but nothing in the Public Health Act, 1875, shall be construed as having restricted the meaning or scope of the Municipal Corporations Act, 1835, or as restricting the meaning or scope of this section, with respect to prevention or suppression of nuisances.

Evidence of bye-laws.

Sect. 24. The production of a written copy of a bye-law made by the council under this Act, or under any former or present or future general or local Act of Parliament, if authenticated by the corporate seal shall, until the contrary is proved, be sufficient evidence of the due making and existence of the bye-law, and, if it is so stated in the copy, of the bye-law having been approved and confirmed by the authority whose approval or confirmation is required to the making or before the enforcing of the bye-law.

Accounts and Audit.

The borough auditors.

Sect. 25.—(1.) There shall be three borough auditors, two elected by the burgesses, called elective auditors, and one appointed by the mayor, called mayor's auditor.

(2.) An elective auditor must be qualified to be a councillor, but may not be a member of the council or the town clerk or the treasurer.

(3.) The mayor's auditor must be a member of the council.

(4.) The term of office of each auditor shall be one year.

(5.) The appointment of the mayor's auditor shall be made on the ordinary day of election of the elective auditors.

(6.) On a casual vacancy in his office an appointment to fill it shall be made within ten days after the occurrence of the vacancy.

Half-yearly accounts of treasurer.

Sect. 26. The treasurer shall make up his accounts half-yearly to such dates as the council, with the approval of the Local Government Board, from time to time appoint; and, subject to any such appointment, to the dates in use at the commencement of this Act.

Audit and publication of treasurer's accounts.

Sect. 27.—(1.) The treasurer shall within one month from the date to which he is required to make up his accounts in each half-year, submit them, with the necessary vouchers and papers, to the borough auditors, and they shall audit them.

(2.) After the audit of the accounts for the second half of each financial year the treasurer shall print a full abstract of his accounts for that year.

Returns to Local Government Board.

Sect. 28.—(1.) The town clerk shall make a return to the Local Government Board of the receipts and expenditure of the municipal corporation for each financial year.

(2.) The return shall be made for the financial year ending on the twenty-fifth of March, or on such other day as the Local Government Board, on the application of the council, from time to time prescribe.

(3.) The return shall be in such form and contain such particulars as the Local Government Board from time to time direct.

(4.) The return shall be sent to the Local Government Board within one month after the completion of the audit for the second half of each financial year.

(5.) If the town clerk fails to make any return required under this section, he shall for each offence be liable to a fine not exceeding twenty pounds to be recovered by action on behalf of the Crown in the High Court.

(6.) The Local Government Board shall in each year prepare an abstract of the returns made in pursuance of this section, under general heads, and it shall be laid before both Houses of Parliament.

45 & 46 Vict. c. 50, s. 29.

Revising Assessors.

Revising assessors in non-parliamentary boroughs.

Sect. 29.—(1.) In every borough whereof no part of the area is co-extensive with or included in the area of a parliamentary borough, there shall be two revising assessors elected by the burgesses.

(2.) Every person shall be eligible who is qualified to be a councillor and is not a member of the council or the town clerk or treasurer.

(3.) The term of office of each revising assessor shall be one year.

(4.) Every revising assessor shall, as soon as conveniently may be after his election, and from time to time as occasion requires, appoint, by writing signed by him, a person eligible to the office of revising assessor, to be his deputy, to act for him in case of his illness or incapacity to act.

(5.) The appointment shall be signified to the council, in writing signed by the assessor, and be recorded in their minutes.

Division of Borough into Wards, or alteration of Wards.

Proceedings for division of borough into wards, or alteration of wards.

Sect. 30.—(1.) If two thirds of the council of a borough agree to petition, and the council thereupon petition, the Queen for the division of the borough into wards, or for the alteration of the number and boundaries of its wards, it shall be lawful for Her Majesty from time to time, by Order in Council, to fix the number of wards into which the borough shall be divided; and the borough shall be divided into that number of wards.

(2.) Notice of the petition, and of the time when it pleases Her Majesty to order that the same be taken into consideration by Her Privy Council, shall be published in the *London Gazette* one month at least before the petition is so considered.

(3.) Where an Order in Council has been so made, the Secretary of State shall appoint a commissioner to prepare a scheme for determining the boundaries of the wards and apportioning the councillors among them.

(4.) In case of division into wards, the commissioner shall apportion all the councillors among the wards.

(5.) In case of alteration of wards, he shall so apportion among the altered wards the councillors for those wards as to provide for their continuing to represent as large a number as possible of their former constituents.

(6.) In either case, each councillor shall hold his office in the ward to which he is assigned for the same time that he would have held it had the borough remained undivided or the wards unaltered.

(7.) In case of division into wards the returning officer at the first election for each ward held after the division shall, notwithstanding anything in this Act, be the mayor or a person appointed by the mayor.

(8.) If by reason of any division ar alteration under this section any doubt arises as to which councillor should go out of office, the doubt may be determined by the council.

(9.) The division of a borough into a greater number of wards shall not affect the qualification of aldermen or councillors.

(10.) The number of councillors assigned to each ward shall be a number divisible by three; and in fixing their number the commissioner shall, as far as he deems it practicable, have regard as well to the number of persons rated in the ward as to the aggregate rating of the ward.

(11.) The commissioner shall make the scheme in duplicate, and shall deliver one of the duplicates to the town clerk, and shall send the other to the Secretary of State, to be submitted by him to Her Majesty in Council for approval.

(12.) The scheme shall be published in the *London Gazette*, and shall come into operation at the date of that publication, and thenceforth the boundaries of wards and apportionment of councillors determined and made by the scheme shall be observed and be in force.

(13.) If Her Majesty in Council does not approve the scheme, as originally pre-

45 & 46 Vict. c. 50, s. 30

pared by the commissioner, it shall nevertheless be published in the *London Gazette*, and shall be in force for the purposes of any municipal election until Her Majesty in Council, on further information and report from the commissioner, definitively approves a scheme in that behalf.

(14.) The commissioner may administer oaths, and may require any person having the custody of any book containing a poor rate made for a parish to produce the book for his inspection; and every person required by the commissioner to answer any question put to him for the purposes of this section shall answer it.

(15.) The commissioner shall have remuneration as appearing by the Fourth and Fifth Schedules.

Supplemental and Exceptional Provisions.

Occupation of part of house.

Sect. 31. In and for the purposes of this Act—

(*a.*) The terms house, warehouse, counting house, shop, or other building include any part of a house, where that part is separately occupied for the purposes of any trade, business, or profession; and any such part may, for the purpose of describing the qualification, be described as office, chambers, studio, or by any like term applicable to the case.

(*b.*) Where an occupier is entitled to the sole and exclusive use of any part of a house, that part shall not be deemed to be occupied otherwise than separately by reason only that the occupier is entitled to the joint use of some other part.

Claim by occupier to be rated.

Sect. 32.—(1.) If an occupier of any qualifying property, whether the landlord is or is not liable to be rated to the poor rate in respect thereof, claims to be rated to the poor rate in respect thereof, and pays or tenders to the overseers of the parish where the property is situate the full amount of the poor rate last made in respect of the property, the overseers shall put the occupier's name on the rate book in respect of that rate.

(2.) If they fail to do so, he shall nevertheless for the purposes of this Act be deemed rated to that rate.

Rules as to qualification of burgess on succession, &c.

Sect. 33.—(1.) Where a person succeeds to qualifying property by descent, marriage, marriage settlement, devise, or promotion to a benefice or office, then, for the purpose of qualification, the occupancy of the property by a predecessor in title, and the rating of the predecessor in respect thereof, shall be equivalent to the occupancy and rating of the successor; and rating in the name of the predecessor shall, until a new rate is made after the date of succession, be equivalent to rating in the name of the successor: and the successor shall not be required to prove his own residence, occupancy, or rating before the succession.

(2.) The qualifying property need not be throughout the twelve months constituting the period of qualification the same property or in the same parish.

(3.) Where by law a borough rate is payable by instalments, payment by any person of any such instalment shall, as regards his qualification to be inrolled as a burgess, be deemed a payment of the borough rate in respect of the period to which the instalment applies.

(4.) A person shall not be disentitled to be enrolled as a burgess by reason only—

(*a.*) That he has received medical or surgical assistance from the trustees of the municipal charities, or has been removed, by order of a justice, to a hospital or place for reception of the sick, at the cost of any local authority: or

(*b.*) That his child has been admitted to and taught in any public or endowed school.

Obligation to accept office or pay fine.

Sect. 34.—(1.) Every qualified person elected to a corporate office, unless exempt under this section or otherwise by law, either shall accept the office by making and subscribing the declaration required by this Act within five days after notice of election, or shall, in lieu thereof, be liable to pay to the council a fine of such amount not exceeding, in case of an alderman, councillor, elective auditor, or revising assessor, fifty pounds, and in case of a mayor one hundred pounds as the council by bye-law determine. 45 & 46 Vict. c. 50, s. 34.

(2.) If there is no bye-law determining fines, the fine, in case of an alderman, councillor, elective auditor, or revising assessor, shall be twenty-five pounds, and in case of a mayor fifty pounds.

(3.) The persons exempt under this section are—

(*a.*) Any person disabled by lunacy or imbecility of mind, or by deafness, blindness, or other permanent infirmity of body; and

(*b.*) Any person who, being above the age of sixty-five years, or having within five years before the day of his election either served the office or paid the fine for non-acceptance thereof, claims exemption within five days after notice of his election.

(4.) A fine payable under this section shall be recoverable summarily.

Sect. 35. A person elected to a corporate office shall not, until he has made and subscribed before two members of the council, or the town clerk, a declaration as in the Eighth Schedule, act in the office except in administering that declaration. Declaration on acceptance of office.

Sect. 36.—(1.) A person elected to a corporate office may at any time, by writing signed by him and delivered to the town clerk, resign the office, on payment of the fine provided for non-acceptance thereof. Fine on resignation, &c.

(2.) In any such case the council shall forthwith declare the office to be vacant, and signify the same by notice in writing, signed by three members of the council and countersigned by the town clerk, and fixed on the town hall, and the office shall thereupon become vacant.

(3.) No person enabled by law to make an affirmation instead of taking an oath shall be liable to any fine for non-acceptance of office by reason of his refusal on conscientious grounds to take any oath or make any declaration required by this Act or to take on himself the duties of the office.

Sect. 37. A person ceasing to hold a corporate office shall, unless disqualified to hold the office, be re-eligible. Re-eligibility of office holders.

Sect. 38. The mayor and aldermen shall, during their respective offices, continue to be members of the council, notwithstanding anything in this Act as to councillors going out of office at the end of three years. Mayor and aldermen to continue members of council.

Sect. 39.—(1.) If the mayor, or an alderman or councillor— Avoidance of office by bankruptcy or absence.

(*a.*) Is declared bankrupt, or compounds by deed with his creditors, or makes an arrangement or composition with his creditors, under the Bankruptcy Act, 1869, by deed or otherwise; or 32 & 33 Vict. c. 71.

(*b.*) Is (except in case of illness) continuously absent from the borough, being mayor, for more than two months, or, being alderman or councillor, for more than six months:

he shall thereupon immediately become disqualified and shall cease to hold the office.

(2.) In any such event the council shall forthwith declare the office to be vacant, and signify the same by notice signed by three members of the council, and countersigned by the town clerk, and fixed on the town hall, and the office shall thereupon become vacant.

(3.) Where a person becomes so disqualified by being declared bankrupt, or compounding, or making an arrangement or composition, as aforesaid, the disqualification, as regards subsequent elections, shall, in case of bankruptcy, cease on his obtaining his order of discharge, and shall, in case of a compounding or composition as aforesaid, cease on payment of his debts in full, and shall, in case of an arrangement as aforesaid, cease on his obtaining his certificate of discharge.

(4.) Where a person becomes so disqualified by absence, he shall be liable to the same fine as for non-acceptance of office, recoverable summarily, but the disqualification shall, as regards subsequent elections, cease on his return.

Sect. 40.—(1.) On a casual vacancy in a corporate office, an election shall be Filling of casual vacancies.

45 & 46 Vict. c. 50, s. 40.

held by the same persons and in the same manner as an election to fill an ordinary vacany; and the person elected shall hold the office until the time when the person in whose place he is elected would regularly have gone out of office, and he shall then go out of office.

(2.) In case of more than one casual vacancy in the office of councillor being filled at the same election, the councillor elected by the smallest number of votes shall be deemed to be elected in the place of him who would regularly have first gone out of office, and the councillor elected by the next smallest number of votes shall be deemed to be elected in the place of him who would regularly have next gone out of office, and so with respect to the others; and if there has not been a contested election, or if any doubt arises, the order of rotation shall be determined by the council.

(3.) Non-acceptance of office by a person elected creates a casual vacancy.

Penalty on unqualified person acting in office.

Sect. 41.—(1.) If any person acts in a corporate office without having made the declaration by this Act required, or without being qualified at the time of making the declaration, or after ceasing to be qualified, or after being disqualified, he shall for each offence be liable to a fine not exceeding fifty pounds, recoverable by action.

(2.) A person being in fact enrolled in the burgess roll shall not be liable to a fine for acting in a corporate office on the ground only that he was not entitled to be enrolled therein.

Validity of acts done notwithstanding disqualification, &c.

Sect. 42.- (1.) The acts and proceedings of a person in possession of a corporate office, and acting therein, shall, notwithstanding his disqualification or want of qualification, be as valid and effectual as if he had been qualified.

(2.) An election of a person to a corporate office shall not be liable to be questioned by a reason of a defect in the title, or want of title, of the person before whom the election was had, if that person was then in actual possession of, or acting in, the office giving the right to preside at the election.

(3.) A burgess roll shall not be liable to be questioned by reason of a defect in the title, or want of title, of the mayor or any revising authority by whom it is revised, if he was then in actual possession and exercise of the office of mayor or revising authority.

Duties of town clerk, deputy, and treasurer, during vacancy or incapacity.

Sect. 43. If there is no town clerk, and no deputy town clerk, or there is no treasurer, or the town clerk, deputy town clerk, or treasurer (as the case may be) is incapable of acting, all acts by law authorized or required to be done by or with respect to the town clerk or the treasurer (as the case may be) may, subject to the provisions of any other Act, be done by or with respect to a person appointed in that behalf by the mayor.

PART III.

Preparations for and Procedure at Elections.

Parish Burgess Lists: Burgess Rolls; Ward Rolls.

Preparation and revision of parish burgess lists.

41 & 42 Vict. c. 26.

Sect. 44.—(1.) Where the whole or part of the area of a borough is co-extensive with or included in the area of a parliamentary borough, the lists of burgesses are to be made out and revised, and claims and objections relating thereto are to be made, in accordance with the provisions of the Parliamentary and Municipal Registration Act, 1878.

(2.) Where no part of the area of a borough is co-extensive with or included in the area of a parliamentary borough, the lists of burgesses shall be made out and revised, and claims and objections relating thereto may be made, in accordance, as nearly as may be, with the provisions of Part I. of the Third Schedule.

(3.) In either case the lists shall be styled the parish burgess lists.

The burgess roll and ward rolls.

Sect. 45.—(1.) When the parish burgess lists have been revised and signed, the revising authority shall deliver them to the town clerk, and a printed copy thereof, examined by him and signed by him, shall be the burgess roll of the borough

(2.) The burgess roll shall be completed on or before the twentieth of October in each year, and shall come into operation on the first of November in that year, and shall continue in operation for the twelve months beginning on that day. 45 & 46 Vict. c. 50, s. 45.

(3.) The names in the burgess roll shall be numbered by wards or by polling districts, unless in any case the council direct that the same be numbered consecutively without reference to wards or polling districts.

(4.) Where the borough has no wards, the burgess roll shall be made in one general roll for the whole borough.

(5.) Where the borough has wards, the burgess roll shall be made in separate rolls, called ward rolls, one for each ward, containing the names of the persons entitled to vote in that ward, and the ward rolls collectively shall constitue the burgess roll.

(6.) A burgess shall not be enrolled in more than one ward roll.

(7.) Where a duplicate of a burgess list is made under section thirty-one of the Parliamentary and Municipal Registration Act, 1878, it shall have the same effect as the original, and may be delivered instead thereof.

(8.) Every person enrolled in the burgess roll shall be deemed to be enrolled as a burgess, and every person not enrolled in the burgess roll shall be deemed to be not enrolled as a burgess.

(9.) No stamp duty shall be payable in respect of the enrolment of a burgess.

Sect. 46.—(1.) If and as far as the council so direct, the parish burgess lists, and the burgess roll, and the ward rolls (if any), and the lists of claimants and respondents, or any of those documents, shall be arranged in the same order in which the qualifying properties appear in the rate book for the parish in which they are situate, or otherwise in such order as will cause those lists and rolls to record the qualifying properties in successive order in the street or other place in which they are situate. **Arrangement of lists and rolls.**

(2.) Subject to any such direction, and to the provisions of this Act as to the polling districts, the arrangement of the lists and rolls shall be alphabetical.

Sect. 47.—(1.) Where the parish burgess lists are revised under the Parliamentary and Municipal Registration Act, 1878, the burgess roll is subject to alteration or correction in manner provided by section thirty-five of that Act. **Correction of burgess roll.**

(2.) Where the parish burgess lists are revised under this Act, any person whose claim has been rejected or name expunged at the revision of the lists may apply, within two months after the last sitting of the revision court, to the High Court in the Queen's Bench Division for a mandamus to the mayor to insert his name in the burgess roll; and thereupon the court shall inquire into the title of the applicant to be enrolled.

(3.) If the court grants a mandamus, the mayor shall insert the name in the burgess roll, and shall add thereto the words "by order of Her Majesty's High Court of Justice," and shall subscribe his name to those words.

Sect. 48.—(1.) The town clerk shall cause the parish burgess lists, the lists of claimants and respondents, and the burgess roll, to be printed, and shall deliver printed copies to any person on payment of a reasonable price for each copy. **Printing and sale of burgess roll and other documents.**

(2.) Subject to section thirty of the Parliamentary and Municipal Registration Act, 1878, the proceeds of sale shall go to the borough fund.

Sect. 49.—(1.) The overseers of each parish shall at the same time that they make the parish burgess list make a list of the persons entitled in respect of the occupation of property in that parish to be elected councillors, as being resident within fifteen miles although beyond seven miles from the borough. **Separate list of persons qualified to be councillors but not to be burgesses.**

(2.) The provisions of this Act as to the parish burgess lists, and claims and objections relating thereto, and the revision of those lists shall, as nearly as circumstances admit, apply to the lists made under this section.

(3.) The town clerk shall arrange the names entered in these lists, when revised, in alphabetical order as a separate list (in this Act called the separate non-resident list), with an appropriate heading, at the end of the burgess roll.

45 & 46 Vict. c. 50, s. 50.

Election of Councillors.

Borough and ward elections.

Sect. 50.—(1.) Where a borough has no wards, there shall be one election of councillors for the whole borough.

(2.) Where a borough has wards, there shall be a separate election of councillors for each ward.

Title to vote.

Sect. 51.—(1.) At an election of councillors a person shall be entitled to subscribe a nomination paper, and to demand and receive a voting paper, and to vote, if he is enrolled in the burgess roll, or, in the case of a ward election, the ward roll, and not otherwise.

(2.) No person shall subscribe a nomination paper in or for more than one ward, or vote in more than one ward.

(3.) Nothing in this section shall entitle any person to do any act therein mentioned who is prohibited by law from doing it, or relieve him from any penalty to which he may be liable for doing it.

Day of election.

Sect. 52. The ordinary day of election of councillors shall be the first of November.

Returning officer at election.

Sect. 53.—(1.) At an election of councillors for a whole borough the returning officer shall be the mayor.

(2.) At an election for a ward the returning officer shall be an alderman assigned for that purpose by the council at the meeting of the ninth of November.

Notice of election.

Sect. 54. Nine days at least before the day for the election of a councillor, the town clerk shall prepare and sign a notice thereof, and publish it by fixing it on the town hall, and, in the case of a ward election, in some conspicuous place in the ward.

Nomination of candidates.

Sect. 55. The nomination of candidates for the office of councillor shall be conducted in accordance with the Rules in Part II. of the Third Schedule.

Relation of nomination to election.

Sect. 56.—(1.) If the number of valid nominations exceeds that of the vacancies, the councillors shall be elected from among the persons nominated.

(2.) If the number of valid nominations is the same as that of the vacancies, the persons nominated shall be deemed to be elected.

(3.) If the number of valid nominations is less than that of the vacancies, the persons nominated shall be deemed to be elected, and such of the retiring councillors for the borough or ward as were highest on the poll at their election, or, if the poll was equal, or there was no poll, as are selected for that purpose by the mayor, shall be deemed to be re-elected to make up the required number.

(4.) If there is no valid nomination, the retiring councillors shall be deemed to be re-elected.

Publication of uncontested election.

Sect. 57. If an election of councillors is not contested, the returning officer shall publish a list of the persons elected not later than eleven o'clock in the morning on the day of election.

Mode of conducting poll at contested election

35 & 36 Vict. c. 33.

Sect. 58.—(1.) If an election of councillors is contested, the poll shall, as far as circumstances admit, be conducted as the poll at a contested parliamentary election is by the Ballot Act, 1872, directed to be conducted, and, subject to the modifications expressed in Part III. of the Third Schedule, and to the other provisions of this Act, the provisions of the Ballot Act, 1872, relating to a poll at a parliamentary election (including the provisions relating to the duties of the returning officer after the close of the poll), shall apply to a poll at an election of councillors.

(2.) Every person entitled to vote may vote for any number of candidates not exceeding the number of vacancies.

(3.) The poll shall commence at nine o'clock in the forenoon and close at four o'clock in the afternoon of the same day.

(4.) But if one hour elapses during which no vote is tendered, and the returning officer has not received notice that any person has within that hour been prevented from coming to the poll by any riot, violence, or other unlawful means, the returning officer may, if he thinks fit, close the poll at any time before four o'clock. 45 & 46 Vict. c. 50, s. 58.

(5.) Where an equality of votes is found to exist between any candidates, and the addition of a vote would entitle any of those candidates to be declared elected, the returning officer, whether entitled or not to vote in the first instance, may give such additional vote by word of mouth or in writing.

(6.) Nothing in the Ballot Act, 1872, as applied by this Act, shall be deemed to authorise the appointment of any agents of a candidate at a municipal election; but if, in the case of a municipal election, an agent of a candidate is appointed, and notice in writing of the appointment is given to the returning officer, one clear day before the polling day, then the provisions of the Ballot Act, 1872, with respect to agents of candidates, shall, as far as regards that agent, apply in the case of that election.

Questions which may be put to voters.

Sect. 59.—(1.) At an election of councillors, the presiding officer shall, if required by two burgesses, or by a candidate or his agent, put to any person offering to vote, at the time of his presenting himself to vote, but not afterwards, the following questions, or either of them:

(*a.*) Are you the person enrolled in the burgess [*or* ward] roll now in force for this borough [*or* ward] as follows [*read the whole entry from the roll*]?

(*b.*) Have you already voted at the present election [*add, in case of an election for several wards*, in this or any other ward]?

(2.) The vote of a person required to answer either of these questions shall not be received until he has answered it.

(3.) If any person wilfully makes a false answer thereto he shall be guilty of a misdemeanour.

(4.) Save as by this Act authorized, no inquiry shall be permitted at an election as to the right of any person to vote.

Election of Aldermen.

Time and mode of election of aldermen.

Sect. 60.—(1.) The ordinary day of election of aldermen shall be the ninth of November, and the election shall be held at the quarterly meeting of the council.

(2.) The election shall be held immediately after the election of the mayor, or, if there is a sheriff, the appointment of the sheriff.

(3.) An outgoing alderman, although mayor elect, shall not vote.

(4.) Every person entitled to vote may vote for any number of persons not exceeding the number of vacancies, by signing and personally delivering at the meeting to the chairman a voting paper containing the surnames and other names and places of abode and descriptions of the persons for whom he votes.

(5.) The chairman, as soon as all the voting papers have been delivered to him, shall openly produce and read them, or cause them to be read, and then deliver them to the town clerk to be kept for twelve months.

(6.) In case of equality of votes the chairman, although as an outgoing alderman or otherwise not entitled to vote in the first instance, shall have the casting vote.

(7.) The persons, not exceeding the number of vacancies, who have the greatest number of votes, shall be declared by the chairman to be, and thereupon shall be, elected.

Election of Mayor.

Time and mode of election of mayor.

Sect. 61.—(1.) The ordinary day of election of mayor shall be the ninth of November.

(2.) The election of mayor shall be the first business transacted at the quarterly meeting of the council on the day of election.

(3.) An outgoing alderman may vote although the person for whom he votes is an alderman.

(4.) In case of equality of votes, the chairman, although not entitled to vote in the first instance, shall have the casting vote.

Election of Auditors and Assessors.

45 & 46 Vict. c. 50, s. 62.

Time and mode of election of auditors and assessors.

Sect. 62.—(1.) The ordinary day of election of elective auditors shall be the first of March, or such other day as the council, with the approval of the Local Government Board, from time to time appoint.

(2.) The ordinary day of election of revising assessors shall be the first of March.

(3.) If the election of elective auditors and that of revising assessors are held at the same time, then at the poll one voting paper only shall be used by any person voting. The names of the candidates for the respective offices shall be therein separate, and distinguished so as to show the office for which each is a candidate, and the provisions of the Ballot Act, 1872, shall be varied accordingly; but in the counting of the votes every voting paper shall be deemed to be a separate voting paper in respect of each office, and any objections thereto shall be considered and dealt with accordingly.

(4.) An elector shall not vote for more than one person to be elective auditor or revising assessor.

(5.) Elections of elective auditors and of revising assessors shall be held at the town hall or some one other convenient place appointed by the mayor.

(6.) Save as in this section provided, all the provisions of this Act with respect to the nomination and election of councillors for a borough not having wards shall apply to the nomination and election of elective auditors and revising assessors.

Supplemental and Exceptional Provisions.

Right of women to vote.

Sect. 63. For all purposes connected with and having reference to the right to vote at municipal elections words in this Act importing the masculine gender include women.

Polling districts.

Sect. 64. The council may divide the borough or any ward into polling districts, and thereupon the overseers shall, as far as practicable, make out the parish burgess lists so as to divide the names in conformity with the polling districts.

Notices as to elections.

Sect. 65. Any notice required to be given in connexion with a municipal election may, as to elective auditors and revising assessors, be comprised in one notice, and may, as to ward elections, comprise matter necessary for several wards.

Time for filling casual vacancies.

Sect. 66.—(1.) On a casual vacancy in a corporate office, the election shall be held within fourteen days after notice in writing of the vacancy has been given to the mayor or town clerk by two burgesses.

(2.) Where the office vacant is that of mayor, the notice of the meeting for the election shall be signed by the town clerk.

(3.) In other cases the day of election shall be fixed by the mayor.

Illness, &c., of mayor or return-

Sect. 67.—(1.) If the mayor is dead, or is absent or otherwise incapable of acting in the execution of his powers and duties as to elections under this Act, the council shall forthwith choose an alderman to execute those powers and duties in the place of the mayor.

(2.) In case of the illness, absence, or incapacity to act of the alderman assigned to be returning officer at a ward election, the mayor may appoint to act in his stead another alderman, or, if the number of aldermen does not exceed the number of wards, a councillor not being a councillor for that ward, and not being enrolled in the ward roll for that ward.

Election of councillor in more than one ward.

Sect. 68. If a person is elected councillor in more than one ward, he shall, within three days after notice thereof, choose, by writing signed by him and delivered to the town clerk, or in his default the mayor shall, within three days after the time for choice has expired, declare, for which of those wards he shall serve, and the choice or declaration shall be conclusive.

Elections not in churches.

Sect. 69. A municipal election shall not be held in any church, chapel, or other place of public worship.

Sect. 70.—(1.) If a municipal election is not held on the appointed day or within the appointed time, it may be held on the day next after that day or the expiration of that time. 45 & 46 Vict. c. 50, s. 70.

Omission to hold election, or election void.

(2.) If a municipal election is not held on the appointed day or within the appointed time, or on the day next after that day or the expiration of that time, or becomes void, the municipal corporation shall not thereby be dissolved or be disabled from electing, but the High Court may, on motion, grant a mandamus for the election to be held on a day appointed by the court.

(3.) Thereupon public notice of the election shall, by such person as the court directs, be fixed on the town hall, and shall be kept so fixed for at least six days before the day appointed for the election; and in all other respects the election shall be conducted as directed by this Act respecting ordinary elections.

Burgess roll to be in operation until revision of new burgess roll

Sect. 71.—(1.) If a parish burgess list is not made or revised in due time, the corresponding part of the burgess roll in operation before the time appointed for the revision shall be the parish burgess list until a burgess list for the parish has been revised and become part of the burgess roll.

(2.) If a burgess roll is not made in due time, the burgess roll in force before the time appointed for the revision shall continue in force until the new burgess roll is made.

Non-compliance with rules.

Sect. 72. An election shall not be invalidated by non-compliance with the rules in the Third Schedule, or mistake in the use of the forms in the Eighth Schedule, if it appears to the court having cognisance of the question that the election was conducted in accordance with the principles laid down in the body of this Act.

Election valid unless questioned within twelve months.

Sect. 73. Every municipal election not called in question within twelve months after the election, either by election petition or by information in the nature of a quo warranto, shall be deemed to have been to all intents a good and valid election.

Offences in relation to nomination papers.

Sect. 74.—(1.) If any person forges or fraudulently defaces or fraudulently destroys any nomination paper, or delivers to the town clerk any forged nomination paper, knowing it to be forged, he shall be guilty of a misdemeanour, and shall be liable to imprisonment for any term not exceeding six months with or without hard labour.

(2.) An attempt to commit any such offence shall be punishable as the offence is punishable.

Offences in relation to lists and elections.

Sect. 75.—(1.) If a mayor or revising asssessor neglects or refuses to revise a parish burgess list, or a mayor or alderman neglects or refuses to conduct or declare an election, as required by this Act, he shall for every such offence be liable to a fine not exceeding one hundred pounds, recoverable by action.

(2.) If—

(*a*.) An overseer neglects or refuses to make, sign, or deliver a parish burgess list as required by this Act; or

(*b*.) A town clerk neglects or refuses to receive, print, and publish, a parish burgess list or list of claimants or respondents, as required by this Act; or

(*c*.) An overseer or town clerk refuses to allow any such list to be inspected by a person having a right thereto;

he shall for every such neglect or refusal be liable to a fine not exceeding fifty pounds, recoverable by action.

(3.) An action under this section shall not lie after three months from the neglect or refusal. A moiety of any fine recovered therein shall, after payment of the costs of action, be paid to the plaintiff.

Revival of former law on expiration of Ballot Act.

Sect. 76.—(1.) If the Ballot Act, 1872, ceases to be in force, so much of this Act as directs that the poll at a contested election of councillors shall be conducted as the poll at a contested parliamentary election is by the Ballot Act, 1872, directed to be conducted, and as applies provisions of the Ballot Act, 1872, to a poll at a contested election of councillors, shall forthwith cease to be in force, and thereupon the enactments in Part IV. of the Third Schedule shall revive and be in force.

45 & 46 Vict. c. 50, s. 76. (2.) But this cesser and revivor shall not affect any act done, right acquired, or liability or fine incurred, or the institution or prosecution to its termination of any proceeding in respect of any such right, liability, or fine.

PART IV.

Corrupt Practices and Election Petitions.

Corrupt Practices.

Definitions. **Sect. 77.** In this Part—

"Bribery," "treating," "undue influence," and "personation," include respectively anything done before, at, after, or with respect to a municipal election, which if done before, at, after, or with respect to a parliamentary election would make the person doing the same liable to any penalty, punishment or disqualification for bribery, treating, undue influence, or personation, as the case may be, under any Act for the time being in force with respect to parliamentary elections:

[*"Corrupt practice" means bribery, treating, undue influence, or personation:*]

"Candidate" means a person elected, or having been nominated, or having declared himself a candidate for election, to a corporate office:

[*"Canvasser" means any person who solicits or persuades, or attempts to persuade, any person to vote or to abstain from voting at a municipal election, or to vote or to abstain from voting for a candidate at a municipal election:*]

"Voter" means a burgess or a person who votes or claims to vote at a municipal election:

"Election court" means a court constituted under this Part for the trial of an election petition:

"Municipal election petition" or "election petition" means a petition under this Part complaining of an undue municipal election:

31 & 32 Vict. c. 125. "Parliamentary election petition" means a petition under the Parliamentary Elections Act, 1868:

"Prescribed" means prescribed by general rules made under this Part:

"Borough" and "election" when used with reference to a petition mean the borough and election to which the petition relates.

Striking off votes. **Sect. 85.** The votes of persons in respect of whom any corrupt practice is proved to have been committed at a municipal election shall be struck off on a scrutiny.

Personation. **Sect. 86.** The enactments for the time being in force for the detection of personation and for the apprehension of persons charged with personation at a parliamentary election shall apply in the case of a municipal election.

Election Petitions.

Power to question municipal election by petition. **Sect. 87.**—(1.) A municipal election may be questioned by an election petition on the ground—

(*a.*) That the election was as to the borough or ward wholly avoided by general bribery, treating, undue influence, or personation; or

(*b.*) That the election was avoided by corrupt practices or offences against this Part committed at the election; or

(*c.*) That the person whose election is questioned was at the time of the election disqualified; or

(*d.*) That he was not duly elected by a majority of lawful votes.

(2.) A municipal election shall not be questioned on any of those grounds except by an election petition.

Presentation of petition. **Sect. 88.**—(1.) An election petition may be presented either by four or more persons who voted or had a right to vote at the election or by a person alleging himself to have been a candidate at the election.

(2.) Any person whose election is questioned by the petition, and any returning officer of whose conduct a petition complains, may be made a respondent to the petition.

(3.) The petition shall be in the prescribed form and shall be signed by the petitioner, and shall be presented in the prescribed manner to the High Court in the Queen's Bench Division, and the prescribed officer shall send a copy thereof to the town clerk, who shall forthwith publish it in the borough. 45 & 46 Vict c. 50, s. 88.

(4.) It shall be presented within twenty-one days after the day on which the election was held, except that if it complains of the election on the ground of corrupt practices, and specifically alleges that a payment of money or other reward has been made or promised since the election by a person elected at the election, or on his account or with his privity, in pursuance or furtherance of such corrupt practices, it may be presented at any time within twenty-eight days after the date of the alleged payment or promise, whether or not any other petition against that person has been previously presented or tried.

Sect. 89.—(1.) At the time of presenting an election petition or within three days afterwards, the petitioner shall give security for all costs, charges, and expenses which may become payable by him to any witness summoned on his behalf, or to any respondent. Security for costs.

(2.) The security shall be to such amount, not exceeding five hundred pounds, as the High Court, or a Judge thereof, on summons, directs, and shall be given in the prescribed manner, either by a deposit of money, or by recognisance entered into by not more than four sureties, or partly in one way and partly in the other.

(3.) Within five days after the presentation of the petition the petitioner shall in the prescribed manner serve on the respondent a notice of the presentation of the petition, and of the nature of the proposed security and a copy of the petition.

(4.) Within five days after service of the notice the respondent may object in writing to any recognisance on the ground that any surety is insufficient or is dead, or cannot be found or ascertained for want of a sufficient description in the recognisance, or that a person named in the recognisance has not duly acknowledged the same.

(5.) An objection to a recognisance shall be decided in the prescribed manner.

(6.) If the objection is allowed, the petitioner may, within a further prescribed time not exceeding five days, remove it by a deposit in the prescribed manner of such sum of money as will, in the opinion of the court or officer having cognisance of the matter, make the security sufficient.

(7.) If no security is given, as prescribed, or any objection is allowed and is not removed, as aforesaid, no further proceedings shall be had on the petition.

Sect. 90. On the expiration of the time limited for making objections, or, after objection made on the objection being disallowed or removed, whichever last happens, the petition shall be at issue. Petition at issue.

Sect. 91.—(1.) The prescribed officer shall as soon as may be make a list, in this Act referred to as the municipal election list, of all election petitions at issue, placing them in the order in which they were presented, and shall keep at his office a copy of this list, open to inspection in the prescribed manner. Municipal election list.

(2.) The petitions shall, as far as conveniently may be, be tried in the order in which they stand in the list.

(3.) Two or more candidates may be made respondents to the same petition, and their cases may be tried at the same time, but for the purposes of this Part the petition shall be deemed to be a separate petition against each respondent.

(4.) Where more petitions than one are presented relating to the same election, or to elections held at the same time for different wards of the same borough, they shall be bracketed together in the list as one petition, but shall, unless the High Court otherwise directs, stand in the list in the place where the last of them would have stood if it had been the only petition relating to that election.

Sect. 92.—(1.) An election petition shall be tried by an election court consisting of a barrister qualified and appointed as in this section provided, without a jury. Constitution of election court.

(2.) A barrister shall not be qualified to constitute an election court if he is of less than fifteen years' standing, or is a member of the Commons House of

45 & 46 Vict. c. 50, s. 92.

Parliament, or holds any office or place of profit under the Crown, other than that of recorder.

(3.) A barrister shall not be qualified to constitute an election court for trial of an election petition relating to any borough for which he is recorder, or in which he resides, or which is included in a circuit of Her Majesty's judges on which he practises as a barrister

(4.) As soon as may be after a municipal election list is made out the prescribed officer shall send a copy thereof to each of the judges for the time being on the rota for the trial of parliamentary election petitions; [*and those judges or two of them shall forthwith determine the number of barristers, not exceeding five at any one time, necessary to be appointed for the trial of the election petitions at issue, and shall appoint that number accordingly as commissioners under this Part, and shall assign the petitions to be tried by each.*]*

(5.) If a commissioner to whom the trial of a petition is assigned, dies, or declines or becomes incapable to act, the said judges or two of them may assign the trial to be conducted or continued by any other of the commissioners appointed under this section.

(6.) The election court shall for the purposes of the trial have the same powers and privileges as a judge on the trial of a parliamentary election petition, except that any fine or order of committal by the court may on motion by the person aggrieved be discharged or varied by the High Court, or in vacation by a judge thereof, on such terms, if any, as the High Court or judge thinks fit.

Trial of election petition.

Sect. 93.—(1.) An election petition shall be tried in open court, and notice of the time and place of trial shall be given in the prescribed manner not less than seven days before the day of trial.

(2.) The place of trial shall be within the borough, except that the High Court may, on being satisfied that special circumstances exist rendering it desirable that the petition should be tried elsewhere, appoint some other convenient place for the trial.

(3.) The election court may in its discretion adjourn the trial from time to time, and from any one place to any other place within the borough or place where it is held.

(4.) At the conclusion of the trial the election court shall determine whether the person whose election is complained of, or any and what other person, was duly elected, or whether the election was void, and shall forthwith certify in writing the determination to the High Court, and the determination so certified shall be final to all intents as to the matters at issue on the petition.

(5.) Where a charge is made in a petition of any corrupt practice or offence against this Part having been committed at the election the court shall, in addition to the certificate, and at the same time, report in writing to the High Court as follows:

(*a.*) Whether any corrupt practice or offence against this Part has or has not been proved to have been committed by or with the knowledge and consent of any candidate at the election, and the nature of the corrupt practice or offence;

(*b.*) The names of all persons (if any) proved at the trial to have been guilty of any corrupt practice or offence against this Part;

(*c.*) Whether any corrupt practices have, or whether there is reason to believe that any corrupt practices have, extensively prevailed at the election in the borough or in any ward thereof.

(6.) The election court may at the same time make a special report to the High Court as to any matters arising in the course of the trial, an account of which ought in the judgment of the election, to be submitted to the High Court.

(7.) If, on the application of any party to a petition made in the prescribed manner to the High Court, it appears to the High Court that the case raised by the petition can be conveniently stated as a special case, the High Court may direct the same to be stated accordingly, and any such special case shall be heard before the High Court, and the decision of the High Court shall be final.

---

* Words in italics repealed by the Municipal Elections (Corrupt and Illegal Practices) Act, 1884.

(8.) If it appears to the election court on the trial of a petition that any question of law as to the admissibility of evidence, or otherwise, requires further consideration by the High Court, the election court may postpone the granting of a certificate until the question has been determined by the High Court, and for this purpose may reserve any such question, as questions may be reserved by a judge on a trial at nisi prius. 45 & 46 Vict. c. 50, s. 93.

(9.) On the trial of a petition, unless the election court otherwise directs, any charge of a corrupt practice or offence against this Part may be gone into, and evidence in relation thereto received before any proof has been given of agency on behalf of any candidate in respect of the corrupt practice or offence.

(10.) On the trial of a petition complaining of an undue election and claiming the office for some person, the respondent may give evidence to prove that that person was not duly elected, in the same manner as if he had presented a petition against the election of that person.

(11.) The trial of a petition shall be proceeded with notwithstanding that the respondent has ceased to hold the office his election to which is questioned by the petition.

(12.) A copy of any certificate or report made to the High Court on the trial of a petition, and, in the case of a decision by the High Court on a special case, a statement of the decision, shall be sent by the High Court to the Secretary of State.

(13.) A copy of any such certificate and a statement of any such decision shall also be certified by the High Court, under the hands of two or more judges thereof, to the town clerk of the borough.

Sect. 94.—(1.) Witnesses at the trial of an election petition shall be summoned and sworn in the same manner, as nearly as circumstances admit, as witnesses at a trial at nisi prius, and shall be liable to the same penalties for perjury. Witnesses.

(2.) On the trial the election court may, by order in writing, require any person who appears to the court to have been concerned in the election to attend as a witness, and any person refusing to obey the order shall be guilty of contempt of court.

(3.) The court may examine any person so required to attend or being in court although he is not called and examined by any party to the petition.

(4.) A witness may, after his examination by the court, be cross-examined by or on behalf of the petitioner and respondent or either of them.*

(9.) The reasonable expenses incurred by any person in appearing to give evidence at the trial of an election petition, according to the scale allowed to witnesses on the trial of civil actions at the assizes, may be allowed to him by a certificate of the election court or of the prescribed officer, and if the witness was called and examined by the court, shall be deemed part of the expenses of providing a court, but otherwise shall be deemed costs of the petition.

Sect. 95.—(1.) A petitioner shall not withdraw an election petition without the leave of the election court or High Court on special application, made in the prescribed manner, and at the prescribed time and place. Withdrawa petition.

(2.) The application shall not be made until the prescribed notice of the intention to make it has been given in the borough.

(3.) On the hearing of the application any person who might have been a petitioner in respect of the election may apply to the court to be substituted as a petitioner, and the court may, if it thinks fit, substitute him accordingly.

(4.) If the proposed withdrawal is in the opinion of the court induced by any corrupt bargain or consideration, the court may by order direct that the security given on behalf of the original petitioner shall remain as security for any costs that may be incurred by the substituted petitioner, and that to the extent of the sum named in the security, the original petitioner and his sureties shall be liable to pay the costs of the substituted petitioner.

(5.) If the court does not so direct, then security to the same amount as would be required in the case of a new petition, and subject to the like conditions,

* Sub-sections 5—8 of sect. 94 Corrupt and Illegal Practices Act, 1884.

45 & 46 Vict. c. 50, s. 95.

shall be given on behalf of the substituted petitioner before he proceeds with his petition and within the prescribed time after the order of substitution.

(6.) Subject as aforesaid, a substituted petitioner shall, as nearly as may be, stand in the same position and be subject to the same liabilities as the original petitioner.

(7.) If a petition is withdrawn, the petitioner shall be liable to pay the costs of the respondent.

(8.) Where there are more petitioners than one, an application to withdraw a petition shall not be made except with the consent of all the petitioners.

Abatement of petition.

Sect. 96.—(1.) An election petition shall be abated by the death of a sole petitioner or of the survivor of several petitioners.

(2.) The abatement of a petition shall not affect the liability of the petitioner or of any other person to the payment of costs previously incurred.

(3.) On the abatement of a petition the prescribed notice thereof shall be given in the borough, and, within the prescribed time after the notice is given, any person who might have been a petitioner in respect of the election may apply to the election court or High Court in the prescribed manner and at the prescribed time and place to be substituted as a petitioner; and the court may, if it thinks fit, substitute him accordingly.

(4.) Security shall be given on behalf of a petitioner so substituted, as in the case of a new petition.

Withdrawal and substitution of respondents.

Sect. 97.—(1.) If before the trial of an election petition a respondent other than a returning officer—

(*a.*) Dies, resigns, or otherwise ceases to hold the office to which the petition relates; or

(*b.*) Gives the prescribed notice that he does not intend to oppose the petition; the prescribed notice thereof shall be given in the borough, and within the prescribed time after the notice is given any person who might have been a petitioner in respect of the election may apply to the election court or High Court to be admitted as a respondent to oppose the petition, and shall be admitted accordingly, except that the number of persons so admitted shall not exceed three.

(2.) A respondent who has given the prescribed notice that he does not intend to oppose the petition shall not be allowed to appear or act as a party against the petition in any proceedings thereon.

Costs on election petitions.

Sect. 98.—(1.) All costs, charges, and expenses of and incidental to the presentation of an election petition, and the proceedings consequent thereon, except such as are by this Act otherwise provided for, shall be defrayed by the parties to the petition in such manner and proportions as the election court determines; and in particular any costs, charges, or expenses which in the opinion of the court have been caused by vexatious conduct, unfounded allegations, or unfounded objections on the part either of the petitioner or of the respondent, and any needless expense incurred or caused on the part of petitioner or respondent, may be ordered to be defrayed by the parties by whom it has been incurred or caused, whether they are or not on the whole successful.*

(2.) The costs may be taxed in the prescribed manner, but according to the same principles as costs between solicitor and client in an action in the High Court, and may be recovered as the costs of such an action, or as otherwise prescribed.

(3.) If a petitioner neglects or refuses for three months after demand to pay to any person summoned as a witness on his behalf, or to the respondent, any sum certified to be due to him for his costs, charges, and expenses, and the neglect or refusal is, within one year after the demand, proved to the satisfaction of the High Court, every person who has under this Act entered into a recognisance relating to the petition shall be held to have made default in the recognisance, and the prescribed officer shall thereon certify the recognisance to be forfeited, and it shall be dealt with as a forfeited recognisance relating to a parliamentary election petition.

* So much of sect. 98 as relates to the principles of taxation is repealed by the Municipal Elections (Corrupt and Illegal Practices) Act, 1884.

Sect. 99.—(1.) The town clerk shall provide proper accommodation for holding the election court; and any expenses incurred by him for the purposes of this section shall be paid out of the borough fund or borough rate. 45 & 46 Vict. c. 50, s. 99.

Reception of and attendance on the election court

(2.) All chief and head constables, superintendents of police, head boroughs, gaolers, constables, and bailiffs shall give their assistance to the election court in the execution of its duties, and if any gaoler or officer of a prison makes default in receiving or detaining a prisoner committed thereto in pursuance of this Part, he shall be liable to a fine not exceeding five pounds for every day during which the default continues.

(3.) The election court may employ officers and clerks as prescribed.

(4.) A shorthand writer shall attend at the trial of an election petition, and shall be sworn by the election court faithfully and truly to take down the evidence given at the trial. He shall take down the evidence at length. A transcript of the notes of the evidence taken by him shall, if the election court so directs, accompany the certificate of the election court. His expenses, according to a prescribed scale, shall be treated as part of the expenses incurred in receiving the court.

Rules of procedure and jurisdiction

Sect. 100.—(1.) The judges for the time being on the rota for the trial of parliamentary election petitions, may from time to time make, revoke, and alter General Rules for the effectual execution of this Part, and of the intention and object thereof, and the regulation of the practice, procedure, and costs of municipal election petitions, and the trial thereof, and the certifying and reporting thereon.

(2.) All such rules shall be laid before both Houses of Parliament within three weeks after they are made, if Parliament is then sitting, and if not, within three weeks after the beginning of the then next session of Parliament, and shall, while in force, have effect as if enacted in this Act.

(3.) Subject to the provisions of this Act, and of the rules made under it, the principles, practice, and rules for the time being observed in the case of parliamentary election petitions, and in particular the principles and rules with regard to agency and evidence, and to a scrutiny, and to the declaring any person elected in the room of any other person declared to have been not duly elected, shall be observed, as far as may be, in the case of a municipal election petition.

(4.) The High Court shall, subject to this Act, have the same powers, jurisdiction, and authority with respect to a municipal election petition and the proceedings thereon as if the petition were an ordinary action within its jurisdiction.

(5.) The duties to be performed by the prescribed officer under this Part shall be performed by the prescribed officer of the High Court.

(6.) The general rules in force at the commencement of this Act with respect to matters within this Part shall, until superseded by rules made under this section, and subject to any amendment thereof by rules so made, have effect, with the necessary modifications, as if made under this section.

Expenses of election court.

Sect. 101.—(1.) The remuneration and allowances to be paid to a commissioner for his services in respect of the trial of an election petition, and to any officers, clerks, or shorthand writers employed under this Part, shall be fixed by a scale made and varied by the election judges on the rota for the trial of parliamentary election petitions, with the approval of the Treasury. The remuneration and allowances shall be paid in the first instance by the Treasury, and shall be repaid to the Treasury, on their certificate, out of the borough fund or borough rate.

(2.) But the election court may in its discretion order that such remuneration and allowances, or the expenses incurred by a town clerk for receiving the election court, shall be repaid, wholly or in part, to the Treasury or the town clerk, as the case may be, in the cases, by the persons, and in the manner following (namely):

(*a.*) When in the opinion of the election court a petition is frivolous and vexatious, by the petitioner;

(*b.*) When in the opinion of the election court a respondent has been personally guilty of corrupt practices at the election, by that respondent.

(3.) An order so made for the repayment of any sum by a petitioner or respon-

45 & 46 Vict. c. 50, s. 101.

dent may be enforced as an order for payment of costs; but a deposit made or security given under this Part shall not be applied for any such repayment until all costs and expenses payable by the petitioner or respondent to any party to the petition have been satisfied.

Acts done pending a petition not invalidated.

Sect. 102. Where a candidate who has been elected to a corporate office is, by a certificate of an election court or a decision of the High Court, declared not to have been duly elected, acts done by him in execution of the office, before the time when the certificate or decision is certified to the town clerk, shall not be invalidated by reason of that declaration.

Provisions as to elections in the room of persons unseated on petition.

Sect. 103. Where on an election petition the election of any person to a corporate office has been declared void, and no other person has been declared elected in his room, a new election shall be held to supply the vacancy in the same manner as on a casual vacancy; and for the purposes of the election any duties to be performed by a mayor, alderman, or other officer, shall, if he has been declared not elected, be performed by a deputy, or other person who might have acted for him if he had been incapacitated by illness.

Prohibition of disclosure of vote.

Sect. 104. A person who has voted at a municipal election by ballot shall not in any proceeding to question the election be required to state for whom he has voted.

PART V.

Corporate Property and Liabilities.

Misapplication of Corporate Property.

Prohibition of expenditure of corporate funds on parliamentary elections.

Sect. 124.—(1.) It shall not be lawful for a municipal corporation, or the council of a borough, or a corporate officer, or a trustee, or other person acting for a municipal corporation, to pay or apply any money, stocks, funds, securities, or personal property, of or held in trust for the corporation, in payment of any expenses occasioned by a parliamentary election or incurred by any person offering himself as a candidate at or before a parliamentary election.

(2.) Any bond, covenant, recognisance, or judgment given by a corporation, council, officer, trustee, or person as aforesaid, for securing payment of such expenses, shall be void.

(3.) Any payment, application, bond, covenant, recognisance, or judgment made or given by a corporation, council, officer, trustee, or person as aforesaid, for inducing any person to labour in a parliamentary election at a future time, or to pay or incur expenses as aforesaid at a future time, shall be deemed to be forbidden and declared void by this section, although colourably made or given for any other cause or consideration.

(4.) Any mortgage or other disposition of corporate land for securing or satisfying any expenses or engagements incurred or to be incurred as aforesaid, and any estate or charge thereby created, shall be void.

(5.) Any resolution, bye-law, or other proceeding of a council, purporting to direct or authorize any payment or thing forbidden by this section, or made or adopted for evading the provisions thereof, shall be void.

(6.) If any member of a municipal corporation authorizes or directs any payment or application forbidden by this section, or assents to, or concurs or participates in, any affirmative vote or proceeding relating thereto, or signs or seals in his individual capacity, or affixes the corporate seal to, any instrument by this section declared void, he shall be guilty of a misdemeanour, and, on conviction thereof in the High Court, shall, in addition to such punishment as the court awards, be for ever disabled to take, hold, or exercise any office in the same corporation.

(7.) If any corporate officer, trustee, or other person as aforesaid, makes, or concurs in making, any payment or application of money or property as aforesaid, he shall be deemed to have done so in his own wrong, and he shall be individually liable to repay and make good the amount or value thereof to the corporation, notwithstanding any release or pretended indemnity given to him in the name or on behalf of the corporation. 45 & 46 Vict. c. 50, s. 124.

(8.) Any two or more burgesses may bring and prosecute any action in the name of the corporation against any officer, trustee, or person making any illegal payment or application as aforesaid, as if they, their executors and administrators, were jointly and severally appointed the irrevocable attorneys of the corporation for that purpose; but the plaintiffs shall, on the application of the defendant, give reasonable security, as the court directs, for costs, as between solicitor and client.

(9.) Nothing in this section shall affect the provisions of the Ballot Act, 1872, or of any other Act for the time being in force regulating the payment by the returning officer or otherwise of expenses relating to parliamentary elections.

PART XII.

Legal Proceedings.

Sect. 219.—(1.) In summary proceedings for offences and fines under this Act the information shall be laid within six months after the commission of the offence.

Prosecution of offences and recovery of fines.

(2.) Any person aggrieved by a conviction of a court of summary jurisdiction under this Act may appeal therefrom to a court of Quarter Sessions.

(3.) Any fine incurred under this Act and not recoverable summarily may be recovered by action in the High Court.

Sect. 220. A conviction, order, warrant, or other matter made or done or purporting to be made or done by virtue of this Act shall not be quashed for want of form, and shall not, unless it is an order of the council for payment of money out of the borough fund, be removed by certiorari or otherwise into the High Court.

Exclusion of certiorari.

Sect. 221.—(1.) Where by any Act passed or to be passed, any fine, penalty, or forfeiture is made recoverable in a summary manner before any justice or justices and payable to the Crown or to any body corporate, or to any person whomsoever, the same if recovered and adjudged before any justice of a borough having a separate court of quarter sessions shall, notwithstanding anything in the Act under which it is recovered, be recovered for and adjudged to be paid to the treasurer of the borough.

Application of penalties in quarter sessions boroughs.

(2.) But this section shall not apply to a fine, penalty, or forfeiture, or part thereof, where the Act under which it is recovered—

(*a*.) Directs payment thereof to the informer or to any person aggrieved; or

(*b*.) If passed since the Municipal Corporations Act, 1835, directs that the same shall go in any other manner and not to the borough fund; or

(*c*.) Relates to the customs, excise, or post office, or to trade or navigation, or to any branch of the revenue of the Crown.

Sect. 222. Where the offices of town clerk and clerk of the peace for a borough are not held by the same person, the clerk of the peace shall perform all duties imposed on the town clerk by the Act of the third year of King George the Fourth, chapter forty-six, "for the more speedy return and levying of fines, penalties, and forfeitures, and recognizances estreated;" and the clerk of the peace shall make all returns, issue all processes, and do all other acts required by that Act to be made, issued, and done by the town clerk.

Duties of clerk of peace as to fines and forfeitures.

Sect. 223. Any summons for appearance, warrant to enforce appearance warrant for apprehension, or search warrant, may, if issued by a justice for a borough, be served or executed in any county wherein the borough or any part thereof is situate, or within any distance not exceeding seven miles from the borough, and, within those limits, shall have the same effect as if it had been issued or indorsed by a justice having jurisdiction in the place where it is served or executed, and may be served or executed by the constable or special constable to whom it is directed.

Service of summons or warrant

45 & 46 Vict. c. 50, s. 224.

Procedure in penal actions against corporate officers

Sect. 224.—(1.) An action to recover a fine from any person for acting in a corporate office without having made the requisite declaration, or without being qualified, or after ceasing to be qualified, or after becoming disqualified, may not be brought except by a burgess of the borough, and shall not lie unless the plaintiff has within fourteen days after the cause of action arose, served a notice in writing personally on the person liable to the fine of his intention to bring the action, nor unless the action is commenced within hree months after the cause of action arose.

(2.) The court or a judge shall, on the application of the defendant within fourteen days after he has been served with writ of summons in the action, require the plaintiff to give security for costs.

(3.) Unless judgment is given for the plaintiff, the defendant shall be entitled to costs, to be taxed as between solicitor and client.

(4.) Where any such action is brought against a person on the ground of his not being qualified in respect of estate, it shall lie on him to prove that he was so qualified.

(5.) A moiety of the fine recovered shall, after payment of the costs of action, be paid to the plaintiff.

Quo warranto and mandamus

Sect. 225.—(1.) An application for an information in the nature of a quo warranto against any person claiming to hold a corparate office shall not be made after the expiration of twelve months from the time when he became disqualified. after election.

(2.) In the case of such an application, or of an application for a mandamus to proceed to an election of a corporate officer, the applicant shall give notice in writing of the application to the person to be affected thereby (in this section called the respondent) at any time not less than ten days before the day in the notice specified for making the application.

(3.) The notice shall set forth the name and description of the applicant, and a statement of the grounds of the application.

(4.) The applicant shall deliver with the notice a copy of the affidavits whereby the application will be supported.

(5.) The respondent may show cause in the first instance against the application.

(6.) If sufficient cause is not shown, the court, on proof of due service of the notice, statement, and copy of affidavits used in support of the application, may, if it thinks fit, make the rule for the information or mandamus absolute.

(7.) The court may, if it thinks fit, direct that any issue of fact on an information be tried by jury in London or at Westminster.

(8.) The court may, if it thinks fit, direct that any writ of mandamus issued shall be peremptory in the first instance.

Provisions for protection of persons acting under Act.

Sect. 226.—(1.) An action, prosecution, or proceeding against any person for any act done in pursuance or execution or intended execution of this Act, or in respect of any alleged neglect or default in the execution of this Act, shall not lie or be instituted unless it is commenced within six months next after the act or thing is done or omitted, or, in case of a continuance of injury or damage, within six months next after the ceasing thereof.

(2.) Where the action is for damages, tender of amends before the action was commenced may, in lieu of or in addition to any other plea, be pleaded. If the action was commenced after the tender, or is proceeded with after payment into court of any money in satisfaction of the plaintiff's claim, and the plaintiff does not recover more than the sum tendered or paid, he shall not recover any costs incurred after the tender or payment, and the defendant shall be entitled to costs, to be taxed as between solicitor and client, as from the time of the tender or payment; but this provision shall not affect costs of any injunction in the action.

(3.) Subject and without prejudice to any other powers, the council, where the defendant in any such action, prosecution, or other proceeding is their officer, agent, or servant, may, if they think fit, except so far as the court before which the action, prosecution, or other proceeding is heard and determined otherwise directs, pay out of the borough fund or borough rate all or any part of any sums payable by the defendant in or in consequence of the action, prosecution, or proceeding, whether in respect of costs, charges, expenses, damages, fine, or otherwise.

45 & 46 Vict. c. 50, s. 226.

Sect. 227.—(1.) Where a person charged with a petty misdemeanour is brought without the warrant of a justice into the custody of a borough constable during his attendance at a watch-house in the borough, at any time (by day or night) at which a justice is not actually sitting for the public administration of justice at the justices' room, or town hall, or other place used for that purpose in the borough, the constable may, if he thinks fit, take bail without fee from that person, by recognisance conditioned for his appearance for examination within two days before a justice in the borough at some time and place therein specified.

Power for borough constables to take bail.

(2.) A recognisance so taken shall be of equal obligation on the parties entering into the same, and liable to the same proceedings for the estreating thereof, as if taken before a justice.

(3.) The constable shall enter in a book, kept for that purpose in every watch-house, the name, residence, and occupation of the person entering into the recognisance, and of his surety or sureties, if any, with the condition of the recognisance, and the sums acknowledged.

(4.) The constable shall lay the book before the justice present at the time when and place where the recognisor is required to appear.

(5.) If the recognisor does not appear at the time and place required, or within one hour after, the justice shall cause a record of the recognisance to be drawn up and signed by the constable, and shall return the same to the next court of quarter sessions for the borough, or, if the borough has no separate court of quarter sessions, for the county in which the borough is situate, with a certificate at the back thereof, signed by the justice, that the recognisor has not complied with the obligation therein contained.

(6.) The clerk of the peace shall make the like estreats and schedules of every such recognisance as of recognisances forfeited in quarter sessions.

(7.) If the recognisor applies by any person on his behalf to postpone the hearing of the charge against him, and the justice thinks fit to consent thereto, the justice may enlarge the recognisance to such further time as he appoints.

(8.) When the matter is heard and determined, either by the dismissal of the charge, or by binding over the recognisor to answer the matter of the complaint at quarter sessions, or otherwise, the recognisance for his appearance before a justice shal be discharged without fee.

PART XIII.

General.

Boundaries.

Sect. 228.—(1.) Every place at the commencement of this Act included within each borough then existing, and no other place, shall be part of the borough, and in each borough then existing which is a county of itself, shall be part of that county and of no other, as if this Act had not been passed.

Boundaries of boroughs and transfer of parts to counties.

(2.) Where under the Municipal Corporations Act, 1835, or any Act amending it, any such county or borough does not, at the commencement of this Act, include a place which, before the passing of the Municipal Corporations Act, 1835, was part thereof, that place shall continue to be part of the county wherein it is situate, or with which it has the longest common boundary, as if this Act had not been passed.

(3.) But nothing in this Act shall prevent any gaol, house of correction, lunatic asylum, court of justice, or judges' lodging, which at the passing of the Municipal Corporations Act, 1835, was, and at the commencement of this Act is, taken to be, for any purpose, in any county, from being still, for that purpose, taken to be in that county, as if this Act had not been passed.

45 & 46 Vict. 50, s. 228.

(4.) Any gaol, court, depôt for arms, and any land thereto belonging, which at the commencement of this Act is parcel of a county shall continue to be parcel of the county, and under the exclusive jurisdiction of the authorities of the county, as if this Act had not been passed.

(5.) Nothing in this Act shall be construed to affect the assessments of the land tax or assessed taxes, as those assessments exist at the commencement of this Act, or to extend or diminish the jurisdiction of any commissioners of those taxes, as such commissioners then exist; but all lands, and all parishes, parts of parishes, and places shall continue to be charged as at the commencement of this Act towards the land tax charged on the county or other district whereof at the commencement of this Act they are part, and to be subject in that behalf to the jurisdiction of the commissioners of the same county or other district, as if this Act had not been passed.

Adjustment between boroughs and counties on change of boundaries.

Sect. 229. If any place, which under the Municipal Corporations Act, 1835, or any Act amending it, ceased to be included in a borough or county of a town or city, was before the passing of the Municipal Corporations Act, 1835, liable to contribute to any rate for satisfying any lawful debt to which the ratepayers of that borough or county were then liable, and if after the commencement of this Act any difference arises concerning the proportion of that debt to be contributed in respect of that place, the Secretary of State, on the application of the council, or of the chairman of a public meeting of the ratepayers of the place, may appoint by writing under his hand a barrister not having any interest in the question to arbitrate between the parties, and by his award under his hand and seal to assess the proportion aforesaid, if any; and the arbitrator shall assess the costs of the arbitration, and direct by whom and in what proportion and out of what fund they shall be paid; and the rate aforesaid shall continue to be levied by warrant of the council and to be paid by the place aforesaid to the treasurer of the borough, as if the Municipal Corporations Act, 1835, or any Act amending it, or this Act, had not been passed, until the proportion aforesaid is satisfied, and no longer.

Time.

Computation of time.

Sect. 230.—(1.) Where by this Act any limited time from or after any date or event is appointed or allowed for the doing of any act or the taking of any proceeding, then in the computation of that limited time the same shall be taken as exclusive of the day of that date or of the happening of that event, and as commencing at the beginning of the next following day; and the act or proceeding shall be done or taken at the latest on the last day of the limited time as so computed, unless the last day is a Sunday, Christmas Day, Good Friday, or Monday or Tuesday in Easter week, or a day appointed for public fast, humiliation, or thanksgiving, in which case any act or proceeding shall be considered as done or taken in due time if it is done or taken on the next day afterwards, not being one of the days in this section specified.

(2.) Where by this Act any act or proceeding is directed or allowed to be done or taken on a certain day, then if that day happens to be one of the days in this section specified, the act or proceeding shall be considered as done or taken in due time if it is done or taken on the next day afterwards, not being one of the days in this section specified.

(3.) Where by this Act any act or proceeding is directed or allowed to be done or taken within any time not exceeding seven days, the days in this section specified shall not be reckoned in the computation of such time.

Distance.

Measurement of distances.

Sect. 231. The distances mentioned in this Act shall be measured in a straight line on a horizontal plane, and may be determined by the map made under the survey commonly known as the Ordnance Survey.

Notices.

Notices on town hall.

Sect. 232. Any notice or other document required by this Act to be fixed on the town hall shall be fixed in some conspicuous place on or near the outer door of the town hall, or, if there is no town hall, in some conspicuous place in the borough or ward to which the notice or document relates. 45 & 46 Vict. c. 50, s. 232.

Inspection and Copies.

Sect. 233.—(1.) The minutes of proceedings of the council shall be open to the inspection of a burgess on payment of a fee of one shilling, and a burgess may make a copy thereof or take an extract therefrom. Inspection of documents.

(2.) A burgess may make a copy of or take an extract from an order of the council for the payment of money.

(3.) The treasurer's accounts shall be open to the inspection of the council, and a member of the council may make a copy thereof or take an extract therefrom.

(4.) The abstract of the treasurer's accounts shall be open to the inspection of all the ratepayers of the borough, and copies thereof shall be delivered to a ratepayer on payment of a reasonable price for each copy.

(5.) The Freemen's Roll shall be open to public inspection, and the town clerk shall deliver copies thereof to any person on payment of a reasonable price for each copy.

(6.) A document directed by this Act to be open to inspection shall be so open at any reasonable time during the ordinary hours of business, and without payment, unless it is otherwise expressed.

(7.) If a person having the custody of any document in this section mentioned,—

(*a.*) Obstructs any person authorized to inspect the same in making such inspection thereof as in this section mentioned; or

(*b.*) Refuses to give copies or extracts to any person entitled to obtain the same under this section;

he shall, on summary conviction, be liable to a fine not exceeding five pounds.

Fees.

Sect. 234. The town clerk of every borough shall cause a true copy of the tables of fees for the time being authorized to be taken by the clerk of the peace (if any) for the borough, by the clerk to the justices (if any) for the borough, and by the registrar and officers of the borough civil court (if any), to be posted conspicuously in the following places: Tables of fees to be posted.

(*a.*) The room where the business of the town clerk's office is transacted;

(*b.*) The room, if any, where the justices of the borough sit for transacting their business;

(*c.*) The room, if any, where the court of quarter sessions of the borough is held; and

(*d.*) The room, if any, where the borough civil court is held.

Seals and Signatures.

Sect. 235. If any person forges the seal or signature affixed or subscribed to a bye-law made under this Act, or the signature subscribed to any minute of proceedings of the council, or tenders in evidence any such document with a false or counterfeit seal or signature, knowing it to be false or counterfeit, he shall be liable to imprisonment with hard labour for any term not exceeding two years. Forgery.

Applications to Treasury.

Sect. 236.—(1.) Where the council intend to apply to the Treasury for their approval of any sale, loan, or other financial arrangement under this Act notice of the intention to make the application shall be fixed on the town hall one month at least before the application, and a copy of the intended application shall during that month be kept in the town clerk's office, and be open to public inspection. Notice of application to and correspondence with Treasury.

(2.) If the Treasury either refuse their approval or grant it conditionally or under qualifications, notice of the correspondence between the Treasury and the council

45 & 46 Vict. c. 50, s. 236.

shall forthwith and during one month be fixed on the town hall, and a copy of the correspondence shall during that month be kept in the town clerk's office, and be open to public inspection.

Deputy.

Acts of deputy not to be invalidated by defect in appointment.

Sect. 237. No defect in the appointment of a deputy under this Act shall invalidate his acts.

Overseers.

Notices to and acting of overseers.

Sect. 238.—(1.) Every matter by the Municipal Corporations Acts directed to be done by overseers may be lawfully done by the major part of them.

(2.) Any notice by the Municipal Corporations Acts required to be given to overseers may be delivered to any one of them, or left at his place of abode, or at his office for transacting parochial business.

Declarations and Oaths.

Power to administer oaths &c.

Sect. 239. (1.) Whereby or under this Act a declaration or oath is required to be made or taken by the holder of a corporate office or other person before the council or any members thereof, or any other persons, they shall have authority to receive and administer the same without any commission or authority other than this Act.

(2.) Nothing in this Act in any case shall require or authorise the taking or making of any oath or declaration that would not have been required or authorised under the Promissory Oaths Act, 1868, or otherwise by law, if this Act had not been passed, or interfere with the operation of the Promissory Oaths Act, 1868.

31 & 32 Vict. c. 72

Forms.

Forms in schedule

Sect. 240. The forms in the Eighth Schedule or forms to the like effect, varied as circumstances require, may be used, and shall be sufficient in law.

Misnomer or Inaccurate Description.

Misnomer or inaccurate description not to hinder

Sect. 241. No misnomer or inaccurate description of any person, body corporate, or place named in any schedule to the Municipal Corporations Act, 1835, or in any roll, list, notice, or voting paper required by this Act, shall hinder the full operation of this Act with respect to that person, body corporate, or place, provided the description of that person, body corporate, or place be such as to be commonly understood.

Substitution in former Acts.

Provision for references in unrepealed enactments to 5 & 6 Will. IV c. 76, &c.

Sect. 242.—(1.) In the several enactments described in Part I. of the Ninth Schedule, a reference to this Act shall be deemed to be substituted for a reference to the Municipal Corporations Act, 1835, and any Act amending it.

(2.) In each of the enactments described in Part II. of the Ninth Schedule, there shall be substituted for the respective provision of the Municipal Corporations Act, 1835, in that part mentioned in connexion therewith, such provision of this Act as is also mentioned in connexion therewith.

(3.) Where any Act passed before this Act, and not specified in the First or in the Ninth Schedule, refers to the Municipal Corporations Act, 1835, or any Act amending it, or to boroughs or corporations subject to that Act or any Act amending it, the reference shall be deemed to be to this Act or to the corresponding provision of this Act, or to boroughs or corporations subject to this Act (as the case may require).

(4.) All enactments to which this section relates shall, except as in this section provided, continue to operate as if this Act had not been passed.

Short titles of Acts partly repealed.

Sect. 243. Such of the Acts specified in the First Schedule as will remain in force to any extent after the commencement of this Act may continue to be cited by the short titles in that schedule mentioned.

Returning Officers at Parliamentary Elections.

45 & 46 Vict. c. 50, s. 244.

Mayor of certain boroughs to be returning officer in parliamentary elections.

Sect. 244.—(1.) In boroughs, other than cities and towns being counties of themselves, the mayor shall be the returning officer at parliamentary elections; but this provision shall not extend to the borough of Berwick-upon-Tweed.

(2.). If there are more mayors than one within the boundaries of a parliamentary borough, the mayor of that borough to which the writ of election is directed shall be the returning officer.

(3.) If when a mayor is required to act as returning officer the mayor is absent, or incapable of acting, or there is no mayor, the council shall forthwith choose an alderman to be returning officer.

Disfranchised Parliamentary Boroughs

Electors in disfranchised boroughs. 30 & 31 Vict. c. 102

Sect. 245. Where a borough has, in pursuance of the Representation of the People Act, 1867, or of any Act passed in the session of the thirty-first and thirty-second years of the reign of Her Majesty, ceased to return a member to serve in Parliament, and the persons entitled to vote for the member or members formerly returned by the borough were by law electors for any other purpose, the burgesses of the borough shall be electors for that purpose, and shall in all respects, as regards that purpose, be substituted for the persons so entitled to vote.

Licensing.

Explanation of terms "town corporate," &c. in Licensing Act.

Sect. 246. In the Act of the ninth year of the reign of King George the Fourth, chapter sixty-one, "to regulate the granting of licences to keepers of inns, alehouses, and victualling houses in England," the expressions "town corporate," "county or place," and "division or place," include every borough having a separate commission of the peace, and the expression "high constable" includes any constable of any such borough to whom the justices of the borough direct their precept under that Act.

Freedom of Trading.

Right of free trading in boroughs.

Sect. 247. Notwithstanding any custom or bye-law, every person in any borough may keep any shop for the sale of all lawful wares and merchandises by wholesale or retail, and use every lawful trade, occupation, mystery, and handicraft for hire, gain, sale, or otherwise within any borough.

Cinque Ports.

Special provisions as to certain of the Cinque Ports.

Sect. 248.—(1.) The boroughs of Hastings, Sandwich, Dover, Hythe, being four of the Cinque Ports, and the borough of Rye, are in this section referred to as the five boroughs.

(2.) The jurisdiction, powers, and authorities of the court of quarter sessions, recorder, coroner, and clerk of the peace for each of the five boroughs shall extend to the non-corporate members and liberties thereof, and to such corporate members thereof as have not a separate court of quarter sessions.

(3.) The jurisdiction, powers, and authorities of the persons constituted justices within and throughout the liberties of the Cinque Ports by virtue of their commission, shall extend to all places being within the limits of the five boroughs or of their members or liberties, corporate or non-corporate, and not being within the limits of a borough having a separate commission of the peace.

(4.) The justices for the five boroughs respectively shall have all the jurisdiction, powers, and authorities of justices for a county relating to the granting of licences or authorities to persons to keep inns, ale-houses, or victualling houses, or to sell exciseable liquors by retail within any of the corporate or non-corporate members or liberties of the five boroughs respectively, not being within the limits of a borough having a separate commission of the peace.

(5.) The non-corporate members and liberties of the five boroughs and such corporate members thereof as have not a separate court of quarter sessions shall be charged by the respective courts of quarter sessions of the five boroughs, with a due

45 & 46 Vict. c. 50, s. 248.

porportion of all those expenses of the five boroughs, to the payment whereof rates in the nature of county rates are applicable; and such rates may be assessed and levied in the manner in which rates of that description were assessed and levied before the passing of the Municipal Corporations Act, 1835, under any enactment then in force, but subject to the operation of any subsequent enactment affecting the same.

(6.) A due proportion of inhabitant householders to serve as grand jurors and jurors at the respective courts of quarter sessions of the five boroughs shall be summoned by the clerks of the peace thereof from the non-corporate members and liberties thereof, and such corporate members thereof as have not a separate court of quarter sessions; and the attendance of such jurors shall be enforced, and their defaults punished, in the manner by this Act directed with respect to jurors in boroughs.

32 & 33 Vict. c. 53.

(7.) Nothing in this section shall affect the Cinque Ports Act, 1869, or the Acts therein recited.

Cambridge.

Vice-Chancellor of Cambridge.

Sect. 249.—(1.) It shall be lawful for the Queen, from time to time, by her commission of the peace for the borough of Cambridge, to constitute the Vice-Chancellor for the time being of the University of Cambridge a justice for that borough.

(2.) He shall not, by reason of being so constituted, have any greater authority as to the grant of licences to alehouses than any other justice named in the commission.

(3.) But nothing in this section shall affect the rights and privileges which the Vice-Chancellor lawfully has or enjoys, or might have lawfully had or enjoyed if he were not so constituted a justice.

Savings.

Saving for existing corporations.

Sect. 250.—(1.) Nothing in this Act shall prejudicially affect any charter granted before the commencement of this Act, or take away, abridge, or prejudicially affect any of the rights, powers, privileges, estates, property, duties, liabilities, or obligations vested in or imposed on any municipal corporation existing at the commencement of this Act, or in or on the mayor, or the council of a borough then existing, or any members or committee of the council, by the incorporation of the inhabitants of the borough, or by transfer from any other authority, or otherwise; but every such charter shall continue to operate, and every such corporation shall continue to have perpetual succession and a common seal, and to be capable in law by the council to do and suffer all acts which at the commencement of this Act they and their successors respectively may lawfully do or suffer, and the corporation and all members and officers thereof and their sureties, and every such mayor, and every such council and committee, and every such officer, shall continue to have, enjoy, and be subject to the like rights, powers, offices, privileges, estates, property, duties, liabilities, and obligations, as if this Act had not been passed, without prejudice, nevertheless, to the operation of the repeal of enactments by this Act, and to the other express provisions of this Act.

(2.) Nothing in this Act shall alter the boundaries of any borough existing at the commencement of this Act, or the number, apportionment, or qualification of the aldermen or councillors thereof, or the division thereof into wards.

(3.) Nothing in this Act shall affect the right of the council of a borough to collect by their own officers the borough rate and watch rate, or either of them, where, at the commencement of this Act, they are authorized by law to so collect, and are so collecting, the same.

(4.) Nothing in this Act shall alter the respective jurisdiction of county and borough justices.

(5.) Nothing in this Act shall affect the right of any borough named in Schedule (A.) to the Municipal Corporations Act, 1835, to have a separate commission of the peace.

45 & 46 Vict. c. 50, s. 251.

Sect. 251. Nothing in this Act shall alter the effect of any local Act of Parliament.

Saving for local Acts.

Sect. 252. Nothing in this Act, except the provision referring to the Ninth Schedule, shall affect the Prison Act, 1865, or the Prison Act, 1877, and nothing in thi Act shall affect the Act of the session of the fifth and sixth years of Her Majesty, chapter ninety-eight, "to amend the laws concerning prisons," or revive or restore any enactment which, being contained in that Act, or in the Municipal Corporation (Justices) Act, 1850, or in any other Act, is virtually repealed or superseded by the Prison Act, 1865, or the Prison Act, 1877.

Saving for Prison Acts. 28 & 29 Vict. c. 126. 40 & 41 Vict. c. 21. 13 & 14 Vict. c. 91.

Sect. 253. Nothing in this Act shall compel the acceptance of any office or duty whatever in any borough by any military, naval, or marine officer in Her Majesty's service on full pay or half pay, or by any officer or other person employed and residing in any of Her Majesty's dockyards, victualling establishments, arsenals, barracks, or other naval or military establishments.

Saving for military and naval officers, &c.

Sect. 254. Nothing in this Act shall affect the watching, paving, or lighting, or the internal regulations for the government, of any of Her Majesty's dockyards, victualling establishments, arsenals, barracks, or other naval or military establishments, or make the tenements therein or the inhabitants thereof liable to any rate for watching, paving, or lighting.

Savings for dockyards, barracks, &c.

Sect. 255. Nothing in this Act shall affect the authority of justices vested in the Commissioners for executing the office of Lord High Admiral of the United Kingdom, or any authority to appoint coroners to act within the jurisdiction of the Admiralty.

Saving as to Admiralty.

Sect. 256. Nothing in this Act shall affect the jurisdiction and office of the Lord Warden in his office of Admiral of the Cinque Ports.

Saving for Lord Warden.

Sect. 257. Nothing in this Act shall—

(1.) Affect the rights, privileges, duties, or liabilities of the chancellor, masters, and scholars of the Universities of Oxford and Cambridge respectively, as by law possessed under the respective charters of those universities or otherwise ; or

(2.) Entitle the mayors of Oxford and Cambridge respectively to any precedence over the vice-chancellors of those Universities respectively ; or

(3.) Entitle any person to be enrolled a citizen of the city of Oxford or burgess of the borough of Cambridge by reason of his occupation of any rooms, chambers, or premises in any college or hall of either of those Universities ; or

(4.) Compel any resident member of either of those universities to accept any office in or under the municipal corporation of Oxford or of Cambridge ; or

(5.) Authorize the levy of any rate within the precincts of those universities, or of any of the colleges or halls thereof, which now by law cannot be levied therein, or make either of those universities, or the members thereof, liable to any rate to which they are not liable to contribute at the commencement of this Act ; or

(6.) Authorize the transfer of any rights or liabilities by a local authority to the municipal corporation of the borough of Cambridge without the consent of the chancellor, master, and scholars of the University of Cambridge ; or

(7.) Affect the rights or privileges granted by charter or Act of Parliament to the University of Durham.

Saving for universities.

Sect. 258. Nothing in this Act shall prevent any jurisdiction or authority exercised in or over the precinct or close of any cathedral from being continued concurrently with the jurisdiction and authority of the justices of the borough in which the precinct or close is situate.

Saving for jurisdiction over cathedral precincts.

45 & 46 Vict. c. 50, s. 259.

Saving for royal prerogative.

Sect. 259. Nothing in this Act shall prejudicially affect Her Majesty's royal prerogative; and the enabling provisions of this Act shall be deemed to be in addition to, and not in derogation of, the powers exercisable by Her Majesty by virtue of her royal prerogative.

Saving as to repealed enactments.

Sect. 260. —(1.) The repeal effected by this Act shall not affect—

(*a.*) Anything done or suffered before the commencement of this Act under any enactment repealed by this Act; or

(*b.*) Any proceeding or thing pending or in course of being done at the commencement of this Act under any enactment repealed by this Act; or

(*c.* Any jurisdiction or practice established, confirmed, or transferred, or right or privilege acquired or confirmed, or duty or liability imposed or incurred, or compensation secured, by or under any enactment repealed by this Act; or

(*d.*) Any disability or disqualification existing at the commencement of this Act under any enactment repealed by this Act; or

(*e.*) Any fine, forfeiture, punishment, or other consequence incurred or to be incurred in respect of any offence committed before the commencement of this Act against any enactment repealed by this Act; or

(*f.*) The institution or the prosecution to its termination of any legal proceeding or other remedy for ascertaining, enforcing, or recovering any such jurisdiction, practice, right, privilege, duty, liability, compensation, disability, disqualification, fine, forfeiture, punishment, or consequence as aforesaid; or

(*g.*) The terms on which any money has been borrowed before the commencement of this Act under any enactment repealed by this Act.

(2.) The repeal effected by this Act shall not extend to Scotland or Ireland, and shall not, as regards the enactments described in Part II. of the First Schedule, operate in respect of any place other than a borough to which this Act applies, and shall not revive or restore any statute, law, usage, custom, royal or other charter, grant, letters patent, bye-law, jurisdiction, office, right, title, claim, privilege, liability, disqualification, exemption, restriction, practice, procedure, or other matter or thing abolished by the Municipal Corporations Act, 1835, or not in force or existing at the commencement of this Act, or otherwise affect the past operation of any enactment repealed by this Act.

(3.) All elections, declarations, appointments, bye-laws, rates, tables of fees, and regulations made, or pending, or in the course of being made, and all other things done, or pending, or in the course of being done, under the Municipal Corporations Act, 1835, or any other enactment repealed by this Act, before or at the commencement of this Act, shall for the purposes of this Act be of the like effect as if they had been made or done, or were pending, or in the course of being made or done under this Act, and shall, as far as may be requisite for the continuance, validity, and effect thereof, be deemed to have been made or done, or may be carried on and be made or done, as the case may require, under this Act.

THE SECOND SCHEDULE.

MEETINGS AND PROCEEDINGS OF COUNCIL.

1. The council shall hold four quarterly meetings in every year for the transaction of general business.

2. The quarterly meetings shall be held at noon on each ninth of November, and at such hour on such other three days before the first of November then next following as the council at the quarterly meeting in November decide or afterwards from time to time by standing order determine.

3. The mayor may at any time call a meeting of the council.

4. If the mayor refuses to call a meeting after a requisition for that purpose, signed by five members of the council, has been presented to him, any five members of the council may forthwith, on that refusal, call a meeting. If the

mayor (without so refusing) does not within seven days after such presentation call a meeting, any five members of the council may, on the expiration of those seven days, call a meeting. 45 & 46 Vict. 50.

5. Three clear days at least before any meeting of the council, notice of the time and place of the intended meeting, signed by the mayor, or if the meeting is called by members of the council, by those members, shall be fixed on the town hall. Where the meeting is called by members of the council, the notice shall specify the business proposed to be transacted thereat.

6. Three clear days at least before any meeting of the council, a summons to attend the meeting, specifying the business proposed to be transacted thereat, and signed by the town clerk, shall be left or delivered by post in a registered letter at the usual place of abode of every member of the council, three clear days at least before the meeting.

7. Want of service of the summons on any member of the council shall not affect the validity of a meeting.

8. No business shall be transacted at a meeting other than that specified in the summons relating thereto, except in case of a quarterly meeting, business prescribed by this Act to be transacted thereat.

9. At every meeting of the council, the mayor, if present, shall be chairman. If the mayor is absent, then the deputy mayor, if chosen for that purpose by the members of the council then present, shall be chairman. If both the mayor and the deputy mayor are absent, or the deputy mayor, being present, is not chosen, then such alderman, or in the absence of all the aldermen, such councillor, as the members of the council then present choose, shall be chairman.

10. All acts of the council, and all questions coming or arising before the council, may be done and decided by the majority of such members of the council as are present and vote at a meeting held in pursuance of this Act, the whole number present at the meeting, whether voting or not, not being less than one third of the number of the whole council.

11. In case of equality of votes, the chairman of the meeting shall have a second or casting vote.

12. Minutes of the proceedings of every meeting shall be drawn up and fairly entered in a book kept for that purpose, and shall be signed in manner authorized by this Act.

13. Subject to the foregoing provisions of this Schedule, the council may from time to time make standing orders for the regulation of their proceedings and business, and vary or revoke the same.

THE THIRD SCHEDULE.

PART II.

Rules as to Nomination in Elections of Councillors.

1. Every candidate for the office of councillor must be nominated in writing.

2. The writing must be subscribed by two burgesses of the borough or, in the case of a ward election, of the ward, as proposer and seconder, and by eight other burgesses of the borough or ward, as assenting to the nomination.

3. Each candidate must be nominated by a separate nomination paper, but the same burgesses, or any of them, may subscribe as many nomination papers as there are vacancies to be filled, but no more.

4. Each person nominated must be enrolled in the burgess roll or entered in the separate non-resident list required by this Act to be made.

5. The nomination paper must state the surname and other names of the candidate, with his abode and description.

6. The town clerk shall provide nomination papers, and shall supply any burgess with as many nomination papers as may be required, and shall, at the request of any burgess, fill up a nomination paper.

7. Every nomination paper subscribed as aforesaid must be delivered by the

45 & 46 Vict. c. 50.

candidate, or his proposer or seconder, at the town clerk's office, seven days at least before the day of election, and before five o'clock in the afternoon of the last day for delivery of nomination papers.

8. The town clerk shall forthwith send notice of every such nomination to each candidate.

9. The mayor shall attend at the town hall on the day next after the last day for delivery of nomination papers for a sufficient time, between the hours of two and four in the afternoon, and shall decide on the validity of every objection made in writing to a nomination paper.

10. Where a person subscribes more nomination papers than one, his subscription shall be inoperative in all but the one which is first delivered.

11. Each candidate may, by writing signed by him, or, if he is absent from the United Kingdom, then his proposer or seconder may, by writing signed by him, appoint a person (in this schedule referred to as the candidate's representative) to attend the proceedings before the mayor on behalf of the candidate, and this appointment must be delivered to the town clerk before five o'clock in the afternoon of the last day for delivery of nomination papers.

12. Each candidate and his representative, but no other person, except for the purpose of assisting the mayor, shall be entitled to attend the proceedings before the mayor.

13. Each candidate and his representative may, during the time appointed for the attendance of the mayor for the purposes of this schedule, object to the nomination paper of any other candidate for the borough or ward.

14. The decision of the mayor shall be given in writing, and shall, if disallowing an objection, be final, but, if allowing an objection, shall be subject to reversal on petition questioning the election or return.

15. The town clerk shall at least four days before the day of election cause the surnames and other names of all persons validly nominated, with their respective abodes and descriptions, and the names of the persons subscribing their nomination papers as proposers and seconders, to be printed and fixed on the town hall, and in the case of a ward election, in some conspicuous place in the ward.

16. The nomination of a person absent from the United Kingdom shall be void, unless his written consent given within one month before the day of his nominatian in the presence of two witnesses is produced at the time of his nomination.

17. Where the number of valid nominations exceeds that of the vacancies, any candidate may withdraw from his candidature by notice signed by him, and delivered at the town clerk's office not later than two o'clock in the afternoon of the day next after the last day for delivery of nomination papers: Provided that such notices shall take effect in the order in which they are delivered, and that no such notice shall have effect so as to reduce the number of candidates ultimately standing nominated below the number of vacancies.

18. In and for the purposes of the provisions of this Act relating to proceedings preliminary to election, the burgess roll or ward roll which will be in force on the day of election shall be deemed to be the burgess roll or ward roll, and a person whose name is inserted in one of the lists from which the burgess roll or ward roll will be made up, shall be deemed to be enrolled in that roll although that roll is not yet completed.

PART III.

Modifications of the Ballot Act in its Application to Municipal Elections.

1. The provisions of the Ballot Act, 1872, with respect to the voting of a returning officer, the use of a room for taking a poll, and the right to vote of persons whose names are on the register of voters, and Rules 16 and 19 in the schedule to that Act, shall not apply in the case of a municipal election.

2. The mayor shall at least four days before the day of election give public

notice of the situation, division, and allotment of polling places for taking the poll at the election, and of the description of the persons entitled to vote thereat, and at the several polling stations. 45 & 46 Vict c. 50.

3. The mayor shall provide everything which in the case of a parliamentary election is required to be provided by the returning officer for the purpose of a poll, and shall appoint officers for taking the poll and counting the votes.

4. The mayor shall furnish every polling station with such number of compartments in which the voters can mark their votes screened from observation and furnish each presiding officer with such number of ballot papers, as in the judgment of the mayor may be necessary for effectually taking the poll at the election.

5. All expenses of the election shall be defrayed in manner by this Act provided.

6. No return shall be made to the clerk of the Crown in Chancery.

THE EIGHTH SCHEDULE.

FORMS.

Part I.—Declarations on Accepting Office.

FORM A.

FORM OF DECLARATION ON ACCEPTANCE OF CORPORATE OFFICE.

I, *A.B.*, having been elected mayor [*or* alderman, councillor, elective auditor, *or* revising assessor] for the borough of , hereby declare that I take the said office upon myself, and will duly and faithfully fulfil the duties thereof according to the best of my judgment and ability [*and in the case of the person being qualified by estate say,* And I hereby declare that I am seised or possessed of real or personal estate, or both [*as the case may be*], to the value or amount of one thousand pounds, or five hundred pounds [*as the case may require*], over and above what will satisfy my just debts].

Appendix D.

COMPENSATION TO CIVIL SERVANTS ON ABOLITION OF OFFICE.

The award of compensation allowances to established Civil Servants on the abolition of their offices is regulated by Sec. 7 of the Superannuation Act of 1859, which provides that :—

"It shall be lawful for the Commissioners of the Treasury to grant to any person "retiring or removed from the Public Service in consequence of the "abolition of his office, or for the purpose of facilitating improvements in "the organisation of the Department to which he belongs, by which greater "efficiency and economy can be effected, such special annual allowance by "way of compensation as, on a full consideration of the circumstances of "the case, may seem to the said Commissioners to be a reasonable and "just compensation for the loss of office ; and if the compensation shall "exceed the amount to which such person would have been entitled under "the Scale of Superannuation provided by this Act, if ten years were added to "the number of years which he may have actually served, such allowance "shall be granted by special Minute, stating the special grounds for "granting such allowance, which Minute shall be laid before Parliament, "and no such allowance shall exceed two-thirds of the salary and emolu- "ments of the office."

In calculating allowances under this section, it is the practice of the Treasury to award as many sixtieths of the officer's emoluments as he has served complete years, with a special addition, on account of abolition of office, not exceeding the following scale, viz. :—

Actual Service.	Addition.
20 years or upwards	$\frac{10}{60}$
15 ,, and less than 20	$\frac{7}{60}$
10 ,, and less than 15	$\frac{5}{60}$
5 ,, and less than 10	$\frac{3}{60}$
Under 5 ,,	$\frac{1}{60}$

When the duties of the situation have not been such as to require that the older should give his whole time to the Public Service, such deduction is made from the amount of compensation allowance for which he would otherwise be qualified as the Treasury may consider reasonable.

It must be observed that all awards under the section are at the absolute discretion of the Treasury, and are subject to modification if the circumstances of the particular case require it.

Non-established Civil Servants who have been employed for not less than seven years in an employment to which they were required to devote their whole time, receive a gratuity not exceeding one pound or one week's pay (whichever is greater) for each year of service, under section 4 of the Superannuation Act of 1877.

No gratuity can be granted to non-established Civil Servants whose duties have not required their whole time.

Appendix E.

Form of Claim.

To the Overseers of the parish [or township] of

I claim to have my name inserted (see note (*a.*)) in respect of the qualification named below [and I claim to have my name omitted from the corrupt and illegal practices list.]

Dated the day of 18

Name of the Claimant in full. Surname being first.	Place of Abode.	Nature of Qualification	Description of Qualifying Property.

(Signed) A. B.

(*a.*) Here insert according to circumstances.

(i.) Among the parliamentary voters for [the parliamentary division of] the county of [and county electors for the county of .]

(ii.) In the list of county electors of the county of .

(iii.) Among the parliamentary voters for the parliamentary borough of [and county electors for the county of .]

(iv.) Among the parliamentary voters for the [parliamentary division of] the county of [and burgesses for the municipal borough of .]

(v.) In the list of burgesses for the municipal borough of .

(vi.) Among the parliamentary voters for the parliamentary borough of [and burgesses for the municipal borough of .]

Form of Notice of Objection to be Given to the Overseers.

To the Overseers of the parish [or township] of

I hereby give you notice that I object to the name of being retained. (See note (*a.*)) [and to the omission of the said name from the corrupt and illegal practices list.]

Dated the day of 18

(Signed) A. B. [place of abode.]
On the list of (see note (*b.*)).

Form of Notice of Objection to be Given to the Person Objected to.

To

I hereby give you notice that I object to your name being retained (*see note* (*a.*)) [and to the omission of your name from the corrupt and illegal practices list] on the following grounds, viz. :—

(1.) That [*e.g.*, you have not occupied for twelve months to July 15th.]

(2.) That

(3.)

Dated the day of 18

(Signed) A. B., of (place of abode.)
On the list (*see note* (*b.*))

(*a.*) Here insert according to circumstances.

(i.) On the list as a parliamentary voter for [the parliamentary division of] the county of [and as a county elector for the county of .]

(ii.) On the list as a parliamentary voter for the parliamentary borough of [and as a county elector for the county of .]

(iii.) On the list as a parliamentary voter for [the parliamentary division of] the county of [and as a burgess for the municipal borough of .]
(iv.) On the list as a parliamentary voter for the parliamentary borough of [and as a burgess for the municipal borough of .]
(v.) On the list of county electors for the county of
(vi.) On the list of burgesses for the municipal borough of

N.B.—In each of the first four cases the notice of objection should, if there is more than one list, specify the list, and if the list is made out in divisions, should specify the division to which the objection refers. In the last two cases the notice must specify the division of the list to which the objection refers. In all cases if the lists contain two or more persons of the same name the notice of objection should distinguish the person intended to be objected to.

(*b.*) Here insert according to circumstances.
(i.) On the list of parliamentary voters [and county electors or burgesses] for the parish [or township] of
(ii.) On the list of county electors [or burgesses] for the parish [or township] of

Declaration for Correcting Misdescription in List.

I, of No. in the parish of in the county of [and in the parliamentary division of the county] do solemnly and sincerely declare as follows :—

(1.) I am the person referred to in division of the list of parliamentary voters and county electors made out in divisions (*specifying the particular list and division*) for the parish [or township] of by an entry as follows :—

Name as described in List.	Place of Abode as described in List.	Nature of Qualification as described in List.	Description of Qualifying Property.
Brown, John	High Street	Shop	2, Shoe Lane

(2.) My correct name and place of abode, and the correct particulars respecting my qualifications are, and ought to be stated, for the purposes of the register of parliamentary voters for the [parliamentary division of the] county of and the county register about to be made up of county electors for the county of (*as the case may be*) as follows :—

Correct Name.	Correct Place of Abode.	Correct Nature of Qualification.	General description of Qualifying Property.
Brown, Joseph	15, High Street	House	11, Shoe Lane

Dated this day of 18

(Signed) John Brown.

Made and subscribed before me, this day of 18

A. B.,
Justice of the Peace for .

N.B.—This form, of course, must be adapted to suit the various cases.

Appendix F.—FORM OF RATE BOOK.

An Assessment for the Relief of the Poor of the Parish of   in the County of   , and for other purposes chargeable thereon, made this 1st day of October, in the year of our Lord One thousand eight hundred and eighty-eight, after the Rate of One Shilling in the Pound, which is estimated to meet all the expenses for the above purposes which will be incurred before the 25th day of March next.

	ARREARS.		RATE.									COLLECTION.							Name of every Man other than the Owner or other Person rated, or liable to be rated, in respect of a Hereditament, comprising a Dwelling-house or Dwelling-houses within the meaning of the representation of the People Act, who is entitled to be registered as a Voter in respect of his being an Inhabitant Occupier of any such Dwelling-house; and Name of every Man being an Inhabitant Occupier of a Dwelling-house in respect of which no person is rated by reason of such Dwelling-house belonging to, or being occupied on behalf of, the Crown, or by reason of any other ground of exemption; and the Situation or Description of the Dwelling-house (*48 Vict. c. 3, s. 9*).	
															Uncollected at Balancing this Book.					
																Irrecoverable at Balancing this Book.				
																	Otherwise not Recoverable.			
No.	Due, or if Excused.	If excused, write the word "Excused."	Name of Occupier.	Name of Owner.	Description of Property Rated.	Name or Situation of Property.	Estimated Extent.	Gross Estimated Rental.	Rateable Value.	Rate at 1s. in the pound.	Amount of Rate assessed upon and payable by the Owner, instead of the Occupier, by virtue of the Statute or Statutes in that behalf.	Recoverable Arrears of former Rates.	Total Amount to be Collected.	Amount actually Collected.	Recoverable Arrear at Balancing the Book.	Amount legally excused.	Amo'nt	Causes.	Name of Man.	Situation or Description of Dwelling-house.
1.	2.	3.	4.	5.	6.	7.	8.	9.	10.	11.	12.	13.	14.	15.	16.	17.	18.	19.		
	£ s. d.						A. R. P.	£ s. d.	£ s. d.	£ s. d.	£ s. d.	£ s. d.	£ s. d.	£ s. d.	£ s. d.	£ s. d.	£ s. d.			

We declare that the total of the above rate amounts to the sum of   pounds   shillings and   pence.

We, the undersigned, do declare that one of us, or some person on our behalf, has examined and compared the several particulars in the respective columns of the above rate with the Valuation List made under the authority of the Union Assessment Committee Act of 1862, in force *in this Parish*, and the several hereditaments are, to the best of our belief, rated according to the value appearing in such **Valuation List.**

A.B }
C. D. } *Churchwardens.*

E. F. }
G. H. } *Overseers.*

Appendix G.

THE CONSTITUTION OF COUNTY COUNCILS.

THE number of County Councillors for each County Council in England and Wales, as fixed by the Orders of the Local Government Board, is as follows:—

ENGLAND.

BEDFORD—

Bedford	6
Dunstable	2
Luton	7
Remainder of County	36
Total	51

BERKS—

Abingdon	2
Maidenhead	2
Newbury	3
New Windsor	3
Wallingford	1
Wokingham	1
Remainder of County	39
Total	51

BUCKS—

Buckingham	1
Chipping Wycombe	3
Remainder of County	47
Total	51

CAMBRIDGE (exclusive of ISLE OF ELY)—

Cambridge	14
Remainder of Division	34
Total	48

CAMBRIDGE (ISLE OF ELY DIVISION)—

Wisbech	6
Remainder of Division	36
Total	42

CHESTER—

Congleton	1
Crewe	3

CHESTER—*continued.*

Hyde	3
Macclesfield	4
Stalybridge	3
Remainder of County	43
Total	57

CORNWALL—

Bodmin	1
Falmouth	1
Helston	1
Launceston	1
Liskeard	1
Penryn	1
Penzance	2
St. Ives	1
Truro	2
Remainder of County	55
Total	66

CUMBERLAND—

Carlisle	8
Workington	3
Remainder of County	49
Total	60

DERBY—

Chesterfield	2
Glossop	3
Ilkeston	2
Remainder of County	53
Total	60

DEVON—

Barnstaple	2
Bideford	1
Clifton, Dartmouth, Hardness	1

DEVON—*continued.*

Tiverton	2
Remainder of County	72
Total	78

DORSET—

Bridport	2
Dorchester	2
Lyme Regis	1
Poole	3
Shaftesbury	1
Wareham	1
Weymouth & Melcombe Regis	3
Remainder of County	44
Total	57

DURHAM—

Darlington	4
Durham	2
Hartlepool	2
Jarrow	3
Stockton-on-Tees	4
West Hartlepool	3
Remainder of County	54
Total	72

ESSEX—

Chelmsford	1
Colchester	3
Harwich	1
Maldon	1
Saffron Walden	1
Remainder of County	56
Total	63

GLOUCESTER—

Cheltenham	6
Tewkesbury	1
Remainder of County	53
Total	60

HEREFORD—

Hereford	8
Leominster	2
Remainder of County	41
Total	51

HERTS—

Hertford	2
St. Albans	3
Remainder of County	49
Total	54

HUNTS—

Godmanchester	1
Huntingdon	3

HUNTS—*continued.*

St. Ives	2
Remainder of County	33
Total	39

KENT—

Deal	1
Dover	3
Faversham	1
Folkestone	2
Gravesend	2
Maidstone	3
Margate	2
Ramsgate	2
Rochester	2
Remainder of County	54
Total	72

LANCASTER—

Accrington	2
Ashton-under-Lyne	2
Bacup	2
Blackpool	1
Chorley	1
Clitheroe	1
Darwen	2
Heywood	1
Lancaster	1
Middleton	1
Mossley	1
Southport	2
Warrington	3
Remainder of County	85
Total	105

LEICESTER—

Loughborough	3
Remainder of County	51
Total	54

LINCOLN (HOLLAND)—

Boston	7
Remainder of parts of Holland	35
Total	42

LINCOLN (KESTEVEN)—

Grantham	7
Stamford	4
Remainder of parts of Kesteven	37
Total	48

LINCOLN (LINDSEY)—

Great Grimsby	6

LINCOLN (LINDSEY)—*continued.*

Louth	2
Remainder of parts of Lindsey	49
Total	57

MIDDLESEX . . 54

MONMOUTH—

Monmouth	1
Newport	8
Remainder of County	39
Total	48

NORFOLK—

King's Lynn	3
Thetford	1
Remainder of County	53
Total	57

NORTHAMPTON (exclusive of the SOKE OF PETERBOROUGH)—

Brackley	1
Daventry	1
Remainder of County	49
Total	51

NORTHAMPTON (SOKE OF PETERBOROUGH)—

Peterborough	20
Remainder of Soke	10
Total	30

NORTHUMBERLAND—

Berwick-on-Tweed	3
Morpeth	1
Tynemouth	9
Remainder of County	47
Total	60

NOTTS—

East Retford	2
Newark	4
Remainder of County	45
Total	51

OXFORD—

Banbury	1
Chipping Norton	1
Henley-on-Thames	1
Oxford	11
Remainder of County	43
Total	57

RUTLAND 21

SALOP—

Bridgnorth	1
Ludlow	1
Oswestry	2
Shrewsbury	5
Wenlock	4
Remainder of County	38
Total	51

SOMERSET—

Bridgewater	2
Glastonbury	1
Taunton	2
Wells	1
Yeovil	1
Remainder of County	59
Total	66

SOUTHAMPTON—

Andover	1
Basingstoke	1
Newport	2
Romsey	1
Ryde	2
Winchester	3
Remainder of County	65
Total	75

STAFFORD—

Burslem	3
Burton-on-Trent	4
Lichfield	1
Longton	2
Newcastle-under-Lyme	2
Stafford	2
Stoke-upon-Trent	2
Wednesbury	2
Remainder of County	57
Total	75

SUFFOLK (EASTERN DIVISION)—

Aldeburgh	1
Beccles	2
Eye	1
Lowestoft	6
Southwold	1
Remainder of Division	46
Total	57

SUFFOLK (WESTERN DIVISION)—

Bury St. Edmunds	6

SUFFOLK (WESTERN DIVISION)—*continued.*

Sudbury	3
Remainder of Division	39
Total	48

SURREY—

Guildford	2
Kingston-on-Thames	3
Reigate	3
Remainder of County	49
Total	57

SUSSEX (EASTERN DIVISION)—

Eastbourne	5
Lewes	3
Rye	1
Remainder of Division	42
Total	51

SUSSEX (WESTERN DIVISION)—

Arundel	1
Chichester	3
Remainder of Division	41
Total	45

WARWICK—

Leamington	4
Stratford-on-Avon	1
Sutton Coldfield	1
Warwick	2
Remainder of County	46
Total	54

WESTMORELAND—

Appleby	1
Kendal	8
Remainder of County	33
Total	42

WILTS—

Devizes	1
Malmesbury	1
Marlborough	1
Salisbury	3
Remainder of County	54
Total	60

WORCESTER—

Bewdley	1
Droitwich	1
Evesham	1
Kidderminster	4
Remainder of County	50
Total	57

YORK (EAST RIDING)—

Beverley	4
Remainder of Riding	47
Total	51

YORK (NORTH RIDING)—

Richmond	1
Scarborough	6
Remainder of Riding	53
Total	60

YORK (WEST RIDING)—

Barnsley	2
Batley	2
Dewsbury	2
Doncaster	2
Harrogate	1
Keighley	2
Morley	1
Pontefract	1
Ripon	1
Rotherham	2
Wakefield	2
Remainder of Riding	72
Total	90

WALES.

ANGLESEY—

Beaumaris	2
Remainder of County	40
Total	42

BRECKNOCK—

Brecknock	5
Remainder of County	40
Total	45

CARDIGAN—

Aberystwith	4
Cardigan	2
Lampeter	1
Remainder of County	41
Total	48

CARMARTHEN—

Carmarthen	4
Kidwelly	1

CARMARTHEN—*continued.*	
Llandovery	1
Remainder of County	45
Total	51
CARNARVON—	
Bangor	4
Carnarvon	4
Conway	1
Pwllheli	1
Remainder of County	38
Total	48
DENBIGH—	
Denbigh	3
Ruthin	1
Wrexham	4
Remainder of County	40
Total	48
FLINT—	
Flint	3
Remainder of County	39
Total	42

GLAMORGAN—	
Aberavon	1
Neath	2
Remainder of County	63
Total	66
MERIONETH	42
MONTGOMERY—	
Llanfyllin	1
Llanidloes	2
Montgomery	1
Welshpool	4
Remainder of County	34
Total	42
PEMBROKE—	
Haverfordwest	3
Pembroke	7
Tenby	2
Remainder of County	36
Total	48
RADNOR	24

INDEX.

Hadden, Best & Co., Printers, West Harding Street, Fetter Lane, London.

REMITTING CASH.

All Cheques and Post Office Orders should be crossed "London Joint Stock Bank."

Post Office Orders may be made payable at Fleet Street.

Customers are earnestly requested in remitting cash for small amounts, not to send stamps without registering the letter.

Where Postal Orders are used they should in all cases be filled up, payable to HADDEN, BEST & Co. at FLEET STREET, and crossed LONDON JOINT STOCK BANK; otherwise they are as easily stolen and cashed as stamps.

SPECIAL TERMS FOR QUANTITIES.

HADDEN, BEST & Co. are prepared to supply any of the within-mentioned FORMS, with the local particulars printed in, at the following reduced rates for quantities:—

Those published	Supplied in quantities		
	of 250	of 500	of 1000
at 4/- per 100	for 10/-	for 15/-	for 25/-
,, 6/- ,,	15/-	22/6	37/6
,, 8/- ,,	16/-	24/-	40/-
,, 10/- ,,	20/-	30/-	45/-
,, 12/- ,,	24/-	36/-	54/-
,, 16/- ,,	32 -	48/-	80/-

1/6 per quire *is equal to* 6/- per 100 3/- per quire *is equal to* 12/- per 100
2/6 .. ,, 10/- ,, 4/- ,, ,, 16/- ,,

COUNTIES—*continued.*

	s.	d.
Form B. No. 2.—Notice as to Rates to be published by the Overseers (County Government) *per* 100	4	0
Form C. No. 1.—Notice as to Rates to be served by the Overseers - - - - *per* 100	4	0
Form C. No. 2.—List of names of Persons disqualified - - - - - - *per quire*	2	0
Form D. No. 3.—Old Lodgers List - *per quire*	2	0
Form E.—Occupiers List—Division I. *per quire*	2	0
Do. do. Division II. *per quire*	2	0
Do. do. Division III. *per quire*	2	0
Form G.—List of Persons entitled to be elected Councillors, though not entitled to be on the County Register - - - - *per quire*	2	0
Form H. No. 1.—Notice of Claim to Vote in respect of the Occupation Franchise (Parliamentary and County Government) - - (general) *per* 100	2	6
Form H. No. 2.—Notice of Claim to Vote in respect of the Occupation Franchise (Parliamentary and County Government) - - (lodgers) *per* 100	2	6
Form H. No 3.—Notice of Claim to Vote in respect of the Occupation Franchise (county Government) *per* 100	2	6
Form I. Nos. 1 and 2.—Notice of Objection to Vote in respect of the Occupation Franchise (Parliamentary and County Government) *per* 100	4	0
Form I. Nos. 3 and 4.—Notice of Objection to Vote in respect of the Occupation Franchise (County Government) - - - *per* 100	4	0
Form K. No. 1.—General List of Claimants (Parliamentary and County Government) - *per quire*	2	0
Form K. No. 2.—List of Occupier Claimants (Parliamentary) - - - - *per quire*	2	0
Form K. No. 3.—List of Lodger Claimants (Parliamentary) - - - - *per quire*	2	0
Form K. No. 4.—List of Claimants (County Government) - - - - - - *per quire*	2	0
Form L. No. 1.—List of Persons objected to (Parliamentary and County Government) - *per quire*	2	0

COUNTIES—*continued.*

		s.	d.
Form L. No. 2.—List of Persons on Occupiers List who have been objected to (Parliamentary)	*per quire*	2	0
Form L. No. 3.—List of Lodgers objected to (Parliamentary) - - - - -	*per quire*	2	0
Form L. No. 4.—List of Persons objected to (County Government) - - - -	*per quire*	2	0
Form M.—Declaration for Correcting Misdescription in List - - - - - - -	*per* 100	4	0

BOROUGHS:

The Forms in the following List are for use in a parish situate in a Municipal, and also in a Parliamentary Borough, *i.e.*, a parish in a Municipal Borough where the Lists are made out under the Parliamentary and Municipal Registration Act, 1878.

Form No. 1.—Form of Precept to the Overseers, including the general instructions and list of things to be done in order of date -	*per doz.*	3	9
Form A.—Requisition by Overseers requiring names of Inhabitant Occupiers, with instructions for filling up the Form - - - - -	*per* 100	4	0
Form B. No. 1.—Notice as to Rates, to be published by Overseers (Parliamentary) - -	*per* 100	4	0
Form B. No. 2.—Notice as to Rates, to be published by Overseers (Municipal) - -	*per* 100	4	0
Form C. No 1.—Notice as to Rates, to be served by Overseers - - - - - - -	*per* 100	4	0
Form C. No. 2.—List of Names of Persons disqualified - - - - - - - -	*per quire*	2	0
Form D. No. 3.—Old Lodgers List -	*per quire*	2	0
Form D. No. 1.—Occupiers List— Division I.	*per quire*	2	0
Do. do. Division II.	*per quire*	2	0
Do. do. Division III.	*per quire*	2	0
Form D. No. 2.—List of Persons entitled to be registered in respect of a right reserved under sec. 31 and 33 of the Reform Act of 1832	*per quire*	2	0

BOROUGHS—*continued.*

	s.	d.
Form G.—List of Persons entitled to be elected Councillors or Aldermen, though not entitled to be on the Burgess Roll - . - *per quire*	2	0
Form H. No. 1.—Notice of Claim to Vote (Parliamentary and municipal) (general) - *per* 100	2	6
Form H. No. 2.—Notice of Claim to Vote (Parliamentary)—(lodgers) - - - *per* 100	2	6
Form H. No. 3.—Notice of Claim to Vote (municipal) - - - - - - - *per* 100	2	6
Form I. Nos. 1 and 2.—Notice of Objection (Parliamentary and municipal) - - *per* 100	4	0
Form I. Nos. 3 and 4.—Notice of Objection (municipal) - - - - - - *per* 100	4	0
Form K. No. 1.—General List of Claimants (Parliamentary and municipal) - - - *per quire*	2	0
Form K. No. 2.—General List of Claimants (Parliamentary) - - - - - - - *per quire*	2	0
Form K. No. 3.—List of Lodger Claimants (Parliamentary) - - - - - - *per quire*	2	0
Form K. No. 4.—List of Claimants (Burgess List) (municipal) - - - - - - *per quire*	2	0
Form L. No. 1.—List of Persons objected to (Parliamentary and municipal) - - - *per quire*	2	0
Form L. No. 2.—List of Persons objected to (Parliamentary) - - - - - - *per quire*	2	0
Form L. No 3.—List of Lodgers objected to (Parliamentary) - - - - - - *per quire*	2	0
Form L. No. 4.—List of Persons objected to (Burgess List—municipal) - - - - - *per quire*	2	0
Form M.—Declaration for correcting misdescription in List - - - - - - - - *per* 100	4	0

BOROUGHS—*continued.*

The Forms in the following List are for use in a Parish within a Parliamentary Borough, but not within a Municipal Borough.

Where the Parish is in a Municipal Borough in which the Lists of Parliamentary Voters have not, before the passing of the County Electors Act, 1888, been made out under the Parliamentary and Municipal Registration Act, 1878, the following forms shall be used, with the substitution, wherever necessary, of "Burgess" for "County Elector," "Municipal Borough" for "County," of "Enrolled" for "Registered," and of "Burgess Roll" for "County Register."

		s.	d.
Form No. 1.—Form of Precept to the Overseers of a Parish situate in a Parliamentary but not in a Municipal borough, including the general instructions and list of things to be done in order of date, *but omitting so much as relates to Burgesses as is described in paragraph 3 of the Instructions to Town Clerks* - - - - -	*per doz.*	3	0
Form No. 1.—Form of Precept to the Overseers of a Parish situate in a municipal borough, comprised in a parliamentary borough, which after the dissolution of 1885, ceased to be such, *or* to the Overseers of a Parish situate in a municipal, but not in a parliamentary borough, and which was not included in a parliamentary borough merged in a county by the Redistribution Act, 1885, including the general instructions and list of things to be done in the order of date, *with the necessary alterations and additions as described in sec. 4 of the Instructions to Town Clerks*	*per doz.*	3	9
Form A.—Requisition by Overseers requiring names of Inhabitant Occupiers, with instructions for filling up the Form - - -	*per* 100	4	0
Form B. No. 1.—Notice as to Rates, to be published by Overseers (Parliamentary) - -	*per* 100	4	0
Form B. No 2.—Notice as to Rates to be published by Overseers (County Government) -	*per* 100	4	0
Form C. No. 1.—Notice as to Rates, to be served by Overseers - - - - - -	*per* 100	4	0
Form C. No. 2.—List of Names of Persons disqualified - - - - - - -	*per quire*	2	0
Form D. No. 1.—Occupiers List— Division I.	*per quire*	2	0
Do. do. Division II.	*per quire*	2	0
Do. do. Division III.	*per quire*	2	0

BOROUGHS—*continued.*

	s.	d.
Form D. No. 2.—List of Persons entitled to be registered in respect of a right reserved under sec. 31 and 33 of the Reform Act of 1832 *per quire*	2	0
Form D. No. 3.—Old Lodgers List - *per quire*	2	0
Form F.—List of Burgesses for a parish situate in a municipal, but not in a Parliamentary borough, and which was not included in a Parliamentary borough merged in a county by Redistribution of Seats Act, 1885 - - - - - *per quire*	2	0
Form G.—List of Persons entitled to be elected Councillors - - - - - - *per quire*	2	0
Form H. No. 1.—Notice of Claim to Vote (Parliamentary and County Government) - *per* 100	2	6
Form H. No. 2.—Notice of Claim to Vote (Parliamentary—lodgers) - - - *per* 100	2	6
Form H. No. 3.—Notice of Claim to Vote (County Government) - - - - - - *per* 100	2	6
Form I. Nos. 1 and 2.—Notice of Objection (Parliamentary and County Government) *per* 100	4	0
Form I. Nos. 3 and 4.—Notice of Objection (County Government) - - - *per* 100	4	0
Form K. No. 1.—List of Claimants (Parliamentary and County Government) - - *per quire*	2	0
Form K. No. 2.—List of Claimants (Parliamentary) *per quire*	2	0
Form K. No. 3.—List of Lodger Claimants (Parliamentary) - - - - - - *per quire*	2	0
Form K. No. 4.—List of Claimants (County Government) - - - - - - - *per quire*	2	0
Form L. No. 1.—List of Persons objected to (Parliamentary and County Government) *per quire*	2	0
Form L. No. 2.—List of Persons objected to (Parliamentary) - - - *per quire*	2	0
Form L. No. 3.—List of Lodgers objected to (Parliamentary) - - - - - - *per quire*	2	0
Form L. No. 4.—List of Persons objected to (County Government) - - - - - - *per quire*	2	0
Form M.—Declaration for correcting misdescription in List - - - - - - - - *per* 100	4	0

FORM CABINETS.

Strongly made in wood, covered cloth.

(*a*) *Twenty drawers, to hold foolscap forms.*

Size—

2ft. 6⅝in. × 2ft. 2½in. × 11¼ in. deep.

Price £3 3s.

(*b*) *Twenty shelves, to hold foolscap forms.*

Size—

18¾in. × 18¾in. × 14½in. deep.

Price £2 8s.

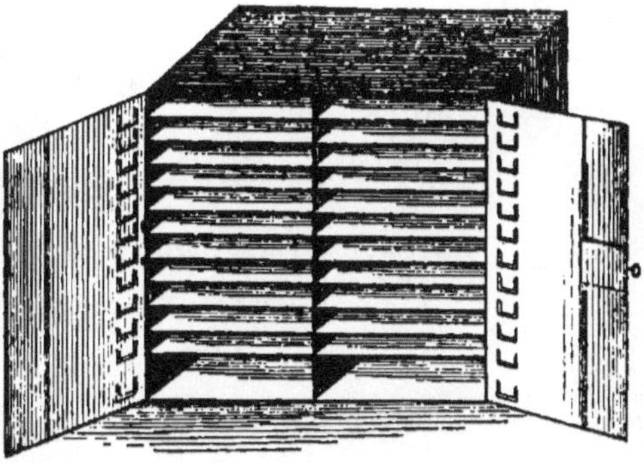

(*c*)

Substantially made in Japanned metal.

	£	s.	d.
12 shelves, to hold Foolscap Forms	1	10	0
24 shelves, to hold Foolscap Forms	2	15	0
24 shelves, to hold Bankruptcy Forms - -	4	3	0

LIST OF FORMS

REQUIRED IN THE

Election of a County Council

No. of Form.		s.	d.
1	Notice of Election - - - - *folio, per* 100	6	0
2	Nomination Papers - - - - - *per quire*	3	0
3	Notice of Nomination—*Rule* 11 - "	3	0
4	Notice of Candidates Elected—*Rule* 45, *per* 100	6	0
6	Notice of Polling Stations - - - - "	6	0
7	Directions for the Guidance of Voters—*Placard for Polling Stations—Rule* 19, *folio, per* 100	8	0
8	Appointment of Presiding Officers, *per quire*	2	6
9	Appointment of Clerks - - - - - "	2	6
10	Ballot Papers - - - } *printed to order.*		
11	Tendered Ballot Papers, *on coloured paper* - } *printed to order.*		
12	Declaration of Secrecy—*Rule* 54 - *per quire*	3	0
13	Declaration of Inability to Read—*Rule* 26 "	3	0
14	Questions to Voters, and form of Oath, *on card, per dozen*	2	0
15	List of Votes Marked by Presiding Officer, *per quire*	3	0
16	Tendered Votes List—*Rule* 27 - "	3	0
17	Presiding Officer's Ballot Paper Account—*Rule* 30, *per quire*	3	0
18	Notice of Time and Place for Counting Votes "	2	6
19	Report of Returning Officer to Clerk of Crown—*Rule* 37 - - - - - *per quire*	3	0
	Instructions to Returning Officers - *per dozen*	3	0
	The Duties of a Presiding Officer - "	5	0
	Offences at Elections; *being Extracts from the Statutes in force, for the use of Returning Officers* - - - - - *per dozen*	2	6

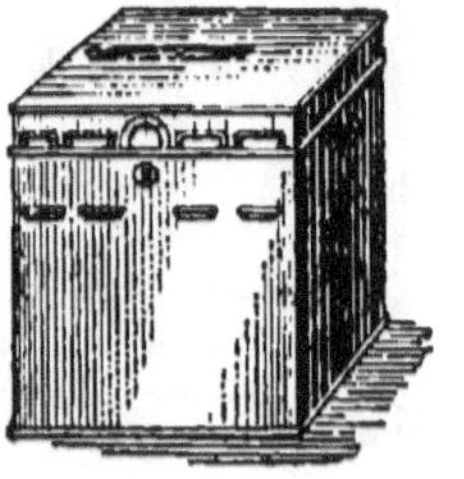

BALLOT BOXES.

Japanned, very Strong.

(*To hold* 1000 *Papers.*)

18in. × 14in. × 14in.

Each, 21s.

THE "WHITEHALL" STATIONERY CABINET.

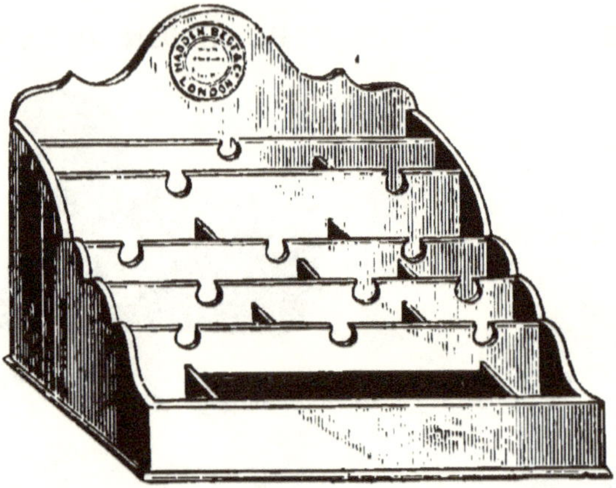

The want of a suitable Stationery Cabinet for strictly Official and Commercial purposes has been long felt; the "Whitehall" Stationery Cabinet is intended specially to meet this requirement.

IT CONTAINS:

1	Compartment	for	Foolscap Paper.
1	"	"	Letter "
4	"	"	Large Note " or Memorandum Forms.
1	"	"	Foolscap Envelopes.
4	"	"	Commercial "
1	"	"	Post Cards.
1	"	"	Ruler.

Also a Pen Tray, &c.

The compartments are made extra wide, so as to be capable of holding a good supply of paper and envelopes, and there being four compartments for each, renders the Cabinet specially suitable for Solicitors and others holding several official appointments with separate Stationery for each.

Substantially made in solid oak,

price 16s. 6d.; *or with folding doors*, 32s. 6d

www.ingramcontent.com/pod-product-compliance
Lightning Source LLC
Chambersburg PA
CBHW021327110726
47900CB00005B/1382
9783337301903